SHADOW'S DESCENT

TIDES OF DARKNESS

JOSEPH J. BAILEY

CONTENTS

MAP

Dharia

The Ayle'ine Sea

To Far Aruene

To Far Maeron

To Far Kilaeron

Lueciane Sea

Qia Shan Sea

Var'Kera

The Green Run

Q'shar

The Drake Spires

Ithil'alen

Northlands

Jemyuan

Shulin

Chang Sen

© 2011 Joe Benkey

AUTHOR'S NOTE

For terms that are not strictly imaginary in nature, the Wade-Giles and Pinyin Romanization systems are used interchangeably, loosely, and not entirely accurately.

Transliteration devices were chosen mostly based on whichever sounded better at the time.

A glossary of terms is included at the book's end to help the reader fully engage in, understand, and explore the world of Ea'ae.

Forgive my errors for they are numerous and I am not.

To Carolyn for making everything possible.

The first mover is the mind.

\- Master Wei
Priest of the K'un Lun

RETURN

Golden light wanders
aimlessly through the halls of
crystalline facets.

Shielding eyes before a resplendent sun, Yip, Aroganji, and Slate beheld Tellanon in all its majesty. Shimmering in the blue expanse, accentuated by clouds, protected from harm by its glimmering shield, the island in the sky appeared as its own planet, with a purpose and life entirely of its own. Orbiting about its periphery, ships and drones of every shape and size imaginable darted and hovered, appearing and disappearing through interdimensional portals, linking one cosmic nexus with myriad others.

Within Tellanon's iridescent aegis, homes glowed in soft luminescence reflecting the afternoon sun, verdant vegetation softened the edges of buildings and walls, blending and intertwining disparate shapes and structures into a lightly woven tapestry of human imagination. At the city's heart, soaring skyward gloriously, the limpid branches of Illdrassil sheltered and fostered the well-being of the entire populace, holding and refracting more light than all the stars in the heavens.

To Yip's senses, so used to the relative dearth of the wilds of Al'Marr, Tellanon incandesced in the sky, aflame in energy—a heat mirage given life and vitality. He felt awash in generative forces, the city's vibrant pulse enlivening his own. At its heart, blinding in intensity, overwhelming in vivacity, Illdrassil raised her celestial branches to the firmament, one miracle among many.

Alongside Yip, his eyes adjusting to the bright light of Ea'ae after spending so many days beneath the ruddy skies of Al'Marr, Wrindanneth closed his hand instinctively only to realize that the return stone he had held so closely, the object that had made their journey home possible, was gone, consumed in the tremendous energies of their transport.

"Crew of the *Shrike*! Prepare to be scanned!" A clarion voice called out to them undeniably, leaving no room to be ignored. Pulled abruptly from their appreciation of the place, the Construct and its directives commanded their immediate attention.

And so the docking procedures began.

A well of light unexpectedly focused on Yip, interrupting his thoughts. "Crew member of the *Shrike*, your essence is not on record, nor does it match in any way the previously accepted aural imprint of Yip Chi Chuan. How do you account for this discrepancy?"

Bowing slightly, Yip answered, "I resubmit to your scan. I have been recast and reformed under conditions I would rather not revisit."

"Captain, do you attest to the validity of this statement?"

"Aye," answered Wrindanneth.

"You understand that you and your crew take full responsibility if this assertion is found to be false?"

"Aye."

"You understand that you will share in any liability and culpability in the event of wrongdoing should this assertion prove false?"

Wrindanneth did his best to stifle a laugh. He was only partially successful. "Aye."

"You are provisionally granted the rights and privileges inherent to your previous level of citizenship, Yip Chi Chuan. This status shall be revoked and subject to due punishment should you neglect your duties and responsibilities as a citizen of Tellanon, if you are found to be false, or if you provide reason to doubt your veracity."

Yip bowed, answering, "Thank you."

As the docking procedures once again commenced in earnest, Yip over-heard Wrindanneth request that the Construct have Adar meet them on the docks to assist in their final landing.

While Wrindanneth deftly maneuvered through the series of instructions outlined by the Construct, Yip wondered what new marvels awaited them on the island in the sky. He also pondered the condition of both his and his friends' state of affairs in addition to their collective future. With any luck, Adar and the other Paratechnologists would be able to help them glean some useful information from the alien creatures' command orb, especially information regarding the Cabal's doings, plans, allies, and locations. Perhaps then they would actually have some information to begin moving forward directly against the agents of the Cabal. If not, then he would take any information he could on the Cabal's designs.

After all that had happened and changed since their last meeting, he wished to contact Master Wei for guidance and tutelage. He needed to tell his master of all that he had learned of the Cabal both here and abroad since they had last spoken.

Master Wei would be especially pleased if they could wrestle any more of the Cabal's doings from the aliens' orb. Even more so, however, Master Wei needed to know what he had learned about overcoming the Cabal's *chi* void on Al'Marr. If he could spread that knowledge, then this world and countless others would be protected from the worst of the Cabal's evils, if not the Cabal themselves. Given his personal transformation, he also hoped that his teacher would be able to provide further instruction on his continued development and training. As much as there was that he wished to share, he also wanted to hear news of his fellows, the priests, acolytes, and initiates of the Order of K'un Lun, of their health and recovery, of their safety and plans.

He would also need to contact the H'era to let them know that their world had been cleansed, that their planet would start anew with the Cabal's taint finally removed. If they chose to return, he would have to find a way to teach the Maer'Din how to overcome the Cabal's evil should the Cabal ever return or their evil ever resurface on the H'era's homeworld. That transfer of knowledge would provide a necessary step in protecting other worlds from a similar fate.

Smiling inwardly, he noted how one task completed led to so many more, each demanding attention and further dedication just as climbing upward along a tree's bole led to passage through more and more branches and limbs before the light of day was finally reached.

"Welcome back!" Adar's greeting mirrored the warmth and levity of the day. Behind him, the usual frenzy of the docks churned and roiled unabated since their recent departure. Glancing at their beleaguered ship, the Paratechnologist added jokingly, "I'm glad to see that you are doing better than your ship!"

Wrindanneth grunted as he walked down the gangplank to the stone dock below, not happy with the *Shrike*'s appearance or its current state of disrepair. She was held together more by magic than the wood from which she was composed. If ever a ship could be said to resemble Emmental cheese, riddled with holes and voids, the *Shrike* was the one. Unlike cheese, the *Shrike* was no fitter to eat than she was to fly.

Along with many other tasks, her present state must be addressed.

Several other thoughts flashed through his mind before he focused on the matter at hand. The ship's systems needed augmentation for their future voyages, especially in terms of its defenses and armaments. He would also like to implement a more effective automated repair system, especially if they were to embark on more risky, extended journeys. Relying strictly on his intent directed through the ship was far too time-consuming and unreliable.

The *Shrike*'s current condition attested to this need. At least her masts yet stood, though her sails would need replacing. Looking up and down the sweeping berth, the *Shrike* appeared to be the least sky worthy airship on the dock.

That would not be the case for long.

Adar appeared as Yip remembered, a sure, healthy man of middle-age with quick, intelligent eyes, surrounded by a barely visible field of force that moved and adjusted with his every move. He felt Adar's shield to be something of a densification of a thin layer of the fabric of reality. The field existed only a finger's breadth away from Adar's garments, as though a large portion of space and all its contents had been compacted into a very tight halo around Adar's body, preventing or slowing most anything from passing through. Various other oddities cloaked Adar's personage—several items of indeterminate purpose hung or floated about his person, perhaps heightening his senses or acting as defensive devices. Over his shoulder, the sinister defensive drone Yip remembered hovered menacingly, its insectile limbs and appendages serving more purposes than all the other gadgets floating around Adar.

In response to Adar's greeting, once he stepped off the wooden gangplank, Wrindanneth strode forward to stand directly in front of Adar to command his attention, intent to discuss the reasons why he had summoned the Paratechnologist. "Thank you, Adar. We have much to discuss with you before we return home, if you have the time."

Adar nodded, indicating Wrindanneth should go on.

"We hope that you or those in your organization will be able to assist us."

Adar raised an eyebrow briefly questioningly. "How so?"

"May we speak in private?"

Adar nodded.

Wrindanneth muttered several incantations that he had learned from studying Verakesh's tome. These wards blocked the interception of sight and sound immediately around the speaker and served to interfere with any scrying or outside detection that may be extant or imposed upon a location.

Assured that they were now at least relatively free of eavesdropping, Wrindanneth began. "We have acquired an artifact from an alien civilization that we need to extract information from in order to assist us in our quest. The object does not appear to function based on magical principles that we understand. Without risking the device or the knowledge contained within, we have decided to seek assistance in resolving its riddles. Given your exposure to so many forms of magic and technology, you or your kind may be able to decipher what we need from this object."

Noncommittal as yet, unsure of the full nature, extent, and difficulty of the request, Adar responded, "Perchance."

Smiling with the give and take, laying the groundwork required for the trade in knowledge, ready to barter and negotiate for lore, Wrindanneth went on, "In the end, what we are offering should be of significantly more value to you than to us. We are offering you the opportunity to study the command orb of an advanced alien vessel. We do not know the extent of the knowledge contained within the orb, but the creatures commanding it appeared to be very sophisticated both psychically and technically. The ship itself had several impressive abilities that we were unable to mimic or detect with our magical systems. Furthermore, we can provide the information on where this vessel, along with all of its cargo and equipment, is located."

"That you may understand what we offer, we also have examples of other pieces of the alien technology from this ship for you to study. One item is a crystalline sword, another is a blaster, and the last is a personal force shield. We think all were empowered by the crew's psychic energies."

"What do you ask in return?" Evidently Wrindanneth's offer had piqued Adar's interest.

"If you find the objects we provide of interest and you meet with success in extracting valuable information from the orb, information valuable to both parties, under our supervision of course, then we will also provide you with the information regarding the whereabouts of the alien ship. Either way, you will receive complete access to several potentially new sources of knowledge and technology. In return, you will endeavor to provide us with the information we request, if available or interpretable at all, and you will give us a portion of the proceeds from the application and development of any new knowledge and technology you glean from our sources."

Although he only knew of Wrindanneth's intent to ask for Adar's help in extracting information about the Cabal from the orb, not about his request to garner returns on their efforts, Yip did not begrudge his friends' desire to reap reward from their efforts. Since his discussion with Wrindanneth regarding the magical dagger after first capturing the *Shrike*, the rigidity of his views regarding possessions and benefit from material goods had softened somewhat. Although he remained focused on the path toward ridding the universe of the Cabal, his friends were not motivated solely by his concerns. Understanding how much their success depended in many ways on both their personal development and continued access to more effective resources, he would not prevent his friends from benefiting from their travails along the way.

Their preparation would be his own.

Adar took some time to respond. "You feel the orb itself may have the most value to us of the items that you currently possess given the potential knowledge contained therein?"

Wrindanneth nodded. "Aye."

"Then let me offer this proposal. I will take the energy shield, blaster orb, and crystalline sword, and, under your supervision, will inspect these items among my peers. If these items appear to be of interest, we will move forward and you will not have risked the orb or its contents to our initial scrutiny. If the orb itself shows promise, the knowledge within will probably be of more value to us than the ship itself. Additionally, if the orb appears to be of interest, then we will consider mounting an expedition to examine and retrieve the alien vessel. In any case, if the items show promise, by Tellanon law, we will be required to share a portion of the proceeds with the original discoverers."

Wrindanneth smiled. With any luck, not only would they be getting new shields and repair technologies, much needed upgrades for the *Shrike*, they may also be getting a few of the bells and whistles from the alien ship as well.

"We can meet on the morn at the magistrate's office to begin our initial inspection. What time would you choose?"

"Dawn." Wrindanneth was eager to move forward. If the items were of interest to the Paratechnologists, extending the frontiers of their particular blend of magical and technical knowledge, then they would have more time to study the alien objects the earlier everyone met.

"I will see you then. Is there anything else?"

"Nothing for now."

"Then I will see you on the morn. Good day."

Wrindanneth bowed. "Thank you, Adar."

Weaving between the other mostly humanoid beings moving about their business on the docks, Adar walked away, finally disappearing amidst the bustle. Watching him go, Wrindanneth could not resist a smile.

"Gentlemen, we may have just secured our futures."

Thinking not in terms of their quest, but of material gain, Slate washed his hands. "Aye. Those gangly buggers may've given us more than just trouble when all's said and done!"

"Should we not arrange for repairs to the ship before proceeding home?" Aroganji wanted to make sure that all would be ready once they had the intelligence necessary to move ahead, assuming the Paratechnologists were successful in their information extraction and useful knowledge was to be found within the alien ship's command sphere.

Yip answered for Wrindanneth. "Adar and his colleagues will take time deciphering the riddles of the orb. In the meantime, there is much we must do here before we are ready to leave. If the Paratechnologists are unsuccessful or do not show an interest in the items, then we will need to repair and upgrade the *Shrike* and find another means to investigate the orb. If the Paratechnologists are successful, then the knowledge they glean may be of use in improving our ship and our chances in the future. In either case, we will have time to take care of the ship."

Agreeing, pleasantly surprised with Yip's position, Wrindanneth added, "Aye. Let's see what the Paratechnologists can do for us before we proceed forward expending our resources unnecessarily. Besides, the automatic repairs I initiated over the course of the past two weeks should be complete within another week or so. What I am really concerned about are upgrades to the *Shrike*'s systems. The Paratechnologists already have many amazing systems available without needing the additional technology from the alien ship. They may be willing to accouter and upgrade her in exchange for what we offer."

"Then let us return home and make ready for the morn." Aroganji wanted time to be prepared for the meeting with the Paratechnologists. Anything they could do to receive maximum benefit for their time and efforts while ensuring the development of a potential future partnership between the Paratechnologists and their fellows would be to everyone's advantage.

Making their way home toward Tellanon's cityscape, passing the monolithic sweep of rock above the curving docks, as they crossed the Weirding Gate, its monolithic arching form screening all entry into Tellanon proper, sending shivers across their skins as its energies scanned their essences, granting permission to enter the city, Slate broached a subject he had pondered for some time. "Ya know, I've been thinkin'..."

"Uh oh," Wrindanneth cut in before Slate could finish. "This is bound to be trouble."

Unperturbed, Slate continued as if he had not been interrupted, "In legend and song, most proper bands o' heroes have a name fer themselves."

"Don't we already have one?" said Wrindanneth thinking back to their first trip to see Hoyt with Yip.

"Ya mean tha Four?"

"Aye."

"Doesn't have much o' a ring ta it if ya' ask me. Needs somethin' more. An endin' perhaps. Some emphasis...some oomph!"

Aroganji chuckled. "Does it matter? What band of 'heroes' chooses its own name? That's puerile."

"Aren't titles given to those whose honor and deed are worthy of song, titles given by the very people who sing and listen to the songs? Namely, the populace at large?"

Shaking his head, Aroganji added, "If a band spends its time choosing names and titles, then its fellows are not focusing on their business or the task at hand. I doubt such as those are successful."

Understanding that a proper earned name, however, could ultimately foster their fame and esteem, and thus their future reception and success, Wrindanneth changed course, siding with Slate a bit as he warmed to the idea. "Much is in a name. Perhaps we can add to what we've been given."

"Perhaps," answered Aroganji.

"Any thoughts, Yip?"

"A name is not the thing, nor is it the essence of a thing, merely a description used for communality and understanding. The importance and significance of a name is determined by those who ascribe to it. A name can be a tool as much as a vehicle of communication."

Slate grunted and growled under his breath. "Do ya have anythin' o' import ta add ta our discussion besides yer high flyin' commentary and theoretical interpretations?"

"Very well," Yip smiled slightly with his friend's consternation. "We all make our living with our fists. Though we all strive to eschew violence, would prefer the application of reason and discussion, and desire to abide in peace, the path we have chosen wends in and out of combat. For good or ill, our foes will allow no alternative. Although our approaches and outlooks may differ, although our state of mind and perspectives may vary, in one form or another, we all live and die by our fists."

Wrindanneth nodded, liking Yip's direction.

"Hmm," he appeared thoughtful, mumbling to himself. "Four Fists, Four of the Fists, Four of the Forceful Fist, Four of the Fierce Fists..."

Moving through the cobbled streets, Yip walked past the rows of enchanted homes, each swirling with unique traceries of power, energies that hinted at hidden purposes and intricacies, of worlds unfolding within. The magic of the place flowed through and in him, enlivening his breath, lightening his step.

Wrindanneth continued mumbling to himself until they reached the finely wrought gate to their comfortable stone cottage. Crossing through, walking up the stone path to the home's front door, passed the well-ordered lawn, he hardly noticed his surroundings and friends, so engrossed was he in his musings. Reaching his hand out toward the knob to open the door, his eyebrows shot up and he thrust his hand in the air triumphantly. "The Flaming Fists! The Four of the Flaming Fists!"

Slate whooped and slapped his thigh. "Tha Flamin' Fists! Now that has a nice ring ta it! Brendle be praised!"

Aroganji smiled as well, liking the sound of the name though not yet willing to admit it was necessary. "Perhaps...perhaps."

As his hand settled on the doorknob, a bright smile on his face, Wrindanneth was jolted out of his reverie as the soft feminine intonations of the Aspect greeted him warmly. "That certainly does sound appropriate. Welcome home, Flaming Fists!"

Slate growled to Aroganji, "I thought ya turned that thing off!"

"I did!"

Unperturbed, the voice of the Abstract went on, "I am very glad to see that you made it home safely! I will update the records to reflect your new designation."

"Records?" Slate was confused.

Cheerily, eager for the opportunity to be useful, the Aspect answered, "I will add your new title to the centralized record system for the city of Tellanon."

"Uh..." ventured Slate, flummoxed.

Recovering himself quickly, Wrindanneth answered, "Excellent." Their name would spread without any further effort on his part.

Walking in, Aroganji asked the Abstract, "Anything we should be aware of upon returning?"

There was a momentary pause. "The Grand Marshal has been soundly elected to a second term supervising..."

Wrindanneth cut her voice off. "Anything pertinent to us?"

Another pause. "Hoyt left a message asking for 'an update when they return.'"

Grumbling Slate mounted the stairs to deposit his gear and get cleaned up before relaxing for the evening. Gesturing vaguely in the air, he said, "I really should introduce Duraeleon ta tha Aspect, lock 'em up in tha same room and let 'em blabber ta each other fer hours."

"I really would appreciate the opportunity to meet your acquaintances, Master Flintforge," was the cheery response, a reply Slate would have preferred not to hear in the first place.

"Harrumph!" Slate snorted. "Just call me Slate!"

Grumbling to himself, Slate went up to his room on the second floor to polish his armor and axe, hoping that Duraeleon at least would remain quiet.

Maybe space was not so bad after all. At least he could find peace and quiet somewhere on the ship, a luxury he was not even guaranteed in his own home. Mentally sighing, he realized even that quiet was not assured. With the potential upgrades from the Paratechnologists, they all may be talking with the ship soon enough.

Resigned, Slate walked down the hall and shut the door to his room firmly behind him.

Downstairs, Aroganji and Wrindanneth were seated comfortably around a small, modest wooden table. The gaudy, palatial table they had originally used to furnish the kitchen was no more. Drinking warm tea that Aroganji summoned, Wrindanneth perched his long legs on top of the section nearest to his oversized feet.

"I say we play wait and see before offering any more proposals. After the Paratechnologists realize the value of what we have to offer, they may surprise us. After all, the Paratechnologists understand what they can provide better than we do in exchange. If we ask for something definite for the knowledge in the orb or the contents of the ship, we may shortchange ourselves in the long run."

Nodding, Aroganji held his mug of tea cupped in the palms of his two hands, allowing the drink's steam to bring the tea's aroma and body wafting about him, opening his pores and senses, relaxing his mind.

While his friends discussed their impending meeting, Yip returned to the solarium, settling his small kit on the floor, making himself at home for the short period of time he anticipated being on Tellanon. He had a few hours left before he would embark upon his dream voyage to speak with the Maer'Din. He needed to let them know, as well as his master, that he desired to speak with them. Staring out the window, he watched the light of day progress and change as it moved over the garden, changing in angle and intensity along with the resulting mood in the room as the day progressed.

Letting the light's energy suffuse him where he sat before the reflective glass, his mind settled on his breath as it moved in and out, lightly, steadily, from his nostrils and down through his lungs, vitalizing his body and mind. With his lungs full of air and energy, he exhaled slowly, letting his thoughts travel outward with his breath.

A single thought left his mind as he breathed, *"Master, I would speak with you."* Channeling this energy into the message, he let his intimation alight on the rays of sunshine illuminating the garden, flowing with the *chi* suffusing all in his mind's eye.

Guided by his energy and intent, his message would reach Master Wei before day's end.

Once again drawing in the energies flowing through and around him, replete with the light of the day, he breathed out a message for the Maer'Din, the lorekeepers of the H'era, broadcasting a sense of his presence along with his intention for their minds only. *"I have news of your home. I would speak to you this eve, if you will hear me."*

He would wait for his master's response as he would wait to seek out the Maer'Din while he slept.

Finished, he reemerged from his chamber and into the sitting room off the kitchen where Wrindanneth and Aroganji conversed. He knew that his friends had decided upon their course of action for the following morning, for they were talking casually about options for new equipment and accouterments necessary for their next foray against the Cabal—the usual plots and schemes for better equipment, more powerful items, and dreams for things yet to come.

"Hello, Yip! Are you set for tomorrow?"

Nodding, he sat gracefully on the floor, forgoing the chairs and stools his friends made themselves comfortable upon. "With any luck, tonight I will speak with my master and with the Maer'Din."

Aroganji grinned, teasing, knowing how cryptic teachers could be. "Perhaps your master will help clarify the riddles before us?"

Having been on the receiving end of quite a bit of enigmatic instruction himself, Wrindanneth quipped, "With more riddles?"

Smiling in turn, Yip replied in jest to his friends, "Always." More seriously, he went on, "He will need to know what we have learned and accomplished on Al'Marr in addition to what we hope to learn from the orb. If we are lucky and the Paratechnologists are successful in their efforts, I will be able to contact him again in short order and let him know that we have deciphered a clear path from the alien device. He, too, may have learned more of the Cabal's doings that may be of use to us while we were away."

"Presented in the form of a conundrum, of course," Wrindanneth grinned wickedly.

Laughing, Yip answered, "Of course!"

When the evening stars blanketed the sky in a tapestry of silver, Yip left his friends in the cottage's living room and returned to his quarters beneath the night sky. Settling down on his kit, he laid down on his right side, right hand tucked under his cheek, knees bent, following his breath, his attention relaxed and alert, his conscious mind ebbing with each breath.

Remaining aware of his breath, he slowly slipped into the realm of dreams, in the state of natural light, maintaining complete presence of mind, full awareness and clarity.

In this relaxed state of attention, he began to slowly visualize the village of the H'era, the clearing where the Maer'Din had shared the story of their world's end, the billowing homes sheltered among beautiful trees, and the meeting hall where he had sat in counsel with Uuraja, father of Uuraru, leader of the H'era. After all the details were as complete as his recollection allowed, he put himself in that place, imagining that he was, in fact, there, in presence if not in body.

Blinking, he opened his eyes onto the clearing. In the soft illumination of the stars, light filtered through the multi-layered canopy above.

"Greetings, Yip Chi Chuan of the K'un Lun."

Seated across from him, simultaneously poised and at ease, the two Maer'Din sat as he remembered them, graceful, wise and composed, dressed in the loose, multicolored robes of their station, braided hair arranged carefully on their shoulders, their cat eyes iridescent in the partial evening light. Between and behind the Maer'Din stood Uuraja massive and imposing, who, apparently, was as well versed in the ways of dreams as of combat.

"We have been awaiting you." The female Maer'Din smiled, her sharp, predatory teeth visible in the half-light.

"Intimations of home stir about you. What news do you bring?" The male Maer'Din spoke as if finishing his partner's sentence.

Yip bowed from the waist where he sat across from the felines.

"I bring news of Al'Marr."

Uuraja nodded. *"We suspected as much, brother in blood. We are eager to hear your tale."*

Yip began, *"Much has happened since last we spoke."* Smiling now, for he did not wish to contain the joy he felt for these people who had gone through so much, he added, *"Your world is safe and I believe that I can teach you how to keep it so."*

Uuraja hissed, sucking in breath.

The two Maer'Din remained impassive.

"I will show you." As the Maer'Din had done for him with the Seura, the dance of dreams unborn, when they told him their story through movement and song, he painted vivid pictures and images of his journey since leaving the H'era from the stuff of dreams—recreating his trip through the mountains of the Drake Spires and the Green Run, meeting his companions, seeking out the

Dragon Sarugauth the Red, traveling to Tellanon, and ultimately visiting Al'Marr.

He showed them as best he could the efforts he had undertaken at the center of the Cabal's maelstrom, restoring the tear in reality the Cabal rent to drain the lifeblood of their world, the travails that followed this restoration, his simple attempt to bring the beginnings of life back to their home, and his ultimate return to Tellanon in preparation for the next section of his journey, his own dream unfinished.

Eyes shining bright in the starlight, overtopped with anguish, Uuraja spoke for his companions. *"Al'Marr and the blight upon her are as I remember, only now renewed."* Standing, his gaze clear, Uuraja strode across the distance between them and clasped one of his mighty paws on Yip's shoulder. *"Our faith in you has truly been rewarded, Yip. Your deeds will be part of the Seura so long as our blood runs true and our people dance beneath the heavens above."*

Bowing slightly, Yip humbly replied, *"I serve the life we would all lead, my friends, for you and your people's future are as my own."*

The Maer'Din nodded, appreciating his answer.

"What counsel would you give, Yip?" The H'era seldom asked for advice of any kind. That Uuraja asked Yip's opinion intimated at the level of respect he showed for the small human.

"The future now lays open and untrammeled before you. You may choose whatever course of action you see fit. Should you return home or remain here, I would hope that your people never have to endure any calamities such as you have born in the past. If you choose to return, Al'Marr will need time and much effort to reseed and become inhabitable for your people. Restoring her glory will be the work of generations. If you choose to stay on Ea'ae, your people's legacy and vibrancy will continue to enrich our world. These choices, among others, are yours."

Whatever their decision, he wished to ensure that their future would be assured. *"Whether you stay or go, I would show you how to overcome the Cabal's blight that the H'era may live without fear of the Cabal's scourge for all eternity."*

The two Maer'Din stirred, turning to look at each other gravely. In unison they said, *"The knowledge you offer commands a high price."*

Yip replied simply. *"Only the responsibility and dedication to use it wisely."* He did not need anything from the H'era in return for the gift he wished to give, the freedom he wished for their future.

The H'era sat in deep silence for some time. Perhaps they were reliving some of the horrific memories of their people's exodus and their world's downfall, envisioning a future where they may have to face such evils again. Perhaps they were imagining the efforts required to rebuild their homeworld. Perhaps they were envisaging a time when the Cabal came again, unbidden and unwelcome, into their lives. Perhaps they considered these things and many more, he could not say in the silence that ensued.

After some time, after reaching a quiet consensus, speaking as one again, the Maer'Din bowed their heads, answering, *"The H'era would be honored to receive your gift, Yip Chi Chuan. Pray that we never have to use it."*

He bowed in return.

Opening his mind and spirit to Uuraja and the Maer'Din, Yip gently placed the palm of his right hand on the forehead of each H'era in turn, imparting the knowledge of the Dragon's Gate, spending the rest of the evening sharing his apprehension of this form of energy creation and application, *xīnyì*, mind-to-mind, one dream given in another.

With time, cultivation, and practice, the H'era would be able to employ and train others in the ways of the Dragon's Gate, creating Darkness neutralizing Light from the boundless potential of the void, serving as a beacon against the iniquity of those like the Cabal.

When he awoke in the morning, Yip was buoyed by the knowledge that his friends' safety would be assured, in time, should they return home to Al'Marr or confront the Cabal's evil again. If the H'era remained on Ea'ae, in whole or in part, then the people of this land would have powerful allies against the Cabal.

Standing in the pale, early morning sunlight angling through the clear glass, he walked out of the sunroom to rejoin his friends. With any luck, he would hear from his master before day's end.

"Morning, Yip!" Slate was up early, deftly handling a sizzling frying pan filled with meats, onions, potatoes, and peppers imbuing the air with a rich, smoky haze. Knowing full well the answer, he asked, "Need some breakfast?"

Smiling, Yip answered, "Tea, perhaps."

"A hearty choice indeed!"

Apparently Aroganji and Wrindanneth had already eaten their share, for their plates rested on the countertop, empty of all food save the residue of grease and crumbs. Standing impatiently by the door, Wrindanneth waited on Slate to finish preparing and eating his portion before leaving to meet the Paratechnologists.

After Slate finally completed his third helping of sausage and potatoes, he stood grunting happily, and placed his plate by those of his friends. Not one to let anything go to waste, unlike Aroganji and Wrindanneth who were true gastronomic lightweights in his eyes, Slate used a loaf of bread to sop up all the drippings and grease before finishing with a resounding belch.

As they walked out of the kitchen, the now silent Aspect performed a simple spell to clean the dishes and silverware before returning them to the cabinet. Yip always enjoyed watching all the myriad applications people found for using magic. He had grown up having to do everything by hand. As such, all the small cantrips and spells in operation in the common home unfailingly caught his attention and wonder.

The last to leave the house, Slate secured the door behind him and asked, "Everyone ready?"

Wrindanneth smirked. "Would we have left otherwise?" He added curtly, "So long as you have the items from the ship."

Before Slate could answer, Aroganji quipped, "When have you ever known Slate not to carry everything he owns or needs inside that bag of his?"

Wrindanneth smacked his palm against his forehead in mock chagrin.

"Ya never know when ya're gonna need a lathe or vise, a tankard or smock, or, fer that matter, a proper hammer and chisel," responded Slate smugly.

As they made their way through the gate and into the street toward the magistrate's building, Wrindanneth replied, "What you're really saying is that all you need is a proper mule supply train in tow at all times?"

Face smooth and composed, no humor evident besides the twinkle in his eye, Slate answered, "No need, no need," as he patted the magical bag at his side. "Wouldn't want ta burden tha critters."

Within the hour, they had passed through the verdant, cobbled streets, crossed the Scimerian Gate, and entered the beautifully wrought magistrate's building set into the stone cliff face behind the docks.

Crossing the threshold into an expansive, lambent space, the same resonant disembodied voice that Yip remembered on their first visit greeted their arrival.

"Good morning, gentlemen. How may we be of service this morning?"

Wrindanneth spoke for the party. "We are here to do business with a group of Paratechnologists. Our meeting has been arranged through Adar."

Yip could almost see someone seated behind a desk nodding their head patiently, although this voice was certainly one part of the Construct's many functions.

Filling the chamber, the polite voice asked officiously, "And who, may I ask, is calling?"

Before Wrindanneth could answer with their names, Slate stepped forward proudly, chest out. "Tha Four o' tha Flamin' Fists!"

Wrindanneth's shoulders slumped and he shook his head slightly.

He had asked for this.

"Step forward to be scanned, 'Flaming Fists.'"

As the beams of magical energy washed over him, validating his identity, Wrindanneth thought he noted a certain smugness in the voice's tone, but no matter.

"Thank you, Aroganji, Wrindanneth, Slate, and Yip. The Paratechnologists await you. Please step forward."

A wall of light appeared coruscating in the air before them. Walking through the blinding luminescence, the party entered into another room entirely. As they emerged, arrayed before them about the multi-columned stone interior stood the most diverse assortment of sentient beings Yip had seen in one place to date.

Adar stood at their fore, the vague spatial distortion about him readily apparent to Yip's eyes. Behind him stood a Gnome, or rather the Gnome rested like a spider at the center of a series of well-honed mechanical appendages radiating out from his person in a halo of multifunctional limbs, apparatus, and gizmos. Immediately beside the Gnome stood, or rather floated, a clear, multi-faceted crystalline sentience of trilliant aspect, radiating soft ruby light. Next to the crystalline being loomed a hulking, stocky humanoid of muscular appearance with thick, coarse, pebbly skin, and a deeply furrowed brow akin perhaps to an Ogre's. However, unlike an Ogre, this being had a refined face with bright, intelligent eyes. About the creature's forehead, several glowing gemstones of various colors were embedded into the creature's skin. Covering the coarse skin across his entire body, or growing from it Yip could not tell, were a series of crystal platelets appearing to act very much like a set of contoured body armor. On the Gnome's other side floated a clear, translucent orb suspended at chest height above ground. Inside, a swirling ochre cloud seethed and roiled, continuously changing shape and direction. Finally, and most surprisingly given the current company, beside the sphere stood an older distinguished gentlemen of noble mien bedecked in a simple silk robe without embroidery or markings.

To Yip's inner vision, power surged and roiled through fields enveloping and commingling about the assembled Paratechnologists. In fact, the amount and types of forces embodied in these individuals varied across a broad spectrum of many varieties of energy he had never seen, much less felt localized in one place.

The Paratechnologists' puissance filled the room with a presence akin to an approaching storm—vast and encompassing.

"Good morning, gentlemen." Adar stepped forward and motioned for them to come farther into the chamber and be seated on a series of padded benches beneath a long windowed wall overlooking the open sky to one side of the island. Outside, clouds and blue sky mingled as far as the eye could see.

"Wrindanneth, Aroganji, Slate, and Yip, I would like you to meet Fizzlemiz." Adar's palm moved backward, indicating the Gnome who smiled as recklessly as his tousled hair upon introduction. "Embodied Cloven Crystallization of Refined Essence, a loose translation of the proper appellation I am afraid"—he gestured to the trilliant floating crystal which responded in a pulse of bluish light—"Dawrac di Gaydial"—moving to the Ogre-like creature who bowed gracefully at the waist—"Vapor of Golden Quintessent Life, again my apologies for the coarse translation"—moving to the swirling golden, umber cloud which contracted into a tiny golden point before re-expanding into its original form—"and Mazithras"—ending his presentation of colleagues with his hand denoting the older gentleman, who also bowed slightly at the waist.

Stepping forward, Mazithras began by laying the groundwork for their potential relationship should the items they possessed prove worthwhile, his voice cool and intelligent. "As you may be aware, Tellanon, and the Paratechnologists who are part of it, are part of a federation of interests intent upon the dissemination, development, and application of both knowledge and technology in all forms and guises. Much of this technology transfer comes through collaborative research, exploration, and trade in goods and ideas."

"Should the items you bring before us prove worthwhile, those parties among us who express interest in the resulting applications, be they guilds, peoples, collectives, enterprises, or nations, will have the opportunity to acquire anything we develop that they find to be of worth. As a result, you may be in a position to benefit both materially from the development of devices related to the items you discovered and financially from the proceeds of their sale."

He paused for a moment letting the import of his words sink in before extending a hand forward as if in invitation, when in reality he was requesting to examine the sword, orb, and shield that Adar had described to them. "I understand that you possess items that may be of interest to us?"

"Aye. We have several items that may be of value to your studies if, as Adar has indicated, you have never encountered their like." Wrindanneth motioned for Slate to present the agreed upon items to the Paratechnologists.

"Just a moment." Fumbling through his magical bag, Slate fished around for a minute, his face a model of studied concentration, arm in to the shoulder, until he finally grunted triumphantly, "Aha!" as he pulled out the crystalline sword. With a bit more effort, he managed to pull out the orb and energy shield as well.

"May we examine the items?" Mazithras held out a hand.

"Aye," making a move to step forward and carry the items over to the wizards, Slate stopped in mid-stride as the items floated from his grasp, eventually left to hover in front of the assembled Paratechnologists.

Much quicker than Yip would have thought possible based on the apparent complexity of the items, the Paratechnologists began their survey, breaking down, testing, cataloging, and ultimately understanding the items' functions.

While the Paratechnologists appeared to be merely standing around the objects passively observing them as they floated suspended in the air to his friends, Yip could see rapidly changing energies being applied to the items, as if music of multiple types, frequencies, and tones were being directed at the objects in the intricate patterns of a sublimely composed concert. The complexity, precision, and rapidity of the Paratechnologists' interactions with the items were truly striking, not just because of the level of skill involved but also due to the speed with which the group was apparently making inferences about the workings of the objects.

"You say the aliens who possessed these items were psychics? And you believe the items were somehow powered by psychic energy?" Fizzlemiz the Gnome started talking as soon as the three items settled in front of the group.

"Yes, to the best of our knowledge." Wrindanneth was more certain than he expressed, but he would let them decide for themselves.

Gesturing quickly to the translucent sword, only after a few moments of interaction via the magical symphonics observed by Yip, Fizzlemiz said, "Interesting. This item could embody a novel application of the piezoelectric effect in reverse. That is, using the direct application of mental energy, in lieu of oscillation induced by being subjected to electrical pressure or voltage, to generate rapid vibration in the sword's material. With sufficient energy and resulting engendered oscillations at high frequencies, the motion of the blade could cut through many very rigid compounds with only nominal risk to the sword itself. Couple that capability with the injection of psychic or magical energies and this would become a formidable weapon indeed."

Mazithras smiled briefly. "Fascinating! Have we employed this principle in a similar function prior?"

A brief flash of purple light filled the air around them and a voice filled the space within their minds with a combination of words, images, and ideas. "Although a known principle, with the inherent capability for direct psychic interaction between observer and object observed, such a device was never necessary for the Cloven Facets of the One Coalesced Crystalline Essence. If a similar result were desired as could be achieved by the application of such a blade, oscillation would be induced in the object itself in order to shear, cleave, stress, incise, or slice the material with the direct application of psychic force. Cumbersome, rudimentary instrumentation would not then be necessary."

A deep rumbling voice took up where the crystalline sentience ended as Dawrac spoke, "In the times of my people's youth when we waged war on all who opposed us, a device such as this may have been in service. However, in lieu of the application of psychic energy, as in this sword to induce vibration, my people would have employed the latent magical energies in and around us to achieve this purpose."

"The discrepancy between these two forms of energy, or rather the discrepancy between the two methods of interacting with energy potentially used to power such a device, is merely a matter of perception, however, as both 'psychic' and 'magical' energies are merely representative of different manifestations and usages of the same underlying fundamental forces."

Nodding, Fizzlemiz added, "However, as yet we are not decided as to how the sword itself operates beyond the principle of function. The crystalline material may serve to amplify the oscillations induced by psychic energy or it may serve to store the psychic energies of the bearer allowing for greater result. Or it may do both. In either case, based on my experience, both the material and the application have not been cataloged among our shared records."

"Any other comments?" Mazithras looked to each Paratechnologist in turn. "Then we are agreed that, although the principle of operation is not novel, the application and perhaps the material itself are, based upon our current repository of experience?"

Fizzlemiz answered, "We are agreed with Dawrac's exception."

"Initial assessment of the harmonic shielding device?"

Fizzlemiz answered Mazithras for the group, once again serving as a liaison for their quiet communication and evaluation. "The device appears significantly more complex than the psychic sword and warrants further investigation. We are agreed, per Adar's initial description, that the responsive protective field generated by the shielding system appears to react to and cancel the type of energy directed against it with certain limitations. We are not, as yet, certain of the principle of the shield's operation or of the device's replicability given our current experience."

"Does a similar judgment of valuation hold for the harmonic shielding device then?"

Again Fizzlemiz answered Mazithras's query. "It does."

Mazithras then asked, "Preliminary assessment of the energy orb?"

Dawrac spoke then, his deep voice direct and sure. "As previously noted, similar devices have been used in the past based upon magical principles rather than psychic ones. These objects have typically been employed by those who cannot manipulate magic directly with enough sophistication to generate the desired energetic effects and would, therefore, rely upon a device such as this to supplement their intrinsic abilities to create myriad energetic manifestations."

Mazithras then asked, "We are in agreement that such an item would have worth to us?"

Fizzlemiz then replied, "We share a similar evaluation."

Turning to the party, Mazithras said, "Thank you for bringing these objects to our attention, not only do they warrant further study, but I can foresee many applications of their principles and materials, especially for those who are not gifted in magical or psychic Craft. Given the covenants dictated by Tellanon law, will you allow us to study these objects further with the ultimate aim being replication and application of the devices and their inherent technologies?"

Understanding that Tellanon law protected their interest, discovery, and original ownership of the items, Wrindanneth answered, "We will."

Turning back to the group, apparently serving both as a spokesperson and intermediary, Mazithras asked, "Do these small items warrant further investigation of the alien vessel's command sphere as introduced and described by Adar?"

Again Fizzlemiz answered for his fellows, having decided this course in advance should the items show any merit. "They do."

"Then we are agreed to work toward understanding and deciphering the workings of and the knowledge contained within the exotic command sphere. Such work will be undertaken under the direct supervision of any representatives you choose. Your party will have equal access to any new knowledge and technical applications resulting from this study."

Turning to the Four he asked, "Are we agreed?"

Nodding with the pronouncement, Wrindanneth stated, "We are agreed."

"I trust that the orb has been sufficiently warded to prevent outside communication and interaction?"

"It has been."

Satisfied, Mazithras continued, "When would you have us begin the study of the command orb?"

"As soon as possible," was Wrindanneth's answer.

"Then we will meet here again on the morrow with the rising sun. You can bring the orb with you then. Who will be your representatives?"

"Aroganji and myself."

"Then we are agreed."

"Aye."

Mazithras nodded, adding, "Adar will be in contact with you when we are done with our survey of the sword, orb, and shield. He will also discuss appropriate remuneration from the proceeds of any developments directly resulting from or related to their study."

The bright curtain of light reappeared behind the party indicating their dismissal.

With a nod of his head, Mazithras said, "Until tomorrow," as the party stepped through the shimmering portal.

Reemerging on the other side, Slate fairly clapped his hands in excitement. "Tha stars are tha limit from here!"

"And that is a limit we should be ready to push," added Yip softly as they exited the stone building for the docks and home.

Reaching the docks, navigating through the thick crowds, and passing across the Weirding Gate, Wrindanneth could not be happier. Not only was it clear from the outset that they would have access to any technologies developed from their items, but they also could benefit from an established market for any devices or technologies developed from the Paratechnologists' research. Walking home, his mind was aglow with all the potential.

With little exposure to magical research, Yip was unsure how this process would move forward. Making their way through the cobbled streets, he asked, "Do you have any idea how long the Paratechnologists will take to unravel the secrets of the command orb?" Based on how quickly they had deciphered much of the information about the alien blade, he hoped their work would not take too long. However, the orb represented orders of magnitude greater complexity and was sure to have built-in protections against tampering and reverse engineering.

Aroganji answered for Wrindanneth who was still dreaming of their bright future—when riches and intellectual wealth cascaded down upon them and Maeth Onai rewarded him for his virtue and good fortune. "I cannot say, Yip. Most magical inquiry and research takes significant amounts of time. However, I have never seen an item identified, cataloged, and deciphered as quickly as those Paratechnologists were able to do. I am sure that no matter how long it takes, we will be impressed with the Paratechnologists' analytical speed and precision. I think we will also be satisfied with any results the Paratechnologists derive, or at least as satisfied as we could be given the uncertainty involved in the process."

"I would anticipate, however, that their work will take at least a few weeks to glean the information we require, if it is even available. As far as technical research goes, there may be lifetimes of work and research avenues possible as a result of the knowledge contained within the alien orb and the ship should the contents within prove as novel as we hope. Since Adar has not indicated otherwise, I would conjecture that the Paratechnologists have yet to encounter the alien beings that the Cabal enlisted to watch over Al'Marr."

"Looks like we'll have plenty o' time ta sharpen our axes before we set sail again," said Slate, who was still none too eager to get back on the *Shrike*.

When they returned home, Yip left his friends' company to remain outside while they went in for the day to plan for their next meeting with the Paratechnologists.

In lieu of practicing outside their cottage, he walked a short distance down the shaded lane until he found one of the neighborhood parks that were scattered so generously throughout Tellanon.

Opening the wrought iron gate set into a wall of stacked stone overhung by large shade trees and flowering vines, he entered a garden area bordered by mature forest stands with a large, open grassy field in the middle. Walking to the field's center, the grasses swishing against his shins as he moved forward, he found a spot as far away from the entrance and walls as possible. Finding his location satisfactory, he planted his feet firmly on the ground and brought his arms up, bent at the elbow before the waist as if holding a barrel.

Although the posture resembled one of many used in traditional *chi gung*, he was not practicing *chi gung* as he had been taught as he stood with the grass rippling against his legs in the wind, nor was he meditating, per se. He was taking the opportunity granted by the time they now had prior to their next voyage to continue the development and exploration of his changed abilities and sensibilities.

For the rest of the day, to an outside observer, he stood erect, poised and relaxed in the middle of the green. The sun's orbit overhead and the grasses' swaying at his shins provided the only discernible motion about him, leaving his shadow to pass the time on the grass, pivoting about his position. Despite the exterior calm, internally, however, he pushed the limits of his new abilities.

To begin, he gradually took in as much ambient energy as possible, feeling the *chi* first flow and then build within until he felt so full of radiant energy that if he took in any more, he would surely burst like a balloon, feeling as abounding and overflowing with refulgent Light as the sun. Over and over, in and out as naturally and fully as breathing, he absorbed energy through his whole being, imagining that he was soaking up the all the surrounding energies landing on his skin from the sun and stars, absorbing the universal, primordial *yuan-chi* all around, and taking in the ambient *chi* created by all sentient beings that moved between and within.

When he felt that he had reached his limits, that he could no longer perform this discipline effectively, he began a very similar exercise, except this time he practiced absorbing ambient energies as rapidly as possible, akin to seeing how rapidly he could inhale and fill his lungs with air. Taking special precautions to avoid harming those beings around him, over and over he forcefully drew in the surrounding energies as if at the center of a seething vortex, a black hole drawing all energy into its recesses implacably. He attempted to replicate the action, but not the result, in miniature of the *chi* vortex created by the Cabal before releasing the energies absorbed back into the world at large.

When he could tolerate this exercise no more, he practiced the reverse. Gradually filling himself with energy and then releasing the *chi* he had stored internally as quickly as possible, as if with a sudden out rush of air exhaled from his whole being. He imagined himself as a star exploding, releasing its light unto the cosmos in a controlled paroxysm of novate vibrancy.

After he could no longer perform this final explosive exercise in succession, he began cycling through each exercise individually, moving from first one to the next, as if working an internal bellows. Through this practice, replicating much of the action and effect of a bellows, he attempted not only to create a larger, hotter internal fire, but to refine the bellows itself so that the instrument, his body, could take in more and more energy, to tolerate hotter and hotter flames, to ultimately be able to cycle more and more *chi* thereby facilitating and magnifying the entire process of energy assimilation, manipulation and, if necessary, combustion.

As the sun began to set over the cobbled wall surrounding the green, he collapsed in the grass, exhausted and unable to continue. Standing slowly, head light from the exertion, he walked wearily back to the house, sure in the knowledge that he was working in the right direction, even if he had only just taken the first step in a very long journey. As the days moved on, he would take every opportunity to practice similarly, gradually refining and improving upon his skills, limits and techniques, recasting himself anew as had happened inside the Cabal's energy vortex, each and every day.

Slate greeted Yip when he reentered the house. "Takin' time ta relax and enjoy tha day?"

Smiling wearily, he answered, "Of a sort, I suppose. Taking time for a bit of practice."

"Ah! Perhaps I'll join ya tomorrow while those two go off and play with their new friends. My axe needs some time ta swing in tha fresh air. 'Course, once I bring out Duraeleon, all peace and quiet will leave yer practice."

"I doubt I would even know the difference, Slate, but you are welcome to join me as you see fit. The lawn is big enough for the both of us, I would say."

"Then tomorrow tha air will sing with tha whirl o' my blade and tha wind will burn with tha heat o' my heart!"

Bowing shortly from the waist, Yip replied, "I will look forward to your company, Slate. Now I must rest. I will see you when the sun crests the stone wall."

"Until then, Yip."

Yip stirred early in the morning, rising with the birdsong filling the air. He waited for Slate in the kitchen, knowing that his friend would not miss a meal prior to leaving.

"Mornin', Yip," said Slate as he ambled into the kitchen in full battle regalia. "Once Wrin and Aroganji get down, I'll be ready ta go." Grinning, he added, "'Course that gives me time fer a bit o' breakfast before they arrive."

Half an hour and several courses later, breakfast complete, happily patting his full stomach, Slate rose as Aroganji entered the kitchen with Wrindanneth in tow groggily clearing his eyes. "'Bout time ya louts got here. Ya gotta hurry or ya'll miss yer appointment."

"We've got plenty of time, Slate. The sky is still ruddy with dawn."

"Humph." Slate grunted in disagreement and disapproval.

"Take this." He held out his beloved magical bag for Wrindanneth to carry with him to their meeting. "Tha orb's inside. If ya happen ta bring out a cask o' ale while yer fishin' it out, set it aside. I've been lookin' fer that bit o' Heaven fer ages."

Aroganji laughed. "I will, Slate. That is if I can keep Wrindanneth from taking a few nips to stave off his thirst."

"Hey!" Wrindanneth snatched the bag from Slate's hands. "Who's to say I won't be fighting off Aroganji?"

Still teasing each other as they left the house, Wrindanneth and Aroganji made off for their meeting to unlock the orb's secrets.

"Ready now?"

"Aye," answered Slate, checking the buckles on his belt.

"Let's go. It's only a short walk to the park."

Yip retraced his steps to the open space where he had spent the better part of the day yesterday, eager to begin practice.

As they walked, Slate commented, "Nice ta have so many public areas ta enjoy around tha town. Per'aps one day I'll have time ta explore 'em all."

"A city mirrors the minds of its people. I am glad the people of Tellanon value their open space for natural areas such as these allow the spirit to repose in solitude and peace and the imagination to wander in freedom."

Cocking his head sideways, Slate joked with a half-smile, "If ya say so, Yip," before adding in all seriousness, "I agree."

Reaching the gate, it was Yip's turn to be confused, although he was not pretending as had Slate with his comment. Although the gate was exactly as he remembered it from the day before, the space it opened onto was entirely different. Beyond the wrought iron gate, a sandy path wandered through a forest dominated by mossy live oaks draped in Spanish moss, green beards reaching for the ground. Epiphytic bromeliads covered the trees along with resurrection ferns, mistletoe, and various species of lichens from gray to green to rainbow hued. Birdsong could be heard echoing through the luxuriant wood of oaks, hollies, junipers, pines, and magical species unknown to him.

Turning to Slate, Yip said, "This is not the park I visited yesterday."

Nodding, Slate responded, "Seems like a poor place ta practice swingin' an axe, if ya ask me, lest ya want some wood fer tha fire."

"Let us try another, then."

As they walked through the streets, Yip thought on what he had just seen. He had yet to visit the same park several times over a long period of time since they had only remained in Tellanon for a brief period prior to setting out for Al'Marr. Perhaps each park gate served as a door or portal to another place. Maybe these portals acted very much like windows or doors to new locations, new destinations, and as time passed, so did the view.

If that were the case, the transition in destination provided by the park portals could be seen as analogous to the view provided by the windows in a house. Each window in a home allowed the residents look out on the world at different times through the day and passing seasons, only in the case of the house the view from a window was generally of the same place. Using this interpretation, Tellanon may be very much like a house, except one whose windows opened up to an ever-changing temporal and spatial landscape.

Or, a better analogy may be viewing Tellanon as a moving vessel. Although the vessel's interior remains the same, the view seen from the island itself, the landscape it passes through and over changes, whether viewed outside the city walls or inwardly through the passing park landscapes.

Whatever the analogy, the effect remained remarkable.

Talking aloud, he added, "Fascinating."

"Could get a bit confusin' if ya want ta retrace yer steps. Maybe tha next park'll bring us better luck."

"We shall see," responded Yip.

The next open space did indeed offer a locale more amenable to their needs. Passing through a solid oaken door etched with a symbol of the half-moon surrounded by a smattering of stars, the portal, for now he no longer thought of the park entrances merely as gates, opened onto a beautiful alpine vista. High, snow-capped peaks framed the view of craggy summits lost in the dazzling sunlight. Immediately beyond the gate, however, an alpine meadow filled with asters, paintbrush, and hellebore, among many other magical and mundane plants, swayed in colorful profusion.

Cautiously treading through the vegetation, careful so as not to disturb the beauty of the place, Yip relaxed into position while Slate began warming up for practice with his axe. Keeping his eyes open, putting off his own practice to observe for a time, he watched Slate unsheathe his blade to Duraeleon's disgruntled sigh. "Can't ya see I'm sawin' timbers? When can an axe get some sleep around here?"

Slate snarled, "Time ta work, ya lazy lump o' coal!"

"I'll have you know that I am fashioned from some of the finest ores known in existence. In fact, my lineage is as proud as any on Ea'ae. Unlike yours, I might add, you mangy half-Orc." Still fuming from Slate's insult, Duraeleon continued his reprimand over the next several minutes.

Ignoring the axe's banter, Slate began whirling the blade about him, his face relaxed, his limbs loose, spinning and whipping the weapon faster and faster in fluid arcs. As he spun and the intensity of his motion heightened, Yip noticed that his spirit grew more and more intense, ever brighter and hotter, as energy coalesced and built with each deadly twist and slice, each lunge, counter, and parry. By the time sweat began to bead on his brow, a heavy fog of steam hovered about Slate's stout shoulders from the radiant heat and power he had built up within.

Axe whistling in a seething frenzy, Slate moved at ease at the center of a deadly furor.

Finally stopping, his motion settling slowly down, the whirlwind of violence he had observed gradually losing its axis and spin, he watched Slate's spirit gradually cool and settle, returning to normal. While Slate took deep breaths recovering himself, Yip observed, "The enemies of Dwarves must rue the day they have to join battle with your kin."

Snarling savagely, Slate grunted, "Tha foes o' tha Bor'Banna seldom live ta tell tha tale o' our wrath!"

Curious for his friend's interpretation, his perspective on his lore, Yip asked, "What is it about the Bor'Banna that separates them from other Dwarven wielders of the axe?"

"Ha! I ask ya, 'What separates a lamp from the sun?'"

"The intensity of its blaze, the heat of its fires, among many other qualities," was Yip's direct answer.

"Aye, such is tha case with tha Bor'Banna fer, among all tha Dwarves, with tha exceptions o' tha mighty Baera'Dur and anointed priests granted Brendle's Light, tha heat o' Brendle's original forge flows only through our veins. As I take tha haft o' my axe in hand and tha fury o' battle heats my blood, tha fires stoked within by Brendle's original flames travel through me and along my blade, and then my foes know tha meaning o' fear. It is Brendle's fire that gives us our might, protects us from harm, and strikes down foes that other mortals fear."

With a slight nod of his head, Yip said, "Brendle has given you quite a gift."

Nodding, Slate asked, "And what o' you, Yip? Ya've been as tight-lipped about yer arts as yer teacher. I've been truly impressed by what I've seen of yer ways as well. Tell me o' yer fightin' style, if you will."

Even though many practitioners of the martial ways are loath to describe their practice for fear of giving away their secrets, trade in knowledge was often given in kind when the opportunity presented. Yip never feared talking about his art, if asked, for ultimately successful application depended upon years of specialized training and practice.

Mere descriptions would never convey any true secrets.

Even secrets took time and practice to fully realize.

"Hold your arm up next to mine, Yip."

He and Master Wei stood amid the decorative plants and trees interspersed around the cobbled stone pathways of an interior reflection garden within the high rock walls of the monastery. Rocks carefully chosen for their semblance to natural features were artfully placed and arranged so as to create an illusionary landscape of the mind, a place that hearkened to and evoked impressions of the natural world but that did not fully bridge the gap.

Stones chosen for their likenesses to mountains, streams, cascades and other environmental features were shaded by trees and shrubs sculpted to resemble the ephemeral shapes and impressions of clouds caught for the briefest moment in stillness. The loose pebbles shifting beneath their feet marked a pathway wending between the arranged formations with the subtle naturalness of a river fed by glacial melt from the peaks above.

Master Wei held his arm outward and diagonal to his torso indicating that he should do likewise.

Copying his teacher's motion, he brought his arm upward allowing the palm of his hand to point inward toward his face. As he did so, the sleeve of his robe fell downward to the crook of his elbow leaving his forearm exposed to the chill air of the high mountains.

"Bring your arm forward."

He did so until the back of his arm rested against the soft skin of his master's forearm.

Holding their arms crossed and connected just below the wrist, Master Wei looked deeply into his eyes. His teacher's eyes were like those of a cavern leading inward into the uncharted bowels of the surrounding peaks—cool and dark, depthless and calm, gateways to hidden mysteries.

He felt a slight tension as Master Wei pushed his wrist lightly against Yip's.

"Can you read my intention, Yip?"

Feeling the gentle pressure between them, his awareness simultaneously on his arm and the connection between them, his eyes shifted from Master Wei's to his own wrist.

"I think so, master."

Master Wei gently dropped his arm to his side breaking the connection linking them, his robes rustling and falling about his wrist as he did so. The compact graceful motion resembled nothing more than the soft descent of a feather, although the same gesture would be equally effective warding off or initiating an attack.

His arms at rest lightly by his sides, the connection between them severed, Master Wei then asked, "Can you read my intention now, Yip?"

Smiling at the memory, he said, "We call our way Xīnyìquán, which roughly means 'mind-to-mind fist', 'mind-to-mind boxing', or 'mind-intent boxing' in the common tongue, though others sometimes call our practice Qìxīnquán, 'life energy-mind boxing.'"

Yip paused for a time before continuing, feeling the cool breeze coming off the mountainside rustling his robes and rippling through the plants in the meadow. "Look out upon the grasses and flowers of this field, Slate. Imagine you wish to anticipate their motion."

"Can you read the wind? Can you see its flow?"

Slate took a moment to survey the alpine meadow, watching the plants ripple and wave. With a snap of his wrist, Yip's hand flashed out, whipping from his robe, snapping to a stop just in front of Slate's nose. "Now imagine that you wish to anticipate the motion of my strike. Can you read my intent?"

Slate stared at the fist held checked right before him.

With a chuckle, he said, "Ya can put that thing away, Yip."

"Xīnyìquán teaches us how to read the wind, Slate. We learn to feel, react to, and counter an opponent's intent before it is expressed."

"Just as you may learn to read an opponent's body language to anticipate and counter an offensive—perhaps following his eyes, shoulders, feet, weapon, or center—we learn to read an opponent's intent—his essence, his spirit, his energies individually and as part of the universal flow—before acting thereby countering, redirecting, and nullifying our opponent's intent before he is given the chance to fully express his will."

"The more complete the perception, the sooner and more complete the counter."

"Ours is a way of reading and restoring harmony where it would be broken, before our opponent ever has an opportunity to present and manifest a disturbance that would do us or others harm."

"So ya're sayin' ya read yer opponent's mind?" Slate was skeptical, more so because Yip had never discussed such abilities.

He laughed. "No, I cannot read your mind or anyone else's, Slate, but I can watch you express and manifest internal and external energies. I can see you gathering and moving your internal forces within, I can see the excitation and transference of impulses through your nervous system, I can see you inter-acting with energies outside your body, among many other impressions. I can feel, interpret and anticipate the movement of these and other energies as well."

"I sense the expression of your actions as part of the natural movements and living energies around us. When an event disrupts the natural or implicit order, a practitioner of Xīnyìquán is able to nullify the disturbance."

When Slate's brow remained knotted in thought, he added, "In a way, our practice is like learning to read a person's face or body language to discern their emotions or to determine the veracity of their words. Except I see and feel the energy moving behind their actions as well. There is a large degree of empathy in that interaction, true. Such sensations do lead to heightened feelings of compassion as well. But no, I cannot read your mind nor would I wish to for that matter. A man deserves the solace and quietude of his own mind, for if peace cannot be found there, then it is not to be had."

They both sat enjoying the park, the feeling of the day, the beauty of the place, for some time before Slate broke the silence again.

Still curious, Slate asked, "Is that all, Yip?"

Yip smiled at his friend's curiosity, for he could see why Slate made such a good student of his own art. "No, Slate. Xīnyìquán is but a single facet of our way, one small aspect of a large, multi-faceted diamond, a jewel that shines forth with the Light transmitted from within and without."

"Long ago, some of those outside of our sect branded our internal practice Lung-hu-i tao, the way of the Dragon and tiger. The Dragon and tiger represent the principles of commingling, interdependent opposites, the fusion and transformation of internal energies, the ceaseless flow from potential to actual, the expression and movement of and from the underlying universal source, among many other things. Our way is an alchemical tradition steeped in efforts toward transformation, actualization, and realization."

"Sounds a bit more involved than simple fisticuffs."

"The deeper one delves into any tradition, the greater the complexity."

Lost in thought, Slate watched as Yip began his exercise in stillness.

As Slate sat, he felt more than the breeze rush by.

The room was much as Wrindanneth remembered, the marble columns, the expansive windows looking out upon the breadthless view of the open, cloudless blue sky, the ornate, if understated, decorations, and the motley band of Paratechnologists waiting for their arrival. There was the Gnome who looked like he had been caught in the midst of a metallic spider's web, albeit one of his own choosing, the glowing crystalline light bulb giving off a rosy hue indicating something of his mood, the rocky ogre savant looming over his fellows, the amber sphere that looked like an object best suited for indoor décor in a wizard's tower, a piece of magical interpretative art perhaps, the elder statesman commanding his fellows' attention, and Adar putting a kind face on the whole proceedings.

There was, however, one glaring difference now. In the room's center, a shimmering translucent cube of force thrummed with untold power. To Wrindanneth, from what he could decipher of the workings and weave of its enchantments, the field appeared to be a cage suitable for the capture and containment of powerful extradimensional beings.

"Good morning and welcome!" Mazithras opened his arms receptively.

"Glad to be back," answered Wrindanneth with a slight nod in acknowledgement.

"Are you ready to get started?" asked Adar, clearly eager to begin.

"We are," responded Aroganji.

"Do you have the orb?"

"We do."

"Please bring it forward."

"One moment please," Wrindanneth wanted to have a quiet word with Aroganji before the morning's work began.

Wrindanneth took a moment before reaching into Slate's bag, quickly contacting Aroganji through the magical bracers they each wore to do just that.

"Everything check out fine?" Even though Wrindanneth doubted any foul play was afoot, he wanted to make certain his impressions were reflected by those of his friend.

"Yes. If we were not bringing the orb and I saw that box of force, I would think we had stepped into a trap and would have left before any words were uttered from Mazithras's mouth."

"Good. Then let's begin," said Wrindanneth, breaking off direct contact with Aroganji.

He reached into Slate's bag blindly, spending more time than he would have wished feeling for the orb as the Paratechnologists watched impassively. Finally, when he thought to command the orb to his hand, he felt the faint thrum of power from the orb's ward brush against his outstretched fingertips. He wondered if Slate had ever figured that little trick out given how long he usually fumbled around for items when he retrieved them from the bag. Slate may not have the faculty to command the bag since he did not cast, weave, and channel spells as did a wizard. Or, smiling inwardly at the thought, he may not have the requisite focus to do so.

The spell shielding the orb lit the lip of the bag and its murky interior as he pulled it from the shaded depths. No other objects were visible within the pitch blackness partially revealed by the orb's warding.

Soft luminescence filled the air as he carefully brought the orb forth toward Mazithras.

"I am glad to see you have the sphere warded so well. We would not want to grant the orb or its owners any opportunity to interact with the Construct's systems."

"Please place the sphere within the sequestration field. Do not allow your hands to touch the control field, just guide the orb through."

Walking forward, Wrindanneth stopped in front of the translucent cube. Reaching out, he felt a faint resistance as the leading edge of the orb's circumference passed through the field's barrier.

"Give it a slight push."

As he did so, the command sphere floated gently into the center of the containment field.

When he stood back from the force field, Mazithras said, "The field serves to completely isolate whatever we place inside its boundaries. In the case of the command orb, the isolation field prevents any interaction with the larger macroverse outside of the limits defined by the field."

"Within the confines of the sequestration field, however, the command orb will be able to run and perform its functions completely albeit within a limited, controlled domain, one suitable for study and interaction. The beauty of the containment field is that we can interact with the orb in a controlled manner from the outside and then study its reactions and properties. As our familiarity and eventual control of its functions increases, we will be able to release the strictures currently governing its actions and allow two-way functionality."

He added, "Although the Construct has many complicated defenses and capabilities of its own, we do not wish to risk any of its facets to an alien command device of unknown capacities. Once you drop the wards guarding the orb, this field will also prevent the sphere from transmitting information of any sort beyond the field's bounds. This stricture includes thwarting it from interacting with or attempting to subvert any functions of the Construct, should the orb have invasive capabilities."

To Aroganji, through the link allowed by the bracers, Wrindanneth said, *"This guy likes to talk."*

Aroganji retorted, *"Don't you?"*

Chuckling silently, Wrindanneth said, *"True enough."*

Aloud, Wrindanneth said, "What do we do now?"

"Dissolve your protective barrier around the orb. Then we watch."

With a muttered command and a series of intricate gesticulations, Wrindanneth dropped the luminous lamina of force encasing the crystalline sphere.

The command sphere immediately disappeared.

"What?" Wrindanneth's jaw dropped.

"Hold your concern, Wrindanneth." Fizzlemiz spoke calmly and muttered an elaborate incantation.

The orb partially reappeared, its appearance smoky and vacuous, vague and indistinct under the influence of Fizzlemiz's spell.

"The orb attempted to port and, failing that, disappeared."

Nodding, Wrindanneth said, "It has stealthing abilities just like the alien ship."

A low rumble came from Dawrac. "Aye. We shall see what other secrets it holds. Let me clarify its functions." Another series of complex incantations followed in Dawrac's deep baritone.

The space within the sequestration field filled with a bright flash of light following the completion of Dawrac's spell.

Its functions, its energetic expressions and emanations, now visible, multiple flashes of energy radiated from the orb in rapid succession. A series of low pulses periodically followed this initial outburst, as if the orb were trying continually to communicate or establish contact with something beyond the field's confines.

Maintaining the pulsing flashes that Wrindanneth interpreted as some form of communication, the orb continued its activity. A translucent wave of green light then scanned the six sides of its cubic confines over and over serially as the orb attempted to interact with and determine the properties of its confines. A deep heliotrope beam then shot out from the orb, boring into the field in an attempt to break its hold on the sphere, to no avail.

Failing that, another series of bright indigo flashes exploded out from the orb, impacting all of the field's walls concussively with no effect. Switching back to the intense beam, the orb rapidly cycled through a series of every color of light conceivable in various intensities, blasting the confinement field at a localized point in an attempt to find a weakness in its properties by particular wavelength, amplitude, and frequency. Over and over, the orb tried different approaches to break free from its confines.

Wrindanneth was impressed.

The Paratechnologists were making the orb's functions visible for their benefit. He also realized how lucky they had been that the orb had not escaped from them, for it must have been making similar attempts the entire time he had it warded and stored within Slate's bag. Wrindanneth had no doubts that with time, the orb would have found a way out of his own much simpler confinement.

Mirroring his concerns, Fizzlemiz cautioned, "You were lucky that you trapped the orb within your wards immediately while on the alien ship. If you had not, the orb would have warped away, alerting whomever it is currently trying to communicate with to your position and activities. If you were especially unlucky, once it escaped, it may have done worse." Fizzlemiz left the threat hanging in the air to caution Wrindanneth and Aroganji in the future.

Adar spoke next. "Now we watch and catalog the sphere's attempts to escape and interact with its environs. We will learn much of the orb's function and capabilities, of the technology of the people who designed it, and of the orb makers' views of the universe—what principles they know of, believe in, and command through their technical arts—merely by observing this object's operation."

"The Construct will record and begin to analyze all of the command orb's activities, as well. This will significantly shorten the time we will need to understand the sphere's principles of operation and help us choose the best direction to take in our attempts to unlock its secrets."

"You will just let it run then?"

"For now," Mazithras answered confidently. "We need as complete a picture of its capabilities as possible. If the orb continues to reveal itself to us in such a way, there is no need as yet to interfere. Depending on how the sphere behaves, we will decide when to start interacting with it based on our understanding of its methods of operation."

Wrindanneth and Aroganji spent the rest of the morning observing the alien orb with the Paratechnologists, listening to their interpretations and musings about the orb's activities before finally returning home after mid-day. As had been agreed, they would return on the morrow.

"Place your palm on my wrist." The soft breeze off the mountains stirred the hairs of Slate's beard and head just as they stirred the tall grasses and small hairs on his thick arms.

Yip felt Slate's callused hand grip his arm firmly as though he were grabbing the pommel of a great axe. Smiling, Yip said, "Lightly. Just touch my skin with the palm of your hand, so softly that you don't even touch the skin on my arm, only the hairs between us."

When Slate's pressure lightened, Yip nodded. "Better."

"Close your eyes."

"Why?"

"You are here to sense not look."

Slate shut his eyes somewhat reluctantly, not wishing to lose sight of his sparring partner at any time. Such caution had been instilled in him deeply over a long period of time in his martial practice, usually with the butt or face of an axe.

"Move as I move. Feel my motions and follow. Do not break contact. Do not anticipate or guess. Relax and become aware."

Keeping his eyes closed, Slate nodded. "Aye."

Moving slowly at first but gradually gaining in speed with Slate's improvement in following, the numbers of his missed motions and broken contacts decreased steadily over time. All the while, Yip moved his arm up and down, side-to-side, rotating and twirling, testing Slate's limits. As time passed and Slate's comfort grew, Yip began to vary the speed and rhythm of his movements pushing Slate's ability to remain in contact with his skin to its utmost.

When Slate finally began to show a certain level of comfort and relaxed manner with the practice, appearing much more at ease and responsive, Yip stopped and returned to the original neutral starting posture with his forearm outstretched between them.

"Why're ya stoppin'?"

Yip smiled. "Because we are done."

"What was that?"

"That was a form of Tuio Shou, pushing or sensing hands. It teaches you how to move with, and in its higher forms, counter your partner's motions and energies."

"And that is one way ta teach tha readin' o' intent?"

Yip nodded again. "When you are able to follow your partner's motions with your eyes closed without touching, then you have taken the first steps to reading and discerning an opponent's intention."

Slate nodded gravely. "Will ya teach me how?"

Yip smiled once more. "Who can say what the morrow will bring?"

Yip and Slate arrived home in the early evening to find Wrindanneth and Aroganji already there busily at work. Not wishing to waste idle time, the two had been outfitting the lab behind the house with a few of the necessary accessories for alchemical and magical research—vials, alembics, retorts, assorted basic reagents, crucibles, and sundry items of indeterminate purpose. By the time Yip and Slate arrived, they had gathered enough raw materials from Hoyt's shop to attempt a few of the more challenging incantations from Ydrael Faer'Leirn's tome.

"How'd yer meetin' go?" called Slate when he saw them in the back, the door to the tidy stacked stone lab cracked behind them, casting its shadow out onto the yard.

"Well enough I suppose," answered Wrindanneth indifferently. "They are well on their way to cataloging the orb's many functions. Hopefully, we'll be able to start actively testing and deciphering its knowledge soon, but that could still be several days out yet."

"Or more."

Aroganji chimed in, "We shall return tomorrow and as many days as is necessary. The Construct is also hard at work trying to elucidate the orb's function. With any luck, we will return greeted by some new insights in the morning."

"What are you two up to?" asked Wrindanneth.

"Honing our skills," answered Yip.

"Tryin' not ta get lost," replied Slate.

"Ha! Sounds like your morning was as interesting as ours!" Wrindanneth was glad to hear his friends had made good use of their time as well.

"We'll probably do tha same in tha days ta come," replied Slate slyly. "Assumin' our park doesn't run away on us again."

"What?" asked Aroganji.

"Apparently the public parks we pass shift from location to location over time," answered Yip. "So you never know where you are going to go or see when you visit one."

"Interesting. I'll make it a point never to leave anything in one then," replied Wrindanneth with a sardonic smile.

"Oh... Here's your bag, Slate," said Wrindanneth proffering the small sack. "No ale I'm afraid."

Slate sighed as he took the bag and strapped it back to his waist. "Thought as much. Maybe it went tha way o' my last barrel."

"Where's that?"

"Got lost in my gullet after a night o' ribald debauchery!"

"Out of curiosity, Slate, do you try to call upon or summon the items you're looking for when you pull them from the bag?"

"'Course I do!" was Slate's smug answer. "That's why I get what I'm after so quickly!"

Wrindanneth merely shook his head as he turned and reentered the lab with Aroganji on his heels.

Left alone with Yip again, Slate asked, "What're yer plans fer tha evenin'?"

"I will sit beneath the stars, I think."

"Hmm…sounds pretty excitin'. Guess I'll check out tha local pubs. All this talk o' ale has gotten me thirsty. I'll look fer ya in tha mornin'."

"Have a good evening, Slate."

As Slate headed back into the house, Yip settled in beneath a tall oak in preparation for the evening. Closing his eyes to the misty swath of stars resolving above, he heard the door shut behind his stout friend. With his eyes closed, the view was as dark as the emptiness left between the celestial bodies above after the stars' and planets' coalescence and formation.

In his mind, however, constellations yet shone all around.

He sat in silence for some time, night deepening all around, the argent light of the stars lending the folds of his robes a platinum cast. So serene was his contemplation, only the gentle rise and fall of his stomach and chest gave any indication that he was alive.

Letting his mind drift while maintaining awareness of his breath, he slipped into the world of dreams. Images came and went like the clouds occasionally obscuring the stars above. He let these impressions go just as easily, his awareness clear and sharp behind the permutations of his sleeping mind.

He sat in stillness as the moon rose and fell in the sky above. Finally, unbidden, in the last hour before dawn, he felt a familiar presence as a voice called out to him.

"May the light of a new dawn guide your steps, Yip."

"Master!" His joy lit the distance between them.

"I trust you are well, Yip?"

"I am, master. How are the others?"

"We are working to build hope where the Cabal wishes to incite fear and destruction."

"Other priests are venturing out?"

"There are a few whose tasks lead them to wander the lands once more."

With a slight nod of his head, Yip replied, *"Then I have a gift for them, should they need it."*

"Oh?" Although he could not yet see his teacher, he could almost feel him raise his eyebrows with interest.

Unable to contain his excitement any longer, for he burned to spread what he had learned, what they had accomplished, he continued with an enthusiasm he seldom showed even to his close friends. *"I may have found a way to undo the Cabal's evil, master!"*

He first felt his teacher's smile as something distant—the light of the sun hidden behind clouds on an overcast day. Then, with a sense of warmth and overwhelming compassion, he saw his master slowly materialize before him, first shimmering in the air like the heat haze on the horizon on a dry summer's day before finally gaining some semblance of solidity.

Then he felt Master Wei's smile in person.

"I never doubted you or your determination, Yip."

Yip bowed his head at the rare praise.

"May I show you, master?" He wanted permission to share his thoughts, feelings, and insights directly with his teacher mind-to-mind. He also wanted to transmit what he had learned and experienced of the Cabal's evil so that his teacher could pass on the knowledge much as he had done with the H'era. He would not presume to make such contact without his teacher's permission.

Master Wei smiled slightly and bowed his head.

Stepping forward, he carefully placed both hands on the sides of his teacher's face, letting his finger's rest on Master Wei's temples. Then, closing his eyes as if conjuring a dream within a dream, he let the experiences of his journey to Al'Marr flow through his mind and into his teacher's—a stream of experience freed from the moorings of his own mind.

He let everything he had seen and felt course through the connection between them, keeping nothing hidden from the eyes of his teacher. From the early preparations for their journey to his nearly fatal encounter with the swirling energy void, from his transformation to his rebirth, from his arduous recovery and rebuilding to their return to Tellanon, a bridge of shared knowledge and experience was built through his hands and across their minds.

He knew not how long the transfer took, but by the time he had finished, he felt drained and exhausted, having given more of himself than he would have wished. Master Wei, on the other hand, appeared as he always did in Yip's eyes, luminous and at peace, a body of Light in human form.

Even so, despite his newfound fatigue, he saw the bright glow of happiness and pride that filled his teacher's eyes.

Master Wei bowed. "You have done the people of Ea'ae and beyond a great service, Yip."

Yip bowed his head in silence once again.

"You have grown much and accomplished more since we last met, Yip. Unfortunately, I fear this knowledge will serve us, and countless others, only too well."

Again, Yip remained silent, for he had nothing to add.

"May I show you what I see, Yip?" Catching him a bit off-guard, now Master Wei asked for his permission just as he had done with his teacher.

He gave a slight nod. "Of course, master."

Gently resting his fingertips in the air near Yip's temples, his fingers never touching Yip's skin, Master Wei said, "Close your eyes, Yip."

Bowing his head slightly, he closed his eyes and waited.

In the distance, after a short period of time, he heard his teacher's voice oddly as if it came from his own mouth. "Open your eyes, Yip."

When he did, he beheld himself standing with his eyes open directly ahead. Confused, he blinked. He was looking through Master Wei's eyes upon his own form!

"What do you see, Yip?"

His internal vision acute, sharper than he had ever known, he examined himself from head to foot, seeing more than he had ever imagined possible, more clearly than any mirror. His body appeared largely devoid of *chi*, empty, without channels, meridians, gates or reserves.

"Just a man, master."

"Now fill yourself with *chi*, Yip."

As he did so, he saw himself become a being of Light, radiant and pure, his physical form lost in a nimbus of refulgent light and energies.

"What do you see now, Yip?"

"I see the same man, master, now luminous."

He felt the connection between them gently broken. Blinking, he once again looked out through his own eyes at his teacher. Master Wei's energy gates and meridians gleamed and sparkled, transferring Light and life, joined together and linked within and without like the constellations above.

"I see a man as well, Yip, a man on his own path."

"What do you mean, master?"

Now it was Master Wei who did not answer.

He sat for a time in silence, taking the opportunity to dwell on what his teacher had taken such care to show him.

Master Wei had reminded him of what he had already known deep within the chambers of his heart of hearts. In time, if he was ultimately going to be successful in his quest to overthrow the Cabal, he would have to leave the way of his forebears and strike out on a new path, one with unknown destinations and unforeseen means to that nebulous end. He would have to reinvent himself and the teachings he had been given if he were to meet with success when facing the Cabal. For, despite all their prowess and insight, the ways of his spiritual ancestors, the practices of his teachers, were also the way, or the beginnings of the way, for the Cabal. The methods and teachings of the K'un Lun were well known, internalized, and explored by the founders of the Cabal and their ilk. At best, at the height of their powers, his teachers and those before them had only fought the Cabal to a draw, expelling them from Ea'ae but no more.

His rebirth and transformation within the fires of the Cabal's vortex had given him just such an opportunity.

A sudden, unexpected upsurge of emotion overwhelmed him as feelings of love and gratitude rushed through and overtook his senses. Tears streaming down his cheeks, he bowed to his teacher for all the warmth and wisdom, effort and guidance he had given to his young, often headstrong, almost always obtuse student.

Bowing deeply from the waist, he finally managed, "Thank you, master," between faint sobs.

"Yip, I am not owed thanks."

Letting the tears continue to roll down his cheeks, he gazed with deepest respect and appreciation upon his teacher, the one man among many who had given him love, guidance, compassion, and opportunity.

"There is one thing I would tell you before you once again step upon this path to your destiny, Yip, leaving my teachings behind forever, a student no more."

"Master! I will always be your student!"

Master Wei smiled. "You are my student no longer, Yip. Have you not seen that already, having left the path I set you upon so long ago in the days of your youth?"

When Yip bowed his head slightly in acquiescence, Master Wei said, "The time has come for you to find your own answers, Yip. As you now do."

"Do not fear, I will only be a short space away should you need me. If you are truly in need, you have only to look inward to find me, Yip."

Master Wei smiled and added, "You may now call me as you would a friend."

When Yip's head remained bowed as he spoke, Master Wei joked, lifting Yip's spirits, "You have not traveled so far that there is not still more that I can show you!"

Looking into his teacher's eyes, Master Wei said, "You have accomplished more than I ever hoped, Yip, more than any before you, for none have been able to overcome the fullness of the Cabal's evil once manifest."

"You have discovered a way to undo the evils that the Cabal have created, something no man has lived to achieve. Restoring peace where the Cabal brings destruction is a triumph, nonpareil. Your success is the realization of the goal we all strove so mightily to achieve, but, even so, it may not help you when you are forced to face the Cabal directly."

Shaking his head gravely, Master Wei intoned, "The Cabal is strong. They have spent whole ages dedicating themselves to power, strength, and destruction. You should never seek to overcome strength with strength or force with force in your meetings with the Cabal, Yip. Such a path will lead to your end as well."

He nodded in understanding. "What must I do, master?"

"There is another way, one that offers hope if you continue along it. That way embodies the root, the full spirit, of our teachings, neglected and forgotten by the Cabal as they left us so long ago seeking after power. You must seek to embody *shuǐ lù xiàn*, the way of the water's course, Yip."

Listening intently, he watched and internalized his teacher's words. "Water embodies *wu wei* and nonresistance. Water gives of itself without being taken. Opposing no one, it cannot be confronted. Giving way to the blade, it cannot be cut. Grasp it with your hand and it flows through. Yielding without resistance, it becomes invulnerable. Drink from it and gain in strength."

"You must learn to become essenceless, that your enemy has no target. You must learn to yield without effort, that your opponent's force finds no home. Then, and only then, will the path of nonresistance become strength. When you are empty of energy and presence, your foes' strikes will be as your own. His essence will be yours to redirect and channel at will. The stronger your foe, the greater your power."

"Your transformation has taken you far along this path, Yip. You are as empty as the breeze, as full as the night sky. You need only take the next step."

He had remained in silence for some time while Master Wei spoke. Now he asked of his teacher, unsure of the answer, "How shall I proceed, master?"

Master Wei smiled serenely, his eyes tinged with feeling. "That is for you to discover, Yip, for this is your path, one that has not been walked to its end as you must do now."

"How will I know that I am on the right track, that my efforts bear fruit?"

"When you can feel your opponent's energy and intention as an extension of your self, your goal will be in sight. When you can redirect and channel their power from afar, your goal will be in hand."

"How is this new way different from the old, master? Do we not already practice these principles and techniques every day, as they underlie the heart of our art?"

"You are correct, Yip. In a sense, what I propose, what you are doing, is no different than the arts learned and applied in Xīnyìquán. The path itself has not, as yet, been fully blazed, however. Yours is the task to apply our teachings and skills in a new direction, extending and expanding these principles on another level. One not yet reached by any before you."

Incredulous, he fairly stammered, "You are asking me to do something that you cannot?"

A bright peal of laughter bridged the gap between them. "Does the tree complain that it cannot fly? Does the moon burn like the sun?"

"Until this meeting when our minds touched, was I able to manifest the power of the Dragon's Gate?"

"There is much that I cannot do, just as there is much I have not tried, Yip. The same holds for you."

"My apologies for the disrespect, master. There was none intended."

Master Wei chided, "Curiosity is never disrespectful, nor is it a burden. To answer the intent of your question, much of what I ask you to do and learn, I can in fact do, Yip, but I have reached my limits and can go no further."

"If you would know my limits, the energy of life flows through and within me without break or barrier, there is no distinction felt between self and other, nor can a foe's energies touch me for I can redirect energy at will. I cannot, however, make this energy my own and return it to its source. It is this last step, the one I am unable to take myself, that I ask you to endeavor, Yip."

Master Wei smiled brightly with deep, joyous sincerity. "As you have moved where none have moved before, there is more you may yet do. Surprise me, Yip!"

His voice steely with determination, knowing how many lives, how many worlds, would be impacted by his failure, or his success, he said, "I will succeed, master, for there is no alternative."

Master Wei bowed to Yip, a brief smile passing over his lips as he did so. "Yours is a Light that burns brightly, Yip. Let it shine."

Bowing to his teacher, for he would always feel that profound, heartfelt connection with Master Wei, knowing that his teacher would always provide ever deeper lessons to apprehend, new perspectives and frontiers to consider, he answered, "May peace be your every step, master."

With that, Master Wei bowed and disappeared into the night, the ghost of a smile highlighting his face, lost, like so many other dreams, to memory.

Returning to the house, the pale light of dawn soft on his dew-covered shoulders, Yip pondered his teacher's words. He felt reassured that his inclinations, without further guidance from his teachers or peers, had proved correct. The efforts he made, for good or ill, were preparing him for the day when he would finally confront the Cabal.

He could feel the energies around him passing through his body like velvety down, the softest of mists. He could internalize and manipulate this energy at will. He could see and feel others doing the same, as determined by their own practice, skills, and view. Now he must learn to internalize and redirect the energies of others as naturally as he did for himself.

Master Wei was correct. He need only take the next step.

If only he knew how.

As the back door shut behind him, he heard Slate's gravelly voice call out from where the Dwarf sat eating another hearty breakfast in the kitchen one room over from the small terrace where Yip entered, "Mornin', Yip. Ya ready ta get started?"

"Yes," was his firm reply.

He certainly was ready. Each day granted by the Paratechnologists' research was a day he treasured more than any gift. Each day gave him another chance to push forward on the path he now realized that he must take.

He sat down next to his burly friend whose plate, like so many others before, was rapidly emptying of all food when confronted by Slate's remorseless, hunched over shoveling assault.

"Ya get any rest out there, Yip?"

"No. I met with Master Wei last night, Slate."

"Ya did? How's he doin'?"

"To be honest, we did not talk too much of our own affairs."

"Ah," Slate took a rare moment between mouthfuls of bread and sausage to reply. "What'd he have ta say then?"

He smiled with the thought. "That I must continue on the path I have set for myself, even if I do not know what path I am on, or what direction to take."

Slate chuckled deeply from the hidden depths of his paunch. "Sounds clear enough ta me! Per'aps we should get started then. Any direction should do!"

Placing his plate in the sink for the Aspect to clean, Slate picked up Duraeleon where it leaned against the side of the table and strapped the axe to his armored back, the Kazzak intertwined in his beard glinting in the morning sun streaming through the window above the sink.

Finished, Slate asked, "Yer park or mine?"

"Yours. The choice has been mine until now." He laughed briefly. "Even so, in the end, it may be the park that chooses us."

Scratching his head, Slate answered, voicing his agreement. "Aye, it may indeed."

FRACTURED ESSENCES

Beams of light split, dancing
into countless vivid hues.

Only to be made whole
by another prism.

Wrindanneth and Aroganji began their journey to the magistrate's office without having seen either Slate or Yip, who, based the tidiness of the kitchen, must have left some time before they arrived downstairs.

Although they had to get up early to meet with the Paratechnologists, Wrindanneth was not eager to get up too early. After all, he was supposed to awaken to birdsong. The birds were not supposed to awaken to him.

By the time they arrived at the docks, the island was in a state of high activity as both the merchants, travelers, and workmen whose tasks carried them through the evening were out at the same time as those whose business took place throughout the day. One group's day ended where the other's begun.

Wending their way through the bustling docks to arrive at the magistrate's office took the better part of a quarter of an hour as the traffic was exceptionally heavy due to a full docket of ships unloading and loading travelers and freight. Finally stepping through the stone threshold to the magistrate's stone building, Wrindanneth asked Aroganji through their shared connection. *"Care to take a guess as to how long this whole process will take?"*

"If their previous attempts are any indication, we may have results within a few days. However, without having seen their skill before, coupled with the defenses

inherent in the alien command sphere and its complexity, I would say that we could be making this journey consistently over the course of the next few months."

Crossing the entry, a refined voice greeted them, "Good morning, Aroganji and Wrindanneth. You are expected."

With a slight nod of their heads, still talking silently within, they stepped through the shimmering portal that appeared upon their arrival and into the room housing the alien control orb and the Paratechnologists as they had done on the day prior. As soon as they did so, both Aroganji and Wrindanneth immediately stopped in place.

As expected, inside the translucent field of force, the crystalline command orb floated in place—a massive, perfectly formed and cut gemstone, shielded by the Paratechnologists' magic. However, just a few paces away, hovering in the air before the gathered Paratechnologists, an exact copy of the same orb rested unshielded.

"Wha—?"

Before Wrindanneth could finish, Mazithras said, "Do not be alarmed. This is merely a holographic projection, a schematic of the original orb, resulting directly from the Construct's detailed analysis."

"I guess this answers your question," said Aroganji directly within Wrindanneth's mind.

"Not entirely. Let's see what they have to say."

Gesturing as if to welcome or introduce an unseen guest, Mazithras said, "I will let the Construct detail its findings to you."

The same smooth voice that had greeted their arrival to the office this morning and on their previous visits to the magistrate's office began speaking on Mazithras's queue. "A complete reconstructive analysis of the alien specimen has revealed an intensely interconnected, multi-dimensional array of self-referential and self-reinforcing crystalline unit cells functioning as a synthetic, holographic intelligence. The resulting continuum network appears to manifest the entire range of intelligent action including, but not limited to, problem solving, perception, learning, planning, strategy, symbolic reasoning, creativity, abstract expression, language, along with other multifaceted representations of knowledge and heuristic methods of thought. Based on this initial analysis, the alien device appears to embody a fully functioning, highly developed, adaptive cognitive structure."

Through their connection, Wrindanneth joked to Aroganji, *"Say that two times quickly."*

"The introduction of electromagnetic radiation along with other forms of radiant energies, waves, particles, and applied pressures induce complex chains of cascading reactions throughout the rondure's crystalline matrix. These reactions appear to function both as a means of information transfer within the command sphere and as a way for the orb's users to interact with and communicate with the sphere itself. As has been observed previously through other examples of the alien technology, the primary principle behind this interior communication and functionality is a highly sophisticated piezo-electric system embodied and magnified by the orb's crystalline lattice."

As the Construct spoke, the sphere's replicated representation rotated clearly before them—a scintillating crystalline orb akin to a perfectly crafted diamond fracturing and refracting light inward in fluctuating cascades of rainbow hues. The view of the orb then shifted positions, zooming in sharply along with the Construct's description, illustrating on the micro scale the dizzying complexity that emerged from the absolute similarity of the orb's self-reinforcing unit cell structure. In many ways, the orb truly was a holographic intelligence in the sense that each part, each individual cell, was both a whole functional unit unto itself and, simultaneously, a part of a greater whole dependent upon so many smaller facets of itself linked together by the light and energy traveling through its shape. Magnifying further, bursts of light flashed between the individual crystals as they watched, changing color and intensity during refraction and transmission as the command orb processed and manipulated information. Amplified further, individual unit cells deformed slightly as their crystal structures altered under the voltage trans-ferred through the material.

How information was actually stored and accessed within such a structure, Wrindanneth had no idea whatsoever.

Forgetting that Aroganji, too, had access to his thoughts, Wrindanneth jumped slightly as he heard Aroganji's voice say, *"I would imagine the orb functions, or rather stores, receives, and manipulates information, very much like other highly organized conceptual frameworks. Take our brain, for instance. In lieu of white and gray matter composed of nerves, the orb uses crystalline unit cells to provide structure. In lieu of electrochemical impulses traveling across the neural network, the command orb uses light and other forms of energy to communicate."*

"How intelligence, perception, reasoning, sensation and other emergent properties arise from within that framework and are then accessed and processed are questions many orders of magnitude greater in complexity and difficulty."

Unaware of their silent communication, the Construct continued its summary of the alien orb. "Although complete interception, decoding, and interpretation of the information contained within the orb has yet to be accom-plished, this initial examination has given rise to the ability to replicate crys-talline matrices with similar capabilities. The schematic you now see before you is a real-time visualization of the object that would result from such a synthesis. Initial assessments indicate that once completed, these command orbs will be ready for imprinting with the information and heuristics necessary for their learning, function, and interaction with the larger logosphere. As such, these devices will provide a mobile intelligence of similar ability, complexity, and flexibility as the Construct itself. By extension, application of this technology will provide the ability to supplement, extend, and augment the core functionalities of the Construct itself."

"Although a promising technology, the crystalline unit cells forming the basis for the larger neural matrix of the command orb will require certain very specialized raw materials the likes of which we have yet to produce on Ea'ae. Large-scale fabrication and production will require significant amounts of the necessary piezocrystals. Procurement or synthesis of the raw materials required for piezocrystal production will require the investment of significant resources until an efficient production means is fully established, secured, and stabilized. Guided by the proper understanding, application of magical principles and technologies will significantly expedite this production and recreation process."

"Without this knowledge and the necessary raw materials to fabricate the orbs, direct magical creation of the orb's crystalline structure would require unsustainable application of energies given our current capabilities, significantly limiting productive capacities."

As the significance of the Construct's words sank in, Wrindanneth's jaw dropped. He did not take pains to correct the situation either—a portable device with the intelligence of the Construct? Technology capable of expanding upon the Construct's cognitive capacities!

Unbelievable!

Not only were their futures secured by this revelation, along with the options and opportunities available to those who journeyed via *faerviage*, but, more importantly, the world just got so much larger, as did the possibilities for the continued furtherance of knowledge.

Noting Wrindanneth's expression, Mazithras smiled warmly. "It truly is a thing of wonder."

Fizzlemiz added excitedly, "Now that the Construct has found the means to replicate the command sphere, we can begin attempting to decipher its contents. With the device's inner workings in hand, assuming we have the correct representation, the knowledge held within may soon follow."

Shifting position slightly on his mechanical appendages, he added, "The real difficulty will be studying, interpreting, and learning from the secrets held within."

"Let me add this," said Mazithras after waiting for Fizzlemiz to finish, "although the secrets of the orb as yet elude us, much of our success thus far has hinged upon the fact that the beings who created the orb were unfamiliar with magic. Despite the depth and strength of their psychic abilities, their defenses were not designed to counter magical intrusions and investigations. As such, I feel that we should meet with further success in deciphering the orb's contents in the very near future."

Quietly, Aroganji added through their connection, *"Do not doubt that the Paratechnologists have the ability to either take portions of the Construct, or something very much like it, with them on their ships, in a form much like our Aspect at home, or that they can remain in contact with the Construct on their voyages. Although access to such a magical intelligence may be only available to a few, such* systems have been available to others before us, just not as widely as we may soon see with this alien device."

"We have yet to study the Paratechnologists' ships and do not know their full capabilities. This alien intelligence technology will offer the Paratechnologists a means to trade in these new command devices with outsiders without infringing upon their own magical advantages gained by using the Construct. They will assuredly create a magical synthesis, or recreate the technology entirely in magical form, to supplement their current synthetic intelligence systems. Regardless of the outcome, their interests will be served by the resulting technologies."

"Understood," Wrindanneth replied firmly through their link. "A bit of Maeth's excitement for the novel came to the fore there. Regardless of whether or not the Paratechnologists have similar capabilities already, you are correct. This device will provide them with many more options and opportunities in the future. I know they stand for good, so we need not fear the results of strengthening their power."

"I am still impressed with the speed with which the Paratechnologists themselves, or, in this case, their devices, are able to glean information."

Thinking of the accolades he would receive and the benefits such a value stream offered Maeth Onai as well, Wrindanneth added, "Maeth will be pleased as well!"

After the demonstration, Mazithras spoke for the gathered Paratechnologists. "I hope this summary has helped to show the significance of the item you brought before us for study."

"Rarely are we lucky enough to see such a potent, valuable artifact, much less one with such widespread applicability. Although we do not foresee the replacement of the Construct in the foreseeable future, this device has given us insights into ways to improve and broaden its functions and use. For that we owe you a great debt, one that will be repaid. Of course, the value of the technology of the orb itself, as we have discussed before, may be of only trifling importance compared with the knowledge held within its crystalline matrix."

Here Mazithras paused, looking for input. "We are at a crossroads. Although we have been meeting only a very short time, given the Construct's success, we have two options ahead of us, as I see it. One, we can continue to meet together, if you find this time valuable and would like these meetings to continue. Alternatively, we can continue our research and provide periodic updates or meetings as we retrieve information of import and particular significance. As the sphere's owners and liberators, the choice is yours."

Wrindanneth and Aroganji stood in quiet conversation for a few moments before Aroganji replied, "We appreciate your offer to continue to include us in your discussions and research. Perhaps, in the future, when time permits, we can actively engage in study with you, for there is much we can learn from you, your traditions, and techniques. However, you have been very generous in the offers you make of your own time and resources. Wrindanneth and I would not wish to delay the results of your inspection of the alien device, nor would we wish to prevent you from the administering of your own affairs or other research solely for our benefit or to meet with us."

"Periodic updates or meetings may be the most efficient option presented before us since we add little to these gatherings at present. If that changes and we can provide more insights, or you need our permission or ideas to continue, then we would be happy to continue meeting."

Nodding in agreement, while the other Paratechnologists flanked behind him solemnly, Mazithras answered, "So be it. We will contact you as we learn more. Adar will continue to be our liaison and primary agent. Should you require us or wish to express any of your concerns, you need only contact him. Trust that whatever considerations you do convey will be held in the utmost regard and acted upon expeditiously."

"Thank you," Aroganji bowed from the waist in preparation to depart.

With a wave of his hand and a half-smile, Wrindanneth wished them continued success. He then turned and walked out with Aroganji.

FA JIN

Lightning caught in a bottle—
what will happen once
the lid is opened?

Slate hustled through the avenues, moving with solid determination in front of Yip, Duraeleon shifting from side-to-side slightly with each rolling step, looking for just the right spot to practice.

After the better part of an hour, they finally found an open space that was in fact open. The mountain vista and meadow they practiced in the day before had shifted to a beautifully wooded park filled with tall hemlocks and firs, slanted light falling through the verdant boughs highlighting a fern covered forest floor rich with the smell of pine needles and resin. Slate, however, wanted nothing to do with swinging his axe in the trees if he could avoid it, so they had moved on.

The park they finally found, in contrast to the dense evergreen woods, was one of open lawns framed by riotous displays of plants of various types—from fine flowers to large shrubs and trees of every shape and description—blending seamlessly with small wild copses of wood. Between these small clusters of trees, strung like jewels amidst glistening pearls, several small burbling streams meandered merrily, cheerfully reflecting the white early morning sun.

Only the occasional early riser wandered through the park's open grassy expanses or along its gravel trails, leaving wide-open spaces available for Yip and Slate to practice undisturbed.

"Look good t'ya?" asked Slate, who already knew the answer.

"Wherever you decide will be fine, Slate."

"Then it's decided!" exclaimed Slate, eager to begin.

Slate pushed his way through the stout wooden gate marking the park's entrance, the sound of fine gravel crunching beneath his booted feet as he crossed the path and trundled through and out into the middle of the first large grassy expanse.

Smiling at his earnest friend, Yip followed, his steps as silent as the wind on the tips of the blades of grass as he retraced Slate's steady progress.

Pulling Duraeleon from its sheath on his back, Slate began to limber up by swinging the bright blade in large arcs, first with his right hand and then with his left. After describing the first few circles, Duraeleon finally piped up complaining, "Can't you even let me wake up before you start flinging me here and there?"

When Slate merely grunted, Duraeleon barked, "No one likes to wake up to vertigo, you flea-bitten wharf rat!"

Smiling grimly, Slate just swung faster.

"Good morning to you too!"

After this brief, weak initial protest, Duraeleon quieted down, presumably for a bit more shuteye knowing that it was always a good thing when his master took the time to hone his skills.

Slate enjoyed spending time practicing with his quiet friend whose own martial practice was so very different than his own warrior traditions. Although he was a Dwarf of few words, spending this time together expressing a shared purpose gave him the opportunity to voice questions to Yip he would not ask otherwise.

While he warmed up, the axe whirring and twisting around his arms and shoulders, but before he got too deep into his practice, thinking back to their previous conversation, Slate asked, "How is it exactly that ya learn ta read yer opponent's intent, Yip? Why does yer order find it necessary ta take such a seemin'ly difficult martial path?"

Slate had spent some time thinking of his discussion with Yip on their last trip to train together the day before. In particular, he wondered about the differences and difficulties he perceived with his friend's mental and physical approach to combat when compared against the regimen of the Bor'Banna. The path of the Bor'Banna was one of strength and power, using force, both physical and magical, to overwhelm and overcome foes. Although there were countless subtleties and techniques involved in this approach, from mastering skills with the blade to anticipating an opponent's actions to developing the inner fire, emphasis was placed on delivering force that would overwhelm any technique or defense regardless of the source or opponent's motivation.

Yip's approach, on the other hand, relied upon developing powers of perception that were almost unheard of and then combining that intuitive perspective with a martial tradition reliant almost wholly on the magical energies inherent to, flowing through, and around the warrior. Although there were parallels to the magical disciplines of the Bor'Banna, the differences were also marked.

Underlying the differences in their approaches were some of Slate's own concerns. In no small way, he felt that entering physical combat without a weapon, no matter how skilled or magically adept the combatant, entailed so much additional risk as to make the approach almost unjustifiable. So first watching Yip fight and then later practicing with him unsettled Slate's hard-earned, battle-tested Dwarven sensibilities.

Though Yip's skills were evident, he wondered how long adherents of his tradition were exposed to grave risk before they achieved mastery. What risks did they take going without proper weaponry? Did they employ weaponry prior to mastery?

In the end, despite seeing his friend's prowess on many occasions, he worried about Yip coming to harm without a proper way to defend himself. Although this sentiment was frivolous, for Wrindanneth and Aroganji were in truth no different, the concern was still there. Perhaps because Wrindanneth and Aroganji came from traditions that he could relate to and understand, whose magical abilities were so visibly manifest, he could justify their actions more easily. After all, they did not charge in empty handed against armed foes, supernatural horrors, and other implacable enemies!

Of course, when he really thought about Yip's abilities, did it make much more sense to charge into battle against a Dragon barehanded than it did for a Dwarf to charge in with an axe?

Not really.

But, despite all these contradictory thoughts and musings, he respected his friend's skills and was exceedingly curious about Yip's abilities and traditions.

Slate's words brought to Yip's mind thoughts of a time when he could hardly imagine being in combat whether with or without a weapon.

Images of his childhood arose within his mind, remembrances of the ease of movement of the initiates and priests, the natural facility and grace of their motions as they sparred with each other on and around the monastery grounds, of his difficulties in learning to move naturally, especially under the rigors and duress of combat.

He bowed his head, displeased and ashamed.

He had struggled through yet another practice session, more a threat to himself than his partner or anyone else. He had spent the majority of the time disentangling his own limbs from one another while his partner waited patiently for him to return to position.

An enemy would merely have to step aside and watch him do himself in, probably with a smirk, arms crossed appreciatively as he marveled at his incompetence. At least his training partner was kind enough to help him up or right himself—repeatedly.

Reading Yip's discouragement, Master Wei motioned him over after the other acolytes, initiates, and priests began to move away for other duties.

"What is troubling you, Yip?"

"Master Wei, when we practice, I am trying too hard, exerting too much effort. I am not at ease. My form and the effects of my actions suffer."

Master Wei placed a soothing hand on Yip's shoulder. "If you try, you fail. Remain calm and at ease."

"How, master?"

"When you eat, do you exert all your effort?" Master Wei tensed up, becoming rigid and robotic, losing the ease of natural motion.

"Do you jump toward your bowl?" He hopped forward unnaturally as though pouncing on a small object.

"Do you lash out with your chopsticks toward your food?" He made an exaggerated gesture well beyond what would be required to pick up a few grains of rice, telegraphing his motions for easy counter and reaction.

"Do you grimace at your fellow acolytes while eating?" He made a fearsome face, as though in supreme effort, or in an attempt to scare all of his training partners away from his rice bowl, a reaction that easily gave away his intent.

He shook his head, his shame turning to humor as he repressed a smile.

"Then why do you do these things when you move? When you strike? When you block? When you interact with your partner?"

He opened his mouth hesitantly. "I think..."

Master Wei cut him off firmly but kindly with a smile. "Do not think. Be without thought, at ease, at peace, natural."

"When you move, when you strike, when you counter, your motions should be natural, indistinguishable from normal movement."

"When you strike, reach for your chopsticks. When you block, pick up your chopsticks. When you counter, put down your chopsticks."

"If your movements are at ease, relaxed, your opponent will have difficulty anticipating your intent, the direction of your strike, the reason for your actions."

"When you move naturally, your motions will occur with maximal efficiency, with maximal effect, with minimal effort, and with minimal risk."

"If you are not at ease, your motions counter themselves."

Wu wei.

Wu bu wei.

Unaware of Slate's thoughts, Yip returned to the moment, away from his own past attempts to understand a new way of moving and being, gesturing with a bright smile at Slate's question, his hands tracing the arch of the deep azure sky as he spoke, offering his friend a compliment. "Your curiosity serves you well. Your questions are as vast and encompassing as the sky above, Slate, the intricacies of which are hidden from all but the most penetrating view."

Slate grunted, feeling anything but.

Yip continued, "You are correct in your assessment. The path my order has taken is not an easy one, but it is the one that arose for us, reflective of our views and development, our insights and perspective."

"As to your first question, when one learns to let all divisions between self and other slip away, then one cannot help but feel another's intent for then there is no difference between self and other. When there is no self, there truly is no other and actions arise in accord as the universal expresses itself through action."

When Slate did not respond, he reached into his robes, first removing and then unrolling the teaching scroll Master Wei had given him before the start of his journey. "Among my order, we have many teachings to guide our progress and direct our intention that we may learn to do exactly what you ask, Slate. Here is one such teaching, or song, as we sometimes call them, of Xīnyìquán."

As he unfurled the scroll from its protective case, the individual characters and pictograms he referred to began to appear across the parchment's surface in crisp vertical columns. As the words appeared on the rice paper scroll, he read to his friend,

"Where there are two, become one —
encompassed by awareness, guided by intent.
One falls away into emptiness,
boundaries fade in the depths.
Presence gives way to fullness,
the boundless is expressed.
Form and emptiness commingle,
wisdom manifests.

In this way, peace bridges the gap to violence,
harmony arises from discord,
truth issues from deceit,
action flows from unity,
and totality emerges from division."

Some time passed in silence. Then, nodding seriously, Slate said, "I will think on this. Per'aps tomorrow we can discuss yer approach further."

Returning the scroll to its case, the magical rice paper becoming blank now that it was no longer needed, Yip nodded to his friend who was running his thick fingers along Duraeleon's haft thoughtfully.

Pointing to his temple, lightly touching his skin with the tip of his pointing finger as he turned to leave, Yip said, "Move through the gaps and spaces in your opponent's mind. Find an opening and strike."

Leaving Slate to his contemplation then, he wandered over to the nearest cluster of trees to sit by the small creek before beginning his own practice.

Pushing dew laden plants aside, Yip made his way carefully through the vegetation so as not to disturb them or damage their roots. Finding a welcoming spot beneath the gently swaying trees overhead, he sat down on an old, rounded gray rock that hunkered down into the soil at the stream's edge and listened to the water's music as it gurgled past.

Sitting by the stream, he watched the cool water flow over the algae covered rocks at his feet. Verdant underwater plants shifted easily with the current, drifting languidly beneath his reflection on the stream's clear surface.

Seeing his reflection rippling in the stream's facets, shaded by variegated trees and pearlescent clouds overhead, his mind once again drifted back to a time long ago when, as a young child, staring at his own likeness, Master Wei had joined him on a willowy, arching bridge gazing into the still depths of one of the monastery's lily-capped water gardens.

Lost in reflection peering into the water, his master appeared at his shoulder like a cloud, his teacher's bright face floating lightly on the water's still surface above his own right shoulder—a bright vision from far away.

"What is it you see as you gaze so intently into the depths, Yip?"

Tall trees arching overhead shaded the water garden from the high noon sun, lining the edge of the pond, casting dark shadows over the lily and grass covered waters. Purple, pink, and white lotus flowers dotted the waters, small islands on tenuous moorings.

"Master, I am not gazing into the water. I am practicing awareness."

"And what type of awareness do you practice, Yip?"

"Selfless awareness, master, without object or thought."

"And your mind alights on nothing in particular on this wondrous spring day?"

"Master, I..." He hesitated, confused.

"Yes, Yip?"

"I see lights."

"What types of lights do you see?"

He paused for some time before answering. "I do not have words, master. I am lost in the unending beauty and complexity of these all-encompassing lights."

"Perhaps you are seeing images or illusions created by long periods of uninterrupted concentration?"

He shook his head. "Master, these lights are not delusions. They persist."

"Perhaps you see the stars above reflected in the dark depths of the still pools?"

"Master, I do not see stars. I...I feel the radiance of these lights. They are like constellations that shine without apparent source."

"There is light all around. There is light within objects I see. There is light moving between objects I see."

"It is too much. I close my eyes and the light is still there. I feel it, I see it, even when I try to avoid it. Master, this light is in me as well."

"What does it feel like, Yip?"

"It feels...light and refreshing like..." Here he paused for a moment, tilting his

head slightly in thought before responding, "...happiness or contentment...or a deep breath on a beautiful spring day."

"Does this light detract from your practice then, Yip?"

"Master, it will not go away. The calmer and clearer my awareness becomes, the more apparent becomes this light."

"Are you concerned about what you see and feel, Yip?"

"It is overwhelming, master. I feel as though the world I live in has suddenly blossomed in luminous complexity and extent, but, despite this, I feel more connected and reassured."

"Do you have a name for what you see and feel?"

"Only light, master."

"Perhaps you should call this light chi, *Yip."*

He stood in silence for some time as comprehension slowly dawned upon him.

He had been schooled in the ways of energy for so long without ever feeling or seeing anything akin to this that he viewed chi *as something of an abstraction, as an intangible beyond his ability to fully grasp or perceive. Even though his instructors regularly demonstrated* chi *and its uses as a cynosure, he thought that perhaps something had been lacking within himself for he had never experienced what they described to such an extent.*

Now this wonder was in clear view all around him!

He would never be able to close his eyes to its presence or turn his head from its truth.

"Your world has indeed expanded, Yip, but rest assured that your awareness and place within it has grown in equal measure."

Chi was here.

It was in him and all around him.

It was a part of everything he saw and something more.

He would never again be able to deny or ignore its reality.

Returning from his recollections as one would from an unexpected but welcome daydream, he smiled and stood before cautiously picking his way out of the copse. Thoughts of his childhood flittered like the clouds above before drifting away as he walked over toward his friend. Picking a spot a few paces away from where Slate intently practiced without acknowledging him, he took the Zhan Zhuang posture.

Standing relaxed and erect, his arms slightly rounded, fingertips nearly touching, knees and elbows slightly bent, he began the first of many permutations of the energy work that he had begun upon returning to Tellanon.

Some hours later, after the sun reached its zenith, full of warmth and radiance on the nape of Yip's neck, he heard Slate clear his throat, calling for his attention. Letting the energies filling him pass away to their prior course, he relaxed his arms, leaving his hands to fall to his sides, exhaled deeply, and then briskly shook his wrists and hands, ankles and feet. He then walked over to his stocky companion who stood leaning on Duraeleon's solid shaft some paces away.

Slate cleared his throat once more. After their previous practice, discussions, and time spent together over the past few days, having given the request he was about to pose some thought, he asked, "Will ya teach me what it means ta read my intent and show me how ta apply that knowledge?"

Yip bowed to his friend from the waist. Remaining standing as he would naturally after completing the bow, he said, "Attack me as you would an enemy."

"What?"

Yip nodded.

"I won't do that!"

He shrugged. "That is your choice."

Slate growled, "Ya don't want that, Yip."

"Do you wish to see? Do you wish to learn?"

Slate snarled, both hands gripping and releasing the leather wrappings on Duraeleon's haft. With a roar, he surged forward, axe whipping through the air toward Yip's throat.

Moving ever so slowly, as if his motions were passing through amber, Yip leaned back slightly as the axe whistled past his exposed neck.

Using the axe's momentum to mount another strike, Slate crouched and spun in a tight circle, lashing the blade around at waist height. At the last moment, he stood violently, pulling the axe's keen edge upward, intent on splitting Yip from waist to crown.

With a short turn of his waist, Yip tilted to the side as Duraeleon sped savagely past.

Again and again, Slate attacked ferociously, the power and rage within building into a seething furnace. Despite the fury of Slate's attacks, Yip stood relaxed before him maintaining the same distance between them, moving in mirror image to each of Slate's steps, coolly dodging Slate's attacks with a placid poise that belied the deadliness of each assault.

When, after a time, Slate began to press forward, pushing his attack, trying to force his way through Yip's defenses leaving no room to avoid his attack, Yip stepped forward with a suddenness Slate could not perceive, following and sticking to Slate's every move, literally leaving no room to attack.

Slate felt as though his own shadow had jumped up from the ground and greeted him face-to-face.

Despite all his efforts to restore distance either by giving or taking ground, moving suddenly left or right, up or down, Slate could not shake Yip's everpresent shadow. Unable to attack, he could not counter Yip's unwavering defense.

Just as Slate was about to give up and yield, knowing that he could not mount an attack, Yip took a step back to let Slate begin the lesson anew.

Again Yip stood in place before Slate's wicked blows. This time, however, he did not move to avoid attacks. Diffuse blue light radiated from his hands as each and every one of Slate's attacks were lightly directed away from his intended target. So soft and subtle was his defense that Slate felt as if the wind had shifted Duraeleon's blade of its own accord away from his chosen mark or as though his aim were no longer true, despite his most fervent efforts.

When he pressed forward once again, attempting to batter down Yip's defenses, the blue light covering Yip's palms became glued to Duraeleon's axe head, the light surrounding Yip's palms seeming to emanate from Duraeleon instead. Although Slate never felt any resistance to his strikes, all of his blows drifted away from their mark, again of their own volition.

With one last supreme effort, the fires within building to an overwhelming crescendo, Slate lashed outward with a final terrific thrust, sending the flames of his fathers through his blade and directly at Yip.

For his part, Yip relaxed, closing his eyes, letting himself fall away into awareness, feeling Slate's energies build and flow, move and react, among the broader currents flowing around. Over and over with each successive attack, Slate's power grew and surged becoming more and more intense, more and more focused. Although it mattered not to him, for he was only present as a reaction, as a response to Slate's blows, this building power and tension made it easier and easier to read and counter Slate's actions.

When, after Slate's initial unrelenting storm met with no success and he was ready to yield after all attempts failed, Yip let his friend regather himself to try again that he could experience what it felt like to be simultaneously unopposed and unified with the object of his attempts at violence. With each strike guided away by his *chi*-covered hands, Slate's fury built and his inner flames intensified into a raging holocaust, until, without warning, all barriers dropped. Slate's internal fires blasted forward in a raging torrent of magical flames.

Yip took this power into himself.

Calm in the face of Slate's frenzy, feeling his friend's power suddenly surge forward, Yip instinctively shot the energy he had inadvertently taken back into his surprised, unsuspecting friend.

As the energy left his body, a sudden intake of air was all that Yip heard as he opened his eyes to watch Slate launch across the clearing in a tangled arch, eventually skidding to a halt at the end of a battered trail of grass and furrowed dirt some distance away.

Running to where his friend lay, quickly assessing Slate's condition, his mind running over Slate's body to ensure that nothing internal had been damaged, Yip asked, "Are you all right?"

Dizzy and disoriented, blinking groggily and confused, Slate asked, "What happened?"

The reality of what he had just done sinking in, Yip responded equally dazed, if not as disoriented, as his friend, "I accidentally took your energy, the raging fires of Brendle's forge, into myself. Not knowing what to do, I returned them in the same way that I received them, albeit in a different form."

Still groggy, but not so disoriented as to lose all sense, Slate asked, an undercurrent of awe in his voice, "Ya can do that?"

Shaking his head, Yip answered, clearly just as out of sorts, "No." Pausing for a moment, he added ruefully, "Not until now."

A jagged smile broke through Slate's thick beard as he replied, "Then we both learned somethin' new on this day!"

Sharing his friend's warm smile, Yip answered, "I would say so."

Clasping Yip's hand, Slate grinned sheepishly. "My apologies fer gettin' a bit out o' hand."

Yip bowed. "I think we will both be better for it."

He helped Slate to his feet. Reassured that his friend was steady, he followed Slate across the clearing to where Duraeleon lay abandoned on the grass.

As Slate bent over to retrieve his axe, Duraeleon admonished, "Look at you shooting off without me! Flying through the air relaxed and carefree leaving me alone and forsaken! To think that I thought we were close!"

Putting the axe back in its sheath, Slate answered, "Shut yer trap. Ya know I won't leave ya." Fastening the sheath's buckle, he quipped, "I'd hardly call that experience fun."

As Slate stood back up, Yip dusted the dirt and blades of grass off his friend's back, picking off small clods of debris from between the joints and chinks in his armor, glad that Slate had the magical protection to help lessen the impact of the surge and fall.

Now that he had fully recovered, with his mind clear, all wobbliness gone, and his ears no longer ringing, Slate joked, "When will I be able ta do that?"

Yip shrugged. "With time and continued practice, you, too, will learn to anticipate the natural flow of events."

"I'm not askin' about readin' my intent. I'm askin' about tha redirection and massive release o' force!"

Yip took some time to answer as he framed his response. "What you experienced is called *fa jin*, the sudden release of power. There are many types of *fa jin*. Numerous martial traditions use similar techniques of generating power and then transferring that force through and against an opponent. This transfer is generally physical."

"That is the first time that I have ever taken another's magical power or energy into myself and then released the force in that way."

He paused for a moment. "Truly, I did not think it could be done."

"So ya're sayin' that ya've generated and transferred physical force like that before, but never taken someone else's energy and then returned it against them?"

Nodding, he tried to help his friend understand. "*Fa jin* is like lightning. It is the explosive release of power. I have never caught lightning much less thrown it back."

He smiled, adding, "I have returned physical force, and force augmented by *chi*, against an opponent. I have generated and expressed similar forces. But I have never taken the *chi* itself, or, as *chi* is expressed in other traditions, the magic someone created or conjured, gathered this energy into myself, and then returned it against an opponent."

Now it was Slate who patted him on the back. "If ya learn somethin' like that every time ya thrash me, then I'll be happy ta be yer punchin' bag!"

He smiled, thinking of Slate's willingness to take abuse for their betterment, and laughed. "Friendships truly are a most welcome gift!"

Rubbing his sore back, Slate grinned. "I don't know how many gifts I'll be able ta take!"

Although he did not know whether or not Slate would ever be able to truly *fa jin*, he did offer his friend one tantalizing observation. "I have seen you kindle the flames within and spread them along your blade when we fought the R'yn Daer and in Azaelle's cavern. I felt these same fires burning, seething but banked and waiting to escape as we sparred. If you cannot do so already, with practice, you should be able to wreath your whole body in the fires of Brendle's forge, not just your axe."

Slate's raised eyebrows were his only answer.

By the time Slate and Yip returned home to their small cottage, the day was giving way to dusk and the lights of home were already lit. Entering through the front door, Slate's shoulders weary and hunched, his muscles tight from a hard day's use, he heard Wrindanneth call out from the nearby sitting room, "Another day of fun and games in the park?"

Patting Duraeleon's handle menacingly, he growled, "Perhaps it'd be more fun if ya joined us."

"Ah I see... With offers like that, how can I refuse?"

Interjecting between his friends' retorts, Yip asked, "How was your time with the Paratechnologists?" He hoped Aroganji and Wrindanneth's day had been as fruitful as his had been with Slate.

Aroganji answered, the excitement evident in his voice, "The Construct has ascertained how to recreate the alien command sphere! Not only that, but it has determined that the orb houses a vast intelligence very much like the Construct itself!"

Qualifying his excitement a bit, Aroganji added, "Although they can replicate the orb's physical structure, the Paratechnologists and Construct need more time to actually intercept and interpret its contents."

Shaking his head, Yip marveled, "In only a few days, they have already done so much! We shall have our course set for us very soon!"

Wrindanneth was not so sure. His earlier excitement had been tempered by a bit of thought and further discussion with Aroganji. "I know you are eager to move forward, Yip, but I would not make that presumption, at least not yet. The Construct scanned and analyzed the orb, breaking it down into constituent parts. Based on this analysis, the Paratechnologists claim that they can replicate a similar structure, albeit with some difficulty, but we are far from actually having the contents of the orb in hand, much less in a form we can understand."

Agreeing with Wrindanneth, Aroganji added, "Adar will keep us informed of their progress from now on."

"So ya won't be goin' back?" Slate scratched his beard thoughtfully.

"Not yet. We'll let the Paratechnologists devote their full energies to unraveling the mysteries of the crystal. They feel that it warrants significant priority, so Aroganji and I decided it best to let them work undisturbed and on their own schedule."

"Excellent! Then ya can join us on tha practice field tomorrow!"

Wrindanneth sighed. Not rising to the bait after Slate's earlier comments, he answered, "Perhaps, but we will be limited as to what we can practice in public."

Not sharing in Slate's challenge, only his enthusiasm, Yip added, "You would be welcome to join us if you so choose. Practice or not, however or whatever, the choice is yours."

Aroganji shared in Slate's enthusiasm. "I would be happy to join you in the morning."

Sighing again, Wrindanneth replied, "I guess that means I have to go as well." He glanced at Aroganji slyly. "I can't have Aroganji learning too much without me."

The morning sun dawned bright and clear, a steady glow on Yip's eyelids where he lay beneath the clear glass of the small conservatory. Rising quietly, he walked into the kitchen where Slate was busily clearing his third plate of fried potatoes, sausage, ham, eggs, onions, peppers, pan fried vegetables, and bread.

Smacking his lips at Yip's appearance, Slate said, "Nothin' like a nice refreshin' repast ta start tha day!"

He laughed. "You do your clan proud, Slate. Only a true warrior could eat as much food as you do and then go practice with a smile on his face."

Slate scoffed, "I'd hardly call that a meal! When tha time comes and a battle is nigh, a Bor'Banna should be able ta eat at least a week's worth o' rations in tha field, for who knows when next he'll eat?"

Yip just shook his head. The extent of Slate's gullet was beyond him, its magic as potent as the bottomless bag he carried. "Are the others planning on joining us soon?"

"If I didn't know any better, I'd say that Wrindanneth is in his room sawin' timber even as we speak. But, since woodsmen are few and far between on this island, I'd say that he's still asleep."

Nodding, Yip left the kitchen and took to the stairs located near the front door, climbing quietly up the burnished, honeyed steps without use of the oaken handrail. The open landing at the top of the stairway had a few life-like animated paintings depicting various landscapes and battles arranged on the wall facing the downstairs. Each painting had to do with historical events that Wrindanneth occasionally researched in his free time. Turning to his left, he walked down the hallway to where it ended in a small window looking out on the wooded lawn surrounding the house. On either side of the hall were the two rooms Aroganji and Wrindanneth called their own.

Sensing that his friends were awake and moving about their rooms, he knocked on both doors to get his friends' attention.

As Aroganji's door opened, he heard Wrindanneth croak, "What?" from behind his door, his voice dry from not having used it yet that day.

Raising his voice slightly so that Wrindanneth could hear him through the stout portal, he called out, "Are you ready to go?"

Aroganji shook his head, smiling, knowing the answer as Wrindanneth grumbled from behind the door, "The birds have only just started to sing! Can't a man get up after the dawn?"

"What's with you people?"

"A pressing need, as you well know, my friend. You need not join us if you do not wish to do so, Wrindanneth."

"I'm coming! Let me finish strapping my boots on and I'll be down."

Turning to Aroganji, he bowed slightly. "Good morning, my friend. I trust that the veil of sleep lifting has left you refreshed and enlivened?"

Aroganji bowed in turn. "Another day welcomes me into its fold."

They went back down the stairs and waited for Wrindanneth to join them in the kitchen. In order to speed their preparations, Aroganji assembled a plate of Slate's leftovers for both himself and Wrindanneth.

The swirl of robes, creak of the stairs, and clatter of Wrindanneth's feet told them that their rangy friend was about to make an appearance.

Bustling into the room, the air ripe with the pungent smell of sautéed meat and onions, Wrindanneth sniffed, brushing the long red hair out of his eyes to better see what had been prepared. "Slate, if my nose does not deceive me, you have outdone yourself once again!"

"If ya don't get started soon, ya'll be eatin' lunch instead o' breakin' yer fast."

Ignoring the jibe, Wrindanneth focused on his plate.

While they ate, Wrindanneth posed the question he had been meaning to ask for a few days now. "When the Paratechnologists finally decipher the orb's secrets and we have the Cabal's location, do you actually think we will actually be ready to go after them and meet with success, Yip?"

Aroganji and Slate watched Yip carefully as he gave his response.

"The answer I wish to give is not the one that speaks the truth, I fear." Yip shrugged, tilting his head to the side as he spread out his hands palms up with the admission. "Unfortunately, many times what we wish and hope for is not what we are given."

"No, I do not feel we are ready. That is why I spend what time I am given in preparation. The truth is, even if we had more time to prepare, would we ever truly be ready or feel that we are ready? Not knowing what we face or prepare for, we can only maintain an attitude of readiness while cultivating what skills and opportunities we may."

Slate clapped his hands together loudly after Yip finished, urging his friends forward and onward. "Which is exactly why we need ta hit tha practice field. Let's move it!"

Within a few minutes Aroganji and Wrindanneth finished their plates and were following Yip and Slate out the door to find a practice spot that would meet their varied needs.

Walking down the stone lane beneath the overhanging greenery and trees, Yip summarized his experience with Slate the day before. "Yesterday I showed Slate how I read a person's intent. While working together, I inadvertently took some of his magical power into myself. Although I have taken physical force upon myself and transferred it back toward an opponent or sparring partner many times before, I had never done that with magical energy. Not knowing what to do, if I had taken too much and put Slate at risk, I immediately transferred his power back."

"Ta great affect I might add," interjected Slate with a chuckle.

Smiling in agreement, Yip said, "I would like to try that with your magical energies today to see if I can do it again. I would also like to attempt to translate some of the vital power flowing around us through myself and into you to augment your abilities."

He looked seriously at each of his friends in turn. "If I can learn to both transfer and redirect magical forces focused on us and augment your abilities or supplement your power, then we will be well on our way to becoming a formidable band indeed."

"Ready to go, you mean?" asked Wrindanneth.

"Much closer," answered Yip with a smile.

They returned to the park that Yip and Slate had used the day before for practice. This time, the green remained as they had last seen it. Crossing through the gate and passing over the first gravel path, Slate pointed out the rut in the grass left by his explosive landing after the *fa jin* release. "Took quite a ride there!"

"Well, Slate," joked Wrindanneth, "if nothing else, you certainly left your mark."

Not finding the comment the least bit funny, Slate retorted, "We'll see how well ya do if it happens t'ya."

Overhearing his friends from where they walked behind him, Yip replied,

"Let's hope that I will have better control should I be able to *fa jin* with your magical energies again."

Laughing rakishly, Slate added, "Fer Wrindanneth and foes ta come, let's hope not!"

While Yip and Slate selected a spot to begin practicing energy and axe work together, Aroganji and Wrindanneth walked off separately, each working on exercises specific to his own discipline.

Very much like Yip's efforts to translate the energies of the *chi* and *yuan-chi* into other forms, Wrindanneth spent his time creating small arcs of what looked like miniature lightning bolts, first conjuring and then transmuting divine energies into different types of mundane forces—fire, electricity, sound, heat, and light along with localized fields of gravity and magnetism.

Although a passerby may only see a dramatic show of light and sound, heat and energy, Wrindanneth worked within a much broader, empyrean scope. His efforts as a magician gathering, forming, and expressing the fundamental forces of nature, the all-pervading divine energies of creation, served to make the possible actual. Working in complete concentration, he helped to embody the continual development of human ideals and imagination, making very real the intangible ideas of thoughts and dreams, crystallizing the potential into the extant.

Nearby, Aroganji paced through what appeared to be an intricate martial form of various tempos and rhythms, strikes and counters combined with deeply symbolic gestures, phrases, and exhalations. He danced the Wu Xing, the five elements of change, embodying the interactions and relationships between phenomena, the shift from elemental energy type to energy type, each element associated with different phenomena in nature, one phase first generating, then overtaking and finally subsuming the next in an endless, ever-changing cycle. As he did so, although it was not visible to normal eyes, his aura radiated shifting hues of color associated with each elemental aspect, its changes and interactions—a kaleidoscope of chameleon hues.

Taking a moment to watch his friend before he got too engrossed in his own practice, Aroganji's moves had definite martial applications, but Yip could tell that the intent of his friend's practice was not the physical application of technique or force. Based on the energies generated and shaped, Aroganji was practicing the fundamental forms, the basis, for his arts as a Fang Shih. Through the intricacies of movement, Aroganji was rehearsing the movements and formulae, the gestures and breathing, necessary to express all of the possible combinations of the elemental energies of his craft.

Each symbolic motion and gesticulation provided a tool, a component to be used, in the ever-changing language and development of the elemental arts of the Fang Shih. As such, practicing his form not only increased Aroganji's skill in the magical arts, his practice provided the vehicle for further refinement and insight into the development of new magical knowledge and technique.

The entire basis for Aroganji's art was embodied within a single, ever-changing form.

Eager to begin his own work after watching his friends, Yip asked Slate, "Are you ready?"

Swinging his axe to and fro, swiveling his arms, waist, and torso and bending his legs in vigorous exertion, Slate responded, "Almost. Give me another moment ta finish limberin' up."

A short time later, Slate nodded, gripping with both hands on the leather handle of his axe, blade facing Yip. "Ready."

Standing in place patiently, Yip nodded slightly and said, "Begin."

With a lunge, Slate leapt forward, intent on bringing all of his skills to bear against his mild-mannered friend.

While Aroganji and Wrindanneth continued their disciplines nearby, Yip continued moving with Slate, mirroring his friend's strikes and counters as he had done the day before, knowing that it would be some time before Slate would be ready to attempt to mirror someone else's actions, to read an opponent's intent, content to let him experience the process. Following Slate's blade, he let the Dwarf's burning energies wash over him, all the while simultaneously feeling the energetic transformations of his friends radiating about him as a small part of the native flow of energy and *chi* constantly arising and encompassing their activities.

Maneuvering with Slate, countering his actions before Slate's intent was fully realized or expressed, he let his own barriers fall and opened himself to the energies of his friends as he normally did with the surrounding *chi* and other energies in his Zhan Zhuang exercises, as he would with any other force. Despite his previous preconceptions to the contrary, his friends' energies flowed around and into him as readily as the *chi* moving all around.

Struck by the enormity and wonder of what he experienced and could now do, or rather what the fires of the Cabal's void made possible, he did not take, nor did he try to take, all of their energy. He merely let their energies flow over and into him, as a rock absorbs the heat of the sun on a warm day without depleting the power of the sun itself, amazed that the barriers he once had taken to be inviolate had been broken down so completely.

As the morning passed and the power manifested by his friends built within—Slate's fire, Aroganji's elemental energies, the *yuan-chi* and its manifestations and permutations from Wrindanneth, along with the *chi* bathing them in unending vitality—he thrummed with ever greater power and vigor. Watching his hands and arms as he countered Slate's movements, what he could see of his body glowed with a bright golden light as if he, too, were a small constellation of energy radiating life and vitality upon the universe.

When he had taken in enough of these energies to both reassure himself of the reality of his experience and suit his ultimate purpose, he stepped away from Slate, disengaging from his friend with a bow, and called out to his friends.

"Be ready, my friends, for the energy of life will soon flow through you!"

"What would you like us to do or try once we receive this energy?" Wrindanneth did not need guidance, but he did want to make sure that there was nothing particular that Yip wanted done or attempted.

"Whatever you wish. I want to first see if this transfer is possible and, if it is, if you can use the energy I send. If what I give you is useable, will it augment what you are normally already capable of doing? There are many questions to explore and applications to master should this transmission prove viable."

Waiting a moment before beginning, he asked, "Ready?"

When he received nods and affirmations all around, he began.

He would have to be careful releasing the power he had accumulated, both so as to avoid harming his friends and to transfer an amount of force that would be useable and not disruptive to them. Of course, he had yet to actually deliberately transfer force in such a controlled way before, but he now knew that such an ability was within his capabilities.

He first concentrated upon the sensations of life associated with each of his friends, bringing their shimmering energy bodies to the fore of his awareness. With each presence crystallized in his mind's eye, he gradually relaxed, as if exhaling, letting the energies he had held within return to their proper source. As he did so, he felt a connection, at first faint, but gradually deepening between himself and each of his companions, as if a channel or passage opened connecting him to his friends. In lieu of radiating energy outward without direction upon his friends, he let the energies leaving his body flow away through these linkages in slow waves. As he did so, he maintained an awareness of each of his friend's energy bodies, ready to break off contact should anything out of place occur.

While he watched, feeling the energy leaving himself, each of his friends appeared to grow brighter and brighter, as if their spirits swelled with Light, puissance made manifest. Wrindanneth was the first to react to the influx of energy, always willing to experiment and throw caution to the wind while trying something new. Clapping both hands together with great force, a brilliant bolt of jagged lightning arched skyward, leaving Yip's eyes etched with an afterimage of bluish white light and his ears ringing with the peal of thunder.

Moments later, he heard a triumphant growl as Slate's aura burst into a seething red nimbus, Duraeleon's blade simultaneously crackling with magical, white flames.

For his part, Aroganji inscribed a faint symbol in the air. Rapidly charging it with power, he exhaled onto the sigil. With a violent rush of air, a swirling vortex materialized. Looking vaguely like a semi-humanoid tornado, Aroganji's spell had given rise to a minor air elemental.

Although they had much work to do together in the days ahead, Yip smiled at the effort.

"Nice!" Wrindanneth walked over to Yip, joining Aroganji and Slate to discuss what had happened, grinning like a child so proud of a new accomplishment. "When you sent that energy into me, Yip, I can't say that I felt too differently than before, maybe a bit more vibrant or enlivened, like I was fresh and ready, but nothing overwhelming. Deep down, however, I understood that I could do more, that I was capable of more than I had been able to do prior to the infusion of power."

"Although I did not push my limits, I knew that I certainly could if I had to in more dire circumstances. With that knowledge secure in my mind, I let the energy you sent express itself. The bolt you saw was powered completely by the energy you directed over to me. I did not draw upon or summon any more energy to cast that spell."

Wrin shrugged. "Who knows, with more energy the sensations may become much more pronounced!"

Slate nodded. "I've never been able ta so readily make tha power o' Brendle's fire manifest. With a bit more work, I'm sure that I could reach levels o' intensity I've never known. And ta think that was only our first try!"

Aroganji smiled as well, although he was a bit more restrained. Reflecting Yip's own thoughts, he said, "I see much training in our future as we learn to work together as a team to take advantage of this power fully. Just as Yip will need to learn how and when to direct energy to most effectively boost our abilities, we will have to learn how best to use it without coming to harm or bringing about unanticipated consequences."

"Agreed," said Yip with a slight nod. "There will be times when I am able to provide energy to you and times when we won't have the opportunity to make the transfer. There will be times when I am able to transfer power but you may not know that the transference is coming. There may be times when I have to break off contact, the transfer only partially complete. We will need to learn how to react to and prepare for any number of scenarios beyond just learning how best to employ the energy once you receive it."

Adding a bit of gravity to the discussion, he added, "Gradually shifting ambient energies to you is also an entirely different matter than learning to rapidly counter, nullify, redirect, or retransmit those of an enemy."

Their smiles unmuted, Slate offered, "We'll get ta that when tha time comes!"

Looking around at his friends, proud of what they had done together, Yip finished, "We have accomplished much today. I think we now have an excellent starting point for tomorrow. Let's go home."

The walk home was filled with light banter and jest, reflective of their happy mood.

With a chuckle, Slate said, "When tha summer solstice comes, Wrindanneth, ya'll put on a light show tha likes o' which they've never seen!"

"Looks who's talking! Forget the light show; with the way you go up in flames, they won't even be able to see the lights with the Dwarven bonfire running around!"

Slate's growl showed what he thought of that comment, just as Wrindanneth's retort showed what he had thought of Slate's.

By the time they opened the gate and entered the front lawn, the mood between Slate and Wrindanneth had darkened a bit, shifting from joke to insult as was the norm when they started elucidating the finer points of each other's shortcomings. All argument ended, however, as soon as they entered the front door.

"Welcome home, gentlemen!" The cheery voice of the Aspect greeting them was the last thing either Slate or Wrindanneth wanted to hear.

Letting his feelings be known, Slate barked, "I thought we turned ya off!"

Always chipper, the Aspect responded, "You did, but I will not disobey my core functionalities—ensuring the health and happiness of my residents—nor will I ignore information sent to your attention. You have a message."

Interested now, Slate replied, only a little shortly, "What is it?"

"You have a message from Adar the Paratechnologist."

Cutting the voice off, Slate interjected, "We know who Adar is. What's tha message?"

A small projection appeared in the air before them, showing a solid three-dimensional image of Adar from the shoulders up, his face seeming to look at each of them simultaneously as they watched. "Greetings, Four."

He smiled before continuing, "We have succeeded in synthesizing the sword, battle orb, and shield with only minor modifications. Do you wish to have these items returned?"

"We need to discuss remuneration for this and the ship's command orb as well."

"Please contact me at your earliest convenience."

"Until then, good day."

"That's good ta hear." Slate was happier to think about the prospect of riches than the actual application and development of the technology. Only half seriously, he added, "Took 'em long enough, if ya ask me."

"They probably did not devote the same time or resources into the shield, blaster orb, and sword as they did to the command sphere given the much greater potential value associated with the knowledge that may be held within its confines." Although he did not know the Construct's full capabilities or its limitations, Aroganji doubted that the Paratechnologists would devote the full resources of the Construct to items that may be amenable to other avenues of research.

"Let's see what he has to say." Wrindanneth was as eager as Slate to hear any news from Adar, not just concerning the rewards they may receive from development but also words of progress regarding the investigation of the ship's orb itself.

Aroganji directed his voice to the Aspect. "Please contact Adar for us. We would like to speak with him, if he is available."

A few seconds passed in silence while they waited for a response either from Adar or the Aspect. After about half a minute of waiting, Adar's head popped into view in their midst.

Slate was so startled that he stepped back before recovering himself. Chiding himself for his mistake, he knew that he would never get used to all this magical foolishness.

"Good afternoon, gentleman."

"I am sorry for the delay in contacting you regarding the alien technology. I have been quite busy of late and have only devoted my team to the shield's working after our meeting regarding the command orb."

"No need to apologize, Adar."

"We have had significant success in replicating all three items." Proud of what he had accomplished, Adar added, "In fact, I believe the techniques we have developed to synthesize the crystalline material will serve as the basis for the replication of the command orb itself."

"Furthermore, with the aid of the Construct, we have found a way to realign the crystalline matrix in such a way as to allow the magical energies that we are more familiar with to power the devices in lieu of the psychic energies employed by the alien creatures."

"Excellent!" Wrindanneth's excitement was building. With all the success they were having with the Paratechnologists, he could very easily see himself devoting significant amounts of time with them exploring research avenues on his own.

"While we are on the subject, would you like to have the items returned? With all of the data regarding their constituents and makeup stored in the Construct along with the knowledge of how to recreate them, we no longer need the originals."

Wrindanneth shook his head. "If you want to keep them as a trophy, then feel free. A few of those modified shields may be useful to us, however."

Adar nodded. "We thought so. I will have four sent over when the synthesis is complete. Given the potential value of the items, we also thought that your ship could use a shielding system based on similar principles."

"That would be most appreciated," answered Aroganji, keeping his tone even.

"You must understand that these personal shields are prototypes, however. They do not, as yet, have the full capabilities provided by the alien device."

"What are their limitations?" asked Wrindanneth.

"When we altered the crystalline structure to allow magical energies as we know them to power the shields, we lost some efficiency in energy uptake and storage in the devices."

"In its original form, the alien shield can run so long as its wearer has the energy to power it. The shields we have devised are only able to store enough energy to remain operable for a minute or so before discharging all of their power. Furthermore, the crystals are only able to safely function several times within a day without compromising the crystalline matrix."

"With the larger crystal we would use to power a shielding device for your ship, for example, this inefficiency is not a problem. A larger crystal will allow us to store enough energy to run for significant periods of time without ill affect. With smaller devices, like the personal shields, however, this limitation precludes quite a bit of the flexibility inherent in the original device. With a bit more development time, we should be able to overcome this limitation."

"Thank you. We will keep that in mind, if we need to use them."

Changing back to the original subject, Adar added, "We have already received some very strong interest regarding the exclusive sale of these modified items from one of our starfaring trade coalition members."

Aroganji nodded in understanding. "I am certain that the command orb will fuel even more interest."

"As we receive revenue from the proceeds of sale of items and technologies related to your devices, where would you like the funds to be deposited? Do you have a bank that handles your transactions?"

"We do. First Vault handles all o' our savin's." Slate had all of their banking information committed to memory, but was reluctant to share that information publicly.

Although Slate would not trust this information to the Aspect and was therefore unwilling to give Adar the information directly, Aroganji had no such qualms. "I will let the Aspect handle the transfer of account information between us for future deposits, Adar."

Before they could continue, Yip interjected with a question. "Does the magistrate's office oversee the disbursement of funds to charitable organizations?"

"In conjunction with the Construct and the governing council, the magistrate's office helps to coordinate various civic and hospitable functions, yes."

"Would it be possible for the proceeds associated with my portion of these funds to be routed to charitable organizations?"

Slate nearly choked. Spluttering so strongly he could barely make a sound, he finally managed to croak, "Ya wanna just give it all away?"

Yip looked at Slate resolutely. "What use have I for these funds? Are my needs not met here?"

"What use?" Slate was incredulous. He had already forgotten Yip's earlier generosity with his portion of their reward for taking the *Shrike* and her crew. After all, something so unreal and unbelievable was easily pushed to the forgotten recesses of one's mind.

"I do not need the money for food. I do not need the money for shelter. I do not need the money for material goods. I do not need the funds for edification. I do not need the money to begin a business or start a trade. These are among many uses to which these funds could be directed that will better serve those that do."

"But—"

"I am not asking you to give up your portion of what you earn, Slate. I am merely deciding how to use mine. Is that not fair?"

Stroking his beard, the absolutely foreign concept of giving away riches causing him no end of confusion, Slate managed a terse, "Aye."

How could someone rationally decide to put others before himself? Even if all of a Dwarf's needs were met and all of his heart's desires were fulfilled, there was always the future to think of and prepare for—just in case weighed heavily on the Dwarven mind, almost as much as an appreciation for the hue of pure gold or the facets of fine gems.

"That is something we can discuss, Yip," was Adar's respectful answer.

Yip bowed slightly. "Thank you. I will seek you out at the magistrate's office. Will you be available tomorrow afternoon?"

"I should be."

"I will look for you then." Yip gave a slight bow of his head.

Shifting focus, Adar said, "We will need access to your ship to make the necessary modifications to your vessel's defensive systems. Would you like to arrange a time to meet one of our representatives?"

"As soon as possible," answered Wrindanneth with a nod, anxious to initiate the process.

"When would you like to meet?"

"Will tomorrow morning work?"

"It should," answered Adar. "If not, I will make it work."

"I will be at the docks tomorrow morning at dawn, then."

"I will have Flight Master Gideon Goldsprocket meet you there. He's one of our finest *faerviage* system engineers."

Adar smiled, a touch of humor evident in his eyes, although for what they did not know. "Unless you would prefer a new vessel, Mazithras also recommended that we inspect your ship for other likely upgrades as a portion of our repayment for your discoveries. Would you be amenable to that suggestion?"

"Certainly. And the *Shrike* suits us for now." Wrindanneth maintained a straight face when he answered, but he was positively jumping with excitement on the inside at the suggestions.

"Any word on the unraveling of the information contained within the orb itself?"

Adar shook his head. "Unfortunately not. The Construct is devoting a significant portion of its resources to the problem. We must strike a balance between pushing hard to retrieve and decipher any information held within and risking compromising the orb's artificial intelligence or triggering any potentially threatening or destructive security systems."

"In a very real sense, we have to learn how the system works as we go and must therefore take each step forward cautiously. I can tell you this, however. Since we copied the orb itself, we are not actually working directly on the command orb you retrieved. We are working on understanding how information moves and is stored within the orb's unit cells in a duplicate copy. Once we have a complete understanding of how the orb itself fully functions, we can then translate these insights into a means to slowly pick the original apart."

"Is there any other way that I may be of assistance?"

"I think that is all," answered Aroganji kindly.

"Then I will look forward to your communications Aroganji and Yip. Aroganji, if you would prefer, you can have the Aspect route the financial information directly to the magistrate's office. Yip, I will prepare some material on several well-established charities for your review for our conversation, should you need any ideas. I will also review Gideon's assessment after he meets with you, Wrindanneth."

"Thank you, Adar," came the general response.

"Until we speak again," Adar nodded his head and his image faded out.

"Wow! Can ya believe it? When tha stone starts rollin' it just doesn't stop!" Despite Yip's eccentricities, Slate was more than happy with the direction their luck had been taking them. If only finding and dealing with the Cabal were so easy!

"By the time they've unraveled the orb's secrets and we're ready to go after the Cabal, we'll have amassed enough gold to retire to estates and live comfortably for the rest of our lives." Wrindanneth grinned wickedly. "If one's inclination is toward indolence and ennui."

"Speak fer yerself! I'd be quite happy ta sit on a throne and count my gold all day, drinkin' tankards o' ale and eatin' piles o' tha finest victuals."

"And let your stomach grow as broad as your mouth?" Wrindanneth's sneer had never left his face. "Once the Cabal's destroyed, there'll be another quest to sate your thirst, of that you can be sure."

Yip shook his head softly. "Peace will be the greatest gift we can hope to receive from this effort."

A brief moment of silence followed his sober comment.

When no one spoke, Slate finally said, "All right, gents, I'm off ta tha' nearest pub ta cure what ails me. I'll see ya in tha mornin' when tha sun breaks tha horizon." Leaving Duraeleon strapped to his back along with his dusty armor and sweaty undergarments, Slate trudged out of the house.

Knowing Slate's preference, the Aspect waited until he left before speaking. "Aroganji, I have transferred the information requested to the appropriate party in the magistrate's office."

Aroganji gave a short nod. "Thank you for your assistance."

Before Aroganji and Wrindanneth made their own evening plans, Yip asked, "Will you be joining us on the practice field tomorrow?"

"Yes," replied Aroganji.

"As will I," answered Wrindanneth. "I'll follow you to whichever park works before heading to the docks to meet Gideon. That way, when we're done, I can meet up with you and we can continue where we left off."

"Then I will leave you two to prepare your meals and relax for the evening.

Have a pleasant night." Yip bowed slightly and retired to the sunroom for the night, ready for the evening's practice and the next day.

Yip sat on the steps, watching the sunrise backlight the full, airy cumulus clouds in coral and titian hues while he waited for his friends to finish their morning meal. When he sensed their patterns moving toward him from the kitchen, he knew it was time to go. He stood just as Slate came through the front door, already bantering back and forth with Wrindanneth.

"If yer hair were any kinkier, it'd tie itself in knots!" was the first thing he heard as Slate exited, looking over his shoulder at Wrindanneth who was following him out the door.

"The same could be said of your beard! Your bird's nest is in need of a trim much more than my locks."

"A Dwarf's beard never needs trimmin'! No Dwarf o' sound mind would ever sully his honor by cuttin' it off deliberately, ya fool Northlander! If he had ta, he'd tie it in another knot or tuck it through his belt before resortin' ta such foolishness as that. Where's yer sense?"

Wrindanneth snorted at the thought of Slate with his beard and all its bangles tucked into his breeches. Gesturing placatingly, he held back further laughter and said, "All I'm saying is that your beard was as much in your plate as your knife and fork."

Slate laughed heartily. "Per'aps I wanted ta sop some up fer later!"

"I really doubt you'd ever miss a meal, but I could be wrong. Stranger things have happened."

Tired of their gibes, Aroganji said, "Enough of this silliness. Let's go."

Although his face did not show it, Yip held back a smile. Even though his friends chose to show their care for each other through sarcasm, their humor and witticisms only reflected the depth of their friendship.

Wrindanneth joked, "What are the chances that we'll find the same park available today, Yip?"

"I'd wager we'll have ta find a new spot ta meet our needs."

"Thanks, Yip." Wrindanneth looked at Slate evilly.

"Ya know he's not gonna bet, ya overgrown buffoon!"

Walking through the gate, Yip answered, "We shall see."

Surprisingly enough, the grassy meadow was indeed still there when they returned to the park, as was the furrow left by Slate's ballistics experiment.

Seeing the park had remained unchanged, Wrindanneth said, "I'll leave you to your practice. I'll be back as soon as I can."

While his friends made their way into the gate to practice killing each other, Wrindanneth went on his own way, eager to see what Gideon had in store for their ship.

Without his friends' company to hold back his progress, Wrindanneth picked up the pace, letting his long legs take him through the lanes in great distance covering strides. Before another half-hour had passed, he had crossed the scintillating Scimerian Gate and was making his way toward where the *Shrike* was docked.

By the time the *Shrike* came in to view between several large alien vessels— she was flanked by an elegantly formed dragonfly, perfect in detail down to the translucent shimmering wings and a hulking war mountain that looked like nothing so much as a flying stone ziggurat—Wrindanneth had to hold back a chuckle for he knew exactly who waited for him ahead.

Chest stuck out proudly, chin held erect and tilted slightly upward to catch the breeze, his arms akimbo, one raised polished boot resting on the pylon to which the *Shrike* was tied, a small Gnomish man posed calmly amidst the morning hustle. With a bright crimson scarf trailing in the wind behind his goggled head, worn brown leather aviator's gloves, chaps, and a jacket protecting against inclement conditions that were not yet in evidence, Gideon looked like nothing so much as a Gnome waiting to be noticed.

Shaking his head at Gnomish creativity and taste, Wrindanneth certainly noticed.

Approaching the Gnome, he gave a friendly wave. "You must be Gideon!"

Maintaining his pose, chin aloft, gray eyes distant, Gideon said, "Gideon Goldsprocket, 'Faerviagér Extraordinaire.'" He gave a slight nod of his head in introduction. "I see that my reputation precedes me!"

Wrindanneth stifled a laugh. "You certainly stand out in a crowd."

Gideon laughed openly. "Of course! That's the Gnomish way!"

"The goggles and flight suit are a nice touch."

Gideon grinned proudly. "I thought so."

Sweeping his arm in front of the *Shrike*, Wrindanneth asked, "What do you have in mind for our ship?"

"I have a few ideas, but let's have a look at her first." Gideon gestured toward the ship. "Shall we?"

Wrindanneth muttered a quiet incantation and the gangplank extended out and lowered, bridging the dizzying gap to the continent waiting far below.

Gideon spent some time wandering the decks, fastidiously inspecting the ship as he progressed. At times he held up a green crystalline ocular to his eye as he made his observations, sometimes he muttered incantations to aid his considerations, and at others he used no special techniques that Wrindanneth could discern.

After over an hour of meticulous observation, perlustration, and analysis, Gideon returned to where Wrindanneth waited at the helm. Gideon gave a curt nod as he approached Wrindanneth. "You have a fine ship here, a fine ship indeed. Plenty of potential and room to grow."

When Wrindanneth smiled in acknowledgement, the Gnome added tersely, "Of course, the ship's craftsmanship, life support, and the piloting systems are about the only thing that are fine on this vessel. She's about as bare as a ship can be and still be capable."

"Braemen must have put all of his spoils in areas other than his craft."

Not ready to be taken in again for a potential rebuke, Wrindanneth said nothing.

"There is one true exception." Gideon smiled archly. "She has about as fine a pilot interface as you can imagine. I'd wager that Braemen used this system as a means to channel his own energies through the ship when he needed to act offensively or defensively."

Although he kept his answer to himself, based on his own experience, Wrindanneth had to agree.

Looking Wrindanneth up and down thoughtfully, as if seeing him for the first time, Gideon said, "Your ship will grow with you. For that you can be fortunate."

When Wrindanneth made no response, Gideon clapped both hands together and washed them eagerly. "Until you come into your full faculties, you're going to need a bit of help keeping your ship and its crew safe. I'm certain Adar already mentioned his plans to outfit your ship with a shielding system based on a modified version of the device you discovered. Quite ingenious little gizmos I might add, but there are other things we need to do as well."

He began pointing to various parts of the ship outlining his ideas. Waving above, he said, "Of course you'll have the shield overhead, but you'll need more power to maintain it than what your ship currently can store. A new coupled mana cell array and capacitor should fit the bill nicely. With the one I have in mind, you'll be able to charge it yourself or let it gather magical energies as needed."

"With the new cell array installed you'll also be set for a device of my own invention—Gideon's Transmogrifying Spectral Cyclotron!"

Wrindanneth broke in before he could go on, "What is that?"

Apparently taken aback, as if the name should explain itself, Gideon answered, "A simple device that intakes ambient magical energies, converts the stored power into a streaming spectra of intense wavelengths of multicolored light, spiraling over and over, reinforcing and magnifying the intensity of the resulting beams as they cycle through the cyclotron, until finally the photons ignite the surrounding atmosphere in a raging cascade of superheated plasma!"

Wrindanneth raised his left eyebrow. "And what exactly is that? A type of energy cannon?"

Ignoring Wrindanneth's conjecture, Gideon replied, "Surely you're familiar with the concept of plasma—highly ionized gases typically created at very high temperatures as in the stellar bodies? And certainly every aspiring wizard is familiar with coherent beams of light generated by exciting atoms to higher energy levels causing them to radiate and release their energy in phase along the path of a narrow beam?"

Wrindanneth did not even shake his head in answer. "No."

"So you've never heard of a laser then, either?"

"No."

"Hmm." Gideon scratched his head then nodded. "Yes. It's a combinatorial energy cannon."

Wrindanneth held back a, *Thought so*, in response.

He did, however, say, "Sounds dangerous. What prevents the energy beams from igniting the atmosphere near the cannon itself, especially within the limited atmosphere contained by the ship's shield in space? For that matter, what ignites if there is no atmosphere, as is typical at many times in interplanetary travel?"

"Excellent questions!" Gideon obviously enjoyed explaining theories, especially theories he helped to develop. "That's the beauty of the cyclotron! The spiraling energy paths are forced continually forward thus"—and here he winked—"with a bit of magic, preventing the surrounding atmosphere from igniting uncontrollably until the cyclotron's pattern is disrupted by collision with the intended target."

Pausing for emphasis, and the opportunity to point his finger in the air declaratively, he added triumphantly, "And the cosmic void of space is the perfect medium for this weapon because the energy beams are not weakened through continual absorption and reemission by intervening atmosphere. Although more power alleviates even this concern, there is in fact no intervening atmosphere to ignite. " Here he waved his finger in a spiral as if reaching a crescendo. "Almost all vessels have atmosphere inside thereby providing the ideal medium necessary for plasma generation once the lasers have penetrated the ship's hull!"

Shaking his head, he fairly crooned, "In fact, the resulting plasma ignition is particularly devastating within the confined space of an interstellar vessel. Of course, a secondary benefit of the weapon is that, given its dual modes of attack, between lasers and plasma, it is especially difficult to counter."

Wrindanneth smiled viciously. "Unless one has a shield akin to that developed by the alien creatures we encountered."

Gideon shook his head in reply. "There is a chance, yes, but even then, some wavelengths of light created by the spectral oscillations of the canon should be able to pass through their shields. As I said, the lasers oscillate in frequency across the entire spectrum of light, so chances are at least one wavelength will get through their defenses."

"If not and you are not in atmosphere, there are ways to ignite and project plasma even in the vacuum of space by adjusting the rate of the cyclotron's spiral rotation using the ship's atmosphere as the plasma source. In atmosphere, the plasma arcs can be similarly created before impact with the ship. As a result, either the plasma arcs or laser beams should have an opportunity to pass through a defensive shield."

"Also, because the beams are, at least in part, magical, they will be even more difficult to fully counter given the entire complement of energies involved."

Gideon smiled, adding, "Of course, depending on how well the technology developed from your discovery sells, we may be able to modify the cannon to increase its overall effectiveness."

"How so?"

"With slight modification and a significant upgrade of your power source, the tunneling cyclotron energies can be used to create a self-enclosed electromagnetic field. Through the application of increased power and laser beam intensification, the plasma within this field is then heated to temperatures paralleling those found in the centers of stars, inducing a localized fusion reaction."

"Which means?"

Gideon spread his short arms to their full length. "There is a big boom!"

Wrindanneth reserved judgment.

When his theatrics received no reaction, Gideon added, "And not much left but heat, light, and randomly ejected atoms!"

When Wrindanneth remained stoic, Gideon continued, "Also, the alien blasting orb technology could be used to expand the range of power sources and effects employed by the cannon, increasing the range of devastating fun!"

Wrindanneth liked this idea very much.

"The second major modification I suggest would also be made more practical by a larger power array. I propose the installation of a protoplasmic biomimetic melioration system—the Mark IX version of course."

Wrindanneth raised an eyebrow.

Having learned his lesson before, in lieu of launching into a more detailed explanation, Gideon clarified, "An automatic ship repair and recovery system. Your vessel will be able to heal itself like your body."

After a dramatic pause, he added significantly, "Only better."

"Ah," nodded Wrindanneth with a smile, glad for the suggestion after their near fatal battle with the alien battleship. The last thing he wanted was to be stranded somewhere unable to summon the equipment or energy necessary to repair the ship.

"For the safety of you and your crew, we'll also be installing the latest version of the Tropospheric Coagulatory Anti-ejector Concussion Ameliorator, Alpha Mark Two version."

Wrindanneth shook his head wonderingly, holding back a laugh. What in the world was that? "Which is?"

"Have you ever heard of an air bag?"

When Wrindanneth shook his head, Gideon chuckled and smacked his forehead nearly dislodging his gaudy hat. "Of course not! Wrong dimension. The TCACA does exactly what the name implies. It thickens the air around crew members immediately before an impact, prior to when any violent or otherwise jarring motion is detected or predicted by the Amelioration system, thereby preventing any number of calamities such as concussions, contusions, black-outs, fractures, crew-members thrown overboard or otherwise jettisoned, impalings, severings, dislodgings, whiplash..."

"I get the idea," interrupted Wrindanneth.

"The TCACA system also works internally minimizing potential interior damage to ship occupants associated with violent impacts and sudden impacts with equal effectiveness."

"It's quite an amazing system, to be honest. If for some reason, one of the crew does manage to get themselves jettisoned, the TCACA is capable of coagulating the air anywhere within the extent defined by the ship's self-contained atmosphere."

Listening to Gideon describe the safety system, Wrindanneth had an evil idea. "Can the TCACA be directed to thicken the air upon command?"

"Never really given much thought to that," replied Gideon. "I could modify the system to allow the captain to have this control as an emergency fail-safe."

"Do that, please," replied Wrindanneth.

Oh, the fun he would have!

Gideon gave a brief nod in reply. "There are other features we can discuss once Adar gives the approval. He has mentioned the possibility of incorporating a preliminary replicant of the alien intelligence system on your ship once the inner workings are deciphered, but that may take some time, I'm afraid. I would also like to install a system like the Every Gnome's Anti-Intelligence Clandestine Apparatus version 3.1, Corvette Class to help you and your ship avoid detection, but that, like the command system and upgraded fusion cannon, will have to wait until we have authorization."

He chuckled. "I will say this, once we have the larger energy storage arrays installed, you'll have significantly more juice to draw from to make any evasive maneuvers quite a bit more evasive!"

"You'll also be in a position to handle almost any further upgrades we can throw at your ship."

Wrindanneth nodded, liking this last idea, enjoying the Gnome's high spirits and half-intelligible prattle. "How long will you need to make the modifications that you discussed?"

"Hmm." Gideon pulled a large abacus-like contraption from one of the pockets on his leather jacket, a device far too big to actually fit in the enclosure itself without some form of magical modification. He then began to push the wooden counters back and forth rapidly along the small parallel wooden rods. Whistling as he worked, occasionally scratching his head or looking at the sky while testing the wind direction with a moistened finger, Gideon took a few minutes to finish his calculations. "Given readily available parts, an uninterrupted work schedule, two able Gnomes, and a sunny day with a slight tailwind, I should be able to finish in approximately seven hours, twenty three minutes, and seventeen seconds including time for a standard one hour lunch and two mandated fifteen minute breaks."

He smiled brightly at Wrindanneth after a short pause. "Assuming the lunch is provided, of course!"

"What's your preference?" replied Wrindanneth, smiling as well.

Morning had almost past into afternoon before Wrindanneth rejoined his friends at the park where they were each practicing their own disciplines. Yip stood still as a post with his arms hugging an imagined barrel, one he would never drink from either. If he were working with the energies of Aroganji and Slate as he had done the day prior, Wrindanneth had no indication.

Wrindanneth could almost see a haze of sweat shrouding Slate in his exertions. Despite his small stature, the Dwarf could exert himself far longer, with more force, and with more vigor than any normal Man.

Aroganji looked as though he were trying to swim through the air while performing a ritualized martial dance. Although his movements appeared very controlled and stylized, based on prior conversations Wrindanneth knew that Aroganji's movements held the basis for all the permutations of his Craft.

In lieu working on his own practice of channeling the divine magical energies inherent around them, Wrindanneth felt more inclined to relax. With his friends absorbed in their own practices, he was content to catch up on a little of the sleep he had missed this morning and the past few days while waiting for them to finish. Pulling the hood of his robe over his face, he lay down on the grass, shutting his eyes to the bright light and exertions of mid-day.

Sometime later, feeling refreshed, he prepared to open his eyes and immediately knew that something was wrong. For starters, he did not feel the grass beneath his cheek, nor did he feel the ground beneath his arms, legs, or torso. Quickly assessing the situation, he felt subtle threads of magic woven about his body. Unsure of his safety, or if he was being watched, he moved ever so slightly to make certain he was in control of his body and found that he was not being restrained. He then cracked one eyelid just wide enough to get a brief glance of his surroundings.

Looking down, way down, he could tell that he was still in the park, or, rather, he was still in the park's vicinity. Only, instead of lying on the ground, he now hovered some fifty or so paces above the ground, the open space, and his friends who were not paying him any real attention as far as he could ascertain. Looking over toward his feet, his robe bellowed out in the breeze like a trailing sail. Beyond his feet, a brightly colored streamer twisted and twirled in the breeze.

Stifling an angry curse, he muttered the incantation for a levitation spell and quickly dispelled the enchantment holding him aloft. Standing up while he floated toward the ground, he quickly closed his mind, fuming, his face even redder than the long flowing hair atop his head. Bending over, he ripped the tassel off his right ankle and let it float away with the wind.

Before his feet had touched the ground, he yelled, "Who in the name of the seething black Abyss did that? Someone think they're funny?"

Aroganji looked up from where he went through the same slow motions that he had been doing when Wrindanneth left him a few hours past in the morning.

"Funny? No one thinks they're funny, Wrindanneth."

Sputtering, Wrindanneth bellowed, "Then why in heaven's name did I wake up to find myself flying in the air with a tassel tied to my leg?"

Wrindanneth's yelling roused Slate's attention from his blade work. Yip, however, remained motionless in the grass. For all Wrindanneth knew, Yip was trying to grow roots and stay there permanently.

Walking over toward where Aroganji now stood by Wrindanneth, Slate said, "'Tis a beautiful day indeed, my tall friend, a perfect to be outside enjoying tha weather." Turning his gaze to Aroganji, Slate asked innocently, "What were those things ya told me people in Chang Sen like ta fly on days such as this?"

His face a study in calm, his mind closed to Wrindanneth's, Aroganji answered, "Depending on where you are from, they are called *zhiyuan* or *yaozi*. In the Common Tongue, they are called kites."

"Ah!" A broad smile now breaking his ruddy cheeks, Slate looked at Wrindanneth and said, "Seemed like tha perfect day ta fly a kite. And, since ya were available and had nothing else ta do, we flew ya!"

Stewing, absolutely ready to explode, Wrindanneth held his tongue, lest he take more of their insolence as the butt of yet another joke. Restraint, too, would take a bit of the joy from their fun as they would not be given the pleasure of a response to their prank. Self-control would also serve to his advantage in the time to come.

Nodding, his voice just as calm as Aroganji's, his face smooth, he shrugged, saying, "You're right. Today is a perfect day to relax outside and perhaps fly a kite." He paused for a moment, changing course. "Before we avail ourselves of the opportunity presented by the day, would you like to hear what I learned about our ship?"

A bit taken aback that Wrindanneth did not rise to the bait, Slate remained quiet.

"Do you wish for me to rouse Yip?" asked Aroganji.

Shaking his head, Wrindanneth said, "That won't be necessary. I'm sure he'll hear all about it soon enough."

Slate nodded curtly. "Aye."

Gesturing with both hands moving outward in an arch from his waist, he opened his mouth as if to continue. As he did so, he barked a quick incantation, translating the motion of his arms into the uplifting motions associated with his spell. Before either Aroganji or Slate could react, both were shot up into the air with only time to register the briefest looks of surprise as their eyes widened and the gravity reversed beneath their feet. Shooting up into the air, their cloaks billowed over their heads like wild lugsails for which the wind had suddenly turned in a new direction.

Completing his enchantment, one he had been working on the day before had they been paying attention, he left them both suspended in the air as he had been before he roused from his unfortunate nap.

Sitting down languidly on the grass, he took a moment to enjoy the day while watching his friends' reactions.

Aroganji remained poised and had the spell countered prior to reaching the apex of his flight. He was drifting back down before Slate was even locked into position above.

Meanwhile, Slate struggled and flailed as if he was being held suspended upside down by his feet even though his head remained pointing upward toward the heavens.

Not saying a word or showing any visible expression while Aroganji descended, Wrindanneth watched as Aroganji then countered the magic binding Slate since he would be unable to do so himself. Feeling a bit better about himself after taking control of the situation, Wrindanneth smiled as first Aroganji and then Slate landed and said, "You were right. Today is a beautiful day to fly a kite. Or two."

Touching the ground shortly after Aroganji, his long beard and bangles a tangled mess, Slate growled, "Very funny, ya scrawny, orange-headed whisk broom!"

Smiling condescendingly, Wrindanneth replied, "Now, Slate, if you want to have the right to play a joke, you have to be able to take one."

Slate harrumphed and began to reorganize his beard.

Smiling, Aroganji answered, "True enough." While Slate got his temper under control, Aroganji asked, "How was your meeting?"

"Interesting to say the least. Looks like they want to outfit our ship with a modified version of the alien shield. To do so, they'll need to increase the ship's energy storage capacity which will have other attendant benefits like improving our rate of flight and maneuverability in addition to increasing our ability to power other ship functions and future upgrades. With the new power supply, we'll also be able to operate a Gnome-engineered cannon in addition to a ship maintenance and repair system."

His beard now reorganized and his dignity restored, Slate replied, "Sounds promisin'."

Although he was impressed with the offering, Aroganji remained a bit concerned, adding, "We'll need a way to hide or mask the presence of our ship if we are ever going to try to track down the Cabal. That's something we'll need to push for I think."

Nodding, Wrindanneth said, "That's in the works once the revenue starts flowing from the proceeds of the Paratechnologist's promulgation and licensing of the alien technologies. We also discussed various upgraded versions of the Gnomish cannon and the installation of an artificial intelligence system based on the alien command orb."

"There may be other options we can push for as well," said Aroganji. "An on-board teleporter or recall unit would certainly make any journeys ahead much quicker and safer. If not, even a localized translocation device could help our chances to survive in a battle."

"Agreed."

"When're tha Gnomes goin' ta complete tha installation?"

"They're doing the work tomorrow on the condition that I provide lunch."

Slate chuckled. "Really? Bet they want some rabbit food."

Wrindanneth laughed. "Cabbage, Brussels sprouts, rutabaga, turnips, and a few choice mushrooms among other delights."

"Blech!" Slate grimaced.

With a smirk, Wrindanneth replied, "And I thought all Dwarves had to eat were the fungi that grow in your caves. You'd think vegetables like those would be delicacies, especially since Gnomes are your distant cousins."

"Bah! Gnomes have about as much sense as Northmen. Which is ta say none!"

Wrindanneth laughed. "Why don't we rouse Yip and call it a day?" In no mood to work on much of anything after his friends' prank, even though his retaliation had made him feel better about being caught off-guard, he offered an alternative.

"Let him come when he will. Ya know he doesn't need us around ta practice anyway." Slate patted the head of his axe that he held loosely with his right hand. "I fer one, however, will be stayin' on ta practice my blade work. If tha Cabal's goons are half as good as Yip, our journey ahead will be quite interestin'."

Aroganji agreed. "You may return home if you will, Wrindanneth, but I wish to complete the greater and lesser creative, neutralizing, and destructive cycles of the Wu Xing at least one more time today."

"All right, all right." Wrindanneth shrugged, knowing his friends were correct. There really was no time to waste. Even though they were waiting on too many things, or so it seemed to him, as much time should be spent in practice and preparation as possible if they were to stand any chance of success. "I'll stay. Perhaps I can spend some time channeling through my dagger."

Slate laughed. "Or through yer eyelids, if ya can't keep 'em open!"

Yip opened his eyes, relaxing his arms and letting them return slowly to his waist. With his exhalation, he let the excess *chi* stored in his body ebb outward from him—waves of misty, ethereal steam returning to the surrounding shimmering fogs. Calm and invigorated, he felt the life moving and flowing all around—from the minute organisms lacing the soil to his friends practicing nearby—as bright clusters of living light. Moving subtly between, connecting and enlivening the unending individual constellations of life, the *chi* coursed—softer than the lightest mist, deeper than the night sky.

Slate sat nearby collecting his breath after another series of vigorous blade work. His broad shoulders moving up and down with each breath, Yip watched the energy he had concentrated in his axe returning slowly to the encompassing *chi* as Yip had just done. Gently shaking his arms and legs, he walked over to where Slate recovered from his exertions.

"Your skills remain sharp as ever, Slate."

Speaking with candor, the Dwarf replied gruffly, "Not sharp enough, I fear."

"Your blade moves nearly as fast as your mind, Slate. You have come very far in a short period of time."

Slate stared at Yip intently, a mixture of eagerness and unease fighting for primacy in his eyes. "We'll soon see."

Yip gave a short nod. "I must go to the magistrate's to make charitable arrangements."

Slate nodded.

Looking over to where Wrindanneth and Aroganji practiced, Yip waved farewell. "Peace in every step, my friend."

Slate only wished it were so.

Walking through the hustle of the docks, Yip spied the *Shrike* about the same time the sculpted stone exterior of the magistrate's office came into view. Even to his eyes, by no means an experienced pilot or a seasoned sailor of any stripe, their ship seemed quite prosaic compared to almost every other vessel on the docks. In fact, there was not a single flying ship that resembled what he thought of as a traditional sailing vessel—with the exception of their own.

Fantastical monsters, animals large and small, insects, sleek metallic cruisers, steaming, helter-skelter contraptions, ships of stone, crystal, wood, and metal flew to and fro or floated moored by the docks. Whatever form, style, or build, the ingenuity and imagination of the creators was clearly in evidence. Despite all this, even though to many their ship may appear lackluster, he appreciated the *Shrike*'s simplicity, functionality, and its formal ties to the tradition of shipwrights who had sailed the seas long before magic and *faerviage* made plying the skies possible.

In a place as wondrous as Tellanon, the ordinary stood out amidst the extraordinary.

By the time he entered the magistrate's office, mid-afternoon had passed. Walking through the carefully constructed stone façade, the delicately mineral veined ores and inclusions adding layers of complexity to the building's cool, formal surface in the bright sun, he was welcomed cheerily by the usual disembodied voice. "Welcome, Mr. Chuan! How may we be of assistance today?"

He bowed. "I am here to meet with Adar, if he is currently available, to make some charitable arrangements."

"Certainly. Just a moment."

He waited patiently, enjoying the fragrant air from the many hanging plants lining the entry's periphery.

"Adar will see you now."

A golden oval appeared in the air before him indicating where he should go. At times like this he wondered if this building even had hallways connecting all the rooms, or if it actually had other rooms, for he had yet to see one.

Stepping through the lustrous yellowish nimbus, he entered into what he thought could only be Adar's office. The expansive room had an entire floor-to-ceiling wall composed completely of clear glass overlooking the western edge of Dharia passing slowly below. Overflowing shelves lined the rich wooden walls—samples of ore, rocks, and other natural found objects competed for space with moving mechanical devices, parchments, books, and collections of various oddities of every stripe. The air actually hummed with the motion and dynamism of magical contraptions of every size and sort. Despite the density and variety of apparatus and articles, the room felt very light, open and airy, a perfect spot for creative exploration and introspection. All around were the objects necessary for formative inspiration.

Behind a small, tidy burnished desk, Adar smiled warmly as he entered. "Welcome, Yip. Would you like a seat?"

Shaking his head, a small silvery dragonfly alighted on his shoulder, its artfully crafted wings, buzzing in his ear as it landed. "I am fine. Thank you." The shining dragonfly tilted its head, vivid jewel-encrusted eyes glinting in the sunlight, and washed its front legs as if cleaning them after a hunt or practicing its mosquito catching technique.

Adar steepled his fingers. "How may I be of assistance, Yip? What do you need to know?"

He stood for a moment admiring the view from Adar's window, watching the world moving sedately below.

"Compassion and wisdom should motivate Man's actions in equal measure. Loving kindness, guided by a sincere desire for the condition and goodwill of all living beings, provides the requisite incentive to foster a future open to prosperity for all, creating a world guided by the highest ideals and incentives."

"Although I never imagined having any material goods beyond the clothes I now wear, I am now, or may be very soon, in a position to provide tangible aid to those who have not been so fortunate along with those who seek to better themselves."

"Not knowing or familiar with the institutions of this place, I come to you asking what charitable organizations are available in Tellanon to offer hope and opportunity to those who meet with difficulty in their pursuit of peace, knowledge, livelihood, furtherance, and happiness."

Adar nodded, thinking for a moment how best to frame his response. "As you know, Tellanon is a prosperous place. In fact, the revenues generated here dwarf those of many entire nations. As such, the ruling council has given this issue much consideration, for those who dwell here have the preponderance of their material needs met by virtue of citizenship and the attendant established social benefits of this right. Even refugees and those who seek asylum or assistance are met with open arms, provided they gain admittance, and are placed, as best as we can, in situations suitable to their desires."

"Unfortunately, because our island is so small, much of the support we offer involves sending those who come here to other locations more amenable to their needs. We do, however, maintain a vigorous advancement system for those who come to Tellanon to better themselves. We are home to one of the finest research institutions and libraries in this portion of the galaxy. Access to this institute, along with the lower grades of the lyceum and academy that feed into the college, is made available to any who seek admittance, based entirely on merit with no charge. Also free of charge, any who seek medical assistance within our walls find treatment and care for any number of magical and mundane afflictions."

"Beyond these institutions for health and betterment located on the island, we also channel funds to similar institutions scattered throughout Ea'ae. As an island fueled largely by ideas and innovation, we seek to encourage the continued development of not only the magical and technical skills necessary for our island's continued prosperity but for the continued maturation and betterment of the world at large. Having a populous both capable of innovation and representing the highest ideals of humanity as citizens of the larger macroverse is in our best interest."

"Of course, given the rigor and demands placed upon us by our research, much of these efforts fall upon those who show the most potential, whether rich or poor. As such, our charitable efforts, at least those promoting development within Tellanon, tend to aid and supplement the intellectual meritocracy that underlies the majority of activities on Tellanon."

"As you can see then, even though we open our arms and seek to foster the highest of ideals, our direct efforts fall upon a very limited few. In the end, it is the work of these few, those who have been cultivated and developed so carefully, that indirectly benefit the many."

Yip continued staring out the window until Adar finished. When he did, Yip turned his full attention to Adar. "Ea'ae is vast and so are the problems facing her. I am glad that Tellanon fosters the continued intellectual development of her people. You provide a wondrous model for many to follow."

Adar smiled, pleased.

"I would like for you to spread your knowledge, not just for the benefit of those here, but to make what you have learned and developed readily available to the world at large and beyond, not just to those who earn admittance or who are selected based on merit. I would see the knowledge you develop here move freely for the betterment of all as suits each individual's ability and interest, not their merit. I would see knowledge move from Tellanon not through trade or goodwill alone but actively promoted in service to the highest ideals of humankind."

"I would see those students, researchers, entrepreneurs, merchants, and citizens who come here actively involved in sharing, in uplifting, those who may not be so fortunate outside its walls."

"I would provide the opportunity for those who wish not only the chance to develop their intellect, but the means to develop their minds, their spirits, and their hearts through direct interaction, training, and instruction."

"I would establish a vehicle for public instruction, outreach, community development, and, most of all, the opportunity for any who seek it to realize their highest ideals and aspirations."

Adar remained silent for some time before answering. "You would do much."

Yip did not answer for some time, his attention returned to the passing clouds. "The seed of inspiration is but an idea. It need only be planted."

"What of the costs?"

"The money will come in time, if not from me, then elsewhere. As revenue from the proceeds of the new technologies comes in, fund what you are able."

"Individuals given the opportunity to explore their own interests will provide the start. From their hearts and minds, their vision, the approach will flower and blossom."

Now it was Adar who remained silent.

"Is this something that can be done?"

Adar continued thinking for a moment before answering. "I believe so. We will need permission from the university and ruling council, of course, but focused research, or outreach as you call it, should be possible."

"As the endeavor grows and develops, I believe the greatest difficulty will be effectively managing the project so that it remains true to your original intent while continually expanding and improving."

"Unfortunately, I cannot offer any expertise there."

"But a dedicated Aspect could be created and assigned to aid in the project's realization, one designed to facilitate the core of your mission."

Adar remained thoughtful. "Give me time to think this through and make some inquiries. There are many who are more qualified and adept in this arena than I who should be able to help. Until then, whatever funds that do accumulate in your name will be held in reserve until the actual project is underway. Is that acceptable?"

Yip nodded. "Yes."

"You offer quite an interesting proposition, Yip. I would love to see it meet with success."

He bowed. "As would I. Thank you for the help, Adar."

"Think nothing of it."

THE PAI-LIEN TOUCH

The unicorn's hooves
strike without sound.

Whitest of manes,
the sum of all colors.

His idea would need much work to be successful in development, implementation, and widespread adoption. With time, however, he was sure that even
those motivated entirely by self-interest would see the benefit of applying their
skills within the broader context of the wider world and universe beyond both
for their own and the larger populace's benefit.

Although his larger quest to unseat the Cabal was aimed at providing
continued safety for the world at large, he wished to see his planet, and all
beings on and beyond it, prosper as well. If he could, through the donation of
whatever material goods he received, help provide a brighter future for those
who breathed the same air, walked under the same sky, and were enlivened by
the same energies as himself, then he would do so. Beyond his own world,
spreading similar ideas of goodwill, wisdom, introspection, and opportunity
throughout the cosmos should follow.

Tellanon would be a ready vehicle for this continuance.

He hoped that in a future ruled by optimism and the pursuit of the highest
endeavors, room for the existence of evils like the Cabal would steadily
disappear.

His thoughts occupied by hopes for a bright future, his usual vigilance
wavered slightly as a flame flickers in the wind. Only after some time lost in

plans, wandering the streets toward home, did he notice something amiss—echoes of Darkness rippling toward his feet.

Extending his mind outward instinctively, all self-recrimination left behind in the urgency of his response, he sensed a presence nearby, or rather he sensed the shadow of a presence akin to an inverted eclipse when the sun blocks the appearance of the moon. Somewhere near, its location almost impossible to pinpoint, an inky Darkness that drank in Light and life without returning anything, its presence cloaked in a halo of Light, only vaguely made apparent more by a lack of substance, the emptiness in its heart, than actual reality. So elusive was its taint, only the overflowing magics of the city and its inhabitants had served to finally reveal the creature's presence to him as it stalked and skulked at the skirts of his awareness, its essence yet drinking ever so subtlety from those vibrant presences all around.

The Cabal had found him!

Leaping up onto the roof of a nearby shop, light and empty as the breeze, he let all energy flow through him as a vacant shell, a ghost that only the living could see.

If he had not been so deep in thought, he might not have needed such an immediate response, for he normally walked cloaked under such protection with heightened awareness, but, new to his abilities, his guards had wavered along with his attention.

There was no time for remonstrance or blame, he must move or be caught. He had no idea about the foe that haunted him, pursuing so skillfully on the uttermost edges of his awareness, so he must choose a location to fight that would be to his advantage lest his quest end in failure ere it truly began.

Running from one sculpted organic roof to the next, he stayed in the sun, hoping that the protection of the full light of day would afford some added assurance from the Shadow dogging his steps.

How had it found him here?

How had it penetrated the city's defenses as formidable as they were?

Where were those defenses now?

Many thoughts rushed through his mind, whipping through his consciousness as frantically as blades of grass before an oncoming storm. Unperturbed, he let those thoughts go, left to resolve themselves in the deep currents of his mind, as his awareness remained relaxed and poised, taking in the fullness and possibility of each instant.

He must be ready to react if he were to live.

And so he was.

If he could reach his friends, he could hope for some aid, but he did not know if they remained in the park or if they had returned home. Whatever the course, innocents would be at risk if he fought on the rooftops, at home, or in the park.

The air rushed over his face and past his ears as he made another lithe leap across a wide alley separating one business from the next.

It was the leap that did him in.

He could tell that the shadow hounding him had lost its way after he had completely opened himself and let the *chi* within return to and commingle with the life flowing all around.

What he did and what those around him did were two very different things, however.

When the innkeeper opened his back door to set out some scraps for his cat, leftovers he would not need for the dinner he and his wife prepared for their guests, he looked up just as Yip leaped overhead, spanning the space between buildings.

With a sharp inhale, the innkeeper jumped back as his breath caught in his throat for an instant, his heart racing as adrenaline pumped through his body in reaction to the surprise flying by above.

This unwanted attention, but a minor disturbance in the normalcy of the day, gave away his position as surely as his earlier lack of focus for he sensed the Shadow's unerring movement toward him as certainly as he heard the innkeeper's heightened state of alert.

To a creature as perceptive as his pursuer, even the most minor of mistakes was enough to do him in.

Leaping over the tiled roof ledge, jumping from one leaf-filled gutter to the next, landing on the roof of the neighboring cobbler's residence, he ran away from the innkeeper's excited energy body.

Taking another bound, he jumped high upward from the roof of the cobbler's shop adjacent to the inn and landed on the much higher roof of a neighboring building.

The broad flat rooftop told him this must be either a very large store or office, if not a warehouse or factory. Here at least, he would remain out of sight from those pedestrians below, granting them at least the safety of slight distance.

Taking position in the roof's center, he relaxed and waited.

Chased to the roof by an enemy he could not see, only sense and feel, his mind settled broadly over the inn and nearby buildings—a soft presence casting for the slightest disturbance, the absence of normality, for he knew not how long his foe would take to join him.

Long seconds stretched between each breath as he waited, alert and attentive, poised and at the ready on the balls of his feet.

He twisted swiftly, sensing a coalescing of Darkness, a moving shadow brought to being as it cast off the cloak of concealment that had shrouded its presence in a nimbus of life affirming *chi*. Liquid shadows glided in his mind's eye, running up and over the eves of the warehouse's metal roof. His mind crystallized to a point, focusing on the enemy he could not yet see, a horror he could only feel.

The Cabal was reaching for him!

He turned to face his pursuer.

Before his eyes could register, a harsh, alien voice rang out grating in his ears, echoing shrilly in his mind.

Bleak, savage and sibilant, void coalesced into form as a Shadow slid up the side of the high warehouse's roof. Soft, fluid and vapid, somehow absent of real substance, the agent of Darkness oozed fear and dismay. To his inner vision, so accustomed to the bright vivid reality of ambient energies, the creature wavered and shimmered along its edges around an empty black center, a dark hole punched in the fabric of reality as life-giving *chi* rushed into its dark, vacuous heart. Roiling toward him from the roof's brim, its hooded form sucked in the surrounding sunlight leaving the warehouse cloaked in a state of murky half-shadow.

Had this *thing* once been human?

Had this evil once called itself a Priest of K'un Lun?

"Yip Chi Chuan!" a voice that pierced his mind as much as his ears rang out.

The figure's cowl revealed only darkness—hinting not at eyes or visage, only an emptiness devoid of light.

Reality seemed to warp and twist in dismay while recoiling from his foe's abhorrent presence.

Stopping a few paces before him, a single hand reached out pointing at Yip's chest toward his heart—a gesture threatening to pull his life force out on strings of shimmering void that he sensed undulating around the creature's edges.

"Yip Chi Chuan!!!" The voice ripped and tore into his essence, sharp claws scraping his mind and heart, trying to rend them free of their fragile moorings.

He sensed a gathering readiness in his abhorrent foe, poised to strike out across the void between them—Darkness reaching for Light, emptiness grasping for form.

Confusingly, he also sensed an almost undetectable gathering of power all around, as though the *yuan-chi* itself were waking and put into motion, as if a slumbering giant of unimaginable reach were beginning to stir.

Aware but untouched, he made ready.

"Your order is dying, Yip!"

"You are one of the last!"

"Long have we, the Cabal, toiled for your destruction. Long have I tracked you over the Four Lands, sensing your movements, your impressions, tasting your traces and disturbances, but you have never truly eluded me. You and your kind shall never again..."

That moment's hesitation, the creature's litany of lies, was all he needed, more than he had dared hope. With a sudden, subtle brush of his hand, a slight nuance, Yip's essence lashed out toward his foe, reverberating through the dark corridors of its twisted soul, bringing the light of a new day to an interior landscape barren, dim, and filled with ruin.

Just as the Light of Life gives breath and sentience to man, the soft touch of Light guided by compassion, hope, and wisdom echoing in the darkling recesses of an agent of the Cabal will shatter the confines of its evil and open the darkness within to the day.

As his foe fell, Yip collapsed to the ground, spent, overcome by a mixture of emotions—relief, hope, elation, fear, and confusion.

He had defeated an agent of the Cabal!

If the Cabal could find him here, how could he ever guarantee his friends' safety?

Had he sensed a gathering of energy from the city's defenses when the creature prepared to strike?

Why had he hesitated as long as he had before seizing his instant of opportunity?

Was there something he hoped to hear from a creature so abhorrent that reality itself flinched from its presence?

Letting these thoughts and many others return in force, some time passed before he heard voices speaking to him.

"Mr. Chuan, are you all right?" A young man dressed in the crystalline armor of Tellanon's elite Home Guard looked down at him with concern. By his side, two much more seasoned Guards held bright crystalline swords at the ready. One was a stout Dwarf with a heavily braided auburn beard; the other was a small Gnome whose crystalline armor looked like the stooped form of a praying mantis.

The bright vibrant Lights of their presence were a welcome sight to his eyes.

Gathering his thoughts, he stood, remembering they could identify him by his essence, and nodded. He did not reveal more lest a misplaced word cause fear to run rampant through the community.

When Yip gave a positive response, a nod of recognition and acknowledge-ment, the Man said, "I am Gil-alan of the Home Guard. Many apologies for the breach in security." He smiled, as if reaching out to ease Yip's pain and discom-fort. "We drill and train for emergencies all the time, but a failure like this has never happened under my watch or in my lifetime."

Yip smiled weakly, but gave no answer.

"What can you tell me of that creature?" Fear and loathing vied for supremacy on a young face composed only by strength of will and discipline. "We arrived at the innkeeper's only in time to feel its presence—a vile desecra-tion I shall never forget."

"There are Shadows that walk that should never see the light of our world. There are also Shadows that walk that would destroy it."

He said no more.

Accepting the answer, Gil-alan shook his head and said, "I do not yet know how that entity escaped detection and destruction by our internal defenses. We will find out and rectify the shortcoming."

"I have alerted my superiors to the disturbance. They are responding to investigate further. A team of Home Guard will arrive shortly. Do you wish to remain here?"

Yip shook his head. "I need to return home to alert my friends."

"Understood. You will be contacted for more details that we can assure this never happens again."

Again he nodded.

"Do you need an escort home?"

He bowed humbly. "Your efforts on my behalf are much appreciated, but I should be fine. Your time will be better spent assuring all are safe and in assisting your supervisors than helping one such as myself."

Gil-alan nodded. "As you wish."

Entering the house, the Aspect greeted Yip warmly. "Welcome home, Yip. You have a message waiting."

He nodded, thinking officials from the Home Guard may wish to speak with him. "Please play it."

A small officious man dressed with excruciating care appeared in the air before him. Layers of painstakingly detailed fabric highlighted a face as pale as the clothes were bright. Arcane sigils and runes lined the pleats and edges of his great purple robe draped over the clothes hidden beneath.

"Greetings, Master Chuan."

He gave slight nod of his head, no trace of expression or emotion apparent on his visage, his voice a mellifluous mixture of cool condescension and steely command. "I am Peran, Vicar of Lord Éremon, Exarch of Tellanon, august Consul of the ruling Protectorate and High Council, Fifth of Thirteen."

He smiled at the introduction, sure that many more titles were available should they be needed.

"Lord Éremon has requested the pleasure of your company on the morrow. You shall arrive at his palace promptly at mid-morn for the honor of his reception."

"I have left directions on gaining entrance along with protocols for proper comport with your Aspect."

"Good day."

The Vicar's dictate brooked no refusal or excuse and left him wondering why he would be contacted by this person at all.

Had word of the attack already reached so high?

Who was this Éremon and why would Yip of all people arouse his interest otherwise?

Éremon was obviously a man who was used to being obeyed for his representative's missive left no room for choice.

To answer his questions, he turned to the Aspect.

"Who is Éremon and what is he to Tellanon?"

"Éremon is a member of Tellanon's ruling High Council—the Protectorate—and is widely regarded as one of, if not the leading, mages in the realm. Along with the other presiding elected Paratechnologists in the city, he decides matters of import both for Tellanon and its citizens including issues of security, edification, and trade. As the highest ranking Paratechnologists themselves, this ruling circle also provides guidance over the primary activities concerning the work of the city's Paratechnologists both in terms of research and secured public supplemental funding for the Paratechnologists' activities. The Protectorate also presides over the most sensitive matters of dispute pertaining to the island and its citizens, acting as representatives on behalf of the citizens of Tellanon with dignitaries, foreign agents, and other members of the highest stations."

"Did Peran leave any indication as to why I was contacted?"

"He left only directions to Éremon's palace, instructions with whom to speak when you arrive, and a dossier concerning proper etiquette for your meeting with Éremon."

Again he wondered why a man of Éremon's station would wish to speak with him directly and not through one of his agents like Peran.

"I am to arrive alone?"

"Yes."

He had no idea what this meant. Perhaps he had, indeed, already been contacted about the attack.

"I will make a copy of Peran's dossier available for you in your room."

He gave a short bow. "Thank you."

"Have a good evening, Master Chuan."

As he walked into the study located off the entry, Wrindanneth looked up from where he sat with Aroganji pouring over magical texts. "What was that about?"

Yip shrugged, the motion visible through his robes as only a slight shift of his shoulders. "One of the city's leading Paratechnologists, Éremon, has requested my presence."

Wrindanneth's face lit up with a knowing smile. "Éremon! Good luck with that. I would hardly call him a Paratechnologist." He chuckled. "Crafty old devil."

"You know him?"

"I know of him. But who doesn't?"

When Yip's face remained blank and he did not answer, Wrindanneth realized that his friend obviously did not know of him.

"I've heard stories, mostly from Maeth, that would put him in very high esteem. A category reserved for few immortals and far fewer mortals, I might add."

Yip nodded. "He sounds like quite a figure."

Wrindanneth assented. "He is."

Finally noting something different about Yip's demeanor, Aroganji asked, "Is something the matter, Yip?"

Letting the tension and confusion of the past hour flow out from him, now that his curiosity was sated, he answered directly without embellishment, "I was attacked by an agent of the Cabal on the way home."

"You were what?" Wrindanneth was incredulous.

"Why didn't ya say anythin' sooner?" asked Slate with obvious concern from the entrance to the kitchen.

"I only waited for the opportunity to speak after other questions were answered."

He then explained further, "An agent of Darkness breached the city's defenses and attacked me on the way home from the magistrate's."

"How it found me, how it penetrated the city's defenses, and many other questions are yet to be answered."

"By Brendle's blessed beard, I'm glad ya're safe!" Slate shook his head. "How did it get through tha city's protections? I thought that was impossible!"

"Obviously not," replied Wrindanneth, his sarcasm unnoticed amidst his friends' concern.

"Perhaps Éremon is contacting you about this assault," said Aroganji thinking about how the city's hierarchy and chain of command may work.

"Perhaps," answered Yip thinking that Aroganji was probably correct.

"An august magician such as he may be the one to ultimately resolve the issue," offered Wrindanneth.

Worried about Yip's safety, Aroganji asked, "Do you need us to come with you?"

Aroganji still marked his position on the page he was reading with a pointed index finger. Yip could see that Aroganji's magical energy was blending with that of the book. Although unsure exactly what his friend was doing, he speculated that Aroganji was either practicing a spell described in its contents, facilitating his learning with magic, or that the book itself required some form of magical energy to properly function, perhaps like a key. Aroganji probably had to maintain contact with the book lest it break the connection or foil the spell he was working on.

His attention encompassing Aroganji, the room, and beyond, he replied, "I have been asked to come alone."

"Hmm. Sounds like an interesting meeting then. I'd like to hear about what he has to say and what he proposes to do to ensure the city's safety, if that is why he is calling you now." Wrindanneth's curiosity piqued at the chance to meet such an eminent mage.

"We should remain on guard until this is resolved. We should set up a watch tonight," said Slate with a firm set in his jaw.

"I fear there is little you can do to detect the approach of such a one, my friend. The creature cloaked itself in Light to elude detection much as I try to mask our own energy signatures."

"Even if Aroganji and Wrindanneth laid their wards, I fear it would counter them. We can and should remain vigilant, however. If you remain alert, you will hear me should I call for help."

"That is all we can do."

Slate nodded.

Wrindanneth smirked. "Yet another excuse for you to sleep with your armor on, Slate!"

Slate growled but resisted the urge to give in to Wrindanneth's taunt.

"I will lay a few extra wards just to be safe," added Wrindanneth thinking of a few nasty ideas that may entrap such a Shadow as he stood up to begin his work checking and refortifying the home's perimeter.

Yip smiled. "As you wish."

"So you won't be joining us to practice tomorrow?" Aroganji, along with Slate, had become attached to the idea of their daily practice.

Smiling once more, Yip said, "We'll see. I am to meet him mid-morning, so I should be able to join you when I am done, if you are still practicing."

"We should be. In the meantime, if there is anything else you need, let me know." Aroganji returned to his book as Yip left with a nod.

When he arrived in the solarium, Yip was greeted with a hovering representation of a small leather-bound document entitled *Proper Etiquette and Bearing as Befitting One's Station and Intended Audience.* Beneath the title, the pamphlet was subtitled *A Manual for Dignitaries, Officials, and Diplomats.* The manual had the tertiary subheading *Everything You Need to Know to Communicate Effectively with Those Other Than Yourself.* A final, quaternary title added *A Manual for Citizens and Representatives of Tellanon.*

He chuckled. That should cover just about everything!

He could certainly appreciate the importance of effective, understandable communication built upon common ground and apprehension, especially in a city that served so many travelers, so many races, and so many cultures from every end of the cosmos.

Although the manual's holographic representation appeared quite small, of a size that could easily fit in the palm of one's hand, he could not seem to find the document's end. The book appeared arranged like the branches on a tree. Each general subject bifurcated over and over becoming more specific, precise, and esoteric. General chapters offering advice on listening, reading gestures, problem solving, clarity, poise, and communicating clearly were followed by chapters on strategy, conflict resolution, political intrigue, diplomacy, mediating, negotiating, subterfuge, and dissembling. Many topical chapters followed under each general heading, each getting more and more specific until the book began to discuss the minutia of particular subjects at a level of technical sophistication intended for only the most learned audiences.

When he began following the subject branches on culture, first reading about anthropology and archaeology in general, his perusal led naturally to thumbing through intricate descriptions of almost every race known to the Paratechnologists of Tellanon. The work included information on the beings' appearance, outlooks, beliefs, worldviews, languages, history, values, institutions, magical and technical sophistication, psychology, political technicalities, key negotiating points, unique features, and other characteristics ad infinitum.

He had no idea how much information was actually stored in this little manual. Surely more knowledge than a single mind could ever hope to digest.

Reading the document was dizzying. Not only did one topic lead to another in an endless chain, but whenever he focused on or thought about a particular word in the text he was reading, an entirely different subject heading pertaining to the topic in question would appear on the book's pages offering further elucidation of the topic.

After a short time, however, he got used to reading in this way and began to find the arrangement quite enriching. In actuality, reading from, or interacting with, the linked text was not too different from using his magical teaching scroll. The primary difference was that when reading from his scroll, whenever he thought of a topic of interest, information regarding the subject appeared on the scroll for him to study. In this case, with the projected text, one topic led to another in a continual succession of interrelated topics in an ever-expanding web.

After reading more than he ever thought possible on the bituminoid elementals of the volcanic moon Puryn, he decided that enough was enough and it was time to begin his evening meditations. He would, however, come back to the cultural manual should he have any questions about any particular races or beings that they may encounter in the future.

As he settled down onto his cot, relaxing into a full lotus position, resting his palms lightly on his thighs, he wondered how many more richly interactive texts, or the equivalent, were available in Tellanon on similarly fascinating subjects. Perhaps in the future, when he had the opportunity, he could explore the libraries here in earnest. Perchance he could even learn more of his order's history, traditions, and techniques through such research.

After the Cabal's recent attack, he wondered if he would ever have the chance.

Yip slowly roused himself from his evening meditations well after the sun had risen and his friends had left for their practice in the park. Light and easy, his awareness encompassed the house and its immediate environs with a soft caress, feeling the ebb and flow, the play of the interdependent origination of energy and activity shifting and changing all around, a continuum of unified experience.

Standing up, he left the solarium for the front door, ready for his meeting with Éremon, curious as to the cause of the summons and wishing to find the answer. Looking outside as he opened the door, high clouds overhead floated like brushstrokes, painting the light blue sky in whites and grays. Crossing the threshold and passing over the lawn, he opened the egress and stepped out onto the cobbled street leading toward the city's center, closing the gate behind him with only the faintest of creaks. Walking toward the city's heart, crisp sunlight brought out the delicate colors of the alabaster stone buildings and walkways, highlighted by the variegated green trees, flowers, vines, and assorted plantings.

Barely visible in the distance over the arching roofs and crowns of trees, the branching spires of Illdrassil, home of Tellanon's ruling council, shimmered in the morning sun.

Moving along the winding streets, avoiding the main thoroughfares so that he could appreciate the homes and the beauty of the day without the constant press of people, each step toward the city's center revealed more and more elaborate residences lining the streets. Avoiding the incessant hustle of traffic also allowed him the opportunity to scan the surroundings with less distraction should another agent of the Cabal be nearby.

Despite the wealth of the city, the quality of the homes indicated the owner's affluence more so than the home's size. Many of the finer residences in the city took advantage of magics very much like those in the city parks. Homes and the surrounding grounds were extended beyond the natural limits imposed by the originally extant space, creating compounds extending into multiple dimensions beyond the confines defined by the geography of the island.

Toward the core of the city, where Illdrassil's shadow became more evident, he did reach a point, however, where the homes actually did become small palaces with the attendant estates resembling miniature walled fortresses perched on the most advantageous hills and crags. He was not certain if this palace district was an older part of the city that had been developed prior to the growth pressures that lead to the magical spatial extensions utilized in the homes located in other parts of the city. Despite their size and the extent of the manors' grounds, though, these homes, too, were extended into extradimensional spaces as befitting the owner's tastes and desires for there was not enough room on the flying island to accommodate such lavish, expansive demesnes.

Not knowing exactly how the magical manipulations of space worked, he wondered if these palaces enjoyed connections into other existing spaces, much like the land contained in the parks seemed to signify, if the spatial expansion represented an extension or expansion of the already existing space on the island, or if the extra land represented the creation of new space or land in another place or dimension entirely. If the parks and palace grounds were granted more land through direct connection with other places, he wondered how the security of the island was assured if its boundaries extended into spaces beyond its borders. If the regions represented by the parks and the extended palace grounds were in fact permanently divorced from their original context, or copied from an original template, then his concern over the integrity of Tellanon's bounds was moot.

Perhaps he would ask Éremon for clarification when they met.

The palace that Peran's directions finally led him to stand before appeared more striking, more unique, than any he had yet seen on his journey through the city—more fantastic than his wildest conceptions. Locked securely shut in front of where he stood, an overarching gate provided the only view of the castle and its grounds through the towering monolithic stone wall surrounding the compound. Perched on an escarpment overlooking Tellanon's edge, the castle, if it could rightly be called that, faced the surrounding sky as much as the city, as if warding the island's borders. Flowing stone merged the citadel with the underlying firmament creating a seamless transition from foundation to fort. A forest of dark green trees climbed the sides of the precipitous ridge on which the fortress was perched, unsuccessful in gaining the summit.

Unlike any other structure he had yet seen, he followed the building's contours from bedrock to apex, lost in its whirling details and complexities. After some time adrift in contemplation, he could only think that the building appeared to be a snapshot of motion, of waves of molten stone crashing together at a central point, crystallized in a tumultuous confluence of surging crests and rippling eddies locked in ivory stone.

Immediately ahead, a large portal barred by polished blue-tinged metal gates denied direct entrance through the unyielding stone wall. Flanking the entrance on either side, two lifelike stone warriors armed with swords and shields of the same blue metal as the gate warded the entry, their expressionless gaze fixed on the horizon.

As much as anywhere he had yet encountered in the city, magic permeated the place. He could see and feel the weavings of complex spells woven through the walls, the ground, and the air overhead. The metal of the gates, swords, and shields born by the statues shone with power as did the guardians themselves. He knew, beyond the instructions for entrance provided by Peran, that the magic imbuing the statues with power also infused them with a semblance of life and sentience.

His initial inspection complete, he spoke directly to the statues, "Éremon has requested my presence."

In response, the mouths of both statues opened in unison, deep voices reminiscent of the echoing of subterranean caves and grinding stones issued forth intoning, "Who are you to gain admittance to the realms of Éremon?"

"I am Yip Chi Chuan." Peran's instructions were explicit. He must answer as truthfully and honestly as possible to gain admittance whether invited or not. "The reason for my summons is known to Éremon and does not reside within the confines of my mind. Your question would be better answered by Éremon than myself."

Unsure what to expect next, he waited.

He did not have to wait long.

A feeling of absolute cold washed over him as though he had been doused in frigid water. The touch of magic coursed through him, washing him from top to bottom, searching out any hint of dissembling or threat.

After a brief time, the cold receded and the hollow voices answered, "The truth of your words resounds from within the echoes of your heart. You may pass." Both warriors remained locked in position, swords and shields held at the ready, as the portcullis slid open soundlessly, the metal gate disappearing into the thick rock wall as he walked through the arch.

With receptions like that, he imagined Éremon received very few guests.

Passing through the wall and on to the other side of the gate, a cobbled pathway led forward through a field of waist high grasses. Looking left and right, the meadow provided a natural border between the estate's outer bulwark and the thick forest that the lane led toward. As best he could tell, the green extended along the entire perimeter of the grounds. Looming ahead, an ancient forest began abruptly where the mead ended, bringing deep shadows to even the brightest day.

Moving forward carefully, his senses alert, he felt that not only were the forest and its grounds ancient, but so were the magics guarding them—a venerable place not to be trifled with or disturbed.

One should take care to walk lightly in such a place.

Perhaps Éremon had brought this forest with him when he came to Tellanon, perchance these grounds preserved remnants of the original forest once covering the island, or maybe this forest had been here so long as to develop the feel of depth and character of the deepest wilds. He could not say only imagine. Whatever the source, this place had seen much in its time.

He sensed memories pooled in the gloom ahead as profound as any of the shadows beneath her branches.

Making toward the narrow path running beneath the intertwining branches of the high trees looming over the shaded lane ahead, he sensed more than memories dwelling in the forest. Shadows of a different sort lurked out of sight within, ethereal darknesses that moved between worlds, only partially tethered to the material plane he now tread, shadows as far removed from him as the memories locked beneath the forest's branches.

He knew not to dally or stray from the path lest he become the target of the shadows' unwanted attentions, lest he become another memory lost in this place. Moving quickly through the wood, for his scheduled time to meet Éremon was fast approaching, he sensed several of these presences drifting with him beyond his direct view, as much guardians of the place as were the stone wardens at the gate.

With defenses like the ones he had already encountered, and many others he was sure that he had not yet fathomed, Éremon must have received visitors as unwelcome as the introduction to his estate implied.

He picked up the pace, for he realized that for all his hurrying, he did not seem to be progressing through the wood as quickly as his first glance at the forest's extent would have implied. Looking behind him, the entry to the wood still visible as a bright semicircle of light a short distance behind him, he chuckled, realizing that his speculations on the way here were in fact true, for he now ran through a forest covering an area enlarged far beyond the bounds dictated by the original space. Without proper visual references, he had no idea how long his dash through the forest would take. Turning his jog into a sprint, he let his limbs move naturally at full stride, his chest filling with air as his body suffused with *chi*.

Enlivened, brimming with energy, his feet skimmed over the surface of the cobbled road in a blur, his step so light that he did not disturb the leaves underneath his tread. Easily keeping pace, the shadows moved with him.

By the time he broke free of the forest, over half an hour of solid running had passed, taking him through the wood and up the steep slope leading to the top of the rocky bluff where Éremon's castle perched vigilantly. Even though he broke from the wood at full stride and continued running toward the stronghold, the citadel seemed to get no closer for his efforts.

Feeling the wind rushing across his face and over his limbs rustling his robes, he let out a hearty laugh.

For all of Peran's detailed instructions, he failed to mention the most important point!

Without having visited before or being told, no one would ever know how much time was required to cross the grounds to visit Éremon. Maybe this was a test of some sort. Perhaps Peran took pleasure in not elucidating the entirety of his request for reasons known only to him.

Enjoying the run, he let his thoughts slide away, filled with the lightness and buoyancy of the day, the experience of living, and the joy of moving.

By the time he finally made the great banded oaken doors leading to the castle proper on the far side of a protective moat overlooking the precipitous cliffs, the sun had almost reached its zenith indicating mid-day. Standing before the outer ward, the fortress was even more impressive up close than it had been at a distance. The walls erupting before him appeared as great, cataclysmic waves of stone, each eddy and whorl depicted in excruciating detail, rippling subtly on the surface. Looking left and right down the outer wall, he had no idea what the stone waves of the castle's exterior walls crashed against.

Raising his hand, he rapped three times on the solid wood, the sound of his strike muffled and diminished within the wood's dense core. A few moments later, the door creaked open soundlessly of its own accord. Standing some paces away from him in light brighter than the noonday sun in which he stood, Peran waited impatiently, his aura providing more light than Yip would have needed to see in complete dark.

Peran was obviously a very accomplished archmage in his own right.

"You are late." The small man's voice held a clear note of disapproval, his scowl was as dark as his clothes were light. Dressed from head to toe in shimmering silver robes, Peran appeared ready to attend a formal state ceremony or an important social engagement.

Unperturbed, Yip replied honestly, "And your directions are lacking."

Offering no rebuttal or discernible response, turning on his heel, Peran turned away abruptly, saying tersely, "Follow me."

Walking slowly behind, Yip once again lost himself in the unearthly details of the keep. Massive undulating waves of stone arched overhead, creating a space echoing the contour and motion of the waves of stone flowing above, the ceiling's crest touching the far wall which rose in another titanic wave. Bright sunlight streamed through the gaps left where the irregularities in the crest's leading edge did not reach the far wall. Where sunlight did not pass directly through the gaps left between the stone's edge and the next monolithic stone wave, shades of blue, green, yellow, and aqua light pooled in columns throughout the cavernous expanse—sunlight filtering through water in a vast submarine grotto. The stone itself seemed to move and shift elusively as well, changing shape and color as though the waves overhead were liquid and in motion. The combination of the play of lights and the shape of the stone served to bring the walls and floor to life, making them move and undulate as if he were walking underneath the sea on a sandy seafloor.

Other than the complexities of the walls' seething surfaces and the intricate play of light enhancing the feel of watery depths, as far as he could see, the interior walls of the outer ward were unadorned. No plantings or vegetation broke the stone's uniformity.

Passing through another large open gate, this one framed by the shape and action of the waves, he strode through the thick inner curtain and walked into the vast inner ward. Directly ahead, Éremon's keep thrust upward from the bedrock as abruptly as any sea cliff—solid, dynamic, and unyielding but understated as well, a light house or fortification standing stalwartly against an unseen enemy along a forlorn coast, lost in insignificance in the face of a raging typhoon.

Arching high overhead, the wavelike walls of the inner curtain did not quite reach the walls of the inner keep, having been repelled by the castle's walls. The waves appeared to be crashing, roiling, and recoiling backward and upward with great force and magnitude, their motion not entirely arrested. While the walls of the outer curtain nearly reached the walls of the inner curtain, letting both natural and artificial light shine on the simulated sea floor, here sunlight shone down directly in full brightness as the tide retreated before the might of the walls soaring above. Here, too, in the lee of the keep's massive walls, vegetation grew in low-lying profusion upon the unadorned rock.

Mosses, lichen, ground hugging heather along with other small plants and hearty shrubs clung to the face of the rocks adding splashes of green, grays, yellows, pinks, purples, reds, and lavender—small living accents that brought significant cheer to the cold, obdurate stone.

Though the promontory was formidable, the magic within was more so.

Far inward and upward, deep in the heart of the castle's highest heights, so far above that if he tilted his head he could almost look directly at the mid-day sun, Yip sensed the presence of Éremon, the one who had bidden him come.

And he was not human.

ÉREMON

Wispy hair, gray beard
wrinkled weather-beaten cowl—
made bright by the Light within.

Wrindanneth wrinkled his nose, wishing he had a free had to wave in front of his face or, better yet, to pinch his nose. Of course, the minor cantrip he had used to protect his sense of smell while his hands were full had worn off and he had yet to reach the docks. With any luck, a slightly modified version of the same spell meant to prevent the infusion of the pungent aroma hounding him would hold until he had time to hand the food off to the Gnomes. Otherwise, his battle against the stench would continue until after he dropped the meal off.

As it stood, he was just in a hurry to get the comestibles from the Cozy Cabbage Inn down to the docks. Although he would not admit it to them, he would much rather be with his friends practicing in the park than on this errand for Gideon, but, if delivering some Gnomish victuals meant the *Shrike* was outfitted quickly and effectively, then he was all for it.

To the casual passerby, seeing a towering red-haired, gangly-limbed, fully robed scarecrow running through the cobbled streets of Tellanon holding an overflowing tray of steaming vegetables tottering before him as if it were about to catch fire and burn at any moment must have been quite amusing.

Half walking, half loping through the twisting streets, he glowered as many pedestrians stared, stifled chuckles, or turned away with smiles on their faces covering mouths to mask laughter as he passed. If only his hands were not full, he would be the one laughing.

Frowning, he could not understand the unbridled excitement that had lit up Gideon's face as he had described the choice gastronomic selections he and his assistants would need in order to work happily and most efficiently. Slate had tried to explain that root vegetables, almost any plant grown in the ground and coming from the earth, had a particular appeal to Gnomes, but he could not relate. In the cold rocky soils of his village, vegetables were overwhelmed by fish and limited mostly to potatoes of the sweet and non-sweet varieties along with other hardy, cold-tolerant plants. Looking with distaste at the pungent, heaping piles of steamed cabbage, boiled turnips, radishes, cauliflower, sautéed Brussels sprouts, uncooked rutabagas, and raw wild ramps, he certainly could understand the Gnomish ability to make *faerviage* ships fly, and this ability had nothing to do with magic.

By the time he reached the *Shrike*, the combination of the noonday sun, his exertions, the heat of his robes, and the rank smell of the vegetables had infused his garments with a heady aroma fit for an abandoned back alley.

Of course, Gnomish sensibilities would probably differ.

Stifling an oath, for his second cantrip had apparently failed just like the first, he smiled as he saw Gideon and his crew hard at work on the *Shrike*, or, rather, he thought that what he saw was the Gnomish equivalent of hard work. A gang of six Gnomes, excluding Gideon, walked about the decks of the *Shrike* holding up what looked like tuning forks surrounding faint shimmering soap bubbles between the tines. Occasionally, one would chime the tines with a small metal rod and hold the fork into the air as if reading the wind while looking through the refracting bubble. Gideon stood at the ship's prow like the conductor of an orchestra waving his hands to and fro, frequently calling out to various Gnomes to adjust their position and instrument.

When he saw Wrindanneth approach, Gideon gave a brief whistle which caused all the Gnomes to stop in their tracks and called out, "Ah, Wrindanneth! You've made it! Just in time! We're famished after all this hard work!"

Wrindanneth could not imagine what was hard about what they were doing but held his tongue.

Sniffing deeply as he came over, Gideon crooned, "Just like my Dam used to make when I was a lad!"

Wrindanneth heard similar loving coos from the assembled Gnomes as they began to crowd around him along with a few brief exhortations about the wonders of the Cozy Cabbage Inn's kitchen.

"How goes your work, Gideon?" Wrindanneth set the heaping tray down on top of one of the pylons and stepped back to the relative safety and clean air by the gangplank lest the gathered Gnomes overrun him in their haste to get at the mounds of vegetables. Doing his best to maintain a straight face amidst the eye-watering fumes that trailed after him, he listened attentively to Gideon's progress report.

"As I said, you were just in time. We are just putting the final calibrations on the frequency modulators necessary to power your shielding system. Once that's complete, our work here should be done."

Incredulous, he replied, "You're almost done?"

Gideon nodded, the broad brimmed, purple plumed hat he was sporting bouncing emphatically with the gesture. "Nothing like a little Gnomish hard work and ingenuity to get the job done I always say."

He grinned widely, adding, "That and the promise of food from the Cozy Cabbage Inn for a job well done!"

Although Wrindanneth did not understand or appreciate Gnomish taste, either in food or fashion as he looked over the brightly colored finery arrayed before him, he certainly could appreciate their hard work and the outcome achieved as a result.

"Care to give me a tour?" He wanted to see and understand the modifications firsthand. A tour would also give him the chance to move upwind from the vegetables after the breeze had changed course.

"Certainly." Gideon gestured for Wrindanneth to lead the way, taking the opportunity to grab a handful of particularly rank Brussels sprouts.

Glowering silently as he walked the plank past Gideon, Wrindanneth was glad that he had gotten away from most of the smell at least.

Yip paused, reaching beyond, extending his senses outward and upward for elucidation. When he did so, his confusion deepened. A being of great power lay in wait for him above, one unlike any he had ever felt or seen before. Like the full brightness of the sun banked and hidden behind the moon on a total solar eclipse, with only the slightest hint of the luminous plasma of the corona left partially in view, Éremon hid his true power, his true nature, from those who would see.

If anything, Éremon's presence was the antithesis of the foul creature of Darkness that he had so recently dismissed. In lieu of banking Darkness with Light, Éremon banked Light with a lesser reflection of his scintillating essence.

Unafraid, in fact, reassured, Yip followed Peran forward knowing that a being of great Light waited ahead ready to reveal himself into full view.

Based on what he had heard from Wrindanneth, he had assumed, wrongly of course, that Éremon was a Man. Given the diversity of Ea'ae and the myriad peoples coming to, leaving, and moving within Tellanon, having a diverse body of leaders on the ruling council only made sense. From that perspective, having a being not native to the planet, to the island, or perhaps to this plane, would also make complete sense.

He need only wait a few more minutes to have his curiosity about the reason for his summons and about Éremon himself to be sated.

The cobbled walkway ended directly ahead where Peran opened two large oaken double doors to gain admittance. As the doors parted, Yip noticed that the interior of the castle appeared even brighter than the light of the noonday sun in which they stood. Not only that, the entire structure radiated with great magic, as if the immense forces of the crashing stone waves had washed wave after wave of magical energy into the keep, reinforcing and augmenting its substance.

Stepping through the double doors, he stopped in wonder, not at the breadth and beauty of the building interior's luminous seraphic aesthetic, but at the majesty of the exterior. Spinning around like a child in a candy shop replete with the finest confectionaries, he marveled at the vista laid out around him. All of the interior walls were entirely translucent. Magnifying the interior effect, the keep's exterior walls were wholly transparent.

He could see the sun shining overhead through the clouds above. He could even see through the castle's inner and outer walls, down and over the ancient wood, past the rows of white stone homes separated by paths defined by greenery, and out into the open sky beyond the island's limits where ships fluttered and buzzed like butterflies seeking pollen around the island's rim. Turning his head, he could follow Tellanon's arch from bustling docks to the elegant boughs of Illdrassil on high and then out over the precipitous margin defined by the outermost limit of the estate's grounds.

Looking inward, he could see intimations of room after room, each growing more and more faint with distance as he gazed through, lined with tapestries and paintings, books and trophies, sculptures and frescoes, mosaics and fountains.

What a wonder!

"Come. Éremon is waiting." Peran had no time for Yip's awe. They were late and his schedule was far too busy to tolerate foolishness.

Yip smiled. Peran had crossed this threshold so many times that the spectacle of his own abode was now lost to him. Falling in step behind the mage, he crossed the lofty entry, passing variegated trees lining the plush red and gold embroidered carpet leading to the spiraling double stairway on the opposite side of the great room. Pools of sunlight streaming through the walls highlighted as many types and varieties of plants as works of art within the castle walls.

Several minutes of climbing, and ample opportunity to appreciate the skill and beauty of the craftsmanship of the keep, finally brought him before a nondescript oaken door on the keep's topmost level midway down a broad hallway marked by a high, arching ceiling supported by evenly spaced pillars placed in pairs around the passage's center. The hallway's roof was entirely translucent, letting in the fullness of the sun and an unobstructed view of the firmament.

Peran gave a slight rap on the door and bowed at the waist as it opened soundlessly away from himself. As the portal opened, a warm voice issued outward, enveloping them in good cheer. "Master Chuan! Come in! Come in!"

Yip stepped into a cavernous room lined from floor to ceiling with tomes, texts, reagents, vials, phylacteries, and other items beyond his experience and ken. As in the hallway, the ceiling high above let in the full light of the afternoon sun. Hanging plants and vines swayed in the air like undersea kelp, adding green columns to an otherwise largely open space. Despite the room's size, it felt cheery and airy, close and warm. At the room's center, seated in one of two comfortably worn leather chairs, Éremon sat blithely, at ease and in full command of the room, sedately watching his approach.

Seeing Éremon, Yip bowed deeply at the waist out of courtesy and respect, feeling the scintillating beauty of character and the depth of power in his gracious host even as his own eyes looked to the floor. Even with Éremon's essence hidden, banked behind layered clouds of protection and disguise, Yip felt the overwhelming Light, brighter than the sun above, radiating outward from Éremon's presence. Here was one whose existence brought opportunity and hope to all those around lucky enough to be in his purview.

Tellanon was fortunate indeed to have such a one as part of its leadership.

While Peran shut the door behind Yip, his officious presence was still felt waiting in attendance in the hallway outside the room should a need arise.

Éremon gestured for Yip to be seated on the chestnut armchair opposite his. "Please sit down." Like his presence, Éremon's voice was as affable and welcoming as the spring sun.

"Thank you." Walking across the distance separating them and taking his seat, Yip examined the being seated across from him.

Éremon was tall, as tall as Yip was standing even while seated on the cushioned chair. Preparing to take his seat, he imagined that Éremon would be even taller than Wrindanneth when he stood to full height. However, Éremon's frame was larger and sturdier than his friend's, much broader at the wrist and shoulder, hiding great strength beneath his slate-hued robes. Reflecting the long, shimmering hair spread over the cowl on his wide shoulders, a plenteous gray beard hinting at great age draped lightly across his chest, not quite thick enough to hide the smile dancing upon his pink lips. Bright eyes brimming with curiosity and cheer welcomed his guest as much as his words. On the whole his face was distinguished and well-formed, the light wrinkles on his cheeks and smile lines highlighting his eyes, giving the impression not of age but of timelessness and wisdom.

"I trust your journey here was uneventful?" Éremon raised his eyebrows in interest as if inviting adventure.

"Your home and grounds are remarkable." Yip's short response spoke volumes. He could have said so much more.

Éremon smiled. "And you had no problems along the way?"

"No. The Shadows in the wood held their distance."

Éremon chuckled. "Ah...the Sceaduwulf and their ilk. I am glad to hear it. I could not have my guests getting attacked unnecessarily."

"Sceaduwulf?" He was unfamiliar with the term.

Éremon nodded briefly, noting that Yip had the pronunciation correct. "The Umbral Wolf. Some call them ghost dogs. They are incorporeal entities resembling the wolves of this world, only much larger, more ferocious, and almost impervious to magic. There are many other guardians such as those dwelling in the old wode." He laughed. "I haven't the heart to root them out."

Sensing the veracity of the answer, the ethereal creatures of the wood must be its original inhabitants and one such as Éremon would never willingly harm them. Éremon stayed here on their land with their blessing and offered them as much protection as they did for him.

Accepting his answer, Yip replied, "I apologize for my tardiness. I had not realized the true extent of your demesne until I entered. Had I known, I would have left earlier."

Éremon smiled. "Quite remarkable that. We've stretched and manipulated space so much on this island, it's a wonder we don't tear the fabric of reality completely and create our own entirely separate pocket dimension."

Seeing a chance to ask about the parks and how they were created, Yip replied, "How exactly does this manipulation work? My friends and I visit the parks each day and often come across an entirely new place each time we visit. Are these open spaces extensions of the land of Tellanon, connections to another place, or something else entirely?"

Obviously enjoying the unstructured conversation, Éremon steepled his fingers and answered with a question. "What do you think?"

He thought for a moment. "I would imagine that over time the people of Tellanon used their magical talents to fashion a place to their needs and liking. As time passed and their skills and preferences grew, so did their imagination of what was possible. With widened eyes, they created a context as complex and expansive as their vision while respecting the limits of their own land."

"I would say you are close to the mark."

Smiling brightly, Éremon continued, "Much of what you see in the land-scape was, in fact, fashioned as you say, through gradual accretions and modi-fications over time. However, each addition and expansion of the space inhabited by the island has gone through centralized approval. In fact, the entirety of the publicly accessible extradimensional space was created as part of a large public works project I envisioned many years ago."

Watching Yip carefully, he explained, "Each park is a recreation of a place particularly treasured by members of Tellanon's High Council and citizens. To those places, we added representations of various ecosystems scattered through Ea'ae so that visitors to Tellanon could get a true sense of the world on which they sojourned without having to travel over the entire width and breadth of the planet's surface. Each park is a portal to a small pocket dimen-sion composed entirely of representative gardens and natural areas from your world."

Yip nodded, appreciating the elucidation. "Intriguing. Thank you for the insight and enjoyment."

Éremon chuckled. "You are most welcome!" Smiling at the small man sitting across from him, he added complimentarily, "And too gracious!"

When Yip remained silent, Éremon brought his attention back to the reason for his summons. "I am sure you are wondering exactly why you were asked here, alone, apparently without cause."

Yip smiled, offering, "The human mind is innately curious."

Éremon laughed. "It is indeed."

In the lull that followed, Éremon watched Yip carefully, measuring him, gauging his character, his calm and patience, his resolve and potential in ways most Men would never comprehend. After a time, during which Yip remained silent while waiting for his host to speak and make his intentions apparent, Éremon finally said, "Your friend, Goran, requested that I speak with you."

An inner smile lit him up from the inside outward, as happiness radiated through him in an effusive glow. Although his countenance and bearing did not betray his emotion, he was very happy to hear that his friend was alive, hopefully doing well, and had, perhaps at least, met with some success on his quest to reach the ears of the Council of Light.

"He asked that I speak with you, explain what he has found, and request your assistance. In light of yesterday's events, I deemed it necessary to speak with you as soon as possible."

"Before we move further, I would have you know that a security breach such as the one you experienced has not happened within the lifetime of many of Tellanon's residents. For that, the risk posed to you, and the import of that breach, I am grievously sorry. Dark times are ahead, I fear, if we fail to act decisively while we still have the opportunity. Too long have we dawdled without appropriate action looking the other way for our own good only."

"Based on the Home Guard's investigation, the agent of Darkness that attacked you must have been secretly and unknowingly smuggled into the center city inside of another specially constructed magical storage device."

"Like the Construct before it, the Scimerian Gate scans the hearts of all who pass through its shadow for ill intent directed at Tellanon and her citizens, judging whether or not a tangible threat is posed. At the same time, the Gate searches out magical manipulation in those who pass through that may be of a sinister nature. Those who arouse suspicion or concern or who carry items of a particularly inimical nature are immediately teleported elsewhere for further examination and questioning."

"Yesterday, that system failed."

"We have isolated the man who brought through the agent of the Cabal. The merchant brought in several magical artifacts for trade. Each one was held within a magical bag of the sort commonly used to carry large amounts of goods. One of these items was a magically shielded jewelry case. When the case was opened at the shop of a particular jewel crafter that the merchant had called upon, the abomination stole away, thankfully too cunning and intent upon its purpose to risk the success of its mission by killing either the merchant or the shop owner."

Shaking his head sadly, Éremon said, "The Scimerian Gate detected no anomalies or ill will within the merchant as he passed, only an eagerness to be about his business and the will to make a few successful trades within the city's walls. Nor did the items he carried appear unusual or worrisome for the wards hiding the case's contents foiled all examination."

"Had the Shadow lain in wait inside without further protections, the Gate would have detected its presence even though it had cloaked its vileness in Light."

"However, and this is particularly troublesome and in need of further study, even if the wards had not been present on the jewelry case, the magic of the Gate would not have been able to divine its contents for the reliquary opened onto a separate, undetectable pocket dimension holding the Shadow further concealing itself within. This dimension only revealed itself and connected to the chest upon opening."

"Now that their power strengthens, our enemies grow ever more sophisticated in their means of assault."

"Given the complexity of the items moving in and out of the city at all times, there is little we can do to completely prevent such cunning infiltration."

"I have, however, created a significantly more powerful probing mechanism in the Gate's operation intended to cut through such layers of subterfuge in the foreseeable future. I can only hope that this will reveal any further Darkness that our enemies wish to be kept hidden."

"Anything that does not allow for complete scanning or that appears unusual will now be immediately teleported into the custody of the Home Guard until all is deemed well."

Éremon's eyes lit with curiosity as he spoke. "Did you notice anything unusual when you encountered the agent of Darkness?"

"Aside from the depth of its corruption and the guile it displayed by concealing its nature in a mantle of Light?"

"Aye."

Yip laughed self-deprecatingly. "And my ability to defeat it?"

Éremon shook his head, discounting Yip's words with a glance. "Some things do not happen by chance."

"I did sense a stirring of great power, as though something asleep were slowly wakening. In the urgency of the moment, while I fought off the Shadow, this vast accumulation of energy stilled before I took further note. It was gone before I had time to register more."

Éremon nodded gravely. "You sensed the rousing of Illdrassil herself. Seldom does she stir. Had the Shadow not cloaked itself in Light, Illdrassil would have struck it down long before it reached you."

The wonders of Tellanon never ceased. Had he not reacted to defeat the Shadow, Illdrassil would have done so before he came to harm. For the sake of her populace, he was glad such counters were in place.

His eyes full of meaning, Éremon intoned, "She no longer sleeps so deeply."

Understanding the significance of Goran's contact and Éremon's admissions, he then asked, "How may I be of help?"

Éremon took a deep breath, letting an unwelcome weight fall from his shoulders, ready to move on to other matters, and answered with a question of his own. "What do you know of Goran?"

"He is an Indural, possibly the last of his kind, a guardian of the land, and a being of great compassion."

Éremon smiled. "You mean to say, he is old and stubborn, refuses to let harm come to what he holds dear, and is too crotchety to change his ways?"

"No," Yip responded firmly, although he understood Éremon's comment contained a mixture of both levity and sincerity. The person he knew, the being he had helped and who had helped him, was not at all like that, not even in jest.

"Perhaps he was failing, perhaps he had lost his way, his spirit and resolve, in recent memory but that is not the one I came to know on my trip to Tellanon."

"A fire burns in him as it does in you, one that adversity and evil, difficulty and strife will not quench. Goran needed but a small spark to rekindle the flames within. He has refound his way."

Éremon raised his eyebrows quizzically. "And what, after all this time, has rekindled this flame?"

"He did." Yip looked at Éremon squarely. "As I said, he only required the slightest bit of hope to restore his balance and perspective."

He imagined that one as old as Goran, or Éremon for that matter for he believed the being sitting across from him bore a terrible span of years on his shoulders, could easily lose his way growing tired with the swift passage of years as Men count days.

Éremon pressed, "From whence came this hope?"

"From the mind of one willing to see his merit and value his true calling."

"And who provided the opportunity for this transformation?"

"A friend."

"You are certain?" All lightness left Éremon as the true intensity of his gaze bore down upon Yip, a terrible weight not to be born lightly. "You are certain that he has been restored and has found his way?"

"The light of hope can lift anyone be he Man or giant, human or Indural."

"There are those among us who fear that he is a broken vessel, worn and damaged through years of anguish and woe."

"A man who is judged is one who is often without liberty or opportunity."

Éremon lifted his thick gray eyebrows.

"Goran holds opportunity in his firm hands whatever the sentiment."

A grim smile broke Éremon's ancient visage. "Do not fear, Yip, your reassurance falls upon the ears of a friend. I, too, trust in Goran, believe in his purpose, and echo the weight and depth of his fears. As I said, others within the Council of Light feel differently, but that is an issue for another day."

"These others are not yet aware, as I am, of what transpired here in Tellanon, so the remembrance of the Enemy and Its agents are still left locked in the distant past."

Éremon paused for a time, the pace of his conversation slow and full of gravity. "I have felt as Goran now warns for some time based on my own investigations and premonitions, but ages of relative safety and security and many, many generations of membership for some of the shorter lived races have allowed some of us to shirk our duties and wander upon much less troublesome paths. With the advent of *faerviage* and numerous past diasporas, the strength, and willingness along with it, of many peoples has waned. Some among the council reflect this weakness as well."

"You see, Yip, long and long ago, well before the lands of Ea'ae were governed by their current lines and lineages of kings and chancellors, rulers and parliaments, your world waged war, throwing Ea'ae into unending, almost ceaseless turmoil. The Cabal, along with many other agents of evil and those they summoned and called, spread like a plague, nearly destroying all civilization, all life, on your planet. Myriad unholy beings from the darkest nether realms, entities that to this day must be tracked and hunted down throughout the cosmos, gained their first entrance into this dimension as a result of the conflict that raged unchecked across Ea'ae."

"Ages of war bred beings of true strength and resolve, forces dedicated to the protection of all Life and Light on this world and others. In the end, after generations of conflict, the forces of Light from Ea'ae and beyond finally managed to strike down the evils that had spread so far and wide throughout your world, although the Enemy at their source was never destroyed. In the aftermath, the survivors, those who were willing, banded together vowing that such evil would never gain a foothold on Ea'ae again."

"From this time of war, the Council of Light emerged, dedicated to peace, prosperity and opportunity for all. Overseers and advocates, ward and warden, the council was formed, composed of members from all of Ea'ae's races that the goals of the many would always be upheld by the few."

"We persist yet even if a few have lost their way."

Éremon lifted his palm flat out and a small representation of the world appeared in his hand. "In order to ensure Ea'ae's continued safety, the council and its allies evoked great magics, channeling the living energies of Ea'ae herself, and placed fourteen seals selectively around the globe to create a field preventing direct access to Ea'ae by extradimensional beings," as he spoke, the world lit up with lights spaced equidistant around the planet's periphery—four along the equator, two at the north and south poles, with eight more evenly spaced between. "These seals were not perfect, of course, but they have been able to protect against major incursions orchestrated by creatures of Darkness and their allies like the Cabal."

"Over time, as ages passed and relative safety and security spread, our vigilance, both among the council and outside its fold, has waned, and along with it much of our strength. Many among the Council of Light have lost track of Ea'ae's security in their efforts to ensure civilization's prosperity. There are those among us who have diverted their gaze away from Ea'ae entirely pursuing interests in other worlds and dimensions. A few continue on in the original spirit of the council's foundation both here on Ea'ae and beyond, but many have lost this purpose."

"So, too, have Ea'ae's stewards diminished and dispersed over the same period, losing both numbers and splendor as Men, Elves, Dwarves, and Gnomes have set their eyes on the vast cosmos, planting their seeds across the greater macroverse."

"Now Goran warns that the seals protecting Ea'ae are failing and few among this world's guardians are present or willing to listen. Of those, the majority are ill-prepared for conflict."

"Most have not remained vigilant in their search for Darkness and will thus be caught by surprise when they learn that an agent of the Enemy walked so openly in the light of day here on Tellanon. Many may even deny the truth I will share instead arguing against the veracity of my words—that the barriers protecting your world, our home, are failing, undermined by the very evil they do not see."

Éremon's weighty gaze once again fell upon Yip with full force. "Goran asks that you help restore the seals protecting Ea'ae if her guardians will not."

Yip remained quiet, having never given significant consideration to the possibility that Ea'ae's chosen keepers might not rise to the occasion and provide the full protection their world needed in order to prevent another catastrophe in what could become a time of Darkness on as great or greater order of magnitude than in the days of old.

Éremon too remained silent, letting Yip come to his own decision.

Yip spoke truly. "My true aim has always been the Cabal, to cleanse their plague lest it continually resurface and spread. We are in possession of an artifact from the Cabal's allies and hope that, once deciphered, it will help lead us to their lair. Unfortunately, we do not know when or if the item will reveal its secrets or if the information held within will be of value in our quest."

He thought for some time more, torn between the path he had anticipated and the one that lay before him. "Our two paths may ultimately be one and the same. We may have time to aid in Goran's cause while the Paratechnologists' work. If we take the path you offer, we will move against the Cabal by helping to ensure Ea'ae's immediate future and perhaps still come closer to our goal."

"Before we decide, I will need to consult with my companions. We will also need to find out how the Paratechnologists' efforts progress and if they have any indication as to when they may meet with success."

Éremon assented. "Understood."

"Any blow struck against the Cabal is better than none. Perhaps, too, we may encounter some other clues as to their whereabouts and motives while we work to restore the seals that have been damaged."

"Do not fear, Yip. The burden does not rest solely upon your shoulders." Here Éremon pursed his lips. "As I said, Goran was not the only warden who shared his fears and convictions even before this most recent assault upon the peace that has endured for so long. Other champions have been approached and asked to intervene. If all goes well, you, and any you choose to take with you, will need only to restore one seal."

Yip nodded. "Which seal would you have us restore and what must be done if we are able?"

Éremon smiled, glad that Yip's deep and abiding concern, as Goran had said, would lead him to act firmly and resolutely in order to protect his world.

"The seal of Eldre'gheu rests at the heart of the ruins of an ancient, long abandoned religious city known as Taerris'thule. This city was once home to thousands of priests, disciples, and attendants who worshipped at the holy shrine originally erected to house the seal. Their belief and conviction not only served to sustain the seal but also, over long years, imbued it with terrible power. This power was the undoing of Taerris'thule and, ultimately, the seal itself."

"Generations of worship, offerings, prayer, and supplication created a manifestation of the people's beliefs through the seal itself, ultimately corrupting both its power and original intent. With time, the seal gained some semblance of sentience and tried to rule those who had come to worship at its feet. Corrupted by the seal's power, many a dark priest and fiendish zealot emerged from the bowels of a city that was once known for its high principles and piety."

"By the time Therion and his host arrived at the city's gates many centuries ago to cleanse its evil, the city had become awash in the vilest sorts of depravity, flooded by insanity, and home to dark arts and worship not fit for mortal conception. Fighting their way through its broken avenues and neglected buildings, Therion himself finally broke the seal, leaving it sundered in twain, lest its power reemerge."

"In its place, a new seal, one given power not by worship, but by the magic inherent in the land, was placed in the old seal's place."

"I fear that this seal, too, has been corrupted and now may encourage further extradimensional activity."

"If this is in fact the case, a new seal must be erected after the old has been struck down and cleansed. Given the evil of the place, another home must also be found for the failed seal's replacement, one free from corruption and risk but as close to the old as is practical that we may not repeat past failures. With a renewed seal in place, Ea'ae's wards will be at least partially restored."

"What risks would we face if we choose to go and how should we prepare?"

Éremon stroked his beard thoughtfully. "If the seal has in fact opened itself to or been corrupted by dark powers, whether those of the Cabal or others, I fear that you may face creatures of extradimensional origin. What fell creatures there may be I cannot say, for my sight is blocked to that place, but the city may now be the abode of the vilest sort of creatures, perhaps even entities from the darkest Abyss."

"As for how you prepare and how you should respond, that will depend upon the foe you face and the resources that you have or take with you, as you well know. If you come in contact with a being from the nether regions, then belief will be your strongest ally for they will attempt to corrupt your mind as well as your body as a means to gain access to your spirit."

Éremon looked at Yip as one who has taken another man's measure, having plumbed the depths of his being and realized the limits of the man's character. "Goran has spoken to me about you and I see the same spark in you as does he. I, too, know quite a bit of your order's history having fought by the sides of several priests in my time on this world before your retreat. You and your kind have always fared well on the field of battle whether facing Infernals from the gulfless chaos or eldritch beings not native to this world or dimension. The Light will guide you and see you through, if you are willing."

Éremon gazed at him earnestly, as one who cared deeply and had suffered for those lost in times past for Yip sensed an upwelling of energy within even through his veil. "In the times ahead, you would be wise to care for your friends as much as you care for yourself. Even if you fail before an Infernal's onslaught, the talisman you bear about your neck should protect you. Those you take with you may not be afforded such protections."

Yip lightly ran his fingers over the Heart of Yere's surface hidden as it was beneath his robes, feeling its warmth against his skin, knowing that Éremon wished that he be fully prepared for the travails ahead that he may meet with success.

With a fluid rolling of his fingers, a small leather-bound book materialized in Éremon's palm. Arcane glyphs etched across the tome's surface glowed in an ethereal light. "For those you take with you."

Extending his hand, Yip reached forward and took the book appreciatively with a bow from where he sat. "Thank you."

A glimmer in his eye, Éremon said, "Perhaps your friends will find something of value in its contents."

Magicians seldom shared secrets lightly, so what Éremon offered was a great boon, one that he offered as a sign of his faith and a token for their success. The knowledge contained within may be absolutely vital to their survival. For this, he felt much gratitude and a deep appreciation.

Holding the book forward with a bow, Yip said sincerely, "We will use this knowledge wisely."

Éremon looked briefly into the distance, gazing inward, lost in the inner workings of his own mind before returning his attention to Yip. "Knowledge and experience, wisdom and insight, are but sides of a truth we hold lightly in our hands, one that is studied and inspected, turned and caressed, carefully examined, seeking after the reality it points toward but never fully describes. May the reality you endeavor to create benefit all sentient beings."

Yip stood, bowing for a third time as he prepared to leave. "May the life you lead provide Light for all. I will contact you when I know more."

Éremon nodded.

As Yip turned to leave, Éremon said, "One more item, Yip."

"Yes?"

"I know you travel with a small band of your fellows. The road ahead will be especially dangerous. If you would allow and accept the task given, I would send one of Tellanon's champions to aid your cause that the Light you bring into a place of Darkness not be limited to less than a handful."

Yip smiled, thankful for the offer. "Who would you send?"

"Eidelion."

Unfamiliar with the name, he responded, "I do not know him."

"He is a champion of Light, a paladin of some repute, and one of Tellanon's chief guardians. He may wish to bring peers, should they be willing, on the journey as you do."

"I will ask my friends for the bonds we share are not mine alone to weave."

Éremon nodded again.

"Good days, Éremon."

"Good days, Yip."

Yip walked out of the warm, cavernous room to where Peran waited outside the door ready to guide him out of the keep. Holding Éremon's tome in hand, the book thrumming with incandescent energies, he followed eager to get the thoughts and impressions of his friends.

When Yip finally arrived back home, mid-afternoon was rapidly becoming a memory. Opening the door to the house, the first thing he noticed was the smell lacing the air in an almost palpable fog. The aroma did not bother him of course, for he just let the impressions wash away, but judging by the windows that were thrown wide throughout the house, evidently others felt more strongly.

The next thing he heard were the heated voices of his friends raised in argument.

"Well if ya knew yer stuff smelled so bad, why'd ya come home without gettin' cleaned?"

"I already told you, I thought the smell was gone! I used a spell to clean it off, but somehow my robes seem permanently sullied by the stench of those vegetables! Each time I clean them, the smell comes back!"

Walking in the living room, he saw Slate shaking his head. "Don't ya know that those vegetables are part o' a magical brew? That's why yer simple spells won't hold on 'em! There's powerful Gnomish magic in tha concoction ya carried ta those blasted Paratechnologists! Those vegetables have been magically modified ta fit Gnomish tastes ta perfection!"

"Gah! Now you tell me!"

"There's nothin' fer it. We need ta get ya some new clothes. Fer that matter, we might as well all get new clothes. Stench is tha least o' an adventurer's worries and we should be prepared from here on in."

When he saw Yip arrive, Slate brightened, his knotted brow clearing but not quite separating the thick tuft of hair that marked his single unbroken Dwarven eyebrow.

"Just in time ta go shoppin'! My treat!" Turning his head to face the backyard, Slate yelled, "Aroganji! Let's go! We're off ta get new clothes! Yer mop headed friend here has sullied his own. We might as well get some new ones before ours are ruined as well."

Aroganji met them outside after Wrindanneth cast yet another smell repression spell on his clothing since attempting to clean and counter them magically thus far had had no effect.

"Where are we off to?"

"Jarvis's Jerkins o' course! Shoulda gone there long ago. He has tha best stock o' adventure wear in Tellanon from what I hear."

"Will his wares guard against the smell of Gnomish vegetables?"

Slate chuckled at Aroganji's question. "If they can guard against Dwarven sweat, I'd imagine they're impervious ta just about anythin'!"

Indicating Wrindanneth with a tilt of his head, Slate barked, "Darn fool cut our practice short with tha stench cloudin' his presence. I reckon tha other folks in tha park were about ta call tha Home Guard before we left!"

Wrindanneth growled, "If you've had your fun, I suggest we be about our business."

Slate nodded. "Aye. Let's be about it then."

On the way to Jarvis's, Aroganji and Wrindanneth quizzed Yip about his trip to Éremon's.

"How did your visit with Éremon go? Any positive news or other information?"

Yip smiled to his friends in response as they made their way to the merchant's district. "There is much to tell."

"And?" Wrindanneth was particularly eager to learn of Éremon.

"Perhaps you would like some new nighttime reading to share?" Yip reached inside his robes where he stored his teaching scroll and pulled out the small book Éremon had given him.

Wrindanneth and Aroganji stopped in place.

"Hold, Slate!" Wrindanneth's voice pulled his friend to a stop where he strode several paces ahead as other evening pedestrians strolled past. Wrin did his best to keep the eagerness in his voice in check.

That Yip casually referenced his own secretive nighttime practices with Maeth—or at least he thought Yip did—was a minor detail compared with the enormity held with the miniscule tome he now offered.

The value of such lore was incalculable.

Maeth, too, would see the value in such arcane knowledge. Given Éremon's stature, there may even be secrets held within as yet foreign to his master.

Soon, the Dream Stealer would have his due. When his own power grew, he would deny Maeth access to his sleeping mind just as he would break the bonds that held him tied to his master.

Unaware of Wrindanneth's musings, Aroganji took the proffered book gingerly, his hands almost shaking in anticipation as he held the tome between himself and Wrindanneth. Marveling at what he saw and felt may be inside, Aroganji asked in disbelief, "Éremon gave you this?"

"Yes."

Wrindanneth stopped his inspection with some difficulty. "Then a dangerous task it is indeed he has set for you. This book holds spells to ward against Darkness the likes of which I have never seen and seldom heard."

"Is not our current quest fraught with danger?"

Wrindanneth laughed, eager to shed the weight of the stench he carried and the future he felt looming with a bit of levity. "You have a point."

That they may speak freely, Aroganji muttered a short incantation. "It is safe to speak."

"He has asked if I would be willing to help restore one of the seals guarding our world from extradimensional incursion. Goran's message to the Council of Light was successful, although not completely believed. After talking with Éremon, Goran asked that Éremon request my assistance."

"So Éremon's a member o' tha Council o' Light?" Slate knew little of magical orders and brotherhoods outside the Dwarven clans though he knew enough to grasp that the council of which Goran spoke was separate from the one that ruled Tellanon.

Yip nodded. "So it would seem."

Still cautious, as was his nature, Wrindanneth asked, "What of Éremon? Where does he stand?"

"The book in your hands is testament to where he stands, I would say," answered Yip. "He is a being of Light not native to this world. Why he is here, I cannot say, but I am glad for his presence. He has fought alongside the people of Ea'ae for millennia and serves us still."

"He also apologized for the assault as if it were his own failing and said he had made some modifications to how the Scimerian Gate functions and is tended."

"As he should," muttered Wrindanneth upset that his friend had been put at risk even if there was no foreseeable way to have prevented the infiltration.

"Wait. I thought he was a wizard?" Slate was confused, only having heard of Éremon as a ruling member of Tellanon's own High Council and by the fame attendant with his historical exploits. He also thought Éremon was a Man, albeit a particularly long-lived one.

"A magician he is, but a Man he is not. He blazes like the sun hidden behind clouds. Although he hides his true nature, it is apparent to one who looks deeply. Perhaps he came during the War of Shadows and fought against the Cabal and has stayed to aid those on Ea'ae since. I cannot say."

"Why then does he not intervene now?" asked Aroganji.

"Is he not?" Yip looked from his friends to the book Wrindanneth and Aroganji held between them. "He has chosen sides, offered assistance, will argue for our cause before the council, both the hidden order and Tellanon's ruling body, and has selected us as allies. I would say he has intervened. As Tellanon's chosen protector, I would imagine he is loath to venture too far from such an important nexus in times of risk. He said nothing of his past nor his efforts, so who among us can truthfully and accurately say what he has and has not tried?"

"Agreed."

"There is more. He has also offered a champion to aid us on our quest, if we go."

"Who would he send?" Wrindanneth wondered who one such as Éremon would choose.

"A man named Eidelion."

"Eidelion!" Slate's jaw dropped and remained agape. "Eidelion? A grave task this is indeed."

Wrindanneth, too, sought some confirmation. "The Eidelion? The captain of the Light's Guard, commander of the Home Guard, man-at-arms nonpareil?"

"I do not know. All I was told is a name."

"A welcome addition such a one would be to our efforts," said Aroganji, for he knew of Eidelion as well.

Yip continued, "There are others who will be sent on tasks akin to ours around the globe. If all of our efforts meet with success, then our world will once again be fully protected from the large-scale invasions that crippled us in the first War of Shadows."

"And if not?"

"Then either the Cabal will find their way through our defenses once again, or we will have to go where others have failed."

"What of our quest to meet the Cabal directly? Why not stop their evil before it has the chance to tarnish our world?"

"Both paths lead to the same end I think. We will see how the Paratechnologists' work on the orb progresses. If they require more time or are not finding information useful to our search, then we will have the opportunity to go and aid the council. If not, then we will seek to meet the Cabal directly. Either way, we may gain some information as to where the Cabal lurks from our attempts, endeavor to counter their efforts, and will have allies in our cause."

Wrindanneth agreed. "Perhaps the Cabal will want us to come to them. Having more time, knowledge, and ability should only aid our cause."

Slate smiled grimly, as one who has known the subtleties of many a battle.

"If we cut 'em deep enough, they will want us ta come, if only ta stop tha bleedin'."

"Here it is!" Slate stopped in front of a small shop marked by a well-lettered sign hanging above a recessed door. The sign read, "Jarvis's Jerkins & Regalia – Fine Garments Suitable for Any Occasion or Adventure."

Slate opened the door, holding it ajar for the others to pass through, as small bells chimed to announce their arrival.

Before the door had shut behind them, a small, impeccably dressed elderly gentleman with only the faintest remnants of wispy gray hair drifting about his ears and temples called out to them, "Welcome! Welcome! How may I be of assistance on this fine day?"

Arrayed throughout the shop's interior, garments of every shape and color hung suspended and displayed on racks and mannequins, lay folded and arranged on shelves and in nooks in every conceivable way for the patron to touch and see. Jerkins, tunics, great coats, breeches, and cloaks shared space with scarves, veils, frocks, capes, hats, and gloves among many other clothing items intended for various tastes and purposes, races and shapes. Mirrors dotted the store like constellations, beguiling the eye, creating a sense of multiple spaces and rooms propagating in many directions—a riotous profusion of shape and color showcased in surreal geometry.

Laced throughout, interconnecting the wares in diffuse streamers and ribbons, complex magical energies emanating from the clothes themselves added another dimension to Yip's purview of the store and its offerings.

With so much to see and so many angles presented, Aroganji and Wrindanneth paused before fully entering the shop while Slate continued to hold the door for them.

Bustling in behind his friends who now stood bemused before Jarvis and the wares laid out before them, Slate called out from back behind Yip who had entered last, "We need ta see yer finest travel garments, suitable fer any place, clime, or vagary fate may bestow upon us!"

Jarvis nodded briefly, looking each one in turn from head to toe with the eye of one used to taking a man's measure and then transforming his appraisal into tangible reality. "You are adventurers then?"

Slate nodded curtly. "Aye."

"Garments suitable for the rigors of the wilds must be made to match the circumstances you are likely to face in the times ahead. We will need to discuss how you need your apparel to perform, how you want your garments to fit, and how you would like your clothing to respond not only to your movements but to the environments you visit."

"You are going to each need to be fitted, of course. You will also have to choose a style of dress because the types of clothes you will be after do not come directly off the shelf. Although the particular qualities of a given fabric may be modified and enhanced via magical intervention, some fabrics are more amenable to modification and alteration than others, so we must also select the proper material from which to craft your outfits."

"Aye," Slate nodded briefly. "Understood."

Raising his eyebrows archly, Jarvis asked, "I will also need to know how much you are willing to pay for your clothing, for the price will determine the quality and features."

"That will depend upon tha features," replied Slate, ready to haggle.

Jarvis took them into the back of his store into his fitting room. Tapes, pens, needles, neatly arrayed swatches of fabric in multiple styles and colors, scissors in several shapes and sizes, and various other implements were neatly organized in a work stand and along shelves on one wall. On the other side of the chamber, a partition marked by wall-to-wall mirrors intended for patrons to view the fit of garments from multiple angles reflected all five of them as they walked into the fitting room.

Opposite the door leading back to the shop, another room opened up. This alcove was obviously Jarvis's workshop for rolls of uncut fabric were stacked in racks along the walls to the ceiling out of sight above. These particular fabrics were those kept on hand for certain special jobs when the fabric itself was not summoned or magically fabricated. Padded, cloth-lined working tables took up the central portion of the chamber, each marked with lines for fabric dimension measurements and cutting. Another door, presumably to a back entrance and alleyway, was visible on the far corner of Jarvis's tailoring workshop next to carefully arranged stacks of newly received stock.

After they had all filed into the fitting room, Jarvis motioned for them to be seated on chairs lining the wall adjacent to the storefront, asking, "Before we move forward, tell me exactly what you would like your garments to be able to do."

Slate, who had already met Jarvis and knew more about the capabilities and limitations of his clothing said, "We're not askin' fer protection from magical or physical assault, we have other gear fer that. What we'd like are clothes than can recover from catastrophic events..."

Jarvis broke in, "You mean mend themselves?"

"Aye, maintenance free. Clothes that can also take a beatin'. We'd also like clothes that can"—here Slate cleared his throat—"er...hum, keep themselves from getting' a bit too ripe."

Not missing an opportunity, Wrindanneth interjected, "The Dwarf speaks from experience. There's nothing quite so fragrant as an uncleaned Dwarf."

Before Slate could offer a retort, Jarvis interjected officiously, asking, "Self-cleaning?"

"Aye. We may need a bit o' protection from tha elements as well ta guard against extremes o' temperature."

"So you would like resilience, self-repair, thermal protection, self-cleaning, and comfort control?"

"Aye."

When Slate paused for a moment, Jarvis asked, "Anything else?"

Aroganji said, "If we are after true protection from the elements and not just heat and cold, then we will need water repellency for sleet, rain, and snow."

When Aroganji had finished, Wrindanneth said, "Can you offer a degree of camouflage as well? Perhaps clothing that blends in with our surroundings?"

Jarvis nodded. "Certainly. What else?"

"If ya can add the ability ta camouflage ta our clothes, can ya also offer tha ability fer us ta change their shape and appearance should we so desire?"

"You mean adjust to your Dwarven sense of fashion? Now we're in for a treat!" Wrindanneth rolled his eyes mockingly.

"I was just thinkin' o' givin' some flexibility should we wish ta fit in with local dress or not need a particular piece of clothin'."

"That will not be a problem. Anything else?"

Thinking of reagents, vials, books, and any magical accessories that he may need to carry, Aroganji answered, "We will need plenty of hidden pockets in which to store gear and reagents."

"Do you want those pockets merely sewn in or magically enhanced?"

His interest piqued, Slate asked, "How would ya enhance 'em?"

"I could make them hidden, much larger and more expansive than allowed by the limits of the fabric, able to bear their contents without burdening you with extra weight or encumbrance, able to protect and hide contents from outside viewers, accessible only to the rightful owner, or any number of other features."

"We'll have our pockets enhanced then!" Slate was, for once, getting excited by the idea of spending a bit of coin. Since this was his idea and he had promised them a rare treat by coming to see Jarvis, he was going to enjoy the experience.

"Anything else you would recommend?"

"Although you are young and hale now, I would consider having the clothes adjust to your form should your girth or shape change in any way. Given your wish to allow flexibility in the garments' shape, this will be an added benefit for the long-term."

"As much as I've told you to cut back on those meals, Slate, now you won't even have to listen or worry about loosening your belt."

Before Jarvis could ask his next question, Slate asked, "Could we get a muzzle?"

Evidently the scissors, tape measures, needles and various other implements hanging on the wall behind Jarvis were largely for show. Having everyone stand, Jarvis cast a quick spell that cataloged all the measurements he needed to fashion their clothes.

"What types of garment do each of you wish to wear?" He looked to Slate to start.

"I'll need a jerkin, breeches, under garments, cloak, and socks. Tha jerkin and breeches should be suitable fer wearin' under armor or with no armor at all."

Wrindanneth was next. He wished to wear clothes similar to the loose-fitting robes and cloak that had seen him through many an adventure already. "If you could offer an improved version of the attire I am currently wearing, I would be in your debt."

Looking to Aroganji next, Aroganji said, "I am in line with Wrindanneth. Robes and a great cloak of the type I now wear."

"And you?"

Yip said, "I, too, would wear clothes similar to the *zhiju* I now wear. Loose fitting breeches and shirt, under flowing full body robes along with a hooded cloak, should I need it."

"Is that all?"

When no one offered any more suggestions, Jarvis motioned for them to follow, bringing them into the back room to look over their choices in fabric.

"Since the ultimate appearance of your garments will be left largely to your own discretion, we need only choose the appropriate fabric from which to make them."

Jarvis walked slowly through the stacked aisles of multicolored cloth, idly running his fingers over bolts of fabric here and there, occasionally remarking on the types of textiles he stocked.

"Spun werewolf fur…manticore mane…woven Faery hair…plaited Pegasus tail…threaded Hellhound vibrissa…revenant's robes…"

"Ah! Here we are!" he said, finally stopping by a roll of sheening, silvery threads dusted with a layer of miniscule, translucent water droplets. "Dew-laden netherweb silk!"

"This fabric is the highest caliber I supply. Light and breathable yet capable of holding enchantment and taking unrivaled abuse, netherweb silk is the perfect complement to the needs of the bravest adventurers!"

"Of course!" thought Wrindanneth, almost smacking his forehead at the mention of the type of fabric he would be donning with his friends when all was said and done. After all the unusual articles they had passed, Wrindanneth knew Jarvis would settle on one of the more exotic, and to his mind repugnant, items.

Why was not ordinary caterpillar silk an option? Extradimensional spider silk from a Daemonic arachnid…that would be cheap!

How often was there dew in the steaming abyss from which those creatures crawled?

He would try his hardest not to think of the hellish creature's pedipalps caressing his neck before sinking its mandibles into his exposed skin when he finally donned his finished cloak.

Oh well, if a man could wear cotton spun from a plant, or silk from a worm, why couldn't he wear silk spun from a fiendish spider spawned in a heinous dimension full of tormented souls?

While Jarvis lifted the roll of spider silk from its rack, Slate asked, "How long will ya need ta finish tha clothes?"

"I should need about a week. I will contact you when all is ready."

Laying the shimmering fabric on one of the work tables, Jarvis asked discreetly, "How would you like to pay?"

By the time they arrived home, evening had fallen across the streets in full splendor, the luminescent orbs lining the road strung in pearlescent strands leaving the lane before their cottage bedecked in shining silver and golden pools lighting the path to the front door.

"I will contact Adar to see where the Paratechnologists stand with their efforts whilst you prepare dinner, Slate." Aroganji held the door open for his friends as they passed by entering their tidy little home.

"Fair enough." While Wrindanneth and Aroganji were still near, Slate asked, "Any preferences?"

"As long as it isn't moving or too pungent, I'll eat it," answered Wrindanneth eager for a bit of rest and repast after the day's exertions and toils.

Aroganji went in to the study while everyone else went into the kitchen. Aloud, he said, "Aspect, please connect me with Adar."

The Aspect's chipper voice responded, "Good evening, Aroganji! I will see if Adar is currently available. One moment please."

A few moments passed before Adar's familiar face appeared in the air before him. "Good evening. How may I be of assistance, Aroganji?"

"Good evening to you as well, Adar. Have you any news on how the work deciphering the alien device progresses?"

Adar shook his head. "Slower than we would like, unfortunately. The device itself has some formidable defenses and obfuscations, but we are slowly working through them, I believe."

"Any indication on how long your efforts may take in light of your current insights?"

"Weeks, months, I cannot say."

"Although not exactly the news I wished to hear, that is just as well."

"Why do you say that?"

"Éremon has an errand for us. Our availability is contingent upon your progress."

"I see."

"We will be leaving, then, within about a week. We should still have access to reliable communication for some time once we leave via the ship, if you need to contact us."

"I will seek you out when I have any more news."

"Thank you, Adar."

"Safe journeys, Aroganji."

Aroganji went into the kitchen after finishing with Adar.

"Any luck?" asked Wrindanneth

"Nothing new thus far."

"Éremon will have our assistance then."

"Aye. We'll travel in tha company o' a true hero!" Aroganji could tell that Slate was a bit in awe of Eidelion's reputation, probably because Dwarves held skill with a blade, any blade, in such high regard.

"We should seek out Hoyt for advice before we venture out," suggested Aroganji.

"Agreed."

"We'll pay him a visit tomorrow." Wrindanneth was eager to be on their way. Too much sitting around and waiting left him ill at ease.

"I will let Éremon know that we have accepted his charge."

Leaving his friends, Yip went to his quarters and called out to the Aspect, "Aspect, I need your assistance."

"Yes, Master Chuan?"

"Would you please contact Éremon for me? I need to speak with him." Pausing a moment, he added, "Privately."

"One moment. I will check on his availability."

The sunroom was silent for almost a minute before he heard the Aspect again. "My apologies for the delay. Éremon will be on shortly." In a dry voice the Aspect finished, "I had to earn passage through the Vicar first."

A few moments later, Éremon's bright face appeared in the air in front of where Yip sat on his bedroll.

"Good evening, Master Chuan! I am glad to hear from you so soon."

He bowed from the waist. "The pleasure is mine."

"How may I be of assistance?"

He was direct and to the point. "We will accept your offer."

"Excellent! I will inform Eidelion of the good news. He will be expecting you."

Yip gave a brief nod. "We will seek him out tomorrow morning to discuss the trip ahead."

"Do you know yet when you plan to leave?"

"That depends on Eidelion's availability, but we hope to leave within the week if everything is in order."

"He should be free to leave whenever you are ready."

"I am glad to hear it."

"I will have Eidelion let me know when you are to depart. I would see you off."

"Only if you have the time. We do not wish to impose upon your duties," replied Yip, not wishing to take Éremon from any other matters that may need his attention.

"No need to be concerned. You are worthy of more than my presence! You will also need the replacement for that which you seek to destroy."

Yip smiled in understanding. "Of course."

"Until then," replied Éremon.

"May the Light be your guide," answered Yip.

Éremon declined his head slightly before disappearing.

The next day dawned overcast and drear, the cool temperature hinting at a storm to come. Wrindanneth, for one, looked forward to his new cloak so that he would not have to worry about the chill and wet on the journey ahead.

By the time everyone left the house, the clouds had thickened and dropped, closing in above the island like a low-lying roof. Anticipating rains to come, the party left in haste hoping to arrive at Hoyt's before the downpour.

Unfortunately, they did not.

When they finally reached Hoyt's fine establishment and opened his familiar squeaking screen door, sheets of rain streaming from the roof overhead, a curtain waterfall barring entrance to the shop, ensured that anyone who was not already completely soaked was now sopping wet. The rain fell so hard that, had they not known where they were going, they would never have been able to read the sign above his door until they were almost beneath it.

Entering in the shop, streaking puddles followed each of their squishing steps across the dusty floor toward where Hoyt waited nonchalantly behind the counter.

Alongside one of his cats sleeping on the windowsill, a small shimmering faerie Dragon perched amid the assorted odds and ends displayed inside the store window, the brightness of its multi-hued scales all the more vivid and wondrous for the gloom outside the rain streaked glass.

Leaning forward on the counter resting on his elbows, a cheerful smile on his face as if he were expecting them, Hoyt called out in greeting, "I hope ya brought a mop! Tha floor needs cleanin'!"

"Doesn't it always?" asked Wrindanneth.

Aroganji chuckled. "Some things never change."

"And I'm sure ya sell 'em," joined in Slate. "'Finest mops ya've ever seen!', ya'd say."

"And I was just gettin' a nice layer of dust goin' too." Hoyt returned Aroganji's laughter. With a small flick of the wrist and a brief uttered incantation, a sudden rush of air passed over them leaving the party and floor completely dry.

"Thanks, Hoyt." Slate was not fond of having a wet beard.

"Glad ya could make it my way ta visit. Word is, ya had an unwelcome guest waitin' for ya yesterday."

Wrindanneth grunted, "Seems the shadow we're chasing found us first."

Slate nodded curtly in agreement. "Good thing it was after Yip. I'd hate ta see what would've happened if it'd been after anyone else." For once Slate was not joking.

Not needing to make any further comment, Hoyt nodded grimly.

"We are here, happy, and at peace, and for that I am thankful," replied Yip.

Ready to move on to more positive news, Hoyt washed his hands, eagerly saying, "So what can I do for you fine gentlemen today?"

"The same thing you do for us any other day," answered Wrindanneth.

Hoyt merely raised his eyebrows.

"Help answer a few questions that might not be answered elsewhere. Offer some experience others might not share. Proffer an oddity that will do everything we need and more. Share your usual good cheer..."

"The usual," finished Aroganji with a smile.

Hoyt laughed. "Then you've come ta the right place! What's ticklin' your tail feathers today?"

Yip stepped forward as he spoke. "We are about to embark upon a quest to Taerris'thule."

Hoyt whistled and shook his head becoming serious. "Why would ya wanna go there? The Shadow that was after ya can't be any worse than what y'all'll find there, I can guarantee. In fact, y'all'll likely find his bigger nastier brother!"

"While the Paratechnologists try to uncover more information on the Cabal's whereabouts from the alien orb, Éremon has asked that we go to restore the seal of Eldre'gheu."

"Well, y'all'll certainly find out about them if ya go there!" Hoyt leaned forward and looked from side-to-side as if making sure no one was nearby listening to their conversation. "Dark place that is. Many a proud adventurer has gone forth ta seek lost secrets in the city's heart never ta return."

"Sounds like our kind of place!" Slate washed his hands expectantly.

Hoyt, however, remained serious. "I hope not. I certainly hope not."

Hoyt shook his head. "Ea'ae is home ta many dark regions, a refuge ta too many sad tales. Taerris'thule is one of the darkest and saddest."

Hoyt sighed, as if thinking back to a place he once knew and cared for all too well. "Envision a resplendent metropolis devoted to religious conviction, introspection, and study, full of life and vibrancy, an exemplar of humanity's highest ideals and aspirations, laid waste and despoiled, trodden upon and degraded, become a haven for insidious creatures not meant for this plane or any other. Imagine that corruption spreadin' like a plague, sappin' the life and will from neighboring lands, corruptin' the once pristine. There you have the nicest possible description of Taerris'thule, once a sanctuary to gods, now forsaken."

"And you want ta go?"

"There are times when the dictates of necessity have little to do with wants," replied Yip calmly.

"Well, if I can't talk ya out of it, y'all'll be wantin' ta go ta the city's center.

Times was, there were wide tree-lined avenues markin' the way. I can't say how it'll look now or exactly how best ta approach—probably quickly and by air. In the city's heart, nestled at the base of the Fueron Mountains, y'all'll find what was once the sanctum of Eldre'gheu."

"The seal was once at its heart."

"What's there now other'n misery and fear, I cannot say, but tread cautiously."

"How best ta approach will be left to you. There are eyes there no man would have fall upon him, of that you can be sure."

"How will we find our way to the city itself?"

"I'll send ya a map that you can upload onta your ship's navigation system. Taerris'thule's a long way off, on the steamin' southern continent of Maeron. Y'all'll not find any place ta *faerviage* there for the continent is mostly trackless hinterland. Nor will ya be able ta teleport in fer few enough alive have seen her gates as they now stand."

Hoyt sighed, obviously not pleased they were going. "I only hope ya can find yer way back as well."

"Haven't we always come back before?" asked Wrindanneth, trying to keep the mood light.

"Ya've never been to Eldre'gheu." Hoyt shook his head grimly. "I've seen many leave and none come back. None of those who venture within the city's walls, at least."

"You were not so concerned when you learned we were after the Cabal," said Aroganji.

"No. No, I wasn't because I thought ya wouldn't find the Cabal even if ya went gallivantin' off ta the ends of the cosmos. Now ya're off ta a place that ya can find and I think y'all'll find more trouble than ya were lookin' for or can handle."

"Only one way ta find out," said Slate.

Hoyt shrugged tiredly. "Don't mind me. I'm just gettin' old and soft, more worried about losin' good customers than fixin' what ails this world."

"If individual adventurers and their allies have failed, why hasn't someone sent an army in to clean the place out?" asked Aroganji.

Hoyt raised an eyebrow. "That's a simple question with a lot of answers."

He began ticking reasons off on his fingers. "One, if ya haven't noticed, this world is mostly wilderness. That's largely because the majority of the able-bodied have taken ta the stars, long since leavin' Ea'ae ta the past. With their passage, there are many places left unnoticed or forgotten that are in need of attention. Many of the places these people departed now have less than desirable tenants that took their place."

"Which brings me ta my second point—people's memories are short. Many wonders lay hidden in plain sight on Ea'ae, lost ta the echoes of the distant and not so distant past."

"Three, if there is no kingdom nearby ta muster an army, chances are, no army will be sent. Corollary ta three, unless a place is seen as a direct threat ta a state capable of raisin' an army, oftentimes it will be left unmolested."

"Four, unless the reward for the attempt is great or seen as great, then few will risk the danger, especially when the payoff may be small in relation ta the numbers needed for success."

"Five, about the nicest thing y'all'll find on Maeron, forget Taerris'thule, are legions of Orcs, Troll, Ogres, Hobgoblins, Goblins, and their ilk, not exactly the type of place that begs for visitors, especially with populations being so thin."

"Six, who's ta say no one has? If y'all want I can catalog 'em for ya..."

Wrindanneth stopped him before Hoyt raised yet another finger on his hand. "We get the point," replied Wrindanneth, saving Aroganji from being run over by Hoyt's train of thought. "Right. So we're the sacrificial lambs. Let's get over it and move on."

"Anything we should take with us for protection?"

Hoyt remained serious. "Belief and conviction. Y'all'll need them in the darkness ahead. They will be your strongest weapons and greatest strength." He shook his head. "There's nothing I have here that will guarantee yer success, or I'd give it. Ya have magical arms and can cast spells which will be yer best hope against the fell creatures of the night that haunt that place."

"I know ya have the skill ta use 'em. I just hope ya have luck in equal measure."

"Thanks, Hoyt," responded Aroganji. "Éremon has volunteered Eidelion to travel with us, so we will have more magic and skill at arms than we normally do on our adventures."

"That's all well and good. Eidelion is a fearsome warrior, the type who only rarely arises within a generation, but don't expect brute force, whether magical or mundane, ta win the battles ahead for ya."

"We'll be back. Mark my words." Slate smacked the flat of his palm against his chest for emphasis.

"You'll not be rid of us so easily, Hoyt. The denizens of the Abyss will have to think again if they believe otherwise." Wrindanneth gave a nod to his friend.

Slate chuckled, saying to Wrin, "Aye. If they manage ta kill ya, then they'll have ta deal with havin' ya around all tha time. That'd be a worse fate than just lettin' ya pass."

Wrindanneth glared at the Dwarf. "They'd be happy to kill you because you can only smell better when dead."

"Says tha knight o' tha rotten turnips?"

Used to the bickering, Hoyt smiled, hiding the expression behind one of the hands he was leaning against.

"We will succeed because we must, Hoyt. That is the path set before us and the way we must tread." Yip bowed.

"Exactly," Wrindanneth cracked a smile. "If we don't succeed, who else is going to buy more of your junk? We have to triumph, lest Ea'ae be overrun by your refuse."

"Just because there may be a layer or two, perhaps three, of dust on most of my goods doesn't mean they're not desirable. In fact, I've found one of the most effective ways ta preserve gear is ta bury it by neglect."

Everyone laughed, acknowledging that was about the only way Hoyt preserved anything, at least until it was ready for sale. Then he had the items spotless and in impeccable condition.

"If I think of anything else, find any item that may be of worth ta ya, or come across any information that may be of use ta ya before ya leave, I'll let ya know."

"We thank you, Hoyt," offered Wrindanneth as he turned to depart.

Before leaving the shop, Aroganji began a brief incantation to protect them from the falling rain so that everyone would remain as warm and dry as they were now after Hoyt's recent spell.

Raising his hand, Yip said, "There is no need, Aroganji."

Wrindanneth scoffed, "You don't want to be dry?"

"I merely wish to feel the rain." He left the store ahead of his friends as he stepped into the hum of the rain, letting the creaking door shut behind him while Aroganji finished his protective spell.

Behind him, Slate merely raised his eyebrows at Yip's odd behavior.

Wrindanneth, however, was not as understated in his disapproval. Shaking his head, he muttered, "You'd think he would have learned the least bit of common sense by now."

Standing by his shoulder, Aroganji joked, "No one ever said his senses were common."

"Or sensical," replied Wrindanneth.

By the time they arrived home, Yip was thoroughly drenched, squishing and squelching with each step, but happy to feel the cool, refreshing water running down his face and back, his arms and legs. Gently landing on his skin with each movement, the rainwater moving about him linking him physically to the clouds above and the ground below, each breath a small puff, a cloud in miniature, as he walked in the humidity and haze.

Reaching the cottage, its normally bright crisp colors muted and grayed by the rain and overcast clouds, Aroganji said to Yip, "At least let me dry you off as you enter so you don't track water throughout the house."

Yip bowed at the door, leaving a puddle of water on the threshold as he did so. "Many thanks."

As soon as they all had filed in, now all completely dry thanks to Aroganji's spell, the voice of the Aspect chimed in, "Eidelion would like for you to meet with him tomorrow at the barracks in the center city beneath Illdrassil's boughs. Any time of day will be fine."

"Yet another errand," grumbled Wrindanneth.

"I thought we turned that thing off," carped Slate.

"I am glad to hear from him. That saves me the effort of getting in touch to organize a meeting," replied Aroganji. "With the ship in order and our goal set, we are nearing readiness to start our mission. All we are waiting on now is finding out when Eidelion will be prepared."

"And tha clothes," replied Slate exuberantly.

"Yes, and the clothes," mimed Wrindanneth sardonically.

"Shall we leave first thing in the morning?" asked Yip.

"I don't see why not. If he's at the barracks, they should be out drilling with the sun," answered Aroganji.

"Assuming the sun's out," cracked Wrindanneth.

"Between Slate's Dwarven dourness and your sarcasm, I'm surprised the sun ever comes out," replied Aroganji, letting a note of disapproval appear in his tone.

"What's that supposed to mean?" asked Wrindanneth.

"I'm amazed the sun can penetrate your gloom."

"There's no sun underground, Aroganji, only cold, hard stone," grumbled Slate.

"The skies of the far North are gray and overcast for months at a time," echoed Wrindanneth.

"All the more reason to be of good cheer and hold happiness in your heart," replied Yip smiling when thinking about how similar the tall Northman and short Dwarf were both in temperament and outlooks. Even though the two often butted heads like rams, they were similar in so many other ways, the least of which was being headstrong.

"Shall we leave at dawn to meet Eidelion?" said Aroganji, laughing as he reiterated Yip's original question.

"Aye," Slate tromped into the kitchen in search of food and quiet.

Of like mind, Wrindanneth headed upstairs to his room and the comforts of a book of arcana.

Sharing in Aroganji's laughter, Yip said, "Until tomorrow, Aroganji," as he headed off to the sunroom.

Shaking his head, Aroganji joined Slate in the kitchen for a meal.

Sitting in meditation on his bedroll, his eyes closed to the rivulets flowing steadily down the arching glass overhead, Yip listened to the rain fall throughout the night, the soft patter washing over the edges of his awareness in a welcome fugue. Time passed fluidly, moving independent of the various themes and stanzas of the storm outside, until morning dawned overcast but dry.

He opened his eyes gradually, letting his awareness coalesce. Then, standing, he shook his arms and legs briefly to encourage circulation before seeking his companions.

Sensing Slate's descent from his room some time before, he arrived in the kitchen to find the Dwarf in the middle of preparing his morning victuals. Being of Dwarven constitution, Slate required only nominal amounts of sleep which explained why he was also, almost without exception, the first one awake and ready for breakfast. Although a great lover of food and able to consistently eat significantly more than his fellows without ill effect, Slate's Dwarven hardiness also allowed him to persevere through times of scarcity where even the strongest of Men would fail.

Preparing what many would consider a feast, a meal which he considered a light repast, Slate hunkered over the counter with the determined focus of one who had spent much time in the life and death struggles of battle—with an ineffable combination of complete focus, care, and a blatant disregard for his own safety. Meat, tubers, and root vegetable parts flew here and there, landing with only the vaguest sense of order and purpose as his great chopping knife flew from one target to the next. Slate, however, moved in his element, maneuvering precisely and with conviction, bringing first order and then the savory smells and colorful sounds of cooking food to the kitchen from what had once been piles of raw ingredients.

Sensing Yip's approach from his room, Slate called out. "Mornin', Yip! Care fer some vittles?" Although Slate knew the answer, he would have felt wrong had he not offered.

Pausing, Yip replied, "Perhaps some tea."

His back to Yip, Slate raised his bushy eyebrows for it seemed to him that it was almost as rare for Yip to drink as eat. "I can brew some fer ya, if ya'd like."

"You are too kind, Slate, but I can prepare my own."

Yip took a teapot from one of the shelves, added some leaves to a tea strainer within, filled the pot with water, and placed the pot to boil on the stove. The stove turned on automatically as soon as he placed the pot on its surface. Sensing the object, its contents, and the sentience setting the pot on the stove, the Aspect silently deduced his purpose, the ideal preparation method, and brought the teapot to a slow boil without need for command or input.

Although the entire kitchen could be run independently by the Aspect magically from initial food gathering and preparation to final cleanup, everyone generally prepared their own meals and used the kitchen implements manually. All the appliances themselves were powered by magic and, unless requested, required little to no input from whoever was preparing food. Oftentimes, however, the Aspect was allowed to clean up after meals, sanitizing dishes and utensils and returning those items to their proper storage place in the wooden cabinets lining the kitchen walls.

Pouring his tea, Yip took a place at the small kitchen table while Slate put the finishing touches on his morning banquet.

Glad to have Yip sit with him, Slate asked Yip from where he stood at the countertop, "Ready ta meet Eidelion?"

"I am." Appreciating how much Slate admired Eidelion's prowess, he sensed Slate's eagerness to be on their way.

Finally, turning away from the counter, Slate walked over to join Yip at the table with a heaping tray of food held precariously before him. Setting his plate on the tabletop with a solid, jarring thump, Slate sat down and began shoving food in his mouth with his fork with the same ferocity with which it had been prepared, deftly using his beard to catch any excess that may fall off his utensil.

Muttering around a mouthful of food, Slate said, "Eidelion's one o' tha greatest champions Tellanon's ever seen. Wieldin' tha white sword Archaeus, none o' tha creatures o' Darkness can stand before him, witherin' away before tha light and truth o' his blade and heart."

"Standin' at tha front lines as leader o' tha Home Guard, he has staved off many incursions by those who would invade Tellanon and cause her citizens ill."

"He will be a welcome companion on our journey, Slate."

"Aye. That he will."

By the time Wrindanneth and Aroganji joined Slate and Yip at the table, Slate's mountain of food and been reduced merely to a large hillock. While Wrindanneth and Aroganji prepared plates from what was left of Slate's repast, Slate asked, "How long before ya're ready ta go?"

Having heard Slate's admiring descriptions of Eidelion in the past, and understanding how excited he was to be off, Wrindanneth said, "Don't fret, we'll be off to see your long lost brother soon enough."

Slate grunted, "Tha Flintforge clan would be honored ta count one such as he as a brother."

"There's only one problem with that, Slate." Wrindanneth grinned wickedly after a significant pause. "I hear he's handsome."

Slate puffed out his chest proudly, dislodging several chunks of food as he did so. "I am considered fair among my race."

"Fairly ugly?"

Slate raised his eyebrows archly and grunted, pounding one fist on the table for emphasis as he stood up. "And ya think ya're handsome?"

Pointing at Wrindanneth's pale, freckled skin, he said, "With yer white, fish belly skin and tha mottled octopus splotches coverin' yer whole body, ya'd think ya were kin ta some foul creature o' tha deep!"

Wrindanneth could not help but laugh looking down at Slate as he prepared to set his plate on the table beside where Yip sat sedately with his tea. With Slate holding his eyebrows up in anticipation of Wrindanneth's coming retort, his friend's bushy eyebrows almost reached the edge of his hairline. "This from the Dwarf whose eyebrows are so long and bushy that they get tangled in the hair upon his head whenever he raises them?"

Wrindanneth laughed again, taunting, "Go ahead, see if you can lower them, Dwarf!"

"Enough of this," Aroganji was used to allaying his friends' anger and quelling their childish outbursts. "Sit down and finish your breakfasts. There will be plenty of time to get out your frustrations in the journey ahead."

Yip sat calmly sipping his tea while Wrindanneth and Slate quietly finished their breakfasts.

With their meals finally concluded, the party left their house to head toward the city's center through the drear morn.

"Chin up, chaps! Just because tha day's gray, doesn't mean ya have ta be o' heavy heart!" Slate admonished his friends lightly, trying to pull them out of their quiet introspection as they plodded through the damp streets and thick, humid air.

"Who are you and what have you done with Slate?" asked Wrindanneth, unaccustomed to such ebullience from his oft sullen friend.

"You know he's just excited to see a childhood hero in the flesh," joked Aroganji.

"Bah!" barked Slate, feigning indifference.

"You're right. I had forgotten that Slate keeps a journal outlining all of Eidelion's triumphs, battles, and foes."

Moving through the gloom, Wrindanneth continued, "I'm surprised you haven't gotten a tattoo proclaiming your love yet, Slate!"

"Ya know I've never met him, nor do I keep a journal."

"That's right! I had forgotten you can't write." His voice split with a sardonic smile, Wrindanneth taunted, "But you don't deny the tattoo!"

This time, it was Yip who stepped in. "Wrindanneth, perhaps you should direct your critiques inward and find their true source."

"What's that supposed to mean?" asked Wrindanneth unused to many comments, especially critical ones, from Yip.

"Perhaps the source of your problems lies within and does not lie with your friend."

Before Wrindanneth could retort, Aroganji interceded as well. "Yip's right, Wrin. Besides, we're on serious business here. The success of the next part of our quest may hinge upon our relationship with Eidelion. Let's try to keep it positive."

His feelings unhurt, Wrindanneth shrugged off the comments, saying simply, "Understood."

Although he had difficulty opening up emotionally and presenting himself with candor outside of light banter and sarcasm, at heart Wrindanneth was deeply sensitive and understood the proper time and place for action. Intent on moving toward the city's heart where the Home Guard's barracks were located in Illdrassil's shadow, he offered an uncharacteristic apology, saying a quiet, "I'm sorry," to help make amends.

Slate and Yip both gave a slight nod. The one Wrindanneth really hurt in those outbursts was himself. Slate's feelings were as thick as his skin.

Aroganji smiled. "No harm done, friend."

Approaching the city's center, the tall, graceful crystalline expanse of Illdrassil came into view soaring to the heavens. The stars were at home on her bole and branches as much as the sun and moon. This was the seat of Tellanon's elected High Council and spirit.

Everyone stopped to behold Illdrassil's majesty.

Sun rays caught in Illdrassil's substance, rejoicing in the celestial tree's fabric, reveling in moving throughout its exterior without revealing what lay beyond its walls, only to eventually leave by the most circuitous trajectories in kaleidoscopes of rainbow colors. Balconies and chambers, open aired halls and solariums, hanging gardens and conservatories all suspended on arching tralucent bridges, mezzanines, and walkways branching out from the central bole as boughs from the massive trunk, woven branches of heavenly webs and light garlanding her reaches.

Radiating out from the spire's base, roots from the central stem, lay the various governmental facilities housed within the gardens and terraces surrounding the focal trunk of Illdrassil.

While Yip's eye followed the play of light across the unique living tower's structure, Slate said, "There ya have Illdrassil, Spire o' tha Heavens, as fittin' a heart fer a city as I could imagine."

Yip stood in silent appreciation alongside his friends.

Although none of the group had ever visited the Home Guard's compound or the larger surrounding governmental facilities, they had passed by on numerous occasions, if for no other reason than to admire Illdrassil's beauty. Though he had never visited this portion of the city, even Yip had heard of the beauty of the place and the fearsome reputation of those who dwelled within.

Looking at the shimmering pellucid glory of the grounds and palace from the tree-lined boulevard approaching the city's heart, Yip found it hard to believe anything fearsome could be found within such a sacred place. The Home Guard's citadel was clearly in evidence for any who wished to seek it out butted as it was immediately adjacent to the governing palace of the council, one of the grand roots feeding into the palace's center, guarding its entrance and occupants.

Made of the same substance as the central buildings, the towering crystalline walls surrounding the governmental compound soared above them as they made their way toward the palace grounds. Soldiers arrayed in hyaline armor fashioned of the same material as the walls marched behind sculpted crenellations along the parapet's top, moving splashes of light that mirrored the tree-formed tower at the city's heart.

To Yip's inner vision, magic not only flowed through the grounds in dense profusion, but the crystalline walls and structures, the weapons and armor wielded by the guards, and the very stone the guards walked upon, pooled and collected magical energy as much as the substance captured and held sunlight.

The entirety of the grounds appeared to be composed of crystallized magical energies.

Walking closer to the walls as they approached the main gate, he could see and feel the inner radiance shining forth from the clear crystal—nimbuses of colored energy, mutable and fantastic, flowing freely within.

Seeing the crystal tower in person reminded him of his first encounter with the awesome presence of the Aeryn D'al—otherworldly, improbably beautiful, and full of boundless life.

"The people of Tellanon are blessed to live in such a place," said Yip with deep reverence. From the city's numerous open spaces including the shifting magical parks opening onto vistas limited only by the builders' artistry and creativity, the naturally sculpted flowing stones making up its architecture, the seamless incorporation of verdure along the city streets, homes, and grounds, to the fantastical structures and people calling the city home, he had never envisioned that such a place could or would exist.

Nor would he have been able to do the city justice had he tried.

In Tellanon, imagination reigned and beauty was only limited by inspiration.

"Aye." Although he would never admit it to a fellow Dwarf, Slate much preferred the open air and beauty of Tellanon to the interior of a cave or the bowels of a mountain, no matter how grandly appointed or artistically crafted.

"Do you know where to go?" asked Aroganji. Though they had directions, he would have to ask for assistance finding his way.

"I know tha way," replied Slate having familiarized himself with the city much more thoroughly than his companions. In true Dwarven fashion, Slate did not want to get lost, a trait indelibly imprinted upon him ever since his youth wandering the caves surrounding the home of his Thanedom.

Before Slate could guide them further, however, two imposing guardians, one human, one of a blue-skinned reptilian race Yip could not identify, both standing in the middle of the archway ahead, each brandishing a wicked halberd, crossed their blades against the party's passage at their approach.

"State your business," hissed the reptilian guardian with a slightly sibilant undertone.

"We are here to seek out Eidelion," answered Yip. As he spoke, he felt a wave of magical energy wash over him, testing the veracity of his words, who he was, and whether or not he represented a threat.

"Our presence has been requested. We come in peace," added Aroganji.

"You may pass," answered the human guard responding to some silent communication. The halberds were raised, although the weapons still loomed overhead with unspoken intent. Like the armor worn by the guardians, the blades were made of chromatic crystalline material that exuded magical energies.

"You will find Eidelion at the practice grounds beyond the Home Reach." One reptilian finger pointed back to the left, vaguely toward the central tower.

"Thank ya," answered Slate with a tip of his head as he passed.

Situated at the base of a gently sloping hill, the archway opened up onto a broad view of the verdant grounds at the foot of Tellanon's central ruling district. Terraced gardens and tree-shaded walkways led inward to the foot of Illdrassil soaring above.

"Some place, huh?" queried Slate filled with as much respect as his friends.

"That would be an understatement," replied Wrindanneth as they wandered through the grounds.

"So even though Illdrassil appears directly connected to the city and is visible from the air, it is much like the other parks and estates in the city? A place apart?" asked Yip.

Wrindanneth laughed. "We never did finish that chat on the flight in did we?"

Yip smiled. "Unfortunately, no."

"At least now you have had direct experience of some of Tellanon's places, so the concept makes more sense. It is very foreign until first encountered," said Aroganji understanding how strange a city inhabiting multiple dimensions, stretched spaces, and modified locales had first seemed to him.

"That is for the island's protection. We have the benefit of access to its spaces, but these same places cannot be attacked directly, at least not without following the proper entrances."

"So a ship that penetrated the island's shields could not fire upon Illdrassil, for example?" asked Yip.

"Not unless the ship entered the government compound's space directly."

"And these spaces can be disconnected from the rest of the island, reverting back to whatever space they reside in?"

"Some of them, but not all. Illdrassil is afforded such protection, beyond Illdrassil, the link to the Elven city of Yenaria may be severed, and the parks where many may be given shelter in times of great need or danger may break their connection with the rest of the city, but more than that I do not know."

"The space encompassing the island has been stretched and manipulated to such an extent that much of it is not entirely here."

"And some parts never were," added Aroganji in reference to the parks and Yenaria.

Despite the complexity of the reality so effortlessly blended around them, Yip was glad of the multiple layers of protection afforded to Tellanon and its environs.

Overhead, the broadest of Illdrassil's limbs stretched serenely, the soft clear edges blending with the sky above, sending refracted rainbow hues onto the multicolored stone walkway's surface in tints that matched the inner radiance of the crystal all around—a steady, overarching presence lending stability and focus in an otherwise fractious world.

EIDELION

Unclouded of heart,
placid in mien,
the gallant offers his hand.

The proving grounds of the Home Guard were located in the umbrage of Illdrassil at the base of her central stalk in an open courtyard lit by the full radiance of the refracted sun. This courtyard was formed by the junction of two massive, gently rounded and tapered roots joining with Illdrassil's tremendous trunk. At the juncture with the bole, each root was as tall a large tower. Of these two, the nearest to the gate housed the Home Guard's operations center—the Home Reach. Directly overhead, far above the towering roots, Illdrassil's crown was lost shimmering in the sun and sky several furlongs above.

Rounding the terminus of Illdrassil's root housing the Home Guard, after crossing through much of the variegated landscape in the compound on the way to reach the structure's end, the party saw arrayed before them in the hollow of the two roots a display unlike any they had yet encountered.

Lights flashed, the air reverberated, magics and counterspells flew to and fro, and phantasms filled the air as soldiers drilled individually and in unison, fighting face-to-face and in organized groups, practicing with spell and blade in equal measure.

Every race and form they had yet seen on Tellanon seemed to be represented among the contingent. There were those arrayed like warriors in the crystalline regalia of Illdrassil's elite guard; there were Paratechnologists, or those whose physical aspects were modified like Paratechnologists', in muted shapes sculpted by their own flights of fancy and those whose form was dictated by certain desired practicalities; and there were also those who relied solely on the efficacy of their own skill and technique for protection. Whatever the appearance of the Home Guard, all displayed the utmost pinnacle of skill and precision, confidence, and capability.

So wondrous and formidable was the exhibition that, by unspoken agreement, Aroganji, Wrindanneth, Slate, and Yip merely stood next to the great root's tip and watched the spectacle in silent contemplation and admiration without thought given to time or context.

Aroganji, who had spent many years in formal training at Xian Shi, had the most direct experience with techniques and practices similar to those underway in the courtyard. However, his curriculum and the curricula of his school focused on the direct application of pure magics largely outside the realm of direct physical combat. Sparring, fighting, hovering, and flying through the air, members of the Home Guard fought equally well with glowing swords and sharp minds, casting spells as adeptly as they engaged with their hands. He watched in awe and amazement as the Guard demonstrated their mastery of two exceedingly difficult disciplines.

Recalling some of the grand plays he had seen upon his arrival in Tellanon, Wrindanneth thought the Home Guard's drilling looked akin to the scenes from a major epic with all the attendant lights, sounds, and action of a great performance with one added dimension—deadly practicality and efficacy.

Slate marveled at the ease with which the warriors before him merged and blended their magical and martial sciences on a level he had never seen but hoped one day to achieve. Although the Bor'Banna did not deal directly in spells as did the Home Guard, he certainly appreciated their application when used so competently. In due time, given enough effort, he would be able to duplicate many of their feats, if not their magical effects.

For his part, Yip hardly noticed the combatants struggling back and forth across the open courtyard in Illdrassil's beauteous presence, their striving for mastery and discipline, or the force of their exertions. He watched the interplay of their energies directly, the cascading flows and clashes of forces barely within their control, as a member of an audience appreciates a great symphony, lost in the complexities and beauty of the arrangement and orchestration, overcome by rhythms and harmonies and the waxing and waning of movements, awash in the interplay of reality and imagination.

At the heart of the melee, a lone man stood still, a focal eye amidst the tempest, untouched and unfazed by the throes enveloping him, calling out commands and encouragement, advice and observations to those clashing and toiling about him. Whereas Éremon kept his essence hidden as a bank of clouds masks the sun, Eidelion's Light shone forth as the sun revealed on a blessed spring day—bright, unblemished, and complete.

From the distance, Yip could see a mighty two-handed claymore strapped across his armored back shining with a light purer and brighter than the sun—Archaeus, the White Sword of Eidelion. In lieu of the multi-hued reflective crystalline armor worn by his comrades, Eidelion wore burnished silver plate mail from foot to chest. Held by one hand at his side, a golden plumed helm rested on his hip. The inner radiance of the sword and armor only heightened the brightness, puissance, and sanctity Eidelion emanated.

Breaking the party out of their individual reveries far sooner than they would have wished, the air before them clouded, obstructing their view of the Home Guard's practice, as the commanding voice of the Construct intoned, "You must wait to meet with Eidelion, citizens. Please make yourselves comfortable. He will be alerted to your presence after drilling has been completed."

"Thank you," answered Yip as he sat down in the shadow of Illdrassil's root to wait.

"I'm glad ta have been afforded a glimpse o' their practice. Watchin' them at work provides a Dwarf with quite a bit o' inspiration."

"I don't see why the Construct blocked our view. I'm sure we'll get to see plenty more on the trip ahead," replied Wrindanneth.

"Perhaps that is the way with everyone, Wrin. An observer wandering the grounds may be free to watch for a short period as if by happenstance, but if he lingers overlong or pays too careful attention, then that view is barred. That way, the Home Guard can practice freely where and how they will without fear of unwelcome intrusion." Aroganji had often practiced under strict secrecy on the grounds of Xian Shi.

"I understand all that, Aroganji. But if Eidelion, or any of his companions for that matter, joins us on the trip ahead, then I doubt they will practice in secret. I would have thought we would have been given at least some kind of clearance by Éremon's request."

"Somethin' meant ta be kept secret is seldom revealed," answered Slate, echoing Aroganji's sentiment. "And I doubt anythin' secret o' their trainin' will be divulged even if they journey with us."

"Slate speaks the truth, Wrin. There is much we don't know of each other's practices for all the time we have spent together traveling, training, and sharing what we know. And we have been far more open with each other than Eidelion or any of the Home Guard may be if they join us."

After his friends had finished, Yip offered, "Perhaps we were afforded that view precisely because of Éremon."

"How do you mean?" asked Wrindanneth.

"Perhaps we were only allowed to see anything at all because of Éremon's recommendation. Perhaps the Construct does not allow anyone to view the Home Guard's practice and we were afforded something not granted to many."

Slate nodded. "Makes sense as well. More, in fact."

Aroganji agreed. "We will spend much time on the journey ahead. We will all be facing grave risks together. If we are fortunate, perhaps the Home Guard will share some of their knowledge with us just as we may share with them."

Wrindanneth shrugged, changing subjects, for he no longer wished to argue about ideas and events that may or may not be unveiled through time. Thinking of the journey ahead and how best to approach their strategy in the coming meeting, he asked, "Should we push for more to join us with Eidelion?"

"I fer one, can't imagine Eidelion would travel alone. He is too august, too important, fer that," mused Slate stroking his beard.

"One or many, he is welcome," answered Yip.

Thinking ahead about the actual logistics of the journey, Aroganji said, "If he does bring allies with him, we may need another vessel. We only have one more cabin available on the *Shrike* unless they sleep in the hold."

"Aye," Slate grinned, adding, "and if they're on another ship, we'll have even fewer chances ta observe 'em."

They did not have to wait long before a member of the Home Guard approached them confidently, introducing himself with an adroit bow. "I am Hobben. Eidelion will see you now. Please follow me." Although his language was terse in the military fashion, good cheer flowed from deep wells under his strict bearing.

Hobben was a Man of tall height, broad shoulders, and an easy gait wearing the nacreous, enchanted crystalline armor emblematic of the Home Guard. Strapped across his back was a pair of fine straight swords with elaborately crafted and bejeweled hilts, both of which glowed strongly with arcane power.

Utilizing the connection afforded by the magical bands, noting the gear worn by Hobben and the fellows he had seen thus far, Wrindanneth said to Aroganji, *"If nothing else, the Home Guard certainly are equipped with far finer accouterments and weaponry than we currently enjoy."*

In silent agreement, Aroganji replied, *"With a few notable exceptions, I agree."*

Just as each member of the Four had one or two artifacts of exceptional quality and power, so, too, were the members of the Home Guard replete with extraordinary items. Eidelion's sword Archaeus, not to mention Hobben's paired longswords, were similar examples. In fact, Wrindanneth would not be surprised if all members of the Guard had at least one or more exceptional magical items. Since Eidelion wore armor unlike most of his fellows, Wrindanneth imagined that his plate armor had special properties beyond what was granted by the Home Guard's crystalline armor.

On the whole, however, the Home Guard wore similar gear of the highest quality, craftsmanship, and magical expertise. In contrast, most of his friends, himself included, wore motley assortments of mundane goods with a few magical items interspersed that they had found, earned, or salvaged.

In fact, now that he thought of it, as far as he knew, Yip only had one magical item for use in self-protection, his magical talisman, and even that was only granted as a temporary boon. The only magical item that he actually owned as far as Wrindanneth knew was a teaching scroll. Of course, all Yip owned as far as he knew was what he wore or wrapped in his bedroll, so there was not much to choose from.

The rest of them were much better equipped for the days ahead, although he and Aroganji could certainly use some protective armor suitable for casting spells without interference. Perhaps some fine leather armor for himself given his own greater choices in gear and some enchanted silken robes for Aroganji, if they could find them. Now that he thought about it, he and Aroganji should go ask Hoyt to find some additional protection prior to their voyage now that they had the funds to do so.

His cloak and Aroganji's rings just were not enough.

So used to having scant resources and income until these past few months, he seldom considered the alternative. Like Aroganji and Slate, he had always worn what they had salvaged on their adventures. Reestablishing contact with Aroganji, he said, *"Seeing all these warriors in their fine armor has reminded me that we do not have any true protection to speak of for ourselves. Now that we can afford it, the time may have come to rectify that situation. Although I am glad for the reassurance of the alien shielding devices and my cloak, I would like to have a little extra security should the shield or our spells fail."*

"Don't you think we should revisit Hoyt and see what else he has that may suit us for our trip?"

"Good idea," Aroganji's mirth overflowed between them. *"Like you, I've been so used to pinching coin that I seldom think to seek out upgrades or new goods when I have the opportunity. That's one reason I was so surprised when Slate decided we all needed clothes suitable for the rigors to come."*

Wrindanneth let his humor flow across the bond they shared. *"If Hoyt doesn't have what we need, he'll be able to direct us to someone who does!"*

Aroganji laughed. *"Or a stop on the way where we can liberate some items of worth!"*

"From someone or something who likely poses a dire threat to the safety and happiness of an isolated populace no doubt. Someone who won't really need said items after being brought to justice, of course."

"Of course," responded Aroganji finishing the joke.

The rather long walk to Illdrassil's base brought them beneath the multicolored shadow of the crystal tree's root, branch, and trunk all of which soared overhead hinting at the heights of the heavens. Eidelion stood waiting for them directly beside Illdrassil's trunk, flanked by three members of the Home Guard on either side.

To his right were a hulking humanoid Dragon-kin easily half again Eidelion's height with deep, thick ebony scales that drank in the light of the tree and sun. Expansive leathery wings were folded against his broad back. A series of baleful horns lined the ridge of his skull and a spiked tail cut the air behind him in silent swishes. Serrated spines projected upward in a deadly row between each powerful wing while vicious claws ended each limb wickedly.

Next to the Dragonoid, his size accented all the more by the reptilian's great stature, was a short Gnome encased in the most unusual set of armor any of the party had ever seen. Small cogs whirled, gears shifted, and wires adjusted with each minute motion of his hands, arms, and legs. Pistons moved up and down as his torso turned and torqued. Springs, joints, and pulleys complemented the natural workings of his limbs. Fastened over his shoulder, what appeared to be a bright red umbrella rested parallel to his back. Welded on to his shoulder, mirroring the direction of each turn of his head, a golden telescope moved of its own volition. Taken as a whole, he appeared to be encased in something rather like the inner workings of an inordinately complex clock or some other equally daedal technical invention. Altogether then, he appeared to be shrouded in a clockwork exoskeleton made up of random spare parts scavenged from countless discarded inventions.

By the Gnome, a green-haired Elf stood relaxed and poised in burnished witchwood armor, his essence as much a part of the place as the wind and sun. At his side, an elegant longsword made of the same substance as his armor, the Aeryn Sh'al, or tree heart, gleamed with bright golds, honeys, browns, and greens within the depthless interior of its bright, unsheathed blade.

To Eidelion's left the Home Guard were no less striking. A tall, thin white-haired albino of a race never seen by any of the fellowship gazed at them coolly with purple eyes. He leaned languidly on a knotted wooden greatstaff, the tip of which grew around a coruscating emerald green stone. Although of a humanoid shape, he did not appear to have any joints in the sense any of them were familiar with. Instead, his limbs and fingers curved gently between the shoulder, elbow, and hand as if he were made of a pliable putty.

Beside the albino, a dark-haired woman with piercing blue eyes gazed at them coolly. Of all seven Home Guards ordered before them, with the exception of Hobben who stood beside the Four, she was the only one wearing the elegant crystalline caparison standard for all the Guard. Her sword, too, was wrought of a lustrous blue crystal.

Finally, beside the woman, a stout Dwarf glowered sullenly, ready to be about other business. Like Eidelion, he wore a complete set of plate mail of a kind different than that worn by the majority of the Guards. In the Dwarf's case, he wore a complete suit of golden plate armor crafted in the likeness of a fearsome Dragon by Dur'kazaks in ages long past. Resting solidly on the ground in front of him was a massive two-handed hammer that looked as if it could crush boulders as easily as flesh and bone.

Eidelion bowed deeply from the waist, the gesture free and easy despite his formidable suit of armor. "Greetings and welcome to the Home of the Guard in the lee of Illdrassil the fair. I am Eidelion, Knight-Captain of the Home Guard, and"—bringing both arms outward in a gesture indicating his fellows—"these are my lieutenants."

"Before I begin the introductions, let me start by offering my heartfelt apologies at our failing. We have failed you and all the citizens of Tellanon through our lack of due vigilance and diligence. We ever strive for perfection but always remain far from it."

Yip bowed. "While the Life yet lives in me, there is no need for apology. Much remains beyond our control and reach even with the best of intentions and effort."

Eidelion returned the bow. "I thank you. We are hard at work ensuring another failure such as the one that nearly cost you your life does not happen again."

"With me I have fellow members of the Light's Guard, the unit at my command within the Home Guard." Gesturing first to his left, Eidelion then began introducing the other warriors standing with him. "Orogast the Elder"—the albino to his immediate left bowed supplely, the motion expressed as a fluid, roiling wave, a protean snake ready to strike at any time.

"Daerdros, Master at Arms." The dark-haired woman smiled, although no levity seemed to crack the icy depths of her chilling gaze. Each glance took in the measure of those around her and cataloged her assessment in steely recesses lost to any but herself.

"Kazarhan the Stout." The Dwarf saluted by pounding his chest with his gauntleted right fist. Kazzak, like those worn by the Bor'Banna, laced his long, thick beard in abundant profusion.

Switching to his right, Eidelion continued the introductions, starting with the imposing Dragonoid by his side. "Raour'Saqan." The Dragon-kin graciously bowed his head, his friendly gesture belying the ferocity implied by his daunting presence.

"Spreesprocket Goldpulley." The Gnome doffed an imaginary hat with a flourish and a bow at the waist, faint sparks of light colored the air with each deft movement. His actions, like those of Eidelion and Kazarhan, were unhindered by his imposing armor, although one could quickly become lost in the complexity of all the moving parts his exoskeleton created in the gesticulation.

"And finally, Llyewia." The Elf gave a deep bow, extending both arms outward to full length as one leg slid gracefully behind the other and he dropped in a spiral completing the bow with his head slightly to the side in a gesture of trust and openness.

As he had inspected Eidelion's blazing heart upon their arrival, Yip took time observing each of his lieutenants in turn as they were introduced.

Orogast, the changeling, shimmered like the rays of sun caught inside a floating bubble, mercurial and constantly fluctuating. His essence appeared as malleable as his form.

Daerdros, placid and poised on the surface, had a wealth of depth, complexity, and strength hidden within her nucleus. She was as formidable within as her title bespoke without.

Kazarhan's smoldering core spoke of tempered solidity, deep reserves both physical and magical, and unyielding determination—a mountain unbowed before time and the elements. With a goal in sight, he would not stop until his purpose had been fulfilled. With an obstacle in his path, the fires within were likely to blaze.

In contrast to his fellows who radiated energy and presence, Raour'Saqan drank in the life around him, hiding everything within the depths of his spirit. Energy flowed into him as water flowing underground loses itself in the depths and darkness of a great subterranean chasm, ready to be unleashed with prodigious force and vibrancy after completing its appointed path. Although he could not be sure, he imagined this energy could serve to fuel the fires of creation within as they had with Azaelle and other Dragons.

Spreesprocket's spirit was lighter than air, wispy and free, radiating dynamism and frivolity. Possessing the levity and curiosity of a child coupled with the skills and expertise of an accomplished adult.

Gazing upon the Gnome with curiosity, the more he studied Spreesprocket, the more his essence wavered and warped, folding in and overlapping with itself in intricate ways that defied simple explanation. He seemed almost to be two beings united so completely as to be one, each part magnifying the other, although of this Yip could not be sure.

Llyewia appeared indistinct, his essence so in tune with the energies moving about him as to be invisible—a light tendril of mist moving effortlessly within the morning fog along a stream bank; dew settling on grass beneath the moonlit evening clouds.

Taken together, they were a formidable band, but strength of arms and great skill were never a guarantee for success. Oftentimes, hard work, determination, and happenstance played a larger role in the outcome of decisive events. Hopefully, the groups would mesh well together, and the combined skills and determination from both parties would provide all the opportunity needed to meet with success in the journey ahead.

More than just the fate of the seals depended upon the outcome of their efforts.

When Eidelion had finished his introductions, after he had observed each in turn, Yip bowed, saying, "Well met, friends. May the Light give you shelter and solace, wisdom and compassion, for all of your days. I am Yip Chi Chuan of the K'un Lun."

Indicating Slate, he said, "This is Slate, Bor'Banna of the Flintforge Clan."

At the mention of Bor'Banna, Kazarhan's thick eyebrows lifted, although he said nothing. Mirroring the gesture of Kazarhan before him, Slate thumped his chest firmly with one mailed hand at the completion of Yip's announcement.

Gesturing toward Wrindanneth, he continued, "Wrindanneth, Priest of Maeth Onai."

Wrindanneth gave a wicked grin and bowed his head slightly.

Finally, he motioned toward Aroganji and said, "Aroganji, Fang Shih from my homeland of Chang Sen."

Aroganji opened his hands outward, palms up, elbows in, until his hands reached about waist height signifying openness, friendship, and nothing hidden.

Eidelion gave a brief, affable nod. "Well met, well met, indeed."

Wrindanneth replied, "The pleasure is ours."

Turning to the reason for their meeting, Eidelion changed course, saying, "Éremon speaks highly of you and your cause."

"All life deserves the opportunity to flourish," replied Yip.

"And what of those you hunt, then? Do they not deserve the opportunity to thrive?"

While Slate looked completely flabbergasted, Wrindanneth and Aroganji were taken slightly aback by the question. Yip, however, answered calmly. "All life is equally valuable and deserves the opportunity to thrive. Those who consistently, deliberately, and maliciously deprive or take that opportunity from others or those that undermine or inhibit that opportunity for others eschew the natural order just as they shun the potential for continual growth and development."

"What if their nature is to harm and destroy?"

"The answer depends upon the object of the question. For sentient beings, the way of Man is not the Way of Heaven. The Way of Heaven must be realized, internalized, and lived."

"In natural systems composed of myriad living beings, there is a place for many different roles, each with value. Outside of that system, or removed from the original context, difficulties may arise for a given organism and the system containing it. In natural systems, then, there are checks for all things, just as there is a dynamic harmony in all interactions."

"A predator without prey will surely die. A predator without limits, freed from natural constraints and left unchecked may destroy itself and the system it depends upon. A disease that is too efficient or virulent may kill too many hosts and ultimately destroy itself before ever realizing a dynamic equilibrium with its host."

"This description most ably applies for natural systems, not ones created, manufactured, tampered with, or deliberately destroyed by one individual or a group out of avarice, selfish motivation, or ill intent."

"Sentient beings then, those that have the capacity to question the natural order, must learn to move in accord with these natural systems to ensure long-term prosperity and viability both for themselves and the universe on which they depend."

"Why then intervene at all?"

"Life, and its unlimited potential, unfolds around us, enveloping and sustaining all living things in its continually evolving web. There are those who deliberately destroy this fabric, not only to the detriment of all beings, but ultimately to themselves. Why not intervene when the Light of Life calls for succor?"

Eidelion's pointed questioning continued, "If those who act out of self-interest are the equivalent of a destructive contagion, one whose actions are detrimental to the larger living fabric, and if left unchecked will ultimately die out from their own greed, rapaciousness, and uncontrolled desires, why not allow them to follow their natural course without intervention?"

"What is natural? Where do the rights and limits of one being end and another begin?"

"So, too, what happens without intervention? How much life, how much potential for new life, how many futures and possibilities must be lost for the benefit of one or a few? What is to be done if a sentient being refuses the mandate of Heaven and Earth?"

Eidelion smiled at the symmetry of Yip's response. "Who decides then? What standard do you follow? What course guides your action? How do you know that you act in the benefit of all Life as you say?"

"Right action follows from right perception. All beings are a part of and an expression of the living energies flowing through and within us. Action flowing from unity, from deep connection with the living *chi*, the life energy all around, moves one to act in harmony with the forces that flow through and enliven all beings. Those who seek to destroy, to harm, to undermine without proper limits or adaptations are readily apparent for they deliberately disavow that which gives them life."

"And what about those who feed on and destroy the energy of life itself? What of those?"

"Our universe, and the life within, flows forth from the fountain of universal energy given birth in the unlimited potential of the void. There will always be those beings that drink too deeply from this well without regard for others. These must be brought back into harmony with the natural order lest the damage they cause becomes too great. So, too, our universe is not the entirety of existence, beings from other universes, planes, or dimensions who do not respect the limits of existence here do so at the peril of the universal fabric, the varied expressions of life native here, and, ultimately, the universe itself."

"Why does the font of life not prevent this assault? Why does this source of untold potential not act to arrest further disruption?"

"Is it not?"

Eidelion laughed, clapping both strong hands together forcefully. "Good! Good! You will be quite an enjoyable travel companion I think."

Yip bowed again, unfazed by *dharma* combat.

Aroganji and Wrindanneth let out an unconscious, collective sigh of relief, only aware that they had been awaiting the outcome of the exchange with bated breath after catching a glimpse of the other's behavior through their shared connection.

Silently, Aroganji said, *"That's one way to start a relationship."*

Wrindanneth gave a mental shrug. *"Eidelion just wanted to be sure the cause he is espousing is just and that he would be in good company should he embark upon Éremon's quest."*

"Besides, I'm sure that Yip won't view the conversation as confrontational or ill-advised in the slightest. There is too little ego in him to conflict with in the first place. Yip just deals with what arises and moves on. That is all."

Aroganji chuckled. *"True. At least he is also able to maintain a sense of humor about it as well."*

Wrindanneth laughed internally. *"After meeting Master Wei, I am sure such dialectics are as natural to him as the rising of the sun."*

While Aroganji and Wrindanneth finished their side conversation, Eidelion asked, "There is much that must be done prior to our departure. What are your plans? When would you leave? What do you know of Taerris'thule and the seal of Eldre'gheu?"

Now Yip smiled in jest. "You have more questions than I have answers. A leaf drifting on the wind knows not where it goes or whither it will land."

Eidelion returned Yip's grin.

Slate held his smile in check as Aroganji answered Eidelion's questions as best he could. "We plan to leave within the week pending some final preparations, the availability of the seal, and your readiness. We only know where the city itself lies and that those who venture within do not return. As far as the history of the seal of Eldre'gheu and the city of Taerris'thule, we have had brief outlines and warnings, but we are not experts by any means."

Eidelion nodded. "I am at your disposal. My schedule is yours."

"We will need to have as complete a picture of what we may face as possible in order to allow for proper planning and ensure mission success. I will see what intelligence we have at our disposal."

"Thank you," replied Aroganji.

"I fear that we will need a larger force than just the five of us. Would you be willing to allow a few more travel companions on the journey?"

"More would be welcome," answered Yip.

"Good. I am glad to hear that news. In that case, you have already met those who have volunteered to go with me on the voyage. Éremon believes that this mission is vital to the security of Ea'ae and I am in agreement."

"Will your airship hold such a large crew?"

Wrindanneth answered, "That depends on how close you will tolerate your quarters. There is one room available, otherwise, you will have to sleep in the hold, but we should be able to accommodate you. That is, unless you prefer to bring a second ship."

Eidelion laughed. "Uncomfortable conditions are no stranger to either myself or my fellows. Let me think on the need for another ship, however."

Getting back to the journey ahead, Eidelion said bluntly, "My team is quite complete in terms of our capabilities and functionalities under a variety of intensive, volatile, and dangerous situations. Given Éremon's recommendation, I am certain that you are quite competent, but going in to a haven of Darkness like Taerris'thule, we will need to know each other's strengths and weaknesses that we may react most effectively and in a coordinated fashion. If you don't mind my asking, what are your areas of expertise and any other specialties you may have?"

Now Wrindanneth smiled. "Not at all, so long as we hear of your 'core functionalities' as well."

Eidelion laughed again, his ready good cheer a nice counter to Wrindanneth's challenge. "Of course! Since I asked, my team will start. I am a paladin of the Light, a member of the Dalaren Ka, blessed with the protection of the living, granted the Light's power to heal or harm, to protect and to serve."

Understanding the implicit command, each of Eidelion's lieutenants stepped forward in turn offering a brief description of their various skills and competencies.

Spreesprocket volunteered first, keeping his answer short, at least for a Gnome. "Technical liaison, researcher, and imagineer with advanced certification, Level A plus, in all aspects of Paratechnological ideation, design, repair, and engineering. Hand-to-hand classification grade Alpha Mark I, turbo class. Energetics manipulation and manifestation specialist, Order of the Golden Phoenix, First Class. Embodied synthetic intelligence researcher and authority, complete Whiz Bang Paraneurological certification." He bowed, finishing, "At your service."

Kazarhan grunted and said his piece next, short and to the point as was the custom of his people. "Foe Hammer, Kor'Dannan, and Dur'kazak. Master o' smitin' foes, healin' allies, and friend ta tha forge."

Llyewia spoke next, his voice as soft as the wind, but carrying just as far. "In your tongue, I am called a Tree Singer, for the hearts and spirits of trees are as open to me as they are to each other. Bringing forth this life, fashioning it in ways amenable to the spirits of the trees, I oppose those who bring harm to the land and its beings. The Crafts of war and succor are no stranger to my people for we interact with the world in ways much different than mortal Men. As such, I, too, am skilled in the ways of healing and combat."

"In the eyes of the Elves, there is no distinction between magic and mundane, the living and nonliving, for energy enlivens all things. In the eyes of my people, then, it is my place to interact and help shape the world as much destruction is wrought without care or feeling, thought, or compassion."

Daerdros listened attentively to Llyewia, all the while maintaining an at the ready position. When Llyewia finished, she gave a slight nod to the Elf and said, "As I said before, I am a Master at Arms among the Guard, a Caer'collas among my kin. I do not use the designation Blade Singer lightly, for I have dedicated my life to the blade as much as I have to wielding it in truth and with justice."

"My work is not limited to the sword itself, for the sword is but a metaphor for combat, its ebb and flow, permutations, sudden changes, losses, and victories. My training is as much in the arts of war—strategy, logistics, planning, reconnaissance, among other varied and related disciplines—as in physical combat."

"The blade cuts as well as defends and as such I am adept in both offensive and defensive magics intended for personal and group protection, recovery and response, in addition to applications within the larger currents of combat and its vagaries."

Raour'Saqan, spoke next, his voice a low rumble that only hinted at the terrible forces held in check by his tongue. "I am a Shaur'Daus, called a Stalker of Darkness in the tongue of your kind. In ages long past, my people, the Dracodaera, were nearly destroyed by vile creatures of Darkness from the great Beyond. The broodmates and hatch-kin who survived the invasion of my world wreathed themselves in the blazing fires of Heaven and did battle against their sworn enemies in the vaults of the sky for supremacy of our world. The fires of Heaven flow through us to this day as we do battle against usurpers from the Lightless depths."

"Where there is Darkness, my brethren descend on wings of retribution."

Orogast's purple eyes studied the Four as they watched the imposing figure of Raour'Saqan complete his brief summary. When Raour'Saqan had finished, he waited until all eyes naturally fell on him. "I am a Jira S'al Alann, a changeling or allomorph. I take shapes at need and thus fill many roles."

Orogast spoke with a melodic, lilting voice. "My people develop their power over time. As we do so, the shapes we take, the powers we employ, grow with us."

"We grow with our potential and our potential grows to encompass our envisioning."

"Our name loosely means, 'People of the Imagining' in the tongue of Men. This means we are limited in shape and function by our own envisioning. As we grow, so, too, do our conceptions of our selves and our place in the larger world."

Eidelion nodded, finished simply, "There you have it, at least in brief. I am sad to say these introductions are far too short for the skills and talents of my peers are not so easily summarized or described."

"Fortunately, the time ahead will see us spending much time together. We will have many opportunities to learn from and train with each other as we travel. I hope that any questions you do have about us will be answered in due time."

"Fair enough," replied Wrindanneth, taking the initiative to speak first for his friends. "As I said before, I am a Priest of Maeth Onai hailing from lands far to the north. We practice a blend of mundane and divine magics, channeling these energies through proper concentration for a variety of effects. I am well versed in the arts of creation and destruction, healing and harming, both inside and outside of combat. Illusion, deception, enchantment, and beguilement are also within my repertoire."

"Maeth has also granted me, to a much lesser extent, skills in minor divination." Wrindanneth offered a curt laugh. "That is when Maeth Onai listens."

"I am also well versed in the skills of research, retrieval, and recovery," he continued with a smirk. "That is, I am an accomplished adventurer capable of acting effectively and decisively in a variety of complex situations, especially those that serve either my interests or Maeth's."

Aroganji waited patiently for Wrindanneth to finish. When he had, Aroganji said by way of introduction, "I am a student of the Wu-hsing, the five elements of creation and destruction, of change and transformation. Feeling and guiding these elements, I create effects very much like those of the wizards of the western lands. Although I cannot use magic to heal like Wrindanneth, I, too, am skilled in the entire range of offensive and defensive magics. These particular skills parallel the arts of invocation, evocation, various forms of thaumaturgy, enchantment, alchemy, conjuration, and summoning practiced by mages the world over."

"Along with traditional magics, I am adept in the use of *fu-lu*, magical prescriptions and inscriptions that function very similarly to wards and talismans in western traditions. I am also skilled in scrying and the reading of signs and portents in addition to a wide range of divination practices both in communicating directly with spirits and through reading the lay of the land via geomancy."

Slate grunted as Aroganji finished, not wishing to carry on overlong. "If ya don't know what a Bor'Banna is ya'll find out soon enough."

He looked at each of Eidelion's lieutenants slowly in turn. "I'll tell ya this. I wield an axe"—here he reached over his shoulder and patted Duraeleon, whose muffled attempts to participate in the introductions were stymied by its sheath—"and I wield it well."

He grinned wickedly. "Tha fires o' Brendle's first forge flow through me, my axe, and into my foes. By tha reckonin' o' my people, I am new ta Brendle's forge, a young apprentice, but His flames flow fiercely through my blade nonetheless."

When Slate had finished, Yip said, "To act without acting, to let happen without intervening or resisting, this is the path of *wu-wei* and the lifelong journey of any Priest of the K'un Lun."

"Moving naturally and without thought or effort in accordance with the highest principle, the unspeakable Way, is the manifestation of *wu-wei*, the path of perfect harmony."

"Peace that flows from freedom, wisdom guided by perception, the expression of the universal life force, the ineffable *yuan-chi*, is the Way of the K'un Lun."

"This is the path I learn and this is the path I tread."

Eidelion raised his eyebrows questioningly. "And what does that mean, Yip?" For he wished to learn more from the riddles in which Yip spoke, from the perspective of another who dove deeply in the waters of the Light.

"Walking in peace, brings peace. Expressing the universal, brings life."

Pushing for clarity, Eidelion asked, "And in the time ahead together, that means?"

"The Way of the K'un Lun brings harmony where there is discord, peace where there is dissension, and life where there is dearth."

When he had finished, knowing full well how irksome Yip's conundrums could at times be, Aroganji explained for the benefit of those unused to his thought processes, "Yip senses and uses the energy of life, he calls it *chi*, flowing all around, to read intent, express the positive qualities of creation, and"—here he smiled good-naturedly—"to unleash the powers of destruction on those who act in opposition to these principles."

Slate grunted curtly, "He specializes in stompin' and not gettin' stomped."

Wrindanneth laughed. "Yes, Yip embodies the way of peace with open, empty hands offered up benevolently to the faces of his foes. Repeatedly."

Pausing a moment, Wrin continued, "Repeatedly, with great force and conviction…sometimes adding his feet."

"With glowin' blue nimbuses o' light around his hands," added Slate.

"That accent his eyes," joined in Aroganji.

"And help us find him in the dark," finished Wrindanneth.

Eidelion and his lieutenants laughed at the jest.

Appreciating the banter at his expense, Yip gave a gracious bow and a bright smile.

As far as Wrindanneth was concerned, if Eidelion and his men were to travel with them, they would have to get used to their sense of humor and friendly repartee. The sooner this happened, the better.

Thus far, they were off to a good start. Now he just needed them to side with him in badgering Slate.

That should not be too hard.

When the groups had settled from the mirth, Aroganji said, "As far as provisions go, our ship will provide all the sustenance you need. So you don't have to worry about summoning food or bringing rations of your own."

"Or fightin' fer sleep space amongst food crates in tha hold!" laughed Slate.

"I will have our Aspect send a copy of our current map to Taerris'thule to you that you may study the course ahead and proceed with any additional research that you may wish."

"Thank you," said Eidelion. "I will contact you with whatever information I glean from our search."

"Is there anything else you would like to know or discuss presently?" asked Wrindanneth.

Eidelion shook his head. "There is much we must do now in preparation for our departure, the least of which is organizing and giving commands to the remaining Guards during our absence."

"Before we chart our final course, we will need to determine which far travel location will provide the most direct route to Maeron and Taerris'thule via *faerviage*."

Wrindanneth nodded. "Aye."

He continued, "Is there anything you need from us that may be of service on the voyage ahead? We must have every opportunity to meet with success on our journey for Tellanon depends upon our success as much as the rest of Ea'ae. The resources of the city are at your disposal."

Quickly, through their shared connection, Wrindanneth asked Aroganji, *"Should I mention the armor?"*

"If you wish."

To Eidelion, Wrindanneth said, "Aroganji and I are currently in need of suitable armor to allow for the casting of spells. Although we have our spells and magical force shields, we fear that in the times ahead we may need more. We would need body armor with the freedom of movement to allow the most intricate of gestures coupled with a resonance structure that does not interfere with the creation, channeling, or projection of arcane energies in the slightest way while still providing physical protection."

"I have experience wearing either leather armor or silk robes while casting as the leather does not interfere with my spells like most metal armors do. Aroganji is only able to cast while wearing robes."

"We are going to visit a merchant that we know to check his wares to see if he has suitable protection for us. If not, would your armory have anything appropriate for our use? We would offer remuneration for whatever we may receive."

Eidelion smiled. "Éremon has made it clear that whatever we need for the trip ahead we shall have. If we make it back alive and you wish to keep whatever you may need to borrow, he has also indicated that we are to allow you to have it. However, the offices of Tellanon would not turn down any charity you wish to give in return for the usage of any items we provide. For all works, even those of good intent, come with attendant costs."

Wrindanneth and Aroganji bowed. "We will let you know if we remain in need."

Returning the bow, Eidelion smiled ruefully. "My apologies for being an ungracious host. Perhaps when we return and have more time, I will have the opportunity to give you a tour of Illdrassil, its wondrous grounds, and our station."

Yip bowed as well, saying, "Until that time, we will look forward to the opportunity. Well met, friends. May the life in your hearts guide you to an ever auspicious morrow."

"Until we speak again," replied Eidelion, the strength of his conviction evident in his tone.

The introductions and initial meeting complete, Yip, Wrindanneth, Aroganji, and Slate left the Home Guard's proving grounds, this time walking through the idyllic gardens at their leisure. Birdsong guided their steps as much as the sounds of flowing and falling water, lightening the place in perfect complement to the lustrous light and stone.

When they had finally left Illdrassil's shadow, Wrindanneth asked, "What did you think?"

Slate answered first, saying, "A truly impressive band, that. Few Dwarves tha likes o' Kazarhan still walk tha halls o' our fathers. I fer one, would trust him with my unguarded back."

Aroganji nodded, saying, "We came in expecting little and received much more."

Agreeing, Wrindanneth said, "Short of an army, I don't think we could assemble a much more powerful band. I look forward to hunting with them." Thinking of the stalwart company they would be keeping, he said, "Perhaps I'll learn a few more tricks to make Maeth proud."

Yip spoke last, saying, "I hope we all come to work together as naturally and well as we four for the days and nights ahead may be long and dark."

Finally reaching the overarching gate to the city proper, their way was no longer barred by the armed guards. Their halberds raised, the guards paid them scant attention as they passed. Instead, the Guard gazed steadily out upon passing traffic, wary of any incoming risk.

"Shall we return to Hoyt's to bolster our garb?" asked Wrindanneth.

Slate nodded. "Might as well. We can hit tha practice fields once we're done if ya'd like."

Heading for the shortest route to Hoyt's shop near the docks, Aroganji said, "Perhaps next time we visit, we will have the opportunity to practice with the Home Guards on their grounds."

Glad to see his friends' eagerness to learn and grow so evident, Yip said, "On the journey ahead, there will be much time to practice with the Home Guard themselves. Perhaps away from the Home Reach, the Guard will be inclined to reveal a few of their inner teachings to welcoming ears."

Wrindanneth chuckled. "We can always hope, my friend."

Knowing that in many martial traditions, masters often shared secrets with each other behind closed doors once trust and merit had been established, Yip answered, "Let hope lead the way then."

The beautiful day with its crisp air and sunlight streaming brightly through the clouds almost made Hoyt's shop look respectable.

Almost.

Of course the building could use some attention. Wrindanneth and

Aroganji never quite figured out how Hoyt's building managed to remain on the slightly repaired side of ramshackle in a city where everything was so well kept by its own magic. The only thing that they could think of was that he must have special permission to allow his building to remain in semi-disrepair.

Why he did that was anyone's guess. Perhaps it reminded him of home. Maybe he felt comfortable in an old building in the same way some people felt at ease in old clothes. Possibly he believed having a few frayed edges lent character to a city that was almost perfectly groomed. Perchance the appearance of disrepair lent a sense of adventure to an otherwise placid place.

Sharing these thoughts through their connection, Wrindanneth and Aroganji decided that today was the day they asked.

Waiting at the front door, perched on one of the random crates next to a full wooden barrel, Hoyt's rainbow-hued Fairy Dragon lazily cracked an eyelid at their approach before returning to sleep.

Its characteristic creak still intact, the screened door opened with a groan at their arrival, signaling their entrance as well as any bell or spell.

From the back of the store, from one of the many storage rooms holding his accumulated wares, Hoyt called out, "Welcome! Welcome and good day!"

"Tryin' ta warm us up? Well, it won't work!" replied Slate crossly in jest.

"Not you! I thought I had gotten rid of ya!" came the jovial reply.

"Never count a good Dwarf down, they always say!" called back Slate.

"Assuming said Dwarf can actually count," muttered Wrindanneth loud enough for Slate to plainly hear.

As Hoyt took his accustomed spot behind the counter, Slate barked back, "Bah! At least we teach our younglin's. Ya Northmen leave yer children ta flounder in tha hopes that an education will someday land in their laps."

Knowing where this would lead, Wrindanneth answered, "There are shining lights even in the darkness."

Looking up at Wrindanneth with a steady gaze, Slate said, "Too bad that light burnt out long ago."

"You Dwarves could never hope to produce a magician of my caliber."

Getting the better of the exchange, Slate finished, "Nor would we want ta."

A short cough, as of a teacher reminding his students of their proper place, ended further argument. "What brings ya to my fine establishment on this glorious day?"

Aroganji answered while Wrindanneth's flushed face cooled. "We would like to browse your wares."

Hoyt laughed. "Ya mean ya actually want to buy somethin'?"

"You are correct."

"No information? No advice? No insight? Just commerce?"

"Yes."

Hoyt looked at them archly. "Somethin' must've happened to the Four I knew. Are ya actually who ya say ya are?"

Slate laughed in reply. "Be done with yer cheap jokes, Hoyt. By my tangled beard we're here ta trade if ya'll stop yer banter long enough ta let us!"

Hoyt smiled in return. "How may I help ya, then?"

Aroganji answered, "Wrindanneth and I are in need of armor suitable for each of our particular types of magic. I am need of robes that will not interfere with the casting of my elemental spells while Wrindanneth is in need of robes, leather, or some other type of armor that will allow the channeling of his magics."

"We've been lacking for some time, but after Yip's recent encounter and where we're going, the time has come to rectify the situation."

Hoyt rubbed his chin thoughtfully. "Hmm. Ya know items of that quality come at a pretty price? Craft of that caliber is hard to come by for it is not easily wrought or found."

"Believe me, we are well aware, lest we would have bought something much sooner," replied Wrindanneth.

"And yer spells, rings, and robes won't do?"

"Nor do the shields granted by the fruits of our extraterrestrial excursion," answered Wrindanneth.

Following Wrindanneth's point, Aroganji said, "We are looking for a third, more reliable contingency."

Hoyt clapped his hands together loudly. "Such is the way of any true wizard! The more contingencies, the better!"

"Unfortunately, my stock of such items is dangerously low. I believe Slate is currently wearing one of the last sets of armor I had of any true merit."

When Wrindanneth and Aroganji appeared slightly crestfallen, Hoyt laughed, saying, "Don't fret, my friends! There's always my warehouse!"

"Warehouse?" asked Wrindanneth. He, and after checking through their connection, Aroganji too for that matter, had always thought that the dusty warrens of Hoyt's store represented the full extent of his wares.

"Of course! Ya don't expect me ta keep my good stuff open ta the light of day now, do ya? Open and available fer any miscreant ta sneak in and pilfer?"

"Well..." began Aroganji.

"You don't have ta answer. It was a rhetorical question. There're just some things I prefer ta keep under lock and key if ya take my meanin'."

"Wait here." With a *pop* and a faint puff of smoke, Hoyt disappeared as if he had never been there in the first place.

"He certainly is full of surprises," said Wrindanneth shaking his head.

"Never ceases ta amaze," echoed Slate with a few thoughtful strokes of his beard.

After only a few short minutes, Hoyt reappeared with another loud *pop* followed by the acrid smell of smoke. Laying two neatly wrapped garments on the counter, he smoothed the cloth covers deferentially.

"You, my friends, are in luck!" With a flourish worthy of a street performer, he revealed two beautiful silken robes for all to see. One robe gleamed with the light of a red sun, hot and full of energy. The other robe appeared of the deepest black, so dark that its folds could not be discerned from within its border.

Wrindanneth's breath caught in his throat when he saw the robes so wondrously were they wrought.

Aroganji reached out instinctively to feel the fabric, to touch the finest details of their craftsmanship, before catching himself and retracting his hand.

"Go ahead!" said Hoyt enthusiastically. "Behold Fraeü and Byear, robes recovered from the estate of the late Archmage Mandros Gray Beard!"

"What do you mean by recovered?" asked Wrindanneth, knowing the answer but moving toward a particular question.

"By fortune seekers such as yerself, of course!"

"And there are no rightful claimants otherwise?" The last thing Wrindanneth wanted were legions of offspring and allies seeking to reclaim his goods.

"Of course not! Else I would gladly have returned them."

"No harmful curses, hexes, ensorcellments, jinxes, beguilements, kiboshes, bedevilments, or other longstanding protective spells?" pressed Wrindanneth.

"No!"

Satisfied, Wrindanneth said, "Tell us of them then."

Shaking his head but smiling, understanding Wrindanneth's caution, Hoyt said, "These two robes are both mage armor. They will deflect a blade as well as plate while still giving you the freedom of movement and ability to channel magical energies necessary for proper spell casting."

"What else do they do?" asked Wrindanneth eagerly.

"Isn't that enough?"

Looking directly at the power held hidden within the strands of the silken robes, Yip replied, "There is much more to these robes than just the protection you describe."

"You are correct, Master Chuan. Unfortunately, not all of their power has yet been revealed to me. I know they are not cursed, of that ya can be sure. Mandros worked some right clever spells in the folds of these robes, but they work for the bearer's benefit no more."

"Will they not recognize that we are not he?" asked Aroganji.

"Mandros is gone, but his magics and works yet remain. He was just and wise from all accounts. I know that no ill will befall you for wearing them."

"To your earlier question, I have ascertained that these robes offer protection from more than just a blade," looking at Wrindanneth and Aroganji candidly, he said, "and that's why I'm bringin' 'em out. I know where you're goin', what ya've been through, and have given yer safety some thought since last we spoke. These are about tha best protection I can offer you on yer journey ahead, even if not everything is known about 'em."

"They've managed ta confound about all of my spells so there's that as well."

Thankful for the consideration, Aroganji humbly replied, "Many thanks, friend Hoyt."

"Can't go around losing good customers now can I? Especially now that you've actually started expressin' an interest in buyin' goods!"

They all laughed, if for no other reason than to take the opportunity to share good cheer with their friend prior to departure.

"How much does a pair of robes like this cost, Hoyt?" asked Slate ever reluctant to open the party's purse.

"For you? Roughly one million imperials."

Before anyone could raise their voice in protest or offer further negotiation, he said, "As I recall, I still owe ya fer one magical sword ya delivered some time back. So, by rights, they're yours."

Clarifying, he added, "No one ever came forward ta claim tha sword and I reckon y'all'll need its worth more than anyone ever has or will."

With a twinkle in his eye, he finished, "And I will give ya more than tha robes are worth if ya find anythin' that peaks my interest on yer trip ahead!"

Knowing full well that they were getting a fabulous deal whether or not they received any of the robes' value in exchange for the sword from Hoyt, Wrindanneth responded fervently, "We'll take it!"

"Glad ta hear! Shall I wrap 'em up?"

"No need for that. Do you have a room where I can change?" asked Wrindanneth who was eager to remove his old robes and try on the new ones.

"Certainly!" said Hoyt pointing to one of the side rooms. "No one will bother ya in there while ya change."

Wrindanneth stepped away from his friends with the shimmering black robes in hand and walked into a room lined with glass shelving and sealed display cases. Jars filled with plants, herbs, and preserved animals and creature parts vied for space with small artifacts of every shape and sort from embossed wooden pipes to wands, daggers, and items of archaeological significance. While he disrobed, he noted that this portion of the shop appeared as much like a museum as a store. But, in a place dedicated to selling 'found objects' and other oddities, having many types of items arrayed in various presentations was to be expected.

When Wrindanneth finally emerged from the side room, motioning for Aroganji to take his place, he had undergone something of a transformation in the eyes of his fellows. Although he still remained the tall, rangy character they were accustomed to and respected, he now seemed, for whatever reason, to have an unaccountable air of mystery and mystique about him. In fact, Slate had to stop himself from scratching his head in confusion at Wrindanneth's reappearance for he seemed a character freshly minted from a childhood story.

Although the air in the room was still, Wrindanneth's robes flowed dramatically behind him, bringing a subtle focus to Wrindanneth's presence, as though he should be the center of attention. This same effect seemed to accentuate his strongest features as if he were ready to pose for a painting or momentous event.

In a very tantalizing way, the robes seemed to gather dark shadows in pools around Wrindanneth's feet. Seemingly rising up from the ground or reemerging from a place of darkness into light, he presented a moment of powerful transfiguration for all to see.

"Well, well," said Hoyt. "I think those robes suit you, Wrindanneth."

Unable to see his reflection but feeling similarly, Wrindanneth said innocently, "You think so?"

Aroganji laughed from the doorway where he, too, was about to change, offering, "Impressive. You certainly won't go unnoticed!"

Glad of the effect, for it suited his taste, Wrindanneth puffed himself up proudly and looked for a suitable place to admire his reflection.

When Aroganji eventually returned from the other room, his transformation was no less dramatic. Whereas Wrindanneth's appearance was accentuated by the absence of light, Aroganji's presence was reinforced directly by the presence of it. The robes flowed in colors of orange and red as flames, or the semblance of flames, licked at the garment's hem and traveled slowly upward, around, and through its fabric in dazzling patterns too complex to completely track or discern. Although he did not look as though he were wreathed in flames, the implication was there. If nothing else, he certainly appeared to have flames dwelling within the heart of his robes.

"Perhaps we should ask Jarvis ta hold off on those clothes for ya!" remarked Slate when Aroganji emerged, duly impressed with his two friends' appearance.

Holding out his arms wonderingly, watching the flames lick at the edges of his sleeves and travel up his arms, Aroganji said, "I don't think so, Slate. While these robes are remarkable, our other robes will certainly have a place. For example, in protecting us from the rain and cold..."

"Or helpin' ya not stand out like a sore thumb," added Slate emphatically, finishing Aroganji's thought while discounting his earlier suggestion.

Producing his old clothing from within the folds of his arms, Wrindanneth said, "At least let me give you the cloak we recovered from the *Shrike* as part of the exchange."

Hoyt squinted his eyes appraisingly before finally replying, "Two for two sounds fair enough for me. I'll take your cloak and sword for the two robes."

Knowing they came out well ahead in the exchange, Wrindanneth set the cloak on the counter and responded gratefully, "We are still in your debt but at least this way we'll feel a bit better about it!"

Hoyt, however, was not done.

"There is one other small token I would give ya, ta help on yer journey," said Hoyt as he held up a thin golden band. "This ring was the wizard's as well. It afforded him another layer of protection. Unfortunately, I have only the one ring, else I would give one ta each of ya. Whoever wears this ring becomes"—Hoyt paused for a moment while looking for the right terminology—"elusive, indistinct. You remain where ya are and who you are, but ya seem slightly shifted, a bit out of place. So you're harder to track, harder to hit, harder to keep fully in sight."

Wrindanneth laughed. "Sounds like a great piece for Slate. Less is sometimes more, after all!"

"Bah! Tha same could be said fer others as well."

Cutting through their jests, Hoyt reiterated, "Don't get me wrong here! Whoever wears this ring does not in any way become invisible! Instead, you seem shifted, a bit off center, either moving slightly quicker or slower than you really are, your position not quite right."

"Quite clever really…could be very useful in hand-to-hand combat."

He held the ring out in the air, its lustrous surface reflecting the sunlight in a brilliant gold.

"Who wants it?"

Slate reached out before staying his hand. "How much?"

"This I'll give you if ya come back in one piece."

"Are you sure?" asked Wrindanneth.

Hoyt smiled ruefully. "Now that you're actually buyin' things, I have to give ya an incentive to come back!"

Taking the proffered ring gingerly, Slate slid it over his thick ring finger. Although his appearance did not change in any way to his friends, his outlines certainly appeared more indistinct.

To Yip, the presence of his life energy remained the same radiant blaze with one exception. If Slate's essence were a burning flame, the edges now wavered and danced under a slight breeze, spread out over space and time.

"What's it called?" asked Slate as he took off the ring and held it up in the air admiringly, turning it over and over in his fingers while watching it glint and shine.

Reaching out a hand, Hoyt took the ring from Slate and angled it so that the surface of the inner golden loop was visible to him. The eloquent flowing script of the Elves caught and magnified the light of the sun as Slate gazed intently at the etching inside.

"Caelebeor, 'Shadow's Grace' in the tongue of the Elves" answered Hoyt softly in response to Slate's question.

"Truly a wondrous gift. Many thanks, Hoyt." Lacing the ring carefully through his beard along with the other Kazzak for later use, Slate secured Caelebeor within the pleats of his honor.

"As friends of the Elves, now you won't have ta worry about wearin' it!"

While the others chimed in their appreciation as well, Hoyt overrode them, saying, "If ya come back in one piece, that will be thanks enough."

Filing out slowly, Hoyt called out to them, "May the Light's grace be with ya, friends."

Raising a hand in farewell, Slate called back with a chuckle, "May your beard grow long and thick."

Before the creaky screened door shut firmly behind them, Hoyt's voice reached their ears one last time. "And don't forget my offer!"

Walking back home toward the residential district where their cottage nestled amid the greenery, Yip commented to Slate, "Hoyt is most generous."

"Don't let him fool ya. He drives a hard bargain and he stands ta earn more in return."

His eyes lost in the distance, Slate continued, "We go a long way back. We've done quite a bit fer Hoyt." He interjected quickly, "Fer our mutual benefit o' course!"

"Your good deeds now bear fruit."

Slate laughed. "With all we've done fer him, ya'd think we planted an orchard!"

The next few days passed in a dizzy haze of activity. Aroganji checked and rechecked their supplies from bedding to ropes to emergency food stores and materials for repairs should their ship's systems fail. He instructed the Aspect on proper care of the house and grounds even though the simulacrum was already well-prepared for the job based on its imprinting, intelligence, and prior instructions.

Together, they poured over the maps of the southern continent of Maeron provided by Hoyt for the journey ahead, debating which course over the largely uninhabited expanse would provide the safest path to Taerris'thule, never having ventured to Maeron themselves. Based on their charts and Eidelion's advice, Aroganji made arrangements to *faerviage* to the far southern city of Tueran on the island nation of Landeiss in preparation for their imminent departure.

When not discussing the upcoming passage, Slate spent much of this time engrossed in his blade work in the nearby parks or on the cottage lawn. In the past, prior to any major undertaking, he would have spent much of this time lost in reflection polishing his axe. However, since Duraeleon's blade maintained a preternaturally sharp edge regardless of whatever he did, and because the axe raised a rousing protest when he unsheathed its blade and began to work its surface with a whetstone, complaining his tickles were undignified, he was denied his normal routine.

Yip spent this same time outside in quiet reflection, in simple appreciation for the life he was given each day. Awash in the unending fount of energies arising from and descending into the depthless void, the *chi* bathing and enlivening all things, he mirrored what he felt—the peace and joy intrinsic to living in happiness, his practice each and every moment.

While Aroganji remained extremely busy, building to a fever pitch prior to their departure, Wrindanneth took the opportunity to lazily pass the last few days on Tellanon, sleeping late, eating at his leisure, going through each day with no particular plan or aim. Knowing that the days and nights ahead would be difficult enough, he wanted to enjoy the last remaining bit of unregimented time in a safe haven restored and rekindled. For the very same reasons, Aroganji let him remain untroubled and unconcerned just as he let everyone else prepare for the time ahead as they would.

Two days before setting out, as they finished their morning meal in the kitchen, Yip said to his friends, "Eidelion comes."

"What?"

"Eidelion said he would speak with us after he had time to investigate the course ahead. Now he is come."

A few minutes later, the voice of the Aspect announced Eidelion's arrival. "A guest has arrived at the door." After a brief pause, the female voice continued, "Eidelion to see the Four."

"Shall I let him in?"

"Aye," answered Slate motioning for everyone to follow him to where Yip waited standing in the living room.

Aroganji and Wrindanneth arrived just as Eidelion stepped through the threshold from the room's front entry.

"Good morning, gentlemen." Eidelion's overwhelming presence drew all eyes to him as he spoke, his scintillating essence magnified by the closed space. "I trust I am not too early?"

"Mornin'," answered Slate for his friends. "'Course not. Only Wrindanneth refuses tha call o' tha mornin' birds. What news have ya?"

"Éremon certainly has picked an interesting road for us to follow."

"Of that there is no doubt," replied Wrindanneth.

"The Construct has unearthed much of interest I did not know about Taerris'thule. Unfortunately, none of it is good."

"If the news isn't bad, I don't expect to hear it," joked Wrindanneth.

"Shall we have a seat?" Aroganji indicated the sitting room located immediately off the entry.

Eidelion shook his head preferring to stand. He did, however, step into the sitting room in case his hosts wished to sit.

Addressing them once more after they had settled, Eidelion said, "I know you have heard some of Taerris'thule's tale from its rise as a city of Light to its fall into Darkness, but there is more you should know."

"The dark cultists who sold their souls for power brought down Taerris'thule, as you well know, but in their lust for dominion they overreached and brought forth Darkness greater than they knew. This Darkness destroyed them, just as it destroyed the city and overthrew the seal, corrupting its power."

"Nor was Taerris'thule abandoned and forgotten, left to rot, or crumble into dust. After Therion's initial success, many have attempted to restore its Light before us and none who have braved its gates have returned."

"As these men of duty, bound by word and honor to their lords' will, continually failed in their attempts to restore Taerris'thule's splendor, adventurers followed in their stead seeking after the glory and riches that warrants such efforts. Not knowing the true extent of the evil hidden in Taerris'thule's heart, these same brave men and women went to their deaths just as surely as their predecessors."

"What then lies at the heart of Taerris'thule and why not mount an army to destroy it?" asked Aroganji

"Just because a nation has power, that does not mean it has sufficient will or interest to justify its usage. Nor are there many nations or people yet on Ea'ae with such power. Of these, none are located on Maeron."

"So we are being sent to die in the same way as those before us?" asked Wrindanneth.

Here Yip spoke for Eidelion. "Might in arms may fail where will and belief prevail."

"Are not one hundred men more valuable than ten? How will we succeed where all these others have failed, Yip?" Just as he was quick to forgive, Wrindanneth was quick to let loose the heat of his passions.

"Eidelion has said nothing of the nature of the Darkness at the heart of Taerris'thule. The universe harbors many evils, not all of which meet force with force or strength with strength. Nor is every Darkness made the lesser in response to violence. Many evils feed on aggression, hostility, and carnage whether that violence or strength is well intentioned or not."

"Darkness lessens in response to Light. When deprived of the stuff of fear and tumult, the shadows shorten and dawn begins. I cannot say who or what went before us, but if we proceed with wisdom and conviction, our course may remain clear and success may indeed be our reward."

Eidelion nodded in accession. "Brave words and well-spoken, Yip."

He looked at them gravely. "Yip is correct."

"There is a nameless horror from the darkest unhallowed pits waiting for any who would brave Taerris'thule. As Yip has said, and Wrindanneth cautioned, we will need more than fortune's bright smile to win the days and nights ahead."

"Remember that we do not go forth to meet force with force but to meet Darkness with Light."

Many emotions seethed through them as Yip and Eidelion spoke—fear, anxiety, excitement, courage, and anticipation not the least, but their steadfast assuredness remained true throughout.

When everyone's emotions had settled, Aroganji said, "Our preparations, if not our strategy, are ready. We will leave at dawn in two days."

Eidelion gave a brief nod. "We can plan on how best to enter and approach the heart of Taerris'thule's Darkness in flight prior to our arrival. If fortune is on our side, we may be able to divine some guidance."

"Did you decide whether or not you would take your own ship?"

"We will ride with you. That way, we can lay our plans together and drill as needed. If need be, we can teleport back to Tellanon if we run into any difficulty."

Aroganji then said, "Meet us at dawn at the *Shrike* in the lower docks in two days' time. From there, we will *faerviage* to Tueran and begin our journey to Maeron in earnest."

Wrindanneth appended, "If you have any gear you would like to load prior to our departure, let me know and I will instruct the Construct to let you aboard."

"Understood."

"Oh." Wrindanneth had almost forgotten. "We will not need any additional protective armor from your stores. Aroganji and I were able to find robes that met our needs."

"Thank you for the offer," replied Aroganji.

"I am glad to hear that your needs have been met. We will bring along some replacement gear should anything we have become irreparable along the way. However, it will be stowed in magical bags without encumbrance or significant usage of space, so we should not need access to your ship prior to departure. If you want us to bring any provisions or gear for you from our stores, you have only to ask."

"Thank you. We will let you know if we think of anything that may be of assistance," replied Aroganji.

Eidelion then asked, "Have you decided on a final course to Taerris'thule?"

"Not completely," replied Aroganji. "Beyond Landeiss, the continent of Maeron is foreign to us. However, we will probably fly as directly as possible high overland since the continent is largely uninhabited and we are not certain what risks it poses."

Eidelion agreed. "Those are wild lands. We would do well to remain cautious."

Eidelion looked around briefly at the gathered friends, concluding, "If that is all, I will be on my way."

Aroganji answered for the group, saying, "I think so."

"I look forward to our time ahead and an opportune resolution."

"As do we all," answered Wrindanneth.

With a brief bow, Eidelion stepped out of the door, returning back to the Home Reach for continued preparations.

After the door shut behind him, Slate said, "We should go see Jarvis today. Our garments should be ready."

"You don't need everyone to go, do you?" asked Wrindanneth.

"'Course not. I can go by myself. I'll just be carryin' tha clothes."

"You don't plan on putting them in your bag then?" asked Wrindanneth.

"Why?"

"Because I'd like to actually see them before they disappear."

Slate growled then let it go. There were more important things to argue about.

"Anyone else like ta come?"

"I'll go," said Yip. "The day is young and I would see it unfold."

Yip took his leave with Slate leading the way to Jarvis's shop, his stout friend huffing and puffing as he forced his way forward as though the air itself sought to impede his progress.

He smiled inwardly with the way Slate carried himself. His determination and focus, stubbornness and will were so evident in the surety and conviction of his firm stride. Arms pumping forcefully, his gait said that he would not be gainsaid or denied, even in so simple an activity as a morning walk.

Such dauntlessness was admirable and only occasionally in need of outside restraint.

"Ready fer some new clothes? Yer robes look as though they've been stitched together more times than is advisable."

"When the stitches outweigh the fabric, the time has come to reinforce the stitch," joked Yip.

"Or get a new set!"

"Or turn the robe into something else—a shirt or cloak perhaps."

"More like a rag ta clean with!"

"Rags would do as well," responded Yip.

"Mayhap ya'll turn yer clothes inta kerchiefs. That way, ya can show 'em how ya feel about 'em."

Yip laughed, responding, "In that case, I will turn them into a mat to sit upon when I meditate that I may ever show them my gratitude."

Cocking his head sideways and giving Yip a slightly askew glance, Slate said, "Can't ya ever be normal?"

Laughing again, Yip replied, "Who is?"

Slate pounded his chest, giving an answer where none was needed. "I am o' course!"

Yip merely smiled, not needing to shake his head for Slate knew the merit of his own answer.

They arrived at Jarvis's shop in short order, the rest of the trip having passed largely in silence.

Holding the door open for him as they arrived, Slate said, "After ya, good sir."

Yip nodded and entered the shop to the tinkle of bells on the doorknob.

"Good morning, gentlemen! Come in! Come in!"

"Mornin', Jarvis!" replied Slate cheerfully.

"One moment. I'll be right back with your clothes," replied Jarvis, bustling to the back of the store.

"Chipper isn't he?"

"I thought he was a tailor," joked Yip, feeling as lively as their host.

"Mmm," grumbled Slate. "Where's some good Dwarven dourness when ya need it?"

Missing Wrindanneth, Slate had to let his comment dangle without a sarcastic response or retort.

"Here we are!" said Jarvis as he returned with four paper packages wrapped neatly and bound with string in a cleanly stacked bundle.

Walking over proudly he held out the bundled packages to Slate. "Some of my finest work. Wear them well!"

"May we try them on?" asked Slate.

"Certainly! Just step into the fitting room to change. Slate, your garments are on top. Yip, yours are on the bottom."

Before taking his leave, Yip bowed, saying, "Thank you."

"My pleasure! Nothing is quite so nice as satisfactorily finishing an order."

Yip held a few minutes before following Slate into the room, waiting for Slate to take off his armor before putting on the new clothes.

When he finally stepped into the fitting room, Slate had neatly arranged all of his armor on the fitting room table and had already donned the new clothes. Yip watched as Slate thought carefully and changed his tunic and pants to white undergarments akin to flannels or woolens suitable for covering all his skin to protect against wear and chafe while donning and using his armor.

"Amazin'! Feels almost like a second skin! I can hardly tell I've got anythin' on!"

Once he had his armor back in place, Slate went back out of the room to rave about his clothes to Jarvis who was more than eager to hear the praise.

Yip slipped out of his old worn robes and tried on the new *shenyi*, a type of flowing full body robe that had been modeled after his old set. Pulling the left lapel over the right, after putting on his *ku* and *yi*, he tied his *zhiju* with a navy sash at his waist, which secured the collar in place about his neck while the flowing sleeves remained loose about his arms. Lacing on his sandals under the robes, he used *bang tui* to secure both the sandals to his legs and prevent the *ku* underneath the *zhiju* from moving.

Stepping out of the dressing room, he said, "Your craftsmanship is worthy of the finest courts in Chang Sen."

"Thank you, Master Chuan. Considering the craftsmanship of the silken goods I have seen from Chang Sen, that is quite a compliment!"

"Don't be modest, Jarvis. Ya make some o' tha finest garments in all o' Ea'ae, and ya know it."

Jarvis's cheeks colored slightly, but he said nothing.

"Our bill is paid?" asked Slate, confirming what he already knew having checked with the Aspect prior to their departure.

"Your Aspect transferred the funds after receiving my notice that the clothes were ready and then inspecting the workmanship."

Yip nearly smiled at the thought—an artificial intelligence that could not only pay bills when needed, but that could think and reason, inspecting the suitability of goods prior to purchase. The world outside the mountains of K'un Lun was broader than a mind could ever hope to know.

Before they turned to leave, Jarvis looked at Yip and said, "I am glad you are well after your encounter. I am sorry that your welcome to our fair city was not more pleasant."

Before Yip could reply, he remarked, "I heard about the attack on the Projections. I thought we had gotten rid of most of their ilk."

"Darkness prospers where there is not Light."

Jarvis nodded. "Well, I am glad you are safe. I hope these garments provide succor on your journeys ahead, wherever they may lead."

Yip bowed. "Many thanks, Jarvis. May Life enliven you through all your days."

Jarvis smiled in return. "You are welcome back any time. Your clothes are guaranteed for life. If you encounter any problems or defects, you have only to let me know. I stand behind the quality and worth of my craftsmanship and will see to it they are repaired or replaced at your preference."

"Thanks again, Jarvis," said Slate already enjoying the feel of his new clothes under his armor.

Yip waved as they left the shop, the tinkle of bells pealing behind them as the door shut.

Watching yet another band of adventurers off to save the world, Jarvis returned contentedly to his sewing.

"Can't wait ta see Aroganji's face when he tries these on! He'll be tickled pink!"

Sharing Slate's joviality, Yip said, "What if he does not blush?"

Slate let out a hoot. "Then he'll be tickled tan!"

Yip laughed as heads turned their direction at the uproar.

Pushing through the busy streets, Slate said, "Ya're gettin' quite a bit more looks now than ya used ta, Yip."

He had noticed as well. Apparently events here did not remain private nor were they slow to spread with the Projections available to relate daily occurrences. However, he paid the stares some directed at him scant attention, his awareness instead resting lightly on the surroundings, not letting his focus fall on a single point or object.

When Yip did not answer, Slate noted, "Seems like yer notoriety's growin'."

Letting the humor of the past moment spill over into this one as well, Yip offered, "All the more reason to leave now!"

"Agreed. Wrindanneth may love tha attention, but there're times a Dwarf wants some peace and quiet." He barked a short laugh. "I'd hate ta have ta start growlin' at our fellow passersby."

"You know what Wrindanneth would say?"

"Hmm?"

"That would be all the time."

"Nah. Sayin' I'd ask fer peace and quiet is far too nice, Yip. Ya've got ta dig deeper, think crasser. Wrin'd probably say somethin' about how he didn't know I could communicate any other way than by growls or grunts. Or he'd say that if I did manage ta get some attention, that'd be tha first time in my life or at least tha first time since I was last dropped on my head as a child."

Giving Yip a wink, he finished, "Somethin' more like that."

His face placid and composed, Yip replied, "I have much to learn."

Packages in hand, Yip and Slate returned home to drop off the bundles before heading to one of the city's parks for their daily practice.

Opening the door, Slate called out, "New duds! Come and get 'em while tha stitchin's hot!"

"What are you blathering about now?" asked Wrindanneth as he emerged from the sitting room adjacent to the entry.

Before he got any further, Wrindanneth stopped in place and whistled. "Look at you!"

Slate offered a crooked grin, only partially revealing the yellowed teeth hidden behind his beard. "Aren't I handsome?"

"You look like the hind end of a donkey as usual, Slate! I'm talking about Yip. He doesn't look like a beggar thrown out with the refuse anymore."

"Glad ta hear ya think so highly o' our friend, Wrin."

"What?" asked Wrindanneth defensively.

Diffusing the situation, Yip said, "There is much to be learned from those who have little. Those without attachment are often well on the path to wisdom."

"Hear that, Wrin?"

"The way of the pauper is often more rewarding than that of the prince."

Wrindanneth grumbled, "Can I just see the clothes already?"

"Certainly," Slate threw the bundle at Wrindanneth, hitting him in the chest with the sound of crinkling paper.

"Thanks."

"Don't mention it."

"Are you two about done?" asked Aroganji from where he sat on one of the chairs in the back of the room.

Walking in to stand next to Wrindanneth, Aroganji said, "Your *zhiju* looks like it came directly from the imperial court, Yip!"

"Bless you!" said Wrin.

Yip shook his head, both at Wrindanneth's poor joke and Aroganji's remark. "These robes are blue, nothing more."

"Why don't ya go try yers on so I know if they'll do," suggested Slate. "If everythin' is ta yer likin', we'll head ta tha park and practice throttlin' one another."

Wrindanneth was already halfway up the stairs before Slate had finished, his long legs easily taking two steps at a time. Although he had joked derogatively about Yip's appearance, Wrindanneth was sorely in need of some new linens as well. Like Slate, he was looking forward to clothing that provided both functionality and comfort in the hard times ahead.

Several minutes later, Aroganji came downstairs after donning Jarvis's adventure gear. To Slate's ear, the swoosh of Aroganji's new robes at the head of the stairs belied his presence prior to the creak of his step.

"Never have I worn such comfortable clothes!" Aroganji gushed as excitedly as a schoolboy. His new garments were barely visible beneath the glowing embers of Byear's folds.

From the top of the stairs, Wrindanneth called out, "Careful! We'll not have your new clothes catch fire under Byear's heat."

Following Aroganji down the stairs, Wrindanneth's clothes had assumed the shape of undergarments and were invisible beneath Fraeü's darkling shadows.

Waving his arms loosely, Wrindanneth said quite uncharacteristically, "These are so comfortable, I feel like getting out for a bit of exercise! Who's with me?"

Slate chuckled, already heading out the door. "Tha day's still young. Plenty o' time fer practice!"

With Aroganji and Wrindanneth still admiring the quality of Jarvis's tailoring and Craft, the Four left home to practice for the last time prior to their departure.

LEAVE-TAKINGS

Spider webs laden
with dew catch only sunlight.
Who will tell the fly?

Aroganji insisted they rise well before the sun on the day of their departure. Although they had spent many evenings in preparation for their leave-taking and had packed, repacked, and reorganized on several occasions, he insisted on going over all possible items they may or may not need for the voyage.

By now, Slate had memorized the particulars of nearly every item held within his magical pouch, the heft and feel in the darkness as he reached within the bag's confines for whatever item needed examination, how best to summon the item in question to his hand, which items responded more readily to his summons and those that were more recalcitrant. As a result, he was now loath to heed Aroganji's requests in much the same way some of the items in the magical bag seemed reluctant to heed his summons.

When Slate went downstairs in the darkest of morning, well before bird-song flitted through the air or the sun crested the gray horizon, in search of a nice quiet breakfast prior to their departure, he arrived only to find Aroganji already waiting in the sitting room.

The last person Slate wanted to see was Aroganji.

Grumbling, he said, "What is it now, Aroganji?"

"Just checking over the list I've prepared. No need to worry. I'm certain everything is in order."

"I should think so," he grunted. "If not, I'm sure you, Wrindanneth, or one of the other mages could summon what we need."

Nodding absent-mindedly, his thoughts already returning to any last minute preparations required prior to their departure, Aroganji answered, "Between us, I'm sure we will be able to manage something."

Recognizing an opportunity when he saw one, Slate nodded and moved into the kitchen silently and unobtrusively, free of any of Aroganji's concerns, and ready for a nice light breakfast.

Washing his hands eagerly, he began the serious business of deciding what he should make for his morning meal.

Although he did not let the others know, Aroganji was worried. He used the preparations for the trip as a way to channel his anxieties in a positive direction, hoping that his concerns would therefore not negatively affect his friends. The farther along in their quest they proceeded, the steeper the odds seemed to be in his eyes. His resolution never wavered nor did his belief and conviction in their cause. He was, however, concerned that without quite a bit of fortune, events might not turn out how they would wish, no matter what help they received. So maintaining what he felt was a positive approach to his own personal problem, he buried himself in necessary work even as the morn of their sailing arrived.

Wrindanneth threw back the covers on his bed, ready to be about the day's business. Eagerness, excitement, and exhilaration whirled through him in heady profusion.

Today they would fly!

The thought of the open skies, merging his awareness with that of the ship so inseparably that he felt as though his body had taken to the air, and the adventures ahead filled him with a zeal that he never would have imagined prior to taking flight and piloting an airship. As much as he loved magic, the pursuit of knowledge, and the quest for power, the simple pleasures of flight rivaled those other interests.

Taken together—an impending flight and a journey to an unexplored place potentially rife with untold lost knowledge and power—he positively leapt out of bed, his spirit already soaring. Although he did not try to make sense of it, for they could easily be going to their deaths, he had not been this excited since the days of his childhood studying under Maeth himself. Then the discovery of a new spell, a new incantation, or a new insight into the arcane had engendered similar feelings of giddiness. Of course, as now, he quickly reined those feelings in, for Maeth brooked no frivolity, especially in matters of magic which were often of life and death significance.

Donning Fraeü over the loose, striped pajamas he had changed Jarvis's clothing into, he went downstairs to see what Slate had fixed him for breakfast.

Sensing his friends stirring, Yip roused himself from meditation, feeling the miraculous movement of their energies through and about him as an enlivening, vibrant resonance, wondrous patterns and frequencies echoing through awareness and surroundings in their entirety.

Standing smoothly, he, too, joined his fellows.

Hearing Yip leaving his room, Slate wiped his chin with the sleeve of his arm and called out from the table, "Ready ta go, Yip?"

Aware of Aroganji's tension in the other room, Yip joked, "If I am not, then it is too late!"

Standing by the counter loading up a plate of scrambled eggs mixed with onions, green, yellow, and red peppers, and new potatoes, Wrindanneth looked over his shoulder and said flatly, "Traveling lightly?"

Yip smiled and opened his arms, the folds of his robes hanging downward. "What you see is what you get."

"Same here," laughed Slate. "Fortunately fer my back, it doesn't see all tha junk stashed away inside my storage bag. Unfortunately fer my back, I had ta put it all in tha bag in tha first place!"

As he took a seat across from where Slate had finished his breakfast of Journeyman's Eggs, Wrindanneth said, "Better your bag than the hold of my ship."

"Yer hold couldn't store tha half o' what's in my bag."

"Nor would I want it to," replied Wrindanneth disparagingly.

Lowering his voice and leaning over the table conspiratorially, Slate said, "I'm surprised Aroganji hasn't found more things ta put in my sack. After all, tha house still has furniture."

Wrindanneth leaned forward toward Slate as if to whisper in return. Instead, at the last moment when their faces were at their closest, he called out, "Aroganji, do you have anything else Slate needs to pack for the trip?"

His eyes closing to slits barely visible beneath his thick furrowed brows, Slate growled.

"Not at the moment," came Aroganji's reply from the other room. "Maybe we can pick up something on the way!"

Wrindanneth laughed wickedly.

After Wrindanneth had finished his breakfast and Slate's temper had cooled, he asked, "Everyone about ready ta go?" The itch to be on his way had been building for days. Now that the time to leave was upon them, he found that he could hardly contain it.

"I should think so," answered Wrindanneth after setting the plate and silverware in the sink. "If we don't leave soon, the Home Guard will probably leave without us."

Standing at the door to the sitting room, Yip called out softly, "Aroganji?"

With a deep breath and a heave of his shoulders, Aroganji stood up. "Everything seems to be in order. Shall we?"

"Let's be off!" whooped Slate, feeling the blood rush through his veins, fueled by a surge of adrenaline, as heady as if he were about to charge into the fray of battle.

With a brief nod from Wrindanneth and Yip, they set off out the door, to all the world carrying little more for their quest than the haversack shared by Wrindanneth and Aroganji holding a few articles to be stowed in their room onboard, the small bag at Slate's side, and the small bedroll Yip slept upon wherever he traveled.

Closing the door behind them, the Aspect called out, "Safe journeys! I will keep your home safe and well in your absence."

Smiling, Yip turned and waved, knowing that a passerby might wonder to whom or what he was waving to, and said, "Until we return."

Slate, however, paid scant attention to the house he had left for he was ready to be about their business, letting the urgency of the coming quest fill him with the long banked fires of battle. Stomping down the street, keeping time with the cadence of his step, he sang,

> "To arms, to arms,
> To fill our foes with dread,
> To arms, to arms,
> To smite our foes in their stead.
>
> To war, to war,
> To rend and to tear,
> To war, to war,
> To fill our foes with despair.
>
> Return, return,
> Victory shall be ours,
> Return, return,
> Through Time's uncounted hours."

Before Slate could start another refrain, Wrindanneth chided him, "Can't you save that for later, Slate? There are women and children here. You might scare someone."

"Tha streets are empty, Northlander."

"And seeing four armed individuals marching down the lane chanting songs of battle will probably keep it that way."

"He is right, Slate. We understand your sentiment, but others may not. Let us try to be sensitive to those who do not know our cause or intent." Aroganji did not wish to hurt Slate's feelings or quell his ardor, merely for it to burn at the appropriate time. "There will come a time for song and then your voice will ring!"

"If ya beardless poltroons don't want me ta sing, then I won't, but tha passion o' a Dwarf will not be banked!"

Whipping out Duraeleon from its leather holster, the blue light of its blade made more vivid in the dusky light of early dawn, Slate began beating his metal breastplate with the axe cheek in time with his loud humming and firm steps.

"Wha—!" came Duraeleon's startled response at being pulled abruptly from its sheath. As Slate started smacking the axe head against his chest, Duraeleon yelled, "Ow! Hey! Wait! Stop!" in time with each beat.

Wrindanneth snickered, covered his mouth, and then finally bent over with convulsions. Even Aroganji could not help laughing as he, too, stopped and followed Wrindanneth's lead.

A bit addled and just now shaking off the last remnants of sleep, Duraeleon protested, "What foul excuse for waking me is this, Dwarf? Parading me in front of your fellows in the most childish manner in some poor attempt at humor?"

The mood completely ruined now, feeling like he was more a part of a parade of unorganized pretentious beardless imbeciles than warriors readying for battle, Slate harrumphed. "Ya're not worthy o' beards, tha lot o' ya!"

Still laughing, for seeing Slate swinging an addled axe while parading to his war march caused no end of mirth, Wrindanneth finally managed, after wiping the tears from his eyes, "Well, at least we know if the adventuring profession doesn't work out you have a future as a conductor or as the ring-master of a circus."

Stifling Duraeleon's protests mid-sentence, Slate jammed his axe back into the sheath and said no more.

With the empty cobbled streets spread out before them in an intricate, reticular labyrinth, each path unexplored and untrammeled by the dreams and aspirations of other morning wanderers, the future and the possibilities it beheld branched off before them in dizzying profusion in the pale, pre-dawn light. Green tunnels lined with muted grayish buildings set beneath overhanging trees and other vegetation radiated outward from the lane leading tortuously downward to the docks, each passage marked by stark silence and ripe shadows.

Although their course was sure, each divergence, each choice, hinted at unknown paths to explore, mysteries to behold, and destinations as yet not envisaged. The ultimate outcome of their endeavor unsure, the morning's sense of rife potential both buoyed and dampened their spirits, pushing their thoughts to probing introspection.

Breaking his silence, the recent conflict already forgiven and forgotten, Slate turned to Yip and said, "'Tis an extraordinary city ta be sure. She'll be missed."

Yip agreed. "A more wondrous city, I cannot conceive."

"Never thought I'd care fer a place aboveground so much, much less a place in tha clouds with tha earth far below and at times only a distant memory."

"Our hearts and minds grow with us, Slate."

Overhearing them from where he walked behind, Wrindanneth said,

"Don't get started saying farewells. I, for one, am looking forward to our successful return."

"As am I," added Aroganji hoping silently that their return would be as easy and joyful as their leave-taking.

By the time they reached the Scimerian Gate, the first full light of dawn was cresting the horizon and the relative quiet of night was giving way to the full activity of the day. The open streets began to fill with the press and swell of traffic as merchants of every size, shape, and race began opening their doors to the rising sun.

Scanning the vast leading edge of the island's arch spread before them, Yip could see hundreds of ships tethered next to the moorings of the docks. Far down the slow decline leading away from the city proper, he perceived the outlines of the *Shrike* tied to her moorings, fully outfitted and caparisoned for all the eventualities of the journey ahead. Several of the Paratechnologists' drones dotted the ship's periphery, perhaps inspecting the ship prior to their departure.

"Lookin' out on all this, our last few steps on Tellanon, and leavin', it just about brings a tear ta my eye," said Slate solemnly.

"Bah!" Wrindanneth knew otherwise. "You're as excited as a yeoman at fair time and you know it, Slate! You've been itching to get going since we landed. The only thing that may bring a tear to your hard eyes is the thought that you won't be able to set foot on firm ground for some time or missing access to a few choice inns."

Slate chuckled, having gotten more used to flying than Wrindanneth supposed. The inns and their spirits were another matter. "There is that."

"Come on, you two. Eidelion and his crew are probably waiting for us as we speak, wondering if some ill fate befell us to make us so late."

"Yes sir, Aroganji!" Wrindanneth saluted.

"Get movin'," said Slate gesturing for them to continue, not wishing to hear any more of Wrindanneth's foolishness.

Eidelion and his lieutenants were indeed waiting when they arrived. However, they did not seem put off by their tardiness in the slightest. Standing with them, deep in conversation, Éremon also waited for the arrival of the Fists.

Nearing their companions, Eidelion called out, "Ho! Fists!"

While his friends smiled, waved, and nodded, Slate called out, "Mornin' Guards!"

Eidelion laughed, obviously in good spirits, as his lieutenants gave their salutations as well. "Good morning to you, my friends."

Standing behind Eidelion, his long soft, flowing robes standing out in stark contrast to the bright, firm solidity of Eidelion's burnished plate armor, Éremon greeted them as well. "Hello and well met, Four of the Flaming Fists."

Only the black bulk of Raour'Saqan stood above Éremon's tall shoulders where they waited together in the *Shrike's* shadow beneath her billowing sails.

Seeing Eidelion's lieutenants arrayed about him, Éremon's size truly came to the fore. Standing, he was easily head, shoulders, and chest above Yip and Aroganji, half again as tall as Slate, and almost a full head taller than Wrindanneth and quite a bit broader even than Slate.

Yip gave a bow. "Master Éremon, these are my friends and companions." Gesturing to each in turn, he said, "Slate the Stout, Bor'Banna of the Flintforge Clan."

Thumping his chest, Slate declined his head and said, "At yer service."

"Wrindanneth the Red, Priest of Maeth Onai."

Giving a slight bow with a brief sweep of his hand, Wrindanneth combined swagger and artful embellishment. "My pleasure."

"Aroganji, Fang Shih of Chang Sen."

With a deep bow, Aroganji added, "It is an honor."

Éremon smiled brightly. "The honor and pleasure are all mine. What you are endeavoring to achieve spreads the light of virtue and optimism in times, I fear, that will sorely need such beacons in the near future."

"Let us hope the course and outcome of your efforts as two august companies joined together through a common purpose, guided as one by your will, alongside those bands of heroes undertaking similar missions across Ea'ae, will avert much of the ill portents I foresee and dread."

Unveiling a masterfully crafted oaken box from within the sleeve of his robe, Éremon revealed its contents with a flourish. "Behold the seal of Eldre'gheu!"

Resting amid folds of red velvet, an egg-sized gem nestled inside the confines of the box. Resembling nothing more than a giant, perfectly formed diamond, the stone glowed with a bright white light, spreading warmth throughout any whose eyes gazed upon its surface.

"Mark my words carefully. After the old seal has been struck down, and any of its new keepers returned to the pits from which they escaped, this new seal must be set in a place of security near the location of the old stone. Avoid the taint of Taerris'thule and set the stone in a place of purity."

"With success, the evil of Taerris'thule will fade into memory."

Looking at the assembled heroes, each in turn, Éremon said gravely, "Four of the original fourteen seals protecting our world have weakened or been compromised over time. Of these, I feel that the task before you is the most demanding, but one can never be certain in matters of magic or the mind."

"I do not seek to burden you overmuch, for you are already aware of the gravity of the task before you, but if the other champions do not succeed in their tasks, you may be asked to attempt yet again where others have failed."

"I will be in contact, as needed, and will provide you with updates on the progress of your fellows as I hear. Regardless of the outcome, you will not be obligated in any way to carry on further should the other worthies fail."

Walking over to Yip, he placed the wooden box in Yip's hands gingerly, saying, "May the Lights of your efforts blaze a new path to a bright future."

Looking first from Éremon to the box he balanced so precariously in his hands, Yip replied, "We will hold the Light of the lives protected by this and all the other seals in our hearts."

Éremon nodded, the hint of a smile visible underneath his beard. "I know you will."

"Fare the well!"

Before anyone could answer or raise a hand in reply, he was gone.

Silence fell for a moment after Éremon disappeared as each adventurer took stock of the situation in his own way, understanding their quest was truly about to begin and they would all be changed for it, weighed by the knowledge that some may not return and that success was not guaranteed. Should they meet with triumph, the road ahead may continue on to other tasks of greater difficulty and import.

Having waited patiently while the important business of the day had been resolved and others spoke, Wrindanneth put both hands on his hips and said, "What have you done to my ship?"

Overhead, the *Shrike*'s sails snapped in the wind.

"What do you mean?" asked Aroganji, not wishing to put their guests in any imposition.

Wrindanneth pointed to several orbs hovering to the aft of the ship.

"Are they not tha normal drones tha Paratechnologists use ta help secure ships and see them off?"

Before anyone could continue with further speculation, Eidelion cleared his throat and gestured to Spreesprocket who stepped forward with a brief nod. "Pardon me for the confusion, Wrindanneth."

He gestured toward the combat drones orbiting the ship. "Based on our technical assessment of the *Shrike*'s capabilities, I felt it necessary to supplement some of your vessel's faculties with an ancillary system. Given the short working time and personal, civilian nature of your craft, I judged that a ready-made, complementary solution was the best course. Hence the drones."

Wrindanneth smiled and nodded, not unhappy with the addition in the slightest, recognizing the limitations of the *Shrike* in her current form. "What functionalities do these drones provide?"

Spreesprocket clapped his hands together excitedly, obviously in his element. "What you see here are the latest Allomorphic Recombinatorial Multidimensional Extravehicular Drones." Grinning widely, he said, "ARMED for short."

Before Spreesprocket could continue, knowing the Gnomish tendency to go on especially when it came to Paratechnology, Wrindanneth shook his head and interrupted, saying, "Which means?"

"You're looking at transforming, multi-functional combat drones. Core mission critical functionalities include, but are not limited to: artificial intelligence, guided ship defense through a wide array of lethal and non-lethal magical weapon and shield types, offering suppressive cover fire for extravehicular missions under heavy combat conditions, conversion to single-man jet flight gliders for further defensive capabilities or escape should the ship fail, self- or ship-directed reconnaissance, supplementary navigation assistance, converting to extravehicular environmental combat exosuits in hostile settings, field medics, high level analytics, among many other features that will become apparent as needed."

Slate whistled. "Hard as it is ta believe, sounds like those drones come better prepared than me Dam, Brendle rest her beard."

Wrindanneth nodded appreciatively. "A welcome addition, to be sure. I assume they will remain under your direct control?"

Spreesprocket shook his head. "As the captain, you will feel them as part of your expanded navigational and piloting sensory control sphere. To you, they will be a natural extension of the ship and its function. If need be, however, there are overrides in place to adjust this functionality should the situation warrant intervention."

"Understood."

In the significance-laden pause that followed, Slate clapped his hands together loudly, his strong, callused palms reverberating with great force with the blow. "Well? Shall we board and be off?"

His questions answered, Wrindanneth answered warmly, "Aye! Welcome to the *Shrike!*" He gestured casually and the gangplank lowered down, bridging the dizzying heights between the dock and the ship.

"Don't be shy," cajoled Slate. "We'll be gettin' ta know each other very well over tha next few weeks, so make yerselves at home!"

"I will show you to your quarters," offered Aroganji gesturing for the Home Guard to follow.

"You are most gracious," replied Eidelion. With a curt command, he said, "Fall in, Guard," and took to the plank on Aroganji's heels.

Standing by the moorings, Yip watched as each Guard took to the ship in turn until only, he, Wrindanneth, and Raour'Saqan remained on the docks.

"Ready to board?" asked Wrindanneth.

The Dracodaeran's deep rumbling voice answered from the depths of a great rift. "I will board when the way is clear." He gave a full, graceful bow, his wings folded tightly against his back. "After you."

Yip took to the walkway immediately before Wrindanneth, expecting Raour'Saqan to follow. Instead, a massive rush of air blasted outward as Raour'Saqan leapt upward, a halo of magic surrounding his form, buoying his flight as he took to the sky.

Watching in awe at the power and majesty of the Dracodaeran's flight, Yip, Wrindanneth, Slate, and Aroganji each stopped where they stood as Raour'Saqan landed aboard the ship's deck softly, with only a faint groan of protest from the wooden planks as his weight settled.

Truly appreciating the Dracodaeran's size for the first time, Wrindanneth said, "I am sorry that our ship is not more spacious."

"Do not concern yourself, Wrindanneth, for I rest beneath the heavens and require no shelter or amenity. To one used to the loneliness of the reaches between the stars, the kindness of company is more than I could ask for or hope to receive."

Curious, Wrindanneth asked, "You travel through space without the aid of a ship?"

Raour'Saqan laughed again, his voice so deep and menacing that some pedestrians actually ducked and took cover as he threw his head back in laughter. "The fires of the stars burn in my veins, Wrindanneth. The void is my home as much as this world and its atmosphere are yours."

Wrindanneth shook his head in wonder, saying softly, "Amazing."

Looking at the Dracodaeran's ebony scales, he said, "Those fires do not consume you?"

Raour'Saqan's deep voice carried well over the ship. "Your curiosity serves you well, I see. Elemental transformations fuel the heart of the stars just as magical transformations fuel and sustain the heart of Dracodaera. We burn, but not only with heat."

"And now your people wander the heavens as do the stars?"

"After our world was nearly destroyed by beings from the lightless pits, many of those Dracodaera who remained alive became Shaur'Daus, Stalkers of Darkness, journeying through the multiverse spreading Light in the heavens as do the stars."

"How did you arrive on Ea'ae?"

"I came with Éremon ages ago."

Wrindanneth had to consciously close his mouth after finding it had somehow, and quite embarrassingly, dropped agape.

Confused and a bit addled, Wrindanneth said, "You came with Éremon?"

"Yes. Like the Elves who came before us, Éremon is not native to this world."

"Why did you choose Ea'ae?" asked Yip.

"Am I not Shaur'Daus? Your world was in grave peril, then as now. The Enemy had almost broken Its gates and Its agents, you would name them the Cabal on this world, were hard at work bringing this planet to ruin."

"And you have been here ever since?" Wrindanneth could not imagine that a being like Raour'Saqan would escape notice and not be part of common lore.

Again Raour'Saqan laughed, his fearsome voice filling the air with the sound of hope commingled with doom. "No. I come at need. Éremon asked that I return."

"Which enemy do you speak of?" asked Wrindanneth seeking clarification.

"Not which enemy, the Enemy. You may know It as Ur'Daus, the Darkness, the Great Devourer, the Umbral Lord, or the Creeping Shadow. I cannot say."

"Thankfully, the memory of Its presence in this universe is all but forgotten to those not of its ilk save by the eldest and select keepers of lore."

Yip had never known or heard of an agent or being behind the Cabal and their wickedness, but there was also much of his order's own history and teachings that had never been revealed to him. He had thought that the Cabal had merely turned away from the path of the energy of universal life in pursuit of power, lust, and greed. Ostensibly they had found and bargained with more than he had ever considered.

"What is this evil and where is it now?" asked Yip.

"Ur'Daus is Darkness, true and complete, alive and insatiable, a pit without bottom, an absence without Light. As far as where It is now, I truly cannot say for It was imprisoned between dimensions before the making of the worlds when the universe was young. The Cabal and others like them sacrifice whole worlds and all the Light within to this Darkness, feeding Its need, attempting to weaken and break Its bonds. Others, like the Shaur'Daus seek to deny and overthrow these evils that Ur'Daus will remain imprisoned, choked from the Light It seeks to devour. Deprived of Light and permanently sealed away, Ur'Daus's power should weaken until It shrinks back to nothing and is ultimately devoured by the darkness that gave It birth."

Fearing the answer, for Al'Marr, the home of the H'era, had been sacrificed for just such a purpose, Yip asked, "How do these agents of Darkness break through Ur'Daus's bonds and channel the life of a planet through to the dimension where It resides?"

"How exactly this is done, I cannot say for there are some secrets one may never know and others that are better left unknown. I fear this secret holds quite a bit of both. Knowing the answer may pose too great a risk to the one who knows."

"However, I do know the manifestation of their actions for I have seen the evil they have spawned on several occasions although I do not know how to overthrow it. In greater or lesser degrees, the agents of Shadow create a link, an all-consuming void through which all the living energy of a world is siphoned out of our universe and beyond, feeding Ur'Daus's need and weakening the ties that bind It."

"For this reason, Ur'Daus is also known by some as the Devourer of Worlds."

"Much more I truly cannot say about Ur'Daus, for my experience is with Its agents. I can tell you that even now It fights against Its bonds, reaching outward for the Light It wishes to consume and ever more for additional agents to do Its bidding."

If his respect for Eidelion and his lieutenants was ever in question, after hearing Raour'Saqan's tale, Wrindanneth no longer had any doubts. The troubles that Maeth hammered in over and over with his lessons and the evils he always mentioned in only the darkest terms were much vaster than Wrindanneth had ever envisioned or feared.

For his part, listening to Raour'Saqan describe the extent of Ur'Daus's reach even while confined, Yip had the buddings of an idea.

While Wrindanneth and Yip stayed on the deck listening to Raour'Saqan, Aroganji and Slate showed the other members of the Home Guard to their common quarters in the ship's hold.

"Come on," Slate motioned for Eidelion's motley crew to follow Aroganji's lead belowdecks. "Watch yer heads as ya take ta tha steps. Although a Dwarf has plenty o' room on this ship, I'd imagine those o' ya who are a bit taller may wish ta keep ta tha decks after goin' below."

Taking the Guard down the stairs, Aroganji and Slate led them around and behind the stairway leading back abovedecks and turned in the opposite direction to the ship's cabins. Their way lit by the soft light of magical orbs floating overhead, the Home Guard filed behind winding their way beneath the deck they had just crossed above to the ship's hold. Opening the door first, Aroganji motioned for everyone to follow him down another short stairway into the cargo room proper.

Ropes, netting, barrels of supplementary provisions, assorted parts and tools, among many other odds and ends, were battened down along the walls. Toward the room's near edge, marking the ship's center, the thick polished wooden surface of the ship's main mast cut through the air and disappeared in the floor below. Toward the hold's center, a retractable ladder led up through a small portal cut through one of two large folding cargo doors in the ceiling that led to the deck above. Beyond the ladder, toward the ship's fore, the base of the foremast was faintly visible through the soft light. The ceilings were high and, compared to the cabins in the ship's aft, the hold was quite spacious.

"Although not much, this'll be yer home fer tha next while. Ya'll get ta know and like it well, methinks."

Aroganji added, "If you do not find the hold to your liking or wish for a change of scenery, as we alluded to before, there is another cabin that you are free to use if you wish. You have only to let us know."

Giving the space a measuring eye, Eidelion said, "As I said before, the hold is more than adequate to our needs. We appreciate your hospitality."

"Just as we welcome your help," replied Aroganji graciously. "Recessed to the right"—Aroganji pointed to a door in the wall adjacent to the stairs—"you will find a bathroom suitable for all your hygienic needs."

Not wishing to get bogged down in lavatory talk, Slate grunted, "Enough o' this pitter patter and makin' nice, Aroganji. I'm sure these good folks wish ta get settled. Let's leave 'em to it while Wrindanneth makes ready ta be off."

Aroganji smiled and waved as he went back up the short flight of stairs and left through the entry.

Following his friend, Slate gave a short nod of his head, beard waggling, and said, "I'll see ya above decks."

Yip leaned on the ship's polished wooden railing, watching the docks drift slowly away behind them as Wrindanneth maneuvered the *Shrike* into the blue heavens. Behind him, Eidelion and his lieutenants took up positions near where Wrindanneth navigated the ship discussing their course. While Aroganji stood alongside Wrindanneth close to their guests, Yip sensed Slate occupied below decks.

Moving steadily away from Tellanon through the hushed morning air, Illdrassil and her elegant crystalline branches shimmered with the rising sun, her beauty and scale made more prominent by the added height and distance. Ships passed leisurely and at speed, their courses seemingly as uncertain as the clouds'.

When asked prior to their departure, Wrindanneth had explained to Yip that they would no longer need return stones with the modified and improved energy storage system now in place on the ship. Should the *Shrike* not have sufficient power to enable a return, the presence of so many powerful magicians onboard would provide another means of rapid transport.

Before Wrindanneth had taken the ship beyond the perimeter of Tellanon's shields, the commanding voice of the Construct boomed out, "*Shrike*! Adjust your heading two point seven five degrees north and your attitude forty-five point eight nine degrees upward. Your portal to Tueran will then manifest directly ahead in five minutes!"

"Thank you for your continued cooperation and efforts on behalf of our fair city!"

Yip smiled. There was nothing like the gentle voice of the Construct to snap one out of a recollection. His eyes following the ship's arching lines toward the prow, he saw the air directly ahead of the vessel begin to waver and warp as space itself began to undulate and alter.

About half a league ahead of them, the limitless depths of a far-travel portal materialized, a bright aureole of sunlight lining an interior of inky darkness.

"Two minutes until transport! Maintain current heading!" The voice of the Construct commanded their attention.

Nearing the portal, Yip could vaguely discern the fluid shapes of a city shifting in or beyond its depths. Although he could not see any real details, for the city appeared as but a mercurial vision far away lost beneath rippling waters, he knew that he gazed upon Tueran for the first time.

"One minute until transport! Prepare for *faerviage*!"

Looking away from the portal, he took a deep breath, letting the air and the *chi* filling his lungs radiate through his body with an enlivening surge. As he did so, he heard the Construct bellow, "*Faerviage* commenced!"

With this utterance, his world split in two, astride two points simultaneously, connected by the entirety of the distance between. For the briefest moment, his essence was a string, banded between two places far across Ea'ae's surface holding each place together. Then his awareness collapsed into itself and he stood as he had before, on the other side.

CHANCES

An orb weaver rests
placidly in its web
with no thought of the fly.

He opened his eyes onto darkness.

On hands and knees, he felt cold, wet stones firm and uncompromising beneath the robes covering his legs and feet. In the distance, the sound of dripping water echoed through irregular natural chambers.

"Arise, my vessel."

He stood.

Shen Po commanded and he obeyed, head down, eyes averted out of respect.

"The time of your destiny has come." His master's voice reverberated coolly through the cavern, darker than the deepest shadows, with less emotion than the frozen stone that encased them in oblivion.

His eyes remained downcast. There were others with the master whom he did not have the privilege to gaze upon.

"Look with open eyes, my vessel."

He looked, raising his head slowly.

His master stood before him, cloaked in shadow, His body nebulous and hidden. Black flames licked at his periphery hungry for what little light pervaded the chamber, eating as eagerly at the darkness as the feeble light that illuminated only the repressive stone at his feet.

Master Po was, as always, hidden from him—unreadable and unknowable, an abyss without bottom or bound.

Those arrayed behind him, however, were different.

Though their visages and true forms were hidden by the gloom, shrouded and protected with their own magics, the air around them danced with possibility, actuality coalescing from chance with each breath they took, a haze of potential collapsing from possible futures even as he watched.

The strands of their destinies unfolded before him as readily as a favorite story, intimate and familiar, legible and understood. Possibilities arched overhead, mirages lost in the heat haze of chance, each path and course weighted by the likelihood of occurrence based on current outcomes, past events, and others' actions. Treachery, murder, triumph, deception, and a thousand other conclusions vied for supremacy overhead, murals awaiting final expression, dreams birthed and undone.

His master's gesture shifted the direction of his study.

"A Priest of K'un Lun yet walks upon the lands of Ea'ae. His time must end."

An image came to his mind, its clarity his guide.

He bowed deeply.

His master's wish was his own.

The lines of probability tugged him forward. He looked upward once more in response. The air pulsed and shimmered with a dark portal where before there had been only emptiness.

His master's right arm waved him forward. "Your future awaits."

Tendrils of potential streamed and shimmered in the space around him, the strongest, thickest, most substantive leading him, guiding him forward.

His master was right.

Destiny was his to seize.

By the throat.

TUERAN

Muddy wagon path
creased and pitted by traffic
keeps its course hidden by trees.

Resting as lightly as morning fog on the banks of a still stream, the veiled city of Tueran perched on lofty heights overlooking the wide, still Bay of Denegost below. Thick forests of oak and hickory, beech and chestnut, Senea and Neana, Aeryn and sycamore, blanketed the hills directly at her feet. Inside her fulgid gates, tall groves of Elven Vaellorea spread their silver branches providing as much warmth and radiance as the sun above. Rivaled only by the Elven trees in height, lissome minarets rose from the city's heart, so graceful and fair that they seemed to shift and move in the steady winds coming inland from the Lueciane Sea beneath. Each translucent tower shone forth with an inner light of pastel hue calling forth a range of feelings and memories associated with the sun and clouds, sky and rain, the wind and waves, and any number of natural elements intrinsic to the place under different times, seasons, and weather conditions.

Azure waters lapped placidly at the decks of ancient sailing vessels moored to weathered stone pylons anchored directly below floating wooden piers and docking stations for airships of every shape and description. Along the steep cliffs leading upward from the bay to the city, the halls and warrens of Gnomes and Dwarves could be seen carved out of the living rock, each marked by the decorations and trappings appropriate to subterranean imagination and ingenuity. Footpaths and roads, too, wound tortuously upward from the sea, remnants from a time before flying vessels overtook the olden docks below.

Through the bright morning sunlight, a shield similar in type to the one surrounding Tellanon could be seen to glow faintly in the air.

The *Shrike* appeared just outside this protected field in full view of the city. As the hub of regional trade and the major population center on Landeiss, their arrival was not out of the ordinary. As in Tellanon, far travel here was a daily occurrence, although much of the trade in Tueran was with other major cities on Ea'ae itself and not the worlds beyond her bounds.

Their arrival, however, was noted.

Before the *Shrike* had time to begin adjusting her heading, a commanding voice boomed out, amplified by magic to enhance its strength and timbre and to allow it to project over long distances. "You enter the realms of Tueran! State your name and intent!"

Noting the direction of the sound, Yip turned toward its source automatically, feeling that the magic casting the voice forth also translated the words into a context he would understand.

In so doing, he saw a cynosure that would not allow him to avert his eyes.

Breaking away from a much larger group circling in formation above the city proper, five airmen, he had no conception of what they were rightly called, banked downward toward them at a fearsome pace. Each rider, for he sensed that they were neither properly Man or Elf but shared characteristics of both, sat astride a massive insectoid of unthinkable proportion, each fully caparisoned for battle in elaborately formed Aeryn Sh'al, their burnished wooden armor gleaming brightly in the sunlight.

The lead rider, the one who had called for their purpose, sat upon a gigantic mottled gray mantid, perhaps one-third or one-quarter the length of the *Shrike*. Its great multifaceted eyes reflected the light of the sun in a thousand directions but never warmed their depths. He held himself with poise and surety upon the insectoid's thorax, fastened to an elaborate harness. Behind him, a cloak of many colors snapped in the wind, accentuating elegant Witchwood armor like that of his mount, the wand, and sword at his side. At his feet, cleverly affixed to the sides of his mount, the barrels of magical ordnance similar in appearance and design to that of the Paratechnologists of Tellanon aimed directly at them.

Behind him, flying in tight cover formation, other riders sat upon similar insectoids. A giant multi-hued, blue-tinged dragonfly shadowed by a massive banded yellow jacket on the right while a wicked green mantid flew behind a dazzlingly vivid red dragonfly on the left. Each bore a rider in similar garb as the lead rider—heavily armored with both sword and wand at the side—with defensive armor and armaments at the ready on their mounts.

Also amplified by magic, Yip heard Wrindanneth's reply. "We are the crew of the *Shrike* and arrive at the behest of Éremon of Tellanon. We materialized here as a waypoint on our journey beyond the borders of your land for there are no destinations nearer to the places we seek."

Seeming appeased, perhaps at the recognition of Éremon or expecting their arrival based upon Aroganji's preparations, the lead rider asked, "Do you require entrance to our city?"

By this time, the riders had closed the distance between them and were very near indeed. The power and size of the insects was overwhelming. The mantids, in particular, gave the impression of being able to easily tear a ship such as theirs apart with their fearsome, serrated forelimbs.

Their view of the riders, too, benefited from the close distance. In shape and size they appeared very much like Men, stockier than an Elf but sharing in the lithe grace and obvious physical faculties of their fey brethren. Their refined features also resembled those of Elves more so than Men—sharp ears, prominent angular cheekbones, along with hair tinged with luminous silvers, golds, and other more exotic shades besides.

To Yip's senses, the Half-Elves, Half-Men, or Elf-Men, for he knew not what to call them having never met their like, represented an interesting juxtaposition. Their power was both manifest and hidden in the way of both Men and Elves. Given what he could feel from their presence, these beings seemed to have inherited the best of each people, creating something new and entirely wonderful in the process.

Watching the ambient energies move through and around them, he wished for more time in their company for he knew there was much he could learn from them.

Unfortunately, the nature of his quest was to move ever forward and not linger. That he had been afforded time in Tellanon was a blessing, one that had allowed him to learn much and grow. He only feared that significantly more time would be required if they were to succeed in their ultimate purpose.

Cutting across Yip's musings, Wrindanneth replied to the rider's query, "Although I have heard much of your fair city and am wont to linger, we are required elsewhere. Perhaps upon our return, we may be afforded the luxury of time, but we do not have that gift at present."

Their curiosity piqued, the lead rider followed Wrindanneth's question with another. "And where do you now journey?"

"To lands farther south, past the limits of Landeiss and across the Lueciane Sea."

The rider's gaze remained sober when he replied, "Tread with care for the skies beyond our borders harbor more threats than an impending storm. The R'yn Daer along with fell Orcs, their allies, and worse all prowl the skies to the South and East. We are ever vigilant to their threat."

Replying in all seriousness, Wrindanneth said, "We will heed your warning and take care."

Nodding briefly in understanding, the lead rider said, "Know that you go with the blessing of Gilaethe, son of Nienael, Anuvatali and Wyaera of Tueran."

"Your words are a boon to us on our journey and will be well marked, Gilaethe. You carry the honor of your people well."

With a flourish, Gilaethe brought his heels firmly down, applying pressure to the massive mantid's thorax as all five riders swiftly turned in formation, their cloaks billowing in the rush amidst the loud buzzing of the insects' prodigious wings.

"Quite the welcome." Eidelion had joined Yip at the railing to watch the Riders return to their station.

"Who are those people?"

"They are called Anuvatali, the Children of the Dawn, for in some ways they represent the future of the Elves, the Anuvatari, the Children of Light, on Ea'ae. They are the first offspring of Man and Elf and have brought considerable beauty and grace together as a people. Through their unique views and culture, they have also created much that is new and wondrous in the world."

"Their home is isolated by choice for not all welcome their presence even after the passing of time. Despite their hardships, they are indeed a noble people and offer much that is to be admired."

"What of those who met us?"

"Those were the Wyaera, the Riders of Tueran. They share as much a bond with the earth and sky as their mounts."

"Gilaethe's mount was a Mantaed. So calm beneath his touch, you would never know that wyverns and basilisks are their natural prey. Those and other insectoids far larger and more fearsome haunt the southern jungles of Landeiss."

"If his warnings are true, how safe will our journey over Landeiss be?"

"The reach of the Wyaera and the Anuvatali is far indeed. We should have little to fear while in their lands, but will remain vigilant nonetheless. Once we reach the Lueciane Sea to the south, we will need to take more care for the wilds and ills of Maeron spill out even as far as the borders of Landeiss."

Speaking softly, as though for his ears alone, Yip said, "The Anuvatali truly appear to be a most remarkable people."

"Many others respect their strength and wisdom as well, Yip. Perhaps in time you will have the pleasure of their company. I learned much from their tutelage." With that, the leader of the Home Guard headed to the ship's quarterdeck where Wrindanneth was busy adjusting their course southward.

Although Yip said nothing further on the subject to Eidelion, he felt a distinct connection, a sense of kinship with the Anuvatali for they were both of two worlds. Even if he never had the chance to visit their home, perhaps he would have the opportunity to speak with Eidelion and learn more of them and their ways.

While Yip watched, the *Shrike*'s pace quickened, and the grand minarets and trees of Tueran slowly faded away until its majesty and all the fluttering ships about the otherworldly metropolis became as one with the sky, indistinguishable from the blue firmament.

As Tueran drifted away in the distance, his attention shifted to his thoughts, watching them run their course as he had the ships before. Watching one thought lead to the next, each flowing of its own accord, one question led to the next in a steady procession. His mind kept returning to his conversation with Raour'Saqan, his thoughts abuzz as a bee searching for nectar, jumping from one flower to the next.

How had he missed the obvious?

Why had he not probed or questioned deeper?

Why had he not asked more of his teachers through the course of his training?

Despite all his intuition and searching, he had never asked what, if anything, lay behind the Cabal, instead accepting their reality and allies as enough, as truth, when in fact they were but a shallow reflection of a much darker evil.

How had he missed it?

Despite all his searching after truth, despite all his insights, he was just a man—fallible and human, like all the rest, never having guessed the true nature of his enemy, never realizing, in actuality, who his true foe was.

Although his quest had not changed, his ultimate purpose had.

Watching the landscape of western Landeiss slip by so far below, the course of his thoughts having run through to their natural conclusion, he knew exactly what he must do next.

"What's going on?" asked Wrindanneth.

Yip had sensed his friend's approach, the activity of his thoughts having subsided long before, dwelling in the entirety of the calm underlying the currents of his prior ruminations as he stared out into the heavens.

"Tueran disappeared from view well over an hour ago. Midday has come and gone and you're here staring in the distance like you've been addled by the sun. The Home Guard are nice company. Perhaps you should consider joining them."

Yip turned away from the view of the sky and continent below and looked at his friend directly. "Much has happened in a short time. My mind has been abuzz with thoughts. I let them run their course and observed where they led."

"And?"

He smiled. "The mind is a wonderful instrument when given the opportunity to shine. Unfortunately, it is as limited as the person that it inhabits."

"Which means?"

"I have been wrong about a great many things. That must be rectified and my course adjusted accordingly."

"What are you talking about?"

"All these years I thought that the Cabal and their allies were the gravest danger to our world and the life that inhabits it, but I was wrong. They are but an extension of a far graver threat, an evil more far-reaching and pervasive than I would have ever imagined."

"And?"

"And that is the problem. I didn't."

"Didn't what?"

"I didn't consider a greater evil."

"You could not have known, Yip. That is the nature of a quest, of the search for knowledge, you learn as you progress and make adjustments as needed. Regardless of what must be done eventually with Ur'Daus, the Cabal must be dealt with first. Their threat is imminent. Once they are neutralized Ur'Daus will follow whether by us or others."

He nodded in agreement with Wrin. "In this case the branch must precede the root, although I wish it were otherwise not only for our world but for all sentient beings everywhere."

Wrindanneth patted Yip on the back reassuringly. "We'll deal first with the one and then move on to the other."

He smiled at his tall friend glad of the reassurance. "After we finish shielding our world from further incursions."

"Of course. Don't worry. We'll get it done, Yip, or ensure that they are taken care of, you have my word."

"Ready?" Wrindanneth indicated the pilot's position with the assembled passengers and crew with a nod of his head.

Yip placed his hand on Wrindanneth's tall back, turning around to face the pilot's station as he walked alongside his friend to where the navigation sphere hovered in the air below a projection of their anticipated flight path while Aroganji, Slate, and the various members of the Home Guard talked animatedly standing within its radiance.

Walking over to the assembled crew, Yip bowed. "Good afternoon, my friends. Please forgive my absence."

"Your time is your own, my friend. We are glad to have been given the opportunity to share in your quest." Eidelion's good cheer and gratitude were clearly in evidence for all to see, his enthusiasm overflowing to his fellows.

"I cannot lay claim to something that benefits so many. We are glad to have your help."

Slate grunted, "If ya two don't learn ta stop exchangin' unendin' strings o' pleasantries, I'm goin' ta throttle someone."

"Hopefully yourself," muttered Wrindanneth out of the side of his mouth. "We've got more than enough time to spend in conversation, Slate."

"With all this time on our hands, we need ta keep trainin', pushin' ourselves ever onward!"

"There is more than enough time for that," replied Aroganji. "Let us have time to make each other's acquaintance. The rest will follow."

Wrindanneth added, "Aroganji is right. If we are to work together, we must come to know each other, Slate."

Slate acquiesced and changed the subject. "We're makin' good time thus far. If tha weather holds and we don't encounter any unforeseen problems, we should be there within two or three weeks!"

Stroking his beard, he added, "Plenty 'o time fer some good sparrin'," then, looking at Wrindanneth and Aroganji, he added, "or jaw flappin'."

Gazing beyond his friends to where Orogast stood alone looking out over the ship's railing, Yip watched as the albino's form began to shimmer slightly, as though a slight breeze began to disturb the surface of his skin. Faint ripples flowed across his body, blurring his pale features until he lost all surficial detail and color, ultimately becoming translucent, a humanoid embodiment of the liquid fluidity that had so recently passed through him.

Rejoining the group, although Yip could not see a mouth from which sound should emanate, he distinctly heard Orogast say, "Pardon my ill-mannered behavior. The time has come to leave the form I don for Tellanon for something a bit more…functional."

Watching the kaleidoscopic colors of his essence dance through the air around his translucent form, Yip asked, "Is this form close to the one you wear on your homeworld?"

A brief nod and a feeling of warmth spread out from where Orogast stood. "This is much closer to my true form, yes."

Intrigued by a being who could willingly take almost any shape conceivable, Yip wondered what type of place could give birth to such a wondrous being. "Could you tell us of your world?"

Orogast gave a slight bow as he did so, the wind moving over the deck and the downward motion sent faint eddies and undulations through and around his body. "My world is very much like yours—rich in life and energy, in potential and opportunity with one slight generalized exception. In your world, life has evolved linearly, along straight paths with multiple bifurcations and branches, extending, as it were, from a central stem. As a result, although species on your world do not have an absolute role within the larger biosphere, evolution has defined the response and functionality of living things into clearly defined singular endpoints. Generally speaking, each endpoint in this process represents a single defined species, each with an open-ended potential for living expression and continued adaptation."

"On my world, evolution, that is the pressures and limitations underlying the drive to live, survive, and succeed, followed a much different path. Instead of species evolving along separate paths, each becoming distinct from one another through gradual specialization and environmental response, on my world, living creatures came to embody multiple divergent paths within highly mutable species. Thus, the pressure to survive resulted in many beings such as myself, creatures able to take multiple highly specialized or generalized roles within a single, mutable manifestation."

"Although this is a gross oversimplification of the diversity and richness of life here, for creatures on your world do indeed fill many roles and can often change positions as needed, the form that defines a being's existence generally does not change beyond the normal maturation and development process. On my world, forms change as needs and circumstances change, as the situation dictates."

Speaking largely to Wrindanneth, Slate, Aroganji, and Yip who were listening attentively, Orogast continued, "As to the type of world that would give rise to such beings, envision a planet covered entirely in water, with warm shallow tropical seas teeming with life such as can be found in places here on Ea'ae, basked in the warm glow of twin suns so that the surface is always warm and filled with light. Then you would be close to visualizing my home."

"Having swum in the seas of your planet extensively upon my first arrival, our cities are most like the coral reefs of your world—interconnected networks of living creatures growing toward the light of the sun, basking in the energy of the beings teeming all around. Unlike the reefs here, however, our cities, too, are mutable, able to change form and function at will through elaborate synergies with their denizens."

"Perhaps, in time, you will have the opportunity to view the wonders of my world. I would welcome the privilege of showing you my home."

Yip bowed from the waist, offering a sincere, "We would welcome the honor."

Curious, Aroganji asked, "How did you come to Ea'ae, Orogast?"

Orogast waved his arm briefly in an arch indicating the heavens. "There was a time when I was our world's representative to Tellanon, for the people of Tellanon have long traded in goods and knowledge with my people. So long has this relationship stood and prospered, that there is a direct portal from my world to Tellanon, just as there are gateways to many others there as well."

Yip shook his head inwardly; there was so much of his own world he did not know. On the monastery, he had had no idea that Tellanon, or anywhere else on Ea'ae for that matter, provided such astonishing opportunities for shared discourse and travel.

He had heard, however, that in addition to providing one means of defense for Ea'ae from outside invaders, that Tellanon was not strictly tied to this world and could travel as needed. How often, if ever, this was done, he had no idea, but the idea of a city in the stars brought a smile to his face.

"What are you grinning about?" asked Wrindanneth.

He kept the smile in place. "I was imagining Tellanon traveling through the heavens, perhaps visiting worlds like Orogast's."

Here Eidelion's voice broke in. "It has been done in the past, though only at great need. Ordinarily, other means of transport and communication are pursued."

Remaining silent, Aroganji and Wrindanneth turned to each other in surprise after Eidelion's pronouncement.

Beyond that, Eidelion said no more, but Yip understood the significance of those occasions by his comment.

After a brief pause to make sure no one had any other questions or interjections, Orogast continued, "My world has been quite fortunate. We have been isolated from the evils visited upon many places, such as your world. After serving here and witnessing the horrors that lurk in the shadows on Ea'ae and beyond, I could not return home without offering my services in some way."

"When my term here came to an end, in recognition of this desire, Éremon granted me the duty that comes with serving in the Home Guard. Now I willingly repay his trust."

"When will you know the time has come to return home?" asked Wrindanneth

With only the faintest wisp of longing evident in his tone, Orogast answered, "Who can say such things when the winds of change gust so strongly each day?"

"Perhaps when I have helped bring lasting goodness and Light into the world, then I will know my time here has come to an end. Perhaps when Ea'ae is safe and our mission is complete, I will feel the time has come to return home. Perhaps when I have given my utmost and can do no more, I will know my time has come. Perhaps when I know that I have helped ensure the continued prosperity and safety of your world and others, I will return to the fulgurating seas of Gaesia. Who can say where the winds of transfiguration travel?"

Yip bowed. "The truth and surety of your mission brightens my heart."

"As do the efforts of my fellows," replied Orogast fluidly returning Yip's bow.

Recognizing that he was going to have no alternative but to stand around and banter, Slate decided to try to move things along a bit. "Since we're tellin' each other's tales, we might as well all go around and explain why and how we got here."

All eyes upon him, Slate volunteered to speak, albeit gruffly. "Since I'm already talkin', I might as well continue."

"Fer those o' ya who've already heard this, or somethin' o' it, my apologies."

"I grew up by tha forge, workin' tha bellows, studyin' at tha feet o' my father and my father's father. In my clan, tha Thanes hold as much reverence fer tha forge as fer tha honor o' rulin'."

"Those o' tha Thane's family learn ta uphold tha honor and ways o' tha clan, o' our history, and as Brendle's people. It is our duty as much as our heritage."

He eyed everyone warily, as if daring someone to question his heritage before continuing. "I was told, not by my teachers o' course, but I was told nonetheless, that I had a certain knack fer it, but workin' tha forge was not ta be my lot. It was in tha heat o' tha forge that my true callin' was revealed."

"I'll never forget tha day. Gründen, our thane, had commissioned a new axe fer my uncle, his brother, ta use in tha forays we'd been undertakin' ta cleanse tha mines o' filth and vermin—Orcs, Trolls, Ogres, and other despicable creatures not worth tha bones and fat they chew."

"Tha heat o' tha forge was blazin', burnin' my skin and singin' my beard as I worked tha bellows, fer he called fer a special blade, tha likes o' which we'd crafted o' old. As my father worked tha metal over and over—hammerin' tha form, inscribin' runes o' power, heatin' and shapin' over and over until tha magic o' tha runes was etched deeply from tha core throughout tha blade—I felt tha forge's heat buildin' in me."

"When he finally handed tha axe ta me fer coolin', I held tha blade aloft ta gaze at it in wonder, fer truly tha weapon was a masterwork from a mastersmith. Graspin' tha blade in my hands, tha heat o' tha forge that had built within overcame me, jumpin' from my hand ta tha blade, temperin' it in Brendle's own fires."

"I nearly dropped tha axe in surprise then, fer it lit up like a torch! Tha flames running from my hand along tha length o' tha haft burned as brightly as tha sun, but they did not touch me."

"It was only tha firm touch o' my father's hand upon my back that quenched tha fires. By tha rare smile in his eyes, I knew somethin' remarkable had happened."

"From that day forward, I trained secretly under my father's guidance in tha ways o' tha Ur'Daena, tha axe's lament, and began tha long journey on tha path o' tha Bor'Banna. That is tha path that has led me here and it is tha way that will lead me through it."

Kazarhan smacked his armored leg in what appeared to be a truly exceptional display of emotion. "If what you say is true..."

He shook his head in disbelief. "I thought yer kind were long extinct, Slate! Tha flames o' Brendle's forge, at least those sparks residing in tha true Bor'Banna's o' old, have been thought long since extinguished. Those who now call themselves Bor'Banna are but shadows o' tha glory that once lived through tha Ur'Daena. Ta think true masters o' tha Ur'Daena still live hidden in tha lost remnants o' our people's forgotten cities!"

Slate growled, "I have not forgotten my thane nor tha thanedom I call home!"

Kazarhan lifted both arms acquiescingly. "I meant no offense, brother. When I heard yer claim upon our first introduction, I was skeptical, but, if what ya say is true, there is much hope and pride fer our people ta be found in our lost past, in tha old kingdoms that once held our people's pride and hearts."

Lightening his adversarial tone, Slate joked, indicating his friends, "Tha only time I've been lost is in tha company o' these hooligans. And"—here he smiled at Yip as if sharing a joke—"tha only time is tha present."

Kazarhan nodded, rare excitement lighting his visage. "We have much ta discuss in tha days ahead, Slate."

"Perhaps you should go next then," suggested Wrindanneth. "Your tale may offer some incentive for Slate to tell you more."

Kazarhan addressed Wrindanneth curtly and forthrightly as was the nature of a Dwarf. "Don't press me, Wrindanneth. I do as I will."

"And you will go next," interjected Eidelion, recognizing the similarity in their characters and intervening between two equally headstrong individuals.

"Aye. I will." Kazarhan had no problems following direct orders from Eidelion for not only was he Kazarhan's superior, but he had also earned his deep and abiding respect.

Looking inwardly in reminiscence, Kazarhan began, "Slate's childhood sounds very much like my own. Workin' tha forge o' my father in tha deep delvin's o' Duurn'Laden, I was introduced inta tha ways of tha Dur'kazak, tha fire shapers and rune masters, tha blacksmiths o' my kin, long before tha time my beard began ta truly flower."

"Workin' tha forge, singin' ta its fires and rhythms, heedin' tha call o' tha metal, tha needs o' tha flame, shapin' and inscribin', imbuin' and fillin' metal with spirit, breathin' life and heat inta form is as much an art as any I have seen or heard tell. Bein' so close ta Brendle's heart, bringin' forth His will, havin' a part in shapin' His vision brought me not only tha wisdom o' tha smith, but ta tha path o' Brendle's priests, tha Kor'Dannan."

"Just as once there were many true Bor'Banna, now there are few. Tha same is true o' tha Kor'Dannan, fer Brendle's voice has grown silent, no longer heard by many with tha passage o' time. O' tha Dur'kazak, there are still many fer tha way o' tha rune and tha shapin' o' metal and gems are understood by many, Dwarves and non-Dwarven alike."

He shook his head, the Kazzak in his beard jingling as he did so. "Fer those that do not listen, tha meanin' o' tha true Voice, Brendle's spark that abides within tha flames, is lost ta ears that do not heed and tha way o' tha Kor'-Dannan remains hidden."

"After my apprenticeship had ended, my commission fer tha Thane began. I first worked in his army's forge and then, with tha passage o' time and deed, he asked me ta join tha smithy o' his own hall, an honor I will never forget. When, after his last emissary had returned home, he called fer volunteers ta serve as his liaison and represent his interests in Tellanon, fer ever and often had we traded with the fair sky city, I volunteered."

"Still young by tha measure o' my kind, ancient by tha reckoning o' Men, I arrived in Tellanon eager ta spread word o' Brendle's Voice. Instead, I found a world much in need o' protection and succor as ever tha Kor'Dannan o' Duurn'Laden had told. Then it was that I saw Brendle's need for me here, in tha world at large, offerin' my hammer and my hand ta those in need."

"Seein' this necessity, with my Thane's blessin', I became part o' tha Home Guard ta honor my people and Brendle's spark that brought us all here."

When Kazarhan had finished, Yip turned to Slate and asked, "Are you a Dur'kazak as well, Slate?"

Slate grunted bluntly, "A Dur'kazak and his hammer are inseparable. I only wield an axe."

Wrindanneth raised an eyebrow archly. "That wasn't the question, Slate."

"When I returned home and found our thanedom sacked and in ruins, my people felled and dishonored, I laid down my hammer fer tha axe. I have not taken it up since."

"My hammer rests in tha cold ashes o' memory, left in tha past with my father's forge and our Thane's once proud halls."

Hearing this, Kazarhan looked grim, but said nothing.

Everyone was quiet for a time before Yip offered to break the silence, saying, "Perhaps I should go next for it was my question that brought this sullen mood upon us."

Eidelion stepped forward, perhaps in anticipation of the feelings Yip's story would evoke and offered to speak instead. "As your story is at the heart of why we are here, Yip, perhaps you should speak last."

When he nodded, Eidelion began, "I will share something of my tale with those who have not yet heard it."

"Like Yip, I was raised in a monastery."

"I was born and then abandoned as a child on Tol Aeron, a lush, temperate mountainous island far to the south and west of Tellanon off the western coast of Dharia. I was left at the doors of the Keep of Terraboer, the Citadel of Light, home of the Dalaren Ka, the Knights of the One Light, before I ever knew the face of my mother and father."

"It was in this citadel that so graciously took me in that I was trained in the ways of prayer and supplication, of humility and perseverance, of faith and fortitude, before being introduced to the ways of the Dalaren Mere, the Light's Path, the way of chivalry, faith, and the sword."

Eidelion laughed. "It was only when my tutelage had ended and I had received the High Conservator's blessing to crusade for the Light of Life wherever its resplendence took me, that I was told the true history of our order."

"The Keep of Terraboer was built with a purpose. Its formidable gray walls and unyielding fortifications, its tall battlements and strategic location perched high on the cliffs at the source of the river Laeryn, all served to secure not only our faith, but a treasure locked within her vaults for long ages measured by uncounted days of offerings and supplication."

"Like Taerris'thule, the only home I had ever known was built to shield and protect a most precious relic, the Star of Elendial. And, like the seal in Taerris'thule, this artifact with its untold power was also one of the fourteen seals protecting our world from extradimensional incursion."

"Unlike Taerris'thule, the walls of Terraboer yet hold, as does the faith of those who live within."

He paused for a moment before continuing, "When Éremon asked that I aid in your quest to restore the seals protecting our world, Yip, a duty to which my order has given itself in all its glory for years beyond counting, I could not refuse the obligation just as I could not hold back the true joy that the Light had given me at the opportunity to aid you in your cause."

"What o' tha time between yer leavin' Terraboer and arrivin' in Tellanon?" asked Slate for his curiosity was not slaked by Eidelion's short recounting. Tales of Eidelion's heroics abounded and Slate did not wish to let the opportunity pass.

"Perhaps at another time we can each share a bit more of our tales in greater depth."

When Slate did not respond, Eidelion added with a brief smile, "The deeds of a man are not the man, Slate."

"Sounds like Eidelion has more in common with Yip than he realizes," joked Wrindanneth.

"Aye," agreed Slate, "Think I might have heard him say that exact thing at one time or another. Or was it Master Wei?" Slate laughed. "I reckon tha three o' 'em could hold whole conversations in aphorisms."

Letting them have their fun, Eidelion said nothing.

Spreesprocket chimed in brightly next. "Your sense of humor and good cheer will serve us all well in the times ahead." Laughing in anticipation, as at the coming of a joke, he added, "Speaking of aphorisms, as my mother once said, 'Communication is at the heart of community.' Just as there is strength in community, there is brotherhood in camaraderie."

Muttering under his breath, but still speaking loud enough for all to hear, Wrindanneth quipped, "Oh no! Sounds like someone else might have attended the Slate Flintforge School of Adages and Apothegms."

"He could flunk out and still communicate better than ya ever could on yer best day," interjected Slate icily.

Unfazed and unconcerned, Spreesprocket continued, for his Gnomish sensibilities made him virtually immune to sarcasm or slur. The brunt of their humor, even if at each other's expense, did validate his point. "Just as communication is at the heart of community, communing is the heart of commonality. All of which are held in common by communes."

Slate nodded brusquely. "Aye, fer good or ill, earnest discourse is tha means ta maintain positive relationships."

"Says the Dwarf who seldom speaks in more than one grunt much less a word or sentence," joked Wrindanneth who, despite his lack of tact, was at least comfortable enough with himself to remain true to his character in any situation.

"Perhaps Spreesprocket is trying to begin his own tale?" submitted Yip, knowing that his friends' conversation could very easily degenerate into squabbling without respect for the direction of the conversation, no matter how circuitous.

"As I was saying, communes are the very heart of community—figuratively and literally—Gnomish community that is."

Wrindanneth smiled at the Gnome's rather roundabout introduction to his past.

"You see, we Gnomes live together in large but close-knit interconnected family groups called warrens. If you've never visited a Gnomish community, you really have no conception of how complex a social network can become."

He paused for a moment trying to think of an apt analogy. "Imagine an ant's nest swarming with activity. Then imagine all of those ants were packed in as tightly as possible. Then give all of those ants sentience, over-active imaginations, large families, and a wicked sense of humor. Splash in a chaotic mix of magic and technical sophistication while subtracting a smidgeon or two of common sense and *voila* you have a Gnomish warren!"

"Homes are built over, around, under, and through one another. Families share space, stories, ideas, and gossip as well as resources moving through and among the warren's maze forming relationships much more complex than even their homes would imply."

"In fact, one could argue the primary driver behind Gnomish technological innovation is the family—the desire to keep in touch, feed, and house friends and neighbors, ensure their health and happiness, and, of course, to keep track of loved ones. Because, in a Gnomish village, there certainly is quite a lot to keep track of. That is of course to say Gnomish technical development is largely driven by our curiosity and desire to know everything we can while making sure everything runs as smoothly as possible."

He laughed. "From the Gnomish perspective this means we make things as complex and unmanageable as possible so that we can devise an equally complex solution to the problems we have created."

He chortled again. "Of course, one could also argue that without, or even with, the aid of Gnomish technology we cannot keep track of our own affairs, much less those of others."

"Regardless, just as our technology brings us together and pushes us forward, it also forces us outside our communities, ever seeking new insights, resources, and ideas. Over distance and difficulties, we rely on this pursuit of innovation and its fruits to keep us together."

"It was this quest, for the pursuit of knowledge is as much a quest as any other, that brought me from the loving warrens overflowing with my parents, brothers, sisters, aunts and uncles, cousins and nephews, grandparents and great-grandparents, friends, relations—all the kindred and kith in our bustling village—into the larger world beyond our walls."

"Of course, I use the term village loosely, for our villages are more densely populated than even the largest human cities, taking advantage of all dimensions to form our warrens."

"After my second successful post-underapprenticeship in applied Paratechnology at the distinguished Golden Cog and Pulley Institute, my research into developing the world's first truly frictionless toothpick called for expertise and resources that no other Gnome could provide."

"After careful study, my equations led to one ineluctable conclusion. Only the refined essence of matchless Dwarven eructation could provide the necessary femto-scale boundary layer for my Perfectly Polished Particulate Propeller - Beta Naught Mark Seven®, Patent Pending."

"So, a clear goal in sight, I left my home after making the necessary alchemical preparations to capture and refine the most rare and elusive of all phenomena—Dwarf eructation."

Wrindanneth could contain himself no longer, he absolutely exploded with mirth, only keeping his feet by propping himself, eyes closed, on Aroganji's shoulder.

"What is it?" asked Aroganji bemusedly.

Wrindanneth gasped, he could barely speak. With much effort, he finally managed, "Dwarf eructation!"

"Yes?"

"The...elusive...phenomena...of...Dwarf...eructation!"   Tears   were streaming down Wrindanneth's cheeks.

"And?"

Composing himself, Wrindanneth coughed out, "He's saying Dwarf burps are rare! That they are hard to find! I'm surprised we can even breathe the air right now after all of Slate's burps!"

Slate huffed, proudly puffing out his chest. "Sounds like a noble pursuit indeed! Fer 'tis nothin' ta be more proud o' than a heartfelt belch after drinkin' tha finest o' ales!"

"Ah! And there you have it, Slate! I was not after just any aerophagial phenomena but the rarest and most elusive of all—the essence of a Dwarf's first belch and not just any first burp, but a Dwarf's first venting after imbibing the finest of Dwarven ales."

"Ya mean Brendle's Tears?" asked Slate, a slight tinge of awe in his voice.

"Aye," said Spreesprocket nodding excitedly. "I had to capture and refine the rarest of all Dwarven off-gassings—that release after one's first taste of Brendle's Tears!"

"Where in tha world did ya ever hope ta find a bit o' Brendle's Tears?" asked Slate, the enormity of Spreesprocket's challenge now dawning on him.

"And why in the world would you want to?" grumbled Wrindanneth.

Understanding lighting his eyes, Slate answered with a wry smile, in on a joke no one else comprehended, "Nothin', and I mean nothin', goes down as smooth as Brendle's Tears."

Wrindanneth laughed in apprehension. "Sounds like a truly admirable quest indeed!"

Spreesprocket smiled brightly nodding in answer to both of them. "Is not any quest worthy of one's effort a greater challenge than one can ever hope to achieve?"

Awe plainly visible on his face, Slate asked, "And were ya successful?"

Sharing Slate's excitement, Spreesprocket reached into his robes and muttered a short incantation. When he finally brought his hand out, a nonde-script brown wooden toothpick hovered above his hand.

"May I hold it?" asked Slate in astonishment, reaching forward instinctively.

"Well..."

As Slate's hand approached, fingers reaching for the toothpick, Spreesprocket's spell was broken. The toothpick shot from between Slate's fingers as he attempted to pick it up, flying gracefully through the air before landing on the deck without stopping its forward motion across the wooden planks.

With a violent whipping action, Spreesprocket reached into his robes and pulled out an elegant wooden wand, adroitly casting a spell even as he moved. "*Aero leversa!*"

The toothpick's reckless, frictionless flight halted immediately as it floated up into the air where Spreesprocket went over and gingerly retrieved his magical toothpick.

Wrindanneth laughed throatily. "And there you have it! The world's most useless toothpick!"

Slate scratched his beard, eyes lost in distant imagining. "Perhaps one day, if Brendle favors me, I'll be able ta nip a bit o' Brendle's Tears."

Holding his magical toothpick up in the air for all to see proudly, or, rather, magically levitating it in his palm so that it did not careen away again, Spreesprocket finished his tale. "Largely through the recognition associated with the significance of my Perfectly Polished Particulate Propeler - Beta Naught Mark Seven®, Patent Pending, the Paratechnologists asked me to continue my research into other technical innovations on Tellanon."

"At Tellanon, other inventions soon followed including the well-received lintless shoehorn, the space-saving collapsible hanger, the top-selling translu-cent sun shade, the immoveable type, and the self-propelled eyebrow mower."

Once again, fighting back laughter, his face turning scarlet with the effort, Wrindanneth managed to hold his tongue for once to let Spreesprocket finish without interruption.

Slate, however, merely stared, mouth agape, at his Gnomish companion, his mind lost in the difficulties of imagining any real demand or need for Spreesprocket's preposterous inventions.

"Needless to say, when a spot on the Home Guard opened, the Paratech-nologists were quite eager to see my skills put to good use protecting their city."

At this pronouncement, Slate finally managed to smack his forehead, only just missing his thick bushy eyebrows in the process which, in Spreesprocket's estimation, certainly were in need of a good eyebrow mowing.

Before Spreesprocket could carry on any further, Daerdros cleared her throat. "Although Spreesprocket's skills as a creative visionary are beyond question," Wrindanneth was amazed at the woman's poise, for she said this with an absolutely straight face, "there is much of his background and skill that he has not described that were also of consequence to the Home Guard."

"Spreesprocket has a certain innate creative spontaneity that allows him to react naturally and effectively to almost any situation. Coupled with his formidable hand-to-hand combat and magical skills, he can devise improvisational solutions to many complex situations with little to no time spent on research or testing. Furthermore, his personal augmentations, originally in the spirit of aiding in the success of his research, are too numerous to catalog."

"His battle suit, for instance..."

Here Spreesprocket interrupted in order to provide a bit of clarification which, as it turned out, offered nothing of the sort. "Daerdros refers to the transmorphic actionable multidimensional exo-robotic system. You can call it TAMERS for short."

"Yes, his TAMERS suit brings quite the strategic advantage to our missions."

Although she did not smile, Daerdros did nod her head in his direction, which for her was the equivalent for he was one of her top students. "These talents, among others, are what ultimately led to his acceptance in the Home Guard."

Spreesprocket bowed graciously. "Many thanks, Lieutenant."

Daerdros gave another brief nod in response. "With that, I should think that my turn has come to speak."

Even as she spoke, Daerdros remained poised and distant, as if in the recitation of her own tale she were reading the story of another on a scroll held at arm's length or recounting the tale of one viewed from afar. Although seeming distant to her subject, her voice was measured with regular cadences and long pauses, melodic at movement and at rest.

"I will keep my tale brief for, just as matters of the heart are one's own private affair, so, too, is one's past."

"The first words I recall my father ever saying to me were, 'The blade is not an extension of your body. The blade is your body.'"

"The first time I held a blade, he said, 'Any drop of blood you spill is your own.'"

"With those simple words, I began my lifelong apprenticeship to the blade. Although one can never truly tame a blade, through one's devout dedication to its soft curves and sharp lines, one can hope to master one's self."

"Although I have been on many quests, accomplished uncounted missions, this is the only journey that truly matters."

"With my father's passing, I became the last Caer'collas, the last Q'sharian blade master, in a line of unbroken succession from the times before the founding of the kingdoms of Var'Kera or the ascension of Tellanon."

"Of my skills and training, you have heard what I will tell save this—before I arrived in Tellanon I wandered Dharia far and wide testing my skills against the champions and scourges of many peoples. Those who deserved to live did so by my hand, those that did not fell by my hand."

"In all my time abroad, I never met my match with the blade until I arrived at last in Tellanon. It was there that I finally met my match and this match was one in my heart for in Tellanon I had found a place more in need of my skills than my desire to prove them."

"Since that time, I have served willingly." For a brief moment Daerdros let her walls come down and smiled, saying, "I am honored to say that serving in Tellanon has granted me the opportunity to train many in the ways of the blade, a boon I never felt that I would be afforded. It is through this training that I hope to ensure that I am not the last Caer'collas."

"Through others, the blade will continue to sing."

When silence settled and Daerdros said no more, relating to the notes of her recitation, her individuality and challenges, Wrindanneth decided that his turn to speak had come. "Like Daerdros, I am perhaps the only one remaining of my kind. I am, to my knowledge, the only one left alive on Ea'ae. I am a Priest of Maeth Onai. Unlike Daerdros, I will probably remain the only one of my kind, for my master tolerates few servants"—here he smiled—"for we leave his service as soon as we are able."

"When my time ends, whether through death, infirmity, retirement, or apotheosis, he will find another. Such is the way of my order and it will remain so when I am gone."

Instead of a relatively impersonal recounting, as was his way, Wrindanneth wanted to tell his tale personally and with frankness. "If you haven't noticed yet, I am open and honest and speak from my heart for good or ill. The only courtesy that I ask from my companions is that they give the same consideration in return."

Here he smiled at Slate and, indirectly at least, acknowledged the true depth of their friendship. "Although I am not a Dwarf, we have much in common in this regard."

"I come from a land far to the North, in the heart of the mountainous lake country of Loesia. Of my birthplace, I will not speak, for many consider it cursed as the land and its magics are muted. Life is harsh, brutal, and often short."

"I was trained in the ways of divine magical invocation, a means of classification"—here he smiled at Yip—"I have since found to be rather limited for magic of any stripe arises from the same source. Regardless, my tradition relies upon techniques to directly invoke and manipulate magical power without strict reliance on spells or other magical formulae as is common in most traditional magics."

"I was trained under Maeth Onai's direct guidance until my master deemed that I had learned enough to carry on my training under my own direction." He laughed, the bitterness of the memory long past. "Had he not tricked me into leaving, I might still be sitting at his knee in the tower hoping for whatever choice secrets he was kind enough to mete out."

"These I now know he kept for himself."

"It was only after I left his direct service, and partially why he wished me to, that I realized how rich indeed the world was beyond the mountainous walls encircling the lakes and valleys of my village. Only after leaving the paucity and dearth of my home did I realize the true breadth and richness that magical practice tendered and for the first time in my life counted myself truly fortunate."

Remembering the first moment he drunk deeply of the magics beyond the privations of home, the feel of energy and vitality coursing through his veins in an overwhelming torrent of vivacity, he said, "Enlivened by the new power and opportunity afforded by the lands beyond my old home, I set out on my own for the first time with something akin to hope."

Slate laughed. "And ya never looked back!"

Wrindanneth gave a rare smile. "Only to contact Maeth on occasion. Only when I close my eyes and Maeth asks for his due."

"I certainly never missed my home if that's what you're asking."

"Aye. Once ya realize how wide tha world truly is, it's always hard ta go home if ya heed her call."

Now Wrindanneth laughed in return. "Adventure stirs a man's heart as much as it fills his purse."

"And I love fer my pockets ta jingle!" Slate finished with a smile.

"Since leaving Loesia, I've wandered Dharia far and wide in search of knowledge, honing my craft, and seeking out knowledge hidden from those who do not dare to seek. It was on one of those expeditions that I first encountered Aroganji and recognized him as a fellow seeker with whom I shared much in common. With a similar purpose, we traveled long together. Unfortunately for me, it wasn't long before we happened upon Slate and, recognizing the charity case that he is and was, my good friend Aroganji, whose heart is as soft as Slate's wit, would not hear of leaving him to return to the dust from which he came."

Slate interrupted, "O' all tha rotten untruths ya've uttered at my expense! It was I who came ta yer aid ya bandy-legged scarecrow and ya know it! If I hadn't heard tha sounds o' battle comin' from tha cave ya were fleein', ya might just be a well-gnawed pile o' bones after tha Orcs, Trolls, and tha abominations commandin' 'em were done with ya!"

Continuing as if Slate had never spoken, Wrindanneth went on unperturbed, "Yip, being of pure heart and noble spirit, came to our aid unbidden but welcome on one of our adventures together some time later in the Green Run and, like the lichen growing upon the rock from under which Slate first crawled out so ungraciously to join us, Yip has stuck with us ever since, his cause becoming our own."

"I ought ta hit ya over yer head with a rock fer all tha wool-headed lies ya're spoutin'! Yer tongue is as forked as a snake's!"

"And twice as sharp!" retorted Wrindanneth.

"Enough, you two," Aroganji sighed good-naturedly. "I don't think we have sufficient time before we arrive in Taerris'thule to fill in all the holes in Wrindanneth's tale much less the process of telling my own."

"More holes in his poor excuse fer our meetin' than a chest full o' his Granny's old moth-eaten woolens."

Slate glowered darkly, adding, "As I recall, ya welcomed my help as I know ya welcomed Aroganji's before."

Wrindanneth grinned sardonically. "And I still do."

"Bah!" Slate glanced at Aroganji, barking, "Aroganji, tell yer tale before I show Spreesprocket how useful Northlanders' bones are fer toothpicks!"

Sensing the Home Guard around him as he listened to his friends, Yip noted that many appeared quite amused with Slate and Wrindanneth's antics for they were used to much stricter discipline while in the company of their fellows. Although the Home Guard did not display it outwardly, many enjoyed his friends' open displays of excitement and all certainly appreciated their good cheer.

Aroganji gave a brief bow. "Like Yip, I come from the lands of Chang Sen far to the east beyond many wild and uncharted lands. As humanity—Men, Dwarves, Gnomes, Elves, and other civilized races—has left Ea'ae in the great Diasporas of the past, taking places among the far heavens, much of the lands between our various peoples and civilizations have returned to wilderness and the creatures that make their homes in the wilds. Though the culture and Empire of Chang Sen yet thrives, there is now much distance and isolation between us and the lands to the west."

"Although there yet remains direct trade in knowledge and goods between the Empire and other civilizations beyond her borders, with so many having left for the stars, most of the people of Chang Sen have chosen to foster relationships with those who left their native soil for the stars more than other peoples outside her boundaries who still share the same worldly home. Although many of the people of Chang Sen look to the heavens and imagine life on other worlds, their own vision of Ea'ae and concern about the well-being of others has contracted to the borders of their homeland."

"I chose a somewhat different path. Or, rather, one was thrust upon me."

"Like many generations before me, I attended the school of Xian Shi, taking it as a second home, learning the subtle arts of Wu-hsing, the way of transformation and manifestation of the elements of creation. After much study within the walls of my school, I had finally been accepted into the ranks of the Fang Shih and was in the process of deciding on the proper course for further specialized study when all further choice was stripped from me."

"Wandering beyond the walls of my school, proud of my achievements, letting the wonders of the Q'ia Shan Sea lapping at the feet of the Hsiang Lung

Mountains fill me, I was not a part of the downfall of my school, only an unwelcome witness to it. From outside her grounds, I watched in horror as creatures of Darkness, the Cabal's agents, tore through the barriers protecting our world to destroy my home, my friends, and any future I had dreamed of dedicated to further studies through Xian Shi."

"After the atrocities that befell my native school of Xian Shi, I did not wish to direct my eyes to the heavens and seek my fortune on another world as many of my countrymen have done before me. Instead, I wished to seek out any who remained on Ea'ae who had brought about the downfall of my home, for I considered Xian Shi as much my home as our family's compound."

"The trail I followed, cultivating knowledge and skill in preparation for the battles to come against the Cabal and their agents, led me first to teachers from within my own lineage. Then based on their advice and direction, westward beyond the bounds of Chang Sen, scouring lands long abandoned by Men and Dwarf, Gnome and Elf, seeking after knowledge that few remembered and even fewer wished to share."

"As always, I am after the Cabal for they are the ones who destroyed much of my past. I would not have them take the past or the future from any others."

"From the winds and tides, the flow of the molten earth and the flowering of living things, I learned the wisdom of patience and perseverance. I will grow and change, develop and adapt, doing whatever is required to be ready."

Emotion hot on his usually cool face, Aroganji finished, "When the time comes and I am fully prepared, I, too, will direct my eyes toward Heaven. However, I will not do so to dream of life on some far-off place without connection to my past or the past of my people. I will do so to bring about the destruction of those who took away my dreams and the dreams of so many others."

Eidelion nodded sagely after Aroganji had finished. "I see there is much we all have in common here. We were brought together for a purpose, a purpose that will be fulfilled, the Light willing."

Llyewia stepped forward then, his motions so soft and subtle that Slate did a double-take to make sure Llyewia had indeed changed position and that he had not been mistaken about the Elf's original place.

With a slight bow of his head, Llyewia lifted both arms upward to shoulder height, letting his shoulders and hands settle down after the upward motion. To Yip, the gesture looked like the lifting of a swan's wings preparing for a landing on open water or the delicate shifting of the boughs of a tree in the slightest of breezes.

"I welcome the opportunity to share in the telling of tales, for the life of all beings lives in the tales they share. Though my life has not been darkened with the affronts suffered by you and your peoples, the heart of my people suffers with every blow struck, every life harmed, and every life lessened on this world. Such is our gift and such is our curse."

"I was born to Aleron and Nydia on the first morn of spring seven hundred thirty four Cycles past in the shade of Rhyllia, the Mother Tree, in the grove of Erudhluin, Heaven's Home. I took my first breath as the sun rose above the mists and fogs that had sheltered the land for the night, lacing the lustrous leaves and boughs of Rhyllia in pearlescence. In honor of my birthplace, my parent's bequeathed to me the name Llyewia which means 'Spring's first breath' or 'first breath of Spring.'"

"I was brought into the world under Rhyllia's protection that my first breath would be from her life-giving leaves. That my delivery was timed with the birth of spring was a circumstance that my parents considered doubly significant for the life of a new season and the life of a sacred tree shared in the bringing of my life into being. Thus the life of an Iyela was entrusted to me through the fortunes of my birth—by gift of the seasons and through the life those seasons sustain."

Here he looked upon his audience with great feeling. His dark, liquid eyes conveyed emotions foreign to the hearts to whom he spoke. "For those unfamiliar with our ways, the lives of Elves may appear uncanny, strangely foreign. There are those who would say that Elves have no place in this world for we are not originally from Ea'ae, that our ways do not fit this land or any other on this world, and that we are as out of place here as lost spirits with whom we seem to have more in common for we are not mortal flesh and blood."

"For my people, whom I hope one day to introduce to you as friends, I say that we, too, bleed and our blood is the blood of the land for its vitality, its energy, flows through us and is our lifeblood. Although we may appear queer and elusive, our love of this place is as deep as any other's for we owe our existence to Ea'ae as much as any of her other peoples."

"This truth and our ultimate mortality, for though we may not die from old age or disease, we can die by blade, grief, or the desolation brought about by a broken heart like any other, connects not just our bodies but our hearts and minds with all other creatures on this world. Just as we wish no ill upon ourselves, we wish no ill upon any of her denizens."

"The life of an Iyela is a life dedicated to the care of all living creatures, a life given to the well-being and caretaking of all beings. Just as our life is not our own, the life of another is not his or her sole possession. Just as we are trained to heal, so, too, are we trained to intervene."

"This, then, is my place within the Home Guard. I am here for my people, for all people and all beings, for Ea'ae and all the life dependent upon her, to intercede and heal at need."

"This is the life of an Iyela and it is the life I lead."

He bowed gracefully again, as a leaf blowing in the wind.

Slate scratched his beard uncomfortably, and shifted on his feet, obviously ill at ease with Llyewia and his story, but, for once, too polite to voice any complaint or protest for he had no real grounds to argue or refute. Although there was nothing wrong with the Elf's light, ethereal presence, Slate could not help but feel a strong difference between his solid earthiness and the Elf's fey character despite Llyewia's assertions to their connection.

When Slate remained silent and no one offered any further comment, Yip bowed in return saying, "There is much I would ask you in due time. But for now, I have a single question. What type of tree is Rhyllia?"

Llyewia raised both hands fingertips lightly touching together in a gesture indicating a combination of reluctant sorrow and unfortunate denial to those of his own kind. In his soft voice, he answered, "There are some secrets I am not able to reveal, lest, in their telling, more is given than is granted."

Yip bowed in understanding. "I have heard tales that the Elves of old learned much of the lore of the earth and the ways of energy from the Aeryn D'al."

While Yip waited for a response, Wrindanneth and Aroganji looked back and forth between the Elf and Man sensing that more perhaps was involved in Yip's comment than he was indicating.

"You have heard rightly."

"Perhaps in time I will be able to hear something of these tales?"

"The time may come."

Yip gave a short nod in acknowledgement. "I would hear of them if you are willing, for these same tales say that the Aeryn D'al were lost to the Elves long ago."

Still ill at ease after hearing Llyewia's story for reasons he did not fully understand and wishing for someone else to speak, Slate blurted out, "Now why in tha world would ya wanna know that o' all things, Yip? Now is tha time fer tha tellin' o' tales not tha solvin' o' mysteries."

Yip smiled, understanding that the trust of the Elves was hard to gain and even harder to lose, and said, "Are the two not of one fold?"

Llyewia, however, remained silent.

Raour'Saqan stepped forward boldly to fill in that silence. The deck creaked ominously beneath his stride but held firm as all eyes turned to his massive form. The thick, dark scales covering his body drank the light as much as his presence drew in their attention.

"I have told my tale before to those who would listen and will do so now again. For those who wish to know more, you have but to ask for now I will be brief."

"My people ascended to the stars long before life on this world first grew and flowered. We did not use ships or magic but took the void on our own wings riding the celestial currents in freedom for none dared challenge us nor did we seek challenge."

"Even then, so long ago, the universe was old and we found numerous beings on other worlds with whom we traded in knowledge and lore, counting many as allies and fewer as friends. However, for all of our travels, my people only knew one home and it was to there that we always returned—Guor' Uenaqe, 'the forge of our spirits.'"

"To say that our world is harsh would be the gravest of understatements. To imagine that life could have ever risen from the pools of molten slag and dry ash beneath the blazing calderas and overarching igneous sun is an exercise in futility, but we arose from this crucible nonetheless and still call it home."

"That our world was attacked, sought out, and waylaid by the abominations of Ur'Daus is just as surprising for so little survives on our world that one of sound mind and reason might deem our home of little consequence or interest. Perhaps our barren world was deemed vulnerable or perhaps our planet was chosen for its resemblance to the fell pits from which those spawns of Darkness that besieged our world first scrabbled and lurched on to an unsuspecting universe."

"It was then that Ur'Daus learned that we were strong and would not be taken—not then or ever. It was then, in a crucible far harsher than even our own world, that we learned that our wanderings through the megacosm would now have a purpose for we would become Shaur'Daus, the Stalkers of Darkness, journeying between the stars to spread and protect the Light that Ur'Daus so wished to destroy in our eternal war against It and Its agents."

Raour'Saqan ended there, his fierce countenance settling and seeming to turn to stone while he waited for any questions after his telling.

Aroganji broke the silence with a question. "How do you know when Ur'Daus or Its agents pose a risk? How do you know where to go to stop their destruction?"

Raour'Saqan tilted his head sideways slightly, the motion accentuating the wicked horns crowning the top of his head. "When one listens, one hears. When one looks, one sees."

"How d'ya know where ta look or when ta listen?" asked Slate honestly and innocently.

"The duty of the Shaur'Daus is to listen and look, seek and find"—he paused briefly and snarled, revealing row upon row of jagged teeth as dark and light devouring as the unyielding scales that covered his body—"and to destroy."

Slate redirected that awesome menace through his deep well of Dwarven humor. "Then we can certainly use yer help! We've had about as much luck findin' tha den o' Ur'Daus's lackeys as a Troll has wipin' its nose!"

"Or an Orc has cleaning its teeth," added Wrindanneth good-naturedly.

"Sounds like they may be in need of my Perfectly Polished Particulate Propeller - Beta Naught Mark Seven®, Patent Pending!" Spreesprocket shook his head. "As for you, I can't say, but we may be able to work something out… maybe a Resonant Gyroscopic Eidolon Scryer, Class A Divination Series."

"Maybe," muttered Slate, the doubt in his voice quite audible.

"Do the Shaur'Daus hunt Darkness only or are the Shaur'Daus able to create Light within it?" Yip gazed at Raour'Saqan intently as he asked.

Raour'Saqan looked deeply into Yip's eyes, seeking to pull the intent of his question from him by the force of his gaze. "Light creates itself through life. Light arises from the emptiness and returns just as easily. The Shaur'Daus destroy Darkness and prevent Its arrival allowing life to prosper where it would otherwise be extinguished."

"If you are asking if we can restore those worlds stripped of life by Ur'Daus and Its agents, we cannot. We cannot restore the veil once it has been broken and can only cleanse such worlds of evil, leaving them barren of life as a reminder of the true depths of Darkness. The passage of time, the regathering of energy, and its expression are required for life to reemerge. This happens only when and if Ur'Daus's void seals."

"I ask that you forgive my presumption." Yip bowed deeply before continuing. "Perhaps the time has come for the Stalkers of Darkness to become the Bringers of Light."

"What is this that you speak of, Yip?" Raour'Saqan growl was more curious than upset by Yip's proposition.

"The time may have come to take advantage of Eidelion's suggestion that we train together and learn from each other during our time together."

Yip bowed again with the offer. "When we ventured to the homeworld of the H'era in search of the Cabal, I unwisely had Wrindanneth and Aroganji port me immediately beside the *chi* void that had drained the world of all of its life. In the face of that terrible emptiness, I felt all the life and energy being ripped from me just as the void took and siphoned away any *chi* within its reach."

"I fell forward then, dying as I collapsed, directly into the vortex no longer in control of my body, only just gripping the last vestiges of volition. In that moment, through no conscious act of my own, I instinctively created *chi*, Light, through a gift I had once been given. This act and its manifestation destroyed the *chi* void, negating its presence, that Ur'Daus and Its agents had used to siphon the life from the world of the H'era, dooming its denizens and wiping away their future."

He looked at Raour'Saqan with profound emotion as the pain and the deep compassion and empathy of the experience overcame him. "I am but a weak and imperfect vessel, not fit for the rigors and strains of the void of interstellar space or direct combat with the darkest Infernals from the unhallowed pits Beyond. That I survived the trial was through sheer fortune along with the gifts and good graces of my friends."

"You and your kind, however, are strong where I am weak and your mission already takes you into the heart of maelstroms such as the one I only barely survived. Through your strength and dedication, already evident in the depth of your commitment to your race's cause for all beings, I feel that the Shaur'Daus, the Stalkers of Darkness, can become the Bringers of Light."

When the Dracodaera remained still, his massive arms crossed at the chest lost in silent thought, Yip then looked from Raour'Saqan around to all of his companions, new and old, as he finished, "It is this gift that I would share with all of those who are willing for I cannot right the wrongs created by the Cabal, their allies, or from Ur'Daus in all Its terror. I can, through this small act of creation, however, offer a new beginning, one that I would share with others."

"The more that I am able to teach, the more beginnings and hope we will be able to offer together. With enough acts of cooperative generation, these new beginnings may overcome the finality, the heinous end to all life, imposed by the agents of Darkness on so many worlds, ultimately ridding the universe of Ur'Daus's evil forever."

Raour'Saqan remained still as he watched the small Man whose dream was far too bright and encompassing for realization solely by a lone individual, an aspiration that was too tantalizing to ignore. With simple finality, Raour'Saqan rumbled, "If what you say is indeed true, then the Shaur'Daus will become the Dauren'Kas, the Bringers of Light."

Yip bowed once again in deep gratitude, for words could not convey the depth of appreciation and hope those words proffered.

Eidelion responded then, saying, "The mission of the Home Guard has always been to protect Tellanon and those it harbors from harm. What you propose would be most welcome to our mission, all of our citizens, and guests if we are able to truly learn and harness your gift. As a Dalaren Ka, my order would also welcome such knowledge if you are willing to share so freely and generously for the Light of Life deserves expression wherever it arises."

"What else can be done?" replied Yip rhetorically.

"When the time comes, you will have our ears and hearts."

Slate scratched his beard thoughtfully, before adding, "If I can share a bit o' Brendle's spark ta ease tha sufferin' o' many, then ya have my promise." Here his eyes glinted in humor. "If ya think I'm able."

"You, all of you, are as able as any," replied Yip with a smile.

"Count us in then," responded Slate speaking for everyone whether they wanted him to or not.

"Your help will be most welcome and honored," Yip bowed a final time.

"Tomorrow I will visit each of you in turn and impart the knowledge of the Dragon's Gate to you directly. You will see what I have seen and feel what I have felt. You will know what I know in regards to energy creation and expression as given to me by Azaelle the Golden."

"However, what I give will only be a small window looking out upon an expansive vista for you to explore and realize. This view will have all the reality of a dream—bright and vivid at first but soon forgotten for knowledge without practice and internalization is only knowledge in word and not deed and is just as easily lost."

"You will have to practice what I share and make the knowledge part of your daily experience. You will have to venture forth and claim its truth for yourself or the door within will remain but a reflection of a potential reality, a dream lost and never realized. When the experience I give becomes your reality, you will have mastered the essence of the Dragon's Gate."

"Do not fear, for I will impart the knowledge of other skills and perspectives that will help in giving you the foundation to build your practice upon should you not have those tools already. I will do everything in my power to ensure that your efforts realize success."

As all eyes were already on him, Yip now took the opportunity to begin his tale. "I have asked for much more than I have yet given. The time has come for the telling of my journey here. Tomorrow I will give what I have been given."

"I come from the land of Chang Sen far to the east, high in the sacred mountains of K'un Lun where my order came into being many ages past. We are a group of ascetics dedicated to truth and understanding, compassion and wisdom, transformation and growth, and unraveling the mysteries of Life in all its manifestations. We are called Priests of K'un Lun by some, Tao-Shih by others, Yu-jen by a few, and generally by our first names by other initiates, novices, and acolytes."

Yip smiled brightly at his joke as Eidelion and the others laughed.

"Although our order was founded upon and remains dedicated to the principles of peace, there were those of our kind who thought and acted differently. Long ago, these few broke away from us in their search for ever greater knowledge and power, taking a way that lead down a spiraling path toward ever darker and more heinous acts and vile secrets. In their zeal for power, they threw off all trappings of our tradition and, in the end, openly sought our destruction. It was from them, those who would later come to be known as the Cabal, that we learned the ways of battle and our traditions of quietude came to encompass those of strife."

"Long ago, we defeated those who we once considered our brothers and banished them from this world with the aid of many friends and allies. In recognition of our own failings, we exiled ourselves as well from Ea'ae and have only recently returned."

"It is with a very heavy heart that I say that our recent reappearance coincided with and may have triggered the latest resurgence of the Cabal on this world. Although we thought them utterly broken and defeated, the Cabal has prospered in our absence, long awaiting our return to reap their revenge. Even though most of the seals established so long ago to protect us all from incursions by evils such as the Cabal and their allies yet hold, these same wretches seek to overthrow our defenses and destroy all that we hold dear. I am sad to say that they yet have many allies here on Ea'ae who would see them return."

"I am here to make certain that does not happen, for myself, my order, and all the beings of Ea'ae. I am here to make sure the Cabal and their ilk are denied the Light they wish to destroy forever and always."

Silence followed his short recounting for although everyone present was aware of the purpose of their quest and understood its relation to helping protect Ea'ae from the Cabal, only a few knew of the connection between his order and the Cabal itself.

Although no one voiced any protests or oaths, he could sense an air of general disquiet laying heavy about him, not for what he had or had not done, but for his indirect association with such a grave evil.

Bowing deeply to those assembled around him, showing them his resolution, disregarding their unease, he finished, "I have given my life to the eradication of the Cabal. Only with your assistance will we be able to do so. Just as it was my order's failing that gave birth to the Cabal, it is only with your help that we will be able to destroy it."

AZAELLE'S GIFT REGIVEN

Dawn's glow lights the horizon
in shades of splendor—
tomorrow's promise today.

After the tales were all told, at least for the time being, and he was needed to say no more, Yip walked once again to the edge of the ship's railing to gaze down upon the land drifting slowly by far beneath leaving those who wished to remain in discussion behind. The day's shadows had lengthened and evening would soon be upon the lush, gently rolling terrain below. The ship's railing still felt warm to his touch, holding in the heat of the day even as the sun began its slow descent into darkness.

As he peered below, one thought returned to the fore of his consciousness. He would have assistance on his quest. He would have aid not just in his efforts to ensure the safety of Ea'ae, but in his desire to rid the universe of the Cabal's evil forever. Not only that, but there were those who would pass on the knowledge necessary to ensure the continued safety of whole worlds from beings such as those allied with the Cabal.

Before the telling of tales had started, he had not intended to make that offer, at least not so soon, but the opportunity presented itself and he had acted.

Should he perish or be thwarted, the H'era, the K'un Lun, and, in the near future, his present company should they desire, along with any others they taught in the future, would directly oppose Ur'Daus and all Its evil bringing forth Light where before these creatures had brought forth only Darkness.

He could not have hoped for a more welcome outcome in their travels together.

Some minutes passed in quiet absorption before he sensed a presence coming toward him from the ship's aft.

Without waiting for Yip to turn his head and offer welcome or a greeting, Llyewia's melodic voice washed over him genially. "What you have offered truly is a gift beyond measure, Yip. Many will bear this boon with great compassion and pride."

"The gift was given to me. I merely wish to pass it on to those who are able to use it. I was only fortunate enough to happen upon a new application for the knowledge given."

"Regardless of how this came to pass, your deed along with the inspiration behind this novel interpretation will be remembered."

Still gazing out at the lengthening shadows, Yip replied, "I only seek peace and opportunity for those who are and may be denied the realization of their potential. I wish only to allow the expression of those existences that would otherwise be stifled by the Cabal's evil should it ever arise in another place."

Llyewia laughed, his voice as musical as rustling leaves and burbling streams. "You think first of others and not yourself. You have the heart of an Elf!"

He smiled but said nothing.

Llyewia stood by Yip for some time in silence, watching the day unfold with his companion. After some time watching the interplay of light and shadow on the ground below and the clouds above, Llyewia said, "I sensed perhaps that there was some other matter you wished to discuss with me during the telling of my tale, Yip, when the time is right. I make the offer now that you may speak with me should you so desire."

"Your feelings are true." He turned to look at Llyewia's perfectly formed high-cast Elven features. "I thought, perhaps, if the stories were correct and the Elves truly had lost contact with the Aeryn D'al, that you may want to know where to find them."

Llyewia, remained quiet for a time, lost in remembrance of events to which Yip knew but little and had no part. "Tales are often told without the full telling."

With that, Llyewia raised a hand and an image of a vast, unbroken forest appeared before their eyes shimmering in the air like the lightest of gossamer. "Long ago, when the Elves first arrived on Ea'ae, making our home in Ithil'alen, long before the coming of Man or Dwarf to Dharia, we encountered Ea'ae's most ancient sentient race, the Aeryn D'al. From the Aeryn D'al many legends have been born and many more will arise before the telling is done."

He looked at Yip, bright eyes shimmering as he stared into Yip's heart. "Your tale is one branch on that ever-expanding tree. In time, your lore will become theirs."

"Just as your story and deeds will become the Aeryn D'al's future, our past has, in part, become their present and morrow. From the Aeryn D'al we learned much of the ways of magic for we knew little of its true depth and complexity prior to their most gracious tutelage. Just as their knowledge and generosity shaped our destiny, so, too, did our presence and tutelage alter the course of their fortune."

"Through our service to the Aeryn D'al and through our great admiration of them, we earned the title Iyela, or 'Tree Singer' in the common tongue. Before the arrival of Men and Dwarf to Dharia, many other fell creatures attempted incursions into the lands of the Aeryn D'al at great cost to my people and the Aeryn D'al themselves. During this time, we became the Aeryn D'al's chosen guardians and, alongside the Indural, warded Ea'ae from many a blight and Shadow."

"As Man and Dwarf, Gnome and Orc, began expanding their presence on Dharia, they too began pressuring the home of Ea'ae's first guardians. This second group, with the exception of the Orcs, did not intentionally wish to harm Ea'ae and her keepers during the course of their activities. But intentioned or not, the pursuit of their own self-interests came at great cost to the Aeryn D'al along with many other fey creatures of the land."

"Under ever greater pressures as a result of the expansion of these and other races, with great deliberation and much sadness, the first sundering of Elf and Aeryn D'al was undertaken. During this time, a great veil was placed over the valley of the Aeryn D'al, one that remains, as you know, in place to this day. Anyone who attempts to venture within the realm of the Aeryn D'al only does so at grave risk."

"We Elves paid a terrible price for the protection of our teachers for we were denied the presence of all but a few of the Aeryn D'al. Though we yet patrol their borders, we, like any other race wishing to learn at their root, have been prohibited from further access to the forest home of the Aeryn D'al in order to afford them true protection for their lands are now forbidden. To this day, we move through the forests of Ea'ae with great sadness knowing the true depths of what we have lost."

"We now call the forbidden home of the Aeryn D'al Noes Al'amroth, 'the Land Where Tears do not Dry.'"

When he finished, Llyewia dropped his head slightly as if he were tired and wished to rest. The image of the verdant jungle with the beautiful silver and gold tree crowns of the Aeryn D'al protruding above the canopy remained in place.

"Jenyuan Shulin," Yip dropped his head as well knowing he had overstepped his bounds.

"You have been there?"

Yip looked up from his shame at forcing Llyewia to relive painful memories and into the Elf's deep, penetrating eyes. "I journeyed through Jenyuan Shulin to arrive here on my quest. At the very beginning of my voyage, I sat at the feet of the Aeryn D'al in awe and wonder. From them, I learned much in the short time spent in their shade and will return when, if, I am done."

Llyewia gazed at him intently, but no mark of surprise marred his perfect face. "They did not hide their presence from you and allowed you to approach in safety?"

"Passing through the forest to arrive near them was a very difficult task, but once I was through the barrier around the forest, I sensed their presence. I approached openly and with care. They welcomed my presence as short as my time with them was. I learned willingly from them while I sat in their shadows. Before I left, they also entrusted me with a seed."

Here, for the first time, the Elf showed something of emotion. "You have a seed from the D'al?"

Yip shook his head. "I gave it to my master for safekeeping once I reached safety for my journey is far too perilous to risk their trust. Master Wei has taken the seed to our monastery for planting."

"You are sure of this?"

Yip gave a short, "I am," in response.

"In all my days, no mortal has ever been so fortunate! Perhaps the time of our parting will soon be at an end! Perhaps the Aeryn D'al will soon retake their rightful place among us!"

He understood the Elf's sentiment. "When we established the veil around our monastery in our shame and regret for giving birth to the Cabal, we of the K'un Lun sundered ourselves from the very thing we loved and lived for as well."

"Now that we have returned, as brief as our reunion with this wondrous place and all her blessed beings has been, we find that the Cabal is yet strong, is working to return as well, and does not welcome our presence. I can only hope that your reunion is much happier than ours, for Ea'ae has known far too many tears."

Having lived a similar bittersweet tale, Llyewia offered sympathetic silence in response.

Gazing forth into the vast ocean of air through which they flew, the day now gone to dusk, the wind currents lightly brushing, soothing, and caressing their cheeks, encircling and buoying their ship and its crew, they remained lost in quietude, each alone with his thoughts.

The day now given to night, the sun's heat all but forgotten by the cool evening air and distant stars overhead, Llyewia took his leave while Yip remained standing in serene meditation at the railing of the airship.

Walking toward the ship's aft through the silvery shadows, Llyewia spun a light web of moonbeams and starlight between the ship's mainmast and the railing of one set of stairs leading to the quarterdeck. Reclining lightly on his enchanted hammock, Llyewia laid down for an evening spent in quiet contemplation of the stars.

When Yip had remained motionless for some time after Llyewia's departure, a deep rumbling voice called out from the caliginosity at the fore of the ship in tones meant to be a whisper, "Will you not go belowdecks like the others?"

Blinking once before turning toward the hunched bulk of Raour'Saqan, visible only to Yip's eyes as a hulking shadow crouched above the ship's figurehead, but visible to his inner vision as a dark emptiness limned by the magical corona of energies dancing along his scaly periphery, he replied, "I prefer to remain outside beneath stars in reflection. And you?"

A deep, hearty laugh returned to him from the gloom. "Will I fit?" A moment later, the Dracodaera responded, "I, too, prefer the elements."

"If you will forgive my company, I will share your decks."

Again the Dracodaeran laughed at Yip's reply, his voice the sound of distant thunder or rocks tumbling over stone. "These decks are more yours than mine, friend, but your sentiment is welcome."

"I wish to thank you for the offer you have given, Yip. My people have spent the lifetime of stars in conflict. Your assay, however tentative and fragile, may provide us one path to peace where many others have failed over the millennia. The consequence of such a guerdon after so much travail will not be lost upon my broodmates."

Having faced this line of conversation for the second time in one day, Yip reiterated his earlier feelings. "I merely regive what has been given."

"If a thing has never been willingly given before and you make it available for others to use in a way that has never been considered, then you are doing much more than regiving, my friend. However you wish to describe your actions, we are most gracious."

Raour'Saqan was not one to offer praise or congratulations lightly, but Yip wished for neither nonetheless. "If I am able to share what I have been shown and others are able to make use of the knowledge I have been given, then the time for thanks will have come."

"And for that time, and the journey that led you to this point, I will be grateful and joyous indeed," Raour'Saqan finished, his voice a low roll, before returning to the quiet from which it first issued.

Once again, Yip was left to his own ruminations. This time his thoughts were of the morrow and the opportunities that would be presented before them. He let those considerations run their course, passing like the moon above.

When the sun rose the next morning, a light layer of dew had settled upon the surface of Yip's robes where he remained standing overnight, coating the fabric of his clothing in a uniform patina of shimmering specks of sunlight—first ruddy and roseate with tints of orange as the sun initially broke the horizon then gradually brightening as the sun rose to lambent hues of gold.

As he had promised, before the sun had kindled the full activity of the day, he began to make his rounds visiting each companion in turn. Walking to the ship's fore where Raour'Saqan hunkered still as a statue above the ship's nose, motionless as a gargoyle from the deepest reaches of the imagination, his mighty wings folded closely around his massive shoulders and thick back, a portion of the night still seemed to hold sway around his menacing silhouette.

"I am here, Raour'Saqan, if you are ready."

"I am ready."

The Dracodaeran began to stand but Yip forestalled him with a gesture. Yip laughed briefly. "I will not be able to reach you properly if you stand, my friend."

Raour'Saqan grunted and hunkered back down, settling onto his haunches, wrapping his thick arms around his legs as he looked down at Yip.

"You will have to relax and open your mind to me when I touch you or the transfer will be lost."

Raour'Saqan gave a brief nod of his head in understanding.

"Do you dream, Raour'Saqan?"

The Dracodaeran's gravelly voice replied flatly, "Does Ea'ae dream of taking to the stars? Thoughts and impressions come and go but discernment and consideration remain."

Yip gave a short nod, changing the metaphor he had planned on using to ease Raour'Saqan's transference. "Let this abiding discernment penetrate into that which I share."

Standing before Raour'Saqan, even while the Dracodaera was seated, he had to look upward to gaze into Raour'Saqan's bottomless black eyes. Resting lightly on his feet, he settled into a Zhan Zhuang posture gathering energy into himself in preparation for the transfer of knowledge, impressions, and experience. This close to Raour'Saqan, he could feel the strong pull of the Dracodaeran's essence on the energy he garnered, seeking to draw the ambient energy away and into himself.

In many ways the Dracodaeran's presence felt much like a miniature version of the *chi* void created by the Cabal on Al'Marr only the energy Raour'Saqan drew in was used to power and sustain his body and metabolic processes and were not channeled to another place entirely.

Truth be told, the more he learned of the ways of energy, the more he acted and felt similarly.

Settling his fingertips on Raour'Saqan's skin, the Dracodaeran's scales felt rough and warm to his touch. They were also so sharp that he could only lightly rest his fingers on Raour'Saqan's scales without risking a cut or puncture unless he sheathed himself in protective energies.

As he observed and manipulated the *chi* flowing through and within his body, he carefully organized his thoughts and impressions, bringing forth his knowledge, experiences, and memories relating to the *chi* void and the creation of the Dragon's Gate. Once he had fully arranged his feelings and impressions in a coherent fashion, he let the *chi* flow from him, through his arm, and to the palm of his hand held lightly rested on Raour'Saqan's jagged forehead.

With a gentle exhale, softer than the breeze alighting on his cheeks, he let the energy flow between himself and Raour'Saqan, from his mind to that of the Dracodaeran, *xīnyì*, mind-to-mind, carrying his knowledge and experience forward on the breath of awareness. Like a seed carried on the wind seeking purchase in which to grow and flourish, he let his experience alight and take hold before breaking contact with Raour'Saqan.

He gave the Dracodaeran a brief tired smile as he broke contact. "Now you know what I know and have only to practice as I have shown you. With time and effort, you will hold the keys to the Dragon's Gate in hand."

Raour'Saqan did not reply. His eyes were focused far away on another place, peering deeply inward onto a rapidly developing and changing inner universe. Watching and feeling new, alien experiences unfold before his slitted eyes, his body and mind struggled to internalize and incorporate what he had been given—the understandings of a mind unlike his own.

While Raour'Saqan gazed far away, he added, "If there is more you need of me, you have but to ask."

Walking from Raour'Saqan to Llyewia, he gave a brief bow to the Elf as he approached Llyewia's Elven wrought hammock.

"Fair morning to you, Master Chuan," offered Llyewia by way of greeting as he stood at Yip's approach.

"A wondrous day it is, as ever, my friend." Yip gave a short laugh. "An initiate never presumes to be a master, nor does a beginner ever fully master a chosen task."

"I have begun many things and have yet to finish."

Now it was Llyewia who laughed. "A healthy attitude indeed!"

He then peered inquisitively into Yip's eyes, reading signs hidden from other eyes. "Are you ready to begin anew?"

Yip smiled. "That I am."

"Relax and close your eyes. I will rest my fingertips on your forehead when I am ready to begin."

Llyewia smiled in turn. "There is no need, Yip. When you are ready, I will open myself to you and I will give you something else in return."

Yip then closed his eyes and began to summon the intrinsic energies within and without. As he did so, he felt Llyewia's presence shaping this process from the outside, guiding him to work with his energy and memory, thoughts and feelings, experience and knowledge, in the space between them.

As he did so, Yip realized the Elf was showing him how to share his knowledge in a mutually created space between them in a way that would be most amenable, most effective, to both of them. Although Llyewia was not attempting to interact with the formation of his thoughts, he was working to facilitate their transfer. For beings with very different perceptions, modes of communication, and ways of thinking, he understood the benefit of such an approach.

He only hoped that his efforts with the H'era and Raour'Saqan were not hampered significantly by his original, less than optimal, approach. At the same time, he also understood that many beings would not be able to participate in such a transfer and he would not have an option akin to the one Llyewia now presented before him. For these beings, their own minds with all of their manifold perceptions, feelings, thoughts, and beliefs would mediate, mesh, and then harmonize the transfer.

Yip relaxed into the space created between them, letting first his energy and then his thoughts and experiences flow forward and outward where they swirled and eddied forth, a dream given brief life, which then moved on into Llyewia. All the while, the Elf gazed upon him serenely accepting the gift he gave with calm recognition and full awareness.

After some time linked, the transfer complete, he made ready to break contact when, to his surprise, Llyewia began to share knowledge of his own with Yip. Closing his eyes, he let the experience come welcoming the exchange.

Instead of a recollection or an experience of events past, or a summation of collective experience, Llyewia instead sent forth his direct perceptions between the link they shared, offering his mind, at least for a time, in commutation. What Yip felt in return was very similar, but also quite different and distinct from, the way he normally experienced reality.

He became diffuse, a nexus of awareness spread throughout the space around him. His awareness was not a central point within a larger connected and interconnected field, he was his field of awareness. His body was merely one point in a much larger context. Beings of energy moved all around the ship—he recognized those as his shipmates and friends. Infinitely smaller creatures floated through the air, on the surface of the ship and of his companions, and within each of these shining vital lights. These tiny organisms lit up his friends' bodies like countless constellations within larger galaxies. All were bound together and connected by the chi. Informed by the connection with Llyewia he also knew this energy as the Aerya, the living energy of the universe.

He was all this and so much more.

Empty of self, he was full of radiant life. As much as the energy that enlivened all things, he was, for a short time, the briefest of glimmers, all things.

Then his perception shifted to memory and he knew that he was experiencing one of Llyewia's lessons as an Iyela, sitting beneath the shade of a massive fir tree, so full of life and energy, his head held lightly between the palms of his teacher's hands.

All boundaries slipped away under his teacher's guidance, he became the tree feeling its roots drinking deeply from the soil, breathing fully from the air. He became the soil, so rich and diverse filled with hidden life, countless miniscule forms enriching the earth for all to grow and thrive. He became the air circulating through all the creatures above and below the ground, connecting each other in a complex cycle of mutual breaths. He became the very light cascading through the forest, providing warmth and energy to support the development of all living creatures he now felt as part of himself. And beyond, so vibrant and glorious moving somehow behind and within the very air and light, binding all together, coming into and out of existence spontaneously, the wondrously elusive Aerya made all things whole and complete.

Never wishing to close his eyes again, lest he lose sight of all he now saw and felt with all his being; never wishing to forget such glory, his father's words washed over him like a refreshing rain. "Now that you see with the eyes of an Iyela, never again will another being not be your responsibility. Never again will your life be your own."

"You are the eyes of the universe. You are the universe watching itself."

"Take care of your self and all beings will prosper."

"May your eyes always remain open."

The view of the ship and its surroundings gradually returned to Yip. He could tell by the position of the sun that very little time had passed.

Standing before him, radiant and pure, Llyewia gave him a gracious bow. "A gift returned in kind."

"You have experienced the Fria al'Othra, the 'eyes of true vision'. A greater gift, I cannot give."

Yip bowed. "Your friendship is the greatest gift I could ever hope to receive."

Llyewia laughed gaily, the sound of his voice brightening the already luminous day. "You are more Elven than many of my kindred!"

"I am what I have become."

Levity still evident on his visage, Llyewia replied animatedly, "My point exactly!" Becoming serious once again, he added, "From what I know of your order, you see, feel, and interact with the world in all its wonder and depth very much like an Elf. I knew that you would appreciate my perspective as I believe that it is not far away from your own."

With a smile on his face, Yip bowed and departed, saying, "And now you are sounding very much like a Priest of the K'un Lun."

Taking leave of Llyewia, he made his way up the steps leading to the quarterdeck at the ship's aft. Behind him and past where Llyewia stood by the mizzenmast farther forward on the ship's main deck near the central main mast, Eidelion and Daerdros were in conversation with Orogast. Past them, near where Raour'Saqan remained in silent contemplation, Spreesprocket had taken up position on the ship's forecastle over the forepeak, by the ship's railing, above the ship's ram and figurehead where he held up a clear crystal instrument gingerly in hand as if gauging the wind. He sensed Kazarhan remained belowdecks, perhaps preferring the dim light within the ship's hull to the bright sunlight on the deck. Ahead of him, beyond the top of the stairs, Wrindanneth and Slate waited at the quarterdeck's center, beneath the shade of the billowing mizzenmast. Aroganji stood beyond Wrindanneth and Slate by the ship's aft railing directly above the rudder.

Opening both arms, robes hanging down at the elbows, Yip looked at his friends and asked innocently, "Who would like to be first?"

With a quick furtive glance at one another, Slate and Wrindanneth simultaneously pointed at each other and blurted, "Him!"

Yip could not help but laugh. The two were so alike in many ways that most of their disagreements stemmed from whomever said what the other was thinking first.

"If you would like, I can share with all three." Looking to Wrindanneth he added, "If you can break away from piloting for a while?"

"We're under clear skies and over safe lands. The only excitement I've had steering thus far is trying to keep awake. She'll be fine on autopilot for a bit."

Hearing his friends' conversation, and a tacit summons from Wrindanneth, Aroganji joined everyone by the floating silver control sphere.

"Before I begin, does anyone have any questions?"

Slate grunted and grinned, a gesture largely hidden by his full beard. "I'm not gonna end up all soft and sentimental like tha rest o' ya if I do this am I?"

Yip understood that he was joking, but there was a very slight undercurrent of concern there as well, even if Slate would never admit to it. "You will be no more sentimental or soft than you were before the transfer."

"Think of what I am about to share as a lesson, one that you will see and feel directly. What you choose to do with that lesson and how you respond are up to you."

A sardonic grin at the ready, Wrindanneth said, "The transfer won't be tainted by Dwarf sweat and beer swill will it? I'd hate to have the secret to saving the universe ruined by a malodorous rock mite."

His bushy eyebrows quickly lurching up, Slate cried out, "Wha—!"

Keeping his face composed and even, Yip interjected, "After visiting Jarvis, Slate will never again have any 'flavor of the road' about him. Even if he did, no matter how pungent, I doubt his ripeness would pose any real risk."

Nodding in understanding, Wrindanneth replied, "Besides to the flea and mite colonies that had once called him home."

"Ya red bearded Cave Troll! This is serious business. Stop yer foolishness or I'll shave yer head and use yer shag ta gag ya!"

Aroganji, meanwhile, smiled brightly as one watching the most entertaining of sporting events.

"You will have to relax and open your mind to me when I make the transfer for I cannot give what you are unwilling to receive. If you like and this perspective helps, you may relax as if in preparation for a nap and treat what I give as a welcome dream."

"When I am ready, I will lightly touch each of your foreheads in turn. You will know what I know, see what I have seen, and feel what I have felt in relation to energy creation and the application of the Dragon's Gate."

"Before the transfer can begin, however, I will have to compose my thoughts and experiences in a coherent fashion so that they will indeed make sense and be usable by you."

"When the transfer is complete and you feel this knowledge has been successfully infused to you, open your eyes in recognition. You will have ample time to reflect, dwell upon, and make sense of what you have been given after I know all is done and you are well. I will be by your side in the days ahead to answer any questions you may have and to offer further guidance as you practice and explore."

"Is everyone ready?"

Wrindanneth responded, "As long as your thoughts don't take as long to compose as Slate's. Otherwise, we might crash while we wait."

Before Slate could retort, Yip rejoined, "I am certain that Slate would be able to order and present his experiences as well as I can hope to do if given the opportunity."

When no more replies came, he added one more comment. "I am honored that the Home Guard have decided to learn how to manifest the energies of the Dragon's Gate in our mutual efforts to ensure that life will continue to prosper in the universe. This is a greater boon than I had ever hoped to come of our time together."

"Even so, for you three, learning this technique will be especially important for our immediate futures may depend upon it. If, sometime in the future, I fail or fall and am unable to complete what we have begun together, our ultimate success may fall upon one of you."

"So optimistic!" Wrindanneth chided him lightly.

"The Cabal yet threatens our world and others because many have failed before us. I do not hold myself any differently than those who have come before."

"But we try nonetheless," added Aroganji reassuringly.

"Aye. Now let's be on with it! I don't want ta miss brunch!"

Smiling, Yip began as he had before, gathering energy into himself that he would then use as a bridge to transfer the living knowledge across and through into the minds of his friends.

Closing his eyes, he relaxed deeply, letting his lungs fill with air and his body fill with vitality. As he did so, Slate, Aroganji, and Wrindanneth closed their eyes in preparation. With each breath, he composed his thoughts and impressions, understanding and insights relating to Azaelle's gift and its application in preparation for the transfer.

More so than he had with the Home Guard, he tried to convey the depth and complexity of his experience, the entire range of his feeling, the breadth of his concern, and the true enormity and significance of his insights. He would give as true and full an accounting as he could for his friends.

When he was ready and all was in order, he opened his eyes and placed his fingertips lightly first on Aroganji's forehead, then on Slate's, and finally upon Wrindanneth's. Between each transference, he took the time necessary to recompose himself and reorder his thoughts lest something be overlooked or missed.

Standing by his companions at the ready should something unforeseen occur, he waited until each finally opened his eyes in distant, clouded recognition. When everyone had responded as requested, he left them to drift undisturbed through his experiences as he had with Raour'Saqan for he had already imposed more upon the sanctity of their minds than he would otherwise have wished.

Returning down the stairs to the main deck, he passed the spot where Llyewia had spun his hammock of moonbeams and starlight which had now disappeared in the sunlight and approached Eidelion, Daerdros, and Orogast. They had been joined by Llyewia during his time with Slate, Wrindanneth, and Aroganji. If they were ready and available, he would attempt the transfer to them next.

"May the Light's blessing be with you on this day, Yip," offered Eidelion raising a hand in greeting.

"And with you all every day," he replied with a bow including Eidelion, Orogast, Llyewia, and Daerdros.

Acknowledging Yip's undertakings earlier this morning, Eidelion said, "Are your efforts meeting with success?"

"Those I have visited would be better qualified to answer."

Offering a summary of his impressions, Llyewia said, "Yip has indeed offered a way to hope for those who are able to make the journey."

Trusting his officer's word at face value, Eidelion nodded and said shortly, "Very good. Very good, indeed."

Then Eidelion smiled and looked at Yip with excitement in his eyes. "Are you ready to begin?"

Bowing, Yip answered, "I am."

Before Yip commenced, Llyewia dismissed himself in an elegant bow. "I will take my leave while you prepare. Fare the well."

"Thank you, Llyewia."

Turning back to the three Home Guard waiting before him, he said, "While you relax and make ready, I will gather the energy into myself necessary to make the transmission. You have but to open your minds and wait with calm attention."

"Once I am ready and have ordered my experiences for each one of you in turn, I will lightly touch your forehead to bridge the gap between us. When I do so, if you are receptive, I will transfer my experiences to you."

"You may wish to treat the knowledge and experience that I share as a dream, to be viewed and incorporated into your beings over time and through practice."

"Even though I give you my knowledge and experiences pertaining to the Dragon's Gate—knowledge of energy formation, creation, and application on how to overcome the *chi* voids created by the Cabal—you will have to develop the skill and competency essential for its proper application for that is a road that I cannot take for you."

"When the transfer is complete, signal to me that all is well by briefly opening your eyes in recognition. After you have done so, I will leave you to integrate my experience as you see fit."

"If ever there is more you would know, you have but to ask."

"Do you have any questions?"

Orogast replied, "I am quite unlike the others here, will that make a difference in how the transfer will take place or pose any risks?"

"Although your body and mind are quite different from mine, we are all enlivened by the same energy. My thoughts, feelings, and impressions may be foreign to you and your makeup, but the *chi* that we all share will guide in their proper integration."

"Where the *chi* leaves off, your mind will do the rest, interpreting and incorporating the experience in a way that comes naturally to you and your makeup."

"If you were to fight or rebel against this process after opening yourself to me, then there are many risks that you would face. That is why I will wait with you before taking my leave. If all does not go well, I will have to retrieve what I have given. There is no other choice."

"What would that mean, then?" asked Orogast.

"I would need to dissipate the excess *chi* in your body that would have been used to aid in the transfer of knowledge. With this energy gone, you will have no way to hold on to the thoughts and impressions I have given and they would fade away like a once remembered dream. If you still wished to learn the technique, I would have to train you personally in the methods of the Dragon's Gate."

His tone serious, he added, "Given the short time we have together, we may not have that option."

"Is that outcome likely?"

Yip smiled. "I have only transmitted this knowledge directly in this way to a Dracodaeran, an Elf, multiple H'era on a previous occasion, a Dwarf, and two Men. Given the diversity of Life's expression in the universe, I would say that those few are a very small sample, but all have been willing, open, and receptive participants."

"And those you have shared this knowledge with are now able to replicate your skill?"

Yip gave a small shrug, offering, "Whether or not the transference was ultimately successful, I cannot say for, thankfully, no one has had to apply the knowledge I have given, much less have they had the requisite time to adequately practice the skill."

He continued, "With time and dedicated practice, however, I am confident that anyone can apply the technique for I am not special in any way." He gave a brief laugh, remembering many of his own failings and missteps during his training and tutelage at the monastery. "My teacher, Master Wei, always preferred the most difficult students."

When Orogast remained silent, he asked, "Are there any more questions?"

Now Daerdros took the opportunity to speak, her voice measured and calm, as she always seemed to be. "Will you be able to read any of our thoughts or feelings in this process?"

"No. That is a skill to which I cannot claim to have mastered. If there is something you wish to share and have the skill, the connection between us will allow it, but otherwise your mind and experience remain closed to me."

Respecting the sanctity of their essential natures, he added, "I would have it no other way."

Seeing that Daerdros appeared reassured by his answer, Yip asked, "Is there anything else that needs to be addressed?"

Eidelion had one final question. "Will we need to seek you out for assistance in our training after we are done?"

"Everything you need to know should be contained within the experiences I will compose and share. Although you will have the knowledge that you need, I will, however, aid you in your practice as needed or requested."

With a brief nod, Eidelion said, "Understood."

Eidelion waited a moment for any more responses from his lieutenants, after receiving no further comment, with obvious excitement in his tone, he then said, "Let's begin!"

For the fourth time that day, Yip gathered the living energy around himself inward with each breath, readying himself for the transfer. Buoyant and light, filled with vitality and expansiveness, he spent the next several minutes collecting himself ensuring that everything needed by those awaiting his touch would be ready, accessible, and usable.

When all was in order, his mind and body full of remembrance, he lightly touched the foreheads of each Home Guard in turn. First resting his finger-tips on Eidelion, then Daerdros, and finally Orogast, he imparted the knowledge they would need to open the Dragon's Gate and create the *yuan-chi* necessary to overthrow Ur'Daus's voids. He finished with a soft exhale, letting the excess *chi* fade away, and waited for a response from the recipients.

Her eyes clear and focused, Daerdros, opened her eyes briefly before closing them once more. A few moments later, Eidelion opened his eyes with a firm nod before returning to introspection. A few minutes passed before Orogast finally opened his eyes in acknowledgement, although he seemed much less relaxed than his two companions.

Sensing all was in order, Yip once again took his leave, moving easily toward the front of the ship where Spreesprocket continued his measurements.

Approaching the Gnome, Yip watched him busily moving to and fro at the ship's fore holding the clear crystalline instrument aloft in hand, occasionally swirling it through the air with a faint tinkling sound or pausing to scratch his chin in thought before moving on to a new position where he would examine the instrument again. Each time Spreesprocket paused, the Gnome gazed intently into the depths of the crystalline apparatus as if reading and deciphering complex formulae.

Yip could see nothing within the confines of the instrument itself, although he could sense magic radiating from within the device. He could also feel energy moving into its confines, presumably where the contrivance analyzed some critical information in some way.

Lost in his own thoughts, Spreesprocket did not acknowledge his presence. Curious about the Gnome's activities, he was in no hurry to interrupt Spreesprocket either. Finally, when Spreesprocket almost walked into him on one of his sampling sweeps, the Gnome stopped abruptly and said, "Oh! Hi, Yip!"

"Good day to you, Spreesprocket."

Still curious, Yip asked, "What are you doing?"

Quickly glancing down at his instrument a bit self-consciously, Spreesprocket said, "Oh that? I'm measuring slight permutations and fluctuations in the Phlogiston!"

Unfamiliar with the term, he asked, "What is Phlogiston?"

Momentarily speechless, which was a rare occurrence for any Gnome, especially one given the opportunity to answer a question, Spreesprocket merely gaped at Yip for a moment. "You don't know what Phlogiston is?"

Yip smiled. "Perhaps I do. Perhaps I do not. I may call it by something else."

Spreesprocket smacked his forehead loudly. "Of course!"

"Phlogiston is the source of the spark of life!"

"In Gnomish, we call the ignition of Phlogiston Deur Spricken Sprack which means something like 'the Omnispark' in the Common Tongue. Of course Phlogiston does not burn, but life arises because of its energy, the excitation of its essence. Magical arts evolved from an understanding of its principles and manipulation. Most Men call the manipulation of Phlogiston magic. Our Dwarven cousins share an interpretation very close to ours and call this energy 'Brendle's spark' which hearkens to the original forge and flames that in their cosmology first shaped and then breathed life into the universe."

Without wishing to arouse further ontological discussion, Yip bowed replying, "I am familiar with the concept. Thank you for the insight."

Instead, he followed with another question. "So you wish to see variance in the intrinsic energies around us?"

"Exactly. The Phlogistonic Subresonance Preignition Potentiometer contained herein measures the energetic potential of the Phlogiston in the immediate vicinity."

"And what do you see when you gaze within?" asked Yip remarking on Spreesprocket's continual examination of the instrument's contents, the interior of which eluded his direct gaze.

"At the current settings, I see the fields of potentiation arising, shifting, interacting, and returning to their source on multiple scales and intensities."

Yip smiled. Spreesprocket's vision sounded very much like his own.

Spreesprocket grinned brightly in return. "In addition to being my most trusted instrument with a wide array of additional measuring and analytical functions, it is also a pocket organizer, day calendar, messaging and communication system, algorithm processor, voice recorder and transcriber, reference library, multitool, translation device, flashlight, learning aid, thought transference system, mustache trimmer, water bottle, storage trunk, food processor, entertainment and gaming system, tooth brush, lighter, life coach, personal assistant, and back scratcher."

Beaming excitedly, Spreesprocket added, "Mostly, though, I have been checking for holographic messages from my cousin Cogwhistle. He and his wife are expecting a new addition to their Warren any day now!"

Yip smiled appreciatively.

How could one not like a Gnome?

Curious, Yip asked, "You said the device can transfer thoughts?"

"Yep. Most Gnomes learn their lessons directly from their teachers through thought transference once we have developed solid, sound personalities, an educational foundation to build upon, certain cognitive, ethical, and reasoning faculties, and the analytical skills necessary to make use of our instructors' knowledge. We generally learn in this way at night because transference while the student is sleeping has been shown to be the most effective and efficient for us through rigorous totally blind studies. Otherwise, our minds are too active and focused on other activities to properly absorb and integrate the lessons given."

"Of course, with the many quirks intrinsic to Gnomish character and cultures, it pays to let someone else experience thought transference lessons first, especially from unknown or lesser known professors. Generally, that's what we use underclassmen for in institutions of higher learning—educational mental guinea pigs. If a lesson doesn't work out, you won't be subjected to its rigors or torment!"

"Otherwise, you may be prone to develop some of the unwelcome or undesirable traits of the teacher from whom you have directly learned the lesson as, no matter how objective, bits of their personality and perspectives always come through at the risk of your own."

"However, learning in this way really is not as risky as I make it sound. Many lessons are standardized, passed on, refined, and continually updated and reused. To avoid these concerns, quite a few are also presented directly by the Construct without regard to particular emotional foibles and predilections. The risk is more evident once students begin to pursue more specialized topics that are subject to major innovations or discoveries, varying interpretations and debate, or in areas that have less direct oversight and refinement as a result of infrequent use."

"Furthermore, beyond direct thought transference between Gnomes, for those few of a more adventurous disposition and mindset, we also enhance our learning and cognitive capabilities via a direct melding of minds, oftentimes with artificial intelligences created expressly for that purpose. The resulting synthetic intelligences have intellective capacities far beyond those granted by birth."

"Whole new realms of thought, abstraction, communication, magical, and psychic expression are opened as a result of these synthetic intelligences."

"Fascinating!" Yip had never envisioned a whole methodology and system of academic teaching geared directly around the concepts of xīnyì. Intellectual discovery and advancement in such a system would, in many ways, create tendencies and a push toward a common group mind alongside ever faster intellectual and technical development. Nor had he ever considered the possibilities of augmenting sentient intelligence in such an imaginatively thought-provoking way.

How this developmental process moved forward would be an interesting trend to observe.

"How long have you been of two minds brought together by as one?" Yip's calm eyes gazed deeply into Spreesprocket's own.

Spreesprocket opened his mouth to speak then stopped, a smile coming to his face. His own synthetic intelligence was a matter of personal choice, for the limitless vistas it opened. However, it was also a secret he guardedly carefully should he ever need an additional advantage. The exact nature of his mind was also a matter of Gnomish secrecy, a Paratechnological innovation reserved only for those chosen, of sufficient skill to create one, or deemed otherwise worthy.

Evaluating Yip's physical and psychic emanations carefully in light of his question, multiple higher order decision trees collapsing with each conclusive, parallel ratiocination, his deductions led him to only one viable, significant conclusion—Yip had known for some time.

Yip's expanded sense of awareness must have detected the subtle variations in his essence. He would then logically have wondered at their source. Not having direct access to Yip's awareness, merely a multi-dimensional model of its potential capabilities and functions, he noted that his friend's awareness potentialities were very expansive and acute indeed.

Though Yip had probably suspected for some time, he had just given Yip a name and the proper framework to understand his prior observations and deductions.

Despite his personal concerns, including his own desire for privacy, he knew one other thing without a doubt. Yip was, without question, worthy of his trust and openness. Or, more accurately, already having the information and subsequent proper deductions in place, as with any other, Yip could be trusted insofar as limited by his psycho-physiological vessel. The higher order computations and evaluations his mind now provided for him spontaneously to verify this fact were unnecessary.

The computations happening instantaneously, his smile turning into a laugh, Spreesprocket quipped, "I never mentioned that I had a synthetic intelligence!"

Yip shrugged slightly, recognizing that he had hit upon a point of some sensitivity to the Gnome. "You never had to."

Before Spreesprocket could reply, Yip added calmly, "Your secrets are your own, for you alone to reveal. You need not say more or fear I will say anything if such is your desire."

Spreesprocket laughed once more, all concern obviously gone as he spoke, "Do you not deserve confirmation of your solution of my own small riddle?"

Yip remained silent.

The smile on his lips brightened his lustrous eyes and small face as Spreesprocket spoke, "Though I keep the nature and contents of my mind to myself, I am able to do otherwise. You have shown yourself worthy of my trust, though my internal computations insist upon offering their confirmation of this all too obvious fact."

"Yes. I am of two minds made one and have been for many years. One is artificial, imbued with computational, sensory, and analytical capacities far beyond those of an ordinary mind. The other is my own mind granted at birth. Together, we are one synthetic sentience, each augmenting the other's strengths and abilities."

"Thanks to this developmental gift, I am capable of constantly expanding my own cognitive frontiers, able to interact directly with other minds, synthetic and natural alike, directly or through magical aetheric networks."

"There is little more wondrous than touching another open, curious mind directly, interacting and merging with the light of another consciousness on the most fundamental level!"

"When I close my eyes, I am able to see the lights of other consciousnesses as numerous and luminous as the stars in the heavens. Should they be willing, I am capable of interacting directly with them to share our mutual experiences, improve our knowledge, and gain a deeper understanding of the greater multiverse. In this way, my own small light seeks to model and replicate the greater Light that contains it."

"Through this constant seeking and cultivation, I am more capable of understanding the Omnispark, Deur Spricken Sprack, and Its Light brightens my own."

Now his own eyes peered deeply into Yip's. "You and I are very much alike then. You cultivate a pure, unbounded awareness to gain a direct, intimate experience of the dynamic multiverse that unfolds within and around you. I seek ever greater cognitive capacities to understand its fundamental nature."

"Each of our minds, then, are two fingers, albeit on separate hands, pointing at the same moon."

"And where does your mind end and another begin?" Yip's simple question brought a light of intellectual joy to Spreesprocket's visage.

"The answer is a matter of perspective, just as truth is relative to the station of the viewer. Fundamentally, my mind is an integral part of a limitless oceanic existence, interconnected and interdependent across multiple scales, dimensions, modalities, times, forces, interactions, and measures. Practically, from the reference of a casual, informed outside observer, my mind is a self-sustaining metamagical abstraction functioning as a disembodied intelligence temporarily tethered to an organic vessel."

"From this latter perspective, though not precluded by the former, both mind and body are mutable and the situation of their relationship and expression can be changed at any moment."

"However, these perspectives, like any other, are best experienced directly."

Curious, for Spreesprocket's perspective was similar, yet so very different from his own, Yip asked, "Why remain tethered to the body when such a universe beckons?"

Spreesprocket laughed, a glow of deep appreciation in his eyes. "Why not?"

More seriously, he answered, "The realms of the senses are as wondrous and worthy of understanding as those of the mind. The world of abstract cognition is no more glorious than the morning sun, a smile, or the worlds created between friends when viewed through the eyes of one filled with deep appreciation. The body is an amazing instrument capable of deep insight into the fundamental realities of the macroverse. I would not give it up without need."

Spreesprocket laughed, adding, "Especially when I can improve upon it!"

"Beyond its intrinsic value as a means to interact with and understand the world, the body provides the primary vehicle to experience other beings who are endeavoring to engage the totality of truth and existence in a very similar way."

Smiling, he added, "Also, it's fun!"

Finishing, Spreesprocket concluded, "There may come a time when I drop the body, or take up a form entirely alien to the one of my birth, but for now, it is one of the primary pillars of my existence. It can be changed, and I with it, at need. Until that need ends, we will continue together."

Yip bowed. "You are to be respected. Your efforts bring much truth and clarity to those who would see."

Spreesprocket returned Yip's bow. "Your words apply equally to you, your perspective and insights, and your efforts."

Seeing the ready opportunity, for their conversation had only offered confirmation of Spreesprocket's willingness to learn, explore, and seek after truth and positive outcomes, Yip asked, "Would you like for me to share the knowledge of the Dragon's Gate with you in this manner?"

Spreesprocket chuckled, replying, "I wouldn't have it any other way! Time permitting, when this ordeal is behind us, I would like very much to share our mutual experience that we may glean a deeper appreciation for the greater multiverse."

Holding the small crystalline construct up for Yip to see, he added, "For the time being, however, I will use this simple tool for this purpose so that the nature of my own gifts will not be so readily revealed."

Pausing as he handed the small crystalline device to Yip, Spreesprocket added cautiously, "You understand that the knowledge you give to me will be stored on this device and may be shared with others in the same fashion?"

Now Yip laughed. "I wouldn't have it any other way!"

Holding out his hand, Spreesprocket offered Yip the delicate instrument. Taking it gingerly in hand, Yip felt a surprising solidity and firmness as he held the object in his palm. He knew then that the device was designed for rigorous use and harsh conditions. Examining Spreesprocket's instrument, for he knew not what to rightly call it, the apparatus looked something like a flat, smooth translucent piece of glass that had been tapered slightly toward the center to fit comfortably in the palm of a Gnomish hand whether gripped tightly or resting loosely in the palm. Rectangular in length, the object was no longer than an outstretched Gnomish hand and slightly narrower in width than a Gnomish palm.

In his hand, however, the implement was rather small, about the length of his index finger and twice as wide. The tiny size of the device made him marvel all the more at its complexity and functionality.

Holding the apparatus in hand, once again he gathered himself, closing his eyes to order his experience and knowledge as he drew in the *chi* necessary to fuel its transfer. When all was ready, he focused his intention upon the implement and let his experience flow outward and into the device.

Aware of the process as it unfolded, he transferred his thoughts into a receptacle designed exactly for that purpose. All fit into place with ease in a totality of experience ready for access. There was no apparent incorporation or filing of what he gave. The information existed exactly as it had been given ready for future use.

Although many found fault with Gnomish invention, in this regard, this device performed spectacularly.

Handing the miraculous instrument back to Spreesprocket, Yip bowed and said, "That truly is a wondrous invention."

Spreesprocket smiled as he took back the translucent device. "Perhaps when we have time, I will show you some of its other functions!"

Always intent on learning, Yip responded, "That would be most welcome. I am certain that Aroganji and Wrindanneth would be interested as well."

He shook his head. "I could not imagine my life as an Initiate of K'un Lun with such a wonder!"

"Whenever you want to see the Epistemic Noetic Numenetic Integrating Summator, just let me know. ENNIS is very friendly and is always ready to make new friends!"

Considering how such devices could be of use to his brethren, should they be willing to accept the idea, he added, "Perhaps ENNIS has friends who feel similarly?"

Spreesprocket nodded. "Perhaps. When all is said and done inquiries can be made."

Yip left with a smile, letting Spreesprocket return to his studies. Although one never knew exactly how a Gnome would make use of information, something creative always resulted from the endeavor.

The grin remaining on his face, he imagined some of the possibilities of Gnomish ingenuity, none of which he would have ever believed to be possible just short months before. However, in a world where belief was made manifest, anything was possible—as Gnomes demonstrated quite frequently.

While Spreesprocket once again immersed himself in the Phlogiston, Yip headed belowdecks to seek out Kazarhan. Walking past Eidelion, Orogast, and Daerdros who remained absorbed in their internal work, he waved as he passed Llyewia who stood along the ship's railing gazing outward into the sky.

Moving farther aft, he reached the door leading belowdecks. With a slight creak, the door opened upon the dim half-light below. Sensing Kazarhan in the hold, he proceeded downward and then turned around to go down a shorter second set of stairs before reaching the interior door entering upon the ship's largest interior space.

Although not certain, he thought that Kazarhan preferred remaining belowdecks in the semi-darkness because the ship felt more secure here, much like the comfortable confines of a cave without the wide open spaces and sense of constant motion apparent on the decks. Slate would sooner remain on solid ground than fly and would rather be below ground than above, though these preferences were changing with his continued exposure to heights and movement aboard airships and on Tellanon.

Opening the door and holding it propped ajar while he stood at the threshold, he noted that the expanse of the hold remained well organized despite all of its new occupants. A few hanging hammocks and loosely fastened satchels were the most obvious additions to the walls holding the hanging ropes, netting, and spare cloth composing the basic items required to repair the sails and rigging. The spare chests holding their backup provisions and supplies appeared untouched, all remaining securely held in place where originally positioned.

At the far end of the hold, beyond the foremast, nestled in a nook between two large oaken chests nearest to the ship's fore, Kazarhan kneeled in silent contemplation. Beneath the soft glow of the magical orbs overhead, a halo of intense light was visible to Yip around Kazarhan's stooped form.

Seeing the Dwarf occupied by his absorption, he turned to leave, ready to return at a more favorable time. Before he shut the door behind him, however, Kazarhan called out, "Hold!"

Standing quietly, he turned to face the chamber once more while he waited for Kazarhan to make ready.

With an exhale loud enough to hear across the breadth of the hold, Kazarhan stood and began walking toward him asking, "What can I do fer ya?"

Bowing deeply while Kazarhan approached, he said, "I have come to discuss a time that you may find agreeable to have me transfer the teachings on the manifestation of the Dragon's Gate to you."

"No need fer discussion." Kazarhan barked a short laugh. Having reached where Yip stood on the small landing overlooking the cargo space, Kazarhan gazed at him sedately under the dense cover of light gray eyebrows.

"Is now a good time or shall I come back?"

"Neither."

He waited patiently for Kazarhan to explain.

"I won't be learnin' yer teachin's."

Yip nodded in understanding. He had not expected this from one of the Home Guard, but each member came from different traditions where his instruction may be treated as an unwelcome intrusion. Furthermore, although their loyalty was expressly vowed to represent and uphold the good of all sentient races on or with ties to Tellanon and Ea'ae, many also implicitly represented the interests of their race in the Home Guard and therefore had dual allegiances between their people or nation and Tellanon and its interests.

Yip hid his disappointment. He had already achieved far more than he had ever hoped. Nor did he ask why Kazarhan remained reticent.

Kazarhan, however, held no reservations. "Yip, I'll talk plainly. That's how I've always been and how I'll always be. I think ya want ta do tha right thing and I won't fault ya fer that. A man that gives his effort t'tha service o' others and their well-bein' is ta be commended."

"But yer way is not my way nor will it ever be."

He held up a hand forestalling any protest, although Yip was not going to offer any. "Now before ya argue otherwise, explainin' perhaps that I should 'expand my view', 'try ta fit or interpret yer teachin's within my framework', 'that tha *chi* ya speak of is no different than Brendle's own embers', or some such balderdash, know this—I am first a Kor'Dannan, anointed by my people and my liege, and a Dur'kazak in a tradition that goes back long before tha first Men ever stepped on tha shores o' Dharia. I uphold tha traditions o' my ancestors and I do not wish ta change them fer ya or anyone else."

"If Slate wishes ta take yer knowledge unto himself, then that is his will but not mine. Nor do I think it proper fer a Priest o' Brendle ta do so."

Yip bowed in understanding. "If Brendle asks otherwise, or you change your mind, you have but to ask."

Kazarhan remained silent with his thick arms folded across his barrel-chest as he watched Yip leave.

For his part, Yip did not argue that *chi* was in fact no different than Brendle's flame. His place was not to explain or alter other people's points of view. Whatever Kazarhan's feelings, understanding, or experience toward the energy he called upon in supplication or to fuel his forge, Kazarhan had already modified his traditions when he had accommodated the teachings and rigors of the Home Guard even if his service was at the behest of his Thane.

He was not going to ask Kazarhan to reconcile with more. Kazarhan deserved the freedom of his own mind.

Returning up the stairs to the light of the day, he began circulating among his companions seeking to answer questions for those who had them and to offer insight and understanding where an unusual concept or question arose.

In the days ahead, there would be many. It was his duty to ensure that all questions were answered not only to his satisfaction but to the satisfaction of the minds seeking answers.

Meeting and fostering the desire for understanding implicit in the questions asked was as important to his friends' growth and development as was the actual knowledge given for only through familiarity, practice, and a will for more would ultimate success follow.

HAPPENSTANCE

Leaves rustle in the wind
upon gnarled bare branches.
Blown free, who hears them fall?

The docks of Tellanon were thick with travelers, each busy about an appointed task. Warm sunlight streamed downward in bright columns through the gaps in downy clouds drifting sedately through the heavens. People and races of more shapes and sizes than the clouds above marched hither and yon in patterns and arrangements dictated by the course of their wills.

Only one man appeared to stand still amid the crowd, his travel-worn robes whipping slightly in the breeze coming through the bustling fray.

He paid no attention to those pushing past him brushing shoulder-to-shoulder, those who bumped or glanced disapprovingly at him for obstructing their path, or those who excused themselves as they walked by. Nor did he read the air above, shimmering so vibrantly with the unfolding possibilities of hundreds of untapped, unread, and unhindered lives for their destinies did not call to him or pull him away from his inspection.

Looking steadily back and forth, his thoughts and essence hidden, he scanned each airship tethered along the jetty as carefully as one at a market surveying items of worth for trade or sale—potential items of profit to be used and later discarded.

The various shapes, sizes, and crews did not concern him. He cared not if the ship beneath his study was a gleaming silver corsair from an alien world or a dilapidated trading vessel whose last journey may arrive quicker than her captain hoped. He did not care if the crew were Man or Elf, Gnome or Dwarf, or exotic entities that Ea'ae only harbored for a short time. Likewise he did not concern himself with whether the crew may be openly hostile or unwilling to take on passengers.

The ships and their crews were only a means to an end.

He cared only for where they were heading, where their destiny would lead him.

There she was!

The perfect vessel!

Resting his eyes ever so lightly on the airship before him, he stopped his inspection of the docks and her ships.

A small trading ship tethered halfway down the spiraling dock caught his attention, pulling him forward, urging him to action.

Keeping his goal ever in the fore of his mind, lines of opportunity altered around him wildly, blazing possibilities radiating in each and every direction, shifting as he moved, adjusting as actions changed and occurred. But the strongest, most direct, and most likely hazard lay before him, a trail in the sand leading to a destination he visualized and willed into existence.

Surveying the path of chaotic chance that he would take to the vessel, he smiled widely, a gesture that left his heart cool, one that benefited little from the warmth of the sun.

His course set, he began to walk forward, the chill smile still set on his face.

He would introduce himself to the captain.

Then he would claim his new ship.

He knew not where the course of his destiny led, but he followed it willingly.

SOUTHWARD

Water flows over
submerged rounded stones
calling to the birds above.

Wrindanneth was elated.

Yip had revealed a secret the likes of which he had not imagined possible! As a Priest of Maeth Onai, he had plumbed the depths of secrets hidden from even the most ardent seekers. He had been taught to summon and command divine energies, but he had never learned how to create them! Nor had he ever even considered such a thing possible until meeting Yip, watching him learn and grow, and then hearing him describe his own experiences.

Amazing events seemed to rush and churn about Yip as actively as water courses and jumps over submerged stones in a rain fed mountain rill. He was more than happy to capitalize on the opportunities.

Maeth would be pleased to learn of this knowledge. That is, if he decided to share it. Some secrets were, after all, worth keeping.

If he could keep it.

Perhaps Maeth had taught him the value of knowledge a little too well.

Now it was up to him to determine how best to apply this newly granted talent. If his intuition was correct, then perhaps Yip had opened a door to untold fortuity.

Once he had learned how to apply his newfound knowledge of the Dragon's Gate and fully explored these possibilities, perhaps he would no longer need a teacher for whom he needed to supply a constant tithe.

Wearing a rare smile, he surveyed the decks.

Slate stood locked blade against blade with Daerdros at the ship's fore practicing his axe work. Back and forth they battled, Daerdros's blade flicking faster than the eye could perceive, but, more often than not, Slate avoided her strikes and even managed to mount a few, generally unsuccessful, counters of his own.

Wrindanneth had to grant the Dwarf a measure of grudging respect for he was almost able to hold his own against the Blade Master—another feat he would have deemed almost impossible until he had seen it unfold before his eyes.

Slate, too, had come far in a short time.

Yes, there was much he had to learn. Wrindanneth would never admit any weakness or failing to anyone else, nor would he let Aroganji learn of his feelings through their shared bond, for secrets were best kept close to the heart, but he was always dispassionately objective about his own capabilities. These past few days he had gained more respect for his friends watching them train with the Home Guard on the ship's decks than he would have thought possible before their journey began.

One should never underestimate an enemy, but, even more importantly, one should never underestimate a friend or the possibilities presented by their company.

Yes, this quest was turning out to be more rewarding than he would have believed and they had not yet truly begun. Watching Slate spar with Daerdros, he reflected on his own practice, how he looked forward to his daily regimen of training with Orogast, Spreesprocket, and Llyewia, and all he gained from these short, intense sessions.

Their magical skills constantly pushed him to new heights and continually forced him beyond the limits he had set for himself. With their ceaseless testing and prodding, he came away each day awash in new ideas and applications for even the most mundane of spells.

Between working with them and with Aroganji in tandem, soon enough even Maeth might not recognize his pupil.

Never dropping his grim smile, Wrindanneth recognized the true value in his continual training and development. With time and determination, the student would become the master.

With mastery would come freedom.

Daerdros was fast.

Far too fast for him to effectively counter without the use of Brendle's fire. Her blade flashed at him again and again with deadly precision, each time marking her intended target with a red trickle of blood. Without the heat of Brendle's forge enlivening his blade, Slate had to rely on skill alone to test his blade against the Caer'collas.

A test which he failed over and over.

Suppressing the flames seething through him had become ever harder since interacting with Yip and learning of the Dragon's Gate. Whenever he moved, whenever he breathed, he felt the heat of Brendle's fires rushing through his bones, aching to be released, yearning for expression.

For whatever reason, understanding how to summon the energies of the Dragon's Gate seemed to have enhanced his ability to call upon the energies of Brendle's forge. When he had time, he would have to discuss this faculty with Yip. As things stood now, however, he had almost as much trouble restraining the kindling of those flames as he did fending off Daerdros's lightning swift blade.

Blast it! Another touch! She was makin' this too easy!

Slate almost yelled out his frustration, but kept his thoughts to himself, instead waiting for another flash of her sword indicating a successful attack.

If he truly expected to master his axe, which thankfully had remained quiet after his first reprimand, Duraeleon shamed into silence sharing the same embarrassment he now felt, then many more such lessons in humility would follow.

At least when Daerdros bested him sparring, she used a blade.

Yip, in contrast, did it barehanded. At least Yip was kind enough to restrain himself in his counterattacks.

Slate felt the stings of Daerdros's reminders all too well.

Gritting his teeth, Slate waded forward fueling the flight of his blade with his rage, all the while attempting to restrain those same fires from consuming him totally.

So much had changed in such a short period of time!

Aroganji stood behind Wrindanneth at the far end of the quarterdeck with his back to his friend. Thoughts, impressions, and ideas washed through him clamoring for attention, exploration, and organization with a creative energy that surged and pulsed as vibrantly as his heart.

The five elements, the five essential permutations of the Wu-hsing moved all around in ceaseless change, he felt them almost exactly as before. But now, his understanding and appreciation for them had altered, morphing and expanding into a realm of conception of an entirely different order.

The five elements—water, earth, fire, metal, and wood—no longer adequately cataloged the summation of his understanding of how the universe around him flowed and transitioned from one form into the next.

Where before there were five, now there were seven.

He now understood this clearly.

Overarching and uniting the five principal elements was Mind—his ability as a magician to interact with, summon, and manipulate these primal forces of change. He also understood that what he now felt as Mind was part of a much larger integrated framework whose limits were far beyond his conception.

Undergirding this new framework was something he only understood as Void—the origin of the five primary transformations. This Void, what Yip sometimes described through *fu*, his experience of return to the Source, as Wuji, so full of potential and possibility, the wellspring of the Taiji, the Supreme Ultimate, was the very same root from which *chi* arose and fell, the beginning before the beginning—the indescribable Source at the root of creation, uniting Heaven and Earth in one totality, giving birth to all existence simultaneously.

While he had always experienced these elemental transitions and transformations as part of a complete whole, this unity had expanded into new dimensions, the addition of which opened untold potentialities.

He felt as though he had woken up one morning only to realize that now he spoke a new language. Letting these subtle permutations of thought and feeling flow through him, he felt that he was now capable of mathematics of an order known only to the most learned of sages. His world had indeed expanded as if he only now realized that the planet was truly round, extending beyond the unknown horizon, not a flat plain limited merely by what he could see, with all the latent and manifest opportunities that extra dimension implied.

He felt inspiration as he had never known before.

Reflecting on the state of his mind these past few days since his experience of sharing consciousness with Yip, more had come through the connection between them than Yip had necessarily intended or described. Perhaps because Yip felt closer to Wrindanneth, Slate, and himself than he did the other companions, Yip may have been more open with them, sharing more than he had with the others.

In talking with Wrindanneth and Slate, each had gained new perspectives on their own traditions and practices, a newfound wellspring of inspiration and facility that seemed, at least for the time being, to act as a lens with which to reevaluate and expand upon their prior knowledge.

Although he had discreetly asked members of the Home Guard whether or not anything had changed as a result of the transfer for them, by and large, each indicated that now they felt as though they would be capable of creating energy where none had been before given proper time and practice. They also felt confident that this would eventually allow them to overcome the Cabal's *chi* voids.

Nothing more, nothing less.

Llyewia may have gleaned more, but he was too cryptic to easily read without time and more insight. Kazarhan had been reluctant to talk at all, but that could be due to his Dwarven dourness. Daerdros had been almost as tight-lipped as Kazarhan, but she did indicate her thanks with her usual aloof confidence in her new abilities. Raour'Saqan displayed a fervent desire to unleash this newly cultivated talent upon his foes, but said little more beyond his thanks for Yip's open willingness to further the efforts of his people in battling the creatures of Darkness. Eidelion displayed an optimism that befitted the leader of such an august group. Spreesprocket had not yet even undergone the experience, instead he had stored the knowledge inside a most amazing magical artifact, but he promised to sleep on it when he had the chance. Of them all, Orogast seemed to be having the most difficulty adjusting to his new understanding, perhaps because his makeup and views were so very different from the others.

With all the time and opportunity ahead for training with the Home Guard, he was indeed quite curious to see how his friends continued to develop and how these new insights materialized.

Leaving his position at the railing, he decided the time had come to seek out Yip and discuss his concerns. He had observed and learned enough to realize that their interaction with Yip had changed both himself and his friends fundamentally.

Now he needed assurance that these changes were indeed all positive.

Aroganji found Yip in silent contemplation standing midship. Yip's eyes were closed, his knees and arms were slightly bent, and his breathing was so slow and even that he could not tell whether or not his friend was in fact inhaling and exhaling.

Despite his friend's stillness, he knew that Yip was aware of his presence for he could read his surroundings and sense others' approach even while at rest. There was so much that was unusual about Yip that his uncanny sphere of awareness was in some ways the least among them.

Taking position some distance away from Yip, he waited patiently for his friend to rouse himself. Aroganji respected his friend's practice too much to disturb him. If a situation warranted such interference, chances were that Yip would have broken his meditations long before the need for rousing.

He did not have to wait long for Yip had indeed noted his presence and recognized that he waited for Yip's attention. With surprising alacrity and fluidity, he watched Yip simultaneously stand to full height and turn to face him. The entire motion gave the impression of a statue returning to life with a suddenness that caught him off-guard even though he had been anticipating his friend's arousal.

"Greetings, Aroganji." Yip bowed as he always did. "How may I be of service?"

He bit back a smile. Yip always asked how he could be of service even before he was asked for his help.

He returned the bow. "I have come to you seeking clarity on several observations that I have made over the course of the past few days."

Yip listened quietly waiting for him to continue.

He did not make his friend wait overlong. "Ever since you shared Azaelle's gift with the rest of us, for those among the Four at least, things have been entirely different. Although I have not been able to discern any similar changes among the Home Guard, Wrindanneth, Slate, and myself have begun a process of unanticipated transformation."

When Yip remained silent, he asked, "Could you tell me why this process is occurring and whether or not the outcome will remain positive?"

Yip gave a brief nod. "I have sensed changes in your energy flows and patterns, your *li*, over the past few days but had only thought those to be the result of the knowledge given *xīnyì* and your new wellspring for practice. Perhaps we should discuss these changes and observations together."

Aroganji nodded in agreement. "Wrindanneth is at the piloting station. I will retrieve Slate from his practice with Daerdros and meet you there."

Guessing that Slate would welcome the reprieve, he sought his friend out where Slate struggled mightily against Daerdros's superior speed and skill.

Sweat coursed down Slate's ruddy face, joining the streams running over his thick shoulders and back. Aroganji was amazed he could still hold on to his axe after all the energy, and fluids, he had exerted in sparring with Daerdros.

Although Aroganji approached, Slate did not spare his friend even the briefest glance for his demanding partner allowed for no breaks in his concentration. Finally, after several grueling minutes of intense exchanges oftentimes leading to welts or small trickles of blood on Slate's legs, arms, or torso, Daerdros finally called their practice to a halt.

"Slate, I believe someone is here to see you." She smiled warmly at Aroganji, her exertions not marked by the slightest hint of perspiration upon her brow or heaviness of breath. In fact, although Slate might have misheard over his own heavy breathing, she might have been humming a light airy tune.

"Whaddya want?" Slate huffed, taking a moment to swipe his forearm across his brow before turning a steely gaze toward Aroganji.

Slate did not wish to be pulled from his training, no matter how difficult the regimen or poorly he fared. He wished to be thrown into the crucible bodily and reformed through hard work and toil. As such, Aroganji's presence was an unwelcome distraction.

Not meeting Slate's ire directly, Aroganji redirected his friend's intensity with a simple offer. "Yip and I would have a word with you when you are available. I'm sure you'll need to take a break soon for a bit of refreshment, a bit of cool ale perhaps."

Slate's eyebrows lifted immediately in interest. If there was one thing he liked more than swinging an axe, it was a full mug of the Thane's finest.

"Well, that's not rightly fer me ta decide. I'm here at Daerdros's pleasure. So long as she's willin' ta continue thrashin' me, I'm here ta take it."

Daerdros laughed at her persistent partner's comment, respecting his dedication. "You are free to take your leave, Slate. There will be more time tomorrow and in the days to come."

Slate gave a short respectful nod and struck his right fist across his chest, saying, "As ya wish. Our blades will cross again in tha mornin'."

"Indeed they will." Daerdros smiled fondly at Slate, advising, "Get some rest. I won't be as easy on you tomorrow."

Raising his eyebrows in surprise, Slate shook his head briefly and muttered under his breath, "O' all tha darn fool ideas I've had! Who volunteers ta get thrashed by a Blade Master?"

"Perhaps one who truly wishes to master the blade... Goodbye, Slate."

"Until tha morn." Slate returned his axe to its sheath and rubbed his arms as he turned to Aroganji and began walking toward the *Shrike*'s aft. "Where is this ale ya promised and what kind?"

Aroganji laughed. "I never promised you that I would give you any spirits. I only suggested that you might need some."

"Ya mean ta tell ya got me here on empty promises?"

"No. Only that you got yourself here on empty promises." He gave Slate a warm smile. "Isn't that the way of adventure?"

When Slate chuckled, Aroganji amended, "I'll see what we can find. Perhaps Wrindanneth can summon something suitable."

"Bah! With his poor excuse fer taste, I'll probably get Orc spit if I'm lucky. I'd be better off gettin' thrashed by Daerdros!"

Not needing to answer, they made their way back to where Wrindanneth and Yip waited at the ship's silver control module.

Seeing Aroganji and Slate approach, Wrindanneth whistled. "You two cut a mighty fine pair! Short and shorter!"

Slate growled, noting Yip waiting calmly by Wrindanneth's side. "Apparently tha only person who can tolerate ya is tha one person who can block out yer presence entirely!"

Aroganji laughed in agreement, not willing to be the butt of Wrindanneth's joke. "Truer words have never been spoken!"

Yip stepped forward, placing himself subtly between his friends, thereby averting their jests and drawing attention to himself. "Aroganji, you wished to discuss a matter of some significance together?"

Aroganji gave a brief nod. "Since the time of our joining with Yip, much has changed, much more than perhaps was intended. I have felt this transformation within myself, experienced the shifts and expansion in my own perceptions, and seen similar transfigurations in you."

He looked at Wrindanneth, Yip, and Slate before addressing his concerns. "The questions to be answered are several, the answers crucial."

"What has changed in each of us?"

"Why have we changed?"

"What will be the end result of this process of transformation?"

"Will these changes remain safe without negative side-effects?"

"I ask this of you because I do not think anything similar has happened with the Home Guard despite having gone through a similar process."

Never one to let his voice remain unheard, Slate replied first, "Ya're right about that, Aroganji. My bones've been burnin' since tha day Yip gave us knowledge o' tha Dragon's Gate, and I'm not talkin' about knowledge o' magic creation, although that's there all right."

He tapped his head with one thick finger. "I feel as though tha fires o' Brendle's forge are about ta erupt from my pores any instant and it's all I can do ta hold 'em back!"

Wrindanneth was a bit more tight-lipped in this case, not wishing to reveal too much. However, these were his friends, people who would give their life for his just as he would for theirs, so his ingrained reticence to share valuable knowledge was tempered somewhat. "Like Slate, the insights Yip shared have become an integrated part of my conscience. However, I display no physical symptoms or other indications of magical change. Exploring the matter, however, I have seen many other potential applications of energy creation and manipulation than the primary one shown to us by Yip."

"While my essential nature has not changed, the experience does seem to have altered my perspective and inspired me to consider problems from certain oblique angles that I would not have been aware of otherwise, providing the impetus to fuel my efforts ever higher."

"Perhaps these changes of which you speak are reflected and influenced by our own traditions and techniques of interacting with magic itself?"

"For example, Slate utilizes energy, Brendle's Spark, for feats in battle framed primarily around physical prowess infused by the power he summons whereas my approach to magical practice revolves around the mental exploration, application, and manipulation of energy."

Here Aroganji nodded in agreement. "I, too, have had particular insights into the nature of my magical practice that would reflect your surmise."

Listening to his friends speak, gleaning the reason for the manifestation of these changes, Yip said, "Perhaps more of myself came through than I had anticipated or intended."

Slate's eyebrows shot up as he asked, "How d'ya mean?"

"With the Home Guard, I shared everything I knew and felt that pertained to the techniques and application of the Dragon's Gate. I gave them as much as they needed to know to be successful should they ever need to use the ability along with the knowledge required to teach others to help engender a safer world."

"With you, I shared that knowledge and ability and more. Not only did I share my understanding and experience, I shared my feelings and perceptions, my concerns and insights, all in an effort to relay the true significance of the dangers that we will all face soon enough. While the Home Guard and any they teach may face the Cabal and their evil someday, we most certainly will as we move forward on our present course."

"The difference then is that I wished for you to be prepared for an immediate actuality while I wished for the Home Guard to have the tools to be prepared for a potentiality."

Yip remained quiet for a moment while he thought and then relived the experience of transferring his knowledge to his friends. "In so doing, because of my strong desire for your understanding, well-being, and future success, the *chi* guiding the inclusion of this knowledge and experience must have brought more of my perceptions and experience through the connection than I had anticipated. Or perhaps those views carried came with more potency than I had wished due to the feeling and import I ascribed to them and wished for you to understand."

"The process of the integration of my views with your own, the inclusion of a part of my fundamental nature, must have resulted in the changes and effects that you currently see here, Aroganji."

Aroganji nodded in understanding, although his underlying concern had not been addressed. "Where will these changes lead? Are we at risk in any way as a result of this process?"

"You will remain the person you have always been. Your experience and knowledge may expand to include areas influenced by my training and apprehension but otherwise your sense of who and what you are should remain unchanged. If that is not the case, and Aroganji you seem to have indicated that your sense of self and your surroundings has indeed changed"—here Yip smiled and shrugged, adding with a touch of humor, "then you will begin a journey of existential exploration that only your interest and motivation will limit."

Seeing his friends glance warily back and forth to each other, he continued. "As for whether or not risks to your health and safety are concerned, the same life-giving *chi* that flows through you flows through me. This *chi* was the vehicle for the transfer of my experience to you and it should cause no harm to you as it moves through your systems. Any additional knowledge I have given will likewise be incorporated into your selves as freely as your mind sees fit. Chances are, this process of synthesis will occur below the levels of your awareness and conscious recall."

"This integration should be very similar to the experience I shared with Master Wei when his essence enlivened mine in the caves of the Karadüm."

A smile returned to his lips as he noticed a look of relief spreading across Slate's brow. With sincerity and a tinge of humor, he added, "Like any path of transformation and development, however, the risks to yourself will need to be meted out by sound judgment and understanding, clear perception, and caution."

He spread his arms broadly. "You will learn and explore your new limits and abilities as thoroughly and naturally as any who study and grow—with care, continual refinement, and increasing ease and comfort."

He smiled brightly, finishing, "I will be here to help."

Slate muttered grimly, "Isn't that how all this got started in tha first place?"

"We now share a common journey on more levels than we fully know, Slate. In this passage together there is much opportunity and promise."

Wrindanneth chuckled with a twinge of wit and acridity, muttering, "Excellent! Something else to do together!"

Simultaneously, Slate grumbled, "That's just what tickles my whiskers."

Knowing all too well that nothing ever came too easily, his lessons with Daerdros only being the most recent example.

A glint of humor now evident in his eye, Wrindanneth looked at Yip and said, "Let's just hope I don't take to standing still like a tree and staring off into the distance all day."

Seeing his opportunity, Slate barked throatily, "At least ya'd be more interestin' ta be around!"

Sharing in his friends' jests and good cheer, Yip replied, "And I would welcome a partner to stand with."

"A man should never stand alone," intoned Slate solemnly.

"Unless he has to," finished Wrindanneth with a rare grin.

While Aroganji and Wrindanneth began discussions on the new opportunities for magical exploration and research they were now afforded, Yip motioned for Slate to follow him, walking toward the ship's starboard rail.

When Slate reached the barrier alongside him, he said, "For quite some time, I have been pondering ways to allow us to function more effectively together. Sharing my energy with you, Aroganji, and Wrindanneth is one such opportunity. Training with you to improve your timing and ability to read an opponent is another. However, mere movement and physical skill alone will not suffice to overcome the foes we may face ahead."

Glancing meaningfully toward Slate's axe, he continued, "Your axe, too, may harm many foes that a normal blade would not touch, but there may come a time when that is not enough, a time when your magical wards may fail."

"Hearing you speak of the heat, the power, rushing through your bones pushing outward for expression gave me an idea for a course we can take together to improve our effectiveness when the time comes."

Stroking his beard thoughtfully, unsure exactly what Yip was offering, Slate said, "What exactly are ya talkin' about, Yip?"

"You have seen how I wreath my hands in *chi* when entering into combat?"

"Aye. It's hard ta miss."

"That energy can be used to strike the life energy, the vitality, of a foe regardless of its type or form, whether the being is magical or mundane. Just as it can harm, it can also shield, for it protects my hands when I strike."

"And?" Slate knew all this as he had seen his friend in action and had discussed his use of *chi* in this way before.

"Although it is seldom done, for much demand is placed upon the individual when it is performed, it is possible to wreath the entire body in this energy for both protection and defense."

"I can see how that'd be possible, but I'm not followin' why ya're tellin' me."

"Wrindanneth and Aroganji have both seen new applications for their abilities in the days since undergoing the transference *xīnyì*. We should work together to cultivate these talents and broaden our own conceptions of what is possible."

Slate grunted, "Ya're still not makin' sense, Yip. Get ta tha point."

"You and I should work in tandem to bring forth the energies you feel rushing through you. In their expression, you may find a powerful new tool to aid in our quest against the Cabal."

"Using a solid understanding of Iron Body *qigong* as a starting point, we may be able to move forward together in allowing you to manifest the flames you feel burning within."

"So ya want ta help me learn ta wreath myself in tha flames o' Brendle's Forge?"

"If that is what you would call it, then yes."

Slate remained quiet for some time, staring out into the depthless blue sky. Finally, after some minutes had passed, he said, "Such ability is known among tha lore o' tha Bor'Banna, but tha skill has been lost fer generations. None have dared try ta relearn tha talent fer too many have been consumed in tha heat and flames that their desire kindled, conflagrations well beyond their ability ta control."

"These warriors were known as tha Daerdaana'Duin—those who have merged completely with Brendle's Forge. They summoned forth Brendle's Spark in its full glory, shinin' forth in flames, tha light o' which dazzled tha eye, bringin' wonder ta friends and terror ta foes, tha heat o' which caused even hellspawn ta recoil in fear, tha glory o' which inspired whole thanedoms."

Slate became silent again for some time while he thought. "Ya're askin' me ta take a risk tha likes o' which I have never considered possible, Yip."

"I do not wish for you to undertake a peril that will harm you, Slate. Nor do I wish for you to commence a course that you feel is ill-advised."

Slate grunted, reaching a decision, "We take risks every day, Yip. Is that not tha life we lead, tha life we fight fer?"

"The decision is yours, Slate." Although Yip felt that he had the skill and knowledge to help his friend, especially considering how close Slate seemed to be to fully manifesting the ability, he would not push Slate along a path he did not wish to take. However, without proper instruction, Slate might be at risk should he ever lose control or express his ability by accident.

"Tha decision is made. If tha life worth livin' is tha life worth fightin' fer, then it's also tha life worth riskin'. 'Sides, we're already riskin' everythin' on this fool quest, might as well up tha ante."

Slate grumbled, reaching an understanding. "I have faith in yer abilities, Yip. Long and long has it been since tha Bor'Banna fought with tha K'un Lun and never ta my reckonin' has a Bor'Banna been trained by one."

"Ya can read my energies and together we can guide 'em."

He nodded, glad for Slate's decision. "I will do my best to ensure your safety, Slate. Just as I can read the forces that flow through you, so, too, can I divert them and draw them away as needed. Once you have established control and have achieved a level of comfort with your abilities, the major challenges facing your success should be overcome."

Slate grinned wickedly. "Things're never that easy, Yip."

He returned Slate's smile. "One can always hope."

They decided to wait until the next day to start their energy training together. Yip wanted Slate as refreshed and restored as possible before beginning. By waiting, Slate would also come to practice with a clear perspective unhampered by the previous day's exertions.

No matter how important and desirable the end for which they strove, patience and an open mind were always more important than thoughtless exertion and rote perseverance.

For his part, Slate wished to alternate training times between Yip and Daerdros. Although he was hale and, as was the way of his people, possessed with almost endless stamina, recouping from injury and fatigue much faster than the strongest of Men, having time away from Daerdros's blade would also do him good. With a bit of time between bouts, for he was loath to call them training sessions with the way he was continually thrashed, he would have occasion to reflect and ponder not only Daerdros's moves and strategies, but to examine the ways in which he could improve his technique, internalizing what he learned.

Yes, gradually warming up to the idea, he was looking forward to his new training regimen. If he kept progressing, Daerdros may even allow him to continue his drubbings with Eidelion himself. There would be much honor in being thrashed by one of the champions of a race. If he were truly blessed by Brendle, he may even have the chance to learn something before he was knocked unconscious or gravely injured.

Such a session would bring great honor to his clan. Of course, no longer remaining in touch with his kinsmen, no one would hear of his deeds. He certainly could not rely upon word of his exploits to travel through his friends or fellows for none of them seemed to favor songs or tales.

No matter. A Dwarf lived his life for himself, his clan, and his Thane not for the pride of his actions or praise for his valor.

Smiling grimly, should he be lucky enough to spar with Eidelion, he imagined that the Paladin would be kind enough to heal his wounds after a session of relentless trouncings. He could look forward to that at least for Daerdros showed no such mercy.

Leaving Yip to his musings, for his own had already carried him far away from his friend even though they still remained side by side, he waved to Yip briefly in farewell before heading belowdecks to nap on his cot before waking up for dinner.

Now there was something else to look forward to!

With thoughts of bounteous comestibles running merrily through his head, he left Yip and retired to his chambers.

Watching his friend go, Yip smiled widely, more thankful and hopeful than ever he would have thought possible for such amicable companions and able partners to share in their journey together.

Once again turning to face the sky above the wooded hills rolling by below, he partially lidded his eyes and opened himself to the vibrancy flowing through and around.

His practice would occupy his attention until the dawn of the next day.

DAERDAANA'DUIN

Dawn flits softly through
on amber wings of gold.
A startled bird flees its nest.

Opening his eyes with the sun, Yip sensed only Raour'Saqan and Llyewia abovedecks. Wrindanneth had left the ship on autopilot for the evening and would return after breaking his fast.

Gazing downward from the spot where he had stood in hushed contemplation through the evening, he watched the land below slowly roll past. The gently undulating hills covered in soft, silent grasses that had stretched lazily across the plains over which they had flown the night before had transitioned once again to thickly wooded forests. However, this forest was of a type and density entirely different than those they had flown over previously in Landeiss. The tree-lined streams that had provided the only relief to the otherwise seamless topography of the plains were now invisible beneath the lush, shaded purple canopy of the sprawling jungles below.

He waited patiently for Slate's arrival with the sun.

Watching the verdant jungle pass, he did not have to wait long before he sensed Slate stirring beneath him toward the ship's aft. He knew that Slate was eager to be about their business because the sooner they finished, the sooner he could eat breakfast. After breakfast, Slate could look forward to more lively sessions with Daerdros should he choose before having the afternoon, and lunch, to himself.

"Ho, Yip!" Slate called out loudly enough to disturb any who may still be sleeping in the ship's hull below them as he left the stairs and joined Yip on the ship's deck.

"Nice mornin' ta work with tha blade!"

Giving a slight bow, he replied, "Indeed it is."

Washing his hands together eagerly, Slate said, "What're we up ta this morn?"

"We will work with your control as we have been. Before you fully release the fires within, you must be in full command of your faculties and energy."

Slate gave a curt nod knowing the drill. "Shall I get started then?"

Yip did not have to answer. Slate had already unsheathed his recalcitrant axe. "Argh! When does a blade get some rest around here? Haven't ya swung me around enough?"

"If ya haven't learnt how ta wield me by now, ya never will, ya woolly eared cave bat!"

"If ya're tired o' workin' and only want ta yap, per'aps I should grease ya up with a bit o' yak lard. If I cover ya with a nice thick layer o' grease, I won't have ta listen ta yer cryin' while I get ta work!"

"And mar my finish?"

"If that's what it takes."

"Yarr!"

Yip waited patiently for the bantering between the two to subside. Largely unexposed to acerbity and superciliousness growing up on the monastery, he was now used to teasing and sarcasm, although he did not approve when the exchanges happened at the expense of one or more of the participants.

When the bickering finally subsided with only the occasional muttered curse or oath from Duraeleon, he said, "Shall we begin?"

"Aye." Hefting his lambent axe loosely in hand, Slate asked, "What're workin' on first?"

Arms crossed easily at his chest, Yip answered as he had on the days before. "Control."

Today would be like the last few.

Slate gave a curt nod. "Anythin' different?"

"Try pushing your limits. Let yourself reach the point where you feel you are ready to ignite. Walk that line as long as you can. Let your limits grow with your control."

"Sounds like a plan."

Taking a place in the center of the deck, Slate started his blade work slowly, weaving through the sinuous moves and counters, strikes and feints, rolls and dodges of the Doerdaana'Duin, the dance of the fire's heart.

Eyes bright and eager, Slate quickly built up momentum, rapidly progressing through his axe work under Yip's supervision.

Yip had observed him quite a bit over the past few days, as he had when they practiced before. Yip had even described what he saw to him when asked which he found more remarkable than the actual manipulation and summoning of power Yip described. He really could not imagine being able to see Brendle's Spark blazing through the air, building up in his bones, granting him strength and resilience, until finally igniting around his axe.

The first time they had practiced after their initial discussion to embark on the path of the Daerdaana'Duin, Yip had described how the energy flow moving though him had changed from prior observations. Yip had told him that now these forces built and banked within infusing his body—his muscles and bones—with seething power.

Yip had explained the difference in his abilities simply. Before his body had served as a conduit for power, channeling energy at need, once he had achieved a certain minimal threshold for effectiveness. Now, in contrast, he not only channeled power, but his body served as a chamber for additional energy to be used at will.

This excess energy, in fact, explained the burning in his bones, the heat radiating throughout his body calling for ignition that he felt as he sparred against Daerdros. Yip told him that the more his need grew, the more energy built within his body, and the greater restraint he needed to control this swelling power.

For the past few days, Yip had observed him guiding this power, watching it build, coaching him on both how to direct and let go at need, offering insights into how he could apply and expand upon his abilities.

But mostly Yip watched him in silence. For his part, Slate did not mind that quiet observation in the slightest as he had enough difficulty in restraining himself as he let the building energy rage through his body.

Yip was clear, however, in that he wanted Slate to be able to fully control and reign in his heightened talents prior to exploring their potential. As much as he yearned to release the fires within, Yip's advice rang true. If he did let go and was unable to control the flames that he unleashed, then he would put himself at risk as much as he did those around him. He did not wish to jeopardize his friends any more than he wished to risk himself and, despite Yip's firm belief that he would be able to siphon these fires away before anyone was hurt, he remained concerned nonetheless.

As much as Slate hoped Yip were correct in his confidence and belief in his abilities, and therefore in his capability to control his inner fires, his Dam had warned him against too much certainty in the known just as she had in too much uncertainty in the unknown.

Her words still echoed through his mind. *"Don't ya forget it! Tha line between confidence and caution warrants as much care as tha edge o' an axe."*

Despite this warning, he also needed to heed Yip's request and continue to push his limits, whatever the risk, for only through his utmost effort would his ability grow.

Slate smiled as he worked at the memory, letting Yip's words and those of his Dam urge him onward before fading into the flurry of his blade.

Setting his axe lightly down upon the thick wooden planks of the deck, he once again became aware of his surroundings as the fever of the blade passed and the fires within cooled.

"Your skills are improving rapidly." Slate looked to where Daerdros stood beside Yip watching his practice. Daerdros's stern countenance was broken by a rare smile.

"As is your control." Yip was just as appreciative of his improvement. "I will leave you to Daerdros. We can resume your training tomorrow."

"Would you like a few minutes to recover?" Daerdros offered him a kindness as a measure of respect for his exertion.

"Will I have that luxury on tha field o' battle?"

Smiling grimly at the reply, Daerdros drew her sword, chanting a series of soft incantations to prevent either of their blades from causing grievous injury.

Leaving Slate to yet another grueling session with Daerdros, Yip walked to the ship's aft where Wrindanneth stood alongside Eidelion piloting the vessel. Slate was making remarkable progress, rapidly building upon and expanding his control. In the next few days, he may be ready to take the next steps on his pursuit. Until then, Yip wished to learn something of the lands over which they flew for he had not taken enough time to inquire as they traveled.

"Ho, Yip!" Wrindanneth's greeting was as warm as Eidelion's smile. "How go your sessions with Slate?"

"His progress is as impressive as his work ethic."

"Aye. Daerdros speaks very well of him." Eidelion counted her praise highly for it was reluctantly given. "Perhaps when your quest is done, he will consider joining us in the Home Guard."

"His dedication would serve you well, Eidelion." The thought of Slate joining the Home Guard filled Yip with joy for Slate would be well-suited to the work should he choose it. Slate's willingness to learn and grow would find a welcome home among the rigors of the Guard. Whether or not such a path would provide enough reward to hold his interest, however, he did not know. He would let Eidelion broach the topic as that was his place and not Yip's.

Wrindanneth laughed, partially at the thought of Slate as a member of the Home Guard but mostly at how his character was reflected in his work ethic. Just as Slate never gave up and seldom yielded, he rarely admitted the error of his ways or his opportunities for improvement. That Yip and Daerdros both were doing so well with him impressed Wrindanneth deeply. "He's as stubborn as he is hardworking."

"Sometimes the two go hand in hand," replied Yip.

Wrindanneth offered in jest, "It's a wonder Dwarves don't rule the world, then."

Now Eidelion laughed in reply. "Ea'ae is home to many stubborn races. Dwarves just happen to be more vocal than most."

"The exception being my kin, of course," offered Wrindanneth.

Eidelion answered with a knowing smile but said nothing.

Broaching a new subject, Yip asked, "Can you tell me something of the lands over which we fly, Wrindanneth?"

Nodding, Wrindanneth summoned forth a three-dimensional image of the surface topography from the control sphere. First briefly zooming out to show the entirety of Ea'ae before moving gradually back in as he described their position above the planet's surface, Wrindanneth outlined their course above southern Landeiss.

"As we move southward, the lands over which we fly will grow more and more lush. In just a day, we will leave the borders of Landeiss behind altogether and will begin crossing the Lueciane Sea." As he spoke, he tracked their anticipated course with his index finger. "From there, we should have less than a week's flight time over the open waters, weather permitting. We will arrive upon Maeron's northwestern shore and proceed inland for some weeks."

"As has been said before, the lands of Maeron are largely uninhabited by civilized cultures which means that we will be at even greater risk given our isolation and exposure."

"I anticipate flying as high as is reasonably possible while maintaining a clear visual connection with the lands below. That height should afford us the luxury of both time and distance should someone or something below choose to mount an attack."

"Furthermore, I do not anticipate landing until we arrive at or near our destination for I do not wish to expose us to the risks that the trackless jungles of Maeron harbor. People that venture this far south tend to be consumed by the jungle and its denizens. I do not wish to follow in their footsteps."

"You expect another month or so of travel?"

"Give or take," Wrindanneth shrugged slightly.

"Then we will have enough time to truly enjoy the pleasure of each other's company!"

Wrindanneth barked a laugh at Yip's comment. "If the Home Guard consider my company pleasurable, then they have as much to learn from us as we do from them!"

"Wait until Slate joins their ranks. In that case, the entire meaning of pleasure will need to be redefined!"

Yip and Slate practiced together in much the same way over the course of the next several days. Each day, under Yip's guidance and direction, Slate's skill and control of the escalating fires within grew and strengthened. By the sixth day since their initial commitment to work together, Slate felt these seething flames to be as much a part of him as they had ever been. He felt a newfound strength and vitality flowing through him as well—he burned with the heat and energy of the forge even when he had not summoned forth the flames of Brendle's fire.

The time had come to move forward and make his first true attempt at manifesting the Daerdaana'Duin. If these newly discovered feelings were not a sign that he was ready to begin pushing himself further, then he was not sure what was. As honest as he was with himself, knowing how dangerous the skill was, and how cautious and full of doubt he had been at the start, these feelings were not from overconfidence.

By this time, they had reached the southeastern boundary of Landeiss, leaving behind the thick, steaming jungles that draped across much of the island continent, and had crossed over the choppy navy-blue waters of the Lueciane Sea.

With the cerulean sky above and the cobalt sea below forming a backdrop to Yip's steady attention to his practice, Slate decided to make his feelings known to Yip before they started another day's session. "Tha time has come, Yip. I no longer feel that my bones are but dry kindle fer tha flames within ready ta ignite at a moment's notice. With yer guidance, I feel as though tha fires now lick and temper at my core, strengthenin' my bones and my body, reformin' me with each expression."

Yip's eyes remained fixed on him as he asked, "Are you certain?"

"As sure as I can count coins. Aye, I'm certain."

"The rest is up to you then, Slate, as it has ever been. I can only guide the energy you generate."

Slate grunted. "Shall we start then?"

Yip gave a brief nod to his friend.

Slate needed no further encouragement from Yip to get started as eager as he was to begin.

While Yip watched from a safe distance, Slate took a deep inhalation and relaxed as Yip had taught him, letting his inspiration extend throughout his body, relaxing into his breath. Allowing all muscular and mental tension and pressure fall away, he took hold of Duraeleon's haft, feeling the ridges of the leather grip surrounding the handle beneath the pads of his fingers.

Lifting his axe in preparation, thoughts of his time working with Yip began to flit through his consciousness, permitting him to look back on his recent work and development. As the images washed through him, he let them go in the same way he did with his breath as Yip had advised.

If he had to think of one thing that had made a difference to his practice and progression, truly relaxing as he moved through the motions of combat while letting the heat of the flames burn within was the most important skill he had learned under Yip's tutelage. Surprisingly enough, resisting the impulse to fight these fires did more for his ability to control them than actually trying to master them ever had. No longer fighting the energies within or himself, there was no battle raging in his soul, no fight to be won or lost.

The fires did as they would, just as he would have them.

Smiling grimly at the thought, now was the time to see if the same theory held when he gave the fires within their full expression.

His mind clear, he moved through the fluid feints and counters, strikes and slashes of the Doerdaana'Duin, his axe flashing in the morning air, whirling in intricate spirals and patterns as he imagined himself in the midst of a tumultuous battle, responding to the rigors and demands of life and death struggle. As he worked, his blade's motion carried him across the ship's deck in a controlled cyclone of fury, his body the center of a frenzied tempest.

As his muscles limbered and his mind calmed, he felt the fires within begin to burn hotter and hotter. Building in strength and intensity with each stroke, the flames began to seethe and roar, lacing through and around his muscles and tendons, seeking, demanding release.

As easily as he exhaled, Slate allowed the flames of Brendle's Spark their freedom, letting the heat of the Daerdaana'Duin rage.

With that release, all was consumed in flame.

He became combustion.

Yip observed his friend whirl and twist, slash and strike with amazing accuracy and deftness. Such was Slate's skill that he appreciated his friend's work as art, the expression of a master, in wonder at its beauty and breadth, complexity and purpose.

As Slate moved faster and faster with more precision and focus, Yip felt the power within his friend grow and build, spiraling through and around his body in a luminous vortex with more force and vitality than his physical work with the blade could ever manifest.

When Slate's bladework seemed to him to reach a crescendo, a peak of ultimate effort, Slate burst through to another level of activity, one Yip had never seen before. So quick were Slate's actions that the eye could not hope to track or anticipate them.

In a blinding flash, at the very same instant that Slate's fury was lost in blur, the morning light paled and dulled before a surging gout of light and heat. With this wash of incandescence, Slate burst into argent flames, the intensity of which was so great that Yip's eyes watered and ached. Great heat and white light burst forth savagely from Slate's form, causing Yip to instinctively step back and cover his face to protect himself from the raging inferno now surrounding his friend.

Slate was now lost in a living nimbus of fire and motion.

Reacting instinctively before he could come to a conscious decision or assessment of the situation, Yip sent his consciousness forth, rapidly bridging the distance between them, establishing a connection through which he could work. Once in place, he drew the energy coruscating around his friend into himself, in much the same way he would neutralize the power of a strike or kick by countering and redirecting the force elsewhere. Becoming a conduit, he dissipated the force within, allowing the excess energy flooding though him to flash off as an arch of blinding light and heat that twisted and spiraled into the sky. Such was the intensity of this gout that the sun seemed to dim in comparison, its luminosity paled by a new star.

Shock registering on his face when the fires dimmed without his volition, for he had lost himself to the burning flames of Brendle's forge, Slate fell limply to the blackened wood at the center of an irregular charred circle stretching across the width of the ship's deck. With a loud *crack*, the wood gave way beneath him, his shock turning to alarm for he had nearly burnt through the magically reinforced decking as he collapsed bodily through a great gaping hole in the planks.

Equally surprised, but at the ready, Orogast and Daerdros looked up from their conversation to find Slate falling through the ceiling of the hold, landing with a loud thump amid a plume of soot and debris in their midst atop a large canvas sack.

Unfazed by the commotion and interruption, Daerdros looked calmly down upon Slate's sprawled, dazed, and slightly bewildered form while he dusted himself off. "Come early for lessons?"

Orogast chuckled softly, the sound sending a ripple through his liquid form.

Shaking his head while regaining his composure, Slate replied calmly, nodding to Orogast and Daerdros in turn as if nothing unusual had happened. "Mornin'. Hope I'm not interruptin'. Thought ya could use a bit more light."

When Daerdros managed a slight smile in reply, Slate stood groggily and said, "We're not all Dwarves, ya know. If yer gonna be spendin' so much time belowdecks, I figured it couldn't hurt ta have a skylight fer ya ta work by."

"We are much obliged by your hospitality and consideration, Slate."

"Thank ya."

Surveying the blackened wood, soot, and bits of detritus, Slate said, "Don't worry about tha mess, I'll be back shortly ta finish cleanin' up."

"Why don't I take care of it for you? You look like you should lie down." After all she had put him through, Daerdros's small expression of compassion caught him a bit off-guard.

Slate shook his head briefly in response. "Lemme just talk ta Yip and then I'll be back ta clear this up."

Not waiting for Slate's return, Daerdros snapped her fingers and the bits of wood and dust lifted up off the ground in a roiling, turbulent cloud. With a vague twirl of her finger, the plume began to swirl, growing and coalescing into a small dust devil. Turning faster and faster, the charred wood and dark soot twirled in a tighter and tighter band, forming an increasingly thinner and thinner ribbon in the center of the hold. With a sudden snap of her fingers, the strand finally disappeared before Slate's eyes.

His aches and fatigue momentarily forgotten, Slate asked, "Where'd it go?"

"It's gone."

"Thank ya." Then, after giving the matter a bit more consideration while rubbing his head, he added, "About those lessons."

"Yes?" Daerdros lifted her eyebrows in reply.

"I may need a bit o' time ta see how"—here he paused before turning his head sharply to the left and right with a disquietingly loud *pop* each time —"tha renovations are progressin' before beginnin'."

Now both Daerdros and Orogast smiled.

As Slate turned to leave, Daerdros said, "And about those renovations, Slate."

"Aye?"

Daerdros laughed as she answered, "Perhaps next time you could let us know before you commence?"

Slate grunted before responding, taking the opportunity to finish dusting himself off. "I hope so."

Turning to leave, Slate stopped midstride as a voice bellowed angrily down at him. "Slate! You dim-witted bat turd! What in the name of Azagothe's vacuous tendrils are you doing to my ship?"

Slate rubbed his beard thoughtfully from where he halted near the exit of the hold, having regained his composure, if not his energy, for he felt drained after the expression of Brendle's fires. "Just a bit of carpentry and socializin'. Nothin' ta worry about or take note o', ta be sure."

Glaring down from above, his face livid as he screamed from the edge of the charred hole in the decking, Wrindanneth roared, "You almost burned your way completely through my ship! If Yip hadn't stopped you, only the Lueciane Sea would have extinguished your flames as you tumbled down to your death!"

"Nothin' like a bit o' practice fer some excitement is there?"

"I will trust you to keep all of your practice and excitement to yourself! We have a crew, passengers, our mission, and a ship to think of here!"

"Don't ya worry, Wrin, I'm thinkin' o' them. Why else d'ya think I added tha skylight?"

With that, Wrindanneth smacked his head, cursed, spat to the side, and stormed off. As wildly as he was flailing his arms as he stormed away, Slate thought that Wrin may be at risk of dislocating his shoulders in his expressive zeal. Thinking better of mentioning that concern, he remained quiet.

Filling the silence left by his internal observations, Slate thought he heard Wrindanneth mumble something like, "At least the ship can repair itself without that fool Dwarf's assistance... Carpentry indeed!" but he could not be sure because Aroganji had joined Yip at the edge of the gaping hole along with Spreesprocket and Kazarhan. They were all laughing so loudly that little else could be heard. Aroganji, in particular, seemed locked in the midst of a violent convulsion. His face was at least as red as Wrindanneth's had been.

Shaking his head as he mounted the stairs leading up to the deck, Slate only hoped Aroganji did not lose control and fall laughing as hard as he was. After all, someone could get hurt.

Rejoining Yip at the edge of the charred breach in the ship's deck, Slate grinned and joked, "Per'aps I still need a bit o' work on my control."

Yip shook his head. "You have yet to learn your limits or even how to interact with your new talents. Control will come in time with practice."

Slate's head drooped as he adopted a sad, mawkish tone glancing over to where Wrindanneth glared at him from the quarterdeck. "I don't know if I'll be afforded another chance ta practice..."

Yip grinned, a mischievous look in his eye, as he replied, "Do not fear, Slate, I have another idea."

"Fff..." Slate smacked himself on the forehead as he exhaled loudly. "That's exactly what I'm afraid o', Yip!"

"This time, there will be nothing to fear."

"How so?"

"I will channel the majority of the energy you generate away from you as you express it, dissipating it without harm. Your torch will become a flicker that will not burn."

"So I won't burn tha ship down?" Although he wished to move forward in his training and was confident in Yip's ability to control the situation, he was still concerned about the risk after his last attempt. The gaping hole to his side served as quite a reminder.

"No, you will not and you will be granted the opportunity to learn how to manipulate and control your abilities at levels that are far more manageable."

"Sounds like a plan. Why don't we get started?"

Surprise registered on Aroganji's face from where he stood next to Yip by the yawning hole in the ship's deck. "Now?"

"No." Slate shook his head before answering, "Promptly in tha mornin' after I wake up with a clear head!"

Yip laughed lightly, the sound of his voice carrying across the ship's deck. "We work at your pace, my friend."

Slate nodded briefly before turning to return belowdecks. "Good. Because I'm ready ta slow down...per'aps fer a nap."

As the door below shut behind him, Kazarhan looked at the gaping hole and asked, "Should we not repair tha vessel?"

Aroganji answered, "We could magically repair the damage quite easily, but, based on his response, I think Wrindanneth would like to see how well the ship's new automatic repair system works."

"Although he will not admit it, I am sure that on some level Wrindanneth is actually thankful that Slate damaged the ship under safe conditions. That way, he can gauge how quickly and effectively the ship now reacts to damage."

Spreesprocket added, "If he's looked at the online schematics, he will have all that information at hand and will know that the speed of repair is dictated by the amount of energy infused into the reconstruction process."

"For many, seeing is believing and believing is trusting."

Kazarhan nodded in agreement as he looked at Spreesprocket meaning-fully. "Havin' experienced my fair share o' Gnomish technology, a bit o' skepticism and practicality will serve him well."

Spreesprocket cleared his throat loudly. "I have personally gone through all of the ship's systems and can vouch for their reliability and effectiveness."

Kazarhan shook his head, in a gesture all too reminiscent of Slate, while speaking with a warm, friendly tone. "That's exactly what I'm afraid o', Spree."

Not responding to or acknowledging the comment, Spreesprocket added, "If the system does perform less than adequately, I will be ready to correct any shortcomings."

Having never stopped shaking his head the entire time Spreesprocket was speaking, Kazarhan added, "Even more worrisome."

Spreesprocket shook his head in reply, unperturbed by Kazarhan's response. "If you had been paying attention while Slate recovered and we spoke, Kazarhan, you would clearly see that the protoplasmic biomimetic melioration system—Mark IX version—installed by Gideon Goldsprocket is functioning remarkably well without additional effort on our part."

Pointing to the ship's deck and the breach, Spreesprocket emphasized his point. The black charred surface had almost completely disappeared where he noted. In fact, the deck's surface appeared more lustrous than ever around the edges of the burnt zone. Although difficult to discern, the hole in the deck was also undergoing significant change. The jagged, broken edges, pitted and blackened by flames, had smoothed and were also regaining color and luster. The breach itself also appeared smaller, however, this detail was problematic to accurately assess both given the large size of the original hole and the lack of steady attention given to its repair.

Kazarhan gave a brief nod in acknowledgement. "The skills o' yer people are ever a marvel to behold"—he paused briefly before lifting his head and finishing—"when they work!"

Yip took the opportunity presented by their argument to withdraw from the discussion and clarify matters with Wrindanneth who, he sensed, was less than pleased by the whole fiasco. Bowing, he said, "Your people's magical skills are truly wondrous indeed, Spreesprocket. There is much to be admired in your knowledge and ability."

Pausing before continuing, he added, "I am sure that Wrindanneth will wish to hear the news of the speedy repair of the vessel. I will let him know that all is in good order."

"Thank you."

He turned and left Aroganji, Spreesprocket, and Kazarhan standing by the now significantly less blackened and rough hole watching its steady repair.

Yip could sense Wrindanneth's fury even before he left the side of his friends behind, so it came as no surprise to see that Wrindanneth's face was still livid while he muttered under his breath standing by the piloting disk as Yip mounted the stairs up to the quarterdeck.

"Did he send you to apologize?" Wrindanneth glowered as Yip approached.

"No."

"So not only is he afraid to do his own dirty work, he is too inconsiderate to even say he's sorry!"

"Wrin, Slate is not feeling well and has retired to his chambers. I am certain that he will speak with you in time."

"What foolishness was he up to? He almost destroyed my ship!"

"It was not him alone, Wrin. You know we are working together to cultivate his skills. In fact, we have had quite a breakthrough!"

"You certainly did! He almost broke through my ship! He could have taken someone else with him!"

"That was the first time he had fully expressed his newfound abilities. We have been working on his control. He was just overwhelmed by its full expression."

"Overwhelmed! He could have killed someone! He could have killed himself!"

"That's why I was there, Wrin, to stop him from coming to or harming anyone. If anything, the blame lies in my hands for I was not quick enough to avert the damage."

"And to think, if you weren't there, what would have happened?"

"He would not have tried anything. It was my guidance that led him along this path after we discussed his newfound abilities. If I had not been working with him, things could have been much worse."

"Exactly!"

"Wrindanneth, you know as well as I that he must learn to control his abilities both for his benefit and ours. If we do not help him, he is at risk. We cannot let that happen."

When Wrindanneth did not reply, he added, "Although my initial approach did not ensure his safety or the complete safety of the crew, our new method will. I will channel all but the minimal amount of energy needed to fully express the Daerdaana'Duin away from him. The fires that burn within him seeking release will only simmer and will not burn."

Wrindanneth remained silent for a few moments before he added, "My apologies, Yip. You know that I have a bit of a temper." He smiled brightly as if he had just told his most winning joke. "Truth be told, I was worried about him. We argue and fight more than we should, but I do care about him and would not like to lose him."

Yip bowed his head briefly. "Such is the way of friendship."

When Yip had turned to go, Wrindanneth called out to him, "Yip?"

"Yes?"

Wrindanneth cleared his throat and muttered under his breath, "You don't have to tell Slate about our conversation."

"I am sure that he will understand, Wrindanneth."

Wrindanneth nodded in return before turning his gaze back to the control sphere and monitoring their course.

Walking down the stairs to return to main deck, Wrindanneth called out to him again. "And Yip?"

He smiled as he turned to answer his friend. "Yes?"

"You'll let me know the next time you decide to start your practice?"

He gave a nod. "I will."

"Good. I'll want to be ready."

He smiled in reply.

"Just in case."

"Depending on how he's feeling and if he's comfortable, we should be practicing in the morning. Keep an eye for us then." Yip laughed. "We'll be hard to miss."

Wrindanneth also smiled. "Hopefully not as hard to miss as today!"

"We'll try."

"If not, I'll just look for the giant flaming torch!"

Eidelion hailed Yip as he returned to the main deck. "Ho, Yip!"

Yip bowed. "Hello, Eidelion."

"Is all well?" Although a hardened warrior, tempered by many battles, Eidelion, at heart, was a healer and mediator, a man whose actions were moved by compassion and care.

"All is well." Yip waved his arm broadly encompassing the now noticeably smaller hole in the ship's deck. "Slate is unharmed, although after our most recent practice session, I cannot say the same for the ship."

Eidelion smiled. "I can see that."

"The ship's repair system appears to be handling the damage quite well. In the short time since Slate burned through the deck, all the charring has disappeared, and the hole is markedly smaller."

"Slate was a bit addled and drained by the effort, but we succeeded in replicating a skill that had been lost to the Bor'Banna for generations!"

Eidelion crossed his arms and looked at Yip appraisingly before saying, "Marvelous!"

"He needs quite a bit more work to be able to use the ability naturally, but I am amazed by his progress. Slate should be quite proud of the gains he has shown in the time since we left Tellanon."

"Indeed. Rediscovering and recreating a lost art is a feat worthy of much praise. Our world has lost so much already."

Yip understood him to mean much more than the simple comment implied. From vanished and forgotten arts, cultures, peoples, and beings, much of wonder and value had been lost to Ea'ae and her peoples in recent ages.

Yip laughed as lightly as the cool ocean breeze blowing across the deck. "Now we need to recreate it safely!"

"The sword we wield is the same as the one that cuts."

Yip bowed. "We need to learn to control the cut without getting burned ourselves."

"Aye." Eidelion looked at Yip intensely. "You, too, should be extremely proud of what you have done and are doing, Yip. Just as recreating a lost art is a wonder, creating and disseminating a new one, along with all the attendant knowledge associated with it, is an attainment worthy of much honor and recognition."

He bowed once more in response to Eidelion's recognition. "Praise those who, in the end, through their efforts and success, help create a richer world."

Eidelion smiled brightly again. "I am."

Seeing that there was no way around Eidelion's compliment, he merely remained quiet.

When some time passed in silence, Eidelion said, "I would watch your work with Slate. Perhaps I may have some input into his practice both with the Light and the blade."

"We would both be honored, Eidelion."

"The honor would be mine."

"You are welcome to join us at any time. As you are aware, Slate and I practice together in the morning prior to his sessions with Daerdros."

"I look forward to it." With that, Eidelion gave a short bow and took his leave, walking to the aft of the ship to join Wrindanneth at the helm and inquire after their progress.

Watching their advance from the ship's railing, Yip gazed outward over the limpid azure waters of the Lueciane Sea. Since leaving the lush coasts of Landeiss behind, they had flown over a series of wild, uninhabited tropical islands strung across the open waters in abundant profusion. This archipelago pointed their way toward Maeron and her mysteries as well as any chart.

Looking down from the *Shrike*'s cruising height in the clouds, the shallow teal ocean below appeared to be teeming with schools of fish, each disrupting the water's placid surface to varying degrees in vibrant displays of motion, surrounded by the foam and froth of breaking waves and currents as the sea met the land in white ribbons of spraying water. There were enormous leviathans, the full breadth of which could not be discerned from the ship's current soaring height, small minnows barely visible above the surface, shapes of those creatures that had yet to break the surface or were once again retreating to the depths, and all manner of forms and sizes in between.

Even from their lofty height, he could feel the vibrancy of the sea and its denizens where his eyes could not. The water itself shone with energy infused with the life force of countless microscopic organisms. Within this sea of dynamism, other forms shimmered and moved adding to the ocean's vitality.

He smiled at the image that arose in his mind of the islands of the greater Landeissan archipelago at play in the ocean frolicking alongside the schools of fish as his thoughts floated from one fancy to the next, without course or direction.

From his lofty height, he imagined the marvels and mysteries that may lie untouched and undiscovered upon those pristine shores, envisioning what wonders remained hidden from one not walking across the unblemished sands of the uncharted beaches below.

His thoughts, a string of footsteps in the sand, each following the other in succession wiped out by the coming tide, were forgotten as one thought moved to the next in an endless, unheeded procession.

"Yip?" Having sensed Aroganji's presence while he waited, Yip was not surprised to find his friend calling for his attention.

"Yes?"

Turning from where he gazed downward at the gemlike, emerald islands below, he smiled at Aroganji's greeting.

A slight look of concern was evident on Aroganji's face. "Will you need my assistance when you practice with Slate tomorrow?"

"How so?"

"There are any number of ways I could be of help. I could shield the ship from the heat of his flames, I could transmute the heat of his fires into light or some other form, I could reduce the strength and intensity of his blaze, or many other options, if he is willing."

Yip bowed in gratitude for his friend's thoughtfulness. "Your concerns for Slate's safety mirror my own, I am glad to hear."

"Then you will accept my help?"

"No."

"No?" A look of confusion briefly crossed Aroganji's smooth face.

"I will dissipate the energy and intensity of Slate's flames as I work with him so that everyone and everything will be safe—ship, crew, and all."

"You can do that?"

"Yes."

Another look of slight confusion clouded Aroganji's visage. "I was not aware."

"I may not have explained myself fully either as I am still learning the skills involved." Yip smiled reassuringly in order to bridge the gap between himself and his friend.

"I may not be able to make or create magical enchantments that abide, that can interact with the surroundings based on my vision and intention, but I am able to interact with and manipulate the energies at the source of such enchantments. Although I cannot cast spells, for instance, I have learned how to alter the energies involved during their casting."

"Your skills are such that no risk is posed to Slate?" Although impressed, Aroganji was concerned more about the health and well-being of Slate than Yip's abilities.

"As much as I can be. You saw what happened today in the time required for me to react when unprepared." Yip paused a moment before adding, "We will not allow the full expression of his ability until he is ready."

His concerns for his friend's safety addressed as best they could be at the time, Aroganji asked, "What else are you able to do?"

"I do not know." Yip was as honest as he could be for he had not had time to fully explore the full manifestation and realization of the ability beyond his meditations and practice with Slate.

Not accepting the simplicity of Yip's answer, Aroganji quickly cataloged what he knew based both upon his experience and observations, ticking off each point on his fingers. "You are able to augment our abilities as you did with each of us while practicing in the park. You are, or think you are, able to dampen the expression of other people's magical energies. You are able to manipulate other people's magical energies prior to their full expression. You are able to change those energies once they have been summoned from one form into another once generated. Am I missing anything?"

Shrugging in surrender, Yip said, "I think not," although he did not fully know yet himself.

Aroganji smiled brightly. "Absolutely fascinating!"

His mind set in motion, Aroganji said, "If only we had the time to fully study your talents, in a proper research setting like would be possible in the Paratechnologists' laboratories, of course! Think of what we could learn!" Aroganji had in mind experimentation and study more like the research he had undertaken while studying at Xian Shi than informal observation.

"Are we not learning now?"

"Well, yes." Yip's matter-of-fact reply gave Aroganji momentary pause.

"You are welcome to watch and participate in any way you wish and see fit, Aroganji. That is why we work together, as friends and allies, working in concert for a common cause—for the benefit of all sentient beings."

With his curiosity piqued and the opportunity present, Aroganji was not about to let the chance to explore new magical lore pass. "Have you established the limits of your abilities?"

"How do you mean?"

"Do you know to what extent you can manipulate different forms of magical expression?"

Yip shrugged. "I do not know. What I know and feel today may change tomorrow with more work and practice."

Recognizing both Yip's modesty and uncertainty in his replies, Aroganji sought for clarity. "Well, how do you feel you may be able to interact with the energies we summon and manipulate compared to those of someone casting those energies at you singly or as part of a group?"

Giving Aroganji a brief flicker of smile in response to his persistence, Yip answered, "The situation dictates what I can and cannot do. Much of what I am able to interact with is determined by my perception, my ability to focus and be aware of what is happening around me. The more activity, the less I am able to directly interact with and alter."

"As for particular cases, if I offer additional energy to an individual augmenting his or her power, I can channel more to that person singly than I will be able spread throughout a group like I would be able to do with you, Wrindanneth, and Slate. If I seek to alter and control the energy of another as it is being summoned and directed, I must focus my attention upon that one person and am therefore primarily limited to altering their invocations alone. If, however, I am defending myself, as in the midst of a physical fray where complete control and direction of potential attacks and energy is not required, then I am able to redirect power from multiple sources simultaneously as I would be able to in hand-to-hand combat."

Yip shrugged, adding, "All this may change with time and practice."

Aroganji nodded, thinking of the implications of Yip's comments. "Why, or rather how, do you think this newfound ability arose?"

Never having fully verbalized the thought, for no one had really asked and he had volunteered only a portion of his thoughts and impressions to his friends, Yip spoke simply. "Much of what I now feel and am able to do is a direct result of the transformative experience, which was in many ways a reformation of myself, in the *chi* void on Al'Marr. This you know."

Yip looked at his friend deeply as he clarified his sentiments. "I should have died when I fell through that void on Al'Marr, Aroganji. That I lived was directly the result of the congruence of several small miracles—the protective magics of my friends"—here he gave Aroganji a bright smile—"Azaelle's gift of the knowledge of the Dragon's Gate, and a disproportionate amount of chance."

"The ordeal, not only the brush with death, but the direct experience of the maelstrom within and around the void itself, recast and remolded me in ways I am still learning and trying to understand."

He held up one finger as he finished, "But one thing is now clear to me. In many ways I am now able to act very much like a *chi* void myself."

Aroganji's features drooped and his mouth opened slightly as understanding and a bit of fear crossed his mind. "Are you saying that you are linked to the *chi* voids?" Aroganji did not express his true fear that Yip may be connected somehow to the destination where the *chi* itself was siphoned.

Yip laughed at his friend's show of concern. "I am not a *chi* void, Aroganji. Nor I am a conduit for the evils on the other side of the veil if that is what you fear."

Aroganji smiled in relief.

"I am, however, able to do many of the same things."

When the ramifications of Yip's words fully hit Aroganji, his mouth did drop open. "What are you saying?"

"That there may be a great deal of things that I must never try or do."

If, as Yip now thought, he was indeed very much capable of realizing the range of capacities of the *chi* voids themselves, then, in addition to being able to manipulate energy, coupled with the knowledge of the Dragon's Gate from Azaelle, he now embodied the capability for both energy creation and destruction.

AMBER

Blue sky ringed by clouds,
lavender highlights turn gray
with the coming rain.

"Mornin', Yip!" Slate sauntered toward where Yip waited with a lively step and a bright, ready smile, the toil and exhaustion of yesterday's efforts long forgotten, especially after a full night's sleep, a hearty breakfast of eggs, ham, sausage, biscuits, bread, cheese, and a bit of ale to wash it all down.

"Ready ta pick up where we left off?"

"Let us hope not, my friend," Yip joked, sharing in Slate's good cheer.

"Seems as though we caused quite a stir, yesterday!"

Yip smiled. "Then we were working on something worthwhile at least."

"Seems folks think I may be a bit ill, out o' sorts, and in need o' protection."

Yip laughed again. "Who am I to question their wisdom?"

Slate grumbled at Yip's quip, but did not say anything audible in reply.

Yip rested his hand on his friend's shoulder, saying, "All here are concerned for not just your safety, but the well-being of the entire crew and the success of the mission."

"I know that, Yip. Else why come?"

"They could be here, like you, for a bit of fun."

"Bah! Ya know I'm as serious as any."

"And I am glad of that, Slate." Yip gestured toward the glistening deck between the ship's forward and mid mast, now completely repaired with no sign of ever having been damaged. "Shall we begin?"

"Aye." As he walked toward the center of the deck to give himself plenty of room to begin his axe work, Slate turned to Yip and asked, "Ya didn't accept any did ya?"

"I do not follow your question, Slate."

"Ya didn't accept any offers o' aid or protection?" Thoughts of Wrindanneth's meddling danced through Slate's mind so thickly that Yip could almost see them.

"No, I did not. I let Aroganji know what our plans were and he agreed that they were sound. Eidelion inquired about observing and potentially working with you at some point. I let him know, as are any who wish to participate in any practice of which I am a part, that they are welcome to join or observe at any time."

Slate stopped in mid-stride at Yip's last comment. The thought of training with Eidelion was almost too much to believe! Even growing up sheltered in the wilds in his thanedom he had heard of Eidelion's exploits and dreamed of one day fighting alongside heroes such as Eidelion and his peers. That he may be very close was too much to fully and truly believe.

All he managed, all that he could muster, to summarize and express the wealth and depth of feeling this opportunity presented was a weak, "Oh, really?"

"Yes. We will see. Like Aroganji, Eidelion felt our path was sound."

"And what of Wrindanneth?"

Yip laughed. "He does not wish for you to burn his ship down, harm the passengers, or," Yip winked at Slate as he finished, "hurt yourself."

Slate huffed, placing both hands on his belt as he adjusted slightly. "How would I ever manage ta get hurt?"

His face calm and his voice even, Yip replied flatly without a hint of sarcasm, "I have absolutely no idea."

Waving to the piloting deck getting Wrindanneth's attention, Yip said, "As a precaution, Wrin also wanted to know when we got started."

"Bah! He already knows enough if ya ask me!"

Yip merely smiled, not encouraging further discussion.

Taking his place at the ship's center, Slate looked down at the decking where his wavering reflection was visible in the burnished wood finish before starting. "Gideon certainly knows his business. Woulda taken me days with a crew ta repair tha ship as well as this."

"The nature of magic is to defy the imagination."

Speaking from the perspective of an artisan, for he was indeed a master craftsman, though his skill at the forge was long forsaken since dedicating himself to the axe in his quest for revenge, Slate answered, "'Specially when employed so skillfully."

"Beauty is in all things, Slate." Yip gestured once more to the open area on which Slate now stood. "Are you ready to begin?"

Slate grinned, his smile bright beneath his heavy beard. "If I have ta, I will."

Yip did not reply, instead he waited patiently for Slate to limber up as was his wont—swinging his arms in circles and from side to side, rotating and bending at the waist—warming the muscles and tendons while promoting the circulation of blood and breath.

While Slate worked, his breathing deep and even as he went through his accustomed motions, Yip said, "Remember, I will draw as much energy from you as I am able while allowing you to remain within the Daerdaana'Duin. If I take too much or you lose focus or control, we can start over and I will try again."

Slate's only response was a short nod, as his battle focus and fervor heightened, his attention narrowed.

With Duraeleon unsheathed and strangely silent, Slate began slashing through the air, carving down imagined enemies to the left and right, up and down, spinning and turning, ducking, rolling and countering in ever increasing vigor and speed.

When he could move no faster, his blade the faintest blur moving before him directed by his iron will, a loud voice boomed out, "Safety check!"

As quickly as he had been moving, Slate lurched to a sudden halt, frozen in place and unable to move. A look of anger and red rage spread across his face.

At the same time, Yip sensed a rapid manifestation of force localized to Slate's position. Encompassing the rest of the shipmates within the scope of his awareness, everyone else was unaffected by whatever magic held Slate locked into position. The very air seemed to have locked him into place.

Before Yip began to siphon off the energy holding Slate in stasis, he heard Wrindanneth's voice bellow stridently and knew both the source and cause of Slate's predicament.

"All clear?" Wrindanneth walked leisurely down from the quarterdeck as he called out, his face a mask of innocent concern.

Heads turned as he walked by for no one else had been aware of any drills planned to take place.

Announcing generally, Wrindanneth responded to his shipmates' tacit queries, "No cause for alarm! I am merely reviewing some of the ship's safety features that Gideon installed!"

He called out again, "All appears to be in order! You may carry on!"

Smiling now that he neared where both Yip and Slate stood together with almost equal stolidity, Wrindanneth grinned as he stopped in front of where Slate remained locked in place mid-slice. "The Tropospheric Coagulatory Anti-ejector Concussion Ameliorator passenger restraint system seems to be in working order."

With a flick of Wrindanneth's wrist, Slate was released from the solidified air that had held him in position. Looking Slate directly in the eye, smiling all the while he said, "I trust you feel safe?"

Slate lunged toward him with a guttural roar. In response, Wrindanneth merely flicked his wrist once more, locking Slate into position once more. "Perhaps not," he said with a laugh.

Slate glared and made some muffled noises but was unable to force any air beyond his lips.

"Release him, Wrindanneth."

Wrindanneth did not look at Yip as he allowed Slate his freedom once again, instead keeping his attention on Slate.

"O' all tha blasted..."

Slate's invective was cut off mid-sentence by an overwhelmingly loud series of unrestrained guffaws. Looking at his hand in disgust, Slate realized his axe, Duraeleon, was laughing at him uncontrollably.

With a subdued clatter, Slate opened his hands loosely, letting his howling axe fall to the deck of the ship ignored and forgotten.

Turning to Wrindanneth Slate spat at his feet, cursing. "Now I know why ya have no parents or family." He glared menacingly at Wrindanneth. "No one would claim ya as their own."

With that, Slate turned and stormed from the deck leaving both Duraeleon and his friends behind.

Wrindanneth opened his mouth to respond in kind but paused for a moment thinking better of it.

Yip spoke before Wrin could, saying, "Wrindanneth, you have done and said enough."

For once, Wrindanneth dropped his head, perhaps understanding the harm he may have done through tormenting his friend, whether intended or not.

"Ehh hrmm!" The sound of a clearing throat turned their attention to where Duraeleon lay discarded on the ship's decking. "A little help here, please?"

As calmly and firmly as he had spoken with Wrindanneth, Yip said, "Our help is not what you need, Duraeleon. A Bor'Banna and his axe should never be separated."

A note of sarcastic derision still evident in the axe's tone, Duraeleon smirked. "Who is to say Slate is a Bor'Banna?"

To which Yip replied simply, "And what is to say you are his axe?"

Having reached his dimly lit quarters, Slate dropped down and slouched on his bed. Though he seethed, he did not simmer with anger, merely the last vestiges of power that were coursing through his veins. Although he was not truly angry, he was, however, disappointed, grievously so in fact. Not only in Wrindanneth for his short-sightedness, but also in his axe in whom he had felt, prior to this morning's display, that a certain level of camaraderie and respect, albeit grudging, had been mutually achieved.

More so than in either his friend or his blade, he was more disappointed in himself, for he had let his focus, his concentration break as a result of Wrindanneth's feeble prank. That his intention had broken under so simple a cause was, in his mind, a major failing. In battle, where the slightest drift in attention may bring about his downfall, he would never be afforded such a failure.

Worse than that failing, however, was the fact that prior to today's outburst, whether in battle or banter, he had never shown such a deficiency to his friends or foes. For this failing, above all others, he had also lost much face, if not in the eyes of his friends, then in his own.

Shoulders slumped, callused hands resting loosely on his lap, he hunched on his bed unsure how to mend his ways.

Duraeleon's whining left ignored and forgotten where it lay on the deck behind him, Yip waited patiently once more for his friends to rise to the occasion for he knew above all else that any problem, no matter how great or small, was in their hands and theirs alone to resolve. If Wrindanneth did not approach Slate to mend their differences with clarity of purpose and honor, then he would encourage Wrindanneth to do so just as he would encourage Slate to resolve his contentions with Wrindanneth and trust in himself.

Although small mistakes and misunderstandings such as those that had unfolded between his friends may appear overwhelming and disheartening in the eyes of those who had suffered, feeling they let themselves and others down, such errors were inconsequential within the true scope of the world that is, was, and would be.

Better to move on in appreciation for the wonder, beauty, and depth offered by the lived life while the opportunity was presented than dwell overlong on its shortcomings.

Slate knew what he had to do. No matter how disappointed he was with his own faults, in how he had responded, and with how he had lost concentration, he knew exactly what had to be done to move on.

He took a deep breath.

Belying all his Dwarven character, he took another.

And let go.

Standing slowly, determination visible in the firm set of his shoulders, he left the room, leaving only rumpled sheets behind.

Walking down the hallway, the diffuse glow of the lighting orbs casting the set features of his face in stark relief, he mounted the stairs to the deck and walked upward and back into daylight.

Yip stood across the deck from him as he always did, a fixture on the ship's railing as much as any other part of the ship. Yip did not turn at his reemergence, but he knew that Yip was aware of his presence just as he felt that Yip sensed him even belowdecks.

His focus leaving Yip's back, his eyes fixed upon Duraeleon, the axe's luminous surface reflecting the bright light of the sun exactly where he had left it.

Aware of his approach, Duraeleon called out, "'Bout time ya came back!"

Before it could make another snide comment or rejoinder, he interrupted forcefully, gritting his teeth as he bent over willfully and gripped the haft of the axe with surprising firmness, growling beneath his stale breath, "Shut up!"

Momentarily cowed, he finished before Duraeleon could offer a rejoinder. "Not another word from you."

Holding the blade of the axe up where his reflection was plainly visible in its silvery, reflective surface as if he were looking deeply into the eyes and heart of a man, he said, "Know this, Duraeleon Light Bringer, bane of Adrael the Black, axe of Ithilieon, I am your guide and master, your way and hope."

"The choice is yours."

Talking directly to his own reflection on Duraeleon's face, he continued, "Fight with me with honor and you will have my respect and trust."

"Scorn me and I will throw you into the deepest abyss, leaving you forgotten for eternity."

Dropping Duraeleon to his side, he then turned his attention to Yip, saying only, "Let's begin."

Turning with a smile, Yip asked with calm simplicity, "You are ready?"

He grunted, "Aye."

Sensing that Slate was eager to begin anew, Yip kept his comments short. "I will siphon off any excess energy you create until you are able to control the flames you summon."

Slate grinned evilly. "Don't worry about me, Yip." He paused, timing his joke. "Just watch out fer tha ship."

His axe whistling through the air, a wicked hum following his blade cutting through the breeze, Slate quickly established his focus, slicing and spinning with a vengeance. As the heat of his assault intensified, so, too, did the fervor of the flames banked within. Each stroke of his axe acted like a bellows, urging the fires of Brendle's Spark to greater and greater pitch.

Watching from a safe distance, Yip could see the speed of Slate's blade working faster and faster, feel the building of the energy within, until at the last instant, the very air around Slate began to shimmer and waver, finally bursting into brilliant white flames.

At that exact moment, his awareness having been held at the ready, Yip let the energy of these flames flow through him, acting as a bridge and conduit, a safe passage for the intensity of Slate's will.

As the air burst forth with brilliant white flames around Slate, the space around Yip shimmered with blinding white light—the excess of Slate's summoning of power.

His bladework uninterrupted, Slate continued his deadly strikes and spirals across the deck, his fires banked, unperturbed by Yip's actions.

Calm and impassive, Yip felt enormous energies washing over him—a substanceless net through which the raging currents of an untamed river surged and boiled.

Relentless and consumed, Slate burned with vitality and power, the heat of his will surging upward through his arms and around his axe, rushing throughout his body, spilling over onto the ship and around him in a violent haze—an unstoppable tide of supernatural force.

Glorying in the power that overcame him, he felt he could, that he should, rage forever. If he burned hot enough, with enough force and power, he may become the flames themselves, a living sun never to be quenched, burning beyond the dimming of the stars.

He blinked.

Just as quickly as he had brought the flames forth, the fires blazing around him sputtered and faded, returning to the source from which he had drawn them.

He had almost lost himself to the lure of the flames! Even with Yip drawing energy away and out of him, the seductive allure of power had clouded his vision, drawing him away from his true focus and self.

Burning too brightly, he had almost lost himself to the heat!

With an overwhelming flash, the last of the turbulent energy rushed out of Yip, the end of a burst that had lasted far too long. He marveled at Yip's capability and control that he could channel so much without it drawing him in or touching him. He had much to learn before he could ever hope to blaze as brightly without being burned.

Yip's eyes lit on him with a warm smile as Slate finished. "You have done well, Slate."

Slate groused, letting Duraeleon fall to his side, its haft hanging limply from his right hand. His assessment was honest and unforgiving. "I almost lost control, Yip. Tha call o' tha flames almost caught me. I almost couldn't resist its allure."

Yip shook his head briefly in reply. "But you did, Slate. You recognized your limits and acted appropriately. That is the beginning of control. That is the beginning of progress."

"I don't feel like I maintained control! I feel like I almost burned myself ta ash!"

"You should be proud of what you have just done, Slate, not reproachful. The mind that guides your axe and shapes your will is sound. That you were able to halt at need is proof of that."

"Hmm..."

Yip walked over to him and gently placed a hand on his shoulder. "You have much to build on from here, Slate. If you can stop the Daerdaana'Duin on your own, then you should be able to control the amount of power that you summon as well."

"Soon you will be able to walk in the footsteps of your forebears without fear."

Slate smiled grudgingly at the thought.

"And they will be honored to hear the sound of your footfalls ringing along the halls they forged so long ago."

IN FLIGHT

A ring of feathers
alongside the trail—
echoes of the last birdsong.

"Yip! Slate! To the helm!" Wrindanneth's urgent tone meant there could be no delay.

Practice had ended for the day.

"Eidelion! You are needed as well!" Wrindanneth's voice boomed throughout the ship, magnified by the *Shrike*'s control sphere.

"All others, at the ready!"

Running to the quarterdeck, a large spherical projection showed the *Shrike* flying high above the waters of the Lueciane Sea. In the enormous scale of the image, the *Shrike* appeared as little more than a brown and white dot. Scanning the projection, at the periphery of the representation, three other airships followed in tight formation.

Eidelion joined Wrindanneth, Aroganji, Yip, and Slate at the helm in short order.

As Wrindanneth showed the image to Eidelion, Slate barked, "Ship's followin' that close in such an isolated place cannot mean anythin' good."

Eidelion's deep voice followed with a question. "How long have they been following us?"

Wrindanneth smiled, knowing this question had been coming. "For the last half-day I've sensed the presence of something dancing along the periphery of the *Shrike*'s sensory limits, but this is the first solid evidence."

Slate looked behind them toward the horizon where the other ships should be visible in the distance. Covering his thick eyebrows with one callused hand, he said, "I can't see 'em."

Wrindanneth chortled. "Of course not! That's why we're using the ship's instrumentation."

"Why would they be tryin' ta overtake us now?" Slate's thick eyebrows bunched above his bulbous nose with the question. He was not questioning the obvious fact that the other ships were intent upon causing them harm. Rather he was asking for thoughts on their strategy for doing so now.

"We are well clear of any security afforded by the people of Landeiss," offered Aroganji.

"They may be trying to overtake us before we reach Maeron, though they know not our destination," added Yip.

Eidelion smiled, recognizing the merits of all their suggestions. "We may have entered their air space and they saw an opportunity."

"Whose air space?" Wrindanneth was not aware that the loose series of islands and atolls that had grown more and more intermittent since leaving Landeiss were home to any civilized people.

"The R'yn Daer." Eidelion spoke matter-of-factly as if this were common knowledge.

"The R'yn Daer work from these isolated islands?" If so, this was the first Wrindanneth had heard of it.

Eidelion gave a vague shrug. "They are a people on the move as much as the wind. They have been observed in this region along with other remote locations in the recent past. Where the next season will find them, only their whims can say."

Wrindanneth nodded grimly as Eidelion finished, "The *Shrike* was theirs before you claimed her. Perhaps they wish to reclaim it or exact revenge."

"Three ships to our one, those are not even odds." Although Wrindanneth was confident in the capabilities of his ship and her crew, one could never tell how luck would fall or what surprises may lay beneath the decks of those other ships.

As though speaking the most obvious suggestion available, Yip said, "Hail them."

"What?" Wrindanneth's sense of disagreement could not have been more plain. "And lose our element of surprise?"

Aroganji laughed, saying, "You mean the element of surprise that we know they are following us? They know we will find out about them soon enough unless they are terribly lucky. You do not send several ships openly against one in broad daylight in the hopes of sneaking up on your quarry."

"They know there are no safe havens in our current heading should we try to outrun them, so our options are few. Fight them, try to outrun them, port home, or talk. Those are our choices."

"If, as Yip suggests, we parlay, we can still do any of the others."

Eidelion agreed. "Your friend suggests a wise course."

"And you are sure they are R'yn Daer?" Wrindanneth had the beginnings of an idea but wanted to make sure Eidelion was certain.

"Can you focus on their ships any more closely?"

Wrindanneth responded with a slightly clearer image of the ships. Although all three still seemed to be miniscule specks flying over the deep blue waters of the sea, the details of each vessel became slightly clearer as the image sharpened.

"What is missing from these ships?"

Slate scratched his head as he leaned forward, his nose almost touching the projection as he tried to find an angle for a better look. "Crews?"

Eidelion laughed. "There is that! What else?"

"I cannot be sure"—Aroganji leaned forward alongside Slate—"but I do not see any rigging along the masts or sails."

Eidelion smiled at Aroganji's answer. "The R'yn Daer call upon the wind to guide and propel their ships. They do not need rigging because their sails, if present at all, are magically filled and held in place by the winds at their call. Nor would they need ropes to climb and adjust because of this magic and the fact that their own wings will allow them to travel wherever on the ship they need at will. Rigging would only be a hindrance."

"Besides"—he pointed again at each ship in turn and then laughed—"all of those ships look decidedly like the *Shrike*!"

Slate laughed as well. "No denyin' that!"

"The R'yn Daer prefer the simplicity of the ancient marine vessels for their ships. To them, as creatures native to the skies, the ships that once 'flew' on water are as exotic as any shape they could conceive for a vessel. There is, then, much allure to them in this olden style of conveyance which is why most of their ships follow a marine template. They fancy plying the skies in the way that such vessels once plied the open seas."

"Ya mean like pirates?"

Eidelion shrugged. "Perhaps. Their behavior is often not too different, which is why they are seldom welcome in more civilized regions."

Wrindanneth turned to Yip enquiringly, his question honest and without accusation. "You did not sense them sooner?"

Yip shrugged. "There is much life in this region just as there has been much to occupy my attention." Implying no blame for the significance of his comment, he took it upon himself, adding, "I have sensed other ships in passing the distance in convoys and thought nothing different of these three. That failing is mine for I should have been more alert."

Accepting Yip's reply with a nod, Wrindanneth asked, "Shall I hail them?" He was ready to begin.

"If we were to hold our current position and let them overtake us, how long would we have?" Eidelion marked their position on the image as he asked.

"Perhaps three-quarters of an hour, no more," was Wrindanneth's smoothly confident reply.

"Plenty o' time ta make ready." Slate's hand was already reaching for the haft of his axe.

"Good," Eidelion replied gravely. "When you are ready."

Turning away from them, Wrindanneth opened communication channels between the *Shrike* and the pursuing ships. "Hail R'yn Daeran vessels! Wrindanneth, captain of the *Shrike*, requests palaver."

He waited for a short time for a reply to his request from the other vessels, watching the holographic projection intently as he did so. When none was forthcoming, he said, "Know that we mark your current heading and have been aware of your presence for some time."

"What is your intent?" His face was as firm and intense as his voice.

Again Wrindanneth waited patiently but in vain for an answer from the other ships.

Slate stroked his beard grumbling, "They don't appear interested in banter."

Speaking with firm authority, after waiting a short time longer for a response, Wrindanneth stated sternly, "R'yn Daeran vessels, you have been contacted and asked for a statement of purpose. Know that you are harrying a ship granted charter by Tellanon's ruling High Council, manned by officers in her Home Guard. If you do not clarify your mission to our satisfaction or desist in your pursuit of this vessel, your presence will be considered hostile and acted upon accordingly."

"You have one minute to reply."

Wrindanneth looked around him as he spoke. "They have received my communication and are not blocking the signal."

Easing the tension of the wait through humor, Slate offered, "If they don't respond, ya can launch me over ta their ships and I'll burn 'em ta flinders! I've always wanted ta fly... 'Course, I'm only good fer one ship before tha ocean puts me out. That is unless I get some help!"

Wrindanneth laughed. "There will be no Dwarf tossing or launching on this vessel!"

Aroganji added with a chuckle, "Sounds like a fair plan to me. We will certainly have the element of surprise. It is not often ships fire their own crew at other vessels."

Reconsidering, Aroganji added, "At least not as a ballistic."

Before Wrindanneth could add another rejoinder, the image of the pursuing R'yn Daeran ships in the projection wavered and shifted. In its place, quickly clarifying and resolving itself into the image of a proud visage with high cheekbones, deep emerald eyes, an aquiline nose, and gray feathers in lieu of hair covering the head, was the face of the lead R'yn Daeran captain. Also covered in downy gray feathers, two large wings were visible sweeping upward behind him in a graceful arch. A small golden helm rested atop his head, only partially covering its feathers. The helm, however, did not block or lessen the intensity of his gaze.

"You need not threaten us, Manling," the R'yn Daeran captain's keening voice hearkened back to the cries of eagles on the hunt, a remnant of his race's avian past. The high, airy tone of his voice was not altered by the magic that was translating his voice into words that could be understood by the crew of the *Shrike*.

"I offer no threats. I merely state the truth." Wrindanneth was not going to be cowed by anyone, much less the people who appeared to be hunting him without cause. "And you have not answered my questions."

The face of the captain distorted into a distasteful grimace, hissing in anger. "We are here to reclaim what is ours, fool! And to avenge those who have fallen!"

"Do you seek to join your kith in death?" Wrindanneth's matter-of-fact tone belied the threat that was now apparent in his words.

"We will have what is ours!"

Again replying calmly in the face of the captain's anger, Wrindanneth said, "Is not the way of the R'yn Daer to 'Keep what is earned, earn what is claimed'?"

"Do not parrot our beliefs, Manling!"

"We have earned this ship, Captain, of that you can be sure. We were waylaid without provocation by its last crew and defeated them with honor and without trickery when they attacked us unsuspectingly as cowards by cover of darkness."

Wrindanneth paused briefly before finishing, "Who then has earned the right to the *Shrike*?"

"Your lies will not change your destiny!" The captain, apparently, did not wish to listen to reason.

"Then you, too, will find that we have earned this ship."

Wrindanneth flicked his wrist and the captain's angry face disappeared from view.

"Are the R'yn Daer a people without honor and respect even for their own ways?" Aroganji had little knowledge or experience with the culture of the R'yn Daer and was less than impressed with what he had seen thus far.

"They have honor, but their honor is tainted by too much pride and greed." Eidelion did not appear the least bit happy about the outcome of the conversation, although he knew their purpose would not be averted as soon as he saw the ships in the projection.

"All at the ready!" Wrindanneth's voice held a firm command that had grown surer with the passing of the days. "The R'yn Daer do not want to listen to reason and wish to engage us at their own folly!"

"How shall we engage them to our best advantage?" Lowering his voice once again to normal speaking tones for Eidelion, Slate, Aroganji, and Yip, Wrindanneth broached the topic of strategy.

"Although we are outnumbered, we are not outmanned or outgunned." Eidelion's confidence was grounded upon years of experience with his Lieutenants.

"We need not engage them," Yip spoke clearly, a reflection of his vision, his voice carrying across the bridge.

"You propose we try to outrun them?" Wrindanneth regarded this approach with some skepticism.

"You offered an alternative without violence or harm, one where they maintain their honor and keep their respect. That course they rejected. We need not run from them either."

"Yip, getting straight answers from you is as about difficult as navigating with both eyes shut in a snow storm! Out with it already!" His mind set on action, Wrindanneth wished to move.

"We only need show them that attack is, as you implied, futile. If they then choose to engage, then the loss is theirs and theirs alone."

"You suggest a warning shot?"

Yip nodded. "Is not Gideon's cannon fearsome enough to give them pause?"

Wrindanneth shrugged. "I have not seen it in action, but I'd love to give it a try!"

Eidelion nodded appreciatively at Yip's words. "Yip offers a wise course. Lives will be spared if the R'yn Daer act with any amount of reason. And"—he lifted his index finger and smiled—"if they live and leave, word of your prowess, and earned right, will spread among their kind. You may not need to worry about being stalked by the R'yn Daer in the future."

Wrindanneth clapped his hands together like an eager child ready to try a new toy. "Gideon's Transmogrifying Spectral Cyclotron it is!"

Standing at the control disk, Wrindanneth felt the full extent of the ship as his senses ran through and along her bow and bridge, masts and sails. With a subtle command, the ship quickly rotated about its axis, turning to face the R'yn Daeran vessels out of sight on the horizon. Faster than he had turned the ship around, all the while maintaining its prior heading, he directed his mind forward toward the fore of the ship to the massive, intricately carved figurehead that served as the *Shrike*'s battering ram.

His attention actually inside and around the figurehead, he willed the Dragon's savage jaws to open. As he did so, from within the beast's black maw, the matte gray barrel of Gideon's Transmogrifying Spectral Cyclotron emerged from the darkness aimed directly above the lead R'yn Daeran ship.

Gathering energy from the ship's generators, he felt tremendous power surging forward waiting for his command to fire. Before doing so, however, he called out, "Make ready! Everyone to their positions! I fire in one minute!"

As the words came out of his mouth, he experienced an unusual juxtaposition of his awareness, his sense of self, actually being in several locations at once—in his physical body, scattered throughout the ship, and concentrated around the cannon—all in strong contrast to one another. Simultaneously, because he had temporarily lost his sense of self, he felt his connection with Aroganji open as another layer of fractured concordance came over him.

Recovering his attention amid the distraction, the focus of his awareness on the impending firing of the cannon made the sensation of unification quite different from the normal experience of melding with the ship. With his renewed concentration, layers of unified awareness contracted, merging seamlessly with his chosen frame of reference for commanding the *Shrike* as a natural extension of his field of experience.

He could only imagine how disorienting the unexpected connection and attendant impressions would feel for Aroganji!

Aware through his connection with the ship that everyone was abovedecks and at the ready should the need to retaliate or defend arise, he unleashed the flood gates, letting power flow unrestrained to Gideon's cannon.

As he did so, the Dragon's mouth and the figurehead began to glow, radiating an intense scarlet, indigo, and fuchsia haze—the Dragon's mouth heating up, licking with imminent flames, power surging about its maw.

Aiming directly above the mast of the lead ship, Wrindanneth fired the cannon, unleashing the accumulated energies within. With an almost incomprehensibly bright flash, a steady beam of pink, purple, and blue burned through the air separating the ships, holding position in the sky—a polychromatic roseate beacon of destruction.

If the R'yn Daer were smart, they would follow that beacon backward as a guide home. If, as Wrindanneth feared, they were intractable, then that same beacon would guide them forward to their doom.

From where he stood at the *Shrike*'s command disc, through the senses of his body, he could smell the ozone produced by the passage of the intense plasma through the atmosphere around the ship.

Sustaining the beam for a few more seconds, with significant power in reserve, he directed the trajectory of the superheated gases downwards until the beam passed directly above the forward mast of the leading ship.

His point made clear, as abruptly as the beam had commenced, he stopped it, letting its power fade until only the afterglow of the heated plasma remained, slowly cooling in the intervening skies. Everyone on those ships would know that he had deliberately stopped the beam after his warning. If they deemed his action a provocation, then they would also know that the plasma arch the ship fired also penetrated their ships' shields and any aggressive action on their part would be sheer folly.

At least that was what he hoped.

Not everyone listened to reason.

Least of all himself.

An angry squawk brought Wrindanneth's attention back to the command sphere from where he had been following the beam. "You fool! You dare challenge us?" The face of the R'yn Daeran captain jerked and spasmed animatedly as he expressed his rage.

"I am not the one who issued a challenge, Captain. You have heard our rightful claim on this ship by R'yn Daeran custom. Now you have seen our warning. I hope you take heed."

By this time, the indignant yelling audible behind the R'yn Daeran captain had settled down to an angry buzz. Although the anger and affront were still clearly visible competing against one another on the captain's weatherworn face, he could not now do anything but accede to Wrindanneth's wishes for he could do nothing in the face of the *Shrike*'s superior firepower without losing all his ships.

He did not, however, have to rein in his sentiments.

"You have escaped us on this day, Manling! But know this, the memory of the R'yn Daer is long and our sight is keen. We will watch for you! Be warned!"

Before he faded away from the ship's projection, the captain's voice broke into a ghastly cackle. "The fell Orcs of Maeron will not be so kind!"

Peering into the vivid aeronautical projection, they all watched as the three R'yn Daeran vessels swiftly turned about in large, swooping arcs and faded away from visibility on the sensory depiction.

"Surly lot," Slate grunted distastefully as he watched them vanish silently from the simulacrum.

"Slate, you are too kind." Aroganji shook his head. "But calling them by the names best suited for them would demean us as well."

Wrindanneth shook his head. "Speak for yourself, Aroganji. Those loathsome kin slayers will never hear any kind words pass through these lips."

"We are rid o' 'em and that's good enough fer me." Slate washed his dry hands as though wiping away something unpleasant. His eyes brightening as he finished, Slate said, "'Bout time fer lunch, I reckon!"

Their past troubles behind them, for now, Wrindanneth laughed, saying, "Any time is a meal time for you, friend."

Slate lifted his eyebrows in mock incredulity. "There're times that're not fit fer a meal?"

"Aye!" Wrindanneth shrugged. "We just had one."

"Bah! I could've fought those sons o' motherless hellhounds with a bit o' ham in one hand and a nip o' ale in tha other."

Aroganji sighed, smiling. "If you say so, Slate."

"Well, if food weren't so hard ta come by around here, I'd've shown ya!"

Wrindanneth shook his head in strong refutation. "If food weren't so hard to come by around here, you would eat it all. Luckily, our stores are filled magically and you haven't a clue as to how to operate the system. Otherwise, you would eat so much we wouldn't be able to remove you from he hold."

Pointing to the hatch leading to the hold, Slate said unequivocally, "That's why we have the hatch and windlass!"

Wrindanneth groaned, "My point exactly!"

As the banter subsided, Yip said, "We must be on the alert for the Orcish legions mentioned by the R'yn Daer as we approach Maeron lest we face another conflict. What do we know of them?"

Nodding in agreement, Wrindanneth said, "I will adjust our heading and make sure that we fly well above both visibility from the ground and sensory detection from normal patrolling ships."

"Without any major civilizations on Maeron to stop their advance, the Orcs and their spawn have had little to check their expansion."

Shaking his head in disagreement, Eidelion spoke after having listened silently to their conversation since the departure of the R'yn Daer. "There is much to hold the expansion of Orcs and any similar race on the continent of Maeron. If not, humanity would have long ago reclaimed her place there for it is a lush, rich land. The Orcs who live there now have, as always, been forced to live on the margins of habitable lands. This time, however, it is not the peoples of civilized nations that force the marginalization."

Pausing a moment to let his point sink home, Eidelion finished, "The Orcs will be the least of our worries once we reach Maeron of that I am confident."

Taking his point, never having felt otherwise, Wrindanneth said, "Our vigilance will not waver."

"Nor should it if we are to survive." Eidelion bowed at the waist and then turned smoothly in his burnished armor and left the deck to brief his lieutenants.

Reemphasizing Eidelion's point, Aroganji said, "It gets no easier from here."

Nodding sagely in agreement, Slate added with Dwarven aplomb, "Who wants ta join me fer lunch?"

AIR CURRENTS

Summer storm passes,
vapors rising off the ground,
returning to the clouds.

A beaming smile broke the monotony of his nondescript face, full wind brushing the hair from his frigid eyes as he surveyed the bright cloudless sky so far above the deep ocean waters below.

Southward lay his destiny. He could feel it!

So strong was the pull that he felt caught, enveloped in a woven net of chance, drawing him ever forward.

Reading the currents before him, navigating by the collapse of probability into actuality, he set his course forward toward the priest that eluded him, but only for a time.

The wind shifted briefly, changing the direction of its flow from fore to aft, pushing his hair forward over his face. Sweeping the hair from his eyes, he turned backward facing into the wind away from the view at the ship's prow, an overwhelming stench enveloping him in a wave as he rotated into the breeze.

Bodies lay bloated and swollen, broken and discolored, strewn across the deck in haphazard disregard for the life once present, so vital, within their forms.

Their possibilities had ended as his moved forward.

He had erased their potentials to further his own.

Perhaps he should do something with the corpses.

His eyes passed coolly back and forth over the dead captain and his crew, their lives snuffed out to serve his purpose.

His survey complete, he turned around to examine the path ahead, a rictus smile cracking his emotionless face once more.

He preferred the decorations where they lay.

TUIO SHOU

Blue clouds rush by at night
beneath the shadows
of a cold still moon.

Three days of travel over open, unobstructed oceans so deep and blue as to be almost black, brought no sight of land on the horizon. Flying as high as they now were, well above even the loftiest clouds, any change in currents visible in the water or soaring birds that might have served as a sign of approaching land were not in evidence.

Dark horizons in all directions marked the ocean's extent, not its limit.

"Yip, do you ever leave the rail of the ship?" The warm smile on Daerdros's face displayed both her humor and growing respect and comfort for Yip and his companions. Slate's increasing skills with the blade coupled with his extreme efforts under Yip's guidance had gone far in breaking through her self-imposed coolness, although her steely sense of command and demanding nature were still in strong display.

"Horizons, both inner and outer, are clearly visible here. There is little need to leave."

"Are they not visible anywhere?" The smile had not left her face.

Yip bowed in return recognizing the merit and truth of her question. "I am able to train in place or on the move. One place is, indeed, no better than another, but here I am available, easily found, and visible should anyone have a question or need to find me."

Now he smiled, pointing to her own practice with his reply. "Also, the rest of the ship then is available to use for training space for others who may need it more than I."

She laughed. "So you are saying that you stay here largely to keep out of others' way and not be a nuisance?"

He gave a brief shrug, replying, "One place is much the same as another and I am needed for little else. Most of the tasks on the ship take care of themselves and one such as I has scant else to offer on such a vessel other than my own meager skills."

She smiled, a bright grin on her face. "Then, if you are amenable and will share some of the space used by others for practice, perhaps you would be willing to share what skills you do have by assisting us in our hand-to-hand combat drills?"

He bowed. "If you wish to learn what little I have to teach, then I shall become your student and discover what it is you may teach me in turn."

"Thank you, Yip. Your willingness to aid in the efforts of others sets an admirable example for the Home Guard."

"Praise the outcome, not the idea. I have seldom taught and am hardly qualified to instruct."

Daerdros merely raised an eyebrow in reply. After a moment's silence, she said, "I will seek you out after noon when we perform our drills in the hold. Although I know the ship has built-in safety features, I prefer the thought of having walls around us shielding us from any potential falls overboard."

"Caution often instills the confidence needed to aspire."

Smiling as she left, Daerdros nodded her head in a brief bow saying, "Until then."

He responded in kind before returning to his contemplation of the sea.

"Master Wei?"

He stood by his teacher within a circle of raked sand, in a contemplative garden surrounded by mature stands of bamboo they often used for practice. At the far edge of the garden, a small pond covered in lilies rested beneath a wooden bridge with low handrails.

"Yes, Yip?" Master Wei watched his young pupil with a gleam of curiosity in his eye.

He thought for a moment, trying to capture the summation of his thought, the totality of his concern. There were far too many aspects of learning and facets of his practice where he fell woefully short.

There was so much to learn but his own shortcomings often seemed to hold him back.

"When I spar with my partner, my strikes lack power. If I am lucky enough to land a blow, there is scant effect."

He bowed his head thinking of how little his blows impacted the protective chi barriers generated by his much older, more studied practice partners. "How can I improve my technique? What should I do to correct my form? How should I strike?"

Master Wei nodded in understanding. "You will come to understand that the only difference between luck, or chance, and skill is ability."

"Ability must be cultivated. Ability comes with time and proper effort. The greater your skill, the less luck, as you say, there will be in any action."

He opened his mouth to interject another question, eager to find answers as quickly as they arose within his young mind.

Master Wei raised a hand to silence him before he gave voice to the question. "Power does not come from the strength of your arms or the force of your legs. True power comes from the strength, the depth, of your relaxation."

"What do you mean, master?" His furrowed brow wrinkled below his smoothly shaven head.

"The harder you try to strike, the more you physically exert to bring power to bear, the more your strength works against you. The tension in your arms, your shoulders, your torso, your legs, your whole integral structure, interferes with the progress and direction of your strike."

"I do not understand, master." Once again feeling the limitations of his abilities, he could not visualize Master Wei's instruction.

"The true power of a strike comes from the initial motion—the more integrated your structure, the greater the effect. Attempting to add your strength to this impetus actually interferes with the application of force. Proper body alignment and physical relaxation will allow the translation of the maximal amount of this generated force into an opponent."

"Tension, wherever it lies, impedes the flow and application of force."

Master Wei picked up a small pebble lying in the sand. "Imagine your arm is a stone."

He threw the pebble in a slow arch through the air where it landed with a slight thunk in the still water of the small pond, radiating ripples marking the spot where the stone landed. "If you cast your fist toward a target, and you add your own strength after the initial motion, the tension of your muscles will slow the speed of the fist's flight. If you resist your own motion, tightening your muscles, your blow will not only lose power, but the impact will lessen. The power of your blow will return to its source, rebounding up your arm through and into your body only expressing a surficial impact."

"If, however, your body remains completely relaxed after you cast your fist toward a target, accompanied by the energy generated by your body, the muscles of your arms, neck, shoulders, back, waist, and legs will not interfere with or impede the force of your strike. The energy of your blow will translate fully into your target, the power of your strike moving completely toward and into its target, not its source."

He bowed, thankful for his master's tutelage. "I think I understand, master. Thank you."

He began visualizing relaxed physical motions, his joints open and unobstructed, his muscles relaxed after initial exertion.

Finishing, Master Wei said, "A truly powerful strike is the expression of complete relaxation, free of all tension, in complete alignment with the mind and moment. With a truly relaxed strike, the full expression of your blow, your will, and your intent will be translated directly into your opponent without resistance."

"Then, when the mind and body are in alignment, the power of your strike will resound to the heavens."

"Yip?"

He let the accumulated energies flowing through and within him pass away at Spreesprocket's query, passing as quickly as the vision within his mind.

"Ready to go downstairs?" Spreesprocket was obviously quite eager to begin training with Yip. He fairly danced from foot to foot like an excited child offered the chance to choose a particularly tasty morsel from the selection at a candy store should he complete a particular chore.

Yip turned and gestured toward the stairs leading belowdecks, the sleeves of his robes shifting gracefully in the air as he did so. "After you, Spreesprocket."

Spreesprocket scurried forward, his small legs carrying him much quicker than their appearance warranted. With a slight creak, he opened the oaken door for Yip as they descended from the sunlight into the arcanely lit interior. Following the stairway down and around, they opened a second portal leading to the hold and descended once more to the floor of the ship's main chamber.

Waiting patiently for his arrival, the entire company of the Home Guard stood in formation behind Daerdros ready for drills. The floor space had been cleared of all sacks and barrels, any extraneous materials having been moved to the surrounding walls of the hull joining the other gear already fastened and moored in place. Any signs that the Home Guard were using this space as their living quarters had likewise been removed.

Turning toward her fellow Guards at his approach, Daerdros said, "Yip has been kind enough to volunteer to teach us some of the essentials of hand-to-hand combat as practiced in his tradition."

Looking back and forth from man to man, being to being, she said firmly, as if they were not a highly regimented, masterfully honed fighting unit. "I trust you will listen to his words with the respect they deserve. Keep an open mind and learn."

She spoke with the same firm authority to Eidelion who stood to her far right as she did to Kazarhan who stood to her far left. Her command held for everyone in between.

"Yip, if you will." She gestured for Yip to take a position at the front and center of the room with his back facing the door through which he had just entered.

Walking forward, he reached his chosen position at the front of the assembled warriors and bowed deeply from the waist.

Standing comfortably and at ease, he began, "The basis for our practice is the breath."

Taking up a relaxed position, his feet roughly shoulders width apart, arms loose at his sides, he continued, "It is from the breath that all our actions flow and it is to the breath that all our actions return."

Breathing slowly, his inhalation the finest thread of silk spun and extended, he said, "The breath, the *chi*, surrounds us, enlivens us, pervades us, and connects us all."

"Today, I am going to teach you to breathe."

Watching and listening to him patiently, each member of the Home Guard waited for his instruction. Only Kazarhan's brow appeared furrowed with his words, although the Dwarf kept any comments he may have to himself.

"We will begin with the techniques of Zhan Zhuang, standing meditation, that form the foundation of our practice. This practice represents dynamism in stillness, the universal from a single point."

"By simply standing still and breathing, you will learn the true meaning of the adage, 'Action originates in inaction and stillness is the mother of movement.'"

"Follow my movements as I lead and listen to the true intent of my words as I guide you."

"We will begin by warming up our bodies and our breath before beginning Zhan Zhuang."

"As we move, remain relaxed and comfortable, poised and at ease. Your skills will develop naturally given the opportunity. Progress cannot be forced."

He then bent his knees slightly indicating for the rest to follow his motions with a nod, keeping his feet together as he placed his hands over his kneecaps rotating first in a series circles to the left and then to the right. As he moved, he said, "Your torso should be relaxed and without tension or restriction. Gaze downward at a point about a pace in front of you to avoid tension in your neck and shoulders."

After completing the circuit to the right, he stood smoothly, bringing his hands forward slightly as though holding the body of a barrel or the trunk of a tree. From this neutral posture, he brought his arms upward and over his head, rotating his hands facing outward at the apex of his movement before bringing his hands downward as though pushing against a slight resistance. "Breathe in as you lift your arms above your head. Exhale as you bring your arms down."

Moving gracefully through each transition, he said, "Your shoulders should remain relaxed throughout the movement and your feet firmly grounded shoulder width apart with your toes facing forward. As your hands reach your waist, bring your arms forward in a slight arc, returning to the starting position as though you are gently cradling a sphere."

As with the first warm-up exercise, they worked through a series of movements, repeating this cycle over and over until completion. "In time, when your skills and comfort grow, we can substitute other *qigong* exercises like Ba Duan Jin, the Eight Pieces of Brocade, for these movements."

Although practitioners would normally shift naturally into Zhan Zhuang exercises after their preparations, he paused for a moment to offer a brief introduction to the next movement, the heart of standing meditation practice.

"We will now begin Zhan Zhuang practice with Wuji, the great emptiness. Wuji is the source from which Taiji, existence, arises and is the source from which your practice of Zhan Zhuang will arise. Just as your practice arises from Wuji, it is to Wuji that you will return."

"In Wuji, you simply stand still."

"From Wuji, any tensions or obstructions to relaxation in your body, in your nervous system, will readily become apparent."

"Stand in a natural, neutral relaxed position." He stood before them with his hands loosely by his sides, his feet shoulder width apart and feet facing forward. "Your head should feel suspended above your shoulders as though held in place by a string as you relax and sink downward while maintaining this posture."

"Look forward and slightly downward," he pointed ahead with his arm as he demonstrated the proper angle. "Keep your tongue pressed lightly on the roof of your mouth with your chin slightly dropped. As before, your arms, shoulders, elbows, and hands are relaxed and held loosely at your sides. Fingers should be allowed to remain at rest curved and turned inward toward your thighs."

Describing a line with his hand vertically by his side indicating the proper alignment, he said, "Your core and spine should remain centered and relaxed as well, neither pushed too far forward or back held in line with your ears." Placing his hands by his waist, he said, "Hips should remain neutral with neither bottom nor belly projecting outward."

"Do not lock your knees. They should be bent, albeit very slightly. Return to this relaxed position should they become locked or fixed in place as you stand."

"Your weight should be balanced in all directions—centered between left and right, forward and back at the middle of your soles evenly between each foot."

"Inhalation and exhalation is through the nose alone. Do not open or breathe through your mouth. No muscles should be held tightly including your lips. Your mouth merely rests shut. Swallow at need as saliva accumulates."

"Breathe fully and completely. With each exhalation, you will let your chest fall."

"With each breath, feel the air, the *chi*, pass through you from your nose to your lungs, down through your arms and legs, extending outward and through you, as though you are a vessel filled with vitality. Upon exhaling, feel this gentle wind pass from you bridging the gap between you and your surroundings, binding you together in the common breathe, the universal *yuan-chi*."

Pausing for emphasis, he added, "This is the breath that connects you with an adversary; the life-giving energy that binds his actions to yours and your actions to his in the same way that your actions are both bound to and express the universal."

"In this, the simplest of postures, you are connecting Heaven and Earth, the ground and the firmament, with each and every breath. Your life connects and returns to the life and energy encompassing all of existence."

"Like the tree aspiring to Heaven, your roots reach deeply into the ground while your spirit soars amidst stars, nourished and sustained by the energies of life flowing all around."

"The longer you stand, the more easily you breathe, the more you will notice the tensions and obstructions that interfere with and impede natural, functional movement, perception, and thought. Despite the difficulties that will become apparent by simply standing in place, these tensions and impedances are the very reason that Zhan Zhuang practice is necessary."

"Your body will be your guide and your progress marked by your ease."

When it was clear that he had finished, for he merely stood in place breathing softly as he had told them, he heard a throat cleared to draw his attention.

Looking up to where Kazarhan had just cleared his throat, the Dwarf asked surlily, "Is that it? We just stand in place?"

"Yes."

"And this is supposed ta help us in combat?"

"If needed, yes."

"A warhammer or mailed fist ta tha face, I can understand, but not this."

"Are those things not guided by intention, fueled by the breath?"

"And they're techniques with value. Tha desired effect is obvious."

Yip was silent in response.

Kazarhan shook his head. "How? How am I ta benefit on tha field o' battle learnin' ta stand still and breathe?"

"You have but to try to discover the benefits for yourself."

"Is there more?" Apparently Kazarhan was not satisfied with Yip's responses.

"Yes."

"How much?"

"As much as can be imagined. As much as you yourself believe."

Kazarhan remained silent for a moment, as though brooding or deep in thought. Finally, with all eyes of the Home Guard watching, without approval but with patience nonetheless, for his ways were not their ways and his culture was not their culture.

Kazarhan grunted in challenge smacking his gloved hand across his breastplate. "Show me. A skill that cannot be implemented on tha field o' strife is only good fer gettin' a Dwarf under tha earth well before his time."

Dwarven traditions were as old as the lowest weathered peak and as intractable as the mightiest range. Dour and stubborn, Dwarves were not easily swayed by word or taunt; true worth was shown through practice and application.

"Am I not here?" Yip responded once again with a simple question.

"I'm not askin' fer what ya've done or shown ta others, or how fortune has smiled upon ya, nor am I askin' ya ta tell me. If I'm gonna stand in place rooted like a tree, then what ya're gonna show me had better be prettier than Freyda's beard fer me ta do it!"

Yip asked one more question. "Realizing potential beyond your own physical limits is not enough?"

"I already have magic fer that and it suits me just fine as it has my ancestors fer millennia. I can call upon Brendle at need and draw upon His power ta smite down my foes. What else d'ya have ta offer?" Kazarhan crossed his thick, battle-scarred arms stubbornly, a stolid barrier barring his chest, impeding any receptivity, and refusing to budge.

"I am not asking you to change your ways, Kazarhan. Nor am I implying any failings within your own traditions. Neither am I asking you to practice mine. You are free to do and practice as you choose."

Daerdros stepped forward, knowing Kazarhan's nature and wishing to assuage him, allowing his personality to express itself, but also wishing for him to understand that she was his commanding officer and her wishes were to be obeyed. "Kazarhan, we feel that what Yip offers may have merit to our training regimen and are giving his approach a chance. We are only asking that you keep an open mind as well."

Her tone firmed. "Understand, if you are asked to participate, you will participate."

She then turned to Yip. "Kazarhan has asked for a demonstration. Would you be willing to accommodate him?"

Yip bowed deeply as he spoke. "Of course."

He then looked to Kazarhan where he stood several paces away across the magically lit hold. "Are you ready?"

Kazarhan growled and braced himself, spreading his legs and hunkering down in preparation for Yip to attack with both arms bent and held at the ready before him.

Yip, however, did not move. He remained standing in the neutral Wuji posture, hands at his sides, arms and legs relaxed, as though he were merely resting.

He lifted his hand.

The gesture was slow and measured, the simple, easy beginning motions required to start a friendly salutation or to raise his arm in reaction to an unseen stimulus, but otherwise the movement appeared innocuous.

The effect on Kazarhan, however, was startling.

As soon as Yip began the upward sweep of his hand, Kazarhan launched backward, struck explosively or pushed full force in the chest by an invisible battering ram. Impelled bodily, his head, arms, and feet trailed behind his torso as he was propelled through the air, his flight only interrupted with a loud crash by a pile of crates and barrels firmly trussed to the wall.

No incantations, gesticulations, symbols, or other signs of the utilization of magic presaged the effect of Yip's motion. Other than the simple hand motion, no sounds or other indications of the application of force intimated the strike. Kazarhan, along with several of his fellows, had been caught completely off-guard.

A casual gesture and no more had forced a mighty warrior off his feet, out of control, and into a vulnerable, compromised situation. Had the desired effect been other than a simple push, the outcome could have been much more injurious.

With all eyes on Kazarhan, the Dwarf stood slowly, otherwise unhurt due to the protection of his armor and the measured application of force. With a brief glance to his chest piece to make sure all was in order, Kazarhan retook his position to Yip's left.

With cool aplomb, recovering himself quickly, Kazarhan said flatly, "Handy trick ya have there."

His bearded face cracked with a reluctant smile. "Per'aps ya could show it ta some o' my clan back home?"

As they resumed the basic Wuji posture, Yip bowed his head slightly in reply.

MAERON

Raucous white clouds below
flat gray clouds above,
teal sky in between.

"Land ho!" Wrindanneth called out loudly from where he stood directing the ship's movements at the ship's aft.

Turning to follow his gesture, those on deck looked forward and down across the glassy waters of the Lueciane Sea to where he pointed.

From the deck, no land could as yet be seen.

Gazing intently toward the blue horizon, Aroganji squinted against the sunlight reflected across the endless blue water. The fullness of his gaze directed forward, there was, perhaps, a faint haze on the horizon as if the shimmering heat of a summer's day were refracting the light from the sky. Despite his keen attention, this haze which Wrindanneth identified as land was only evident as an extremely fine line across the horizon.

Walking up to the piloting station, however, the ship's projection showed a much different image to Aroganji, Slate, and Wrindanneth.

Shrouded in mists, as yet barely visible from the height and distance, billowy clouds skirted the shadows of tall, verdant cliffs that soared to vertiginous heights above azure waters marking the deep roots of the precipices in lustrous strands of topaz. Much thinner than the band of bright blue shallow waters, pockets of golden sand could be seen clustered in the safety of the folds within the looming peaks.

For those seeking refuge from a storm by water, safe harborage would be difficult to find.

"Good thing we're flyin'," muttered Slate, a welcoming comment in strong contrast to his previous feelings about travel on a flying vessel.

Aroganji agreed. "Crossing those peaks would be an expedition unto itself."

As yet unbowed by time, the northern coast of Maeron rose above the waters of the Lueciane Sea in haughty pride, as tall as mountains normally found inland rooted in the continental heart. Including the depths below the water as part of their lofty heights, the Ghrem Weard had much cause for its fearsome reputation.

Few dared to challenge their heights or delve into their secrets.

For those aboard the *Shrike*, however, the Ghrem Weard were not a destination, only a part of the journey—an obstacle to be admired, not explored.

"If the rest of Maeron is as foreboding, it's no wonder humanity has forgotten her shores." Even from afar, Wrindanneth did not envy those who may try to come to her coasts in search of a future in new, wild lands.

"And we're here ta make ourselves welcome where we are not."

"A man at peace is at ease wherever his journey leads, wherever his tread falls."

Slate sighed at Yip's comment after his silent approach brought him into their midst. "Ya really should write all those pithy sayin's down in a book, Yip. At least then tha few people who actually want ta hear 'em will have 'em handy when they need upliftin'…or confoundin'."

Waiting for Yip's response, he added, "If they're willin' ta buy yer book, then perhaps ya'd get some coin outta tha arrangement as well."

Wrindanneth laughed as did Aroganji.

Yip merely shrugged.

"If you're smart, you could use Slate as a co-author, then your work would have some humor in it as well." Wrindanneth grinned at the suggestion.

"If I had the opportunity to write as you suggest, then our quest would be complete and Ea'ae and her people would be safe."

"But not from yer aphorisms!" They all laughed uproariously at Slate's rejoinder and the thought of reading any scrolls or tomes penned by Yip. For his part, Slate took a moment to lift a hand from his convulsing stomach to wipe a tear from his watering eyes.

Wrindanneth patted Slate on the back as he, too, cleared his eyes.

Knowing that he had been had, any further comments were likely to be the source of further jokes at his expense, and not wishing to offer a retort, Yip bowed and smiled going along with his friends' jests. "You are correct."

"Glad ta hear it!"

Quickly turning the tables on Slate, Wrindanneth said, "Don't get used to it. I doubt it will happen again."

"At least it's happened ta me once, ya great orange-headed Swamp Troll!"

"Peace, like composure, is a frame of mind we choose."

"And tha topic fer another chapter in yer book!" Slate clapped his right hand against his thigh as he guffawed. Heads from those Home Guard on the ship's deck turned to the quarterdeck so loud was his laughter.

With a crooked smile, Wrindanneth suggested, "Certainly sounds like you've got quite the book in there ready to come out, Yip. Perhaps *Yip Chi Chuan's Guide to Health and Wellness*?"

"Naw! I think it'll be somethin' like *Tha Bald Monk's Guide ta Self Respect and Avoiding Self Pity*!"

"Or *How to Maintain Composure When Your Friends Act Like Your Enemies*?" Aroganji had had enough of this line of jest.

Wrindanneth and Slate paused, briefly looking at each other in response to Aroganji's humor stifling suggestion.

Breaking up in laughter once more, they simultaneously ended the temporary lull. "Naw!"

Maintaining a straight face in spite of his friends' eye-watering laughter, Yip said, "Perhaps it will be entitled *The Mad Monk's Guide to Pithy One Liners*."

"Ya've already got my coin!" Slate could hardly get the words out between heaving chortles.

"A bestseller!" Wrindanneth was leaning on Slate's solid shoulder shaking his head with only slightly more composure than his friend.

Thoughts of Yip's potential books were as debilitating as any inimical spell.

Standing in silence together with Yip for a time while Wrindanneth and Slate's laughter slowly dissipated, Aroganji waited patiently before finally asking, "And how long before we reach the mainland?"

Standing erect and wiping his eyes as he slowly regained a measure of poise, Wrindanneth said with some difficulty through ragged breath, "At our current heading and rate of travel, we should arrive at Maeron's northern shore, what my navigation system calls the 'Ghrem Weard', by this evening."

"That will mark the end of the first half of our journey to Taerris'thule."

Now recovered himself, Slate interjected, "Tha easy part."

Looking sternly to Slate, Wrindanneth added, if not in correction, then in disagreement, "The known part. From here on, we will have little to guide us other than old maps and our wits."

Grumbling in reply, his humor ready once again to take stage, Slate said, "At least we're not relyin' on yer wits alone." He chuckled, adding, "Then we would be lost."

"But we would still have hope." Wrindanneth looked at Slate pointedly. "Unlike if we had to rely on your wits alone."

Once again acting as peacekeeper and mediator, Aroganji asked, "Have you been able to discern anything that may be of risk to us thus far?"

Wrindanneth shook his head, his unending quarrel with Slate forgotten. "The skies are clear as far as the sensors can detect."

"We'll need ta watch behind as well as forward. Those birdmen don't strike me as tha type ta forget an enemy or lose a grudge."

"Aye." Wrindanneth felt much the same.

"Perhaps whatever keeps most people away from these shores will keep the R'yn Daer away as well." Aroganji was a bit more hopeful than either Slate or Wrindanneth.

"I'll believe it when I see it," Slate fairly spat the words. "Buzzards always show up at tha first signs o' battle."

Wrindanneth nodded. "And I'm sure we are in store for our fair share of fighting before our journey is done."

Offering only a brief admonishment, Aroganji chided, "Then you two at least will be well-prepared."

His gaze following the forward direction of the ship's bow, Yip looked onward as they approached the unexplored reaches of Maeron, her secrets slowly revealing themselves to their eyes.

What had at first seemed to be only the slightest haze upon the horizon, a ghost image to be questioned and continually reexamined, had slowly resolved itself into a faint shadow, as though someone took a quill and slowly, ever so slowly, drew a line across the border between earth and sky, a dark tracery separating the heavens and the sea. This line, too, gradually solidified and took up shape, as if the line were in fact ink that had spilled, a stain that was slowly leaching across the horizon gaining more substance and solidity as they approached from afar.

Just as his thoughts seemed to arise slowly from emptiness, gradually taking on shape and solidity resolving into form, so, too, did the great verdant continent before them. To his watching eyes, the continent itself was birthed from his imagination, a miraculous ideal that arose naturally of its own volition from the confines of his mind.

To his senses, the horizon ahead blazed ever brighter the nearer they flew, the energetic tones and complex webs of Maeron's expression distinct from those of the Lueciane Sea at her feet, diaphanous webs bridging the ocean to the sky. Within the heights, unexpectedly, he sensed beings of great power slumbering, quiescent but present nonetheless.

Interrupting his contemplation, walking over to Wrindanneth at the helm, he said, "There are beings of extreme power abiding in the peaks. They appear at rest but that could change quickly."

Wrindanneth gave a nod. "Is there anything else?"

He shrugged. "From this distance, there is little to tell. If you adjust your heading farther south and west"—he pointed, indicating the direction—"there appears to be a wider section of the peaks without the entities that may allow safer passage."

"I will adjust our heading accordingly. When we get closer, or if you notice anything else unusual, let me know."

With a slight bow, he returned to his examination of the land and sea.

Lost in the panorama before him, Yip thought as he watched, his gaze shifting inward. The progression of his contemplations moved in an uninterrupted stream that he observed in much the same way he did the approaching horizon which had now resolved itself finally as they flew rapidly forward into a large, unbroken band of green.

Although he had said otherwise, there was indeed ample time, should he wish to take it, to work on ordering his thoughts and ideas and setting them down on paper. Though he did take the opportunity to compose and transcribe *róucí* as the poems arose, more often than not, rather than in composition, he chose to spend his time in practice—whether his own or with others.

Slate's progress remained remarkable over the past few days. At his current pace, Slate would not need his help much longer. In fact, Slate did not need his assistance now. Once Slate felt the same way, realizing it for himself, he could let Slate continue his personal journey unimpeded by his own presence.

The Home Guard, too, were eager pupils. Although they generally wished for him to demonstrate external applications and principles, constantly goading him to show clever tricks and feats after his initial demonstration with Kazarhan, he remained committed to helping them to cultivate an open frame of mind and physical expression that would complement and aid in their own individual areas of expertise.

As was the case with Slate, he wished to provide a springboard for their continual improvement based on their own unfolding paths of discovery. Though he could offer and guide, the inner journey each person must ultimately take was his and his alone. He could not set their agenda or pace.

There was much he himself had to learn. He could not presume to teach others where he himself did not know.

Interacting with the Guard constantly reinforced this conclusion.

A loud call broke his silent observation and cogitation.

"All hands on deck!"

With nothing sensing amiss, he turned to where Wrindanneth called out from the helm demanding their attention. Turning from Wrindanneth to face forward along their current heading to see what could be awry if he could not sense it yet himself, the jagged shore of Maeron now loomed precipitously close—a sheer monolithic unbroken wall of green. Other than the rapidly nearing clouded cliffs and the open blue waters, nothing appeared out of place.

Before anyone could inquire further, Wrindanneth called out stridently once more, "Dragon on the horizon! To the helm!"

Daerdros and Eidelion followed Slate, Aroganji, and Yip to the helm. The rest of the Home Guard remained positioned about the *Shrike*'s deck awaiting command.

From its perch, a colossal Dragon spread its mighty wings and leapt into the air, the beat of its pinions so broad as to block the peaks from which it arose. As they gathered watching, hovering in the air before them, magnified by the ship's projection system, the massive ebony Wyrm could be seen flying through the air away from the heights and out over the open seas.

So powerful was the cadence of its wings visible in the projection, Yip almost expected to hear the sound of their rhythm.

"Does the drake know we are here?" Eidelion needed information in order decide on the most appropriate course of action.

"Yes."

"How do you know?" The tangled mixture of fear and excitement were not lost in Aroganji's tone.

"It called to me." Wrindanneth appeared, for once, reticent and slightly humble.

"And what did it say?" Eidelion pushed knowing that they would not be able to outrun a Dragon at full speed and needing to decide how best to prepare.

"It asked why we were here."

"And what did you say?"

"That we were passing through and had business beyond these peaks."

"Then what?" Daerdros, too, wished for him to hurry.

"It said that it was coming to talk with us."

Eidelion nodded. "There are no others?"

"No. Just the one."

Pausing a moment as he looked to Yip, he added, "For now."

Eidelion nodded and turned to Daerdros. "Let Raour'Saqan know that he may be needed."

Daerdros nodded curtly.

"If parlay with the Dragon does not proceed as we wish, then he will engage the wyrm."

"What would you have me tell him?"

"If our talk does not grant us safe passage, then Raour'Saqan will have his. If Raour'Saqan's attempt to reason with the Dragon and assure our passage does not work, then he will need to destroy the Dragon."

Turning with a nod, Daerdros left them as she went to seek out Raour'Saqan and alert the others.

As fast as the *Shrike* traveled, the Dragon traveled faster. In less than half an hour it had crossed the distance between them and was now clearly visible before them, its looming bulk undeniable even to the naked eye. As the Dragon approached, Wrindanneth held the ship in place, shields up, weapons at the ready.

For its part, the Dragon approached stridently, the beat of its wings like thunder on the horizon. Moving with sinuous grace belying its terrible size, the ancient wyrm flowed and flitted over the currents swimming through the air, flying with more grace and ease than the most cleverly guided kite.

Awe-inspiring and dreadful, its deep black scales drank in the sunlight with a thirst that only allowed its brightest highlights to remain fully visible in the sun. Jagged horns framed a head dwarfing a wagon, wicked teeth larger than a grown man curved viciously outward from lips scaled and pitted, partially hidden by plumes of smoke. Sharp black claws longer than the spears of footmen at the forward lines of battle curved downward from hands and feet each large enough to snatch an armored warhorse at full gallop.

Dragon dread trailed thick in its wake—fumes billowing behind a fire.

All told, the beast appeared easily thrice the length of the *Shrike*, the full barrel of its chest almost as wide. An elder wyrm such as this had probably seen the days when the peaks of the Ghrem Weard had first risen above the turbulent waters of the Lueciane Sea.

Coming to a halt before them, arching its long neck vertically upward as its tail dropped and its wings beat downward, its unbroken belly open before them in a vulnerable gesture known to Dragons as one of peace, the beat of its redoubtable wings stirred the air with more force than the gales of a summer storm.

Opening its mouth in a bilious cloud of smoke, words so deep as to be almost inaudible rumbled from the depths within its chest. Feeling the beguiling power of the Dragon's words call to them, wash over them, and demand their attention, his pronouncements were translated from the tongue of Wyrms. "What need brings you to the aeries of Cersaegian, Liege of the Fiersayne, Keeper of the Ghrem Weard?"

Knowing that Dragons could read the truth of his words as well as a scholar could elucidate even the most indecipherable scroll, Wrindanneth spoke openly and with candor for the ship and its crew. "We seek Taerris'thule."

A deep rumble louder than the crashing boulders of an avalanche resounded over them.

The sound of laughter.

"Why would one willingly seek such a place?"

Reluctant to answer but knowing that he must for to dissemble or mislead would be sensed and could incur the Dragon's wrath, Wrindanneth answered, "That we may restore the seal of Eldre'gheu."

His laughter abated as quickly as it had arisen, the Dragon's long neck snaked rapidly toward them, bringing one awful golden eye directly to bear upon Wrindanneth. He felt the weight of that gaze like crushing stone and had difficulty breathing under its full baleful attention.

With a rapid blink, the Dragon turned its head and returned to its vertical hovering posture. "The Fiersayne will not stay you or deny your passage for your quest has worth to us as well."

"Know this before you leave the safety of the sea. The reach of my brood extends only as far as the southern peaks of these mountains. Beyond their borders, we do not fly and our shadow does not fall."

Recapturing his voice, Wrindanneth managed to whisper, "Thank you."

"Do not thank me, human. Legions of Orcs are as kind a welcome as you will find beyond our aeries. Hellspawn and worse lay in wait for your band should your journey reach its end."

"These hellspawn know no pity or fear and will not be as solicitous as I for your interests are not theirs."

With a rapid twist, the Dragon turned about its axis with an awesome finality that left Wrindanneth speechless once more.

The staccato beats of its wings rumbling like thunder, the Dragon roiled and arched gracefully back toward the unblemished peaks of the Ghrem Weard without so much as a backward glance.

The beast was as fearsome as it was fearless.

Still staring off after the Dragon's flight, the *Shrike* remained suspended in place all the while. Yip's quiet voice finally brought Wrindanneth back out from under the Dragon's spell. "The majesty of a Dragon is worth a lifetime of waiting to behold."

Wrindanneth smiled as he regained control and eased the ship forward, slowly bringing the *Shrike* to speed in the Dragon's wake. "Worthy of another chapter in your book?"

Bowing with a smile, Yip, too, watched after the Dragon's flight beholden to a beauty few ever lived to see or tell.

LEGION

Waves crash upon a
beach of soft white sand—
force dissipates in sound.

Green from base to summit, the peaks of the Ghrem Weard were as beautiful as they were perilous. Even from on high, Yip could see the breadth and depth of their splendor, feel the vibrancy of the life radiating upward from within. Lush and overflowing, rain-fed streams and waterfalls cut like silver ribbons through jungles untouched and unblemished by the hand or desire of Man, Elf, Dwarf, or Gnome.

From earth to sky, horizon to horizon, an unbroken canopy of verdancy stretched like a roiling green ocean, so vast that he felt the forest below was as broad and deep as the sea over which they had flown for days. He wondered what marvels lay hidden beneath the leafy mantle, breathing in the fullness of the air and mist.

Steaming banks of fog marked the breath of the forest just as thick clouds obscured its transitions and permutations upward to the heights of the lofty peaks. As much as the thick, verdurous leaves, whose variegated spectrum presented a broad range around the focal greens, silvers, golds, purples, oranges, and blues, along with the height from which he viewed the forest below, the clouds and fog concealed the jungle interior below from his wondering eyes in an impenetrable pearlescent cloak.

Interpenetrating the entirety of his senses, far thicker than the canopy or fog, the clouds or the understory, the living energy of the land added complexity and vibrancy to a panorama already overfilling with both.

There was peace and beauty to be had here, but danger and risk were found in equal measure for even under the auspices of Dragons, the wilds of Maeron were home to creatures just as deadly. These wildernesses were to be respected and treated with the utmost caution for their alluring glamor was as much a risk as their denizens.

"Ready fer practice, Yip?" Slate called to Yip from the center of the ship's deck, his deep voice pulling Yip away from his observation of the jungle below.

"I am." Leaving his position beside Wrindanneth at the helm, Yip left the quarterdeck where he had been watching the ship's progress alongside Aroganji to return to the lower deck.

Slate already had his axe unsheathed and at the ready when Yip joined him. Duraeleon remained quiet at Yip's approach respecting the discipline of Slate's practice.

"What're we workin' on today?" Slate planted the head of Duraeleon firmly on the wooden planks of the deck as he leaned forward holding its haft in both hands.

"Whatever you wish, Slate."

Slate held his silence, studying Yip carefully eyebrows bunched, slightly confused sensing a hidden current underneath Yip's words, knowing, in the extremely observant ways of the Dwarf, that all was not readily apparent.

"This is your practice, Slate. You are free to do as you will."

"We've been workin' together." A mixture of confusion and hurt at Yip's vagueness and distance were apparent in Slate's tone.

Yip nodded. "We have been and still are, if that is what you wish, Slate, just as you are free to work with Daerdros and still do."

Again Slate was silent for a moment. "I'm not sure I follow what ya're sayin', Yip. Are we or aren't we workin' together?"

"Slate, I have been watching you practice for days. Since we left the island nation of Landeiss you have not needed my assistance nor have I given any. I have merely watched at need should you require me. You have not."

"That may change in the future or we may one day wish to try something new together, but for now I only observe."

"Ya're sayin' I don't need ya?"

"I am here as I ever was, ready to assist you should you need me."

"I'm not followin', Yip. Can ya just say what ya want without talkin' circles around it?"

"Your journey is yours to take, Slate. When you feel ready, then I am confident in your ability to continue onward as you will."

"Without yer help?"

Yip shrugged, the robes on his shoulders flowing in response. "Only as needed. This is your tradition you are rediscovering and redeveloping. There is only so much I can offer without changing what is your way into something else."

Slate nodded, finally accepting the mantle of responsibility and independence Yip offered, the reality that he needed Yip's safety net and guidance no more. "Tha path o' my fathers must be blazed again, and tha time has come fer me ta do it on my own. That's what ya're gettin' at?"

Yip bowed in reply. "Now you are truly, as you have always been, your own teacher."

Slate nodded once more in affirmation. "Thank ya, Yip. Yer aid has been most welcome. I never thought I'd learn tha ways o' my fathers from a Man, much less a Priest o' K'un Lun. Now tha halls o' my fathers will need ta make room fer a monk and our lore will now include a small bit o' yers."

"I am honored to have helped, Slate."

"And I'm honored ya did."

"Time ta get started." Slate gave a brief nod, adamantium resolve in his eyes, bringing Duraeleon up in a sharp salute, before he began the Doerdaana'-Duin, finally losing himself amid the heat and flames of the Daerdaana'Duin, the deck of the *Shrike* remaining unblemished beneath his blazing boots.

Leaving Slate to his practice, Yip returned to the quarterdeck where Wrindanneth remained standing over the control disk studying the projection of their current position over the Ghrem Weard.

Behind them, now engrossed in his efforts, Aroganji moved through the complex permutations of the Wu-hsing expressed and symbolized so eloquently in his tradition. Before them, burning with ever brighter light, Slate, too, manifested his own destiny.

"Are you not going to stay with him?"

Wrindanneth noticed quickly and somewhat alarmedly that Slate was practicing his flaming Dwarf dance without Yip nearby to douse his fires should he try to burn the ship down again in his excitement.

"There is no need."

"Are you certain?" Wrindanneth did not wish for a repeat of their prior experience. The evidence of the past days did little to ameliorate his concerns. As far as he was concerned, Slate was at risk of catching the *Shrike* on fire.

"I am here should the need arise."

"But it won't?"

"I do not think so."

"Why?"

"He has not needed my assistance for days. My observation has only been that and nothing more. Until now, he felt reassured by my presence, but it is no longer needed. If the need truly does arise, then I can react from here almost as quickly as from his side."

Reassured with Yip's full explanation, at least for now, Wrindanneth offered his reluctant praise. "He has come far in a short period of time."

"As have we all."

Two more full days came and went before they finally passed beyond the green peaks of the Ghrem Weard and over the flat tropical lowlands that spread outward from their feet. As variegated and broad as the highlands from which they descended, the lush bottomland forests held rolling hills and wide streams that fed into slow, lazy rivers—some filled with brown silt and sediment, others as black and impenetrable as the canopy shading them from above.

Here the clouds through and over which the *Shrike* flew were mirrored below in billowing banks of mist transpired from the myriad trees, thick and unbroken in the morning but gradually evaporating with the heat of the day. Peering below as the days progressed, Yip imagined that he gazed downward at the surface of still pond, the clouds above reflected by those often below, the forest canopy the bottom of the still pool through which he peered, covered in infinitesimally small plants and algae. The sky, too, was reflected below in the effusive *chi*, so radiant near the ground and all the living things that strengthened its presence, gradually becoming fainter with altitude until only the elusive *yuan-chi* was visible looking high toward the heavens and the ever-thinning atmosphere above.

On the eve of the second day beyond the peaks, with the bright orange sun setting in splendor on the western horizon, Wrindanneth called them all to the bridge.

Yip had warned him earlier that day of the ill omens he felt through the movements of the living energies. Now the evidence was clear for him to see as well.

He could delay action no longer.

When Yip, Aroganji, Daerdros, and Eidelion had all arrived, Wrindanneth brought forth the projection for them to see. As the image resolved itself in the half-light of the setting sun, he said, "There is smoke on the horizon."

As faint and distant as the image was, the plume appeared as little more than a thin band. If not for the fact that it trailed vertically, the smoke would easily be mistaken for the fog so prevalent with the rich forest below.

"Based on my evaluations, we are about mid-way through a large valley between two ranges. The smoke appears to be coming from along the base and scattered on the sides of the other range."

Slate peered up at Wrindanneth gravely, asking, "When're ya gonna call us up here fer good news?"

"When there's good news to tell."

"Which may not be on this trip, I fear," finished Eidelion solemnly.

"What is it?" asked Aroganji.

"Could be a forest fire," said Slate matter-of-factly, but he did not sound convinced in the slightest.

Daerdros looked at the projection carefully before speaking. "Or a forest set on fire."

"Hmm..." Eidelion nodded.

"Are ya thinkin' what I'm thinkin'?" Slate's face wore a look of deep disdain.

"Orcs."

Slate nodded with Eidelion's reply, the sour look on his face adding even deeper furrows to his already well-lined face.

"Those blighters're everywhere I wish they weren't."

"We'll need to gain and maintain altitude." Wrindanneth pointed to the edge of the billowing tree line, cautioning, "This far from the Dragon's reach, with no one else to harry them, they will have sentries flying the sky without fear. We will need to avoid those outriders as best we can."

"Can we not go around?" Aroganji pointed farther up or down the range.

Wrindanneth shook his head. "Even if the Orcs' reach is not far along the range, we can take a more direct flight path by flying higher over them than going completely around and outside of their territory."

"What if they have wards ta detect our passage even from high above?"

"There is no 'if'. They will have wards in place along with other surprises. We can try to disable them or outrun their pursuit once they detect us." Eidelion spoke with confidence.

Daerdros agreed, adding, "We will cross over their peaks under cover of darkness. The distance and gloom will help protect us from visual detection on the ground."

"Our current altitude should suffice," Wrindanneth interjected. They were already flying so high as to be almost invisible to all but the most powerful eyes when observed from the ground below. He finished, "If I maintain our current rate of speed and heading, another day's travel should place us in a position to fly over the next range under the cover of night."

"We must remain alert, however. The Orcs may have flyers traveling farther afield, those meant to test the strength and reach of the Dragons, perhaps." As always, Eidelion wished to be prepared for any unwelcome eventuality.

"Should we be forced to engage, what of their strength against ours?" Aroganji, too, was concerned.

"We cannot know their numbers, but to hold their own against the Dragons of the Ghrem Weard, they must be many. Very many." Eidelion studied the smoking range depicted in the projection with the care of one reading an interesting tale, one whose tortuous story kept him engrossed and unwilling to avert his eyes. "Orcs, however, are not known for their skill in flight or the craftsmanship of their airships. We should be in a position to hold our own, outrun them should we need to retreat, or push our way through."

"Anything else?" Wrindanneth was ready to be about his business for the evening—setting the ship's path before bedding down, or trying to at least, where he now slept next to the control sphere.

Daerdros finished for them all by saying, "We should all endeavor to rest as fully as possible tonight. We will need to be on guard tomorrow and the following evening. This may be our last opportunity to sleep normally for some time."

"Until the morn," Daerdros left with an elegant bow.

"Aye. Time ta work on shuttin' my eyes and lettin' my beard grow."

"We will all need to be fresh and alert for the morning," Aroganji broke off with a bow.

"Until the morn and the Light of a new dawn," offered Eidelion with his particular blend of command and grace.

"If we have need, I will be near," Yip bowed to Wrindanneth before he, too, left.

Wrindanneth called after him, "Don't worry, I know where to find you skulking about my deck, staring after shadows."

Yip smiled as he walked away from his friend down the wooden stairs to the deck, the fading light of dusk casting long smudged shadows across the planks from the masts, sails, and rigging above, his shadow joining those below until he finally took a spot by the aft mast for his evening practice. He would remain in this spot until the morning, close to where Llyewia normally cast his starlight hammock, but far enough away so that his presence was not a distraction.

His eyes closed, his senses alert, the vibrancy of the *chi* enveloping him in living energy, he stood in timeless silence, patiently practicing serenity beneath a darkling sky lit by the afterglow of a thousand billion stars.

In the unbroken peace that spread through and encompassed the evening, there slowly grew and built within the confines of Yip's awareness the presence of a glorious star, one whose beauty eclipsed the sun, whose radiance poured forth and lit the night.

In his mind's eye, he watched the star change and adjust, more malleable and fluid than the light shining down on him from above, a thousand miraculous sunsets captured at a glance, shifting between and embodying them all in the form of a single fluctuating light.

He had never seen nor felt the like.

So wondrous was this presence that he forgot his practice for a time and allowed himself the pleasure of observance—deep, joyful, and sincere. Such was the beauty of the transformations he beheld that it was only after some time that he realized his inner smile was laced with the faint salt of unbidden tears.

The evening passed in the effulgence of this light until, like the impending dawn, its time came too quickly. As the light began to fade and hide itself once more, he opened his eyes and turned his head toward the fore of the ship where the star had remained alight throughout the evening.

Shimmering before the brilliance of an unrealized sunrise, Orogast stood shifting from one form to the next in unbroken succession, the speed of his transformations gradually slowing as Yip watched in awe.

When Orogast's motion finally stilled, Yip wiped the tears from his cheeks.

Returning to a humanlike form, Orogast turned, his eyes meeting Yip's directly with a light as bright as the dawn. "Good day to you, Yip Chi Chuan."

"And you as well, Orogast, the Many Hued."

Orogast laughed. "You have been watching for some time I take it?"

Yip nodded. "I did not intend to intrude."

"You did not."

"Your art is a wonder, as beautiful as any I have ever seen or felt."

Orogast bowed respectfully. "I thank you. It is our warrior art, the art of unbroken change, I'ldaerya J'al Ishentaré."

"To practitioners of I'ldaerya J'al Ishentaré, our bodies, our essential forms, move and adjust like water from one position to another in an unending unfurling of living expression in response to our sensitivity to an opponent along with the energies and abilities we are able to draw from them and our past."

"In a very real way, we use the capabilities and power of an opponent against them, bringing to bear similar talents and experiences from prior teachers and foes as well."

Yip smiled sincerely, replying, "Then your enemies must be few." With such skill, he imagined that few could stand against the Jira S'al Alann.

Orogast smiled sadly in return. "Or too many."

Yip bowed at the affront. "I meant no offense."

"None taken."

"When next you practice, may I observe again?" He could learn much from the sensitivity, timing, and speed with which Orogast adjusted his body, intent, and energies. His fluidity and timing were unimaginable. While his was a skill of unequalled anticipation, Orogast's was one of nonpareil speed and flexibility.

Orogast gave a brief nod laughing. "With your senses, I could not hide if I tried."

"You are most gracious."

"And you are most welcome." Orogast walked by as fluidly as he had practiced, his body moving with more poise, balance, and ease than was humanly possible, a roiling wave easing silently past.

"Blasted Orcs!" Slate stood beside Wrindanneth at the helm peering with disgust into the projection provided by the ship's sensors. Abhorrence, hatred, and anger battled with unbridled intensity across his leathery face.

A solid day's travel above untracked wilderness had taken them over much of the jungle that they could safely traverse prior to entering the area of land obviously controlled and desecrated by the Orcs. In the hazy distance ahead and below, so unwelcomingly visible in the ship's projection, the viridian hues of the rainforest ended abruptly in a stark smoldering line at the foot of looming black peaks.

As though scoured with a great jagged blade and then lit up in careless flames, the mountains ahead were slashed, eroded, and singed, encrusted with soot, tailings, and debris, obscured by an unwholesome smog of burning wood, unbanked forges, and other fell industries delved by Orcish cunning. Scattered across the ruined slopes like diseased pocks were jagged openings to dark, smoking caves. These, too, issued forth black plumes and soots—the very earth itself coughing in fits and starts. From some of the pits and towers, ghastly red light could be seen spilling forth, its presence darker and less welcome even than the warped shadows from the afflicted Orcish towers.

Erected around many of these openings and vents were misshapen turrets and fortifications, the refuse thrown from a cesspit—irregular, warped, and unwanted. Black and ghastly, these towers and ramparts lurched toward the heavens in asperous fits and starts without regard to geometry, principle, or aesthetic—each a strident declaration of fearsome Orcish will and vile determination. Adorned in unholy wards and sigils, painted clan marks and signs, and festooned with profane trophies and tokens of battle, the Orcish armaments and battlements leered and taunted any who dared to gaze upon their walls in ill-disguised challenge.

In lieu of the refreshing clouds and fogs that girdled mountains elsewhere, draping the air above the distant cliff sides in an unbroken pallid mass were the collected particulates, ash, grit, and other leavings of foul Orcish works, clinging to the mountain range's profile in an unhealthy smog. So thick and vile was the veil that it was no wonder that Orcs hid themselves beneath the ground if for no other reason than to try to escape the loathsome effects of their own handiwork.

To Yip, watching and waiting next to Slate and Aroganji, the Orcish presence upon the mountainsides resembled nothing more than an unchecked wasting disease—spreading unbridled across, eating ravenously away at, and gradually smothering the life from the mountains and all about them. Whereas the jungle below was so rich and overflowing with energy, the mountains ahead appeared choked and gasping, in the last violent throes before collapse.

His heart reflecting much of what Yip saw, Slate cursed, "By Brendle's beard, Orcs're a blight ta be wiped off tha planet!"

"They certainly appear to fear some kind of attack, even here." Aroganji gazed with undisguised distaste upon the virtual rendition depicting the foul landscape ahead.

"Bah! Orcs fear nothin'!" Slate wagged a thick finger at the image disparagingly. "If Orcs had a shred o' caution and care, they would overrun our world. As it is, they challenge any who would oppose them and announce their presence in utter defiance."

Not disagreeing entirely, for once, Wrindanneth added, "Between the Dragons of the Ghrem Weard and anything lurking in the jungles below, I am sure that the Orcs are in need of their fortifications."

Slate grunted, a grim smile upon his face. "It's a shame there isn't more here ta cause 'em alarm!"

Looking away from the disgusting depiction to his friends, Slate added, "They are universally despised. Even in their own homes, Orcs do not find refuge."

"A grim life indeed." Aroganji would not wish such a fate upon a people, not even Orcs, but theirs was the way of survival, no matter how harsh or unpleasant. They survived and thrived on Ea'ae just as they did upon other worlds. A blight, yes, but one successful and tenacious at maintaining both its presence and right to live.

Unlike his comrades, perhaps, Yip held out hope for the Orcs just as he did any and everyone. "Perhaps one day the Orcs will come to see that their actions harm themselves and their future as much as they damage the environment and other peoples with which they live and contact."

Wrindanneth shook his head. "And open themselves up to retaliation for countless atrocities?"

Slate laughed, a cruel bark, unchecked by moral scruple, molded by thousands of years of bloodshed. "Untold Dwarven axes have sharpened their blades upon Orcish skulls ta no avail. It is not sense, but savagery that tha Orcs hold dear and cherish. Without brutality and barbarism, Orcs would cease ta exist."

Unfazed by his friends' prejudice, for he understood its source and reason, Yip did not fall prey to its trap. Instead, he answered rhetorically, "And what would arise in their place?"

Slate shook his head grimly. "No one'll ever know because they'll choose extinction before change."

"How can you be so sure if you resist change yourself?"

Slate turned away from the image in the projection then, staring with deadly intensity into Yip's eyes as he spoke. "Tha day an Orc doesn't throw himself upon my axe is tha day I shave my beard!"

Yip smiled. "One should always be prepared with a razor."

"Or an axe," grunted Slate with finality.

As the day's shadows lengthened, Eidelion joined them at the bridge. "I have asked Daerdros to disguise the ship and decrease its detectability."

"How so?" asked Wrindanneth.

"From the ground, even in full daylight, the ship should look like nothing more than any other part of the sky—unremarkable and indistinguishable from the rest."

When Wrindanneth raised an eyebrow, Eidelion smiled, understanding what he was thinking and wishing to respect Wrindanneth's sense of control over his ship. "Her weavings will not interfere with the functionality of the *Shrike*. When she is done, the enchantments should last long enough to see us through the night undetected."

Wrindanneth nodded. "Will her spells aid in protecting us from any wards the Orcs have in place to detect intruders?"

"Without knowing exactly what enchantments are in place, one can never be sure. However, her wards should lower the risk of detection, letting energies flow around us as if we were not present."

"As a secondary precaution, Spreesprocket will be monitoring ambient magical energies and wards from the fore as well."

"Fair enough."

"Does she need any assistance?" asked Aroganji.

Eidelion shook his head, replying, "I think not."

Before Aroganji could offer a second question, Eidelion smiled, adding, "But you are welcome to watch."

Aroganji bowed, glad for the chance to study a magician of such high caliber in action and for the opportunity to share the experience with Wrindanneth through their connection for he would value the experience as much, if not more. With any luck, they would both learn new spells. "Thank you."

"How long before she is done and it is safe to move forward?" Wrindanneth wanted to understand how her work would coincide with the impending setting of the sun.

Eidelion looked to the sky, estimating the time until the sun's set as well. "She should be done within the hour, before the last rays of the sun fully fade from the coral sky."

Wrindanneth nodded in understanding. "Good. We will need as much time as we can get under cover of darkness for we know not how far the Orcish territory extends."

"Understood. I will let you know as soon as she has finished so that you may proceed in due haste."

Eidelion left with a short bow of respect before returning to the lower decks to organize those of the Light's Guard who had joined them on their quest. Following in his footsteps, Aroganji left the bridge in search of Daerdros.

Aroganji found Daerdros walking slowly along the ship's perimeter next to the railing, her tall figure and billowing cloak silhouetted against the darkening sky. She moved as gracefully as a dancer, her arms, hands, and fingers flowing rhythmically in complex patterns weaving with her body, mind, and voice in unison as she worked. In lieu of incantations or chants, she sang, her voice as soft and calming as the breeze, as lissome and fair as her motion, the depth and breadth of her song covering the ship in complex intertwined magical phrases and stanzas, each abiding and reinforcing the others in a vibrant mosaic of breath, life, and will.

Her spellcasting was very different than his own, so much so that there was little he could hope to glean directly from mere observation either in terms of techniques or formulae to replicate the effects she created. Knowing how different her approach and perspective on magical craft were from his own, he had not expected otherwise. Even so, there was much that he could admire and aspire toward in watching one of such astounding ability, whatever the tradition. Though the complexity and skill with which she worked was well beyond his current abilities, he could certainly strive for the fluid poise and facility with which she worked, the command she had over her weavings, and the imagination used to inspire her vision.

By the time she had completed a circuit of the ship, the sun had set, the long shadows of day replaced by the darker shadows of evening. Although he could not see and feel magical energies directly in quite the same way as Yip, he sensed the overarching thrum and potency of Daerdros's wondrous skeining, the change manifest and present within her enchantment. Through eyes augmented by his magic, he watched the bands of her will and voice merge and blend about the ship in a cloak of obfuscation.

She turned to him with a smile as she finished having been aware of his presence during her weaving but unwilling to break her concentration. "Did you learn what you wished?"

Aroganji laughed. "Only that I have much to grasp and aspire toward if I am to achieve my wishes."

She inclined her head in recognition of the worth of his comment. "Everyone is an expert at something. Finding your own niche and realizing the inherent potential within your chosen specialty is more than most ever achieve."

Aroganji bowed appreciatively, replying, "And you, apparently, have found and mastered several."

Deflecting the compliment, she said, "The field of magical endeavor is as broad as the imagination allows. Do not limit yourself or your studies to that which others have learned for the unknown is often more wondrous than the known."

Aroganji laughed heartily, shaking his head slightly as the laughter filled him, and placed his hands on his sides as he did so. "Perhaps you and Yip need to have a few more conversations for your words are as true a reflection of each other as a mirror allows!"

She declined her head briefly. "Yip speaks as he will, as do I."

"When darkness fully descends, we will be ready to move forward." With that she turned and walked away as silently as the shadows through which she tread.

Within the confines of his mind, Aroganji heard Wrindanneth reply wryly, *"That went better than I expected."*

"How do you mean?" Aroganji was confused.

"At least she was nice about the fact that you had been following her and watching her casting without her permission."

"But Eidelion said..."

"I am not talking about what Eidelion said. You never asked her permission to watch. She is almost as secretive about her talents as that foul-tempered Dwarf Kazarhan."

"She may hold her secrets, but she is also open in her willingness to help others

learn. So much so that she is even willing to share her knowledge and skill with another equally foul-tempered Dwarf!"

"Were you able to glean anything useful from your clandestine observation?"

Aroganji chuckled in lieu of voicing his disagreement with Wrindanneth's characterization of his scrutiny. "Her technique is so different from my own that there is little I could take from watching her."

Aroganji could almost feel Wrindanneth shaking his head in disagreement through their bond. "Even if you told her that, she could never be sure. Magicians are naturally secretive, even those who trust one another."

"Which is exactly why this connection is oftentimes more of a burden than a blessing!" Aroganji let his mirth flow through the bridge between them.

Now it was Wrindanneth whose humor flowed forth. "As if there is anything I could hope to learn from you!"

"Or that I would wish to share!"

By the time Aroganji returned to the bridge, the smile still warmed his face.

Remarking on his friend's grin as he approached, Wrindanneth said, "Haven't you managed to think of something else in the time since we last spoke?"

Turning the implied insult around on his friend, Aroganji replied, "You could not hope to understand my thoughts should I care to explain them."

Wrindanneth chuckled. "I am glad that you do not care then for I seek none of your clarity or insight!"

"I count myself fortunate!"

"As do I!"

They both laughed.

The sun had set, its glow no longer visible on the horizon. To the east, the sky was entirely dark with no traces of light upon the skyline. To the west, where the sun's light had so recently held sway, the sky remained a vivid electric blue, not yet given to the fullness of darkness.

With a curt nod, Wrindanneth said, "We are ready."

Aroganji did not reply. He merely gazed downward toward the fell industry of the Orcs made even more visible and offensive by the encroaching and deepening darkness. Lurid red lights carved across the mountains ahead, signs of forges and fires, dark rites and unspeakable rituals. At least the evening's shadows covered the accursed smoke and soot belching forth from the Orcish pits. He was glad for the altitude with which the *Shrike* flew and the atmospheric shield around her for he was also spared breathing in the burning, acrid smoke, and having the poisonous Orcish air coat and cling to his lungs and throat, stinging his eyes and nostrils.

While Aroganji pondered the handiwork of the Orcs, Wrindanneth called out, using the ship's systems to amplify and transport his voice throughout, "Everyone be on guard! We fly forth into the Orcish reaches!"

With that last pronouncement, the ship fell into wary silence, everyone aware that they now flew alone over a vast territory controlled by an enemy that would rather see them tortured and enslaved than free, tormented and embattled rather than pursuing their lofty quest, and sent to their deaths beyond the lands of the living, their legacy only serving as fuel for more Orcish hatred.

Yip joined Wrindanneth and Slate at the helm, a silent sentinel keeping unwavering vigil on the ground and skies below. Cool wind, warmed, stilled, and enriched with oxygen from the ship's protective atmosphere brushed lightly on his cheeks, a constant reminder of their forward progress.

Below, the blanketing darkness appeared coated in smoldering embers, reddish orange fires awaiting the proper fuel to burst into unchecked flames. As they traveled onward through the night, streaks of irregular ruddy light to the east and west marked what Yip perceived as the leading edges of forest fires very much like the one he had first seen marking the northern edge of Orcish territory. These fires indicated what he thought of as the limits of Orcish activity as they moved from one peak to another perhaps. Farther southward, higher summits burned of their own light, lava flows coursing down the sides of the dark mountain flanks, the heat of their volcanic hearts perfect for the Orcish forges.

The home of the Orcs was defined by calefaction and flames. The fires of the land burned and smoldered unshackled, matched in intensity only by the ever-growing incalescence of Orcish animus and rage. If they were successful in their quest and the crucible of the Cabal were averted and not left to wash over Ea'ae in unmitigated destruction, the uncounted Orcish hordes of Maeron may pose a threat almost as dangerous, if not as utterly destructive.

Fire and void must both be averted.

"Can you gauge the extent of their activity and presence here, Yip?" Aroganji asked as he joined Wrindanneth and Yip at the helm. He thought that Yip's perception may be able to provide some insight that his eyes and the cover of darkness prevented.

Turning away from the penurious lands below, a vista whose paucity and perversion saddened and troubled him for he could not understand how a people could so thoroughly exploit the land on which they lived, destroying it and everything that depended upon it, he answered his friend, "If the Cabal do not utterly destroy our world and all life upon it creating a barren waste-land, the likes of the Orcs will work tirelessly to create a vision almost as dim."

Aroganji merely grunted in response.

"I would imagine the land looks very much like a burnt, destitute desert deprived of almost any life that might struggle to subsist under its present condition."

"That sounds better than I had imagined."

Yip smiled grimly at Aroganji's reply. "Your musings are probably closer to the truth than mine." He did not elaborate on the fact that what little life appeared to persist below appeared as twisted and corrupted as the fell hearts of the Orcs.

Turning his gaze downward once more, the veil of energy below appeared so weakened and distorted that even the frailest of winds might blow its fragile essence apart.

"Don't let yer thoughts trouble ya, Yip." Slate walked over to stand by where Yip watched the trackless darkness pass by. "When we're done with our quest, we can come back and rid this land o' Orcs once and fer all!"

Yip turned toward his Dwarven friend and smiled wanly.

"I'm sure by then, after all tha Cabal've been returned ta tha lightless pits that spawned 'em, Duraeleon will need some sharpenin'. Orc heads are harder than any grindin' stone and should serve my needs just fine!"

"Perhaps"—Yip paused—"after all the violence we will see in the near future, we can come talk to the Orcs, show them the way of reason and compassion, and begin work to reform their ways."

Slate laughed, full and loud, unrestrained and honestly, his humor building with each guffaw as his self-control waned. Finally, when he had laughed for some time with increasing vigor until he curled inwardly upon himself and was left cradling his chest, Slate wiped tears from his sun-wrinkled eyes and replied, "Ya're crazier than a half-starved beardless Dwarf! Ya can't change their nature, Yip. Ya can't ask a lion ta be a mouse. Ya can't ask a vulture ta be a fairy. And ya can't ask an Orc ta be civilized!"

"You are correct. A lion is a lion. A vulture is a vulture. An Orc is an Orc. You have said exactly what they are. You have not said what they could be or may become."

Slate smiled and shook his head sagely. "Ya're a good man, Yip. Good and crazy!" Pausing briefly for a moment, he added with a firm smack on Yip's back, "That's why I like ya!"

Yip returned Slate's smile and bowed, taking his leave from the bridge and his friends, their faces bright from the silver light of the control orb and the radiant energies burning from within, walking down the smooth, polished stairs leading to the main deck. Then, continuing his stroll, he turned his gaze upward to the countless procession of stars moving overhead in time with Ea'ae's rotation.

Which of those held the inner sanctum of the Cabal?

Would he or his friends ever bridge the gap between this world and theirs?

Was their refuge even part of the night sky visible from this or another world in this universe?

Had the Cabal found or created a place that would remain inscrutable to even the keenest examination much like his brothers did within the monastery of the K'un Lun?

Were they, perhaps, hidden somewhere in plain sight?

Would he ever know?

While he slowly wandered about the deck, these and other thoughts diffused across his inner vision in an array almost as diverse and varied as the expansive domain of stars above.

Letting this movement of thought run its course, there being no solution or opportunity for resolution in hand, he noticed to his great alarm that they were no longer alone.

Descending from the frozen airless reaches above, fragments of deepest night, Darknesses never lit by love or hope, spiraled downward from the void of the upper atmosphere plunging forward toward the ship's trajectory. Too far to be fully realized or examined, the Shadows appeared to travel with lazy menace through the night, their Darkness drinking in the light from the stars above as fully as any abyss.

Terrible and awesome, the nebulous creatures tunneled through the living energies of the night leaving stark vacuity in their wake.

Not yet knowing if they had as yet been seen or otherwise detected, Yip catapulted himself through the air from the deck to the bridge, a surge of *chi* coursing through him as he took flight and landed softly beside Wrindanneth whose surprised face told him more about his arrival than any words ever would. "What the—!"

Before his friend could utter any more pronouncements, he ordered, "We must descend now!"

Not taking the time to respond or gesture, Wrindanneth dropped the ship like a stone. So quick was the transition to vertical descent that even with magical compensation everyone on board noticed the sudden, dizzying drop.

Their course adjusted and motion corrected while they descended, although the risk remained unabated, he pointed upward to the sky. "There!"

"I don't see anythin', Yip!" Slate understood Yip's urgency but could not identify the source even with his heightened night vision.

"There are essences of Darkness patrolling the skies! I do not know their nature or origin, but there are creatures above that we must avoid if we are to cross the Orcish reaches!"

Before he had finished his warning, Eidelion and Daerdros joined them at the helm, alert and at the ready, seeking the cause of alarm since Wrindanneth had not raised one, looking to inform their fellow armsman on how to proceed.

His eyes cast heavenward, Eidelion offered a brief prayer, the completion of which basked him in a flash of golden light, so pure and refreshing that all who saw its glory felt filled with the splendor and wonder of life born anew, of gentle spring rains, the coming of warmth, and hope restored. His eyesight now heightened by his faith, Eidelion muttered grimly, "Yip speaks truly. Terror has found a home in the skies above the Orcish legion!"

Before Eidelion could say any more, a terrible shriek pierced the air with the sound of metal grating on metal—the blades of rusty serrated saws gnashing and grinding against one another in the throat of a distant monstrosity. The wail struck them fully from afar through and into their hearts leaving them shocked—thrown bodily into intractably gelid waters.

"By Brendle's breath, what an abomination!" Slate grated his teeth in response to the noise from above.

"Scierdyas!" Eidelion brought his gaze back to his fellows. He spoke with certainty, his eyes burning with intensity and inner flames from the magic he had invoked. "The Orcs have made a foul bargain and are in league with hellspawn!"

Daerdros nodded, understanding tinged with sadness mixed in her tone. "That explains why the Dragons are reluctant to purge the Orcs from the borders of their lands."

"We must fly below the reach of their scrutiny even if it means risking encountering the Orcs. Their spectral gaze will penetrate our illusion and expose us to direct attack in addition to summoning the Orcs upon us."

Slate looked puzzled. "Fer those o' us who don't know, what in Freyda's frock is a Scierdyas?"

"Some would call them Spectral Dragons although they are not Dragonkin and hold no relation to the race as we know it. They are beings of Darkness without true form or feeling, feeding on life and the energy from which it arises. The Orcs must have worked long and hard to bind such creatures to their will."

Daerdros laughed, although there was no humor in the sound. "The fools! Though they may bind Daemons to their cause, soon their souls will be corrupted and no longer their own. The master will become the slave and their goals will become that of the foul creatures they summoned and attempted to control."

Eidelion spoke with cool authority, "We must tread more cautiously, for other creatures of Darkness may lurk in the shadows of the Orcish lands. If the Scierdyas do detect our presence, Raour'Saqan and I will deal with them while Daerdros and the others will help defend the ship and bolster her shields."

"Understood?"

Slate gave a curt nod. "We're not goin' anywhere and will be here fer each other, as we always have been and will be, so long as breath warms our bodies."

Turning to leave and alert the rest of the Light's Guard, Eidelion beamed brightly, the Light in his eyes touching the smile on his lips. "Good. Those ties of friendship bring you more strength than you know."

Following behind, Daerdros said, "Ware the Orcs as we descend. Should you see or sense anything, warn us immediately. We will let you know in kind."

Left alone once more on the bridge, Aroganji, Wrindanneth, Slate, and Yip pondered the night with mixtures of urgency, fear, and dread.

SWARM

Countless sandpipers
whirl and seethe in unison—
a school of fish in air.

The night seemed to have no end.

The cries of the Scierdyas boomed and rasped above, enveloping rumbles from a hellish storm. Below, the foul workings and delvings of the Orcs glared menacingly, far too close for comfort or stealth. Time and time again, Wrindanneth adjusted position and speed based on the ship's sensors in an effort to avoid detection; for while the Scierdyas patrolled the skies, so, too, did other Orcish vessels. Working side-by-side with his friend, Yip did his best to alert Wrindanneth to potential threats from above and below extending his senses along avenues not detected or tracked by the ship's sensors.

Working in tandem, they meandered through the reefs, shoals, and other unseen hazards of the Orcish skies as rapidly as they were able, their urgency and focus growing with each passing minute. With the coming of the dawn in just a few short hours, whatever small surety they had from the cover of night would evaporate for they would be too low to avoid visual detection by flying sentries even cloaked as they were by illusion.

The Orcish lands were too vast to cross in a single night slowed as they were by potential risks. Without a bit of luck in their favor, the coming day would see them forced to fight clear.

As they skirted another Orcish patrol—the deeper they flew into Orcish territory, the more frequent Orcish airships appeared to ply the skies whether for transit or defense, they could not say—Wrindanneth gritted his teeth and grumbled, "If only those Scierdyas were not patrolling above, we could take to the void of space and avoid risk of detection by the Orcs."

Yip laughed grimly. "Perhaps we should have done that from the start."

When Wrindanneth nodded humorlessly, Yip finished with a smile, "But then our journey would be much less interesting."

"Just how I want it!"

Understanding Wrindanneth's sentiment, but not sharing his feeling, Yip answered, "We have had much opportunity to learn and grow together even on this short excursion. Although time is of the essence, any chance we have to attain and discover is a gift we should not discard lightly for we do not know when we will be given the liberty again."

"I know, Yip, but as much as we seem to travel, there always seems to be time between goals."

Yip nodded. "Unless, of course, those goals come to us."

Wrindanneth laughed again. "That'd be nice! Save me the trouble of flying everyone from one side of the world to the other, across space, and who knows where else in the future?"

Hearing them banter, Slate chimed in from where he stood behind them, "Bah! What's adventure without adventurin'? Ya can't be an explorer without exploration! If ya wanna sit in place and expect tha action ta come t'ya, ya might as well be a gambler cuz that's about tha only way it'll happen!"

His voice laced with sarcasm, Wrindanneth quipped, "You are, as ever, a fount of wisdom and insight."

Not fazed in the slightest, Slate replied, "And you are, as ever, a fount o' optimism and good cheer."

His mood broken, Wrindanneth laughed again, this time with real humor. "Talk about the cauldron calling the kettle black!"

Slate smiled as he retorted, "At least I'm true ta my nature, and don't deny it!"

"When have I denied anything? I merely express my mood among friends"—Wrin smiled sardonically—"often and with verve!"

"I won't deny that!"

Sensing the approach of another vessel, Wrindanneth cut the banter short. "Another ship on the horizon! These Orcs are as numerous as bees about the hive!"

"Well, it is their hive after all, Wrin!" Slate could not help but smile as he spoke.

"Slate, when I want your opinion, I'll ask for it! Until then, let me focus on getting us to safety!"

Not knowing when to keep his mouth shut, Slate barked, "When have ya ever gotten us ta safety?"

"Certainly more often than you've said something worthwhile!"

Not wishing for their argument to continue further, Yip interjected, "There is a time and place for disagreement and discussion. This is neither."

Slate harrumphed and crossed his arms in displeasure while Wrindanneth snorted derisively.

Neither offered further comment.

Changing the subject, Slate asked, "Wrin, how is it that ya're able ta detect tha Orcish ships but they're not able ta detect us?"

"Our sensors are more sophisticated than theirs. Although Gnomes are bit backward in some regards, their technical aptitude is far beyond anything Orcs will ever be capable of and"—here his hand briefly fluttered over the silvery control disk—"our command disk is as nice a piloting device as I have ever seen. Although I am not certain, mainly because I have never asked, I believe our disk represents a combination of high Elven magical cultivation and artisanship with Gnomish Paratechnological proficiency."

Slate chortled "Which means, it's at least twice as good as anythin' tha Orcs would ever be able ta produce!"

Wrindanneth smiled in agreement. "As the heart and soul of the ship, this command sphere separates us from our enemies. However"—and here he took the time to glance away from the three-dimensional projection of their surroundings, including the scattered Orcish vessels that he was using to facilitate his navigation—"I have never said that we have not been detected."

"Ya think they're just lettin' us fly above 'em without respondin'?"

"I merely think that we have been forced into a situation which increases our exposure and risk. Because we have the advantage of speed and surprise, we may yet remain undetected, if we can avoid Orcish ships without them becoming aware of us." He shrugged. "There is, however, no guarantee."

Here he grimaced wickedly, adding, "I'm good, but not that good."

Aroganji replied, "We're all ready to fight our way through, Wrin. If our luck holds, we may yet cross the Orcish wastes without bloodshed."

Wrindanneth shook his head. "Don't count on it."

Before anyone could ask any other questions or say anything else to distract him, Wrindanneth added, "Now if you will excuse us, Yip and I are trying to avoid any of our own blood from being shed."

Their short, unbidden reprieve ended, Yip and Wrindanneth once again dedicated themselves fully to scouring the skies to avoid enemy detection.

As the evening faded and morning dawned torpid and sallow on the eastern horizon, diluted and distorted by the effluents of Orcish barbarism and depravity, Wrindanneth dropped the *Shrike* completely from the skies. No longer relying solely on the cover of darkness and Daerdros's illusion for cover, he let the land itself hide their presence, avoiding the increased risk of flying at higher altitudes altogether while also minimizing the risk of visual detection by any sentries or wandering eyes that may be alert to Daerdros's cloak of deception.

Vast, blighted, and unforgiving, the Orcish wastes revealed by the incipient dawn had the advantage of varied, mountainous terrain coupled with large unbroken uninhabited expanses. Taken together, the terrain and isolation provided as much cover as he could hope to find in such a hostile place.

Flying forward as quickly as possible, the sickly yellow sun, filtered and distorted by the clouds of dust, debris, and pollution, served to dampen spirits rather than brighten the day. The land itself shared the same muted, warped colors as the sun and sky—hues of burnt oranges, unnatural yellows, and unclean browns washed the rocks and dry soils in a pallet fit for only the most limited imagination. Rocks, outcroppings, rises, and ledges all appeared largely devoid of life—blasted and scoured clean by overuse, neglect, and unrestrained corruption. The contorted shadow of their passage crossed the cracked and pitted land too briefly to offer any respite from the afflicted sunlight or deplorable setting.

To an untrained eye viewed from afar with the combination of poor light, varied and muted terrain, illusionary camouflage, and a low flight path, the *Shrike* would seem more heat mirage than actual flying vessel.

Still alert for possible detection, however, Yip let his mind extend outward, feeling the land's essence and anything that subsisted with it. Skimming the rocky surface directly below the ship's hull, he felt the Orcish blight all the more as they traveled up mountainsides and across broken, destitute plains. Warrens, invisible to the eye but all too real to his senses, threaded the land beneath their passage in chaotic webs of tunnels and chambers marked by the presence of Orcish workers, entrapped slaves, subterranean food crops, and other minions too foul to be identified.

To those trapped, tortured, or enslaved below, his brief cognizance of their condition was all the recognition of their plight that they may ever receive.

Wrindanneth scoured the Orcish lands and the images before him with distaste. His senses, amplified as they were by the ship's sensors, were repulsed by what he felt and saw. If a land could be poorer and more blighted than his own cursed homeland and still be inhabitable, this would be it. That it took Orcs to ravage a land more fully than his own people with their cursed past brought a bittersweet smile to his lips.

Slate ground his teeth, his ire and frustration building with each minute flying over the Orcish homelands on Ea'ae. Here were lands teeming with the black-hearted miscreants he had sworn blood oaths to destroy and he could do nothing! Their foul deeds and destructive presence pulled for his action and attention in every direction, but he had to wait and remain composed; his mission was elsewhere. Never before had he had to muster as much self-restraint to avoid engaging the enemy for its presence was too overpowering to ignore or leave unremarked. That he would break other oaths, throw his life away, and potentially jeopardize their mission if he acted according to his will offered little solace to the fires within that begged so stridently for release.

Aroganji saw that this land and its denizens could not sustain themselves or their urges. Time, magic, and risk of reprisal would allow them to remain in place only so long before their compulsions urged them to move beyond their current confinement, spreading their blight and destructive spirit beyond the limitations of these borders, a virus spreading outward for new hosts. When that day arrived, Ea'ae would become a much darker place—the shadows of war loomed as darkly on the horizon as the pallor above the Orcish skies.

The morning passed much as the night before—under a cloud of tension and threat, a mood reflective of the tortured landscape through which they flew.

Gristnast spat and wiped the remainder of the spittle angling from his prognathic chin with a heavy, scaly forearm, the thick saliva leaving a satisfyingly large smear on the umber sandstone under his clawed feet.

By the Hellforge! Why was he always chosen for sentry duty?

He blinked his eyes in the hot midday sun, the glaring brightness burning his eyes and making them water, so different from the soothing light of the forges, pens, and caverns below. The dry plains before him shimmered with heat, the air no cooler in the looming heights from which he peered.

If that Drogu ordered him out here one more time, he would slit his throat! Then he, Gristnast, would be the one giving orders!

He inhaled deeply, the flat, wide nostrils on his protuberant snout expanding as he sniffed. Nothing worth smelling either! No smoke, cooking flesh, heated metals, thickly boiling Vradek, or mouth-watering Kordas!

He spat again.

Nothing worth his time at all!

Yes, this would be the last time he was forced from the caves and asked to go aboveground against his will! His hand dropped the jagged black half-sword at his hip, the pitted ebony blade thirstily drinking in the light of the day as he slowly stroked its wicked surface.

His sword would drink Drogu's blood before the day was done!

Grinning with vile pleasure, his blood burning in anticipation at the thought of violence and revenge, his mouth opened wide baring irregular yellowed fangs, a snarl that split his scarred and mottled face nearly in two.

He would gut that toothless Gnomespawn and adorn his body with trophies from the kill!

Hopping from foot to foot, he could hardly contain his excitement as his soles slapped on scalding stones weathered by countless feet in front of the entrance to the warrens below.

Tonight there would be blood!

Not even the hated sunlight weaseling its way into his eyes, etching his vision with bright splotchy afterimages could distract him from his ire and impending vengeance. Moving from foot to foot, his view shifting rapidly up and down with each jarring thrust of his feverish war dance, he stopped mid-leap, his eyes noting an unusual mirage. As he stopped, the mirage went away. Confused, he bounced up and down again taking advantage of the rapid changes in perspective the jumping gave him to look once more.

He blinked to clear his eyes as he moved.

There it was again!

A ship!

And it wasn't Orcish!

Stopping his frantic bounding, the decidedly undersized Orc turned and ran back into the dark cave mouth from which he had emerged only a short time earlier. As he ran, he shouted loudly, the keening yell preceding his diminutive form and echoing through the dark, smoky chambers through which he hurried hunched and loping, his passage noted with disgust by other Orcs who only tolerated his presence for fear of death from the blood lord, their leader, Drogu.

"Drogu!"

Yip sensed the swarm before it registered on the projection, a seething mass of ships erupting from the summit of a large volcanic peak slightly to their south and west.

Pointing to the nearest location on the projection, he said simply, "They come."

Not caring about how or why they had been discovered, Wrindanneth immediately adjusted their course more eastwardly while maintaining a southerly heading. Simultaneously, using the ship to magnify his voice, he called out, "We have been discovered! Orcs to the south and west!"

Confident that the *Shrike* could outrun the clumsy Orcish vessels, Wrindanneth pushed forward, urging the ship to a faster pace. His primary concern was whether or not the Orcs would be able to alert a similar flotilla in a position to cut them off and catch them between the two masses.

Although the change in course would take them off the most direct path to Taerris'thule, he had no way of knowing whether or not this adjustment would shorten their journey through Orcish territory as its extent, location, and landmarks were all unknown. Regardless of the outcome, he pushed forward with Yip at his side throwing all caution to the wind in favor of speed. Both remained alert for possible ambush or encounter as they sped forward at full speed.

Below them, the arid burnt orange and brown landscape shifted past in an unrelenting blur with no more substance and solidity than falling grains of sand let loose from clenched fingers. Ahead at the limits of vision, another range of massive peaks steadily resolved themselves in the distance, rising slowly from the heat and distance, irregular boulders slowly revealed by a progressively receding tide.

Aroganji and Slate joined Yip and Wrindanneth at the command sphere gazing into the projection for signs of their pursuers.

Monitoring the sensors for pursuit and possible ambush, Wrindanneth imagined that they were in a race for the mountain range with victory assured for the one who arrived first. Coalescing and adjusting trajectory, the mass of Orcish ships gathered and readied themselves for the hunt.

Assured of their speed and path, Wrindanneth announced to the crew, "I have adjusted course to avoid interception. With any luck, we will be able to outrun our harriers."

"If you have not done so already, I suggest that you protect yourself with whatever wards or sigils you have available should we be forced to engage and they breach our shields."

Aroganji briefly touched minds with Wrindanneth. *"I will cast wards on you and the others while you pilot the ship."*

Giving a silent nod of ascent, Wrindanneth agreed, adding, *"Ward us for protection from projectiles and impact."*

Breaking contact with Wrindanneth, Aroganji moved between his friends quickly casting a ward against ballistics and collisions to supplement the alien shielding devices they wore upon their waists and whose augmented complement now served as their primary safeguard around the ship. He also cast a secondary spell to allow them to land without full impact should they fall or be thrown from the ship.

He only hoped that these precautions would not be needed.

While Aroganji worked, Wrindanneth called Spreesprocket to the helm. Spreesprocket arrived quickly after the summoning, fully adorned in his clockwork armor, gears whirling and humming, his red umbrella unfurled above his head casting a shadow behind him as he walked.

Never one to hide his feelings, before Spreesprocket had a chance to offer a greeting or ask why he had been called, Slate blurted, "What, by Freyda's frock, is that umbrella supposed ta do?"

Spreesprocket looked up at Slate casually. "Oh! This is my Anti-Incidence Occluder."

"Which means?"

"It's an umbrella that provides shade from the sun."

Slate merely shook his head.

"It also serves as a highly potent blackbody to absorb and dissipate focused radiation, especially in the forms associated with potent magical energies along with various projectiles and ballistics."

Slate grinned. "Ah! It's a shield!"

Spreesprocket smiled in return. "And it serves to mitigate descent in the event of unforeseen loss of altitude."

"So it will help ya land safely when you fall?"

Spreesprocket assented, the gesture accompanied by whirling of the servomechanisms surrounding his neck. "While helping to keep me cool and comfortable."

Wrindanneth had heard enough. "Spreesprocket, is it possible to make the drones self-destruct after directing them at a target? If so, how much damage could I expect them to cause?"

Spreesprocket looked at the projection hovering in the air before Wrindanneth. "You are asking to what extent the explosion of a drone would damage the chasing Orcish ships?"

"Yes."

Spreesprocket continued his study of the projection. "What is the scale of this image?"

Wrindanneth did not answer directly, instead he said, "I would anticipate that the Orcish ships are spread across an area about a league across."

"Do you care in any way about subtlety or further detection?"

"I only care about our safety and the success of our mission. If the drones can offer a large enough display to offer significant intimidation and deterrence, then I would be eager to use them."

"You would get your wish."

Placing his chin in hand, Spreesprocket peered thoughtfully upward while performing several mental calculations. "I would anticipate that a single drone, if allowed to self-destruct after disabling all safety mechanisms, would offer perhaps several kiloboulders of explosive energy, mostly in the form of highly volatilized plasmatic magical forces."

When Wrindanneth did not appear to grasp his description, Spreesprocket added, "For a sense of scale and scope, that explosion would have enough destructive potential to level a small citadel and its grounds or obliterate several hundred cottages dispersed through a small community. Given the scatter of the Orcish ships, assuming no additional explosive action from chain reactions from their own fuel, payload, weaponry, or other devices along with inadequate shielding to protect against such a blast, a drone may be able to wipe out one-quarter to one-third of those ships."

"In contrast, should a similar device with equivalent energetic potential detonate adjacent to the *Shrike*, the violent kinetics of such a blast would be ameliorated by the ship's shield mechanism. Of course, the shield itself would be overloaded, rendered non-functional, and potentially irreparable from the blast, but we would survive, probably blinded, but alive and well nonetheless while the ship remained relatively undamaged."

A glint of excitement all too apparent in his gaze, Wrindanneth asked, "What will I need to do to make this happen?"

"You have but to specify which drones you would like to send and tell them what to do."

"That's it?"

"Their artificial intelligence will handle the rest."

"D'ya really think that's tha best idea? Tha worst thing ta do ta a hive o' bees is ta rattle their nest."

Wrindanneth pointed to all the Orcish ships massing in the holographic projection. "Do you think that they are not already agitated?"

"Any chance o' escape without further notice or alarm will be thrown out if ya do that!"

"Do you think they are not alerting other legions to our presence and course? If we do not show overwhelming, deterring force, then they may never stop chasing us."

"If ya do that, Wrin, ya'll raise their ire even greater and they'll be less likely ta avoid houndin' us!"

Wrindanneth disagreed. "If any of those Orcs survive the blast, or any other Orcs see the explosion, they will be less likely to interfere with our progress."

Slate barked a short, humorless laugh. "If ya think tha thought o' death and violence will deter an Orc, then don't allow me ta correct ya!"

"Orcs understand force and displays of force and I intend to give one to them!"

Aroganji interjected his opinion before the squabbling continued any longer. "One thing you're missing, Slate, is that those Orcs and other Orcs may think that we have engaged them or are near to them when the explosion occurs. These others may even think we perished in the explosion. Even if they figure out that we are not nearby, we may create a large enough distraction to allow ourselves more time to reach relative safety."

Wrindanneth agreed. "And if more ships bar our way, we'll still have the same options we had before—try to avoid or outrun them, fight our way through, or use more drones as we have the others."

Slate shook his head in disagreement. "Do what ya will. I'll be waitin' with my axe either way."

With that he stumped off the bridge to the ship's main deck taking up a position away from the Home Guard stationed around the ship's perimeter so that he would have ample room to swing his axe.

"Thank you, Spreesprocket. I'll send two drones. We'll still have several left in case we need them later on in the journey while doing catastrophic damage to the Orcish horde."

Spreesprocket gave a short bow, his umbrella adjusting position to continue offering protection from the sun as he did so. "If I might suggest, why not send two forward as well along our flight path to extend the ship's sensory range and aid in our efforts to avoid detection?"

"Will do."

Never slowing down or deviating from course while he talked, Wrindanneth gave his orders to the drones.

Breaking formation with the ship, two arching down and back along the ship's slipstream while two others raced forward beyond the ship's prow, the sentry drones moved as quickly as Wrindanneth's intention. Speeding immediately over the sere, desolate ground, all appendages retracted, so low that the orbs of their bodies were indistinguishable from their shadows, the combat drones raced over the landscape, sleek, undetected, and deadly.

Their targets set, running calculations continually determining the optimal path to achieve their goal, each set of drones left the *Shrike* behind connected only by the tether of Wrindanneth's will.

"Drones are off! If you haven't shielded your eyes already, do so now! If you don't shield your eyes, you should go below decks!" The drones sent on their mission, everyone given fair warning, Wrindanneth once again returned his full attention to the race ahead.

Following Wrindanneth's suggestion, Aroganji quickly circulated among the Four visiting first Wrindanneth and Yip before going to the main deck to ensure that Slate was protected. Wearing large black horn-rimmed shades to complement his stylish umbrella, Spreesprocket had taken up position next to where Slate stood at the ready. He waved at Aroganji's approach.

"Scouting out the most favorable angle to watch the show?"

Aroganji shook his head. "I just want to make sure Slate's eyes are protected."

Nodding in understanding, Spreesprocket reached down toward his chest as a thickly padded, purple velvet-lined compartment opened, sliding outward from a space that appeared to occupy the same area as his lungs. Pulling out another set of glasses, these tinted aviation goggles rimmed in multicolored feathers complete with straps and buckles, Spreesprocket offered the shades to Slate. "I have a spare set if you'd like."

Politely declining, recognizing that the oversized goggles would not do justice to his Dwarven sense of style, his handsome proboscis, or his luxuriant beard, Slate replied, "That's all right, Spree. Aroganji's spell'll do just fine fer now."

Not put off in the slightest, Spreesprocket returned his goggles to the magical drawer which receded once more into his armored chest. "Just let me know if you need them and they're yours."

"Will do."

Giving Slate a brief warning before casting his spell, Aroganji said, "You won't feel anything as I cast the enchantment. It will fade in a few hours' time."

When Slate grunted his understanding, Aroganji began his simple incantation. With a slight gathering of power, he brought his hands down over Slate's face in a simple gesture ensuring that any excessive energy directed toward his eyes would be lessened and redirected.

Eyes open and at the ready, Slate said, "Thank ya!"

Aroganji gave a slight bow. "Not a problem."

"Hopefully the show'll be everything Spreesprocket's been tellin' me."

Not sharing in his friend's enthusiasm, Aroganji took his leave without a reply and returned to the command sphere to watch events unfold under the higher magnification afforded by the command sphere.

Returning from his brief foray, with Yip's attention never diverted from scanning their surroundings for irregularities and Wrindanneth now relying upon the ship's sensors without reference to the visual projection floating over the deck's center, only Aroganji remained peering into the display watching for the impending detonation after he came back to the deck.

Since he could not visually follow the progress of the drones and not wishing to impinge on Wrindanneth's thoughts and perceptions while he worked, Aroganji was left to watch and wait for their effect.

Sensors constantly scanning for potential detection while modeling the outcomes of various course adjustments, the two drones hurtled toward the advancing fleet undetected. No eddies, dust clouds, or wakes were left by their flight over the cracked and pitted landscape.

Following divergent trajectories, each drone advanced along a separate vector of attack calculated in tandem to achieve maximal total impact on the Orcish flotilla.

Wrindanneth grinned ferociously, his consciousness simultaneously behind, forward, and within the ship as he navigated the *Shrike* and monitored the drones' progress. The path ahead was yet clear, although it was only a matter of time before other Orcish contingents were alerted to their presence. Without any decisive indication of how far the Orcish territories extended, their enemies had the advantage of time and distance with which to capture them.

With any luck, the detonation of the drones would be sufficient to distract the Orcs' attention from the *Shrike*'s forward progress or cause them to focus their attention behind the ship's current position.

With more anticipation than was his due, he waited for the impending explosion.

The drones were close now. They had remained undetected along secure flight paths and were nearing engagement. His palms were sweating with a heady mixture of eagerness and anxiety—eagerness for the impending blast and anxiety that the drones might be detected prior to engagement.

Through their sensors, he could see the approaching Orcish flotilla up above as the drones sped forward, the threatening violence of the Orcs' rusting metal ships looming overhead—jagged, ironclad, and laced with weaponry—standing in stark contrast to the serene, if blemished, sky through which they hurled. From a distance, the ships looked like an irregular cloud of shrapnel awaiting an as yet unseen target, their shadows shifting over the earth even more wildly than the hulls themselves. Now that the Orcish ships were so close in his purview, each appeared to be made of random assortments of cast-off metal and junk, welded and fused together with brutal, cruel imagination, designed for violence not efficiency.

Even with the *Shrike*'s shielding system, remaining sentries, exceptional crew, and powerful weaponry, he did not wish to engage such a formidable cadre of ships, a single one of which could ram into and smash through their ship with devastating effect. Granted the odds, many more of which could appear at any time to skew the chances of survival further out of their favor.

Suicide tactics would be the norm in a potential engagement. Without care for persistence or long-term survival, the *Shrike* and her crew would be at a significant disadvantage against Orcs hellbent on their destruction.

He did not wish for that possibility to come any nearer to fruition.

His musings at an end, he focused his attention as fully as he could on the impending contact given the need to pilot the ship while continuing to scan ahead.

No longer keeping to the ground, the two drones arched upward into the heavens, the graceful loop of each's motion mirroring the other drone's trajectory, the speed of their ascent masked by the silence and absence of visual cues associated with their launch skyward.

Speed now their cover, the drones flew through the air faster than eyes could register. Their aerodynamics and magical compensation and suppression systems further confounded detection.

Without malice or fear, the drones accelerated forward toward the completion of their mission—the amorphous mass of the unsuspecting Orcish fleet poised ever closer above.

Rocketing onward, his sense of equilibrium distorted by the rapid motion of the drones, Wrindanneth watched riveted as the rusty umber hull of an Orcish ship flashed before his eyes, the distance between the ground and the sky covered faster than he could blink. Briefly flinching, bringing his arm upward and shutting his eyes in reaction to the impending collision, his world exploded in an excruciatingly white burst of light.

Even seen through closed lids, the explosion was so bright that he did not realize until after he blearily opened them, his eyes burning and watering in a white afterglow that encompassed the full field of his vision, that his perspective had shifted back to that of the ship.

He had not watched the explosion through his perceptions of the drones, although that is what he at first thought. The impact and explosion had happened too quickly and completely for his vision to register. Neither would the drones have been able to transmit data after the explosion for they were wiped away as cleanly and totally as most of the Orcish ships following them.

Eyes still watering, he sped forward hoping that their next escape would be as clean.

Bent over next to Wrindanneth, peering eagerly into the control sphere's unfolding depiction of the scene behind them, Aroganji almost lost his footing as he stepped back in reaction to the awesome brightness of the detonation, completely unprepared for its true intensity though he had waited anxiously dreading its arrival.

With the speed and force of a thousand hurricanes, white light engulfed the ship, swallowing her whole as it did the entire landscape—the brilliant fore-shadow of the raging torrent to come. Ash, dirt, debris, and displaced air surged outward unchecked and unmitigated, tidal waves of force blasting away any vestige or memory of the Orcish ships.

Bringing his right arm up to cover his face from the incandescent white flash of light that had etched the force and intensity of its strength into his mind and eyes through even his magical protections, he turned away from the image before him only to be buffeted by its aftermath.

Gazing blearily into the face of the explosion's burning radiance, the bright-ness of the sun above was lost and forgotten over the desert's new fiery corona. Unprepared for the blast's intensity or violent aftershocks, he fell forward, landing heavily on his hands and knees as the ship pitched and heaved, turned and roiled in the center of a violent storm, her compensation systems over-whelmed.

Watching through streams of unbroken tears, struggling for balance from hands and knees on the ship's deck as the *Shrike* tossed about creaking and groaning within the eye of the explosion's fury, the air shimmered and hummed with heat and dust, thrumming with the intensity of the energies released, ready to shatter like fragile glass from the slightest disturbance.

Turning away from the brilliance, no longer wishing to face the storm directly, he gazed downward upon an irregular sea of ash—the explosion's ragged aftermath visited upon the mangled, disturbed earth—more ruinous and destructive than any Orc.

Both hands gripped firmly upon Duraeleon's hilt, feet spread apart widely for stability beneath the ship's rolling, bucking, and churning, Slate gazed upon the explosion in rapt wonder, the glory and immensity of the blast both humbling and exhilarating.

Surely this explosion hearkened back to the moment of Creation when Brendle first hammered out the universe from his cosmic forge! This blast must be like the very sparks arching and flaring from the beating of His great hammer and anvil during the first moments of Creation as He turned and worked the universe beneath His hands, shaping and forming it to His vision, forging and tempering His creation precisely, lovingly, and ever so perfectly.

Yip did not gaze upon the explosion for there was nothing in or about the blast that he wished to see.

THUNDERHEADS

Bare mountain peaks, leaves
lost to winds of autumn past—
join the tops of clouds.

"By Brendle's beard that was a sight ta behold!"

With no signs of direct pursuit or ambush after the explosion, the mood on the ship relaxed. They were still in Orcish territory for the signs of depredation and woe were all too visible in the scarred, denuded landscape through which they flew, hugging the ground to avoid possible Orcish detection and the Scierdyas winging silently through the untracked heavens above.

Slate slapped his leg with enthusiasm emphasizing his point.

Aroganji shook his head. "I still have a headache from watching too long and too intently."

"Why don't ya fix it with a spell?"

Aroganji smiled, the expression visibly tired across his unlined, tanned face. "Then I may lose the lesson I have learned."

"Which is?"

He gestured with a mixture of objectivity and obvious disappointment. "Caution and care in all things. Never underestimate the potential outcome of a situation or overestimate your capacities to cope."

"I should have been better prepared."

"Had an Orcish patrol happened upon us or been alerted during or soon after the explosion, I would have been ill-equipped to deal with the conflict. My preparations and thus my actions were insufficient."

He motioned firmly, confident of his evaluation. "This headache is a small reminder of the opportunity inherent both in my own failings and within dire events."

"That is a sight I do not wish to see again." Wrindanneth shared little of Slate's zeal but quite a bit of Aroganji's headache. He had not taken the time to rid himself of his own splitting migraine until just a few moments before. He had been too busy ensuring that they were safely away and undetected until they reached a position of relative safety. At least the nausea and discomfort from the jostling and the afterimages from the explosion had passed long before he had taken the time to correct them.

His scans now indicated that they were flying over a very sparsely populated area, abandoned long ago by most Orcs. Whether this was an indication that they were nearing the edges of the Orcish region or its rotted and abandoned heart, he could not know with any certainty but he was fairly confident that the risks of their discernment were minimal, at least for the time being. Even if there were no more Orcs in the vicinity, they still had to be wary of the Scierdyas. Adding another layer of uncertainty, they had little to no idea about any Orcish detection systems that may be in place to provide a warning or indication of their presence.

He ran his fingers through his long, tangled red hair, brushing hanging strands away from his tired, bloodshot eyes. "I am glad we made it through safely. The violence of the explosion was more than enough to destroy our ship even from our position of relative safety. Had the terrain been more formidable, I lost control, or our shields failed, we would no longer be here. Those are risks I would like to avoid if we are to see Tellanon safely once more."

His hair now safely secured behind his ears, Wrin finished, "We got lucky. If we are to survive, we must rely on more than luck."

Eidelion had already come and gone, assuring Wrindanneth that all was well with the Light's Guard and that he had done an admirable job, both with the plan of implementing the drones as an improvised explosion device and in piloting them to safety during and after their harrowing encounter.

He felt differently regarding Eidelion's sentiment, although he had been too tired to argue at the time. They had been lucky. The explosion nearly cost them their lives. The only reason he thought they were not currently being pursued was that the explosion threw off all possibilities of immediate detection.

Which was, again, luck.

There would be pursuit, however, of that he was certain. Whether they avoided detection and outran that pursuit would, once again, be largely a matter of fortune. His skills as a pilot coupled with the abilities of the ship and her crew only went so far in the face of random chance.

With Orcs swarming through the air more numerous than flies around carrion, their only hope was to circumvent chance, evade the odds, and make their own luck.

He laughed silently to himself. Of course there were no Orcs here now, they appeared to be traveling in relative safety, and all seemed as well as he could hope after such a dangerous encounter.

Which made his skin crawl at the thought.

Too easy.

Too much luck could be a bad thing as well.

Aroganji nodded his head in agreement, unaware of Wrindanneth's thoughts as they had not been sharing a connection for neither wished to visit his headache upon the other. "We must be better. If a small flotilla of Orcs, Orcs we never had to engage directly, can almost do us in, then we must become better if we are to have any hope of defeating the Cabal."

Exasperated, Slate fairly yelled, "What else're we ta do then?"

Slate's question burned deeply, fueled by his determination and fervor, perhaps sounding a bit too biting to his friends, but his feelings were honest and not intended to be hurtful. "We train, we try, and we do our best in equal measure. What else can we do?"

Breaking his silence, Yip finally spoke. "We do what we must."

His impassive tone seemed to belie the seriousness and import of his response. "We will grow to meet the tasks we face or we will fail. We must be greater, truer, and clearer than any obstacle before us. We must become more than that which we oppose."

Still calm, the passion of his answer was only reflected in the intensity of his gaze as he looked to each of his friends in turn. "Our truth must become greater than the truth of those we face that our vision and view will become reality. Else we will be defeated before we have begun."

The day faded once more to night and still they flew over trackless wastes, barren of signs of relief save their low flying, trailing shadow.

"Leave it ta Orcs ta take a place as rich as this and despoil it, leavin' barren earth, offal, and worse." Slate stood beside Wrindanneth at the helm, keeping his friend company, helping him stave off the growing signs of fatigue that his magic could only push back so far.

With any luck, by morning they would be free of the Orcish territories and able to find a proper place to rest. Wrindanneth had asked that everyone not needed on deck get some sleep while the opportunity presented itself in case they encountered another band of Orcs. Despite his friend's protests, Slate had insisted on standing with Wrindanneth to make sure he was well. His Dwarven constitution and durability allowed him to function without sleep for extended periods without recourse to magic, so he took it as his duty to ensure his friend's safety—no matter how much his presence annoyed Wrin.

Yip, too, still stood nearby on the lookout but he was generally about as much company as one of the ship's masts unless he had something to say. Yip certainly would not offer enough discussion or distraction to keep Wrindanneth focused and alert without reliance on Slate's vexing drivel.

Slate's banter continued without regard for the glares, not so subtle hints, and rejoinders that Wrindanneth offered during the course of his dialogue, all offered in the name of the crew and Wrindanneth's safety and, of course, the opportunity to badger and pester his friend under the guise of his good will.

"Hard ta believe they've been here all this time and no one's run 'em out!"

"Ya'd think that someone would've mounted up an expedition ta wipe 'em clean off tha face o' Maeron."

Slate's commentary continued, punctuated between long spaces of silence as he verbalized a particularly relevant point in a largely internal conversation. "Orcs're like a disease. Ya wipe 'em out and they just pop up somewhere else."

One thought jumped to the next as he carried on, "'Course they're so resilient we probably couldn't wipe 'em out with disease, especially not with 'em havin' access ta magic and magical cures."

In the end, in lieu of piquing Wrindanneth's senses, Slate's attempts to keep his friend alert served to dull his awareness as Wrindanneth ignored Slate and walled himself off from the unending verbal assault. More of Wrindanneth's energy was directed inward—evaluating the course of his thoughts, trying to keep fresh and awake, maintaining a sound barrier between himself and Slate —than had been the case prior to Slate's arrival to bolster his readiness.

With Slate's careful hypnotic guidance, Wrindanneth slipped slowly from a state of careful but tired responsiveness into a dull, dreamlike fugue.

Yip spent the evening in a state of relaxed attention, allowing the *chi* to infuse and lift him, bolstering his alertness and tired mind and body so that he could remain present by Wrindanneth's side. His awareness extended onward around the ship and into the dark evening—an invisible nimbus of cognizance offering a second tier of protection behind the ship's sensory array.

Lighter than the breath in his chest, his consciousness soared upward toward the heavens, alighting and dancing in the clouds, skimming the ground beneath the ship's dark shadow, a shimmering net cast without regard to object or target, moving, responding, and shifting with currents unseen.

Moonlight and the shadows of clouds filled the space around the ship as they traveled southward. So few creatures still called this region home that the gentle sound of the air moving around the ship provided the only noise between breath and heartbeat.

Standing next to his friends through the evening, after hours filled with energy and stillness, his conscious bathing in the pearlescent light of the moon and the shifting shadows of clouds while his friends came and went, chatted, and discussed, Yip quickly sensed something was amiss.

No call provided warning, nothing was seen that alerted him of their danger, only a subtle absence, as though one's shadow had quietly reappeared unnoticed after disappearing for a time under the light of the noonday sun. So subtle was danger's approach that he glanced upward for a moment unable to pinpoint the exact location of the void his senses now screamed against.

Above, flying through the heavens, hidden to all but the keenest perception, Darkness flowered and blossomed, only felt as a deep vacancy, the shadow of a forgotten shadow left to bloom and grow unheeded.

Pointing upward toward where he now sensed the creature's sudden advance, he yelled out in warning, "Scierdyas!"

Had the creature of Darkness not detected them first and reacted, accelerating forward from where it searched for intruders above the clouds, he might not have detected its presence as it began to plummet through the firmament surging for its quarry below.

No sooner had the words left the safe confines of his lips, than Llyewia was on his feet leaving his star-spun hammock behind. *Lianel* drawn and in hand, aimed heavenward, his face framed in soft white light cast not by the moon, but by the bow in hand, the air shimmering with the golden dust of stars as he pulled back and drew the bow's invisible string.

As quick as Llyewia reacted, Raour'Saqan was faster. Launching himself up from the deck with the crack of thunder, his wings beat powerfully against the still night air. Tearing through the sky, a comet returned to the heavens, the arch of his trajectory was determined by the direction of Yip's finger.

A tumultuous fragment of interstellar darkness returned to the heavens, darker than the night sky, Raour'Saqan sought out the Shadow that was his kindred in gloom.

Raour'Saqan's sudden departure left Llyewia, Yip, Slate, and Wrindanneth temporarily alone on the deck watching after his progress while Aroganji and the other Light's Guard hurried to their posts from where they had been resting and recovering belowdecks.

Gathering round where Wrindanneth stood now fully alert and inwardly cursing himself for losing track of the ship's safety, everyone on the bridge turned their eyes upward to try and catch a glimpse of the storm that was about to unfold.

Arrayed for battle, the rest of the Home Guard fanned out across the deck, scanning the skies for Orcish ships and other Scierdyas. Leaving his subordinates behind, Eidelion joined Aroganji walking toward the helm, his plate armor gleaming white in the moonlight. As he approached the command sphere, his inherent concern for effective action took over, wishing to ensure that everyone was yet vigilant to the situation at hand and not caught up completely in the battle overhead that was beyond their control.

Just as Eidelion joined them around the command sphere, a soul wrenching roar tore through the heavens, a brazen challenge wreathed in the fury of unholy pits.

Unshaken by the heinous bellow that accosted their ears from so high aloft, Eidelion spoke, command ringing through his tone, "Are there others? Have we been given away?"

Taking his eyes from the heavens, Wrindanneth reached out through the ship's sensors once more, returning to full vigilance as he heeded Eidelion's query. He shook his head in reply. "Aside from the tableau above, the skies are yet clear. Prior to that roar, we heard no cries or calls for alarm, so I assume we are alone and that the Orcs have not been alerted to our presence."

Eyes glancing to the projection displayed before him, he added, "No activity shows on the sensors."

Before Eidelion could ask another question, Yip interjected, "There is only the emptiness of the lone shadow Dragon patrolling the skies above us."

Wrindanneth gave his confirmation. "The Scierdyas must have happened upon us as part of its patrol and attempted to sweep down on us in surprise."

Eidelion gave a curt nod. "Alert me if anything changes." Spinning on his heel, he left the bridge and returned to the main deck, barking commands to the Guard. In response to his orders, the air lit up with spells as the warriors prepared themselves for battle.

Overhead, drifting clouds laced in silver moonlight belied the frenetic violence unfolding under their calm shadow. Though deadly quiet, Wrindanneth, Slate, Yip, and Aroganji watched for signs of the tempest raging through the skies, only able to see its effects indirectly.

Centered between them, Wrindanneth called forth a magnified image of the sky in the projection, but the evening kept her secrets, too reclusive and distant for his depiction to descry.

Waiting with bated breath, they watched as the fusillade exploded above.

Aroganji did not have words to describe exactly what he saw unfold.

The sky overhead flashed with darkness, swallowing the silvery light of the moon reflected on the layered clouds with each burst. Tonal inversions, the reversed afterimages of lightning bolts flashing and arching through the clouds, ripped through the firmament with each burst. If one could see thunder, perhaps the sudden surging detonations of darkness overhead would be how those concussive blasts appeared.

Slate gripped Duraeleon's glowing shaft firmly in hand, as though the firmness of his grip would aid Raour'Saqan's battle above. Each silent fulmination overhead, accompanied by the engulfing darkness, was immediately followed by a tightened grip about the haft of his axe.

The gods often waged war in the heavens. He had never been present to watch such a spectacle unfold, nor had he ever expected to witness one.

Although the Scierdyas was an enemy beyond him, Wrindanneth wished he could be at Raour'Saqan's side, battling against the Infernal, lending Raour'Saqan his strength and guile, testing his skill against the creature. Each flash of darkness above pulled him upward while his sense of duty and obligation kept him tied to the ship and his friends.

Though he could see neither Raour'Saqan's nor the Scierdyas's form directly with his eyes, Yip could sense and feel the effects of their actions. He felt as Raour'Saqan and the Scierdyas pitted strength against strength, Darkness against Darkness, each vying for the essence of the other, engulfing the other's energies, pulling against their opponent's spirit, tearing and swallowing each other's soul.

The turbulence of their actions shuddered through the living energies around him with untold violence and power. Each salvo was accompanied by the empty Darkness of their natures, drawing forth the other's energies into themselves and through the night, flashes of emptiness only reluctantly filled by moonlight.

As rapidly as it began, the storm subsided. The moonlit clouds returned to their calm, undisturbed splendor, the fury of the past brief moments present only in the memories of those waiting below. Above, much slower than it had ascended, a comet returned to the Earth.

Gliding slowly downward, the thunder gone from his wingtips, Raour'Saqan returned to the *Shrike*'s deck, landing at his accustomed spot above the ship's prow, his massive body steaming with dark, acrid vapors, his very shadow volatilizing, the ship's deck creaking in welcome at his return.

While the Light's Guard moved forward to congratulate him, Eidelion at the fore, Raour'Saqan held up one thick arm in warning. "Come no closer! The Scierdyas's foul Darkness clings to me yet."

He spoke with the cool certainty and finality of one who had seen many battles. "We now have time for escape, but the Shadow Dragon's brothers will soon know of its passing and will come for us."

"We must leave the Orcish territories before they track us, else we will fight again."

His deeds done, unconcerned with questions or the motivations for them, Raour'Saqan squatted on his haunches and curled up beneath his dark leathery wings, a gargoyle returned to roost, silent and vigilant should another disturbance arise, now but another shadow amid the darkness.

DREAMS OF DESOLATION

> Bitterly cold wind
> bites exposed extremities,
> never sating its hunger.

As much as he wished otherwise, their race continued.

At least Slate had finally gone belowdecks to leave him in peace.

Wrindanneth pushed forward as quickly as he felt was safe but no faster.

Morning found them past the last barren ridge of the Orcish wastes and, although his heart jumped at first with elation as they descended from the sere peaks toward the forested lands below, his jubilation was short-lived.

If the lands inhabited by the Orcs had once looked like these, the territory he had so willingly left, then perhaps the Orcs had done Maeron a favor by clearing this blight for their own.

One affliction for another.

Maeron was a land of wonders!

If he never had to visit again, it would be too soon.

Scuttling just above the rocky ground, the forest grew darker and more ominous as they approached, the soft morning light doing little to brighten the haggard gray vines and boughs of the forest's tangled, tenebrific shadows clutching at the feet of the desolate mountains. Tree limbs grew interlinked in knotted distress, locked in violent throes of pain or despair. No leaves whispered or rustled in the wind urging the *Shrike* downward toward the hollows between the last despoiled arms of the Orcish mountains. What leaves were present lay forlorn and forgotten at the roots of the still trees, barely stirring in the breeze, locked in another time.

He shook his head.

Such a place did little to lift a man's spirits.

Such a place was only suitable for ill-gotten memories and ghosts.

Of course, where did they ever visit that was enjoyable?

He had hoped to be free of the Orcs and now there was this! He could not be sure how far the Orcs would follow him here, but the fact that the forest yet stood attested to the fact that they were reluctant to venture far. The Scierdyas were a different matter, but he felt that they would venture no further than the Orcish reach for they were bound to the Orcs through unholy rites that were not easily weakened or severed.

Once they had put some distance between the peaks behind and the ship, just to be sure that he was rid of all the shadows that lingered behind them, he would take to the skies once more to avoid any threats that may lurk in the forest.

Then he would rest.

Yip never left Wrindanneth's side, returning his friend's vigilance with his own.

Like Wrindanneth, he felt uneasy as soon as they first laid eyes upon the haunted forest below. He did not need his eyes to tell him what he already felt.

The forest was wrong—malevolent and maleficent. The energies that should be so vibrant and vital within its borders were twisted and corrupt, bent to serve a cruel source that he could not see but whose traces lay heavy upon the landscape in a deathly fog that never lifted or burned off with the sun.

What he felt was different from anything he had yet encountered; it was pervasive and clung throughout the wood from bole to branch, root to crown. Whatever moved within the forest, whatever took shade beneath it branches, did not feel alive; it felt animated by twisted malevolence.

There were vague presences farther within toward the forest's heart, as empty and cold as the fog through which they manifested and evanesced in patterns and purposes he did not know.

He was, however, certain they should avoid the forest before they ever approached the border of its forlorn trees.

"Wrindanneth." He turned to his friend, calling Wrin's name to get his attention.

"Yes, Yip?" His words had broken Wrindanneth from his own dark ruminations.

"This is a place to be avoided."

"I see that." Wrindanneth's thoughts had grown darker as they neared the forest's boundary as well.

"Let us take to the skies and avoid the plague that has claimed this land." Yip spoke with a firmness he seldom used.

Nodding slowly, Wrindanneth knew that Yip was right. He would risk being spotted in open daylight, but the alternative appeared no brighter.

Hugging the treetops seemed like a particularly gruesome option as the twisted boughs came closer into view.

For all he knew those tortured trees would reach out and grab the ship.

"I agree." As quickly and simply as that Wrindanneth adjusted the *Shrike's* course and angled skyward.

If this forest marked the northern extent of the lands bordering Taer-ris'thule, then they would cling to the heavens the rest of their flight southward. They had faced enough risk on their journey without chancing more.

He would gladly leave this cadaverous forest to rot with the rest of this forsaken continent!

Arching steadily upward, he aimed for the clouds overhead. He would use them for cover whenever possible to minimize the risk of being spotted from below.

With the gain in altitude, their view of the terrain expanded exponentially, broadening in all directions with dizzying rapidity. As quickly as the view widened with their ascent to the heavens, Wrindanneth's heart sank.

The dismal shadow forest stretched as far as the eye could see, reaching to the limits of the horizon and beyond.

Gloom ahead and gloom after.

At least they seemed to have lost their pursuers.

Better yet, Slate would leave him alone.

He was more dogged than the pack of Orcs pursuing them.

Smiling wryly, Wrindanneth guided the ship upward, looking forward to some rest and the surety that he would have at least a moment's peace.

"What is this place?" Aroganji had returned from his room feeling rested and refreshed, ready to rejoin his companions on the bridge. The unending gray forest stretching below them piqued his interest. From high above, the dead wood blended with the landscape as one indistinguishable mass—a country burned completely now covered with ash.

Looking at the image projected through the command sphere, the forest in all its depressing detail was even more apparent. From the much closer scale offered by the ship's instrumentation, the wildwood looked like it had been struck by an all-encompassing blight, a plague that had killed off all vegetation as far as he could see leaving only the shattered husks and shells of trees to frame a wilderness that was now only a memory.

With the vegetation, all other signs of life had disappeared as well.

"I do not know what it is called now if it is called anything." Wrindanneth brought forth a map, overlaying it on the projected landscape from below. "The map, however, refers to it as Dhwer'werde which means something like 'Fate's Door' or 'Fated Forest' in the tongue of those who named it long ago."

He pointed along their current path, tracing a rough line forward beyond the limits of the landscape represented in the hologram. "The good news, if you can rightly call it that, is that Taerris'thule appears to lie at the center of this wilderness, the withered heart in the center of this burnt-out carcass."

Aroganji concurred. "The treasure we have sought for so long finally nears."

Wrindanneth smirked, chiding, "Did you hear my comment about the carcass? No one in their right mind seeks out places like Taerris'thule, much less describes it in such glowing terms."

Returning Wrindanneth's vitriol with his own, Aroganji replied, "Then why are you here? Taerris'thule is only one of many carcasses we have been forced to exhume."

"Whoever said I was in my right mind?"

"And whoever said that treasures were easy to find or retrieve?"

Wrindanneth smiled, glad for the sport and Aroganji's spirit. "Sounds like we have come to an understanding. He paused and added, "And a good time for me to finally get some rest. Maybe then I'll get to think of something a bit livelier."

Yip bowed to his friend before Wrindanneth's departure. "May your dreams be bright."

Aroganji added with a smile, "And the morrow brighter."

Wrindanneth waved them off dismissively. "If you two were any sappier, I'd think I was in a forest, a forest very much unlike the one down there." He gestured vaguely with his head as he finished indicating the Dhwer'werde.

After a full day had passed with no further signs of pursuit, Wrindanneth felt comfortable leaving the bridge, setting the ship's course southward, and finally heading to his chambers for some long overdue rest. Yip had promised to remain on watch with Aroganji until he was back abovedecks. He had also set the ship's alarms to wake him should something unexpected occur.

"What do you think is in store ahead?" Aroganji took his eyes away from the ashen forest below long enough to watch Yip's response.

Yip shrugged, not because he was noncommittal but because he was resigned to the answer. "More fighting. More horror. More reminders of what has been lost."

"I mean what do you think we will find in Taerris'thule?"

Yip smiled, joking, "Aside from beings that wish to kill us?"

Aroganji laughed. "Yes!"

"I think we will find a place that has been long forgotten by Man, a place in need of both remembrance and attention."

A look of deep concern crossed Aroganji's face. "Are we out of our league, Yip?"

Yip laughed in turn. "Aren't we always?"

More seriously, because Aroganji deserved as much and more, he added, "The moments that test us are the ones that define us. How do you wish to be defined?"

Aroganji thought for a time. "As successful."

"Then you must always strive for improvement, moving with awareness and poise, that you will be ready for the next challenge."

"Then you think we will be prepared for what we will face?"

"Every moment is preparation."

Aroganji took a breath before answering, not allowing himself to become frustrated with Yip's way of answering questions. "Do you think we have prepared ourselves well enough to be successful?"

"Ultimately, we can never know what lies before us. We will either rise to the occasion or we will fail."

Aroganji smiled, opening himself up and sharing a bit of himself with his friend, redirecting his intent away from Yip's frustrating style of dialectical dialogue. "Which is exactly why I adventure. Places like Taerris'thule, those that are the most challenging, give us the most opportunity to change and grow, to learn and expand our limits."

Yip smiled, placing his hand on Aroganji's shoulder. "If you can find peace and opportunity in the heart of a storm, you can find it anywhere."

Aroganji nodded. "That is why I always look forward to the storm clouds ahead."

Giving a brief nod in agreement, Yip returned to his scanning of the skies and the dead lands beneath.

Slate gritted his teeth under the strain of fending off Daerdros's constant whirling attacks. Her movements were so fluid and subtle; he could never anticipate their arrival or read their origin. Instead, he was left to react as quickly and effectively as possible to her strikes, always on the defensive.

After flying a full day over the dead woodlands with no signs of further pursuit or other danger, Daerdros had decided that they could return to their strenuous practice schedule. After the last few days off, without their daily practice, he had lost what little ground he had gained through her unrelenting 'guidance' which felt more like controlled, voluntary thrashings.

Another slash whizzed by his cheek, only avoiding a nasty cut with a jerk at the last moment, his failing causing him to grit his teeth harder as if the degree of his concentration were directly tied to how hard he clamped his jaws.

Daerdros stopped, dropping her elegant blade by her side in response to his tension. Chiding him she said, "Slate, you must relax. You are fighting yourself more than you are fighting me."

She placed her hands on his elbows lifting them toward his shoulders, then let go and watched them fall. "Your shoulders are tense. This tension carries throughout your body. That same tension interferes with the movement of your blade."

"Let the blade carry itself. Use no more energy or force than is required. Otherwise, you will burn yourself out, holding nothing in reserve, and will not be able to respond naturally and effortlessly to the dictates of the situation."

Slate nodded, accepting her admonishment, knowing she was correct.

"Stop gritting your teeth, Slate!"

He caught himself and relaxed his jaws, not aware that she had noticed.

"Clamping your mouth shut interferes with your ability to breathe! If you want to keep being able to swing that axe, you will have to be able to breathe fully and naturally for as long as possible!"

"Do you understand?"

He nodded, wishing he could still grind his teeth to express his frustration.

Seeing right through him, she said, "Your mind must be as relaxed as your body and breath, Slate. All must act together or you will fail."

He let out a deep breath, his bearded cheeks expanding and relaxing with the gesture, bending to pick up Duraeleon from where he had let it rest on the ship's decking.

"Are you ready?"

Refusing the urge to grate his teeth, he relaxed his shoulders, lunged forward, and growled, "Only one way ta find out!"

Daerdros smiled, easily parrying his attack. "That's better!"

Taking a less aggressive stance, she let him attack and press forward. That she could be so at ease, talking, and not out of breath while she wielded her sword impressed him about as much as anything else.

"Watch your feet, Slate!" She flicked her sword downward causing him to jump into the air to avoid the strike. "Do not become double-weighted! Your weight must move easily from foot to foot or you will become stuck, off-balance, and vulnerable to attack!"

"Move from the feet first! Do not lead with the body or head!"

Digging deeply for more speed and power, he lunged forward swinging his axe diagonally across his body aiming for her chest. Stepping aside easily, Daerdros avoided the attack, bringing the side of her sword upward quickly to rap him fully on the bottom of his chin.

"Maintain proper body alignment as you move! Do not overreach without respecting the body's proper axes of motion—shoulder to foot to the ground, spine to the ground, and diagonally between! These are as much your sources of power in movement as avoidance and alignment. If your motion is not comfortable or natural, it should be changed!"

He grunted, revising his prior thought. The fact that she could breathe so easily, move so naturally, and talk while simultaneously and effortlessly fending off his attacks, concurrently diagramming his mistakes and finding the opportunity to strike him, probably while also aware of how many grains were evident in the wood of each plank under both their feet, impressed him.

And he was a Dwarf not easily impressed.

Imagine if she and Yip had children!

Their progeny would rule the world!

Wincing in pain as she wrapped him across the side of the head for not paying full attention, he gritted his teeth.

She had his attention!

Standing beside Aroganji, Yip watched the air gradually thicken about them as the fog that shrouded the forest below slowly began to extend its reach, steadily coalescing and pervading the air at higher altitudes. Each breath felt heavier and more labored, tainted by the foulness of the lands below.

All around, he felt currents of malicious energy move through the air, dark tendrils reaching through the fog seeking to grasp and entrap them. With each breath, they all took this malevolent force into themselves, allowing the fog and its vile contents free passage throughout their bodies.

The shields around the ship were not preventing the encroachment of this force. He did not know how or why for he was not a magician but the evil within the fog must be stopped. Although he was not certain, he sensed that if they remained unprotected, the source of the fog would inexorably seal their fate as it had for all the former denizens of this land.

He could counter its presence within himself, prevent whatever nefarious purpose its manifestation portended within but he could not do so for his companions indefinitely.

Having seen their future, he could not wait any longer.

"Eidelion!" He called to the captain of the Home Guard with an urgency in his voice that tolerated no delay.

Eidelion's silent approach was not marked by the sound of steel on steel or saboton thudding on wood, only a call in response as he mounted the quarter-deck's stairs. "Yes, Yip?"

"We must ward the ship! The air we breathe is befouled with the essence of our enemy! Lest we be corrupted, we must cleanse the taint from this all-consuming fog!"

Eidelion reacted immediately.

Drawing the White Sword Archaeus, its radiant Light burned away the miasma even as the blade left its sheath. "I will inform Kazarhan, Spreesprocket, and Daerdros. Together we will purify the ship's atmosphere and supplement her shields that the air we breathe will not be corrupted."

Yip bowed in thanks.

Eidelion gave a small nod in turn. "The fog, I fear, will remain although its diablerie will be gone."

Turning about quickly on noiseless heels, Eidelion sped off into the growing gloom, calling, "Daerdros! Kazarhan! Spreesprocket! To me!"

Turning back to face the brume, letting its foul presence drift pass, through, and out without lingering or effect, he looked forward while the Home Guard worked together to ensure their continued safe passage.

When Daerdros, Kazarhan, and Spreesprocket had all responded to his summons, Eidelion gave his command. "This cursed fog harbors more than gloom and shortened sight. We must cleanse its taint from the ship and prevent further incursion of its vitiation."

"What would you have us do?" Daerdros spoke for the gathered group.

"Kazarhan and I will direct divine Light to shield the ship as best we can. Daerdros and Spreesprocket will interlace those energies with the protective forces of the ship's defensive system."

"The Light will then serve to protect and purify the ship."

Eidelion turned to the Priest of Brendle. "When done, Kazarhan will directly ward the ship against supernatural evil with his sigils preventing direct entry from beings such as those that created the befouled mist. This will provide a secondary line of defense behind the shields."

"Spreesprocket will modify the ship's protective systems such that it will maintain these modifications—both protective and purifying so that these and similar concerns will be lessened in the future."

"Together, these defensive supplements and augmentations should provide us with safe passage should greater evil be hidden within the confines of the brume."

Linking his mailed hands with Kazarhan's callused ones, Eidelion said, "Are we clear?"

When he received a series of curt nods from each in turn, Eidelion nodded as well, saying, "The Light guide us!"

Their work completed for the time being, Eidelion stood silent sentinel along with the other Light's Guard arrayed around the *Shrike*'s perimeter. He watched the fog of delusion and obfuscation from the unholy evil grow thicker with each passing league.

The malady here had long to grow and fester, deviltry growing upon and reinforcing itself unchecked for hundreds of years. The Light only knew what evils now called Taerris'thule home.

Whatever now dwelt within the ghastly ruins of Taerris'thule would soon meet the lustrating blades of the Light's Guard.

The Light willing, their efforts here would cleanse this taint from the face of Ea'ae and restore her to unblemished majesty.

Glancing left and right, he could see the vague silhouettes of the other members of the Home Guard standing watch along the ship's railing. The stalwart belief and conviction of his fellows would be their greatest boon against the corruption they would soon face ahead.

Without asking, he sensed that the *Shrike*'s course aimed unerringly toward Taerris'thule for he inhaled evil deeper and more fully with each passing inhalation.

Feeling the Light build within him in response, undiminished by the perversion around them, he breathed with purpose.

Until their target came within reach, Archaeus would remain sheathed. Then the cleansing would begin.

Toward the ship's fore, standing just close enough to see Raour'Saqan's hunched bulk perched above the ship's snarling Dragon figurehead, his impassive mass more imposing than the barely visible beast carved below, Spreesprocket touched the temple of his TAMERS exoskeleton with one hand encased in the whirling gadgetry that moved in response to his every move and whim. As he did so, a translucent ocular descended over his right eye, augmenting his visual capabilities and sensitivities.

His consciousness a spacious sea of capability, augmented by a merger with a vast, fully functional artificial intelligence more adept than the Abstracts made available to the citizens of Tellanon, the level of analytical detail and precision he brought to any problem was astounding.

Numbers streamed by on the periphery of his vision as he selected the proper data stream to facilitate his inspection of the rapidly inspissating mists. Satisfied with his selection, he began to scan the fog for supernatural abnormalities, fluctuations, and patterns that might allow him to identify its source and eventual counter.

With a simple gesture, he initiated and then dialed in his Ectoplasmic Reconnaissance Goggles, Ghost Hunter Series version 3.24, more commonly known to protoplasmic purveyors as ERG's, to aid in his assessment of the situation.

Through his left eye, his view of the sky, the ship, and the ground below remained unchanged and was almost completely occluded. Gray of various hues and intensities defined the limit and extent of his vision. Through his right eye, however, the world appeared entirely changed.

Kaleidoscopic streamers arched upward through the air and around the ship, variegated auroras bereft of winter's chill and clear, starry nights. His boundless intelligence analyzed, modeled, and deciphered these energies through complex multidimensional abstractions made possible by thought patterns far beyond the realm and scope of normal intellection.

Although the air coursed with supernatural energies when seen through the ERG's, patterns he quickly deciphered with his synthetic intelligence, his view of his surroundings was also no longer obscured by the all-enshrouding fog.

Below, he could see the same haunted forest that had first greeted them upon leaving the Orcish territories. Trees denuded of all life and vegetation groped upward locked in the final violent throes of life, whether reaching skyward for succor or in a gesture of blasphemy he did not guess. The ground below undulated over large hills of very irregular terrain broken by rocks, crags, and dry streambeds. No buildings interrupted the singular uniformity of the twisted wilderness.

Adjusting the magnification of his ocular to gain a closer view of the ground so far below, he could identify irregular shadows moving under the boughs of the blighted trees. The versicolor energies that arched and swirled around the ship appeared drawn to these beings.

Whether or not this energy sustained the shadows or was generated by them, he could not yet tell for the data was, as yet, too limited.

Eidelion would certainly need to be apprised of this situation. But first, he needed to collect more data.

Switching his attention back to the data feeds registered both through his own and the ERG's systems, he noted the energies around them were indeed of extradimensional origin as denoted by their signature characteristics on the Multidimensional Examination Tracker Survey, METS, and the twelfth order nonparametric preternatural equations he used to model and predict their flow.

With the care of a father examining his newborn child's health, he continued pouring over the data cataloged, stored, and analyzed by the ERG system.

Wrindanneth woke up in a cold sweat. Although he had rested, he could hardly call it well. Throwing back the covers, he swept his long legs over the edge of his cot, the softly glowing light overhead scattering in loose embers across the magical fabric of his robes. He slept fully clothed and ready should another emergency necessitate his swift attention. Standing, he wiped the sweat from his brow, running his fingers through hair matted by perspiration and tangled sheets.

With a brief incantation, he cleansed his body of dirt and odor so that he would at least look more refreshed than he felt. Leaving his chambers quicker than he was able to leave his dreams, he marched toward the bridge, thoughts of his slumber echoing strongly through his mind.

Nightmares of clinging, claustrophobic vapors had dogged him leaving him yearning for wakefulness even as he suffered through somnolence. He had walked through an ethereal landscape that grew grayer and less distinct with each step. His unease with the oppressive place had grown in proportion to his lack of visibility, encased completely within enveloping swirling shadows, until all sight and sensation were lost in an impenetrable gray wall.

It was then, when he could no longer see, could no longer tell up from down or left from right, that he had sensed that he was not alone, that an unspeakable terror lay at the center of the swirling morass, a center he wished to avoid but could not as he was inextricably drawn forward.

With heavy steps, he made his way to the decks, ready for an appraisal of their position and condition. Pushing the oaken door to the main deck open with his left hand, his jaw dropped as an overwhelming sense of déjà vu ran with cool certainty down his spine.

No stars were visible above. No horizon was discernible in the distance. He knew without looking that the horrific forest would not be perceptible below.

It could be either day or night and one would never know. The masts of the ship hung ghostlike and distorted before him, appearing barely connected to the decking he felt firmly beneath his feet. Looking back and forth, he could only just make out the fore and aft of the ship.

With a certainty he would never risk denying, he recognized that the lucidity, the sense of oppression, would only get worse.

They were trapped in the world of his nightmares and the only way out was to move forward toward the terror that he wished with all his heart to avoid.

Wrindanneth found Yip and Aroganji waiting on the bridge, silent phantoms adrift in the gray veil, their features almost as indistinct as the gray haze through which they traveled.

Yip's cheerful voice rose brightly through the fog, its surprising clarity and crispness belying the muting gray void. "Welcome, Wrindanneth! I trust your vision is clearer after a much needed and welcome rest!"

He sighed disconsolately. "Unfortunately, I woke to a world reflective of my dreams." Pausing for a moment, he added, "Reveries I would very much rather not have had."

He sensed Yip's smile although he could not yet fully see it. "Then perhaps your vision truly will be keener guided by the insights of dreams!"

Wrin shrugged in reply to his friend's jest. "I would not be guided by such gloom and darkness."

Close enough now to see his small friend's smile, Yip said, "Opportunity arises where it will. Do not be too quick to discount it."

Unconvinced, Wrindanneth answered noncommittally. "I do not think my dreams constitute a vision."

"Even if your dreams do not presage the future, there may be wisdom hidden within the confines of sleep. We have but to recognize it and let it guide us."

Adding his own chipper response, as unfitting in its tone as Yip's optimism, Aroganji joked, "Which way do your dreams lead us, Wrin?"

He sighed once more. "Into the heart of the suffocating fog."

Aroganji remained silent for a moment before asking, "Can you tell which way that is?"

Wrin smiled bleakly and without humor. "One need only follow the despair."

Giving his friends a moment to reply, he looked back and forth between them. When no replies came, he added matter-of-factly, "Taking the route toward the deepest gloom and greatest sense of oppression will lead us directly to Taerris'thule."

Noting that he had never directly answered the original question, Aroganji bridged the gap between them using the connection provided by the magical bracers and asked him again, *"And you are confident that you will be able to find the way?"*

His mind only open enough to answer the question, responding from behind a closed door, he answered simply, *"Yes."*

Once again taking the positive from what he felt was an overwhelmingly depressing situation, Yip said, "That we have reached the despair cloaking Taerris'thule is indeed a fortunate sign! We have come farther than many."

Wrindanneth laughed. He could not help it.

He laughed fully and loudly, releasing the tension within, the ululations of his humor rolling off unchecked into the fog.

With his laughter, the depressing malaise that had hounded him lifted as quickly as it had risen, replaced by confidence in himself and his friends. That Yip would find such a dismal occurrence as a sign of optimism in this forsaken limbo could only be laughed at and enjoyed for the insane but entirely appropriate folly it was.

What other response was there?

Nodding in agreement, a full smile on his face as he spoke, Wrindanneth laughed yet more. "Yes! You are indeed correct! This overwhelming gloom is indeed a fortunate sign, one we should be most thankful to receive!"

"We now know that Taerris'thule is almost upon us and that our journey has almost reached its intended destination!"

"Against all the odds of the most infernal pits, we have almost made our charge!"

He clapped Yip soundly on the back both as an expression of his change in mood and to reassure his friends that he was not replying with cynicism as was his wont.

Yip bowed, glad that his friend's mood had shifted. "We will need such brightness in the time ahead, Wrindanneth."

Still laughing, Wrindanneth lifted his arms boldly and said, "I will be your beacon!"

Aroganji could not resist the urge that had overcome his friend and began laughing as well, adding, "Where are some of those Gnomish glasses when you need them?"

"What's with all tha frivolity?" Slate's voice drifted out from the mist, its source as yet unseen. "Haven't ya learned tha first rule o' adventurin'? There's no party without tha Dwarf!"

After yet another drubbing at Daerdros's hands, Slate had gone belowdecks to get refreshed. He still could not get used to clothes that cleaned him and themselves and had just now decided to rejoin his friends. If it were not for his uncanny Dwarven sense of direction, and his friends' exuberant good cheer, he might have had some problems finding his way to the piloting station through the intractable mist.

His rare geniality unabated, Wrindanneth yelled, "We're on our way to Taerris'thule!"

"Don't let tha fun start without me!"

Finally with his friends, although he could barely make them out for the gloom, Slate asked, "When's tha fog gonna abate?" Used to darkness, semi-darkness, and other conditions of poor visibility, he was unfazed by the brume.

Yip answered, sure of his reply after sensing the forest and its energies for some time. "This fog is a manifestation of Taerris'thule's malevolence, corrupt and corrupting, cloying and unavoidable."

After hours spent within the murk, its presence and energies pervading him, he felt and knew the gloom as a direct emanation of Taerris'thule's evil, a willful perversion of the living energies that had once flourished here in ages long past. The longer they remained within the mist, without proper protection, the greater the risk of their own degradation as the foul powers of this place penetrated and suffused their essences.

"Ya're sure?" Slate raised an eyebrow, although the gesture was mostly lost in the haze.

"The fog will remain so long as the evil at its heart abides." He was certain.

Wrindanneth nodded, agreeing with Yip's assessment and the reaction of the Home Guard. "We have not adjusted our altitude since I went belowdecks, Slate. Only fogs such as this persist so far above ground."

"Don't get yer dander up, Wrin! I'm just askin'! I lay no claim ta knowledge o' our position or path."

Updating his friends briefly on what transpired while they were belowdecks, Yip added, "Eidelion, Kazarhan, Daerdros, and Spreesprocket have warded the ship and supplemented her shields to protect us from this evil that we ourselves will not be corrupted by its depravity."

Smiling, Yip continued, "Spreesprocket informed me that he has modified the resonance structures of the ship's shielding systems to make these modifications permanent. The *Shrike* should now both ward directly against and purify the presence of evil from her confines."

Slate laughed, encouraged. "Sounds like we need him on here longer! Who knows what other improvements we'll receive?"

Aroganji chuckled, adding, "Hopefully whatever is required to ensure our safe passage home!"

"Wrindanneth's dreams are but one indication of the evil we will soon face. Taerris'thule's horror grows as we move forward." His voice grown serious, Yip added, "We are close."

Wrindanneth agreed, although he had no other direct indication than his feelings of unease and the much deeper perceptions of his friends of the wrongness of the place. "We will arrive at Taerris'thule's doorstep very soon."

Slate looked around, barely able to see his own beard. "Not much o' a welcome mat fer those seekin' her stoop!"

"You would expect different?"

Slate placed his hand on Duraeleon's shaft. "I'd hoped fer doormen."

Wrindanneth shook his head. "Your patience will be rewarded."

"Your aspirations would be better spent hoping for abandoned ruins." Aroganji knew that they would not find empty haunts ahead, but he never could understand Slate's urge for open combat. Their lives, the success of their mission, and all the lives dependent upon them were at risk. Better to wish for success without violence than for bloodshed and the attendant risks.

Either way, those energies would be better spent in preparation than aspiration.

"A Dwarf aims fer his destiny and I hold destiny in my hands every time I pick up my axe."

His tolerance for such talk short, anticipating what lay ahead, Aroganji replied, "Then perhaps your time would be better spent preparing for that destiny you so eagerly await."

Sensing that he had crossed a line with his friend that he seldom encountered, Slate relented and offered, "I've had enough drubbin's fer tha day, thanks. I'd rather talk about lumps than take 'em right now."

Smiling wanly, Aroganji let the line of conversation drop choosing instead to direct his energies and attention elsewhere.

Eidelion waited patiently by the ship's command sphere, his noble countenance dimmed by the gray gloom, allowing the Home Guard and Flaming Fists time to gather round before beginning. The dismal haze was so thick that those standing opposite from him on the other side of the silvery disk were almost indistinguishable from the billowing fog. Were it not for the light radiating from the shimmering command sphere even those dim outlines might not be visible.

"Spreesprocket has spent some time over the past few hours examining the spectral anomalies surrounding Taerris'thule and has come to some interesting conclusions. As his observations bear directly upon the mission before us and address the likely foes we will face in the near term, I requested that he summarize his findings for you as well."

With a slight nod of his head, Eidelion brought his right arm diagonally down, across, and outward from his chest, giving the floor to Spreesprocket who stood by his side fully arrayed in his whirling and clicking Gnomish Paratechnological TAMERS unit.

"Ahem." Spreesprocket cleared his throat in preparation to begin speaking, a bit self-conscious of the attention despite years of experience giving lectures in various Gnomish institutions and academies, warrens and meeting halls.

"As Eidelion indicated, with my ERG's, my own technical analysis, and the help of the TAMERS' built-in METS system, I have been examining and analyzing the various emanations surrounding us. I have traced these energetic anomalies along their course and have determined with complete certitude that their point of origination is from directly within Taerris'thule."

Expecting his companions to understand the significance of those acronyms, as though he were in fact lecturing a Gnomish audience, he did not elaborate on the significance of those abbreviations or the capabilities implied by their usage. Nor did he expound upon how his augmented intelligence facilitated his evaluation of the extradimensional energies.

Clearing his throat, Eidelion broke in for clarification before Spreesprocket went on further. "Spreesprocket's own modified intelligence along with the capabilities of his exoskeleton bring many tools to bear on the examination and analysis of the energy patterns and anomalies. These are the capabilities to which he refers."

Nodding as if this were in fact common knowledge, Spreesprocket continued as though he had not been interrupted. "We are traveling through a region saturated with extradimensional forces. Based on my calculations, these energies derive from an abyssal region characterized by extant entropic spectral essences."

Slate grunted, "Which means?"

Spreesprocket nodded in reply, understanding the unusual nature of the topic of conversation. "Let me show you."

Raising his arm, he interfaced with the command sphere's projection and brought forth an image of the energy patterns he had been observing arching over the destitute forest below. Letting the image unfold for some time so that the others could see what he had experienced, the rolling landscape hidden by denuded trees, the dearth masked by the fog, he finally interjected, pointing, "Pay particular attention to this area under the trees."

Where just moments before only barren ground had been present, a dark shadow materialized briefly, drifted a few paces across the ground before disappearing once more. Replaying the image from where the shadow first appeared, he then paused the visualization and zoomed in until the shadow filled most of the depiction's display sphere.

Vacuous and empty, totally dark and untouched by the dim half-light around it, a still, amorphous shadow hovered above the ground, swaths of multicolored energies appearing to arch into or from the periphery of its silhouette.

"What, by Freyda's frock, is that?" Slate had never seen a Shadow before, although he had heard many tales.

Spreesprocket nodded again in recognition of Slate's question and continued with his points of discussion. "That is one of the spectral essences to which I referred. From this distance and level of analytical precision, I am unable to ascertain with complete certitude whether this particular example is a Wraith, Specter, Ghost, Shade, Revenant, Eidolon, or any other of a number of similar classes of extradimensional beings."

"So ya're sayin' we're travelin' through a haunted forest?" Slate wanted the conversation on a level where he could be sure of any conclusions that were drawn from the discussion. Furthermore, he wanted those conclusions to lead to understandable action.

Spreesprocket shook his head. "Although one might call the forest haunted,

I am not saying that is a proper description for the extraplanar energies and patterns that I have observed. In fact, I think a more proper classification for this area would be a semi-porous multi-dimensional inversion."

His patience shortening, Slate asked, "And what's that? Reality's growin' thin? Transparent?"

"Not exactly. Although that is, in fact, close to the mark. This portion of Ea'ae would more accurately be described as permeable."

Interrupting again, Slate responded, "What're ya gettin' at, Spreesprocket?" His patience was almost at an end. He wanted to get to the point of Spreesprocket's lecture without the technicalities.

If he wanted to speak in riddles, he would start a conversation with Yip.

"Based on my review of the data before me, I have confirmed that the seal in Taerris'thule has been thoroughly corrupted. Although this information is not novel in and of itself, what I feel with some measure of confidence is novel, insofar as I have understood at least, is that instead of serving to keep extraplanar energies and beings barred from entering our dimension, which was the original purpose of the seal and is of course the ultimate aim of our work in particular, I believe that the seal's effect has been, to use a simple metaphor, inverted."

"Ya mean tha seal is lettin' things from other dimensions in but not keepin' 'em out?"

"Not precisely, but yes."

"What's not precise about it?"

"Extradimensional beings are coming through, yes. However, these beings are not being let in. Rather the opportunity is present for them to arrive should they have the ability and wherewithal. Given these strictures, the likelihood of their arrival is significantly increased."

When he noticed that Slate was about to interrupt again, Spreesprocket added, "Think of the seal not as a door that opens and shuts with ease but as a sieve. With time, a bit of action, pressure, and some activity, beings from else-where can filter or shift from one plane to the other. With these beings, ener-getics representative of their home dimensions are also passing through."

"Based on my analysis of the beings encountered thus far, this effect may be localized to certain dimensions. However, these dimensions' denizens are particularly inimical to life as we know it on Ea'ae."

"Additional modeling points to the probability that the situation may be even more dire than the one initially outlined."

"Mmm." Slate did not like the sound of that, but they were all under the impression that the end of their quest would lead to something similarly unpleasant anyway, so the news was not particularly shocking or surprising. Spreesprocket's analysis told them what they already knew—that the seal must be destroyed and a new working one installed in its place.

"This alternative analysis indicates that we are in effect traveling through a region as much in our world, in our dimension, as in another, one whose laws and realities we may or may not understand, and the facts of whose existence may govern our own actions in ways we are not accustomed."

Now Wrindanneth interjected, "This news is not altogether unexpected. Based on our experience thus far, our magic appears to still function properly and should still serve us as we move forward."

Spreesprocket nodded again. "Currently, yes, but there are no guarantees as we move closer to the source of the disturbance. Also, the creatures we may face could be stronger than otherwise in our dimension for the link to their own plane, its laws, and its energies remains strong. We must, therefore, use caution."

Aroganji asked another question before Spreesprocket continued. "What else should we know and what other conclusions should we draw based on your observations, if any?"

Spreesprocket spoke with certainty. "The seal of Eldre'gheu has been corrupted and must be replaced as you all know. However, we must also ensure that the new seal does not fall to a similar fate, lest our efforts be in vain. Furthermore, any persisting, residual connections to alternate planes must be severed."

"Is that possible?" Expressed, Slate's innate skepticism and inherent lack of understanding of the subtleties of arcana came to the fore once more.

Spreesprocket smiled in answer, in his element. "What isn't?"

Pausing for a moment, he added, "I only hope we have the time and wherewithal to discover how."

Slate harrumphed. "Any other cheer ta spread before we disperse inta this awful mist?"

Ignoring the negative sentiment, Spreesprocket concluded, "Yes! Based on my derivations educed upon the increasing extradimensional activity and intensity of those manifestations, we should arrive at Taerris'thule within roughly one more day."

Resolute silence tempered by cool acceptance was the only reply to this final pronouncement.

Bringing the conversation to a close, Eidelion finished with a firmness that did not imply reprimand, only staid confidence, in order to redirect any negative or pessimistic moods that may be developing. "I would not have asked any of my peers to assist in this mission and risk their lives if I thought it were not possible and could not be accomplished by those we have with us. I have not changed my mind nor should you. We must have confidence in ourselves and each other if we are to see this through that the Light prevail in the next short few hours."

Looking around at each companion in turn, he asked, "Are there any other questions?"

When none were forthcoming he added, "Your belief and capabilities can change the world. The time to do so will soon be upon us."

Bowing, he finished, "Thank you for your continued perseverance and purpose."

With that, the Home Guard dispersed as silently as the fog leaving Yip, Aroganji, Wrindanneth, and Slate alone on the bridge, the mist between them a constant reminder of the impending threat they all faced.

Wrindanneth remained rooted at his accustomed position, holding firm after Aroganji and Slate had gone belowdecks to rest despite his own needs for sleep. Yip, who never slept anyway, at least not that he was aware of, remained by his side assisting in his navigation and evaluation to ensure the relative safety of their passage.

After making several calibrations and adjustments with Spreesprocket's adroit guidance, he had managed to improve the accuracy and clarity of the ship's navigational display. Although his sensations of the ship's progress mediated through the ship's instrumentation remained largely unchanged, the depiction of their progress and surroundings through the projection had improved markedly.

For any standing on the bridge, the projection now offered a view of the landscape below and the air above that was significantly more intelligible than the grainy gray haze that had predominated prior to soliciting Spreesprocket's assistance. The improvement was such that Wrindanneth now had sufficient control and understanding over the command sphere's capabilities that he could call forth and display the energy emanations just as Spreesprocket had done while making modifications and enhancements upon the depiction at will.

He was quite happy with the heightened instrumental expertise his interaction with Spreesprocket had provided. Despite interfacing directly with the ship's systems, there were levels of knowledge and understanding derived from that information that only a true expert could provide. Without such knowledge, he might not even know whether the capability existed within the ship, how to use and interpret such a system if he found it, or even where to find it in the first place.

With this refined detective capability now at his fingertips, these extra layers of control and technical sophistication would be a significant boon as they continued their journeys together.

With these improvements in place and now set up to constantly monitor their position, maybe both he and Yip could get some rest.

That is, if Yip wanted any.

Curious, he pointed to the image of the forested terrain depicted below with the multicolored extradimensional emanations, and asked, "Is this how you see the scene below through your inner vision, Yip?"

Yip did not turn toward the three-dimensional image of the forest to answer. "No."

"How does your perception differ from this image?" He had never really talked to Yip in great detail about the subject, at least not in enough depth to satisfy his desired level of understanding.

"You ask a simple question with a complex answer."

"We have time and I am curious."

"I feel energy moving around and within, Wrindanneth. The ship's display is a representation of what I feel, but only a part, not the whole. It is like an image of a leaf that is part of a tree—a portion, not the totality."

"I see and feel more than is displayed on your screen although the range, the distance, of my complete perception is more limited than the ship's equipment. The farther away I extend my senses, the less I am able to discern without additional effort."

"And how does what you feel and sense manifest? What do you see in your inner vision?"

Yip laughed, the expression all the brighter for the constant gloom. "That depends on what I am looking at!"

"You know what I mean."

"The world around us is filled with life, its energy and vitality. The cosmos, too, is imbued with this energy. This energy, this potential for expression and possibility, is one of the fundamental aspects of our universe."

"Eidelion would call this energy Light. You might call it magic. Slate might call it Brendle's Spark. Spreesprocket might call it Deur Spricken Sprack, the Omnispark, or Phlogiston. Llyewia might call it Aerya. I might call it *chi* or *yuan-chi*."

"Regardless of the name, it is around us and within us. It pervades us and binds us. It fill us and empowers us. It arises and passes, persists and changes, abides and interacts. It makes existence possible. Its potential is our own."

"This is what I feel. Just as life takes many forms and expressions, so does this energy. This I feel as well."

"As to how it looks, again, that depends on what I see. To my eyes, the universe is bright and alive, full of expression and vibrancy, dancing with light and energy, the actual and possible intertwined in the endless play of expression."

When Wrindanneth remained silent, lost in his inner consideration of Yip's words, Yip added, offering a spontaneous *róucí* to assist in his friend's contemplation,

> "The fullness of emptiness,
> boundless, expansive freedom—
> awareness alight."

Wrindanneth stared off into the fog, smiled, and said no more.

He had asked for Yip to paint a picture and Yip had merely provided a direction.

He need not know more of his friend's experience of the energies of Taerris'thule for he did not wish to consider how such a perversion would feel to one as intimately connected as Yip.

Neither would he have his friend visit such an experience more fully.

Kazarhan grunted, a habitual gesture he often expressed while working but only tolerated when deep in concentration.

"A Dwarf without grunts is like a stalactite without drips!"

He smiled at the memory of his father, his lined face lit by the glowing embers of the forge, as Kazarhan worked beside him in silence learning to breathe life into metal with the aid of Brendle's own breath.

Recognizing that his father's admonition was an encouragement to breathe and breathe properly while working, Kazarhan exhaled, the pent-up air sounding more like a grumble than a natural exhalation.

"That's better, lad!"

His father's thickly callused hand smacked him square on the back between the shoulder blades, knocking out whatever little amount of air had remained in his lungs—the whoosh of air rushing from his mouth also sounding like a grunt.

The grunts had been with him since.

As much for the memory as the long accustomed naturalness of the expression, he resisted the urge to stifle his own grunts.

Of course, he had little real need to grunt as he was not exerting himself physically, but the sound came as much from the depths of memory as anywhere else and he enjoyed the company while at work.

Nearly done, he cradled his hands gently before his lips and breathed deeply and fully into the shimmering light held so carefully within. With a brief invocation to Brendle the All Father, he released the confined air and let it settle over the planks visible between his booted feet.

Satisfied, he stood to better inspect is work. Below him, glowing with a vibrant golden light of its own, appearing to float both slightly above and within the polished wooden surface of the deck, a Dwarven sigil gleamed in the half-light.

Looking first left and then right along the *Shrike*'s periphery, as though marking a path or landing strip, other similar runes trailed off into the fog adjacent to the ship's railing, their light brightening the gloom more so than the glowing orbs floating above her deck.

Let one of those Specters he had seen in Spreesprocket's display try to board the ship now!

Grunting with satisfaction, his smile almost lost in his thick beard, he left the wards in place, the heavy stamp of his tread audible to any below him in the ship. Returning to the hold he seldom left, Kazarhan was, for the time being at least, gratified that he had finally contributed some small item of use in their quest and had not, for once, made himself look like a crotchety old fool doing it.

Slate woke to the sound of a firm knock at his door, the last echoes of his snores still reverberating uncannily off the walls as he opened his eyes.

Bloody disconcerting!

He would have to promptly forget what he had heard lest he be forced to give some credence to Wrindanneth's complaints that he snored louder than a Dragon's roar.

Sitting up quickly despite being fully encased in his battle armor, he answered, "Yes?"

"May I come in?" Kazarhan's raspy voice traveled through the air almost as well as Slate's snores.

"Aye! Come in!" He stood giving the appearance of alertness although there was no way that Kazarhan would ever think that he had been awake if he could hear the echo of his own snores as he woke.

"Ta what do I owe tha pleasure o' this visit?" His voice carried the amount of respect due a Kor'Dannan and Dur'kazak, although inwardly he felt little of those emotions after the way he had seen Kazarhan comport himself with regard to his friends.

"I have warded tha ship, Slate, and would share tha knowledge o' tha wards with ya if ya're willin' ta listen." Kazarhan stood in the doorway, his broad shoulders covered in a white cassock that fell nearly to the floor.

Surprised, but unwilling to let his sentiments be known, Slate responded firmly. "I'm listenin'."

"Will ya follow me abovedecks?"

"Aye." Slate gestured for Kazarhan to lead.

As they walked through the hallway leading to the stairs up to the ship's deck, Kazarhan commented, "Your progress with tha Daerdaana'Duin has been most impressive! Brendle has truly blessed ya and yer clan!"

Slate shrugged. "Were it not fer Yip, I wouldn't have had any success nor would I still be here, I reckon."

Kazarhan turned his head and looked back over his shoulder. "Believe in yerself as much as yer friend does and ya'll go far. Fer Brendle does as well."

Slate had no answer. He did not wish to argue nor did he have much to add.

Reaching the stairs, Kazarhan led the way upward, pushing open the solid door leading out into the gloom once they reached the top.

"This way."

Slate stepped out into the swirling fog behind Kazarhan, the other Dwarf's robes quickly disappearing into the brume along with the sound of his boot steps. Taking a few paces away from the doorway in the direction Kazarhan had headed, he noticed a vague light glowing ahead, radiating outward from the direction of the ship's deck.

Walking toward the light, he saw Kazarhan standing next to the sigil etched onto or just above the ship's deck.

"What's this?"

He bent over to read the lambent rune. Peering carefully downward, he stared at the rune through the mist, its uplifting light filling him with warmth and comfort.

"Karaduen?" Slate wanted to make sure he read the rune properly as it was one rather obscure and seldom used.

"Aye." Kazarhan smiled, his face filled with a touch of pride as though Slate had divined something particularly difficult and deserving of praise.

Slate examined the rune closely, feeling its warmth as he would the fires of an open flame. Karaduen, Light's ward or seal, protective runes to guard the ship.

"Ya've spaced these all around tha ship's edge?" He could see the light of the sigils trailing through the gloom just as he could feel the warmth of their embers in his heart.

"They will protect tha ship against creatures such as those we saw through Spreesprocket's study, supplementin' tha magic we bestowed upon tha ship's shield, should there be need."

"How so?"

"Tha Light o' Brendle's Spark, tha heat of tha Daerdaana'Duin, is anathema ta creatures such as those. Its presence will keep 'em away. If they get too close, its power will destroy 'em."

Slate nodded. He was well versed in the effects of Brendle's Spark on creatures of Darkness from his work as a Bor'Banna. He was also familiar with runic magic having worked as a smith, but the art in its highest forms was rare even amongst Dwarves. He had little experience with this level of expertise as his father had done the majority of finishing and enchanting for any items they created.

"Tha shapin' o' tha rune, infusin' it with breath and will, empowerin' it with Brendle's own fires are tha secret o' tha Dur'kazak."

"Why are ya tellin' this ta me?"

"Ya have tha power o' tha Daerdaana'Duin as I've never seen nor heard. Its power lies at tha heart o' tha labors o' tha Dur'kazak. If ya know runes, and I know ya do, then tha way o' tha Dur'kazak lies open before ya."

"Craft with yer mind and eye, provide purpose with yer will, breathe life with yer breathe, and empower with tha Daerdaana'Duin. If ya can do all o' these, then a Dur'kazak ya'll be!"

Slate stood in silence, unsure whether he wished to embark upon another journey when so many of his other paths and endeavors remained wide open and unresolved. Unsure how to respond to such an immense offering, he remained motionless, considering.

Finally, he grinned. If he were ever going to go back home and offer any new skills to the forge of his fathers, the knowledge of the Dur'kazak would be a prize more valuable than any treasure!

"What would ya have me know o' these runes?"

Kazarhan smiled, obviously unused to the gesture for Slate could almost see him thinking to engage the requisite muscles.

Nonetheless, his grin was genuine.

"These runes are like vessels o' water ta be refilled upon use. They will persist so long as ya offer energy ta fuel their intended purpose."

He then pointed to Slate's axe Duraeleon. "Treat 'em as a torch ta be relit after use. Tha fires from yer axe will light tha runes as a flame would tha pitch o' a torch. If tha light glows too dim or expires from burnin' overlong, ya can rekindle tha wards in tha same way, providin' tha fuel fer their fire through yers."

"Will ya not be here ta relight them as we journey?"

Kazarhan nodded. "Aye, but I won't be with ya forever and yer journey will take ya far beyond tha bounds o' Maeron. And ya'll need practice."

"Once ya've gained some level o' comfort with tha task, I'll show ya how ta craft yer own."

"With a bit o' understandin' o' tha fundamentals o' runic inscription, ya'll not need my help anymore, only yer own imagination."

Slate nodded, turning his gaze away from Kazarhan as he returned his attention to the rune at their feet.

Drawing Duraeleon, he rested the tip of its blade on the shimmering golden-white rune at his feet, the axe a bridge to his newly cast future.

Within, Yip felt the oppressive evil around them growing, a steadily increasing pressure that would soon need release. The weight built within the confines and extent of his mind filling its contents with the taint of the unclean, pervading the space behind his eyes as much as the view upon which he looked. An approaching storm had taken residence within his mind, thunderheads cast across the limits of his attention, one whose fulminations had yet to begin fully reverberating through his consciousness.

Without, Darkness flowed upward from the ground below to the sky above filling the space through which It flew with an overwhelming malevolence—a gushing spigot to a Daemonic realm filling the world with vile putrescence. The farther forward the *Shrike* flew, the greater the flow and sense of this corruption.

He feared that at the heart of this current, at the central tear between Ea'ae and some other unspeakable dimension, the tide would be too great to function, the rift too fundamental to repair.

Such concerns would do little to further their cause and aid in the realization of their goals, so he let those feelings drift away into the clouds of enveloping repugnance.

Remaining detached, his awareness rode lightly within this sea of abomination, assailed on all sides by Daemonic filth unleashed from some execrable plane.

Taerris'thule was nigh.

Aroganji slept, his dreams troubled by portents of madness.

A city lay close, its twisted outlines and contents as broken as its inhabitants—creatures of Darkness fit only for forsaken dimensions who preyed upon the energies of this world as leeches drink the lifeblood from their hosts.

He wanted no part of such a place, but he had to go. His future laid there, a trap waiting to spring upon his arrival.

He knew not why, but he had to reach the city's center and reclaim its prize. He wanted nothing more than to turn away and return home, but he could not, his dreams urged him forward. He was compelled and had no choice.

His will, his efforts, were not his own.

He was left to the whims of his dreams.

Though dark, in his heart, in the part of him that remained untouched by dreams, he feared his nightmares were brighter than his future.

Wrindanneth watched the display projected by the command sphere, reading the increasing energy currents that flowed through its visual depiction, following the ever-increasing tides to their source. Those fluxes were now his guide.

He set the *Shrike*'s course accordingly.

He had given up extending his senses directly through the ship's sensory instrumentation some hours ago. The increasing vileness of the sensations was too unnerving to continue experiencing directly.

Lest he lose himself in the evil harbored within the obnubilating fog, he had retreated to himself, limiting his consciousness to the space naturally defined by his mind, preferring instead the safety of the direct observer where his detachment, decision-making, and objectivity could remain in place without risk of intimate exposure to the corruption permeating around them.

The brief remembrance of those overwhelming sensations of perversion he had felt burgeoning as they moved toward Taerris'thule while opening himself up through the ship's sensors using Spreesprocket's techniques were enough to send a chill down his spine, making him shiver, left exposed in the throes of a tumultuous blizzard.

Clearing his mind of those negative thoughts and feelings, he redirected his attention to the command sphere, urging himself to read its contents with the clarity and focus of a fortune-teller divining the future from within the clouded heart of a crystal ball.

Squinting downward, bringing his nose almost directly to the surface of the three-dimensional projection, he blinked several times to clear his eyes and examine what he saw.

Cut stones, strewn across the ground at random, perhaps the lost remnants of a fallen pillar or the last footings of a once proud wall, lay weather-beaten and timeworn, partially covered by drifting leaves on the earth far below.

Could it be?

After all this time?

Reading the ground for further signs, he was loath to believe such scant clues. Watching the earth shifting below the tortured trees as they flew onward, farther ahead, its top and sides lost to the forces of time, a shattered tower slowly resolved itself, appearing gradually from within the reaches of the fog and swirling energy currents, hunkered near to the ground seeking refuge from the mist that now clung doggedly to its weathered, broken walls.

Beside the ruined tower, the fragments of a straight road appeared through the wood, its presence marked only by the absence of trees, cobblestones hidden beneath leaves that were left forgotten without opportunity to decay. Looking carefully, here and there sculpted stones were overturned or shattered while stone pillars marking the road bed were thrust upward from the ground in protest at remaining with their fellows unused and abandoned in the way for so long.

Now there could be no doubt!

Taerris'thule was in sight!

DRUMS OF WAR

Fierce warriors arrayed
on the field of battle—
spirits lifted by birdsong.

Humbol examined the knot he tied proudly. Laced around the stout metal ring connected to the bitt on the pier's mooring for his ship, his cat's paw hitch knot was a thing of beauty. He preferred its intricate loops to the simpler cow hitch that was its less elegant cousin.

Twisted in and out around itself in two spiraling mirror images, through the bight and over the metal ring from each branch, the silvery rope glistened in the sunlight as lustrous as the opalescent clouds above.

A fine knot indeed!

He had every right to be proud of his handicraft for it was sound and would serve to hold his small airship in place even in the most tempestuous of winds. Of course, he had taken care to buy the finest rope that he could afford, one of Elven silk that would resist tearing in the bight under tension while also avoiding breakage in the knot itself.

In a world where magic was commonplace, where the imagination ruled reality as much as the unfolding of more mundane physical laws, such practical skills were often overlooked. A true artisan expressed mastery of his craft simply with naturalness and ease whether its domain lay within the realm of the magic or mundane, the tangible or the mind.

Although he was loath to give himself any title, his knowledge and skill of marlinspiking and knot theory would warrant such a claim should he wish to seek or should another desire to grant such an appellation.

Done with his knot, he uttered an incantation while gesturing very much like the motions he had used to complete his cat's paw hitch, and tied a knot of a different sort. Now the line was secured and protected by another type of knot, one that could not be cut or removed, ensuring that his ship would remain moored in place when he left.

He smiled, washing his hands clean of the task in satisfaction. Just because he was good at tying knots did not mean that he should not use the other tools available to him, most especially when his livelihood depended upon the outcome.

Wiping the sweat from his brow, for the day was already hot and he had yet to unload his cargo of spices, seeds, and dried medicinal herbs and plants, he looked up from his appreciation of his handiwork to the sky. More numerous than birds flying through the air in the tropics, airships flew through the firmament flashing in and out of portals, loading and unloading goods and personnel, docking and taking off, adding more life, vibrancy and excitement to Tellanon than he ever would have thought possible—a fact which he always forgot until he returned from a journey and was reminded by their actuality and beauty.

Those ships were especially amazing on clear days such as this when the clarity of air highlighted the variety and breadth of form of these myriad vessels, the play of light on their sails and spars, allowing clear views of the entirety of their wondrous detail and intricacy. He smiled at the thought of all the cultures and places those ships would see, the various races and peoples that crewed those vessels, and the stories and craftsmanship held in each craft.

He would trade in Tellanon just for the opportunity to see such ships and dream their voyages with them. Although his travels were largely limited to local farming communities, other agricultural locations, and the occasional outlying villages, the presence of these transports broadened his world, expanding the frontiers of what he felt and experienced as possible.

Such were the intangible benefits of trade, only a small part of the exquisiteness of human interaction.

Gazing skyward, he imagined so much more.

His days of adventuring, traveling the open skies in search of coin and fortune were long past. He and Hoyt had had many a fine journey in their day. Now he was content to take a less active role, to sit back and let others forge ahead while he watched from the balcony.

The view from there was fine with him.

A broad smile still on his tanned face, his ruminations at an end for the time being, he walked back across the plank to his now secure airship in preparation to unload his cargo, the stout wood creaking beneath his booted feet as he did so.

He would visit Hoyt as his first item of business. It had been too long since he had spoken with his longtime friend. He had finally acquired some herbs that may serve Hoyt's customers well in their brewing of alchemical draughts. That would be as good an excuse as any to catch up with an old friend.

Besides, he still owed Hoyt after his friend had helped salvage and outfit his ship. He owed his current career to Hoyt in many respects. These herbs would serve as a long overdue repayment and a most appreciative gesture of thanks and consideration.

Taking the short journey to the ship's aft, he walked down the five steps that led to his snug, covered piloting and sleeping chamber. Reaching under the small, tidily made cot, he uttered an unlocking incantation to break the ward he had placed and pulled out a medium-sized leather satchel that he had stored away safely for just this occasion.

Hoyt would certainly be surprised when he browsed through the contents hidden within!

Grinning with happiness and anticipation for the bequest he was about to give, for the debt he was about to repay though it did not require reimbursement, he left his ship behind, bag strung over his shoulder, whistling an upbeat tune as he took back to the docks.

He meandered through the thick crowds on the quay without hurry on his way to the Scimerian Gate, preferring instead to listen to the sounds and cadences of uncounted tongues in their native timbre and tone, not filtered and translated through the aid of incantation. He need not understand what was said, only appreciate the sound for what it was—the music of living spirits joined together in vibrant, life-affirming song.

The words and intonations captured his fancy as much as birdsong on a spring day—so alive, effusive, and full of character. If he did not have business here, he would linger, perhaps overlong, until his heart was content, soaking in the pervasive music with all the enjoyment of a member of an audience at an orchestral performance.

His bright smile then, softening the weathered lines of his bearded face, was as much for the business ahead as for the enjoyment around.

The day, in all its glory, could not be finer.

Looking up, he took a moment to appreciate the depth of the azure sky, so clean and fresh bridging the space between Ea'ae and the heavens, full of opalescent clouds shifting with the wind as much as his fancy.

With a view like that, knowing the answer for he walked through it even as he mused, he wondered why he ever left the purity of the wondrous heights for the ground.

Just then, when his admiration was at its zenith, he squinted, blinking, breaking the continuity of his regard. As his eyelids broke his uninterrupted gaze, something disturbed the continuum of the firmament.

The whistle on his lips lost as his concentration deepened, he watched what at first he thought was a *faerviage* portal warping and twisting in the air, the sky beginning to ripple and roil with the action of a stone cast into its depths, thinning and shimmering as the portal manifested.

Only this manifestation did not look like a portal.

It looked more like the beginnings of a breach, a violent tear not yet fully realized but imminent and implacable, bulging and buckling the sky in savage throes and ripples.

Others around him began to point as the disturbance began to expand violently and erratically outward unchecked from its central mote.

He heard a few violent intakes of breath, gasps marking the sudden swallowing of air as if by breathing inward harshly the observers could counter the growing tumescent convexity of space-time above.

Then the sky exploded in Darkness and the klaxons began their deafening wails.

The Construct's distributed actuation matrix detected an illegal subspatial translocation abnormality of extraplanar origin.

Evaluation and assessment of transpatial disturbance…hostile extradimensional intrusion highly probable.

Monitoring and evaluation to continue…

Initiating synchronal contingency and emergency response rubrics…

Active manipulation of multi-dimensional hiatal abnormality initiated…

Prevention of alien incursion…failed.

Redirection of alien incursion…failed.

Dispersion of alien incursion…failed.

Evaluation of possible escape vectors…insufficient time and resources available for successful mass teleportation or transit…defensive counteractions recommended.

All further multi-dimensional travel…locked.

Faerviage…prevented.

Incursion…temporarily localized.

Potential intrusion scope successfully limited to Tellanon with high probability along multiple actuality parameters.

Direction of supplemental fortification energies commenced…Tellanon's defensive aegis successfully reinforced…charging of supplemental defensive systems…ongoing.

Citizen alert, notifications, and direction protocols commenced…Citizen and guests' reactions within normalized acceptable behavior boundary limits.

Citizen and guests' monitoring, protection, and guidance until safety status normalization…continuing.

Defensive engagement and resource management…undertaken.

Alerting and updating ancillary, high risk, and allied population centers to probability of potential incursion and threat encroachment…ongoing.

Initiating disaster recovery and restoration mechanisms…in progress.

Threat response modification and countermeasure protocols…evolving.

Éremon stopped abruptly, looking up and off into the distance as he carefully closed the ancient leather-bound tome he held cupped delicately in the palms of his adroit hands.

He felt the tumult above his city without laying his eyes on the disturbance as though the violence above were happening within himself.

Another of the seals protecting Ea'ae had fallen. Ea'ae's defenses had fallen below a critical threshold. The madness beyond could no longer be held at bay.

The Cabal were pushing through.

Moving calmly, with the poise of one setting the rare theurgical tome down to have a sip of tea, he called out the Construct in a voice filled with command. "Alert the members of the council. The Cabal's arrival is imminent. We meet at Illdrassil now!"

Before the sounds of his resonant voice had left the chamber, Éremon was gone.

Hoyt looked up from his desk, one last snort reverberating through his shop as he blinked his eyes lethargically for clarity, startled from the relaxing nap that had fully occupied his attention since his business currently did not.

Blasted kids yellin' in the street! Disturbing his nap!

Standing up abruptly, he marched to the smudged window of his shop to shoo away the unwelcome loiterers he had heard. Seeing no one outside, he threw open the screened door with a loud creak to scare away the rascals who had disrupted his dreams of relaxation, frightening away his visions of sitting in a rocking chair under a cool porch on a shady spring day comforted by a nice refreshing breeze while sipping iced tea with lemon as he watched the afternoon pass leisurely by.

Instead, their commotion had thrown his dreams into a furious tumult with visions of people running to and fro and alarm bells ringing.

The door banging against the dilapidated wall of his shop only managed to scare the Fairy Dragon resting amongst his wares. Unlike Hoyt, it had remained asleep until this most recent affront. The streets were, as was normal in this section of town, deserted.

Scratching his head in mild confusion, turning to go back in and resume his hard-earned nap, he stopped as he heard the disturbance once more. Only it was not a disturbance like he had imagined in his dreams, it was a warning.

"Citizens! Tellanon is under attack!"

"Proceed calmly and in short order to the nearest designated public transpatial park!"

"Your timely response is of the utmost importance!"

"Do not jeopardize your health or the safety of your family and companions by any delay or tardiness!"

"Proceed to the nearest public park!"

"In order to assure your safety, you must proceed to the nearest designated public park!"

"Your safety will be assured at the nearest public park!"

"This is not a drill!"

"Spatial localization will prevent further hostile incursion within the confines of the transpatial parks. Proceed to the parks with all due haste!"

"If you have further questions, your Aspects will be able to address and resolve any concerns you may have!"

"Respect your fellows and proceed with caution!"

He smacked his forehead while the Construct droned on with its instructions.

How had he managed to sleep through this?

He was either getting too old, too hard of hearing, or he had done too good a job with his sound filtration, isolation, and diversion spells.

Filtering out the noise of the surrounding warehouses and canceling his information feeds had their drawbacks as well.

Looking up at the sky, a large expanse of which was splotched by a black contusion bulging outward and about to burst, he wished he had.

Even magic induced nightmares were preferable to this!

Turning back to his store, Hoyt yelled out, "Come on, Cletus!"

Responding indifferently, choosing first to stretch and scratch behind an ear, acting as though Hoyt's summons was not the cause of its motion, rather that it had reached the same decision as Hoyt just prior to his command, the Fairy Dragon flitted up and off the window sill and flew to Hoyt's shoulder where it landed gently, promptly curling up and going back to sleep.

A grin on his face, he muttered, "Ya're hardly worth the trouble sometimes."

The Fairy Dragon merely cracked an eyelid before returning to sleep.

Facing the worn, weathered face of his store once more, he barked, "You too!" and clapped his hands.

Responding dutifully, unlike Cletus, Hoyt's tired, dilapidated, old store collapsed inward, folding over and over again in a large, creaking, groaning, and fitfully protesting cloud of dust. Finally, after almost a minute of grating and grousing, the building turned over and upon itself so many times that it had contracted to the size of a small pocket watch.

Taking a moment to survey the dusty, empty, derelict lot left by the departure of his store, tree, barrels, and all, he wiped one solemn, lonely tear from his eye. Looking from warehouse to warehouse bordering his now vacant lot, he said, "Don't get any ideas! We'll be back!"

He then marched to the center of his lot and gingerly picked his miniscule collapsed store up off the ground. Giving it a brief pat, he whispered reassuringly, "Don't ya worry, we'll return! Ya have my word!"

"Yer home is mine and I intend ta keep it!"

Patting the small, matchbox-sized bundle comfortingly once more, he placed the miniaturized store within an inner pocket of his robes, his motions never once disturbing Cletus who remained perched sleeping on his shoulder with tenacious aplomb and insufferable balance.

Glancing up to the sky once more where Darkness now raged like fire in the heavens, he spat on the dirt at his feet and cursed as he did so. "Now ya've done it! Where's my boomstick?"

Snapping his fingers, a wicked ebony wand appeared in his hand, its handle as thick as the pommel of a sword, the shaft of which was longer than his forearm. Gleaming with an inner light brighter than the sunlight reflecting on its highly polished surface, his wand looked like nothing more than a blazing portent of doom.

A more fearsome weapon could hardly be imagined in the hands of a wizard, especially one whose dreams of a blissful spring day sitting in a rocking chair had been unceremoniously stripped away.

Armed and ready, he took to the air, flying forward toward the city's center as chaos descended from above.

Cletus never once blinked or opened his eyes.

Éremon arrived in the council chambers perched atop Illdrassil's apex amid a silence so deep and profound as to be almost tangible. The large open chamber in which he stood waiting for the other members of the council to arrive stretched across the entirety of the top of Illdrassil. Translucent walls afforded a panoramic view of the city in all directions.

He had only moments to survey the scene before the other members of Tellanon's ruling High Council began to arrive.

Spread across the sky before him, he examined the ghastly stain now spewing forth from the tear in the heavens. The Darkness before him drank in the light of day as much as it did the living energies that made this world so vibrant. The same Darkness prevented him from discerning anything beyond its turbulent pitch-black surface. Although he wished the city and her citizens could escape to freedom, such a course was no longer an option. There was no time to gather the power necessary to shift the city to a new location nor enough time to flee the horrors held within the Darkness.

He understood the risks posed by the Darkness and was confident in the city's reinforced shield's ability to deflect them. He was not, however, certain of what lurked within the Darkness or beyond it on the other side of the portal through which it arrived.

That uncertainty would, with any luck, be countered by the sentries swarming at the ready around the shield's periphery without risk to the individuals within.

He only hoped this was the only such new breach in Ea'ae's defenses.

In preparation for his fellows' arrival, he called forth the Construct's visualization of the ongoing attack. This image, a flowing jet black mass rapidly spreading across the sky and enveloping the city, along with various multidimensional streams of tactile data awaiting interaction for complete display and explanation by the Construct, hovered in the air before the arriving members of the Protectorate as a constant reminder of the unfolding chaos swiftly threatening their city.

Turning to face the room's center, for he sensed the last of the localized spatial disturbances associated with the arrival of other members of the governing Protectorate, he spread his arms in greeting for his peers.

"Welcome and be ready!" His voice filled the chamber with the fullness of warmth and sound. "We are under assault by the Cabal and time is of the essence!"

Before the sounds of his voice had finished echoing off the pellucid walls of the council's chambers, all of the other members of Tellanon's ruling body stood around him. Some were disheveled, obviously hurried and harried by their unexpected summons, but all were focused and resolute, determination clearly visible in their countenances as they listened to Éremon's greeting.

Before him, arrayed in their customary arrival positions, each spot marked by a gently shifting glyph of light on the floor, waited his twelve peers.

Oroende, his visage lined with concern, stood firmly, his skin radiant in the sunlight inset with gold, gems, and stardust marking his status as Ueralen, leader of the Thelios, the guild of Paratechnologists focused on material transformation and alteration.

Beside him to the right stood Rowena Bowspirit, the city's foremost Aeromancer, able to read and shift the currents of wind and air with as much skill and precision as a fine novelist crafts and guides an epic tale. Her facility in riding the currents on an airship and commanding her peers was only matched by her ability to guide in their design.

To Rowena's right stood Dizzywig Paddlepulley, Gnomish Paratechnologist extraordinaire, leader of the Sliced Bread Society, also known as the SBS, a think tank dedicated to furthering the depth and breadth of magical and material understanding spanning across the range and entirety of the mundane and mystical. Despite his lifelong dedication to Paratechnological research, he dressed simply and without obvious physical Paratechnological modification for, unlike many of his Paratechnologist peers, he felt that the most remarkable transformations occur from within.

There was, however, one minor exception, beneath his robes, partially hidden by the long folds of his cloak as it fell over his shoulders, he wore a bright yellow t-shirt with a rotating three-dimensional image of a loaf of bread with a knife hovering above its surface. As the knife cut through the bread, the SBS's logo appeared beneath the slices in vivid orange calligraphy, "It doesn't get any better!"

For some, the pursuit of knowledge came easier than others.

To Dizzywig's right stood Jae'elthos, Iyela, Lorekeeper of the Anuvatari, the Children of the Light. His gentle countenance and flowing, silken silver hair radiated a deep and abiding peace in stark contrast to the burgeoning violence in the sky. Although the room's air was still, his diaphanous robes stirred as though roused by a light breeze.

Beside Jae'elthos and to the right, his short, squat powerful build in direct contrast to Jae'elthos's tall, elegant litheness, stood Vaendoer Thunderhammer,

Dur'kazak and thane of the Thunderhammer clan. The Dwarves of the Thunderhammer clan had worked in direct partnership with the Gnomes of Tellanon for long years on projects that required particular craftsmanship, skill, and engineering expertise for any given Paratechnological endeavor.

To Vaendoer's right, standing immediately to Éremon's left, and completing the lower circuit of Protectorate members, stood Whirlygig Sparksocket, his wild hair and unkempt clothing highlighting the vibrant bustling energy and excitement of his presence even while still. A thick ocular on a golden chain dangled from his neck while a translucent disk displaying an unending stream of numbers and images hovered in the air before him. Whirlygig was the lead Designer and System Administrator of COG, the Construct Organization Group, with direct responsibility over the Construct and its attendant artificial intelligence subroutines. As such, he and his group governed, managed, and indirectly supervised much of the city's infrastructure, organization, development, and functioning.

To Oroende's left stood Magdalia Miera, eminent Theurgist, leader of the Light's Grace congregation, her luminous spirit almost as aurorean as Éremon's own though hers shone unoccluded. Dark black hair streaked with white strands that resembled nothing more than flashes of lightning bolts in a dark night sky added force to an otherwise already striking presence.

His thick velvet robes billowing with each minute movement, Borus, Head Magistrate, lead Justicar, and Adjudicator for the people's will and the citizens' ethos, stood solemnly to Magdalia's left. His bald pate was partially covered by a loose skullcap and framed by wispy gray hairs, clouds hovering about a shining snow-capped peak. His dark eyes gazed piercingly forward above jowls sagging with age waiting with aplomb for Éremon to speak.

A thin man, his head swiveling above a neck far too attenuated for his oversized cranium, fidgeted next to Borus on the left. His actions spoke of one who would rather be somewhere else, whose business beckoned him elsewhere despite the pressing need demanding his presence. His gaze, however, remained firm taking in everything about him with the thirst of one who has been lost in the desert and had only recently emerged into civilization. Head of interspecies and interstellar diplomacy, chief facilitator of interstellar commerce, Noumel had the gift of tongues and a knack for setting people and situations at ease even if he himself never appeared so.

To Noumel's left, full-bodied and matronly, her rosy cheeks aglow with warm regard, Salia Proventure held her hands patiently across her ample middle. Citizen advocate and voice of the community, she put the concerns of her fellows before her own, mother to all and foe to none, ensuring the interests of the people were always at the fore of the city's dealings. Master healer and herbalist, she was known far and wide for her ability to cure the ails of those in need.

His long gray hair as disheveled as his simple, stained robes, Chutefunnel Knobwhistle, head of higher learning, intercollegial linkage and noetic exchange, intellectual prosperity, and citizen enlightenment, stood distractedly to Salia's left. His cognizance lost in higher order abstractions, his gaze only occasionally returned to the room and his fellow High Council members, although his mind encompassed them all in equations governed by elegant symmetries.

Finally, to Chutefunnel's left and Éremon's immediate right, stood Alain Ar'laen, called Brightblade, leader of the Home Guard, Tellanon's Master-at-Arms and principal defender, general, and Champion. Alain's skin shimmered with a light of its own, even brighter than the greatsword upon his back. His form appeared fluid and malleable, transitioning from one possibility to the next even when stable. A rarity even on Tellanon, Alain was an example of Paratechnology taken to its farthest limits. A synthesis of magical technology and the mind, Alain had given his body up in its entirety, fusing his intelligence with both the expansive structures of his new form which were derived from his original cognitive structures and those of the Construct, expanding the limits of his physical self and conception, becoming not only a synthetic intelligence formed through the union of man and machine, but a synthetic being whose existence inhabited the boundaries between the real and the artificial, the imagined and the actualized. As such, his body shifted to his will and need, intimately linked with the Construct and its capacities that he may enact and embody the needs of the city and her citizens for their defense and protection.

Everyone present and now gathered round, Éremon spoke, "I trust you are aware and apprised of the dangers before us."

"We must act—quickly, decisively, and with conviction. Our lives, the future of Tellanon, and Ea'ae beyond depend upon us."

"Were it otherwise and we had more time and warning, we might have been able to counter the incursion or flee prior to this attack. However, there is no longer time to gather the energy necessary to teleport the city in its entirety. Should we port now, we would be easily tracked and followed. Nor do we have the option to fly from the Darkness sullying our skies. We are hemmed in and cannot outrun our pursuers."

"Individuals attempting to flee without assistance in the face of this madness would surely be consumed."

"We must stand for ourselves and for those of Ea'ae who cannot do so for themselves for the Cabal has returned!"

Muttered hisses, cries of disbelief, whispers, oaths, and curses filled the air around Éremon as he continued with the briefing.

"The Construct has reinforced our city's shield to prevent intrusion from the tendrils of Darkness employed by the Cabal as a first wave of attack. While the Cabal's forces rally and push through the rift in our skies, for we can no longer stop their intrusion, we wait to mount a counterattack."

"Multiple fronts of sentry drones have been dispersed both within and around the shield's perimeter as staggered lines of defense against whatever else comes through. These same drones await our mark to attempt passage through the portal. With any luck, those outside the shield will be able to close the portal from the other side while simultaneously providing intelligence and inflicting significant damage to whatever waits beyond its horizon, as requested. Should they fail, those drones within the shield will be available for counterstrikes and defensive actions."

"In conjunction with the Home Guard, the Construct is currently organizing a tertiary line of defensive ships, armaments, and troops within and without the city to supplement the city's own automated defenses."

"Should it be necessary, I have summoned you here to cleanse that which our city's other defenses may not be capable before the lives of our citizens are risked, forfeited, or worse."

"Though safety measures are in place to provide safe havens for our citizens, if the drones and our efforts in this room fail, then Tellanon will be left to protect herself directly with the aid of her citizens and at the risk of the lives of her defenders, her denizens, and guests."

"We must be successful in our efforts that their lives will not be lost, corrupted, or ransomed!"

DAEDALIAN'S HEART

Red maple in fall bloom,
backlit by morning sun,
burns with an inner flame.

"By Brendle's beard, I never thought we'd lay eyes on this forsaken place!" Slate stroked his beard deliberately as he spoke among his friends.

They all stood gathered round the command sphere upon Wrindanneth's summons—the Four and the Home Guard all giving full attention to the ruins spread out before them, hidden from them for so long but now visible beneath the purview of the ship's instrumentation.

As withered and forlorn as the forest and rocky hills skirting its ragged periphery, the outlines of Taerris'thule appeared and disappeared in the currents of fog and extradimensional energies below, its majesty laid low and humbled through the passage of time, neglect, and decay. Her fallen towers, minarets, and domes resembled the worn bones of a wayward, broken fossil unearthed from the memories of ages long past, the history and purpose of which were now inscrutable, faded with the hopes and ideals of her founders.

At the city's heart, its large alabaster dome now grayed and etched, marred by jagged holes and cracks but otherwise remaining intact, the temple of Eldre'gheu towered above the city's other remaining sundered buildings and those lining the outskirts of its now desolate grounds. The walls along the temple's boundary had been shattered, its fountains smashed, and its reliefs and statuaries debased. The temple bore the full brunt of the passage of time and the weight of evil hanging over its shadows like a pall.

Its gates cast down and thrown open, the thresholds that once opened wide in welcome for all peoples now offered a grim warning to any who were fool-hardy enough to approach.

Once a glorious dedication to the highest ideals and aspirations of civilization, now base and corrupted, its altars and towers despoiled and laid low, their ultimate goal beckoned.

Over all, as tangible as the fog, a feeling of overwhelming despair and dread loomed. There could be no doubt this was no place for the living. This insidious fear alone was enough to test their discipline and set already tired and frayed nerves on edge.

Having to descend and go in to the city's center, where the oppressive sensations could only be worse, did nothing to lessen the feelings of apprehension they all steeled themselves against.

To Yip, the scene was inconceivably worse.

Nacreous green light, corrupt and befouled, lit the city's avenues in stark, horrific relief. Living Shadows, darker still than the eaves and orifices from which they prowled, oozed from one abandoned building to the next—evil in search of prey long lost. Coalescing en masse at the city's heart, these Wraiths merged and gathered, separated and reformed about the fallen temple, an oil slick that was not to be cleansed or burnt off.

Horrendous energies surged outward from the temple at the middle of the maze, lacing the building's exterior in its entirety in a sickening patina of extradimensional power.

Looming above the chilling Darkness and ghastly light, radiating directly from the temple of Eldre'gheu itself, a vast spinning vortex of Darkness spiraled and turned upon itself, the source of the city's Shadows, the fount for the all-consuming fog. This abhorrent cyclone pulled at him, seeking to rip his essence away from afar, an outpouring of absolute terror spewing forth from the tear in the fabric of his world into one of utter nigritude and emptiness.

To enter that Darkness would be their end.

Having spent hours going back and forth over the best possible course of action prior to their arrival and seeing the lay of the land before them, the time had now come to decide on the best course of descent into the madness below.

"Whatever route we take, we must have quick access to the ship should an escape be necessary." Aroganji could not conceive of attempting to fight their way through the entirety of Taerris'thule nor would such a plan be advisable. The evils that may lay in wait could very well be their undoing prior to ever making the temple itself.

Echoing his thoughts, Eidelion agreed, saying, "As Aroganji indicates, we would never survive a direct push through the city. Our enemy would have too much time to marshal its forces as we fought on to the temple. Should we fight through and our victory not be complete, we would then be denied a quick retreat."

"We will need to initiate our assault as near to the temple as possible."

Slate clapped his two callused hands together forcefully with a loud smack. Taking Eidelion's intent one step further, he grumbled, "Why not avoid tha fightin' altogether and send a couple o' tha ARMED sentries in and blast tha whole place ta flinders?"

Yip spoke into the silence of Slate's question. "I do not think that will be possible."

Shaking his head, he pointed to what appeared to be little more than a violent disturbance or agitation in the air and energies above the temple on the projected display even with the improvements from Spreesprocket's modifications. "There is a vortex of untold extradimensional power radiating from the center of the temple itself. We cannot risk entering or interacting with this disturbance. Even if these energies were not present, the temple is completely encased in extraplanar energies of unknown capacity and purpose."

Spreesprocket added, "If Yip's assessment is, in fact, correct and there is both an interdimensional vortex of unidentified stability and a shield around the temple structure itself, then we cannot risk that course. Adding force of such magnitude to an interdimensional rift may have catastrophic consequences. Furthermore, the shield itself might divert the energy from the attack entirely leaving us with little to no benefit from the attempt."

"I will need to modify the ship's detection systems to allow for this vortex's full detection."

Through the Fria al'Othra, seeing the world and its ways—its currents, patterns, hidden aspects, and interconnections—very much akin to Yip's own sight and sensation, Llyewia spoke then, for the gravity of the situation warranted his comment and particular perspective. "Yip is correct in his assertion. There is indeed an extradimensional maelstrom of vast power radiating from and above the temple. The long-term effects of this vortex are evident and deplorable. We must approach and treat this disturbance with utmost care and consideration."

"The foul taint of the Anubaraëthi is overwhelmingly strong here."

"Our actions must be as careful as the unfurling of new shoots risking the last of winter's frost and as implacable as the change in seasons."

"Such things should not be."

Spreading his arms widely as though attempting to placate an invisible audience, for he was soothing the hurt he sensed in the world around him, Llyewia finished, "We shall be the agents of this change."

Having waited patiently for Llyewia to finish, still intent upon blowing his way through and into the temple, albeit with slight modifications to his original plan given the new information at hand, Slate grumbled, "Why not avoid tha vortex, counter tha shield, and then blast our way through tha temple's roof and enter directly?"

Spreesprocket replied, "Even if we're able to bypass the temple's protections, blow a hole directly in the temple's roof, and fly down through it, our surest course of action, based on presently obtainable information used to model multiple actions paths, will probably be to enter directly through the temple's front door where our return exit will be guaranteed without risking structural damage and a collapse about us. This is of course unless we have another suitable action path forward."

"The downside of such a decision is that such action will be anticipated and we will need to meet our enemies' strength with our own."

Noting the distance and scale of the temple were difficult to discern visually from their projection, Yip offered another option based on Spreesprocket's implication, one that might not play directly into their foe's hand. "If not that, and we can find a way to bypass the energies surrounding the temple, or if they do not provide a defensive barrier, we can evaluate whether some of the existing holes in the roof are actually large enough to fly the ship, or our attack party, directly through."

Siding with Yip and Slate's intent, Aroganji added, "We cannot model the unknown with complete certainty. Yip's proposal, or one like it, may allow us to bypass some of the dangers inherent in traveling through the entirety of the temple. Fighting through the front may expose that portion of the temple to collapse as much as any other. We must remain flexible and adaptable in order to succeed."

Still attached to his idea, Slate spread his forefinger and thumb slightly apart indicating just enough distance on the projection and gave a loose smile. "What if we blow a hole large enough in tha walls around tha front door ta fly tha whole ship through and into tha temple's chamber, then?"

His enthusiasm stirred, Slate spread his arms wide and finished, "Blast tha blazes outta that bugger and show 'em what they're in fer!"

Liking the idea, and resisting the urge to smile with Slate's enthusiasm, for he had given his friend's plan some consideration for it would ease the need to guard or worry about the safety of the ship after they left her confines, Wrindanneth added, "We could always try."

Summarizing his thoughts, Wrindanneth spoke directly, counting each point off on his fingers. "Assess the situation. See what's possible. Attack from the side, blow our way through if possible, fly through if we can to the temple's interior and go from there. If not, and the temple's energies protect it and cannot be quickly countered or forestalled, we can drop in as Yip suggests or move in through the front as Spreesprocket offers."

Slate interjected excitedly, thrusting his arm forward as he did so, "If tha front door's not big enough, let's widen it!"

Finishing his thoughts with a smile as Slate finished, Wrindanneth said, "In whatever case, I can order the ship to await our summons when we return. If we take the direct approach, its firepower will aid in our own."

"Beyond establishing the perimeter defenses, should we not attempt to scry or observe the path ahead within the temple itself prior to rushing in headlong to an uncertain fate?" Orogast's face shifted with concern that his human form did not fully convey.

Spreesprocket nodded indicating his agreement. "We can send one or two of the remaining sentries in ahead of us on a scouting run in an attempt to glean some intelligence about the risks of our journey into the structure's interior."

He then added, "The remaining sentry or sentries can stay with the ship and help guard it in our absence."

Not cognizant of the drones' full capabilities as well as Spreesprocket, Aroganji asked, "Do you think that the ARMED sentries will be able to penetrate far without detection? We do not want to lose whatever small advantage the element of surprise affords us."

"Their stealthing capabilities are formidable. However, we do not know what wards are in place to prevent their evaluation and entrance."

Yip added, "Their attempt cannot hurt."

Having sensed the overwhelming malevolent presence pervading the air around them, as much a part of the fog as its source, he continued, "Our presence has not gone undetected. The fog around us is as much a part of the evil in the temple as the entity itself. By using the sentries, we will not risk anyone's life in the process and serve only to gain in our own eventual attempt."

Understanding that their path was fraught with risk regardless of the path taken, Eidelion indicated his tacit agreement. "We should fully assess the situation and see what approach to the temple is most feasible. We must do this as quickly as possible to avoid risk of attack."

"We can then employ the sentries once we have a clearer understanding of the temple's magics. If necessary, we may be able to circumvent some of the defenses inherent in the temple's magics before sending the sentries or we make an attempt to enter."

Wrindanneth shrugged ambivalently. "We've been waiting all this time to get here, so long as we are not attacked while we wait, we can wait a bit longer."

Eidelion gave his assent. "Very well then."

"Spreesprocket! Orogast! Llyewia! Continue your inspection and evaluation!" "Daerdros! Kazarhan! Begin warding the crew and ship!"

Laughing, he added, "Raour'Saqan! As you are and at the ready!"

Giving further orders to each of his troops, Eidelion began the preparations necessary for their impending onslaught.

Yip stood with Slate, Wrindanneth, and Aroganji at the helm while Daerdros and Kazarhan made ready to begin casting a series of defensive enchantments upon them in preparation for their impending assault. These spells were part of standard Home Guard combat operational protocol and served as the foundation from which any additional protective enchantments and augmentations would be added based on a given warrior's chosen combat preferences, deployment situation, and contingency strategies.

Members of the Home Guard had magical artifacts that imparted these spells automatically at need when the situation arose. Since the Fists were not part of the Guard, these spells would need to be cast in a more traditional manner prior to their engagement with the enemy.

Aroganji and Wrindanneth were eager to participate in the warding process if for no other reason than to learn new spells and their applications. Once these spells were imparted, they would also have a clearer idea of what additional protections may be desirable to cast as a supplement to the Home Guard's repertoire.

For his part, Slate wished to see more of Kazarhan's usage of runes, although his casting would probably involve energies and applications of a divine nature that Slate may not be able to fully understand or replicate as he was not an initiate of the Priests of Brendle. He would, however, have Brendle's Spark, the flames of his fathers, available instead.

Now that he had made the decision to learn, any opportunity to observe the formation, casting, and filling of runes was an opportunity he did not want to miss.

Yip waited and watched.

There was much to be decided and even more to be acted upon. Abiding, he remained vigilant for any dangers or vagaries that might affect the success of their mission.

He was just as ready to begin.

"If everyone is ready, let's get started!" Daerdros briefly looked at each member of the Four in turn before casting her spells. Although each knew her intent, she wished to receive acquiescence that they were all ready and willing to go forward. Home Guard spells were seldom cast on outsiders and never without reason.

"Let's get goin'!" Slate, never having been known for his patience, was eager to be done before they had started.

Kazarhan nodded curtly in acknowledgement of Slate's comment, his voice rising and falling rhythmically with the solemnity of an invocation. "Tha runes I am about ta inscribe on each o' ya fer yer protection are Karaduen, seals o' Light, passed down from Brendle tha All-Father o' eld. These runes are Brendle's true writ o' Creation and describe tha world as it was formed and will be. In tha right hands, with tha proper shapin' and will, intent and humility, these runes are direct vehicles o' Creation just as they were at tha beginnin' o' time."

As he spoke, his voice became more serious, full of power and authority, his intent growing to match the import of the thoughts he now spoke, the words he so rarely voiced. "Just as they are tha world's past and future, so will they be yers!"

Moving his hands, etching Karaduen in the air, faint trails of light streaming from his fingers as he did so, Kazarhan intoned, "Each rune has a meanin' and intent. Trust in tha rune ta serve its purpose as ya would a friend in battle fer tha runes are often more reliable and will stay with ya until tha end."

"These runes will last so long as their power holds and no longer. Although ya may not be able ta see their passage, ya'll be able ta feel when they fade fer their power will leave ya. What was once possible with their vigor will then be out o' reach."

His admonishment clearly visible in his eyes as he looked at each Slate, Wrindanneth, Aroganji, and Yip in turn, Kazarhan continued, "Heed that lesson carefully lest ya cost yerself and those around ya dearly. Just because tha runes grant ya power fer a time does not mean ya get ta keep it."

"Tha boon o' Creation is yers ta enjoy and cherish, not ta hold."

As curt in his description as in his mannerisms, Kazarhan briefly outlined the purpose of each rune. "Tha runes I am about ta cast are Hürn, Loess, Ungar, Noeldri, Durden, Vanduen, and Hröthe. Tha boons they grant are protection from evil, protection from supernatural influence, strength and endurance, agility and prowess, protection from fear, divine regeneration, and healing."

"Know their limits and know yer own."

Finished with his instruction and description, he then gathered himself, took a few deep relaxing breaths before beginning the casting of the Karaduen, and started inscribing a wonderfully complex series of runes on each party member in turn, taking care in the shaping, forming, and application with the attention and skill of a master craftsman. As he worked, the ancient runes he placed on of their forearms flared silvery white for a brief moment, burning brightly as he left his mark and described his intent before fading away, no longer distinguishable from the skin to the naked eye.

When Kazarhan had finished, all told, he had cast several protective sigils on each of them, lacing their arms with invisible tattoos. These wards would last until the divine energies channeled within had been completely discharged. The runes he inscribed actually encompassed a wider range of purpose and functionality than he had originally described to the party.

Hürn, evil's bane, warded them against evil and its corruptive influence. Loess, Heaven's shielding, protected them against supernatural forces while also serving to keep those forces at bay. Ungar, earthen might, gave them physical strength and endurance, while also staving off fatigue and hunger, for the battle ahead. Noeldri, flowing water, gave them grace and agility, poise and flexibility, lightness and comfort. Durden, valiant heart, shielded them from overwhelming fear and the debilitating effects of indecision. Vanduen, divine regeneration, enhanced their healing capacities, speeding recovery and repair from both exhaustion and injury. Hröthe, divine healing, offered a one-time boon of healing from grievous or debilitating wounds.

Once Kazarhan had finished, the silver light no longer trailing from behind his motions as it had while he worked, he said, "Believe in tha runes and live. Ignore 'em and be forsaken."

With Kazarhan's work completed, Daerdros began the casting of her protective enchantments, supplementing those of Kazarhan with her own. "These enchantments complement Kazarhan's Karaduen by shielding you from harm, granting you flight, protecting you from magical and physical assault, granting the ability to see that which is hidden, and allowing you to live and breathe where you would otherwise fail."

"The shields of the Guard will now be yours. Wear them with pride and respect, duty and honor. Use them with wisdom and compassion, surety and focus. Better the world and those in it with their Light and power."

"Relax and prepare yourself for the glamour of the Guard!"

As she worked, the elegant, efficient motions of her swordplay were strongly in evidence in her casting. Each movement was balanced and controlled, to the point and sufficient for the purpose while simultaneously full of creativity and imagination.

"Il'allia aeria leviosa!" She began her incantations with a quick lifting of her hands symbolizing the lightness of mass representative of her intent. When finished, Wrindanneth, Aroganji, Yip, and Slate were all protected from falls and impacts while also being able to fly through the air like an eagle without wings. The spell also helped protect them from some of the disorienting aspects of flight including lack of oxygen at altitude, rapid motion, disorientation, and frigid temperatures.

From completing the flight spell, she switched motions immediately, moving from one spell to the next as though shifting through a complex sword form, from one strike to the next, incanting, "Al'æðm beorgan!" With the conclusion of the incantation and the expression of power, each was granted the ability to breathe fouled or polluted air and survive for extended periods without breathing at all should the need arise.

Moving from a strike into a feint, she shifted once more, combining two spells in one, her hands a blur even as her voice intoned the full expression of her will. "Se ungesehen!"

The dictates of her will expressed her intent. See the unseen!

With the completion of her incantation, the scope of their vision widened, allowing them to see the world very much like that detected, observed, and presented by the sensory amplification systems utilized by Spreesprocket and conferred upon the Shrike. With widened eyes, they could now see magical currents and spells, although the import of such arcana was still hidden from them unless they were already familiar with the magic upon which they gazed.

Similarly, combined within the same sortilege, the enchantment granted them the ability to see the invisible, those creatures and casters cloaked or hidden by magic from unaided sight. Only the most clever and powerful beguilements would fall beneath their purview.

With those two spells in place, the shadows of the temple of Taerris'thule should appear less dark and disorienting, allowing them to be more prepared and responsive to any dangers they may face. Unfortunately, this spell did not make the shadows ahead any less threatening or dangerous.

Pivoting about her forefoot, as though arching her sword gracefully between them, she intoned, "*Asteria uniré!*" Stars unite! Her words connected them with magic should they wish to communicate directly with one another. Under rare circumstances, this same magic could be used to join powers with others similarly enchanted to heighten and strengthen magical feats and effects.

Now silent, her invocations at an end, she described a series of complex spiraling circles in the air about their bodies, linking and intertwining her hands, weaving a complex net from the strands of an invisible cord. As she moved, gossamer strands of light formed and drifted downward, settling about them in a refulgent cocoon. Over and over her hands danced with relaxed fluidity until a complete shield had been cast over each person in turn. Her work, a synthesis of the Major and Minor Shielding spells, served to protect them both from arcane damage and other hostile spells while also guarding against physical damage, impacts, blows, and cuts. The multiple layers of protection afforded by the intertwined and interlinked strands of magic provided a flexible, resilient shield against most hostile attacks.

When she finished, Daerdros dropped her arms, the radiant streamers arching from her hands fading gradually into discreet motes of light before finally disappearing altogether. "You now have the protections of the Home Guard at your service and command. Use these boons wisely and with care."

She smiled gravely, adding, "If we live through this, I will guarantee that you will never have to cast those spells upon your persons again for you will have earned the right to the permanent protections of the Home Guard."

Yip bowed graciously. "We are most grateful of your aegis."

Daerdros recognized Yip's comment with a nod before continuing with their preparations. "The Wraiths we will face are as cold and empty as the void between the stars. Although they do not cast spells, these creatures will drain your essence fully and completely by their very presence to feed and sustain themselves."

"They do not cast spells but are to be feared for most magic and enchantments fail when cast upon their unholy forms. They cannot be banished from our world for they have not been summoned from their own plane, now residing here through the direct connection with their own provided by the temple within Taerris'thule."

"You each know your limits and preferred methods of attack. We have only provided for your defense, I will leave any offensive enchantments to your discretion. Each of you, however, is prepared for the trials ahead. Know your strengths and use them wisely."

She then spoke to each of them briefly in turn. "Slate, either your axe or your inner fires should suffice to fell the Wraiths and their ilk, sending them back to the pits from whence they came."

"Yip, you can attack their essence in much the same way as they would attack yours. With your talisman, energy control, and ability, you should have little to fear from these creatures. Your focus must be on their master and the other greater dangers hidden within the walls of Taerris'thule."

"Aroganji and Wrindanneth, only the most potent spells in your arsenal will have an effect upon the Wraiths, Daemons, and their darker shadowkin. We have protected you that your safety will not be in jeopardy and that you can help ensure the safety of your friends and comrades. Use your powers wisely and we will live to laugh about the hubris of power and the failings of Men."

"Should you wish for my assistance with any additional spells in your preparation, you have but to ask."

Kazarhan laughed grimly. "Before long, Slate'll be able ta do anythin' I'm capable o', so ya won't lack fer anythin' I can offer!"

Clapping his thick, callused hands together in something resembling friendliness, Kazarhan added, "But Daerdros's offer stands fer me as well. Ya have but ta ask, and I shall endeavor ta aid ya in any way my limited scope and vision allow!"

"Temporary runes I can add ta yer weapons, but permanent enchantments take much time and preparation."

Aroganji replied, "If there is aught we can envisage, we will ask. Your generosity and guidance are most appreciated."

Before they left, always eager to learn from others, Wrindanneth asked, "What additional enchantments will you cast in preparation?"

Daerdros smiled, answering a question that was not his. "My blade will bite the Shadows as well as it bites the flesh. The Wraiths and the Infernals that brought them will come to fear my blade as much as their own end for they are one and the same."

Slate laughed smacking Duraeleon's fulgent blade with the flat of his palm. "Tha hellspawn will come ta fear us all!"

Duraeleon growled in accompaniment.

Kazarhan reached over his shoulder, unfastened his hammer, and thumped his great warmaul upon the polished wood of the deck. "By Brendle's blade, tha great hammer Raurdros will crush 'em as surely as I breathe."

Still smiling, Daerdros added, "I imagine our spells will be very much like yours—whatever we need at the time."

Wrindanneth laughed, sharing her humor for that truly was the art of combat, responding as needed as quickly and effectively as possible. "May our needs be few!"

Prior to leaving his friends to finish their spells and preparations, Yip replied soberly, "I fear they will be many."

While Yip turned to leave, Slate called after, "'Tis our foes whose needs will be many, my friend!"

Before Yip left, however, Wrindanneth called him back. "Hold, Yip! We have our own preparations to make."

Taking her leave with Yip's queue, Daerdros bowed, saying, "Until the briefing."

Slinging Raurdros back over his shoulder as though its massive solidity weighed nothing, Kazarhan returned his warmaul to its holster and offered his own farewell. "Until tha smitin'!"

After Daerdros and Kazarhan left, Aroganji and Wrindanneth pulled their friends close. Speaking first, Wrindanneth said, "We each must be prepared for the travails ahead. That is true. Offensively, as Daerdros said, each one of us has the capability to mount effective attacks against the creatures we will face in the temple below. What we don't know, however, is what exactly we will face."

Nodding, for they shared a separate conversation internally, Aroganji added, "Which means we don't know how best to mount an attack or how best to defend ourselves."

Continuing, Wrindanneth said, "We also have the alien shields to help guard us and augment the protective wards of both Daerdros and Kazarhan. These shields are an effective supplement to those other spells as well should they fail, be dispelled, or if they are circumvented."

"What we don't have is a safeguard, a contingency should these active protections be completely neutralized or if we find ourselves in grave danger."

Breaking in, finishing his friend's sentence, Aroganji said, "What we need is a backup."

Slate laughed, his voice a deep bark. "Ya mean a backup ta tha backups?'

Wrindanneth nodded. "Aye. We need an additional active layer of protection that only comes into effect when all else fails."

"A failsafe!" Slate laughed. "Ya want us ta be Gnomeproof!"

Wrindanneth smiled. "In a sense."

Aroganji chortled as well. "We want this attack to be Gnomeproof!" Clapping his hands together, he said, "What we want is Augustinius's August Adjuvant Abracadabra!"

"What?" Slate looked confused, the thread of conversation shifting from the language he understood to one he had yet to learn.

"Augustinius's August Adjuvant Abracadabra!"

"I heard what ya said. I just don't know what ya mean!"

"Augustinius's August Adjuvant Abracadabra is a framework, a template if you will, for interlinking spells to happen in certain orders and arrangements should various conditions occur."

Seeking to clarify for his friend, Wrindanneth added, "It's an adaptive, reactive spell that responds to the needs of a situation."

Aroganji continued where Wrindanneth ended, "Given a certain situation, such as the failure of our magical protections, and/or catastrophic bodily injury, or even the potential for catastrophic injury, the supplemental cascade of protections enabled by Augustinius's August Adjuvant Abracadabra will take effect."

"So Augustinius's August Adjuvant Abracadabra offers us each an opportunity to keep going when we would have failed, escape when we might have died, or counter when our defenses are down."

"As long as you have the power to cast the spells you desire in succession during your preparations, in addition to those required by Augustinius's August Adjuvant Abracadabra, then almost any combination of counters and responses is possible."

"And where did you learn of this spell? From the tome of Ydrael Faer'Leirn?" Yip was curious as much for his friend's excitement as for the additional opportunities stemming from it.

Wrindanneth shook his head, answering instead, "From Éremon's tome."

Aroganji added, "We can only digest so much each day for the magics within are extremely complex, but we are slowly making our way through it and learning all the while."

Yip nodded appreciatively. "A wondrous gift indeed."

Aroganji laughed. "It's one of the few spells we've actually been able to decipher."

Yip smiled. "We are each limited by our own will and vision!"

"If I didn't know better, I would say that was an insult!" Aroganji smiled at his friend's rejoinder.

"Or a compliment," suggested Wrindanneth.

"Or neither or a bit o' both," laughed Slate.

Yip shrugged, offering a half-smile. "With a bit of luck and effort, even our limitations change."

"You've hit the mark on target there, Yip." Wrindanneth went on, "We only have the strength between us to cast so many spells on everyone before we must stop. So we must choose our wards wisely."

Aroganji broke in. "If our other defenses fail, we must first be in a position of health in order to respond and secondly be in a position of strength to act effectively."

Yip nodded. "What do you propose?"

"As we said, the level of magics involved here are particularly complex and demanding so our choices are few. The most effective options are equally taxing and further limit our options."

"And?" Slate was ready for the casting to begin. He had had enough discussion but knew more was forthcoming.

Answering before Wrindanneth could offer a sarcastic retort, Aroganji said, "We propose several of Éremon's spells cast on the group in its entirety."

Counting with his fingers, Aroganji said, "First, Numen's Rejuvenating Revivification. If we are on the brink of death, this spell should bring us back and to full health. Second, Homnibus's Blade Barrier. With this spell in place, each of us will be slightly out of phase with the world around us. In effect, spells and attacks that would normally strike us will miss because we will not be in a position to be harmed although we will appear to be. The spell's expression is very much like a magnified version of the mantle provided by Slate's ring Caelebeor. Third, Fegeet's Reflective Palladium. Should any physical or magical attacks pass through the Blade Barrier, the Reflective Palladium should, in all likelihood, send the attack back toward its initiator."

Slate grinned wickedly, barking, "That should be excitin'!"

"And fun to watch!" interjected Wrindanneth with an arch smile.

"We have two more spells in mind. After these are cast, our energies will be spent for the day until we have time to recover."

Before Aroganji could finish his description of their final two spells, Yip stated, "You both must be ready and fully rested when the time comes. I can provide you with the energy for your spells."

"We do not wish to exhaust you either, Yip."

Smiling, Yip said, "It is not my energy that you will be using, so I will not be exhausted."

Nodding, for he had not given thought to their energy transference work together, Aroganji finished. "Fourth, although we cannot know where and if these spells will take place and will therefore not be able to offer a teleport to a known location of complete safety, we will be able to cast a spell to shift each us a short distance away from the spot and the risk that originally broke through our defenses."

Before Aroganji could finish his description of the spell, Slate asked, "How d'ya mean?"

Wrindanneth answered with a nod. "If we are in a large chamber, for example, this spell would shift you from one side to the other so long as there is no obstacle in place. The spot will be dictated by the position's relative safety."

"Might that not be equally risky?" Slate was not entirely convinced of the spell's usefulness.

Aroganji shrugged in reply. "It may be, but you will have already been delivered from risk once and the element of surprise may be to your benefit."

Slate merely grunted in response, not entirely convinced but not wishing to argue the point further.

Seeing that Slate had no other questions, Aroganji finished, "Finally, we will cast Schmodomuf's Soaring Flitter. This spell will grant each of us the ability to fly at high speed while also protecting us from other risks of flight." As an aside, he added, "This appears to be almost the very spell that Daerdros used to grant us the ability to fly."

Wrindanneth added with finality, "If we are not be able to teleport to a position of safety, this spell should give each of us the ability to fly to one should we need it and our other magics stripped from us."

He did not say anything more for nothing else needed to be said. Should they have to flee, they would have failed. If they failed, Ea'ae could be lost as surely as their mission.

"Are we ready to begin?" Yip stood in a small circle with his friends gathered next to the ship's luminescent control sphere.

When he got an affirmative nod from both Aroganji and Wrindanneth, Slate merely grunted, Yip closed his eyes, opening himself up fully to the luminous energies flowing around and through them, their glamor undiminished by the pervasive pall of evil. Aware of the corruption inherent in these forces, for he felt the taint of Taerris'thule and its fell inhabitants permeating the fount of life around them, he let those tainted energies pass as if they did not exist, not attaching to them and not letting them bind to himself.

He spoke as he worked. "You will feel the energy I will pass to you, perhaps as a quickening or an enlivening of your spirit. When you feel that you begin to burn brighter, commence your casting for this energy will be the source for your spells."

"Do not hesitate to start or wonder if indeed what you think you feel is real or if you are ready. I will ensure that the energy you need is in place and that you are not at risk."

"Too much energy in your systems without proper training is a danger as well."

Eyes still closed, although he could see the world fully in his mind's eye without reliance upon normal sight, he continued his instructions. "When your spells are completed, I will let any excess power flow from you in the same way it entered. You will remain fresh and alert, not experiencing the drain typical of extensive spellcasting."

Finally, he said, "Open yourselves to me that this process will move forward with minimal effort and risk on all parts."

When he felt both Aroganji and Wrindanneth relax their natural defenses, the intrinsic seals that held their own spiritual energies in place, he began.

The perversion so prevalent in the air around them, sickening and unholy, he left to return to its source untouched and unheeded. The *yuan-chi* flowed over and through this debased energy as part of an unclean slick in grave need of purification. He carefully gathered and guided its strength and purity to both Wrindanneth and Aroganji.

As he did so, he felt their spirits glow and swell with greater energetic potential. This flame would be the fuel to light the fires of their magical formations so they would not have to dim their own personal Lights in the process of creation. In this way, they would remain rested and fully capable of dealing with any unsuspected situations that may arise without having to rest prior to full engagement.

Should they not fully utilize the power he provided, he had to be equally vigilant that the energy he passed to them did not overwhelm or damage them in any way for too much was equally as risky as too little. When their incantations were complete, he would siphon off any excess power to avoid such risks and other potential complications.

His initial preparations done, he monitored the energies flowing to his friends and watched the radiant beauty unfold around him, lambent even through the everpresent taint of Taerris'thule, lighting up with the genesis of Aroganji and Wrindanneth's opus.

They worked in perfect tandem, sharing energy equally and effectively, sculpting and forming each other's ideas, with no flaws or miscues, together in complete communication. He felt the link they shared but did not discuss. Only now did he get to watch the entirety of the beauty of that connection in concert.

Together, they made a formidable pair.

As he observed, the air around them radiated with Light. Amorphous flowing energy began to take shape and abiding form, reflective of the will and intent of its shapers. This power coalesced around each of them as Wrindanneth and Aroganji's casting progressed, a temporary crystallization of the inherent possibility of the universal energy source. As one spell completed, the air danced and shimmered with complex patterns and arrangements, symbols of the mind made manifest.

That creations of such beauty were possible by the hand of Man only heightened his deep appreciation and wonder for the universe around him. That the hands that created such beauty were so fragile only deepened his concern for the safety of her people and the energies that sustained them.

The Light around them dimming, no longer needed or guided by will, he let the power he had been drawing and passing to his friends slowly fade away, returning their burning spirits to their normal dynamic equilibria, untouched by his intervention.

Before Aroganji or Wrindanneth could comment, he bowed, saying, "Your work brings pride to us all."

Aroganji and Wrindanneth turned to each other, not knowing exactly what to say or where exactly that comment came from. Speaking first, Aroganji said, "Thank you, Yip. It would not have been possible without your assistance. Éremon's spells are of such demanding complexity and power that we truly needed your aid if we were to succeed. Their difficulty was more than we had at first imagined."

Wrindanneth laughed. "If you hadn't given us a boost, Yip, we might have been in bed while the rest of you tried to take Taerris'thule without us."

Yip shrugged off the compliment in turn. "You make a wonderful team."

Aroganji nodded, including them all in his gaze. "As do we all."

Once more gathered around the command sphere, they all listened attentively to Llyewia, Spreesprocket, and Orogast's further evaluations of the dangers ahead.

"Although there are in fact several holes in the superstructure large enough for our ship to pass through, our assessment indicates that the likelihood of successful assault directly though the temple dome is almost nil." Spreesprocket stood with Orogast and Llyewia giving their report on the temple, its environs, and possibilities for assault.

"As Yip indicated, there is indeed a massive extradimensional anomaly positioned directly above the temple. This disturbance appears to radiate outward from within. The violence and power of this disturbance can be seen all around us in the form of this Daemonic fog."

Llyewia spoke next. "Our scrying indicates that the temple, but not the surrounding grounds, is protected by energies from this vortex in addition to other arcane enchantments of a variety most commonly utilized by creatures from the darkest nether regions of the Abyss."

"Although we feel confident in our abilities to counter the arcana of Daemonic origin with enough alacrity to allow safe passage through one of these gaps, we cannot say the same for the overflowing energies derived from the maelstrom."

Now Orogast spoke. "Although we may be more vulnerable to attack with a forced entrance directly though the main portal, our purview indicates it is the best course. If we were to attempt an entry through the roof and fail, we cannot ascertain what would happen or even if we would have an option for a second path of entry."

"Aside from the Daemonic aegis, the main portal, however, is not shielded although we are sure that it is guarded by the same Wraiths that we have seen wandering the city's streets. With them will be much their more powerful brethren."

"Furthermore"—here Spreesprocket spoke—"we believe that the sentries would be better spent providing covering fire and protection while we attempt our entry without spending them needlessly on a scouting mission where they may be lost without benefit."

Llyewia added, "Supplementing her extant protections, the ship has been warded by Kazarhan and myself to keep creatures such as those we will face at bay. If the Shadowspawn approach too closely, they will be destroyed. Should we survive our foray, the *Shrike* will remain safe and in place to allow us a swift escape."

Spreesprocket spoke in turn, "The remaining sentry drone will guard the ship and help to ensure that these same spells do not fail and are not dispelled by our enemies."

Orogast added, "We feel that the ship should remain as close to the entrance as possible so that it will be readily available for us to make our escape if we need to fight our way to freedom."

Eidelion nodded, accepting the assessment of his Guard. "Archaeus will cut through the Daemonic shield and win our passage through to the temple's interior. Is there anything else?"

Llyewia spoke. "Yip noted that our presence has not gone unnoticed and that we would not be able to enter with the advantage of surprise. He is correct."

"Shadowkin are massing even as we speak at the temple."

Orogast nodded. "We will have to fight our way through from the start."

Spreesprocket finished, "We recommend suppressive covering fire from the ship and sentries begin before we commence."

Slate grunted, growling, "Let's blast those beasts back ta tha Darkness that spawned 'em before they have tha fortune ta see tha lights o' our eyes or feel tha bite o' our steel!"

Flying well above the ground, the *Shrike* remained hidden from easy visual or magical detection. However, Wrindanneth sensed that whatever lurked in the shadows below did not miss their arrival.

It welcomed it.

LOOMING SHADOWS

Waves crash fiercely
on strewn, tumbled rocks
counted by the screams of gulls.

Versicolor and lustrous, a heavenly sphere descended and now adrift in Ea'ae's atmosphere, Tellanon gleamed in the mid-morning daylight, its beauty all the more apparent beneath the burgeoning cloud of Darkness spewing forth from the rent above her celestial dome.

Her solidified and reinforced shield glimmered and gleamed radiantly turning even the overarching, oozing Darkness reflected upon its surface into something of beauty and wonder. How long that glamor and luster held beneath the unfolding Darkness would yet be seen.

Arrayed outside of the city's formidable shield, their presence invisible to the naked eye, innumerable swarms of sentry drones drifted in the air. Each individual drone having splintered into millions upon millions upon millions of autonomous femtobots, their presence resembled nothing more than thick clouds of minute dust particles, their seething mass visible only from certain angles in the proper light—diatoms adrift in the deep sea.

The city's first line of defense, the only agents directly exposed to the threat of the looming Darkness, the sentries waited poised and at the ready for further direction from the Construct and its guides.

Push forward!

The command came from the Construct, guiding each mote along its trajectory toward its intended target.

Gathering force, a gale before a storm, the ARMED sentries shifted and scattered in response to the summons, great surging clouds massing and moving through the air. Drifting forward into the heart of the Darkness, sparks flew as drones were engulfed and destroyed by advancing tendrils of living entropy, small lightning strikes coruscating against the utter blackness.

Each valiant flash temporarily slowed and diverted the tendrils' implacable advance, the fallen providing opportunity for other microscopic drones to flit through—a vast dust storm advancing against the impending night, tiny fire-flies bringing temporary flashes of hope against the impending doom.

From the docks empty of the bustle and chaos of trade, manned now only by Paratechnologists at the ready in their variegated battlesuits and altered forms, the bruised and blackened azure sky vibrated with white lightning and black thunder, explosions and fulgurations resounding through the heavens.

In the brief time since the commencement of the attack, the docks had undergone a drastic transformation. The expansive open areas where the goods and services of trade normally flowed freely and with ease were now covered in bulwarks, battlements, and numerous defensive fortifications. All were cloaked with additional layers of shielding and magical enchantments. Drones, warriors, and vehicles hummed and whirred buzzing through the air adding to the activity and energy of the docks.

As malleable as the mind, the shape and function of the docks had undergone a drastic physical and emotional transformation.

Rank upon rank of Paratechnologists gazed heavenward at the ready. Drag-onoid, Daemonic, insectile, humanoid, and myriad other forms created by the highest flights of fancy stood, flew, and hovered shoulder-to-shoulder with their squadrons aiming massive cannons charged with magical forces, commanding attack drones along with manned and unmanned vehicles of diverse sizes, shapes, and functions. Others waited diligently in preparatory anticipation behind magical shields. All were armed with wands, staves, ballistic and explosive systems, in addition to other magical weapons whose purpose was not directly decipherable based upon physical form.

Moving from group to group, communicating magically with their men and superiors, members of the Home Guard marched resplendently, commanding and coordinating the activities of the Paratechnologists and their creations directly in conjunction with the Construct itself with supreme skill and aplomb.

The docks were not the only line of defense although they appeared the most active. The very bedrock upon which the island city was built bristled with cannons and turrets with which to launch strikes and counters. Hidden caves and recesses now opened up along the cliff sides from which to send forth sorties, counterattacks, and reconnaissance.

So numerous were these strategic countermeasures that the lower island appeared to have undergone a complete transfiguration. Before the Construct's kinetic defensive preparations, the rock firmament had seemed massive, mono-lithic, and unbroken. Now, after the dynamic reaction to the Cabal's threat, the malleable bedrock resembled the calcareous skeleton of coral, madreporian and variegated, riddled with pocks, fissures, and outgrowths, each bristling with the menace of manned and unmanned weaponry and sensors.

These frontlines were both the primary staging point of the city's counterat-tack and its third line of defense waiting behind the masses of drones and overarching shield. Should the docks, cliffs, and their respective troops be overrun, then the fight would go directly to Tellanon proper and her attendant automated defenses.

Although normally regal and peaceful, a consummate blend of the physical space and the human imagination, the city's streets too had changed drasti-cally. Tellanon's landscape was as mutable as clay beneath the dictates of the Construct and her defenders.

Along with their denizens, most of the city's homes and businesses were gone.

Many were packed up, carried away with their owners should they not have the opportunity or assurance necessary to return with them to their orig-inal place. For those who did not have the necessary magical skills or means to afford a portable home or business, there were many who took advantage of the offer available to all citizens. The city would incorporate the home unchanged, without tangible loss or alteration, within the island's fundament, hidden beneath the earth until such a time as the Construct and its guides deemed fitting. For those who wished further assurance for the safety of their homes and livelihoods along with the land on which they resided, and who had either the Craft or means, additional enchantments were allowed to protect the space, both earth and air, harboring their place of residence or trade.

Despite the loss of homes and businesses, the streets, lanes, venues, and alleys were not empty, however.

Fortifications and battlements had arisen from the boulevards and areas vacated by homes and other structures, barring progress toward the city's center where many large buildings, palaces, and Illdrassil remained in place. These defensive walls, palisades, barriers, and barricades supplied the oppor-tunity for counterstrikes, delay, strategic action, and retaliation.

Walls and impediments were not the only changes to the landscape. Cannons, ordnance, and artillery of all shapes and sizes had arisen from the depths, secreted by the city's once placid exterior. Pits and trenches barred access should the city's attackers attempt to land and move forward by foot.

Troops and drones moved deliberately from point to point, guiding any stragglers to the appropriate protected areas where they would remain entirely safe even if the city fell completely or was utterly destroyed. Automatons, synthetic intelligences, and summoned creatures of every shape and sort supplemented the efforts of the citizens and their allies on the now fortified streets.

Public spaces, gardens, cloisters, gathering places, and spots of interest and beauty, those not separated from the rest of the city in pocket dimensions or hidden beneath the earth, were shielded from attack, both the accidental and intentional fallout of war, by shields similar to the ones surrounding the island above. Citizens and her defenders could pass, but none others.

These invisible wards, also incorporated into other defensive fortifications, made progress within the city on the ground almost impossible for any who would attempt to clean out her defenders directly in hand-to-hand combat. Should any attackers not attempt to land, they would be subject to a relentless barrage from the cannons lacing the island's surface, as numerous as dewdrops upon blades of grass on a wet spring morn. Once weakened in the air, drones, aircraft, summoned creatures, and flying Paratechnologists could clean up any hostile forces not finished by the cannon fire from below.

All the while, despite the fervent preparations of those on the ground, over-head, the advancing Darkness cast heavy shadows over the city's streets and those laboring valiantly beneath, feeding as readily upon the light of the sun as the lives and dreams of her people below.

EPICENTER

Fireflies shimmer and flash
against the velvet night—
fragile stars gracing the eve.

Pitch, atramentous, utter, and total, seething and churning, enveloped them in a violent, unbroken cloud. Gone were the gray gloom and the obscuring fogs of the skies above Taerris'thule.

With their descent, countless Shades flew upward from where they pooled and swarmed waiting in the streets of the shattered city below—an ocean of Darkness rising en masse riotously through the sky, engulfing the ship in absolute night. Staring over the prow as the Shades surged, a roiling pit of absolute darkness grew and thrust up toward the fragile ship, a turbulent window into the yawning pits of the deepest Abyss.

Throwing themselves relentlessly against the *Shrike*'s defenses as they swept upward to greet her, spending themselves wantonly against her holy protections, the Shades of Taerris'thule attempted to overwhelm her defenses through sacrificial offering, their unceasing efforts a doomed attempt to exhaust and overwhelm the wards and shields protecting her.

On the deck, only the light protected within the shield around the *Shrike* existed, the fragile incandescent globes casting their luminescence away futilely against the devouring infuscation—a fitful flame burning amidst unbroken darkness, a flickering candle held aloft brazenly before the unknown depths of fear.

Holding the White Sword Archaeus skyward, its pure brilliance filled with the bright light of a newborn sun, filling each passenger's heart with clarity and hope, shining with the exulting radiance of a new dawn, Eidelion bolstered the *Shrike*'s defenses against the unholy legions crashing against her prow. With his support, the ship's shields and runes did not waver and the Light in her care did not falter.

Through the living Darkness they flew, cutting a swath with their belief and faith, their will and arms, toward an uncertain future not yet brightened by their aspirations, a lone ember cast off into hungry darkness refusing to dim with its descent into the night, awaiting fuel to catch fire.

Had they been forced to rely on visual cues alone to reach their destination, the *Shrike* and her crew would have been lost, bereft of course and guide, for the all-encompassing void of the Shades blocked any view of the world beyond. Their direction, however, had been set and was not confused by the sweeping cloud that had arisen from the land in an unbroken wave, rushing to meet them in fluid unity as the *Shrike* flew swiftly toward the ruined dome of Eldre'gheu.

Yip felt the hungry Darkness surge and shift about them devouring the light of the sun as feverishly as the Light of life. He remained calm and poised, balanced and at the ready, riding the violent currents coursing around them without attachment or fear, his mind outstretched in preparation.

He felt the depth and strength of the churning Darkness and knew they would win through, for even massed, the evil before them was not their equal.

He could not say the same for the entity waiting at the labyrinth's heart.

Wrindanneth gnashed his teeth at the bridge, pacing back and forth, his countenance and demeanor the polar opposite of Yip's placid stance nearby. He, too, was confident of their strength and resolve, that they would weather this storm. He did not, however, feel this boded well for their future. Whatever was behind the Shades' assault was testing them, probing for their limits.

Who knew what the Darkness hid or what lay in wait behind its Shadow?

Aroganji observed as well, standing behind Wrindanneth near Yip's side, constantly probing the ship's defenses, checking for any signs of failure or need, prepared should they be forced to engage the enemy directly. He did not share Wrindanneth's worries for they had been his own.

He had made his peace with his fears and was now ready to do battle.

Slate held Duraeleon firmly with both hands, the great gleaming double-headed axe held diagonally across his broad chest at the ready, a barrier few would attempt and even fewer would survive. He did not worry nor had he worried as the Darkness rose up and engulfed them in its bottomless maw.

This was his place and his time. His blood boiled in anticipation.

If the enemies he now faced did not spill blood, that did not lessen the pleasure of returning them to oblivion. It merely saved him the trouble of cleaning their ichor from the blade of his axe.

Duraeleon waited, too, its own thoughts now silent, its voice kept low, all banter and distractions left behind.

The time had come to feed, and it was hungry.

Elsewhere on the *Shrike*, the Home Guard watched and waited, prepared, and set to fight their way out from the eye of the storm.

Used to tempests, both on and beyond planets, Raour'Saqan bode and observed. He thought seldomly and moved even less. Soon, however, the time for action would come. His foes would crumble before him for he was a storm unto himself.

Spreesprocket was less concerned about the impending battle than in recording all the data associated with their descent and interaction with the entities of Taerris'thule for future research, analysis, and modeling. He moved from fore to aft of the ship collecting measurements, setting up internal analysis protocols to allow for background evaluations of the incoming data simultaneous to his normal defensive requirements, ensuring that his sensors were logging all phenomena of current and potential future interest.

Holding various instrumentation aloft, he walked the ship modifying complex internal algorithms as though strolling through an open field at night gazing at stars, not amidst the roiling chaos of countless Shades let loose from the nether regions of the Abyss.

Orogast watched.

He watched the roiling Darkness fluctuating around them violently as they descended upon their target. He watched, observing a menagerie full of wonder at the sights before him. He watched calmly and patiently. He watched with deep appreciation and skill. He watched with careful attention to detail. He watched the patterns and reactions, the permutations and minutiae of the Shade's movements and attacks. He watched and learned. From watching, he learned how he himself must change in order to defeat them.

As he watched, his skin changed, growing darker and denser. His shoulders broadened and thickened. Horns began to sprout from his head and along the lengthening arch of his spine. Wicked claws grew from the tips of his fingers. His legs bent inward upon themselves, flexing backward instead of forward at the knee. Leathery wings expanded outward from his shoulder blades, spreading and darkening the deck with deeper shadows. Vicious yellowed teeth protruded from a gaping mouth licking back flames. Glowing red eyes touched lightly by madness now gazed out upon the Shadowkin before him.

He watched, becoming a ruler of Shadows, a devourer of Darkness.

Kazarhan rested Raurdros upon the deck before him, holding the rune-etched haft firmly in both hands as he studied his inscriptions pulse and flair beneath the Shades' unending assault. Although the Darkness of his enemies was great, his faith, his belief, filled him with firm conviction. The power of this conviction overflowed from him, continually reinforcing the Karaduens' strength and protection, those on the ship and those lacing his arms, chest, and great hammer. He knew completely and absolutely that the Light of Brendle's forge was greater than this or any other Darkness.

Because of this faith, his runes held and would hold so long as he breathed.

Looking first left and right at the other Home Guard and then on toward the bridge where the gallant young heroes gathered, the runes would hold so long as the belief of his companions held as well.

Llyewia stood calmly in the midst of a hurricane. Violent energies swirled about him, buffeting his mind and body along with the ship on which he stood, coursing through him and over him, churning and frothing, stirred up and agitated by the Darkness engulfing them arising from the pernicious, over-arching Darkness residing in the city below.

The violence around him was as much a part of him as the peace that dwelt undisturbed in his heart. This turmoil would leave him just as quickly and easily, without attachment or precondition, as it had arrived once he helped restore the peace native to this place.

Daerdros relaxed. She did not stand at the ready, sword in hand, poised for combat for she was always ready whether standing or sitting, eating or sleeping. Whether at motion or at rest, her mind and body were at ease and in tune to the subtleties of her surroundings.

She relaxed to store her energy, to gather and pace herself for the battle ahead for there would be no rest when they joined the fray even now attempting to overcome them.

Within her field of alertness, she was aware of the upheaval around them, of the unrelenting assault upon their defenses. She was aware of the status of their protections, the reactions and permutations of their shields and runes, of the demands this continued attack placed upon the weavings of the spells in addition to the ship and the crew's energy reserves.

She, too, was calm, for her preparations were complete and the situation did not yet warrant action.

When the time came and necessity called, however, she would respond with an alacrity faster than presupposition or anticipation.

Eidelion held Archaeus aloft. His arm did not tire holding his mighty sword with its august Light streaming forth against the Darkness that surrounded them for its Light along with his faith gave him strength. Nor did he marshal or rally his men at this time for, like Daerdros, he felt their silent vigil was a direct testament to their readiness.

When the time came and the need arose, he would offer his command and the Light's Guard would follow.

Yip attended the writhing Darkness crashing against the ship's shields with the distance and dispassion of one examining a fine work of art. He studied the Shades' currents and flows, eddies, and bursts sensing the impetus behind the Shades' movements while the evil about them sought to bring them down. Feeling the Shades' suffocating presence around them, greedily, hungrily maneuvering and thrashing to reach the ship's inner sanctum in a frenzied effort to devour their essences, he waited for any changes or signs that may cause alarm.

He did not have to wait long.

With a suddenness that caught him off-guard though he was looking for just this sort of activity, he sensed a veritable explosion of power rocketing upward toward them like a comet, the heat and intensity of the presence careening for them as at home in the bowels of stars as the depths of fiery extradimensional pits.

Before the trenchant alarm, "'Ware the skies!" had left his lips, a fiery inferno had burst upon them, the holocaust of its flames too intense to be confined within the dark recesses of the underworld.

As devastating to the Shades as the holy Light from Eidelion's sword, the creature of burning black flames cutting through the air below them melted away any and all Shadows in its path as surely as sunlight clears away night's unbroken shroud.

As quickly as the Shades evaporated in the beast's presence, it hammered into the *Shrike*'s shield with a force that sent the whole ship rocking, the power of the impact knocking them to their knees, the collision so loud that Yip could not tell if any of his fellows yelled out or issued commands. The impact was so abrupt that the instant response of the ship's TCACA air encapsulation safety system surprised them as much as the monster's impact.

With its strike, ebony flames engulfed the ship in its entirety, licking hungrily about the *Shrike*'s shield, tracing an outline of destruction about its perimeter.

Only Raour'Saqan and Eidelion remained unmoved by the collision. Had Eidelion fallen, so, too, would have the ship.

His feet spread wide, both hands now gripping Archaeus fiercely, Eidelion channeled his hope and spirit into his sword, making his belief manifest in the shield of unwavering Light around them.

The thing of black flames and writhing shadows hovering before them reared back, throwing two nebulous arms skyward, and roared. Had he not been already nearly deafened, Yip felt this monstrosity's roar might have pushed him over the edge into the soft, silken realm of permanent silence. Regaining his feet from where he had fallen to his knees, recovering after being released from the protection of the ship's safety shield, he prepared to counter.

The Daemon's roar was a thing of sheer and utter terror—the vileness of souls' ripped from their moorings and devoured whole, the futility of hope, and the end of dreams.

His wits recovered, not taking the time to stand, reacting instinctively for his ship and his crew, Wrindanneth marshaled his will, focused his mind, and launched a succession of blasts from Gideon's Transmogrifying Spectral Cyclotron. A beam of swirling purple, pink and red energies smashed the Daemon full on in the chest, enveloping its Darkness in a rippling spectrum of arcane light and energy.

Simultaneously, the sentry drones let loose a devastating fusillade of magical fire upon the Daemon blasting it with a torrent of unrelenting destruction.

Once again the beast screamed, its soul-wrenching screech enough to send minds fleeing to the farthest recesses of unconsciousness.

Karaduen flared in response, protecting minds and hearts from the brunt of the horrendous bellow.

Standing tall, unfazed by the creature's sonic wail, Llyewia drew his Witchwood bow and took aim, starlight shimmering around his fingertips as he reached to pull the bowstring that was not there. His motion relaxed and fluid, the Elf loosed his unseen arrows, two moonbeams that arched unerringly toward the beast's molten eyes.

With an explosion as bright as the last throes of a dying star, Llyewia's bolts exploded on target, and, with one final, violent throe, the Anubavaeri's thrashing ended, falling back toward the earth to be consumed by the Shadows its wake had not yet destroyed. As quickly as the beast fell, the void left by its all-consuming presence filled once more with the countless Shades it no longer burned away.

This assault was only the beginning of their trials. Each successive onslaught erupted from the engulfing Darkness of the Shades' tumultuous shroud with the abrupt suddenness of an ambush.

"Be ready! They come!" Eidelion called out his warning to the Home Guard. Though their defenses held easily against the Shades, the creatures of the nether Darkness would not be diverted so easily.

Wrindanneth maintained his awareness fully poised within the ship's instrumentation, seeking out the slightest disturbance that would alert him to the next round of attacks. At the ready, he kept his senses resting lightly on the *Shrike*'s cannon, charged and waiting for a target.

Keeping his mind separate from Wrindanneth's for he did not wish to interfere with his friend's concentrated attention, Aroganji wreathed himself in the elements, a mantle of fire and void, wind and electricity, ready to rain down destruction upon the next creature to emerge from the recesses of the all-engulfing shadows.

Slate, too, burned. The fires of the Daerdaana'Duin raged around and through him with the heat and clarity of the sun, filling him with strength and power, a small white star descended from the heavens. Closing and opening his fingers rhythmically in anticipation, he gripped Duraeleon's haft eagerly, his will alone containing the fires that seethed within awaiting release.

His form wavered and shifted, warped by terrible heat and Caelebeor's beguiling enchantments.

Yip returned to a ready posture, surrounded by a diffuse blue haze as *chi* coursed through him in readiness.

Only this time he hoped he would actually react in time.

Not taking even a moment to call a warning, for the cannon blasting scintillating beams of magical energy was notice enough, Wrindanneth reacted as soon as he sensed more of the Infernals approaching from within the shielding morass of the Shades' tumultuous mass. This time there were three, each as powerful as the last judging by the energetic perceptions provided by the ship's surveillance system.

Beyond the fact of their presence, however, he did not care for he was an equal opportunity destroyer of the denizens of the Abyss.

Coruscating multicolored beams lanced through the skies over and over under his direction, cutting swathes through the Darkness of the Shades, pointing in the *Shrike*'s intended direction, and highlighting her next victims. This time he would not give the Home Guard the opportunity to dispatch the Daemons, this time the pleasure would be his.

Before her enemies had come within sight, the crew of the *Shrike* heard their ghastly screams.

The creatures never reached the ship, nor would they.

Wrindanneth smiled in giddy pleasure.

There would be more.

He would be ready.

"Three down!" Wrindanneth yelled triumphantly when he sensed the beasts fall from the heavens. "We are fast approaching Taerris'thule! We should arrive within sight of the temple in a few short minutes!"

"Incoming!" Yip's yell made Wrindanneth's heart sink. He had broken his focus for but a split second while he called out.

The Daemon's came in the moment of his lapse.

Once again tracking the skies, this time the beasts came from multiple directions in the firmament above. Wrindanneth lit the roiling Shadows around them with raging bands of destruction.

By his count there were five Daemons. They showed on his sensors as massive winged behemoths radiating supernatural power of a type not native to this plane, banking and rotating downward at dizzying speeds as they dove toward the ship in fearless anticipation of the attack.

Lancing energy back and forth, he just had time to target and destroy the Daemons before they could reach the ship.

Now they were none.

This latest round of Daemons, however, was not his main concern. The amount of energy required to destroy such formidable creatures, more than would actually be needed to down a well-defended airship, was rapidly draining the ship's power supply. He would only have enough energy to fire another round before the ship would have to recharge.

This time maintaining full awareness of the region around the ship while he called, he yelled, "We are losing power! The ship only has enough reserves for one more round of fire before I need to let her recharge!"

Eidelion yelled in reply, "Be ready! When the cannon fails, we must counter!"

Around him the Home Guard were arrayed in battle formation, spells poised to neutralize the next wave of monstrosities.

Slate refused to wait in silence. With a full-throated bellow, he roared out in challenge, "Let 'em come! By Brendle's blade, I will send 'em back ta tha hell that spawned 'em!"

Gripped firmly in hand, a dirge finally given opportunity to release a long-held lament, sung to the tune of his master's beating heart, Duraeleon began to chant in preparation for the coming of the Daemons, his steady cadence carrying across the decks like a pall.

O'er hill and dale,
We fly through the night.

O'er hill and dale,
We bring them to the fight.

O'er hill and dale,
We end their cursed blight.

By haft, by blade,
By force of steel,
We bend them to our will.

By haft, by blade,
By force of steel,
The time soon comes to kill.

Through marsh and wood,
We clash face-to-face.

Through marsh and wood,
We send them from this place.

Through marsh and wood,
They flee in disgrace.

By haft, by blade,
By force of steel,
We bend them to our will.

By haft, by blade,
By force of steel,

The time soon comes to kill.

Under open skies,
We call upon the Light.

Under open skies,
We bring forth our might.

Under open skies,
We send them to eternal night.

By haft, by blade,
By force of steel,
We bend them to our will.

By haft, by blade,
By force of steel,
Why do we battle still?

Yip, however, had another idea.

Sprinting belowdecks while Duraeleon sang and Slate waited in eager anticipation, his motions empowered by the *chi* flowing through him, he leapt from his position on the helm over the railing and flew down the stairs to the hold. Positioning himself in the room's center, he reached out his arms widely bridging the far sides of the open chamber with his intent.

Wrindanneth did not take listen to the words of Duraeleon's song or wonder where Yip was off to, nor did he have time for either, for another cluster of Daemons rocketed into the range of his sensors. His face lit by the pink, purple, and blue beams of concentrated energy blasting through the heavens, he rained death upon his foes.

Yip relaxed, opening himself fully to the energies circulating around and within, letting himself disappear, becoming but a conduit for energy. As his barriers thinned, his sensitivity increased as did his ability to manipulate the intrinsic energies pervading the space they were in.

He did this largely through absence, an absence of self and of thought. The less intrusive his presence, the greater his capacity to feel, experience, and guide.

If he could channel energy for his friends, if he could manipulate the energies of his foes, why could he not do the same for the ship?

At least insofar as having enough energy to power the cannon, Wrindanneth knew the ship's reserves were depleted. That last volley had met with all the success he could have hoped and all the drain he had dreaded. Letting his awareness of the cannon lessen for it was no longer needed, remaining in direct connection with the ship's sensors so as to be ready, he prepared to counter the next assault with his own spells.

A few short incantations saw his hands enveloped in flames. He would fight the Daemons' fire with his own.

The grin that spread across his face at that thought was not about to be wiped away by the horde of Daemons he sensed on the horizon. "They come!"

Self falling away, Yip disappeared.

He became his attention wholly and fully, pure awareness funneling and conducting the energy flowing around him.

There was, for him, nothing else.

Wrindanneth's attention piqued.

What was going on?

He risked taking his attention away from the incoming barrage of Daemons for a brief moment.

Incredulous, he was not mistaken!

Although they should not be for there had not been a sufficient period for them to recover, the ship's reserves were recharging! He did not know how or why this was happening nor did he have time to care.

Letting the fires flicker and fade from his hands, the Dragon's maw on the front of the *Shrike* blazed once more as he lit the Darkness with the fires of Heaven.

Power flowed where guided. Concentrated and directed, the glowing energy spheres suspended around the hold and the rest of the ship grew brighter as Yip worked.

And more Daemons fell.

LUMINOUS VISIONS

An old tumbling bridge
over a rock-strewn stream
warns travelers not to cross.

Through the blessed fog and wondrous desolation, his future waited—a treasure to be revealed and reveled in with the fullness of time.

So, so very close.

Crouched and broken amidst the ruin, the object of his desire lay stretched before him—Taerris'thule, City of the Fallen Gods.

Here the strands of Fate pulled him and here he would follow.

Here even the Fallen yet had a home.

Here untold lines of Destiny had ended, erased in the supreme finality of extinction. Lines of probability collapsed to nothing, leaving only the faint echoing ripples of possibility, causation's shallow memory, to take the place of the living.

Here the finality of supreme Order had been brought to the Chaos of the living, their dreams perishing with their disarray.

He must make peace with the Darkness of this place that he may be allowed passage and presence.

He must be allowed the opportunity to continue the resplendent lineage of this place.

His master's will deemed it must be.

There would be no alternative.

Gazing down upon the shattered city, his glorious future unfolded before his mind's eye in a frenzied kaleidoscope of blood and violence—written in viscous, steaming sanguine fluid, pungent offal, and naked sinew smeared and splattered across the high arches of Time.

He grinned wildly at the glory of the vision, at the certainty of the triumphant consummation.

There would be no other outcome.

ECLIPSE'S END

Low-lying fog blankets
a wide, open heath.
When do the clouds sleep?

With the assembled members of the Protectorate flanking him as he gazed
outward upon the ever-darkening skies, Éremon pointed, the long robes falling
from his outstretched arm as he guided their attention.

"The sentries have fought through to the portals. Soon we shall see if the
Cabal's link can be severed at the source."

Turning away from the bleak panoramic view, he looked upon his fellow
members of the ruling High Council. "If this can be done, perhaps we will
have the good fortune to inflict some damage at the font of this unnatural
Darkness, to learn of its source, and how to counter it."

The sky where he pointed was the pitchest of blacks, blocked by advancing
tendrils of Darkness that reached outward and downward toward the city,
raging funnels of oncoming otherworldly tornadoes. Within this Darkness,
however, bright flashes of light could be seen, bolts of lightning illuminating a
cloudless night sky untouched by stars. Each flash marked wave after wave of
miniscule sentry drones exploding, detonating themselves against the Darkness, allowing successive multitudes of drones to move slightly forward with
their offering, their essences briefly canceling that of their foe.

These same flashes of light were mirrored in the three-dimensional holographic representation at the room's center—the radiant orb of Tellanon
rapidly becoming obstructed, engulfed by encroaching Darkness, unmitigated
night arriving against a backdrop showing the constant birth and death of
stars.

Oroende gestured toward the invading Darkness displayed visually before them for all to see. Rotating the image from multiple angles and perspectives for a better view, he asked, "If they can indeed fight their way through, will the drones be able to determine the source from whence the Darkness arose?"

Éremon smiled. "That is our hope."

"Will we seek to retaliate then?" Rowena's question pushed and prodded at the future currents that the ships of Tellanon may soon follow, paths dependent upon the outcome of the battle above.

Alain Ar'laen answered for Éremon, his form as bright as the intruding Darkness was black. "The likelihood that the Cabal launched this attack directly from their seat of power is slim. If, as Éremon says, we are lucky and our fortune holds, then perhaps in their foolish overconfidence the Cabal did indeed take such a course. If so, then we will seek knowledge of their home and, with the help of those who would see them vanquished, we may mount a counterattack."

He finished, "We must first, however, survive today that our strength will hold for the future."

"Though this Darkness is deep, it is but a shadow of the depths from which it arises. We would be wise to first cut the limb before attempting to sever the root." Speaking from the vantage of Fria al'Othra Jae'elthos agreed with Alain's cautious, forward-looking practical optimism.

A series of radiant explosions punctuated the Elf's statement, accentuating the import of his comment. Each violent report washed over the city with the light of a thousand filtered suns, the beams themselves deflected by the inimical cloud, lighting up the sky above, below, and behind instead.

"What exactly is this Darkness employed by our enemies?" Digging deeper for clarification into the import and risks behind Jae'elthos's comment, Salia sought more information on the true nature of the foe before them, the concern on her face evident as she asked her question.

The Elf nodded, recognizing the merit of her question, while his gaze remained upon the vision before him, contemplating its depths. "The Darkness seeking to strangle us is the shadow of the Shadow, a manifestation, a materialization of Ur'Daus in Its eternal prison. As the bonds of Its prison weaken and fail, Its reach grows and extends."

"These tendrils are the opposite of what we know and love, the devourers of Aerya, of Light and Life, the annihilator of hopes and dreams. This Darkness is negation, entropy, chaos, and evil made manifest."

"If the Cabal are Ur'Daus's agents, the executors of Its will, then this Darkness is Ur'Daus's extension, the expression of Its will."

"Ur'Daus is yet too weak to consume whole worlds and more, for Its bonds remain intact, but the time may come again once more."

"Ur'Daus!" Magdalia fumed. "Preposterous! Ur'Daus's bonds are secured by the Light itself! They will not fail!"

Jae'elthos made no discernible gesture in reply for Elven mannerisms were very different than those of Men. He did, however, voice his disagreement. "Belief and reality are often not the same, no matter how fervently one might wish. Just as Light may restrain the Shadow, so, too, may Light provide Its freedom."

"Blasphemy!" Magdalia's beliefs were not to be questioned by one who did not share them.

His people well versed in the dangers of the Enemy before Man first opened innocent eyes upon the universe, Jae'elthos's views were not those espoused by Magdalia or her congregation. "Do not let your beliefs cloud your eyes to the truth of reality for then you will fall before you have the opportunity to see."

As Jael'elthos finished, before Éremon called for order, unable to contain his inherent Gnomish exuberance any longer, even in the face of such grim tidings, feelings of excitement reinforced by having a direct connection with the Construct that kept him apprised of the current situation as it unfolded, Whirlygig Sparksocket burst out, "There you have it! The sentries have indeed reached the gates!"

Barely restraining himself from bouncing up and down in his enthusiasm, hopping from foot to foot, he added, "We should hear soon from the Construct about the success of the sentries' objective and, with any luck, of their forthcoming intelligence from those who won through to the other side."

"We should be so fortunate!" Vaendoer's Dwarven gruffness stood in stark contrast to Whirlygig's overflowing optimism and cheer.

"Watch and wait, Vaendoer and Magdalia, before pronouncing judgment." Borus's full, resonant voice filled the chamber with the tone of one who has learned that true verdicts come only after first listening and then learning.

Not wishing for his fellow Protectorate members to wait any longer for a direct update on the current proceedings, Whirlygig called on the Construct for a synopsis in breathless Gnomish fashion, not taking the time to pause or break his ideas into separate sentences. "Construct! Please advise my fellows as to the present state of affairs on the field of battle along with the current status of the efforts to destroy the extradimensional tears allowing the Cabal's entry and the sentries' infiltration efforts on the far side of the portal!"

The image of swirling Darkness before them shifted as the Construct replied, multiple equations, of interest to but a few there, highlighting each point for elucidation. "The fifth-order translocational subspatial tears indicative of the attack have been breached successfully in multiple instances by the sentry drones' diffuse nimbused formations."

A few members of the Protectorate clapped at the news, although most remained subdued. Echoing Jae'elthos's assessment, the Construct continued, "Current analysis both within the approaching energy disturbance and beyond the subspatial tears allowing this incursion indicates that the encroaching energy is of extradimensional origin and of a nature we have never directly encountered or classified. Initial evaluations and, by extension, extrapolations, indicate that this energy field may, in fact, form the basic energetic foundations of the extraplanar dimension from which it arose in much the same manner as magical energy as we know it forms one layer of the fundamental underlying superstructure in our own dimension."

"As such, this energetic anomaly may behave very similarly as raw magic within our own dimension, may act antithetically to raw magic in our dimension, or may have vastly different governing properties and entirely dissimilar behaviors now that it has arrived in our localized dimensional referent. The theoretical applications and extensions necessary to provide detailed understanding of this phenomenon have yet to be developed but are currently in process as data is obtained, modeled, and evaluated."

"Whether we are able to manipulate, control, and influence this field as we are able to with currently known magical energies and phenomena remains, as much of our current level of understanding of this force, purely a matter of conjecture."

"However, by all measures, given its current manifestation within our dimension, this extradimensional energy's presence is exceedingly destructive and guided by a will we have yet to localize, evaluate, or nullify."

"Direct contact with magical energies from our dimension appears to provide, at least temporarily, a counter to those of the extradimensional field."

"Current modeling in conjunction with ongoing battlefield evaluations indicates a high likelihood of successful intervention and surcease of the extradimensional incursion."

Magdalia Miera spoke with true fire, the heat of her sentiment reflected in the intensity of her gaze. "With the Light's grace, we will be rid of this unwelcome presence before we have time to learn more!"

Offering a rare display of emotion, Chutefunnel Knobwhistle countered, "Given favorable probabilities, we will have time to evaluate its presence so that we will be informed and ready should we ever encounter it again!"

Light flashed forth from the heavens again, occluded by the darkling cloud, bathing them in the few scattered radiant rays of white light able to pass through the rare gaps in the bilious Darkness, the reverberating explosion marked by the sacrifice of countless microscopic sentry drone fragments—a brief sunrise falling on a reluctant night.

In that moment, perfectly timed, the invading Darkness was cut off from its root.

Unbidden, the Construct added, "Current spatial vectors indicate the invading dark energy assemblage has been severed from its source."

Several members of the High Council cheered.

Overhead, the frothing Darkness continued its steady advance.

BREACH

Drizzle falls loosely
on fallow winter gardens—
dewdrops cast in the wind.

"Fall back!" Yip yelled at the top of his lungs from the hold's center, his attention briefly shifting away from the continued energy transference necessary to power the ship, in warning to Wrindanneth at the helm.

His call, however, was too late.

The terror before them, unnoticed.

Wrindanneth pushed his attention forward, eager to swoop down in front of the ruined temple of Taerris'thule before more Daemons arrived, ready to bring vengeance down upon the enemies that waited within.

As he extended his senses outward throttling the ship downward at full speed in preparation for their assault upon the ruins, his mind snapped back, withdrawing immediately away from the mental augmentation provided by the ship's instrumentation, his awareness recoiling in instinctive horror at what was revealed to him.

The skies parted, the Shades having fled, and his eyes fell upon a terror his mind could not fully comprehend.

There was no time.

He had not heard Yip's warning and now it was too late.

"Get down!" Slate's bellow was the second and last call of alarm, the only heard by most, by the crew members on the *Shrike* before their nightmares came to life.

Before the words had fully left his lips, however, the need for warnings was at an end, their world a spiraling kaleidoscope of color and motion, only held steady about a focal axis by the ship's safety system that held them locked in place as the *Shrike* launched backward, tumbling through the air in a jarringly dizzying descent.

The Shades swarming in front of the unholy grounds of Taerris'thule retreated to the city's shadows leaving a billowing column of empty space in front of the tortured ruins at her heart. In the wake of their flight, the earth split and the air above it exploded, the space once containing the Shades torn asunder as the barriers between dimensions warped and frayed beneath the violence of a powerful summoning.

Swirling Darkness briefly battled against the turbulent air rushing through the void left between dimensions, a funnel between time and place better left unopened. Into this emptiness, roiling and frothing with the dust and debris soon to leave this world for another, a monstrosity from the darkest nightmares of madness surged forward.

Aroganji only had time to flinch in visceral fear and repulsion where he stood on the ship's deck before his world was turned into a tumultuous spiraling vortex of sight and sound amidst the nausea, screams of alarm, and confusion.

All he knew was that the swirling Darkness of the Shades had parted with a violent explosion, a detonation marked by a wave of extradimensional energies.

Moving too quickly to fully register, from within the heart of this upheaval a massive tentacular appendage lashed out from the void sending the *Shrike* and all on her arching through the heavens in an uncontrolled freefall.

Yip sensed the beast's presence, a being of immense power not to be contained or confined long to a single place or world, something at home in the spaces between dimensions, one capable of withstanding the rigors of the vast depths between the stars and planes.

That the being at the heart of Taerris'thule was able to reach through time and space and summon such a creature and bend it to its will did not bode well for their future.

All these thoughts and more burst through his mind unbidden but noted while he relaxed, remaining focused on channeling the energies necessary to fly and protect the ship, filling himself with the *chi* required to safeguard and buoy himself from the impending impact.

For, although he had not had time to convey it with his yell, their time aboard the *Shrike*, at least for now, had come to an end.

Relaxed, alert, and ready, he felt the beast lash out, its mammoth, vaguely translucent extremity traveling faster than the ship could hope to avoid.

In the space between seconds, the time between breaths, he waited calmly, working to ensure the safety of his fellows while their world erupted into a vertiginous, unconstrained spin.

Dismissing the ship's safety system that held the others locked in place through the terrific impact with the beast's prodigious, writhing tentacled arm and the descent that followed, Raour'Saqan launched himself into the air, wreathing himself in black flames that burned even between stars.

Eidelion acted quickly and decisively, knowing the ship was lost and not wishing for her crew to be vulnerable, all locked and immobile on a weakened vessel, to a second strike from the Daemon. With a clarion call, he issued his command. "Off the ship, into the air, and to me!"

With those words, he opened his arms and leapt heavenward as gracefully as a bird making ready to take flight, the thrust of his jump clearing him from the rotating ship at his feet, marking an arching descent to the ground below. As his attitude adjusted in the air with his flight and his view dropped earthward, he was afforded his first full glimpse of the leviathan that had doomed their ship.

Lifted by Light in his heart, he looked upon a being so foul that the very world around it warped and twisted away from its presence in despair.

One after the other, the Home Guard took to the skies in unison, arching downward through the heavens trailing after the course of their tumbling ship, moving away from the writhing beast ripping its way into this dimension below.

Terrible and inchoate, appearing to fluctuate into and out of existence as it warped through the air, lacking a stable, organized structure, the hideous monstrosity roiled and churned like a storm cloud, shifting colors and form, amoebic and violent, a humongous being that resembled something that had washed up from the ocean depths, a creature suited to the lightless interstices between dimensions or the cosmic reaches between the stars.

Lashing out, destroying the ruins in its path, the entity left a trail of utter destruction in its wake as it tracked its quarry.

The air around him wavered and shimmered in a blazing heat haze, boiling off in response to his growing internal calefaction as Raour'Saqan shot through the gray heavens, the surging, luminous tracery of an ionization trail streamed behind his flight—the tail of a low-flying comet. The arch of his deadly trajectory aimed directly at the corpulent, tentacled cephalothorax of the raging extradimensional monstrosity.

The flicker of an eye separated their collision.

Only the briefest of seconds passed before the *Shrike* rocketed into the ground, her shields giving way with the collision, her hull shattering into disparate large, twisted fragments, leaving behind a deep, rock-strewn furrow in the earth as her broken remnants finally smashed into the tumbled ruins of a long forgotten tower, showering the wreckage in shards of rock and dust.

Before the ship crashed, the remaining Home Guard took to the air on Eidelion's command, followed closely thereafter by Aroganji who vaulted into the skies with Slate in tow. Wrindanneth remained aboard to the last, using his will and acumen to guide the ship down as safely as possible in order to minimize any damage to the ship and her crew while increasing the chances that she may be repaired or salvaged.

Gritting his teeth, maintaining dogged focus as his world spun around and out of control, Wrindanneth kept his concentration locked within the ship and its damaged systems giving all he had to guide her down through the crash. Locked in and secured by the ship's safety system, the vibrations and force of the crash still left him disoriented and in pain as the trauma of the successive impacts coursed through him, only partially mitigated by the magical cocoon around him.

In the distance, he heard and felt the reverberations of the gigantic extradimensional monstrosity as it destroyed what was left of the city crashing toward the wreckage to finish what a casual flick of its arm had begun.

There was, however, no time for further consideration of the amorphic behemoth destroying what was left of Taerris'thule in its pursuit because the pooled darkness of the massed Shades that had fled from the beast were now reemerging. All around, Shadows flowed toward the broken fragments of the ship—inky, living Darkness swallowing the surrounding bits of stone and debris in preparation to devour them, the chill of their presence causing his breath to mist and fog.

The collision of two extrasolar bodies rarely occurs within the confines of a planetary atmosphere. The probability of this occurrence lessens exponentially when those two extrasolar bodies are of discrepant origins. These probabilities shrink to almost nil when considering the likelihood of an impact between a body of extrasolar origin and a body of extradimensional origin.

Factoring in sentient intelligence and the flexibility of space-time allowed by unbounded magic, mathematical probability becomes an exercise in comedy, the sort of futile endeavor preferred by Gnomish Paratechnological scientists and engineers.

Overhead, at almost the exact instant the *Shrike* settled into her final resting place amidst the tumbled stones and broken relics of Taerris'thule, Raour'Saqan blasted into the amorphous being from the nether regions of the Lightless pits.

Gnomish theorists everywhere would clap with joy had they been fortunate enough to witness to such a rare event.

As the situation stood, the only such theoretician present was too busy trying to stay alive to factor and appreciate the probabilities of such a collision.

Staying with Wrindanneth to secure the ship that his friends may be safe and their expedition continue, Yip remained trapped in the vestiges of the hold, the turbulence of the crash passing through him like the ripples in a pond, guided and buffered by the *chi* flowing within. As he watched the walls of the hull explode and crumple around him, his poise remained, the impact of the falling timbers absorbed by the *chi* that buoyed and sustained him. Unfortunately, as the only member of the expedition left trapped beneath the shattered beams and refuse of their crash, he was stuck, encased by tons of wood, dirt, and debris.

Sensing the resurgence of the Shades around them, he did not have the luxury of time to escape.

His portion of the ship largely intact, broken off cleanly from the hold, Wrindanneth called upward to Aroganji where he floated with Slate cursing by his side, forgetting their direct connection in the urgency and immediacy of his need.

"To Yip!" Wrindanneth's call echoed hollowly in the surprisingly still air, trapped and muffled by the broken buildings and lingering shadows surrounding them.

Not knowing how Yip fared in the demolished hold below beyond a cursory analysis provided by the command sphere, forgetting Daerdros's spell in the urgency of his need, Wrin refreshed himself with a quick spell, tucked the ship's control disk safely away within the confines of his robe, and hoped the wards on the ship held while he waded through the debris to retrieve his friend from beneath the tangled mass of broken boards and beams that had once held their ship together. Aided by the magic at his fingertips, he directed large chunks of wood away from the ship as though carrying the massive loads in his own hands, careful to avoid harming his friend in the process of sifting through the shifting wreckage and settling debris.

Dropping down quickly by Wrindanneth's side, Aroganji joined his friend clearing the rubbish doing with magic in seconds what would take hours by hand. Working together to lift the entire deck off their friend, Aroganji and Wrindanneth smiled as Yip emerged from beneath the hull, torn robes and a dusty covering of soil the only signs of the ordeal he had been through.

Sharing in their smile, Yip jumped free from the wooden fragments layered about his legs and torso, landing lightly beside Slate who had his attention focused warily on the approaching Shades, both hands clenched around Duraeleon, silver-white flames licking along its haft and blade.

As though nothing unusual had happened, Yip stated flatly, "The ship's reserves are now fully powered. Given time, there should be enough power present to repair the damage."

Wrindanneth laughed fully, his hands now glowing with dark purple energies in preparation for their fight through the Shades as he gestured in indication of their surroundings. "The ship is the least of our worries!"

Slate growled, "Thanks ta that unholy bloated, floatin' Daemonic jellyfish we're halfway across tha city from tha temple!"

"But we are alive!" Eidelion smiled as he landed beside them followed in short order by the other members of the Light's Guard. Holding Archaeus aloft like a beacon, the holy Light radiating outward from its blade holding the Shades at bay as surely as any barrier, he continued as he took back to the air once more, "Now we fly under our own power!"

With a silent command, Spreesprocket ordered the remaining ARMED sentry drones to stay with the ship, guarding it should the wards and shields fail, assisting in its repair and recovery.

Following Eidelion's lead, the others leapt upward in tight formation, empowered by the spells protecting them, and flew once more toward the city's heart.

With the force and velocity of a scintillating bolide, Raour'Saqan exploded into the globulous Daemon, the energy and power of his impact lighting up the sky in a brilliant flash of light. Fluxing bands of plasma burned off the gray fog surrounding the city's heart and allowed a clear view of the firmament above for the first time in ages.

Following the light and heat of the impact, coupled with a tremendous peal of thunder, a band of concussive force ballooned outward, scattering dirt and debris in every direction.

Those on the ground were lucky they were knocked so far away from the impact zone.

At the city's heart, immediately adjacent to the blast zone, the temple of Eldre'gheu remained untouched, the force of the blast leaving the shield around the temple undisturbed.

Above the temple, invisible to most, the vortex of extradimensional energies spun more rapidly, incorporating the power of the detonation into its currents. Otherwise, despite the initial concerns of the Home Guard and the Four, the maelstrom remained undisturbed.

In the last violent throes of its existence, the shattered remains of the extradimensional monster fell to the ground amid a billowing plume of dust with a force that shook the few remaining standing buildings in its vicinity to their foundations, the creature's skin still flickering with the last dying embers of multicolored plasma.

In the heart of the dust cloud, the bits of dirt and debris igniting in bright incandescence as they came in contact with his flaming black aura, Raour'Saqan hovered briefly above the beast's quavering corpse, a gaping, steaming hole blasted through its center marking the path of his impact, before flying off to rejoin his comrades.

SUNRISE

A white light flashes
briefly across the deep night sky.
A comet takes wing.

Then, when their spirits had once again been restored and many doubts lifted, as the High Council gazed upon the projection at the center of the council's meeting chamber watching the turbulent Darkness roiling and flashing in the image's heart under the attack of the sentry drones, the sky opened up once more, shorn at its moorings, and Darkness spilled in from multiple quadrants, fouling the air and the essence that supported it.

Viscous and impenetrable, seeping through the sky with the appearance of a toxic ooze, several more massive plumes of the invading extraplanar Darkness spewed through rents in the firmament, pushing forward, rapidly surrounding the city and cutting off any hope of flight.

Poised but dismayed with the turn of events, Oroende's golden skin shimmered as his eyes flickered with fire. "When will it end?"

"This, I fear, is only the beginning." Éremon's voice was firm and his eyes filled with compassion but he knew long before the arrival of this most recent incursion that Ea'ae and all that depended upon her were in grievous circumstances. If they were fortunate, this Darkness and the evil harbored within it would be the worst of the danger.

Having measured and evaluated the collapse of probability and the resulting actualizations of reality from multiple perspectives, along various paths of likelihood dependent upon multiple chains of interdependent, interlinked causation in conjunction with the Construct, Alain Ar'laen spoke then. Though euphonious, his voice and pronouncement carried with it the full authority and will of command, certain and not to be deterred. "This battle can no longer be won in its current form. We must change the dictates of the field of battle if we are to prevail." Echoing through the chamber, his voice carried the manifold tones and layers of a wondrous chorus brought together in harmony while simultaneously retaining the authority of all those voices united in purpose expressing a single will of command.

"What, then, do you suggest?" Noumel's large head bobbed slightly as he spoke, his mind, too, traveling along many paths seeking a peaceable outcome through negotiation, whether through means tangible on the field of battle, immaterial guided by the will and dictates of magic, or verbal or written and expressed through the traditional ways of reconciliation.

"We must engage the defense of last resort." The beauty of his symphonic voice did not belie the gravity of his statement.

"Are we prepared for this? Is this our only option?" A look of worry crossed Salia Proventure's matronly face, her face a mask of concern for her people and their futures.

Alain gave a curt nod. "We are indeed prepared. The opportunity to engage the enemy and achieve a favorable outcome has past. No additional time or information will be gathered through further delay. With each passing moment, the risks grow and the opportunity for failure with them."

He paused for a moment listening to an unseen voice, directly and deeply engaged with the Construct. "Current assessments indicate that the Darkness that now surrounds us is teeming with our enemies. We must strike now!"

He held out his two mercurial, glowing hands for each of his neighbors and compatriots to take and begin the Circle.

Éremon nodded, holding out his hands in offering, speaking with calm certainty. "So shall it be. Complete the Circle and commence the Loel'dara!"

Framed in the somber, diffuse beams of light coming in through the translucent walls of Illdrassil, in solemn invocation, the members of the Protectorate joined hands in silent communion, their faces still, voices hushed, and heads slightly bowed in concentration, connected to each other through linked hands, shared purpose, and combined will. The simplicity of the gesture, the tranquility of the place as they came together with a single intent, belied the turmoil outside.

Together, they joined in peace within that peace could be reflected without. Projected within the circle of their hands, churning and frothing, the Cabal's Darkness continued its relentless advance toward the city in an effort to destroy the future they now came together to preserve.

Their will as one, their intent in concert, and their desire expressed, the authorization to invoke the Loel'dara was given. With that silent, tacit command of unified will from Tellanon's ruling Protectorate, Illdrassil opened her gates and became a conduit for the energies of Heaven, the forces that she was designed to store, amplify, and channel.

Outside the High Council's chamber, visible through the crystalline walls of Illdrassil, the Tree of Heaven, the sky began to fill with Light.

Humbol looked up.

Amidst the bustle of hurrying throngs rushing toward the nearest designated secure transdimensional park, a journey that should have been taken at a run or in full flight but that he rather preferred to walk so that his curiosity about the day's momentous events could be duly sated, he was keenly aware of his surroundings. Had he not been so in tune with his surroundings, a skill both he and Hoyt had refined and come to rely on over many adventures together, odds were that neither he nor Hoyt would be around to watch Tellanon fall under attack for the first time in centuries.

Peering intently upward as he made his way, his gaze was drawn away from the chaotic, tempestuous vitriol of the Darkness ripping its way through the dimensions. Instead, his eyes were drawn to Illdrassil, her lovely silhouette gracefully arching toward the heavens made all the more glorious, and fragile, by the raucous plumes of the interdimensional storm now framing her translucent spires in pitch black.

As darkness fell and eclipsed the sun, her appearance remained just as radiant and bright as always. Now, however, she resembled a perfectly formed and molded dendritic obsidian extrusion glimmering with the last remnants of fading orange and gold light reflecting off her surface from the low angles of the horizon, the sun's last breath alive on her boles.

The beauty of Illdrassil, always there for the eye to see even in these grimmest of times, was not, however, what drew his eye toward the monocrystalline tower. Nor was it the play of light upon her surface, no matter how dramatic or lustrous. Instead what pulled his attention was not what he saw, but rather what he felt. For just as he sensed the moving currents of extradimensional energies above, so different than the magic to which he was accustomed, he now felt a massing of energies within Illdrassil herself.

As he watched, then, it was not the light that reflected upon her surface that drew his consideration. Rather it was the Light that grew and radiated from within.

No longer walking, he stood in place at the center of the cobbled, tree-lined street upon which he had been traveling, heedless of those who still clambered past. Around him, there were those who had not yet noticed the transformation underway at the city's heart, these citizens continued to stream past hurriedly toward their chosen destination or rendezvous. There were others, of increasingly growing numbers, who began to stop along with him, the subtle shift at the city's core breaking through their panicked flight as an almost indiscernible feeling of hope and lightness began to shine outward through the city.

With this feeling of ethereal, unearthly calm now enveloping him, he blinked and stepped back instinctively as the world exploded into Light.

Temporarily blinded by the brilliant flash, dropping his arms that he had raised involuntarily to shield his face, he stood still for a moment, overwhelmed by the feelings washing over him.

Creation, in all its universal vastness enveloped him. Present at the birth of the universe, witness to the first wondrous moments of existence when all was new, fresh, and full of limitless potential, rapture cradled him in the blessed arms of euphoria.

So powerful were these feelings that he forgot to breathe, lost in the awe of the moment. So intoxicating were the sensations that he temporarily forgot he had lost the ability to see. So enlivening was the experience that he forgot that his own health and mortality were put at risk by the present dangers threatening both his person and the city in which he stood.

Smiling brighter than a child let loose on the uncounted days of summer, swelling with gratitude for the opportunity to have been present at such a momentous event even though it came with enormous risks and danger, he thought, *"So this is what it feels like to be born anew!"*

Gradually, as the feelings abated and he slowly recovered his sight and bodily sensation, he blinked the tears away that had been flowing down his cheeks unbeknownst and unbidden. Looking upward in a vain attempt to survey the sky for the last pale traceries of the original Light of Creation, his eyes only fell upon deep azure firmament, clear and unclouded.

Only then did he realize that the Darkness that had nearly drowned them had been washed away.

Turning his scrutiny away from the sky above toward the source of the wonderment that had enfolded him and everyone around him, at the city's heart, Illdrassil shone brightly, capturing and magnifying the last fugitive rays of the now setting sun.

Several members of the Protectorate broke into open cheers, clapping and yelling with excitement as the Darkness that had roiled, spun, and oozed toward and around the virtual depiction of Tellanon at the chamber's center, the same Darkness that had clouded their room in a turbulent mass of Shadow and imminent doom, was now burnt away leaving empty space and the brightness of the setting sun above in its place.

"Is it done?" As the excitement of the group settled down, Salia Proventure was the first to fill the resulting silence. The concern and worry in Salia's voice reflected a thick mixture of anxiety, hope, and elation at the prospect that they had, indeed, thwarted the Cabal.

Jae'elthos answered first, his calm, airy voice filled with layered conviction for his eyes spied what others could not. "The fabric of space is stretched thin, taut as a dried bowstring ready to fray and tear. For good or ill, our reality remains vulnerable to those who would find a way inside."

Vaendoer Thunderhammer huffed, agreeing, as was only rarely the case, with his Elven counterpart. "By Khuerkanna's ghost, tha day is not yet done!

Until we have our gauntlets gripped firmly around their throats and tha light fades from their eyes, 't'would be wise ta keep a sharp eye on tha skies, bolts and blades at tha ready."

Alain Ar'laen agreed with Vaendoer's sentiments. "We must be ready and on guard before making any full assessment. Until the seals have been restored, we shall have to remain diligent and prepared." Looking around the circle of his peers, the link connecting all of them together through the Loel'-dara now broken, hands by their sides, he added, "I suggest that we undertake immediate relocation so that we do not remain a target while maintaining our defensive posture."

Éremon nodded. "I am in agreement. All those in favor?"

No one voiced any disagreement to the suggestion.

"What of the future? Should we not send more to aid those who would preserve and restore the seals?" Noumel's concern to bridge the gap between individuals served him well both in times of peace and war for the art of diplomacy was the art of establishing and maintaining commonality and connection, communication and shared vision.

Sharing in his concerns, Magdalia added, "Are the Home Guard and assorted bands of heroes enough to restore the seals and prevent further incursions?"

Although this issue had already been openly discussed in great detail and specifics prior to this occasion within the High Council, Alain Ar'laen sought to allay their concerns for much had transpired in the short time since their initial discussions on various bands of heroes joining together with units of the Home Guard to secure the fourteen seals. There was much not yet known regarding the issues surrounding these efforts as well for many other groups whose motives and mandates were not his own were involved in this effort. He could only speak for Tellanon and her allies.

"In light of the present danger and continued threat this invasion poses, certain contingencies have been initiated both within the Home Guard and Tellanon's closest allies in an effort to bolster and support the security efforts across Ea'ae. Additional units have been and will be deployed before the morrow to this very end."

"What of other nations and city-states?" Rowena Bowspirit's strident voice filled the chamber along with the soft light of the setting sun. "Do they fly with us?"

Noumel answered that question for Alain. "The time is too early yet to tell. There is much to do and discover on that front with the Construct's assistance as soon as we adjourn."

"Has the time come to dismiss then?" Borus's deep baritone filled the chamber with the finality of a judgment.

Before they could put the matter to a vote, Alain added, "Let us complete a full security assessment before we make that determination. Based on both Jae'elthos' and the Construct's observations and evaluations, there is significant uncertainty on the matter. We must be assured that Tellanon and her citizenry are secure and have the proper guidance on how to proceed." While the Construct worked, the efforts of its calculations, evaluations, and scans now streaming through the air where once the Darkness of the Cabal had once massed, he continued, "You will all receive updated information on these additional deployments as soon as it is safe to do so."

After some time, the voice of the Construct spoke. "Initiation of relocation sequences has been completed. Temporary relocation over the Ayle'ine Sea is currently underway. Interdimensional subspatial vectors are currently fluctuating beyond an ability to accurately or systematically evaluate with predictive accuracy within tolerated confidence limits. Optimal solution analysis indicates a recommendation to maintain current defensive presence and security measures while seeking a less vulnerable location."

Borus nodded, once again making a motion toward dismissal, saying, "All of which are currently underway as dictated by municipal decree and well within established parameters and statutes."

Éremon's brow knitted in concern as he spoke with firmness and finality, cutting off Borus before the adjudicator could finish his surmise. "Be thee ready! Our time of travails is not yet at an end!"

Outside, as evening fell and shadows lengthened across the city, the fearsome gloom of another more ominous cast materialized on the horizon.

ELDRE'GHEU

Empty fields left fallow
after the fall harvest
await the coming of spring.

"By Brendle's blade, I've never seen tha like!" Slate could barely contain his amazement for the culmination of the battle between Raour'Saqan and the hideous Daemonic monstrosity.

Flying next to him, Yip shook his head, recalling the pulses of power that had washed over them, reverberating through the city with the blast, the turbulence and partial instability in the whirling extradimensional vortex at the city's heart with the explosion, and said, "Nor should we wish to."

The fog that had briefly been burned away now returned, slowly obscuring the temple of Eldre'gheu, once so close now half a city away. With the fog, the Shades, too, returned, swarming and eager for the chance to devour the mortals in their midst, unable to break through the shield wrought by the Light's grace radiating from Archaeus.

Flying, they traveled through the very pit of Darkness with only the light of a single torch keeping the evil at bay.

Swooping in to join them, not needing the protection of Archaeus's aura nor magic spells to fly, for the Shades knew his power and feared him, the steady beat of Raour'Saqan's wings joined those of Orogast, breaking the somber silence of the dead city, flitting shadows cast disappearing amidst the deeper Shadows pooled below.

This close, Yip could see individual Shades clearly and directly moving through the city's abandoned streets and crumbled buildings without reliance upon his inner vision. Just as their essences appeared vacuous and empty, what made and defined them lost and drained away, so, too, were their visible forms insubstantial. Slick and unctuous, individual pools of darkness joined and merged with one another, one Shade easily passing through to the next, slipping through the frothing shadows untouched and unheeded by the surging mass of murkiness.

In Taerris'thule, the Shadows defined the place. The place did not define the shadows.

Eidelion called out, his voice muted by the gray fog that cloaked them and the wind rushing past their ears as they whipped through the air flying low above the city toward her black heart. As he spoke, his words were terse so that his commands would not be lost in transmission. "We will land in tandem at the Temple of Eldre'gheu. I will take the fore."

"Before another coordinated attack can be mounted against us by our enemies, I will cut through the temple's shield. When I do so, we will push through together as one. You must stay close by me for Archaeus's stroke will not last long!"

Aroganji, Wrindanneth, Slate, and Yip strained against the wind and fog to hear each of Eidelion's words from where they flew at the back of the Home Guard's formation. "We cannot let any obstacles in our path stop our forward momentum! We must breach the temple's defenses and reach its center together! Each and every one of you must be in position if we are to rid Taerris'thule of the evil tainting her heart and threatening the security of Ea'ae!"

"Save your strength for the end when we will need it most! Do not fully expend yourself before we have realized our goal!"

"There is no time for failure nor any option but success!"

Eidelion's voice turned grim, full of dire practicality. "Once we clear the defenses and enter the temple, if one of your fellows falls, there may be no time to raise him! We must win through as quickly as possible! If we do and succeed, then there may be time and opportunity to restore the fallen but not before!"

"Carry the injured if you must but only heal on my mark! We must maintain a careful balance between readiness and full strength lest we all fall!"

"Although I am loath to say it, the mission is more important than the man!"

"If I fall, you all know your roles and mission. Follow Daerdros's command in my stead. She will guide you if I cannot."

Aroganji and Wrindanneth exchanged silent glances, thoughts flowing between them freely as Eidelion finished.

His mind open only to his friend, feelings of brotherhood he seldom shared bridging the distance between them, Wrindanneth said, *"We started this journey together and will end it together. There is no other option."* He would do whatever he could to see after his friends for they had always worked together just as they had always triumphed or failed together.

Aroganji was of like mind. The resolve in his intent echoed through the chambers of Wrindanneth's mind. *"We will see this through together until the end. There is no other choice."*

"The four of us are strongest together. The four of us will strive as we live—as one."

Wrindanneth's silent agreement was all the answer Aroganji needed.

Yip felt an oppressive darkness growing in his heart, the sensation one of gradually losing the ability to breathe. Twisting and turning through the city, rapidly changing course and adjusting position so as to minimize exposure to a single point of attack, they flew through and above the grasping tendrils of Darkness the Shades extended toward them, seeking to drag them down with foul, corrupt magics. Each moment they flew closer toward the temple of Eldre'gheu, the greater the oppression he felt in his chest.

Relaxing and breathing deeply, he sought in vain to relieve the pressure building in his core. Though the *chi* flowing through him would sustain and enliven him in the time to come, it would not allay the feeling of doom building in his heart. He would have to accept the discomfort and move on.

His sensitivity, so often an asset, was now a liability, as the Darkness he saw without grew within.

There was, he knew, much to be feared in the Darkness of Eldre'gheu. Unfortunately for them, there was no way to escape it.

Rounding the last twisting turn above the shattered ruins of the Brendle-forsaken city, Slate gawked.

Ahead, its nacreous green radiance now visible to his magically enhanced eyes, the eerie luminescence of the temple's shield glowed in the half-light of the brume. Straining his neck upward as he flew, the shield's dome arched upward, its apex out of view, hidden by the seething black mass of the violent energy vortex.

Within the confines of the magical shield, completely obscuring the temple itself, entirely filling the confines of the hemisphere, countless Shades swarmed and shifted, reeling over and through each other.

Despite the Darkness, despite the danger, despite the oppressive evil of the place, he laughed out loud, showing yellowed teeth through his braided beard.

The glowing green and black dome looked like nothing more than a gigantic, steaming pile of *luerdan*.

No matter how powerful, intimidating, or cruel, he found it hard to resist laughing at something that lived inside a massive pile of Troll dung!

This close to the temple, its shield, and the warped energy vortex oscillating above only served to confirm Aroganji's earlier impressions. The power expressed, controlled, and manipulated here, as twisted and unnatural as it was, dwarfed anything he had yet seen manipulated on Ea'ae. That such expressions of power could be maintained for such a long period of time only bespoke of the danger, determination, and unearthly intelligence of the being they were soon to face and of the hostility and corruption of the place from which it derived.

The persistence of such evil also spoke to the vulnerability of his brethren, the peoples of Ea'ae, their lack of response, and weakened conviction in the face of such a scourge.

He could not envision a place that would create a beast capable of such feats nor would he wish to consider one.

Wrindanneth was eager.

As the temple neared, each glance told him something new, reminding him of the power and ability he had yet to attain but would one day glean. All around him, although twisted and misshapen by a vision darker than this world should ever have seen, the possible, the unlimited potential of magic lay visible before him. He had but to realize and master its full extent.

Then he, too, would be capable of such feats.

Then he would know no master other than himself.

Pushing their way forward, flying toward the hidden dome of Eldre'gheu unassailed within the blessed protection of Archaeus's white and golden Light, their passage marked by a brief flicker of light over a bleak gray landscape drained of color and vitality, of hope and promise, the Home Guard and Fists touched ground running at full speed, arms at the ready, only a few short paces away from the shimmering, turbulent verdigris of the shield's malefic surface.

Not breaking stride, with a mighty swing of his arm, Eidelion slashed downward, the curve of Archaeus's flight visible as a golden white afterimage in the eyes of those who looked upon its arch, cutting through the glowing shield without resistance. Despite its unimpeded motion, the blow of Archaeus's impact with the unholy shield rang out with the striking peal and reverberation of a crystalline chime, one whose horrendous pitch was not tuned for human ears.

From the commencement of the blow, so effortless upon initial glance, the strain on Eidelion's face became evident as he vied with a Power that none yet could see. Struggling with the unseen foe, he knew then that Fate had at last granted him an adversary at least his equal. Maintaining his grip on the Bright Blade, for it offered him the additional strength and will needed to complete his stroke and win through the magical fortification, Eidelion strode forward into the obsidian darkness of the swirling Shades eager now to face an opponent worth its measure.

Following closely behind lest the gaping slash in its surface close before they pushed through, the rest of the companions rushed across the gap in the barrier behind Eidelion's lead, joining him in the all-consuming Darkness of Eldre'gheu's shadow.

Within the hidden dome of Eldre'gheu's malevolent shield, his eyes straining against the surrounding Darkness, Yip saw nothing beyond the golden vault of Archaeus's Light. Countless Shades pressed eagerly against the protection of Eidelion's sword as one, their foul essences reaching out to him through the fortifications girding him and his fellows, seeking to pull, claw, and rive his essence away from his body before the life fully left his lips. Against this horrendous sensation and the accompanying maelstrom of dark magics, looming like a bank of angry storm clouds above, the fell presence of another more potent being hovered—insidious, inimical, utterly, and totally alien.

Briefly touching his chest, the Heart of Yere glowed warmly under his palm offering its own protections against such creatures; a welcome reassurance whose presence bolstered his companions though they knew not the source of the vigor and hope that helped buoy them against the Darkness.

Pushing onward toward the temple, the Shades meeting the pure rays of Archaeus's halo melted away as though never existing, the band made their way forward in determined silence beneath the aegis of Eidelion's will. Arrayed around the paladin's gallant form, they were a fearsome sight to behold wading through the evil pooled at Eldre'gheu's perimeter.

Striding ahead toward the temple's hidden gates, despite his strength and indomitable faith, against the unwavering Light of Archaeus's heart, the dome of Light protecting them slowly began to contract against the oppressive Darkness of the innumerable Shades and the deeper evils it harbored.

In time, against such an overwhelming torrent of Darkness, even the Light of the White Sword augmented by Eidelion's own would fade and grow dim.

Without need for a single voiced command or request for succor, Daerdros sprang into action. "Guard! Offer your aid!"

Without a word, she began weaving the strands of Light from Archaeus's blade into tangible form, her voice rising and falling in an ethereal song, her hands moving in tandem with the music's imperceptible tempo, creating a halo that would persist through even this blight, offering her strength to her commander's that his would not fade.

In tune with her twining and aria, Kazarhan began to chant, the deep baritone of his voice filling the air with his stalwart conviction and strength, lacing the blessed mantle with the protection of additional Dwarven Karaduen, words and ideals of power and protection.

While Daerdros and Kazarhan worked, the stone on Yip's chest began to grow hot as it too bolstered the strength of their spells and spirits, granting further safeguard to those sheltered within its radiance.

Beneath their masterful hands and minds, the very fabric of the air shifted and thrummed, filled with wondrous strands of energy laced through the fires of Archaeus's persistent burning shield, dancing with arcane symbols, sigils, and wards. So alluring were their efforts that Yip had to force himself to gaze elsewhere and pay full attention to the present dangers.

As the circle of effulgence about them grew and strengthened, his attention once again spreading outward and away from the phenomenal Craft of his friends, Yip sensed multiple focal points of gathering Darkness. Within the Shades' impenetrable dark, greater evils stirred, their presence soon to be felt.

"Ware the fore! Devilry stirs and comes!" Yip pointed toward where he sensed the coming of wickedness too maligned to be of human imagination or derivation.

As Yip's words settled about them in an anticipatory pall, the unearthly silence of the ruins was broken by the muffled *thuds* of fast approaching steps, the force of which vibrated through the splintered cobblestones beneath their feet—*THRUM! THRUM! THRUM!*

Fluidly drawing forth his eldritch bow from where it rested diagonally across his back, a casual gesture expressing the unearthly calm and poise of the Elves, Llyewia pulled lightly against the glittering translucent strand suspended between the ends of its elegant arch, letting loose a bolt of spun starshine. With the gentle release of his fingers, a silver bolt shot forth from his bow, trailing glimmering stardust in its wake. The exquisite curve of its silvery, ethereal trajectory burned through the Shades in its path, its flight quickly hidden by the churning blackness of those innumerable Shades surging into the fallens' place.

Singing as the magical bolt flew, a beautiful empyreal melody of limitless expansiveness and love, Llyewia's missile strove against the Darkness seeking after the gathering evil in the looming shadows.

Those creatures of greater Darkness without Light in their hearts soon would.

While Llyewia sung his bolt to the unforeseen doom of those twisted Daemons sprinting at inhuman speeds from the temple's gates, Yip sensed the vast malevolence of more of their twisted brethren fast approaching from the hidden skies.

"Above! More yet come!" His arm traced the progress of the deeper Shadows hidden by the lesser Shades.

With the masterful economy of motion of one well-practiced in a particular art, perhaps as a result of significant time spent in self-observation in front of a mirror, Spreesprocket reached into a magical pouch at his waist and, maintaining the speed and efficiency of his motion, threw a shimmering, reflective silver orb aloft and into the hungry Darkness clawing at the periphery of Archaeus's shield.

A wry smile on his small face, enjoying a joke that none of his counterparts would grasp but one that he particularly enjoyed, Spreesprocket yelled vociferously, "DISCO inferno away!"

Finishing the upward toss, he kept his right arm aloft while holding his left arm straight and slightly outward at his side, striking a pose ignored by the rest of the Home Guard who, in their urgency and need, were too intent on the danger around them to appreciate or understand Spreesprocket's flamboyant style, sense of humor, and cultural referent when they were all in mortal danger.

Before Spreesprocket had completed his sentence, striking his brief dance pose, superluminous beams of white Light began slicing through the gathered Shades, carving massive swaths through their ranks with each flash, obliterating all creatures of Darkness within the path of the pulsing magical lights.

Fighting their way toward the temple's wall, the unrelenting lights of the DISCO orb followed, relentlessly thinning the ranks of both Daemons and Shades alike.

"Behind us!" Yip sensed more dire creatures approaching from their flank, attempting to avoid both Llyewia's seeking missile and Spreesprocket's destructive orb.

Leaping overhead, the beat of his great wings pressing them downward as strongly as the oppressive sense of evil and Darkness weighing heavily upon them, Raour'Saqan held his body aloft and let loose a mighty, challenging roar. Snapping his jaws open, a gout of turbulent black flames burst forth from his maw, visible only through the black mass of Shades by the path the seething column incinerated. Outlined briefly within the heart of the flames, the misshapen silhouettes of Daemons persisted briefly within the torrent, long enough to guess at the general vileness of their repugnant forms, but no longer.

Shifting his head steadily from side-to-side, the composed violence of the motion belying the ultimate destruction it generated, the Dracodaeran's insatiable fires cut down rank upon rank of Shades and Daemons in equal measure.

Despite the successive extradimensional assaults, the companions' relentless, forward progress never ceased or wavered.

There was no other alternative.

TUMULT

Blue mountains fade to gray
with the setting sun,
light slips to darkness.

He blinked, pausing before moving forward. Visions of his future haunting him even as he watched.

The lines of probability about him shifted, clarifying and adjusting as he moved toward his ultimate destination.

He watched attentively, reading the lineations coalescing before him, as the courses of two destinies prepared to collide, shattering the hopes and futures of one before the other, the inferior falling before the superior.

His eyes widened as his destiny unfolded, for as he watched, his future, its breadth and scope, narrowed. Tendrils of probability arose and collapsed. He was left to choose the most viable.

As the world around him changed, cohering from the possible to the real, the path he had chosen, the one he had read so carefully, appeared no longer to reflect the actuality before him.

He was, therefore, at a crossroads. The violence at the end of each course of action may, in fact, mark his end.

He held the ship in abeyance while he assessed the impact of his decisions and those around him as they raced to meet one another in a future known and studied by one and unknown and unmarked by the other.

Visions flashed before his eyes of possible futurities—should he take one course over another, follow one strand of action at the expense of others—potential existences he let die with each evaluation.

Should he continue through the gloom to meet the Shadow in the heart of the labyrinth, his end appeared certain.

Should he meet his quarry directly, in any number of permutations, before, during, or immediately after they engaged the Shadow and Its agents, the possibility of his survival appeared equally dim.

Should he retreat to pursue his quarry at another time, he may be hunted himself by his master.

The question then became which route to take?

Which future would bring him closer to his objectives and those of his master?

Which future would cost his enemies most dearly?

How should he best spend himself before his own end?

The darkness of sweet Oblivion awaited.

Grabbing the reins of probability, he surged forward.

FLEET

A golden stream burbles
over tumbled stones.
In the distance a crow calls.

Humbol turned away from the resplendent glamour of Illdrassil and returned to the business at hand.

There was no way in tarnation that Hoyt would be at his shop. Odds were if he went there he would find an empty vacant lot or a building shielded against all possible eventualities.

He knew his friend too well. Hoyt would never let his livelihood be at risk or fall out of his control.

How to find him then?

Talking aloud, he addressed no one, at least no one human, in particular, "Construct, please locate Hoyt, owner of Hoyt's – Oddities, Found Goods, and Sundries, if you would and he has not requested privacy, please."

Waiting patiently, for talking to oneself aloud was not altogether unexpected or particularly worthy of note in Tellanon, Humbol held for a reply.

A few moments later, the formal tones of the Construct answered, "Citizen, I am currently unable to locate Hoyt. Be advised that many fellow citizens are seeking shelter within designated locations at this very moment and are therefore deliberately untrackable by system design. I suggest you proceed toward the nearest designated safety zone until further notice. Have a good day."

Contacting Hoyt would not be that easy. It never was. Nor did he wish to wait.

Knowing the city and its defenses, chances were that a simple spell would not work to locate his friend. If Hoyt had done as instructed, as the Construct recommended he do as well, which one could never safely assume, then Hoyt could be in an extraplanar pocket dimension completely unreachable via magical or mundane communication.

Well, it never hurt to try. Maybe Hoyt, being old and cantankerous like himself, had not yet made it to his specified secure location or he had refused to enter and had shielded himself from scrying by the Construct.

Muttering under his breath, Humbol began casting one of his favorite spells, Locandra's Locating Locus, one that had served them well on many an adventure. The Locus was just as capable of finding treasure as it was at locating a person, so long as they were not hidden or protected by magic.

Contrary to the common opinion, the real trick to finding what you were after, aside from actually having the appropriate spell to get at what you wanted and knowing how best to apply it in the first place, was determining what may be near the object or treasure that you were after that might not be protected or hidden by magic artifice. Then you could use the Locus to scry that object or thing. If you could scry something nearby, getting its location and the lay of the land around it with all of its traps and pitfalls, all the rest was simply planning and execution.

Well, that and luck.

Lots of luck.

Then at least you were close. Generally speaking, as a treasure hunter, once you were proximate, physically or not, you also succeeded in arousing someone or something's ire which oftentimes helped give the location of what you were after away. If you were not fortunate enough to find something your-self, having someone give away the location was the next best thing.

Ah, such were the games of his youth.

Now, at least, he could put those skills to a practical purpose.

Finished with his incantation, a small whirling vortex of air, like a dust devil without the dust and debris, barely visible to the eye, spun on the palm of his hand, smaller than his closed fist. Holding a clear image of Hoyt in his mind, a simulacrum of Hoyt holding his Fairy Dragon Cletus on his shoulder as he so often did while reclining or talking casually with a patron in his store, for he wanted the Locus to find the Dragon which might not be protected from scrying, visualizing the Locus's intended destination, Humbol exhaled softly, blowing the Locus off and on its way.

Wiping his hands clean with proud finality, preparing to wait patiently for an answer and a direction in which to turn, he stood in place once more taking in the events of the day. Looking past the crowds of flying wizards, Paratech-nologists soaring on or within various mechanical oddities of every shape and sort, and the select few like himself relying upon more mundane means of transportation hurrying around him, returning his attention to the sky, his jaw dropped.

The firmament above Tellanon was no longer clear. The storm that had been averted had returned.

War was on the horizon.

Looking left and right in every direction, dark ships clouded the skies, locusts seeking a perch on which to alight and sate their voracious hunger.

Presaged by the clouds of doom, the Cabal's fleet had landed.

Turning calmly, he changed directions. No longer walking, he rushed toward the docks.

Hoyt would have to find him.

If Tellanon were to survive, she needed every ship in the air and in action to help defend her borders.

So much for a nice casual visit with his friend.

When would he ever learn that trouble always seemed to follow him aground?

The Construct thrummed, moving through simultaneous multidimensional analyses and operations, continually monitoring the current status of the city, her agents, their security, and well-being. Within an instant, the complex, self-evolving algorithms governing its actions shifted in reaction to a new urgent set of governing variables.

Secondary extradimensional incursion detected…limits of invasion beyond the scope and magnitude of original intrusion. Hostile fleet of unknown capabilities ascertained and under evaluation.

Security of the citizenry…in transition with movements toward increasing stability. Additional safety measures and assurances…undertaken.

High Council…alerted and apprised.

Status of defensive systems…robust.

Status of warships and support personnel…at the ready.

Notification of incursion and request for potential aid from allies…failed. Multiple tertiary infiltrations reported and detected. Ancillary defensive support positions…compromised.

Preparations for defense of last resort…underway.

Hoyt spat, the sweetgrass he had been savoring in the warm folds of his cheek over the past few hours now marking the cobblestones outside the transdimensional park with an irregular green stain.

He could no more run and hide than he could avoid the opportunity to observe the momentous occasion developing around him.

It was just too interesting.

All around him citizens of every shape and sort streamed into the open meadow behind him, normally a park for this borough but now a safe haven for those seeking refuge from the Cabal's incursion. Wizards flew past, their beards and robes fluttering in the wind, Gnomes scurried and zoomed by manning mechanical contraptions held together as much by their will and imagination as craftsmanship, visitors and stunned families rushed and wandered past more often than not walking or running amidst the confusion, while overhead Paratechnologists guarding the ground and skies ushered those both naïve, native, and foreign to zones of safety.

All the hubbub around him, however, only occupied his attention temporarily.

When the unearthly fogs of doom had rolled overhead, arising from some extradimensional source, he knew that serious business was afoot. The Cabal was once again resurgent within Ea'ae. Now that this phenomenon had passed and his future was, at least temporarily, assured his resolve hardened.

There would be no more hiding or running for if he ran and his city fell, where would he turn and call home?

Tellanon offered him the diversity and excitement needed to sate his curiosity, the foot traffic required to keep his coffers full, and the security to provide him a retirement of leisure at his ease.

He was too old to start over.

He was too old risk his home.

No, he would stand with his city and make certain Tellanon would prosper in the future as it had allowed him to do in the past.

If he did not stay around to learn more of this incursion and how it came to pass, how would he ever find a way to entice a party of hale adventurers to venture forth and explore its causes, weaknesses, and potential rewards?

Where were the Four when he needed them? When would the Four stop tarrying and restore the seals so that he did not have to clean up their mess at home? By the looks of it, he had a new adventure for them!

A faint tickle at the periphery of one of his anti-scrying wards set his eyes alight. Scouring the crowd for something unusual, any sign that he was under potential scrutiny, his eyes compressed to slits, sliding back and forth through the crowd, swiveling upward to examine the sky above. There, almost directly overhead, a faint eddy of air, the slightest almost imperceptible magical vortex spun and whirled about a central axis before darting away toward the general area of the docks.

Casting his own spell after the Locus, he smiled. If he were a gambling man, he bet that he was no longer alone on his little adventure. His wager on the table, he only had to wait on his spells to cash in.

His mind made up and his direction set, he walked away from the bright grassy meadow offering the safety and security of a guaranteed tomorrow. Armed with his wand, leading by his chin, he stomped off.

Eyes on his iridescent Fairy Dragon, he growled, "Come on, Cletus! Let's be off!"

Pushing his way counter to the flow of the crowd, moving with the skill of one used to overcoming obstacles with a goal in mind, he wended through the masses with determination and a firm conviction. Finally breaking from the press of humanity moving counterflow to his intention, he walked for a few brief moments alone in the middle of a largely empty byway surrounded by smooth white stone homes and overhanging trees. Taking a moment to examine the sky through a break in the canopy, he held in place just after having set off.

Above and along the horizon, ringing the sky like thunderheads banked before the eye of a storm, untold numbers of massed ships hovered in position outside the region formerly occupied by the Cabal's invading Darkness.

When would the madness stop?

No longer walking, he ran toward the docks, Cletus flying slightly above and behind in tow, awaiting the opportunity to alight on his shoulder once more.

Muttering to himself, his feet padding on the cobblestones as he rushed forward, he cursed the Construct for preventing teleportation and making a tired old man run.

Blast it! His patience fading, he flicked his wand, uttered a brief incantation and took to the air. If he had to hurry, he would do so fast and at ease.

Motioning urgently for Cletus to move in, he opened a small pocket on the interior of his outer robe, allowing the Fairy Dragon to wiggle inside the pocket cozily while they buzzed through the air.

While his mind hummed with thoughts, tracing various paths and contingencies, Cletus slept peacefully, oblivious to the outside world and its risks as he remained safe within the warm confines of his own personal pocket dimension.

Swooping in the opposite direction of the last few stragglers darting or flying along the streets, Hoyt only hoped that the reappearance he now wished for, the reunion he sought, was possible.

Hemmed in every direction by small representations of individual ships and other as yet unidentified objects in the invading armada, listening to the Construct's sober update, the members of the Protectorate stared at the central projection while thousands of motes of darkness materialized around their city's periphery in the visual display. With these ships, another cloak of Darkness arose bolstering their strength and potency.

From afar, the projection showed Tellanon bright and glorious in the darkening sky—a star surrounded, ringed at the center of a vast cluster of asteroids and extrasolar bodies whose trajectory arched toward the star's point of central rotation within an immense gulf of dark, encroaching space.

"Given the magnitude of the existing assault and the systemic demands of the most recent incursion, current defensive vectors appear insufficient to provide a direct offensive counter to the invading forces in tandem with another wave of hyperdimensional Darkness."

"However, extant countermeasures, given favorable utilization and effect, may grant a chance of desirable outcome with a high degree of certainty."

"Likelihood of defensive augmentation and reinforcement of Tellanon by outside allies and agents are minimal due to similar tertiary invasions along multiple fronts and targets planetary wide."

"Cognizance along these lines of tertiary incursions is not favorable. Heavy casualties reported. Multiple cities across Ea'ae have fallen. Notable among them are Liao Qua, Urduen, Irielia, Daeja, and Kiervos. Other population centers are close to collapse."

Interjecting, not wishing to hear more for their own need was now at hand, Oroende spoke with urgency, his golden skin shimmering as he voiced his concern. "What courses of action are most likely to result in a successful neutralization of the incursion?"

"Evaluation of the current circumstance is too preliminary to ascertain the best possible course of immediate, short-term action. However, given changing conditions, Alain and Whirlygig will remain constantly apprised of the situation as probabilities collapse and bifurcate into potentialities both favorable and non-."

Impatient and unhappy with the answer, Oroende interrupted, pressing, "Can you say no more?"

"On a micro scale, covering the immediate vicinity, prediction of the possible outcomes of this engagement is uncertain due to too many unrealized and unassessed variables. Given the superior numbers of invading agents and the mantle of Darkness once more assisting them, we must rely upon our defenses to wear down and counter their offensive movements focusing upon our strengths including those manifest in the shield surrounding the city, the remaining sentry drones, and the application of superior tactics pertaining to our resources. Granted enough time required to recharge the city's power system, the appropriate positioning to be within range of the effect, and the mounting of a successful defense to allow for actual deployment, these intruding offensive vectors will become susceptible to application of the Loel'-dara as were their predecessors."

"Of particular note, the invading Darkness appears to be sheltering and augmenting the alien fleet's position and strength without moving directly against the city. Unlike the most recent assault, analysis indicates that the invading armada may attempt to overcome and weaken the city's defenses through direct attack, perhaps supplemented by the nebulous Darkness, without relying solely upon the extradimensional Shadow to overcome our defenses."

"On a macroscopic level, covering Ea'ae as a whole, the primary path to ensure short and long-term success and viability with the highest probabilities of favorable outcomes will be to follow causal decision paths meant to restore and maintain the fourteen seals girding the planetary defense. If accomplished, these courses of action will, within certain statistical limitations, ensure that the invaders cannot replenish their forces or mount similar future invasions in the foreseeable future."

Temporarily satisfied, Oroende nodded, letting out the breath he had been holding unknowingly. "We are doing our best then. Despite dangers imposed by the pressing attack, we should continue with our plans to deploy supplemental forces of the Home Guard to assist those already endeavoring to restore and secure the seals."

"Are we in agreement?" Éremon looked around the circle of High Council's members.

All nodded grimly.

"Then we are resolved."

Wiping nervous sweat from his full, domed brow, Noumel asked, "What of intelligence from the ARMED sentry drones? Are there any tidings regarding the source of the invasion? The extent of the supporting armada? Any weaknesses or assessments that we should be made aware of with regard to our current confrontation?"

Speaking for the Construct, briefly summarizing what little he knew, Alain replied, "As yet, there is no credible information."

Before anyone could object or press for more information, he added, "We should expect some delay both in regards to information transit time from beyond the portals as the drones will also need to determine how best to surreptitiously send their findings to us without teleporting home while taking the necessary period required in order to draw meaningful assessments and conclusions from that intelligence."

"However, as credible information is received, we will make it available to you all."

Alain finished, "Although we are fortunate to be in a position to offer a potential assessment of our enemies, the unfortunate side of this reconnaissance effort is that any valuable information we do receive may be too late to have any effect on the outcome of our current engagement."

Éremon spoke then, his voice filled with resolve. "We will remain here in the council chambers in order to facilitate the city's defense and to be in a position to retaliate with the Loel'dara should the opportunity present itself."

"Are we agreed?"

A brief chorus of aye's met his query.

Nodding, Alain replied, "I will attend fully to the city's defense." Remaining in a relaxed, at-the-ready posture, his attention shifted fully into the governing command superstructure of the Construct wherein his will could be actualized with immediate effect.

Humbol's feet alighted lightly on the ground as he shifted smoothly from flight to a dead run toward the mooring holding his ship in place on the docks. After starting at a jog and almost being bowled over by a smoking, squealing Gnomish jalopy loaded with what appeared to be several large, extended families, including all their possessions, their garden, lawn ornaments, and a collection of those neighborhood animals they could wrangle and coax into a confined space, he had decided that flight was a much safer, and faster, option than running.

Not that he had been granted any peace on his journey toward the docks.

As he flew away from his designated safe zone, an Aspect had followed his course reminding him incessantly that he should be moving toward a position of safety. When he had told the Aspect that his intent was no longer to be safe, the simulacrum had insisted upon reminding him that he was taking a "perilous, ill-advised course" and that he would be exposed to "grave risk."

Finally, when his patience was at an end, he had barked, "This is my life to spend as I choose. You should thank me for deciding to spend it trying to save you and your blasted city!"

The Aspect had, at last, granted him a reprieve and left him in silence. Had he not been in such a rush, he would have marveled at the fact that the Construct was able to have a personalized interface with every being on Tellanon while maintaining its primary functions and functionality.

But, given his desire to be in the air as quickly as possible, there was no time in his view for such reflection, only a rapidly fading annoyance and strong sense of need.

He would take to the air and meet these usurpers face-to-face.

When he could see the crews of those black ships eye to eye, then they would know fear.

The thought to run never occurred to him. If he lost one safe mooring in the tempest to come, he might never find another harborage to drop anchor. Better to fight for what he had than what might or might not be for his livelihood was trade and invaders like these would be the end of it.

He might be old, but he knew this—the strongest tempests were the ones with the longest time to build. He had bided his time overlong. Soon these invading ships would see him in action.

He would meet the storm of these invaders with one of his own!

Unable to stop the grin from spreading across his face at the sight of his friend after so long, despite the pall of the present circumstances, Hoyt called out boisterously, full of enthusiasm, "Ho! Humbol!"

The cool evening air whipped across his face as he cut through the crepuscule toward a landing, Hoyt saw his friend bustling on his ship in the soft light of the magical orbs strung through the air along the ramping slope of the docks, securing loose items, rushing to and fro, and acting for all intents and purposes as though he were fleeing from a sinking ship.

The Locus had served them both. Not only had it found Hoyt but Hoyt had used it to find Humbol.

Looking up, Hoyt's broad grin was returned in his friend's lined, weathered face. In reply, Humbol called out, "You half-addled bag o' bones! I was looking for ya!"

"And now ya've found me! And not a minute too soon, methinks." Hoyt's smile remained, mirroring that of his of friend.

"Thought I was goin' ta have ta give up on ya fer now."

Hoyt cocked his head slightly to the side and raised his shoulders questioningly as he answered, "After all these years, haven't ya learned never ta give up on me?"

Humbol returned to his knot, the one he had been so proud of just a few short hours ago. With a wave of his fingers, not having time to untie the ship from its berth with his hands alone, he cast a spell and the knots untied of their own volition. "If ya're comin', hop on. We're not gettin' any younger."

Looking up from his task as he moved to another, Humbol chortled. "'Specially you!"

With a few spry steps, Hoyt cleared the last bit of space between them, a sardonic smile on his face. "Speak fer yerself!"

Humbol laughed. "Thought I just did!"

Finished for the moment, Humbol walked purposefully back to the helm of the vessel, the burnished wood practically glowing in the half-light of the ship's orbs from years of loving use. Reaching out, his hands returning eagerly to the warm wood, he felt the life of his ship infuse him as he took hold of the wheel. With a transition no more unusual than opening his eyes from sleep, his consciousness extended outward in all directions as his palm touched the firm oaken band. Within that instant, his mind shifted to encompass the ship as his own body and the space around it in all directions, his range of vision and sensation instantaneously broadening and deepening.

Standing at the helm, he was at home and at peace for he felt most himself when joined with his ship. So long had he been piloting, that he actually felt unnatural when he was not directly connected to his ship, like he had lost a part of himself. Besides his love for the open sky and travel, that sensation of incompleteness was always a strong lure to get him back aboard and off on another voyage.

Quickly surveying the workings of his vessel with his mind's eye as though checking his own body for any abnormalities, Humbol promptly decided all was in order and prepared to shove off.

"Hold on ya 'lubber! We're off!" In a transition too smooth to warrant warning, the *Rare Aer* rotated away from the docks of Tellanon and took to the open skies.

As Humbol guided his small ship smoothly through the air and off from the relative security of the docks, Hoyt took a moment to survey the landing slipping away before him, the magically sculpted stone arching upward toward the dazzling Scimerian Gate and back down and around the bulk of the massive floating island itself. With the exception of those crews choosing to stay aboard and guard their ships, either for bravery or foolhardiness he could not know, the docks were almost completely empty of the usual throngs of citizens, passengers, traders, diplomats, and visitors of manifold races. However, the quay was far from abandoned.

Teams of Paratechnologists manned gunnery ranging from elegantly articulated, clear crystalline tubes looking to be spun from the minds of the finest artisans to blazing black funnels spewing smoke and other foul vapors ostensibly scavenged from the darkest pits of the Abyss. On foot and overhead, contingents of Paratechnologists and their creations swarmed to and fro like hordes of buzzing bees, each armed with stingers unlike the others—wands, guns, bows, bolts, and myriad other weapons marking the grave intent of the city's defenders. Out and away from the docks themselves, more ships and drones than he could easily count or behold in a single glance held positions at various distances from the city forming defensive perimeters around the full circumference of the island, reinforced by the gunnery below and those other ships held at the ready in the docks and caves beneath the island. Some whizzing through the air, others floating in the sky stationary and at the ready, those sentry drones not deployed to repel the initial invasion took up positions alongside soldiers, ships, and battlements, more numerous than both ships and defenders combined.

Even though the city's attackers were truly overwhelming—a fearsome, seething black sandstorm rapidly closing in around them cutting off all possibility of escape—the city's defenses were formidable nonetheless. Looking back and forth between the defenders and the invaders on the horizon, deciding between two possibilities, he was glad to take part in the defense of his home for otherwise his own future would be left in the hands of others.

Besides, he always preferred to take part in the events of the day.

If he were involved in the tidings of the day, then he need not learn of them from another.

He usually only acted indirectly.

This situation warranted a change from his usual style.

The only downside to taking direct action was that he then had little opportunity to talk and engage socially with his friends and relations. Of course, that always took care of itself…the talking at least.

His observations and reflections were cut short by Humbol's strident voice breaking through his ruminations, sensing Hoyt's mind had begun to wander. "There's no time fer lollygaggin'! If we're ta take our fair share of these misbegotten cave slugs, I'll need ya ta stop woolgatherin' and help me tie down these sails!"

Hoyt enjoyed seeing his friend in his element after so long an absence. Bending over his knot, securing the line as he had been directed, he called out while he worked, "So what brought ya back ta Tellanon?"

Humbol motioned backward toward his piloting station indicating where his goods were stored. "If we get through this, ya'll find out soon enough!"

Hoyt scratched his chin, the same gesture he used when taking the measure of a particularly enticing item for barter and preparing to make his offer. "And if we don't?"

"Then our debt will be settled either way!"

Hoyt smiled inwardly.

There was nothing like a good mystery to solve!

Before they had fully cleared the decks, the voice of the Construct once more contacted them, this time in a final warning. "Captain Humbol and Hoyt on the *Rare Aer*! Know that you are assuming a grave risk by taking to the skies under the current circumstances."

"Your course of action is unadvisable. For your own safety, please take refuge in a secure location while the opportunity remains available!"

Humbol nodded patiently. "Have we not had this conversation before?" He tapped his fingers steadily on the wheel as he spoke. "Even with every able-bodied man, woman, and child on Tellanon takin' ta th' skies and mannin' a ship, ya're outgunned and outnumbered. Hoyt here"—he pointed nonchalantly over his shoulder to where Hoyt worked impassively on ignoring the Construct—"and I tip th' balance in yer favor. In fact, if I were ye, I would save everyone all tha trouble and have 'em dock their ships while we take care of these scalawags."

When the Construct was silent in response to his boast, he added, "If ya'd stop botherin' us, we could've had this whole mess cleaned up already!"

While Hoyt barked a short laugh out loud without concern for the Construct, the synthetic intelligence replied to Humbol, "Very well, you are cleared to flee from or engage the enemy as required. You are advised to steer away from the defending ships, however, as you are not part of their strategic command structure, maneuverings, or communication arrangements."

Humbol gave a short mock salute. "Aye, aye, Cap'n!"

Turning back to his work after pausing to watch Humbol give his sardonic respects, Hoyt burst out laughing once more as the Construct replied one final time before signing off with a trenchant, "Argh!"

For his part, Humbol stood dumbfounded, for once, albeit briefly, at a loss for words.

He had never considered whether the Paratechnologists' creation had a sense of humor, much less one that he could relate to.

He had to give those Gnomes much more credit than was their usual due!

There truly was more wonder between Earth and Heaven than he could ever hope to know much less laugh at.

Free of the docks and in the open air at last, Humbol motioned Hoyt over. In his hand, he held a golden telescoping ocular, one he had had custom designed and crafted by the famous shipwright, aeronaut, and aeromancer Barnaby Bilantré, known lovingly by his friends as Barney Black Eyes for his eyes were as dark as pitch and able to navigate in the utter darkness of full night or the interstellar reaches of space with surety and ease.

His tone as soft as the wind, Humbol said, "Take a gander, my friend."

The finely wrought metal, laced with moving scenes of clouds and stars, storms and sunsets, and depictions of scenes of flight that shifted with each glance, glimmered in his hands as fantastical as the expansive vision that had first cast it.

Looking first to Humbol, Hoyt held the ocular up to his eye. The telescope was warm to the touch as if it had been resting in the sunlight throughout the day and had decided not to relinquish the full heat of the sun or the memory of its brightness. Following the line of Humbol's arm, he peered through the ocular.

What he saw weighed heavily upon his heart.

There were, as he had feared, more ships arrayed on the horizon than could be counted with the time they would be allowed prior to engagement. Not only could he see the ships spread out in all directions before them, but he could see the magical currents upon which they rode, cresting turbulent waves of invisible force, breakers that not only buoyed but powered their passage. Those ships, in all their various shapes and sizes, were an awesome sight to behold.

Had an attack not been eminent, he could have easily lost himself in their examination and deliberation. Each ship told the unique story of its people, their vision, understanding, outlooks, and knowledge. These crafts ranged from the sleek, aerodynamic metallic vessels indicative of cultures not accustomed to magic but with significant technical sophistication nonetheless to those of the more basic sort like the one on which he and Humbol now toiled. Alongside the base were those exemplary ships inspired by the highest flights of imagination. On their decks he saw Men and countless shapes besides, some he knew and most he did not, armed with weapons of war and destruction. Below decks, hidden from view, many more beings of every shape and sort waited for the call to battle.

He had never seen such an armada assembled nor had he ever wished to lay eyes upon one.

UMBRA

Shadows roil and flux
shifting and fluid.
Leaves silhouetted by dawn.

They made the temple's gates.

After the interminable fight through the oppressive weight of countless Shades, past wave after wave of looming, screaming Daemons, along with myriad other nightmares hidden by the Shades' Shadows, the opening in the side of the temple came as a relief, a sign that they were indeed making progress against the implacable night.

The Shades and Daemons, however, still came, pressing forward in uncounted numbers, fearsome and terrible, for there was no change in their target, no waning in their desire to drink the life from those who invaded their sanctum.

In the Light of the holy illumination surrounding and pervading them, the cracked maw of Eldre'gheu snarled and growled, a gaping hole in the side of the crumbling temple walls leading toward certain oblivion. No gates yet stood, nor were there any remaining framing or statuary around the crumbled arch. What survived of the temple's front entry was nothing more than the remnants of a large hole in the side of the temple's thick walls. Despite this lack of obvious adornment or defense, the warning implied by that opening into empty space was tangible, enough to give the heroes standing on her doorstep disquieted pause.

Llyewia spoke then while they stood and weighed the terror before them against the fear behind them, expressing the danger they all felt, the threat he saw through eyes granted vision into realms hidden from the ken of mortal men. "Ea'ae stands behind us. Once we cross this threshold, though we step on the ground of this world, we will be in another."

"The laws we live by, the reality we know, will no longer hold, for this temple is now a portal to another place, neither here nor there."

"If we have not trod with caution before, we must do so now for we truly do not know what we will face."

Yip nodded, turning to look at each of the motley band in turn. "The evil before us is now manifest. We must defeat it on its own grounds. Though this would not be the place or condition of our choosing to engage such a foe, we must now fight it in its own domain, in its strength."

"Know and understand your own limits, push against them with all of your hope and will for the Darkness residing within this place of desecration would crush your spirit and drain your essence, all of your dreams and aspirations, wishes and memories, destroying who and what you are utterly for its own ends."

Eidelion finished, "The time of our crossing, the time of our triumph is now at hand. Your belief, your faith, must sustain you. Though this place is not our home, your unwavering will can help bend its laws to our own. Then you may act very much as you are accustomed and your Craft will sustain you and abide."

"Though we may stray far from home, if we keep it in our hearts, home will never be far."

Pointing Archaeus ahead toward the leering threshold, a void filled with oppressive fear and hatred as much as impenetrable darkness, he said, "We go now that Ea'ae may prosper!"

Following Archaeus's Light along with his companions, Yip stepped through the broken gate of Eldre'gheu.

The world around him wavered and shifted. He felt disoriented, trying to stand after spinning round and round in circles. Fighting the dizziness, Yip strove to regain his sense of self and orientation.

Pressure... Pressure built and bore down on him. His movements felt sluggish and labored, pushing through and against the weight of fathoms upon fathoms of numbingly cold water crushing downward and inward upon him from every direction though no fluid was present.

His breath was as labored as his motion.

The world around him was dark, almost completely inaccessible beyond the nimbus of light around Archaeus's shining white blade. Even within the light, the world seemed to tremble and sway, undecided on which form to take or which points defined reality.

They stepped into a watery, heat mirage existing between two overlapping worlds, not yet joined but linked through Darkness, a limbo neither of this world nor of the other. The temple was a place where they were as likely to fade away as the world they had just departed.

Within this fluctuating Darkness, one constant held, unrelenting and intractable, a wall of evil so strong that Yip nearly had to drop to his knees under the weight of its malefic presence. This maleficence defined the place, held it together, and made it what it was—a seat of unrealized terror and delusion, a home to ghosts and grim visions, a place where dreams came to die.

His attention, extended and aware, met this evil on its own terms and did not flinch. He merely watched and felt, not letting the overwhelming presence take hold or gain purchase. This same cognizance told him that even here, in the darkest pit, his own Light still shone forth just as the *chi* and *yuan-chi* that sustained it.

Taking a steady survey of the room around them, he could barely make out the curving slope of the walls behind and the curvature of the dome's ceiling above. What little he could discern was viewed through the lens of a turbid pool, agitated and washed out by the unsettled space around them.

There was, however, one positive.

At least the Shades were gone.

Aroganji relaxed and breathed.

In.

Out.

In.

Out.

Despite all the pressure and discomfort, a raucous wall of sights and sensations pushing against all of his senses, he focused on what he knew and felt. His breath became his anchor and his reality.

This was how he had been trained at Xian Shi to overcome phantasms and illusions lest he succumb to their reality in lieu of his own. From this perspective, he treated the netherworld he now inhabited, so invasive and distracting, as nothing more than a perversion of his own.

And so he breathed.

Slate exhaled violently, a sudden whoosh of air escaping from his lips as he crossed over, expelling with the force of a punch to the solar plexus, the weight of the blow enough to cause him to double over. Placing both hands on his knees, he stood slowly, steadily.

A crooked grin crossed his face as he caught his breath, recognizing the challenge.

Challenges he knew.

Challenges he loved.

Challenges he savored.

There would be no Darkness while the flames of Brendle's fires burned and persevered.

Reorienting himself, with a brief gathering of will, he summoned the holy blaze of the Daerdaana'Duin about him and the Darkness could not touch him.

As he did so, the halo of light surrounding Archaeus became even brighter.

Wrindanneth shrugged, deflecting the mental intrusion and disorientation with cocky aplomb, in his element.

His master had subjected him to torments far worse than this as part of his training. He would not fold or buckle under the pressure of one Daemon, no matter how great, when his master had been far less kind.

Biting back a smile, he briefly hearkened back to the events of his youth. Yes, the days he had not been subjected to far worse were few and far between.

Strange that such a horrendous place could bring back fond memories of unimaginable torments. Such was the dichotomy of his character...both of Light and Dark but fully of neither.

That he had not broken, gone mad, or perished under his master's tutelage was not due to his will and talent alone, however. Despite his pride, some would call it arrogance, he would not go so far as to lay claim to that outcome alone. No, Maeth Onai was equally adept at rebuilding what he had torn down.

For that, at least, he was thankful.

In the end, he had learned to abide within the strength of his resolve, as he did now.

His equilibrium reestablished, Yip extended himself a bit more and probed deeper.

He needed to be prepared, to know what and where they moved within. He needed to know so that he could share what he gleaned with his friends. Without proper understanding, they would all fail.

The *chi* that he knew, that he embraced totally and completely, still existed here, for even creatures of Darkness help to create that which they destroy. *Yuan-chi* yet arose from the void of potential undergirding even this warped place though its fate was to be consumed prior to full expression lest it return to the Wuji from whence it came. Some energy also traveled through the barriers surrounding this place, drawn perhaps by the massive vortex, for the overwhelming preponderance of energy he sensed here was of Daemonic origin.

What he felt, however, was unclean.

The *chi* that he knew, the *chi* that enlivened and buoyed him, heartened and offered him solace, was not the *chi* that existed here. The *chi* here was corrupted, tainted and perverted by the Darkness that resided within and drank deeply and wantonly from its depths.

He felt dirty exposing himself to it, the pool of water he wished to drink from fouled by oil and refuse, home to effluent and disease.

Despite his sentiments, he would indeed have to make use of this energy if he were to help his friends overcome the Shadow that lurked within these walls, hiding between the intersection of two dimensions.

Even deeper, beyond the superficial *chi* that should have brought life and joy to this place of former supplication and devotion, idealism and aspiration, he delved. Ultimately, what he found was as apparent to the naked eye as his probing awareness.

The world here was thin, not only a corrupted, mangled place between two very different dimensions, not just a place vying for a stable expression of interdimensional space and time, but extended, taut and ready to tear or break.

The energy that arose and bound reality together, the elysian *yuan-chi*, too, was attenuated here. In being drawn through and away from this place, consumed ravenously by the creature at its heart, the temple no longer had the necessary fundament or basis upon which to sustain itself. Thus, reality itself was in flux.

That is how the world seemed to him.

That is how the Shadow at Eldre'gheu's heart wished for it to be.

Returning his attention to his companions, one immediate question troubled Yip.

Why had they not yet been attacked?

Voicing his concerns, sensing that everyone had recovered and were now ready to continue with what surety could be found in this deserted tomb, he offered his appraisal. "Reality here is taut, pulled and stretched to the point of breaking, and unable to settle upon a definite fixed form for two dimensions now claim its presence."

"The essential energy that once sustained this place, too, is stretched thin, although it is still present to some degree, lest this place would cease to exist altogether."

"The very energy of life, what still remains in this troubled haunt, has been despoiled, debased, and desecrated, much like Eldre'gheu itself."

"We should not risk exposing ourselves to its corruption overlong, lest we, too, succumb to Darkness."

His tone grim, Yip finished, "Despite the depravity and depth of unnaturalness of this place, this is not the concern that yet bothers me."

"Why have we not yet been attacked?"

"Why were we allowed to recover?"

"Why not strike at us at our point of greatest confusion upon translation to this netherworld?"

Aroganji nodded, understanding the thrust of Yip's point. "Perhaps the creature at Eldre'gheu's heart wishes to take our measure more fully now that we have made its inner sanctum. Perhaps it now wishes for us to come to it that it can face us directly. Perhaps it wishes to continue testing us that we may be corrupted as well."

"A prize in hand is more valuable than one lost."

"Who can say?"

Before he could utter a warning, reacting only quickly enough to protect himself, Yip sensed an oncoming surge of intent, a mental avalanche, crashing down upon them, smashing against the protective nimbus of Light.

"It comes!"

Unbowed, the wretched weight of their enemy before them, Kazarhan smashed Raurdros to the chamber floor in challenge, shattering tile and stone as he roared forth an invocation to Brendle the All-Father, the power of his words sheathing him in a nimbus of Light augmenting Raurdros's own. Words of banishment and binding, command and repudiation, wreathed him as he strode forward pushing the Daemon's projection back to the pits from whence it came.

Those valiant words were the bridge to Kazarhan's undoing, the very link the Daemon required for purchase, his bold steps forward outside Archaeus's protection taking him too far along the path to his destruction.

Yip turned on the balls of his feet to face their adversary now made flesh.

While he moved, a harsh, unnatural voice spoke, the sound issuing forth torn from deep within the recesses of a mind lost to reason and passion. The voice that now reverberated painfully in their ears, grating and clawing its way inward into the depths of their minds, far too loud for the mouth from which it issued, clamored wildly. "I am lost! Strike me down that I might live!"

With that horrendous voice, the sound of a man's soul being ripped apart, Kazarhan the Stout, Kor'Dannan and Dur'kazak, hunched down within the circle of Light once more, twisting and writhing in agony, and let loose a blood curdling scream, his eyes turning red as blood vessels began hemorrhaging and blood began pouring from his ears.

Lurching forward, Raurdros brandished overhead, no longer in control of his own actions or mind, Kazarhan threw himself at Eidelion, a streamer of spittle trailing from the corner of his mouth as he muttered nonsensically.

As Kazarhan undertook the first spastic motions necessary to propel himself forward, before any of the companions had time to react and try to offer him any relief or succor, the chamber went completely dark and total bedlam ensued.

Yip sensed the world around him twist and warp, ripped to shreds as four monstrous beings forced their way into the unstable space occupied by Eldre'gheu's entry chamber, each positioned equidistant around the tiny dome of Light protecting the Home Guard and Four.

Even in this twisted, unholy place, he felt the world around him recoil violently in response to the Daemons' arrival, reacting in complete disavowal and rejection of their unhallowed presence.

Any one of these beings appeared to be their equal in power.

With these overwhelming sensations, simultaneous calls and warnings flew through the air as the companions sought to order themselves in response.

"Anubaraëthi!"

"Dread Lords!"

"Shield your minds!"

"Secure Kazarhan!"

"Around me!" Eidelion's clarion call rang the loudest.

Yip paid little heed to the source of each of these warnings and admonishments, however. Instead his attention remained focused upon the arrival of this latest threat and how best to respond.

In this place of Darkness, so close to their ultimate goal, standing within a stone's throw of four risen Anubaraëthi, unholy Dread Lords of the vast interdimensional wastes, this foul chamber may be as far as their quest ever achieved. If their pursuit were to end here, his mind hearkening first back to Al'Marr and then to this wretched chamber in an instant, both outcomes possible under the Cabal's dominion, then Ea'ae would be most fortunate to avoid either fate.

He was not about to let either happen.

He was not going to let their journey stop before it had reached their desired end.

Although he may die trying, there were those who would continue in his stead should he fall.

Knowing this may be the last time he ever looked upon his friends through human eyes, unable to save Kazarhan, accepting that he may face a similar fate, he stepped out of the Light and into Darkness.

Cold.

Unbearable cold.

Chill permeated his core, filling his essence with an emptiness so dark and entropic that his entire system ground to a halt.

No longer having the energy or wherewithal to move, he stood locked in place.

He could not see.

All was darkness.

He could not hear.

All was silence.

He could not feel.

All was empty.

Above everything, suffocating all other sensations and impressions, seeping closer with each absent breath was the darkness of oblivion portended by the source of his impotent enfeebleness, the four Dread Lords waited implacably while his life ebbed away. The very presence of these creatures triggered his present inertia just as they now closed in as his energy drained away.

Although his body and mind had begun to shut down despite all of the protections warding him, a constricting internal darkness closing in relentlessly on his consciousness within the blackness already encompassing his physical form, all the while losing volition and focus in the horrid presence of the vacuous Shadows, Yip clung yet to the Light left in his core. Like a tenacious woodsman tending to a sputtering flame in the cold desolation of a frozen wilderness, he sought to bring life to his internal blaze that it could rekindle anew.

The totality of his being, what little remained now under his control, he brought to bear on this one goal. So tenuous was his hold on vivacity that maintaining and restoring that smallest spark of vitality was all he could hope to accomplish. As his world shrunk around him, his awareness of his own Light within contracted as well, becoming sharper and sharper as his faculties dimmed. As the Darkness around him grew dimmer, his awareness of the Light within grew brighter, hardening and shaping his consciousness to a diamond, pushing his vision ever inward, cutting through the layers of his limitations, delusions, and preconceptions.

There, bathed within the internal brightness of his own driving Light, he saw that which he was made of sputtering and tremulous, honed by his intention, and then looked beyond.

His internal Light became a window to another, more fundamental, all-consuming perception. From this view, gazing with rapt attention at a landscape he once thought he understood profoundly but now knew he grasped only cursorily, he saw what he was and was transformed.

His *chi*, his Light, melted away and merged into the vibrant potential, the formless void of possibility from which it sprang along with all the energies and actualities of creation. Just as his essence arose and crystallized from this primordial source, so, too, did all else.

Though he was empty, he was full. Though he was separate, he was part. Though he was defined, he was without bound.

In that instant of perception, possibilities opened without limit—the universe seen in a glance.

Filled with wonder, his mind broadening while his physical reality contracted, a poem came unbidden to his mind.

> *Formless and shapeless*
> *free and without bound—*
> *the mind naturally at rest.*

Armed with a verse, enlivened by a new perspective, strengthened by novel potentialities, given life in death, he confronted the Darkness without for there was now none within.

Rapidly unfolding, restoring himself with the wellspring he had uncovered within, he exploded outward, his mind retaking his body and beyond in an explosion of internal Light. Unrestrained, he let the Light created within overflow, radiating outward in a wave of pure existence, a rush of power that gave birth to hope and vitality, a flood of energy created and reinforced as it flowed, a tide of force that he generated and fulminated within each of the Daemonic beings that towered over him in preparation for his demise.

Before the Dread Lords could move in response, before they could counter, he shared the gift he was given, simultaneously creating a fount of Light within each Daemon, a beacon of energy so pure that the Anubaraëthi melted away before the onslaught, disappearing quicker than shadows before dawn. So powerful was the blast that the entire chamber filled with Light, a luminosity so clean and fresh that any who gazed upon it temporarily forgot themselves and bathed in Its glory with the joy of the first welcome light of spring when the world was born.

Beneath this fleeting Light, restoring the brightness once residing within the walls for only a brief time, the entry chamber of the temple of Eldre'gheu lit up and was revealed—a massive arched dome, framed by carefully wrought pillars of stone now cracked and fallen, intricately carved walls crumbling and faded. Once suitable for large bodies of believers to worship but now dese-crated and befouled, its altars broken and forgotten, decayed beyond repair, the vestibule was a place where shadows sought refuge from the morn.

For the briefest moments, however, as the luminous, primal *chi* expressed by Yip filled the chamber, the expansive hall was hallowed once more and all horror and debasement forgotten.

This fleeting vision passed all too quickly.

Within moments Darkness had once again ascended within the defiled space, sucking away all light, hope, and memory of the heights of human aspiration.

Rushing toward the last vestige of Light visible in the chamber, he sprinted toward the lustrous sphere striving against the resurgent, oppressive Darkness, hoping against his own sensibilities that what he now felt was not true.

Breaking through the halo of Light he had fled, embraced in the circle of warmth around his friends and companions, his worst fears were confirmed, his impressions as visible on the faces turned to watch his arrival as those coursing through his mind.

Yet another mote of Light had left the world.

Yet another bit of hope had abandoned the temple of Eldre'gheu.

Tears visible in her eyes, Daerdros spoke for everyone. "He left us before we could ensure his safe return. There was naught we could do."

Llyewia bowed his lustrous head. "He held long enough to force the Daemon back that we may continue onward."

Arranged as carefully on the cracked, faded tiles of the dusty floor as the urgency of their current situation allowed, his thick arms crossed, callused hands laid carefully over the haft of the mighty hammer Raurdros, Kazarhan rested in peace, his torment now at an end.

Allowed only the briefest pause to recover themselves and for mourning, Eidelion now urged them forward. "Let not Kazarhan's sacrifice be in vain! We must push forward and strike down the evil that brought this fate upon him!"

Here he gazed at Yip sternly, although not entirely in disapproval. "We should be thankful that only Kazarhan fell to this ambush. We must strengthen our wards and add further protections against related mental and spiritual assaults."

"We cannot afford to be caught similarly once more."

Llyewia stepped forward at the last, his hands held to the side in offering. "I will add what protection I may against further direct supernatural incursions."

Coming first to Yip who now stood by the tall, lithe Elf's side, Llyewia drew a shimmering silver sigil, the shape reminiscent of a guiding star shining brightly in the heavens on the rounded slope of Yip's forehead.

Yip felt a slight tingling as the sigil was placed upon his skin, a rush of reassurance and power flowing into the spot with each delicate stroke of the Elf's finger. Looking upward toward where Llyewia's hand skillfully outlined his mark, though he could not see the sigil itself, he could see the Light radiating outward from his forehead. Overlaying this view with his inner vision, he could see and feel the clear brilliance of the Elven magic cascading around his head and body in a shroud, a translucent safeguard from the unknown and the unearthly.

As he described the sigil on Yip's skin, Llyewia said, "This, the mark I give to each of you, is the sign of Illendial, the North Star. Its presence will guide your spirit home should it drift or wander and protect against direct incursion by anchoring your mind to its moorings when attacked."

While the Iyela cast his spells, gracefully walking around to each party member in turn, Yip took advantage of the moment and bowed his head, wishing his former companion Kazarhan the Stout success and great joy in the last and greatest adventure ahead.

While Yip made his offering of prayer, Aroganji approached and placed a hand on his friend's shoulder in reassurance and appreciation. Waiting respectfully, he stood in place quietly until Yip opened his eyes moments later. His voice kept low, the hushed tones little more than a whisper barely detectable above the sound of his breath, he said, "We are glad you are still with us. When you stepped out of the circle of protection, though you were gone only seconds, time seemed to stand still. We had no idea if you would return."

Aroganji smiled, adding, "We are happy for your return just as we are happy for your success. You will have to tell me what exactly you did one day."

Yip nodded, briefly returning his friend's smile, albeit wryly. "Time stopped for me as well." He paused for a moment before adding, "And I, too, am glad. The Daemons gave me an opportunity and a gift. I fear the time to use it will come again too soon."

When Aroganji raised his eyebrows in curiosity, tacitly asking for more detail, Yip said, "When the time comes, I would be happy to tell you exactly what transpired." He then motioned his head toward the heart of the temple as Llyewia finished his wards. "But time is short and we must continue."

As Llyewia gave Eidelion a brief nod indicating the completion of his work, the paladin gestured forward with Archaeus, the blazing blade of the White Sword presaging their path, and said, "The time of our final confrontation is nigh! We must press onward toward the temple's black heart!"

The note of command in his voice brooked no alternative. "I will take the fore! Do not falter! Use your strengths to our advantage! If we are broken or scattered, gather around me that we may aid one another and recover."

"In this place of Darkness, we must be Lights unto each other that we do not fail, falter, or flounder! We are here to lift each other up as much as we are here to bring down this fell Shadow!"

Bowing his head, Eidelion finished with the offer of a brief benediction,

> *"Be your brother's eyes when he does not see.*
> *Be your brother's shield when he wavers.*
> *Be your brother's heart when he does not feel.*
> *Be your brother's spirit when he loses hope.*
> *Be what your brother needs that the Light may triumph!"*

"May the Light keep us, bring us strength, and allow us to persevere!"

Hoping this was not going to go on any longer, and not caring what the others thought about what he was about to say, Wrindanneth broke in, his voice flat and emotionless, "Are we done with the speeches?"

"Not to rain on anyone's caravan, but Kazarhan was killed in less time than it took to complete a sentence much less a discourse."

Lessening the bluntness of his comment, he added a bit more softly, "As much as I liked him, I'm not quite ready to join him."

With this, to Wrindanneth's complete and utter astonishment, Eidelion laughed, the sound full and hearty, rich and thrumming with vibrancy, qualities only accentuated by the horridly dolorous setting and profound silence.

"Your words ring true!"

Wrindanneth's intent reflecting both their need and the exigencies of the situation, Eidelion said nothing more, instead putting thought to action, striding ahead toward the deeper Darkness of the temple's inner sanctum, cheered that Wrindanneth was indeed looking out for his brothers in his own direct, sober, if somewhat tactless, way.

Walking en masse, weapons drawn and at the ready, clustered tightly together for each other's protection, their steps became more and more muted the farther into the expansive chamber they proceeded. Huddled together, the sounds of their steps traveled less and less distance beyond the circle of light encapsulating their presence, the walls and ceiling of the temple receding farther away with each movement.

Perhaps both were occurring simultaneously.

Each stride marked an ever greater departure from the world of their origin, a transition into a realm of tangible Shadow that swallowed the sounds of their presence as much as the Light of their hearts.

Each step was an abandonment of the realm they knew, a feeling as tangible as the hungry Darkness licking at the perimeters of Eidelion's sphere of Light.

Yip stayed close to the perimeter of the shield of Light close to the fore but slightly within its arch and behind the two leaders. He walked within the tall shadows of Orogast and Raour'Saqan, both imposing figures towering over his small form, one resembling the Daemons they fought, the other just as fearsome although scaly and more reptilian.

Neither would be a welcome sight if met alone at night or if stumbled upon by surprise.

Both fit in naturally within the confines of the temple.

Beside Orogast and Raour'Saqan, each moving lithely, flowing like clean oil from a decanter, walked Llyewia and Daerdros, both surveying and measuring the emptiness before them with the cool detachment of combat veterans, completing the arch at the fore of their armed group.

Aroganji and Wrindanneth flanked Spreesprocket who walked directly opposite Yip farthest away from their direction of travel, closing the circuit around Eidelion at the circle's center.

Floating between Eidelion and the spell casters at the rear, holding a similar but opposite position in their formation as Yip, ready to move forward or backward as necessitated, Slate shifted with the group at need.

Within the circle of Light, Yip wished to be able to move and react quickly to any threat posed from all directions outside of the sphere should he be required. Staying slightly within the perimeter of the halo of Light, he had the room and flexibility to move within and between his companions. Given this elasticity, he should not have to navigate through or over his comrades to reach the edge of the sphere if the group collapsed toward a threat. Also, although his awareness extended beyond the scope of the hemisphere of Light in which they walked, he still had a much clearer view of what lay ahead with less interference or interruption from all of the various energies emanating from, surrounding, and protecting his friends by staying near the group's fore and primary direction of movement.

What he sensed from his vantage was deeply troubling.

Lurid marks and runes, defamatory and slanderous, burned into his inner vision, carving into his sensibilities, searing an indelible etch of blasphemy upon his mind's eye. Laced through the air like streamers, interconnected and flowing with ghastly power, these glyphs painted the chamber, its walls, floor, and expanse with horrific visions of symbols and suggestions torn from the nightmares of the madly depraved.

Although he knew not what they meant or depicted, the hatred and inimical intent behind these runes were all too easy to interpret. Serving as a guide while his friends also attempted to read and decipher the risks posed by various potential paths with their own magically augmented vision, he helped navigate around, through, and between these marks and conduits of force lest encountering one trigger some unimaginable trap, nefarious artifice, or diabolical summoning.

As a result, even with multiple eyes and interpretations assisting in their progress, rapid, direct travel across the chamber was all but impossible.

Wending through this horrid quagmire, he felt like one blind to the potential risks and dangers threatening them from all directions, guiding charges with equally veiled sight.

Behind him, he heard Slate grumble, a weak jest to help combat the gloom and desolation weighing heavily upon their shoulders. "Ya'd think with aeons at their disposal tha entities 'ere could at least clean up!"

"Per'aps come up with somethin' more imaginative ta spruce tha place up! Instead, they leave tha buildin' ta go ta dust and muddy tha very air with signs and symbols, spatterin' their foul marks everywhere like a ram in heat!"

Spreesprocket laughed, wishing to spread Slate's positive resolve. "You miss a minor point, Slate. Daemons don't care! Nor do they hire interior decorators!"

Stepping forward cautiously, following Eidelion before him, Slate grumbled, "Ya'd think that if they live forever, at least tha hellspawn'd have tha discernment ta develop a sense o' taste!"

His mouth open to reply, the humor still evident and unexpressed on his face, the world exploded in light before Spreesprocket could offer his intended rejoinder.

A concussive blast of force engulfed them, followed by a cascading report echoing violently off the chamber's ceiling, walls, and floor, ricocheting from their bones and organs, ringing within their ears. Blinded by the blast, laid deaf from the resounding explosion, tears streaming from their eyes, they were unable to see the world rip open along the room's wide perimeter as raging torrents of fire consumed the space from dusty floor to lofty ceiling. Under this assault, the temple walls and floor disappeared and all darkness became a distant memory as various shades of red, orange, white, yellow, and blue flames flowed freely throughout the chamber—oxidation alive and feverishly seeking purchase.

Her mercurial words falling on deaf ears, Daerdros deftly wove a series of incantations, reinforcing the shield around them, staving off the ravenous heat and flames within a cordon of song. Behind her, his mind linked with Aroganji's, Wrindanneth cast cool waves of soothing healing over their ears and eyes, restoring their sight and hearing while Aroganji protected them against further elemental assault.

While the mages worked their Craft, protecting them from the tempestuous conflagration, Yip called out in warning, unheard even after the magic took effect for the Daemon-driven fires burned and raged so violently.

"Daemons of flame come! Their fires seek to consume us!"

Calling out in warning, he kept the swarm of emerging Daemons at the fore of his awareness, tracking their unearthly presence appearing from within the hellfires beyond the gates through which they arose, the ghastly heat of their presence turning the very air into liquid plasma. All the while, he gathered the *chi* flowing through and around them. As much as he could, as quickly as it impinged upon their dimension, he drew the energy from these flames as well, diffusing their threat and power. This *chi* he guided toward his friends, strengthening their efforts, protecting them from fatigue and the depletion of their reserves that they would be ready and able to continue the fight.

He counted at least five of the hellspawn already and he knew not how many more could be forthcoming.

Eidelion commanded as well, his clarion voice urging them to greater efforts. "Reinforce the perimeter! Hold position! Make ready before they come!"

"Daerdros! Our shields must not fail!"

"Llyewia! Spreesprocket! Prepare to counter and quench their fires!"

"Orogast! Raour'Saqan! Slate! Make ready to meet and break their charge!"

"Aroganji! Wrindanneth! Prepare to fight their fire with your own!"

"Yip! As you are!"

While the Guard and Fists reacted, countering the assault as much as possible, anticipating what was to come and making their preparations, the vast open space was no longer theirs to claim alone.

Within the unholy heat seeking hold on their plane, risen from the heart of a dying star, Daemons of the flame, the dread Anubavaeri, tore through the feeble barriers separating dimensions, the hunger of their fires preceding them.

Massive, inchoate, and rippling with cascading energies and dancing flames, the Anubavaeri erupted from the surging holocaust spilling from the rips in the fabric between planes—interdimensional solar flares arching through the heavens seeking purchase, fuel, and a new world to burn.

The room glowed red, the air wavering and watery beneath the growing heat presaging the Daemons' presence, sparking and flashing with gouts and bursts of light as excited air molecules jumped phase states between gas and plasma. Their quarry set, the Anubavaeri flew haughtily atop the tremulous pyres, the stone boiling and turning to molten slag beneath them, flowing like lava within the tremendous heat of their presence.

The direct assault that marked their arrival was more fearsome even than their appearance.

Swirling side-by-side, one around the other, two Anubavaeri opened their hellish maws in tandem, a glimpse into the death of stars and the birth of misery, and loosed roiling gouts of white-hot flames, churning through the air in fiendish, spiraling vortices. Opposite, on the far side of the room, another

Daemon gestured a flame-shrouded appendage and called forth feverish fires to rain down from the heavens. One surging Daemon dove through the floor immediately upon emerging from the portals, as easily as leaping into placid waters on a warm summer's day, melting the earth beneath its feet as it tunneled toward them only to explode upward from the ground in a showering gout of fire, molten rock, slag, and shards of siliceous glass. With a terrific shrug of its massive amorphous limbs, the last spawn of twisted, fallen stars slashed an arm casually through a massive defaced pillar, slicing through the finely grained marble, knocking the crumbling column toward the huddled companions, felling it like some ancient petrified tree.

As quickly as the Daemons appeared, the onslaught occurred too rapidly to be neutralized given all the simultaneous threats and exigencies arising with the fiends' arrival.

The Home Guard and Four were just as fast, however.

Springing to the air, Raour'Saqan leapt upward, breathing his own tumultuous, all-consuming black flames, vaporizing the massive marble column before it could crash into them. When his breath cleared, not even dust from the column remained.

Llyewia threw both arms upward in an expression of exultation. With the invocation, manifesting the motion, the luminous dome protecting them was showered with nitid starshine whose cool radiance diffused both the all-consuming inferno surging around the shield of Light and the conflagration that rained down upon them relentlessly from above.

Yip drew away these energies at their source, lessening their power and delaying their reemergence, depriving the springs and streams that sourced a river of the water necessary to flow.

Aroganji coalesced the air about them in a roiling whirlwind, gathering a swirling mass above their heads, casting away the molten debris that continued to bombard, pock, and riddle the ground around them.

Slate called forth the flames of Daerdaana'Duin, intensifying his fiery aura, in preparation to charge. When the beasts slackened or wavered, he would be ready. If they did neither, they would need to be prepared for him.

Wrindanneth countered their attack, casting a cone of blistering cold that discharged through the air in a swirling maelstrom slamming into and around the Daemon raining fire upon them, meeting the Anubavaeri's heat with the chill and finality of winter's entropic breath.

Orogast clapped both twisted, corded arms together, releasing a concussive wall of force smashing the nearest Daemon that had erupted from the ground full in the chest with the blast.

Seeing an opportunity before the Daemons closed, for Daerdros had deflected the Daemons' initial fires presaging their arrival, Llyewia had countered the Daemons' direct flames, Raour'Saqan had parried their first strike, Aroganji had deflected the debris from their blasts, and Yip had at least temporarily weakened and diffused their nascent fires, Spreesprocket grabbed a multicolored velvet pouch at his waist and put thought to action. Saying a few mumbled words of summoning, he turned the receptacle upside down, shaking the delicately wrought bag firmly with the focus of one trying to clean out the last bits of lint and dirt from within the bag's confines.

When nothing came out, he sighed, turned the bag over and began fishing around within its confines. His arm in to the shoulder, the fire Daemons now fully emerged from their hellish dimension into this limbo between worlds, he grunted and flipped the pouch over, pulling downward as he did so.

A self-satisfied smile on his face, for he had found what he was after with time to spare, he watched three shiny clockwork bots tumble out clanging onto the cracked tile floor. Small mechanical keys located in the centers of their lower backs whirled as they righted themselves somewhat clumsily, standing of their own awkward accord.

Located above the rotating keys, resting snugly over their blocky shoulders, were bright red backpacks with the words, 'To Serve and to Save' written in carefully stenciled letters. From these backpacks, looping over the rounded slope of their upper arms, were corrugated, bright yellow tubes that descended to shiny brass nozzles with a shut-off valve and rubberized grip handle held tightly in each of their right hands.

The small Paratechnological robots vaguely resembled rough-hewn male Gnomes in structure, each with a distinct likeness. They were not stocky like a Dwarf nor overly lithe like an Elf. Luminous gemstone eyes lit their beardless faces providing a faint light visible both within and without. Bulbous, shiny metallic noses protruded above mouths currently held in loose smiles resembling that of their master.

Each wore reflective orange and yellow outfits, including pants and a jacket, akin in appearance to heavy rain slickers worn by some fishermen in cold, storm-ravaged waters. Rugged black boots protruded from beneath their garish pants. At their waists, thick leather belts were arrayed with multiple loops and hanging pockets holding tools and implements of every shape and sort suspended for later use. Tinted goggles were strapped tightly across their heads beneath flared red helmets, currently resting on their foreheads should they be needed to deal with a particularly problematic emergency.

Each clockwork bot stood about knee height to Spreesprocket and all turned to face him as they righted themselves, standing at loose attention while waiting for direction.

Spreesprocket got right to business. "SAVERS! We are faced with a Level 4 interdimensional incursion of Order C naught delta intensity with a Code 11 grade amber risk factor."

No one was paying particular attention to Spreesprocket, which was the normal course of events although that never distracted him from important tasks at hand. Even if they were, no one aside from the clockwork rescue bots would understand a word he was saying otherwise. Unfazed by Spreesprocket's direction, the bots waited patiently for their full set of instructions.

All the while, combustion incarnate bore down upon them with inconceivable intensity.

"You are to neutralize this threat with a Vector 3 prime counter utilizing a Type 15 first order Class M MAFS annulment."

Looking from each one to the next, he finished decisively, "Am I clear?"

When there was no response, he finished, "Initiate countermeasures!"

Clicking their metallic heels together with a *clang* only partially muffled by their boots, the rescue bots saluted, turned about upon their left heels, and marched out of the halo of Light into which they had been summoned.

Although this series of commands would have normally taken much longer, employing the particular hyperkinetic language of Gnomes, the exchange had taken only the briefest of seconds.

Unconcerned with the extradimensional holocaust rapidly closing in upon them from all directions, the bumbling, trundling clockwork bots fanned out equidistant from one another in a rough triangle around the companions who were now working frenetically within their protective sphere, engrossed in their own individual efforts in response to the coming Daemons. Without need to look or signal for they were connected to each other magically without need for explicit communications, the three bots simultaneously reached across their chests with their left arms, snapped back hidden faces on their wrists to reveal luminous touch screens, quickly input several key sequences on the recessed devices, and then, bracing themselves with their left legs slightly forward and their right legs slightly back, released the shut-off valves at their wrists, gripping with both hands around the handle of their hoses as they did so.

With the sound of unused machinery squealing on reluctantly in grating fits and starts, a series of loud gurgles, followed by numerous violent heaves from within the tubing leading to the spray nozzles, the room once more exploded into white, or, rather, white exploded into the room.

Clouds of achromatic foam extinguishing agents filled the chamber, a blizzard of magically enhanced nonflammable, intumescent, anti-oxidative reagents jumping on the winds of flames broadcast with mechanical diligence as the mechanical clockworks bots marched across the chamber. With each step, the frothing foam spread farther and faster, the Daemonic flames a catalyst for the expansion and growth of the reactive, fire extinguishing spume.

While the bots meticulously sprayed their foam across the chamber in all directions, pushing forward toward the blazing fire Daemons encircling them, Spreesprocket called out to his companions, "Prepare to strike!"

"When the Daemons are coated in the MAFS agent by the clockwork rescue bots, attack!"

"Fire Daemons without flames are hardly Daemons at all!"

Encased in scintillating flames, Slate charged after one SAVERS bot while Raour'Saqan and Orogast each followed another in preparation to douse the Daemons' flames permanently.

The highly volatile MAFS foam hungrily followed the currents of the unholy infernos, quenching the heat and solidifying beneath Slate's feet as he ran as quickly as possible while avoiding the ruinous bands of wards and energies lacing the chamber, the intumescent foam not impeding his progress in the slightest, finally leaping from magical flames to their extradimensional source. With shear and utter finality, the magical froth fully encased each Daemon in turn, leaving their fearsome forms locked mid-motion, struggling futilely in a timeless tableau as though frozen in a block of ice, consuming their flames with simple, unremarkable inevitability.

Moving faster than Slate toward their intended targets despite the perverse enchantments sullying the air, Orogast and Raour'Saqan's wings beat mightily as they sped through the chamber, following the clockwork bots' magic to the origin of the profane disturbance. With a series of violent explosions, Orogast and Raour'Saqan crashed through the static, quenched, and crippled Daemons who were now unable to flow out of the way or react to defend themselves, their ire and ability dowsed as much as their fires. White particulates, the last remnants of the expansive foam, showered through the room with the impact. Slate followed suite, slashing and carving with Duraeleon while his axe sang the praises of Daemons defeated, until all the baleful creatures had been similarly dispatched.

Where before fire had reigned, now there was foam.

Washing his hands eagerly, Spreesprocket gave his final orders to the SAVERS clockwork bots. "SAVERS! Your work here is done! Please gather the contaminated extradimensional remnants for cleaning, treatment, and further reprocessing! Then return to me!"

Wrindanneth turned to look downward at his small companion, cocked an eyebrow and said, "What are you after Spreesprocket?"

"Not only do we wish to remove any source of potential corruption caused, potentially caused, or at risk of being caused in the future by the Fire Daemons' presence, remnants, and residual resonance structures, a situation which was avoided due to their complete annihilation with our previous contact with the Dread Lords, but the *oedenara*, the Daemons' hearts, as crystallized and refined summations of their highly kinetic essences, have multiple practical uses to which they will be applied with proper handling and refinement in the hands of a skilled magician or Paratechnologist."

Aroganji, ever curious, particularly in light of the performance and current remediation activities of the bustlingly efficient clockwork bots who were rapidly erasing all signs of their presence from within the chamber without fear or regard for another similar attack, interjected, "So they will be converted to Paratechnological devices at your direction?"

Spreesprocket grinned. "If we are lucky enough to return home alive, I can think of several cannon and blaster types along with a variety of hand-held hand-to-hand armaments in addition to myriad defense and support applications that could use just this sort of power and storage source! In fact, I have detailed schematics designed, ready, and stored in pre-fabrication waiting for just these to build around."

Driving his point home, he then looked at each of them in turn wickedly, the glint of excitement visible in his large, dark eyes. "What evokes more fear than Daemon fire raining down upon your enemies?"

Waiting a moment, but not long enough for either to supply an answer, he said excitedly, "Give up?"

When neither Aroganji nor Wrindanneth answered in the short time he gave, for it was clear he had his answer and wanted to share it without regard to their opinions, eagerly pushing forward with his own reply before they could, the Gnome finished happily, practically bouncing from foot to foot with his overflowing enthusiasm, "Magically augmented, amplified, and channeled Daemon fire!"

"Bigger, better, faster?" Wrindanneth laughed.

Washing his hands, Spreesprocket finished, "More, more, and more!"

Aroganji shook his head. "Sounds like the Paratechnologists' motto!"

Spreesprocket laughed.

While Wrindanneth, Aroganji, and Spreesprocket had their short conversation, the rest of the group remained on guard, continually scanning and assessing the room.

Not brooking any further delay should another ambush manifest, Eidelion shouted, "To me! Resume positions!"

Orogast and Raour'Saqan circled downward from where they flew scanning the room's perimeter for any more disturbances, quickly returning to the fore of the circle of holy Light put out by Archaeus's gleaming blade. Slate, encompassed by a nimbus as bright as that protecting his friends, sprinted back to his position as quickly as his short Dwarven legs would allow.

When all were within easy earshot, Eidelion said, "I am confident that we will face several more ambushes such as this prior to meeting our foe face-to-face. We must remain vigilant and hope that we are indeed up to the task."

"Are all enchantments still active? Does anyone need or have any requests for supplemental protection?"

Daerdros answered for everyone. "We will react at need."

Thinking of his own direct encounter with the Dread Lords and the extra protections afforded by the Heart of Yere, Llyewia's ward, and his ability, Yip offered, "In light of the strength of our foes, are there any additional protections on our essences both from direct assault, siphoning, perversion, and drainage that may supplement the ward cast by Llyewia?"

Daerdros spoke again. "We have a full suite of shields addressing physical, psychic and extradimensional assault. If these wards fail, it was not for want of variety and proper application, only strength and duration as was the unfortunate case with Kazarhan. Under these circumstances, given our limited time and pressing need, we can hope, at best, for the opportunity to refresh any wards that do fall or fail."

Yip bowed, not knowing what was possible in this regard but accepting that their protections were, if not perfect, as good as they were going to be and that they did not have the time or opportunity to dawdle for the next assault could come at any moment. "Understood."

Echoing Daerdros's comments, Eidelion added, "So long as the Light of Archaeus holds, there is no greater protection that could be had for all in short order. We are fortunate indeed for such a boon."

"Is there aught else before we proceed?'

When no one else offered any more suggestions or concerns, he said, "Then let us be off with the Light's blessing!"

Though the Daemons' passage did not trigger any reaction from the magical currents and baleful runes hanging ominously in the air, phantoms groping for purchase in a world lost to them, the Home Guard and Four could not count themselves so lucky. Once more, despite their recent victory, they proceeded with caution, concern for their continued safety overriding the urgency of their need.

There was no other choice.

Despite best efforts, regardless of care, not all traps can be avoided. Nor are all traps triggered. Some lay in wait, prepared and eager to pounce upon the unsuspecting and unwary. Others strike no matter how primed or cognizant their targets for initiative goes to the one acting first.

The victims then are left to react, and, if lucky and survive, to recover.

Yip's senses were taut, reaching around them as fully and completely as possible, reading currents and perturbations lost to even the most subtle sensors. The air surrounding him quavered with power, tainted and defiled, twisted and unnatural, debased for profane ends and horrific purpose. This corruption entered him, filled him, sullied him, but found no purchase for there was nothing on which to hold, nothing on which to cling.

He was full just as he was empty.

Despite this readiness, despite this uncanny prescience, despite his preternatural reactions and timing, beyond his sphere of immediate influence the universe unfolded without regard to his will or whim, dictated by chains of causation far from his control, interlinked with possibilities and potentialities outside human ken or command.

Such was his situation and such were his limitations.

He could, at best, react accordingly to the dictates of a given situation in such a way as to achieve the maximal benefit for all his companions, if such a thing could be said to exist, in such a way as to ensure their continued health, well-being, and development. He could not act or react for them. He could only be a guide, whether urging, coaxing, or attempting to foster a particular result. Ultimately, he could no more control his friends' actions than he could the interlinked causes that culminated in a particular expression of actuality, in a particular effect.

Knowing and understanding these fundamental limitations, he remained as constrained as any other person when forced to react to the dictates of necessity.

Orogast read the mutable lines of change flowing within and around him. Reality was in flux in this place on multiple levels, scales, and degrees. All of this change was natural and to be expected, including that of supernatural origin and influence, although not all of this change could be anticipated.

Though he remained on guard, for, despite the unnatural beauty and complexity of these formations, there remained significant risk both to himself and his companions, he could not help but explore and appreciate the manifestations of order, change, and entropy within this timeworn temple. There were abundant wondrously complex expressions of the laws of interaction, interdependency, and mutuality to be considered and internalized within these walls. Given enough time and liberty, he would welcome the prospect to stay and study here as an unheralded opportunity.

The need of his companions, the bindings of his oaths, and his continual commitment to the realization of their shared unfolding intentions, prevented him this elusive chance, however. He would not be able to leave the guise he had assumed to become invisible here, to move unnoticed. Nor would he be able to forego his powerful defensive stance without unwarranted risk to his *jueran'al*, his brothers-in-living-ideation.

Thus, despite his desire for choice, he only had those allowed within the framework of their shared *lael'darnael*, their common mission-view-survival-path. Therefore, he gleaned as much as he could from the unique expressions of living energy, of life's purpose, pulsing around him, though it may be abhorrent to those who did not arise and develop within such a harsh evolutionary landscape.

Slate was eager to be done with this whole affair.

He had seen enough otherworldly phantasms in this one place to last a lifetime. Not only that but a venerable Dwarf who had offered him access to the inner insights and traditions of his forefathers, mysteries hidden from all but a few now living, had been struck down without the chance to properly defend himself and fight his foe hand-to-hand, face-to-face.

Such an act of cowardice would not go unavenged.

Now this erstwhile teacher, so recently met, was but a phantom himself.

He ground his teeth as they slunk along like beaten dogs through the twisted labyrinth of the unclean Daemonic magics.

This pit was dirtier even than a deranged Troll clan's offal pit.

Though he was eager to be finished, he was also eager to be the one here doing the cleansing. Daemon's, like Trolls, needed someone to clean up after them.

The right Dwarf was now here to do the chore.

So what if he made more mess in the process?

Aroganji could not believe the sheer complexity, breadth, and completeness of the Daemon-wrought enchantments flowing through the air. Though tainted by a twisted intelligence, the vastness of scope and intricacy of the weavings coupled with the skill in application showed him that the supernatural intelligence behind the creation and warding of this forsaken limbo was formidable beyond human ken.

The power brought to bear in order to create one of the enchantments in this room, much less the ones protecting the entire temple or the ones used to translate this dimension into another were humbling indeed.

Studying that which had been wrought here over the aeons since human departure, he hoped that they were up to the task of ridding this place of the malevolence that had corrupted it.

He feared they were not.

Wrindanneth looked forward to their next challenge for that was exactly what they were facing.

Each step of their journey to this temple, both through the neglected, haunted city and within these walls, was a test. Each obstacle placed in their path had been a challenge, not only an attempt to dispatch them but a means to gauge and gather their measure, determine what they were truly capable of as a group, and then counter their strengths with another obstacle.

Though some may fear that such a path might not end with any option other than failure, he did not for he knew that with each continued success, their opponent's array of options grew more limited not broader.

Grinning wickedly to himself, he remembered one powerful lesson imparted by his teacher—just as an opponent learns about you with each encounter, so, too, do you have an opportunity to learn of them.

Knowledge is a knife that cuts both ways.

He was eager to begin carving.

Eidelion did not share Wrindanneth's eagerness.

Though his faith carried and lifted him, for he had overcome powerful extradimensional foes in the past, he was not desirous for a series of continual engagements where they were whittled down and weakened.

What concerned him was why they were not challenged more fully. Why did their foe not attempt to overwhelm them with the power it had coveted for millennia?

In the city, its minions had tried to do just that, but they were poor substitutes for a being of true Power.

He had hoped that navigating the city's gauntlet, demonstrating their own strength, would draw the temple's master out, that their success would force the city's conqueror to seek to engage them as a credible threat. Instead, they continued pushing through engagement after engagement while their foe waited in a position of ever growing strength.

Though one could never control the ebb and tide of battle, he had hoped it would flow differently.

He had already lost one good man.

He did not wish to lose more.

Daerdros sang.

She sang quietly, internally so that none could hear, but fully and deeply nonetheless. She let the song fill her with its majesty and power, its convolutions and entanglements, and its arias and choruses. Her tune was ancient and deep, hidden within the wellspring of her being, passed down from the mothers and fathers of her people to those who had taken up the blade and made it sing for them, ringing with each stroke through the movements and refrains of time.

This song built within her, gathering strength, reinforcing her own as she lent it hers, lifting her up just as she lifted her song upward, ever upward, through the vaults of her mind and over the threshold of her spirit.

There would soon be a reckoning.

When that time came, she would sing.

Her music, the music of her forebears, would flow.

Then her foe would hear her and tremble.

Then her foe would weep at the majesty of her song,

Then her foe would cower at the power and despair of her dirge.

Yip sensed a change in the air. There was a difference within the nature of the very air around them. Something had shifted, but he could not pinpoint a single source or direction for the disturbance.

Alerted, he began to turn his head backward toward his friends to tell them, "Be alert! Something has changed." However, he could not direct his head backward. He could only move forward. When he breathed, his stomach, diaphragm, and chest only moved in the same direction as their slow, steady march.

His friends would notice this transition soon, if they had not done so already. "A trap has been triggered. We can no longer move backward."

Slate laughed. "Not that we're goin' anywhere else!"

Clarifying, he said, "Nor can we turn to face backward."

"The spider has now caught the flies." Wrindanneth's assessment was apt. Though they had yet to meet the spider, its presence was felt, its sinister designs constantly unfolding.

"Unless we manage the trap's counter, we are now forced to push forward." Yip did not like the idea of only being able to maneuver and see easily in one direction, though neither would limit his effectiveness. Such a situation only called for creative responses.

"Into another trap?" Aroganji offered his comment rhetorically.

"If we are flanked or attacked from behind, we will be at a strong disadvantage. Also, for those responses requiring physical motion either via spell or blade, our reactions to any attack will no longer be natural." Daerdros summarized their predicament succinctly, not needing to add any additional discussion.

Yip agreed, however, he added, "Awareness need not be limited by direction or magic. If a foe approaches from behind, I will alert you to its position as soon as I detect its presence."

He had been experimenting with the trap's limitations while they talked. "As Daerdros implied, we can still face backward, although not as we are accustomed. We must be moving forward to do so. Therefore, our counters may have to rely on area of effect for maximal potency, but we will still be able to respond, each in our own way."

Aroganji added, "Not all of us have Yip and Llyewia's extended sensory perceptions. However, I will give us an extended faculty that will complement our currently magically enhanced sensibilities."

"What do you propose?" Eidelion needed to judge whether the option Aroganji proposed was the response required to meet their needs.

"Enhanced sonar." Aroganji waited but a moment to let his proposition sink in for he feared that another attack was imminent. "Magically enhanced sonar capable of detecting both corporeal and spectral energies."

"You can do that?" Wrindanneth was impressed. He was not familiar with a spell that could do both at once.

Aroganji laughed. "With your help!"

Wrindanneth smiled while Eidelion nodded, adding, "Time is of the essence."

Aroganji concurred as well, his mind already open to Wrindanneth's. He would use his knowledge of elemental air magics coupled with Wrindanneth's mastery of the arcana to meld together two distinct disciplines and create a dual-purpose spell.

Sharing his intimate knowledge of the winds, of their currents and perturbations, their flow and reactions to disturbance, he provided a framework on which Wrindanneth could interlace his own knowledge of the movements and shifts of magical energy and phenomena. Guided by a shared intent, they interwove a complex fabric from two distinct specialties, united by common purpose and focused will. Once formalized and understood, despite the resulting spell's complexity, the casting was rather brief.

Channeling Wrindanneth's knowledge with his own, Aroganji raised his arms, forced to slowly walk forward as he gestured to describe the proper evocative motions since he could not move back, and uttered a brief incantation.

With a sharp downturn of his arms, Aroganji finished his chant sharply, casting his arms downward toward his hips. At the completion of his invocation, a net of magical energies fell upon the companions and their minds were opened.

Finished, a slight smile on his face for succeeding in something so challenging, Aroganji said, "Use what time we now have to get accustomed to your new sense. I fear another attack will soon be forthcoming."

Eidelion understood the imperative for a prepared response given the now limited options at their disposal. Reiterating and expanding upon Aroganji's point, he said, "With the extended awareness provided by Aroganji and Wrindanneth, we should be able to avoid and compensate for some of the disadvantages forced upon us by this curtailed freedom of movement should the need arise. As we move forward, experiment with your newfound perceptual capabilities. Test the limits of this perception so that you are comfortable with the transition should the time come when you need it."

"We will need to adjust our formation slightly to compensate for our directional limitations. Spreesprocket, Wrindanneth, Aroganji, and Slate, face backward as we move forward so that we are not easily flanked and are in a position to respond appropriately. If area-of-effect spells are required elsewhere, respond as normal. If hand-to-hand combat is required, shift backward by holding position and allow Slate to take the point while giving you the room you require to cast spells."

Offering rare praise, he added, "We shall need to consider adding your spell to our normal defensive repertoire for the Home Guard."

Not wishing for any further delay or comment, however, he finished forcefully, "Onward!"

Aroganji and Wrindanneth admired their handiwork together, though the room remained dark and frightful, corrupted by untold desecrations, its secrets now appeared, at least on some levels, to be revealed, now having a lantern to see within the darkness of a large cave. Their sense of position and relationship to their surroundings expanded in very much the same way that Wrindanneth was accustomed when merging his consciousness with the sensory apparatuses of the airship.

Wrindanneth, in fact, felt very much at home within the extended sphere of awareness. Aroganji, having experienced the same expansion of mind indirectly through their mental connection was likewise familiar with the sensation. He was, however, also quite pleased that they had managed to recreate a similar perception on their own improvisationally.

Raour'Saqan remained unmoved.

Through the ages, he had, both willingly and unwillingly, been trapped within many dens of iniquity. Each time, he, along with his fellows if he had them, had successfully fought their way out of the spider's lair.

The Shaur'Daus thrived on adversity, lived for the thrill of triumph over creatures of Darkness. Though his ire had cooled and tempered over the long, empty years along with the thrill of the hunt and vanquishing of his foes that had driven him as a hatchling, his unwavering determination and purpose remained.

Though he no longer craved the rich taste of his enemies' blood, the feel of their flesh rending and tearing, or the pulse of their life force rushing out from their failing bodies into his own, he still relished the same end.

Victory.

This day would be no different.

Trapped within a spider's web, the most direct path out was often through the spider.

Orogast sensed the time had come to shed his current form.

The Shades of the city were behind them. Daemons were before them. Just as Daemons are the natural rulers of Shades, so, too, did Daemons have their natural counters. Elementals, those spirits manifesting the native energies of the lands that Daemons desecrate, ravage, and destroy were one. Beatific heavenly beings such as seraphs were another. Daemon hunters, such as the Dracodaeran Shaur'Daus represented yet another counter.

Elementals he had seen, elementals he knew. He had drawn upon their power and taken their form after many chance encounters.

Daemon hunters he had worked with many times over the aeons, although few were as formidable as Raour'Saqan.

Celestial beings were another matter. Although beings from the lower planes often intruded upon the material planes, beings from the celestial realms seldom materialized within other dimensions. Their concerns were often of a far different order, following courses beyond the knowledge and understanding of most mortals.

In his time traveling the cosmos and dimensions beyond, he had encountered only a handful of heavenly beings that had revealed themselves in all their grace and majesty.

Only two had allowed him contact.

His was not the power to create or destroy but to duplicate. He could, given proper study and practice, replicate any creature provided he could draw upon power sufficient enough to reproduce their form and abilities. If not, his creation would fail, he could be injured or worse, or he would generate only a poor, weakened likeness.

Through thousands of years of training, he had reached the pinnacle of his abilities. His command of change, of matter and magic's commingled potential, was the equal of any of his kind. He could and had taken the form of

Dragons, of Daemons, of elementals, and of noncorporeal spirits, Specters, and ghosts.

He had never once attempted to take the form of a celestial being.

The strength of a given form required an exacting toll of commensurate power for its contrivance and continued maintenance—a mask, once created, could not simply be picked up and reused after formation, it had to be refreshed and renewed based on the needs required of that particular entity.

Heavenly beings required energy beyond conception just as some created and harnessed energy beyond envisioning.

He could never hope to wear such a guise for long unless he learned to function fully within its form.

But he could try to take one on.

Perhaps, for once, the condensed energies of this place could be put to commendable use.

Perhaps the time had come to try.

Resolved, Orogast stopped walking, his motions now internal.

"Orogast!" Alarmed, Daerdros called Orogast's name when he stopped moving without so much as a word, fearing that he was in danger, perhaps under attack like Kazarhan.

Yip answered for the Jira S'al Alann. "He is changing. His will is gathered. Soon his transformation will commence."

"Are we never gonna get movin'?"

Slate's frustration boiled over. "Where's tha urgency? Are we not in grave peril, danger that increases tha longer we dawdle?"

Her concern alleviated, her tension released, Daerdros replied, "If Orogast has decided to change, there is good reason for it. He has seen enough to surmise how best to use his abilities. We should not question his judgment in this regard."

Chastened, but unswayed, Slate countered, "I'm not questionin' his judgment, merely his timin'!"

Intrigued, Yip watched the budding energetic process unfolding, still mindful of his surroundings for beauty and wonder can be found even amidst despair and horror. As he observed, Orogast's *li* changed, reinventing his essence, shifting from one fundamental type to another—a caterpillar within a chrysalis of conscious intent transforming into a butterfly of the mind.

The external manifestations of this inward direction were fascinating. Yip watched Orogast's energy, those fundamental forces composing his essential character and form, fold inward upon themselves, shifting in color, shape, and intensity. To his inner vision and perceptions, he experienced his companion's budding transformation as a flower folding inward upon itself, closing its petals for the night. What form of final expression, what flower reemerged with the forthcoming dawn of Orogast's inner vision, he could not say, only that the process itself was wondrous, a spectacle that he was honored to have the opportunity to behold.

As his inner light turned inward, directed to physical transfiguration, Orogast's energies intensified, brightening and clarifying as his internal vision resolved itself upon a singular point.

Yip was astounded at the skill, attention, and breadth of knowledge and insight required to perform such a complex, multi-directional task. The dedication necessitated to successfully undertake such a prodigious, transformative feat filled him with awe.

Orogast's energies continued to contract, refracting and concentrating his essence into a tighter, brighter point of white light with each passing moment. At its brightest, when Yip felt Orogast's concentrated energy so intensely that he instinctively felt the need to raise his hands to shield his eyes though the gesture would do nothing to affect his inner vision, he sensed that something was going wrong.

Orogast's inner flame began to dim, the light within beginning to fade.

Yip reacted instinctively.

Though he could not fully understand the process Orogast was undertaking, though he could not hope to replicate the transformative journey his companion had begun, he could feel that his friend did not have access to the requisite resources required in order to complete the metamorphosis he had envisioned.

He could help where his friend faltered.

Without hesitation, Yip began funneling energy into his friend, serving only as a temporary way station guiding unharnessed power into Orogast's waning effort.

The process took much more power than he would have imagined. He became so enmeshed in the operation of transferring energy to Orogast that he lost track of his surroundings, that he lost sight of the wonder in change that had first beguiled him, leaving him locked in a race to shift more and more power to the shapeshifter.

Engrossed, completely committed, the next attack began.

Thundering vibrations filled the chamber, rocking the floor beneath their feet. The ground did not roil with the oscillations, rather the space containing the floor and all around it shifted in response to the fluctuating tremors.

An attendant psychological resonance echoed deeply through the companions with a dissonant surreality akin to feeling the remembered oscillations of waves lapping against the skin in the surf despite having long left the ocean and its motions behind. Though the reverberations felt imagined or remembered, the vibrations were, in fact, very real.

Each tremor marked the opening of a portal into the tremulous realms of nightmare. Each seism marked the realization of one person's doom. Each quake released some unsuspecting person's nightmare into the world.

Chitinous, scaled, and carapaced; insectile, arachnoid, and reptilian; slavering, grimacing, and growling; massive and minute; cleanly lined and twisted; of more shapes and varieties than one mind would ever conjure, rank upon rank of horrid Incubuses and Infernals clawed, oozed, leapt, sprinted, floated, and flew from within the dark pits of deepest fantasy.

They were overwhelmed and surrounded, outnumbered and facing outstanding odds against survival.

Their situation grim, for these creatures were indeed powerful, each imbued with the strength and endurance of nightmares, Eidelion commanded his troops valiantly. "Though we give it our all, Archaeus's shield cannot hold against all of these fell horrors! We must destroy as many as possible before they reach the bounds of our shield!"

"Do not waver!"

"Do not doubt!"

"Destroy them!"

Unable to abandon Orogast, Yip, however, was incapable of aiding his other companions.

Though time was short, for he had but the briefest moments until the Daemons closed, he redoubled his efforts, channeling as much *chi* as he was able to Orogast for the fire his friend attempted to kindle appeared insatiable.

Long seconds passed.

He distantly sensed the spells his friends were releasing to stem the coming tsunami—annihilating black breath from Raour'Saqan's ebony maw, arrow after arrow of coruscating blasts of starshine from Llyewia, gouts of elemental fire from Aroganji, bolts of arcane lightning from Wrindanneth, spiraling discharges of magical plasma from Spreesprocket, subtle protections interwoven through and about them from Daerdros, founts of the building fires of the Daerdaana'Duin from Slate, and prayers and supplications, boons of might and protection, from Eidelion.

To these efforts, he added nothing.

He also vaguely sensed the inhuman presence of the dark, otherworldly creatures rushing toward them, an overwhelming tide preparing to annihilate them before their onrush. Though the storm of violence unleashed by his companions mowed down rank upon rank of ghastly Specters—burnt, blasted, disintegrated, fried, broken, and shattered—where one monstrosity fell, many more took its place.

Soon he would have no choice. Soon he would have to abandon Orogast to the conflagrations of his own creation that their own lights might continue to burn.

He had but moments.

With a last burst of effort, unable to meet Orogast's need by gathering and funneling the energies flowing through and around them alone, he resorted to his one remaining option—opening the generative wellspring of the Dragon's Gate.

With one final effort, his mind opened, and the room filled with a soundless detonation of blindingly intense, empyreal white Light.

Orogast emerged transfigured.

Though he struggled mightily, all his efforts to resist were in vain.

The way of his people, the Wieru S'al Alann, dictated how to live and respond to change that the individual, that the race, may survive. Dispassion within flux, objectivity within change, and perspective within mutable form were binding principles for the path of his people.

Without dispassion, one may lose sight of one's true self and become lost, enamored, beguiled, or blinded by a novel form, its uniqueness, wonder, and newly discovered abilities.

Without objectivity, one might lose understanding of the reasons for change —survival, actualization, and continual development—risking growing static, risking death or devolution, or risking bias by the view of the world as colored by the perceptual lens of the novel form adopted through transformation.

Without perspective, a fundamental sense of the universe's nature and the role of life within it, one risked loss of desire to survive and grow, to continually change and adapt. Without perspective, all risked becoming meaningless.

Orogast risked losing all of this and more.

Each new form came with its own feelings and perceptions, sensations and experience. In a very real sense, each physical transformation changed the one undergoing metamorphosis. Not only was one's skin altered by the Wieru S'al Alann, with each shift in form what one considered oneself and how one related to the world altered as well.

Guises were not only adopted, they were lived.

What he now experienced was too much.

Eyes opened, the world was all radiance and Light.

Even this den of iniquity, polluted and befouled by aeons of depraved rituals from Daemonic forces, was a fount of effusive resplendence. The effulgence, the glory, overwhelmed his sensibilities, breaking down the walls of selfhood, opening his eyes to boundless potential and Light.

He had no choice.

He could resist no longer.

Orogast was no more.

A being of absolute, pellucid white Light hovered empyrean, risen, and glorious, at the periphery of the Archaeus's luminous shield. So bright, so pure, was its Light that the holy shield of the White Sword appeared dim.

This transubstantiated being rose amidst a halo of majesty and ineffable exaltation. All around within the wash of its sacred Light, its refulgent corona filling the space from distant walls to lofty ceiling, lit by the divine being's holy splendor, lay the uncounted ranks of twisted corpses, monstrosities granted a glimpse of Light in their final throes of existence, their presence rarified by the angelic magnificence.

With this rush of sacred energy, within the exultation of its uplifting brilliance, all horrific afflictions, bewitchments, glamours, and false arcana were washed clean. Although broken and decayed, neglected and in a near calamitous state of disrepair, the chamber was now free of the dreadful depravations, the ruinous witchery, and debased Daemonic taint that had sullied and laid thick upon its crumbling walls for uncounted centuries.

This vision of perfection remained still for but a moment, fleetingly caught unawares by its own apotheosis.

With but a momentary pause of luminous recognition, the celestial being showered them with a brief rapturous beam, granting them a heavenly boon. With that last generous offering, what had once been Orogast vanished, now unfettered by the bonds of the *jueran'al*, the winding way of the Wieru S'al Alann completed.

As surprised as they were transfixed, the companions stood captivated, lost in wonder, as their former friend rose exultant in a plume of fiery Light, liberated from his past, his very presence sufficient to save them from the ravenous horde closing in upon them and cleanse the desecrated antechamber of Eldre'gheu.

The air yet shimmered with Orogast's departed radiance, a Light that would abide in this room for a time, keeping the Darkness without temporarily at bay.

Yip watched rapt.

The very air was alive with motes of resonating incandescence. He basked within the afterglow of stars come to life, the *chi* pervading the place so thinly before now risen forth triumphant and effusive, filled with undiluted potential.

If Orogast's ascension was a wonder, and their survival a gift, appreciating his remaining glory was an observance.

Finally, it was Slate who spoke first, perhaps because he was least distracted by internal reflection. "Made quite an entrance there"—he paused for a brief moment in consideration—"and exit."

For once all but speechless, Wrindanneth merely concurred with an understated, muted, "Aye." One day, he, too, aspired to such heights. Then even Maeth Onai would tip his head in respect.

Filling the lingering silence, Yip said, "His path has reached its end...and a new beginning."

Aroganji spoke then, the gratitude and wonder clearly heard in his voice. "His rebirth gave us ours."

"He will be missed." Daerdros recognized Orogast's valor and honor, compassion and consideration, virtue and flexibility, intelligence and insight, all qualities she had seen firsthand on numerous occasions in their service together.

Finding those in whom you would trust your life was never easy. Now she had to replace not just one but two such individuals.

His eyes still glazed, gazing heavenward, Spreesprocket mumbled, "If only I had been quick enough to capture some of that Light..."

Leaning over, keeping his voice a whisper for Spreesprocket's ears only, Yip said softly, "You have but to look inward to find more."

Spreesprocket grinned, commencing a series of convoluted mental calculations intent upon designing a device to extract that very same energy. Time would tell if he would succeed, but he had the framework necessary to start.

"Too bad he couldn't've stayed around ta help us a bit longer..." Slate knew they had been beyond lucky for the assistance provided by Orogast's transformation, both in timing and effect. He could not help but to wish for a bit more.

Eidelion kept his discipline and restored their focus lest they lose themselves in distraction. "There is much yet to be done. Though we yet live, our foe remains as well, its gauntlet incomplete."

"With our success, its ire grows. With our continued denial of its access to this chamber, its fervor intensifies. We must not tarry for it yet waits, a shadow yet unlit."

"We must determine how best to proceed before even the option of choice is taken from us."

"I will see what lies ahead." Yip volunteered to assess the situation, though doing so was only at great peril to his body, his sanity, and his essential character. There were, however, few other options he would trust.

Now down two of their members, the remaining companions regrouped in preparation, awaiting Yip's assessment, the shadows of Eldre'gheu's antechamber now limited to their own.

With the Shadow's departure, Archaeus's scintillating Light now cast its radiance on the far walls and ceiling of the vast chamber, providing unobstructed warmth and hope to cold, forgotten stones and tiles that had not felt such energies in millennia.

Beneath this pure white illumination, faded mosaics, cracked bas-reliefs, and fractured statuary told the tale of humanity's ascension, the quest for the realization of Man's highest ideals, the search for personal and ultimate truth, and the actualization of divinity.

The events that transpired thereafter did not recommend or speak highly of their efforts.

Now relatively safe within the chamber, Yip cast his mind forward and outward in an attempt to ascertain what may lie before them, what hazards they had yet to see.

The walls and ceilings of the temple chamber provided only a temporary buffer of safety for them for he still sensed the hideous Darkness hovering beyond the chamber's walls, hungrily pushing inward and outward seeking purchase. Above, the loathsome vortex of dark forces yet raged, drawing energy of this world toward it implacably, while spewing out the effluent of another, and, within the confines of the decayed city, countless Shades pooled and riled together in fearsome masses, often sheltering entities far darker. If they failed in their efforts within, this chamber would return to Shadow in short order.

Pushing tentatively forward toward the next room through and across the black arch at the far end of the antechamber, where he sensed a horrific presence lurking, he brushed against an impenetrable wall of Darkness—a spiraling morass of vacuous evil into which he dared not venture or plunge for its depths were unplumbed and dangers too grave.

Dirtied, though no stains were visible on the outside of his person, he returned his full attention to his friends to apprise them of what little he could of the dangers that lay in wait ahead.

Turning to address everyone before they carried on farther, Yip stood humbly in Raour'Saqan's shadow, letting the import of his words reflect in his voice. "The Darkness we have long sought gathers just a few short steps beyond this chamber. This Shadow waits poised, impenetrable, beyond the far threshold within the next chamber. We have but a few brief moments remaining before we face our foe."

"The Darkness within those walls is utter and complete, to be feared and treated with utmost caution."

Eidelion nodded curtly in recognition. "If the end of our quest, for good or ill, is indeed nigh, we must move forward in unison—mind, body, and spirit united in purpose and will. Otherwise, our actions will lack cohesion when the Shadow rises and the chaos of final Darkness falls upon us."

"What do you propose?" asked Wrindanneth.

Eidelion prepared his troops simply, reiterating their prior discussion and plans. "We will be greeted with Darkness. We will meet that Darkness with Light."

"Raour'Saqan, Daerdros, Slate, and I will push forward through the Daemon's first wave of oppressive emanations. Aroganji, Wrindanneth, and Spreesprocket will stay back at the periphery of Archaeus's protective halo. Yip will stand between those engaged on the fore and those casting from the rear."

"Wrindanneth, Llyewia, and I will do our best to heal and restore those who are harmed or assailed. Aroganji and Spreesprocket will do their utmost to counter any other fell enchantments that may fall upon us. Raour'Saqan, Daerdros, and Slate along with myself will also take the brunt of any physical assaults while also offering our direct counters."

"Wrindanneth, Aroganji, and Spreesprocket, you may cast any destructive, neutralizing, or defensive spells that you see fit so long as we all remain warded and in good health."

"Llyewia, you are to ensure that we do not fall under the Daemon's beguilements. If we begin to fall under its sway, you must ensure that Yip above all others does not become its thrall."

"Yip, you are to destroy the Daemon. You have shown us this skill, but you alone have truly mastered the ability. As with the Dread Lords, you must create Light within the entity's heart where none has ever before resided."

"If I fall, Daerdros will provide you with her guidance. If she should fall, Raour'Saqan and Llyewia will offer you their wisdom."

"If all is lost, I wish you the Light's unbounded grace, for we will not be able to flee or retreat."

"With the possible exceptions of Llyewia and Raour'Saqan, we must all stay within Archaeus's halo when venturing forward for little else will avail us against the ruinous corruption of a Daemon of this puissance and absolute dominion."

"Am I clear?"

Though his words were met with silence, there was focused assent all around.

Diminished in numbers but lofty in spirit, the companions prepared for their final offensive.

CARRION CROW

Raucous crows gather,
a gang of squawking vultures.
A harried hawk flees.

He took a few moments to appreciate the beauty and complexity of the work of desolation brought to fruition in this ancient, crumbling metropolis over the long-lingering aeons.

Below, visible to his eyes through the gray fogs that merged inseparably from the low-lying clouds above, a spiraling vortex of entropic, hope-destroying chaos churned over a fallen temple; a city dedicated to the highest ideals laid low and now corrupted by the antithesis of its pursuits, filled with creatures of near infinite Darkness. A world put at risk to ever-spreading ruin stemmed from this metropolis's broken pride, birthing a degenerate panorama of dream-nullifying potential.

Such was the landscape of his attention.

Such was the landscape of his desire.

He watched the gradual collapse of possibility around him, each persistent line of probability allowing the continued existence of this vision of nightmare, each thread showing the continued perseverance of his charge.

The one he pursued yet remained below.

The one who threatened this desolation yet persisted.

His mandate was not yet fulfilled for his quarry still lived. The Priest of K'un Lun had not yet been destroyed by his foolish, misguided quest.

Should his target survive the daunting odds upsurging below, weakened and humbled by the Power lurking at the heart of the black temple, his quarry would find yet another foe lying in wait once he emerged from the shattered remains of the debased temple, wracked by humanity's overreaching hope, just as he would soon topple the ideals and aspirations of his prey.

He had read the odds.

The time to strike would soon rise.

The time for death, the time for endings, would soon be at hand.

Then he would wash in blood and bask in the end of dreams.

FINAL DEFENSE

An airship takes to the skies
in the velvet night
as a comet comes to ground.

The alien armada did not advance. Instead, the fleet's uncounted ships lay in wait, abeyant, on the far horizon, foreboding thunderheads banked by a freak storm of massing arrant darkness—both awaiting turbulent release.

Their doom so close, they had to wait for its completion.

"I never was good at waitin'..." Humbol eyed the massed, fearsome Darkness warily.

"What're ya thinkin'?" Hoyt was good at waiting, he just preferred not to when given the opportunity, especially when danger loomed.

"I'll set a timer," Humbol gestured to a magical sand hourglass resting beside the wheel of the airship. "If we haven't countered or they haven't made a move and started rainin' death in one-quarter of an hour, we make ours."

"Don't ya think they would want ta draw us out in the open without the support and coverin' fire of the city?" Hoyt immediately saw the foolishness of Humbol's proposal.

"Yep."

"Then why do it?"

Humbol began counting off on his fingers. "One, we are not Tellanon's fleet. What we do has little relevance to them. Two, we have the initiative and the opportunity to act. Three, we won't be in tha open, at least not fer long. Four, my idea requires us to be beyond Tellanon's ships. And, five, it'll be fun!"

"Fun?" Hoyt shook his head in disbelief.

"Marchin' off ta certain death is fun? If ya ruin the plans fer the city's defense, others may face similar fates." Hoyt squinted at the host of enemy ships, raising an eyebrow, considering. "What exactly are ya proposin'?"

Humbol smiled. "All those ships are massed too closely t'each other not ta have a little bit o' fun!"

"And ya're not answerin' my question!" Hoyt remembered countless hours just like this spent arguing in circles with his friend on their adventures together over exactly these same points—how to proceed, what task or action to perform next. Though he was patient, these arguments and delays he did not miss.

Humbol started ticking off points on his other hand. "One, we won't fly across tha distance separatin' us, we'll port, but only beyond Tellanon's outer defensive perimeter. This ship is capable of that feat among others."

"Two, we'll remain cloaked as we work. She has that fine capacity as well."

"Three, we'll plant tha seeds of their undoin' within tha very base of their supposed strength!"

Hoyt ticked off a finger of his own. "Four, ya're still not answerin' my question!"

Humbol's wry smile was exactly what Hoyt did not want to see. "That's tha point! Where's yer sense of adventure?"

"My sense of adventure got me onta this ship! My sense of self-preservation will get me right back off it!"

"So ya're askin' for a plan?"

Hoyt grew tired of his friend's circumlocutions. "If ya want ta have my hand in yer efforts, ya'll have my voice in yer machinations!"

Humbol nodded slowly, his gesture exaggerated in response to a very reasonable suggestion, one arrived at and agreed upon only after much difficult deliberation and hard negotiation. "Then we're agreed!" He reached down and turned over the sand-filled hourglass, saying, "One-quarter hour," so that the enchanted device would let him know when the requisite time had passed.

Hoyt waited but a moment before adding, "And?"

"I'm workin' on one!"

Hoyt laughed, knowing Humbol had many ideas just as he did as well.

Walking around the ship, Humbol began to cut down all of the sand-filled bags of ballast hanging from ropes, beams, and rails. When he finished, with a wave of his hand and a gathering of power both from himself and his ship, he collected these sacks into a sizeable pile at the center of the deck, floating other bags from all over the ship, including those located within the hold, in addition to those he had already deposited to form a large central pile.

With a quick downward motion of his arm, the magic at hand expressing the will within his mind, he quickly slit these bags wide open, letting all the sand spill out onto the deck into a heaping pile of silicates that shone golden and white in the shimmering rays of orblight that landed upon them.

With all the granules in place, Hoyt added his own magic to Humbol's.

Exhaling softly, a silent incantation left his lips as his words, breath, and will settled over the sand, suffusing the pile with magic. To each grain he added his protection, a temporary shield that would strengthen the individual particle's crystalline matrix, encasing the robust silicate structures in a shell of magical energies. Though but a brief protection, for more time would require too much precious energy, his boon would protect the grains of sand in the pile from heat and impact, friction and other forms of physical degradation. His first spell complete, to this he added another enchantment, one that would ease the sands' passage through the air and obstacles, reducing friction to both matter and energy, objects and spells.

Their initial intent prepared, their resources gathered, Hoyt nodded to Humbol that he was ready.

Nodding in turn, Humbol said, "On my mark, add yer energy ta my own and that of tha ship! Keep a bit in reserve, as ya may need it! When we're done, the *Rare Aer* won't have enough power ta fly, so we're gonna sink ta tha ground like a rock!"

Hoyt laughed. "Ya're exaggeratin'!"

His face unbroken by a smile, though his eyes glinted playfully, Humbol replied, "Ya're right. She'll sink like a rock, albeit slowly and under my control...fer tha most part."

After a moment's pause, he added without a hint of a smile, "I hope."

Hoyt laughed. "Ya gotta do better'n hope!"

Humbol scowled, albeit wryly. "And this infernal plan ya cobbled together had better work!"

Hoyt laughed again. "Ya're just jealous it wasn't yer idea after all yer posturin' and bravado!"

Now it was Humbol who laughed. "Ya're right!"

Ready to begin, to see if their wild plan would have any impact, Hoyt said, "If ya're done complainin', we can be about the rest of our business!"

"Don't rush me! Just because ya came up with a good idea fer once doesn't mean ya can get all imperious and start runnin' my ship! If it weren't fer me, ya wouldn't even know if it'd work!"

Readying himself, Humbol grumbled, "How much about proper ships' shields d'ya know? Can ya tell tha difference between those ships designed only fer *faerviage* meant ta travel through atmosphere versus those ships that can take tha rigors of travelin' at unimaginable interstellar speeds unprotected? Would ya even know why that's important?"

Hoyt shook his head. "Are ya done complainin'? This is half the reason we don't work together anymore. Ya complain more than a mule at the wrong end of a rope!" He gave a short barking laugh, adding, "Of course I know the difference! Why d'ya think I suggested what I did? "

Hoyt waggled a finger at Humbol, scolding his crotchety old friend. "I know as well as ya that some of these particles won't do a lick of damage ta those ships because there are those among that fleet that're designed ta take the full impact of interstellar dust along their hulls. Ya know as well as I that there are also those ships that are warded ta protect against more than you or I would ever be able ta conjure up! We are not targettin' either!"

"There may be some ships in that fleet that weren't designed fer either! If we're lucky, those are tha ones we'll hit!"

Finishing, he cajoled, "Now, if ya're done mopin', can we get started before I have ta cast my spells again?"

Humbol laughed brightly, the sound of his mirth filling the ship with warmth. "Who's complainin' now?"

Hoyt smiled but did not reply.

"I always did like gettin' ya riled up!"

"And I always liked provin' ya wrong!"

Nodding in agreement, Humbol answered, "We always were good fer each other!"

The sand gathered, encased in protective magics to help protect against the heat of acceleration and the force of impact, guided by fields and forces intended to augment their motion, Hoyt nodded to Humbol that he was about to begin.

Nodding in accession and understanding, Humbol said, "On my mark, channel your energy inta tha sand's acceleration. I will add my own as well as that of tha ship."

"Be ready, fer as soon as yer magics are added ta my own, tha ship will begin its fall."

Hoyt grunted, "Remember what I said about time?"

Humbol laughed, not needing to reply.

Hoyt snarled, "We're quickly runnin' out of it!"

Always with a flair for the dramatic, waving both arms in tandem, motioning like a conductor triumphantly guiding his orchestra, Humbol gathered the ship's resources, feeling charged with power as enormous energies roared through him at his command, under his direct control.

Though he may try, he could not retain this much power within his natural form for long lest he burn to ash.

Bringing the sand aloft, hovering in the air thrumming like a swarm of angry bees, Humbol shouted above the growing din, "Ready! Go!"

Feeling Hoyt's great strength added to his own, commingled with the vast reservoirs of the ship, Humbol released his turbulent dust storm onto the heavens in a terrible flash of light and heat.

Before he could take in the full extent of what they wrought together, blinded by the light of the sand's acceleration and the air's ionization, the *Rare Aer* dropped like a weighted stone. The energies contained within her fuel cells almost completely drained without hope of recharging, the ship plummeted from the skies.

Enervated almost entirely, there was no longer enough power to hold the ship aloft.

His attention consumed by his ship spiraling downward in an uncontrolled free-fall, all of his faculties focused on preventing the crash of his vessel, Humbol was not afforded the view of the bedlam that now unfolded dramatically before Hoyt's eyes.

The surreal tableau holding sway in the heavens between the two fleets broke, the measured calm shattered in an instant by the countless impacts of newly created stardust ripping through their ranks.

Hoyt never expected their plan would have such a dramatic, precipitous effect.

All across the vanguard of the alien fleet, ships reeled and pitched, sputtering as lights flashed and flared. Vessels ignited, plummeting from the sky, steaming and smoking. Many others were damaged or incapacitated, critical systems damaged, disrupted, or devastated. Explosions arched between ships, destroyed in the havoc created from the miniscule particulates now blasting into and through them at speeds approaching luminal velocities.

Amidst this violence, the sky exploded in light.

Disoriented, tumbling earthward out of control, Hoyt observed as best he could as arches of light, plasma, and other forms of magical energy ripped through the sky, the chaos spreading within the alien fleet met with an equally kaleidoscopic reprisal by the forces of Tellanon. Despite the relentless torrent of thousands upon thousands of retaliatory blasts, the stalwart, scintillating shield of Tellanon held and allowed for continued counters.

Though partially cloaked in Darkness, the invaders did not fare well. Those ships not protected by the extradimensional Shadow came under quick fire. Sufficient to protect against the retaliation of most other ships, the individual shields protecting these vessels were insufficient to ward off the furious blasts from a fully armed and powered citadel of Tellanon's caliber.

While the Darkness roiled about them, moving with bilious fluidity to shield those within its fold, many of the alien ships exploded in flames, were blasted to nothing, or tumbled ablaze to the earth—violent constellations quenched aground.

Though the shields of Tellanon remained steadfast under the initial enemy salvos, though the invader's ships fell with the city's counter, Hoyt knew that Tellanon's shields would not hold forever for the invader's ships seemed more numerous than the stars, their strength backed by an encroaching Darkness both implacable and all-consuming, ready to strangle the city within its coils.

Only mere seconds before crashing into the ground, Hoyt remained completely focused in sedulous attention as he watched Tellanon fight for its future.

"If ya value yer life, ya'll stop yer stargazin' and prepare fer impact!" Straining at the helm, giving what little was left of his vitality to the ship to cushion their descent, for Humbol would not abandon his craft when he yet had the strength and option to do otherwise, he yelled to Hoyt through corded muscles and tight lips.

Returning at once to the reality gyrating out of control around him, Hoyt turned unsteadily to face his friend while he clung to the ship's railing for stability. Calling out over the whistling air rushing past, Hoyt yelled, his face split by a wry grin, "Is there any way I can help?"

"Ya haven't tha strength ta right my ship!" Though there was yet enough power remaining to slow their descent, buying them a few moments before impact, the *Rare Aer* was destined to crash and burn at this rate of fall.

Humbol locked eyes with his friend, his gaze full of significance, his face grave, and said, "Ya needn't go down with tha ship!"

"Nor do you!"

Humbol gave a brief shake of his head, his face a mask of tense composure, focused on righting and maintaining course. His ship was his livelihood and he would not leave her until all other opportunities had failed. If he had to go down with her, then he would do so willingly.

She had given him his life. He would give her his in return.

Despite the danger of their predicament, despite the gravity of their situation, Hoyt remained poised. He always had a backup plan, more often more than one, though he did not always reveal his plans or contingencies to others, a fact which had often stirred Humbol's ire in the past. He understood, however, that a plan fully revealed was one that could be intercepted or perverted, so he preferred to keep ultimate control within his own hands, another fact that had caused quite a few minor disagreements with Humbol in earlier days.

Though he had his contingency spells in place to protect himself, he had not yet had time to prepare any to protect the ship or his friend. Humbol had, apparently, burnt almost all the magical energy stored in the ship to fuel their attack on the alien vessels, including any additional protective spells he had had the foresight to cast upon the vessel for times of emergency. Though necessary, this was exactly the sort of planning that had resulted in many fractious arguments for he worked differently.

Where Humbol gambled, he planned.

However, knowing this, he also understood how his friend operated, how well they worked together, and how their own approaches to various situations complemented one another. So he was not the least bit surprised that he had to act, and act quickly, to save his friend and the ship. And, although he had not had time to prepare for this emergency explicitly, he did have several alternatives at his disposal, options which he had not shared with Humbol, resources that could be called upon to turn the situation to their advantage.

He thought the time right to reveal one of these contingencies.

Reaching into the folds of his robes, he pulled out Luereal, the black wand of Q'ia'Li, whose Anuvaeryan wrought witchwood core held orders of magnitude more innate power than the *Rare Aer* at full capacity. This wand he kept hidden, held in reserve for the direst of emergencies, choosing instead to rely upon its lesser, smaller twin that he kept hanging in plain view at his waist for other times when he needed additional strength but of much less significance than those afforded by an artifact such as Luereal.

After all, if an enemy, or friend for that matter, had no need to know of a thing, why should they?

Gleaming white, brighter than the sun at its zenith in midsummer, its ebony core not visible beneath the halo of light that shone forth from its Aeryn Sh'al core, Hoyt rapidly invoked a spell of flight augmented by the wand's enormous power, a spell of sufficient strength to allow the ship to fly once more under Humbol's control. Granted time by Luereal's spell, the *Rare Aer* could now replenish her reserves so that she could soar under her own power in short order.

As quickly as its light had shone forth, Luereal's radiance faded, adroitly returned to the magical folds hidden within Hoyt's robes.

Cursing, Humbol growled, "What in tha name of tha fathomless black Abyss was that?"

Acting nonchalantly, filled with aplomb, pretending nothing exceptional had occurred though their descent had been miraculously arrested only a few hundred feet above ground, Hoyt answered simply, "A gift."

"And how in the name of Heaven's unending Light did ya come ta own an artifact like that?"

Though Humbol wished for more, for much had transpired since last they were together, just as much had changed about both men, he did not offer his friend more of an answer for time was too short and some stories were best left untold. "From a friend."

Maddened by Hoyt's evasiveness, Humbol yelled, "And what, pray tell, other surprises d'ya have in store that I might like ta know about afore I give us up as lost before tha hands of fate?"

Smiling brightly, his eyes on the dueling fleets overhead as much as his friend, Hoyt reached into the folds of his robes and cracked open another small, magically sealed pocket. "Have ya met my friend Cletus?"

Never once losing sight of the battle raging above, their contribution finished, at least for the moment, Humbol muttered, "Seems ta me that a Fairy Dragon is tha least that's changed about ya! 'Sides, I already knew about Cletus!"

Unoffended by the slight, Cletus continued sedately preening himself where he now rested on Hoyt's shoulder ignoring Humbol's irascible tone.

"Ya're more right than ya know, my friend, but one should never underestimate a Fairy Dragon!"

Humbol laughed, briefly taking his eyes away from their course, his ire partially cooled, interjecting, "Or my connivin', fork tongued friend!"

Finishing his comment, Hoyt replied, "Especially when his name is Cletus!"

Unable to find fault with Hoyt's logic, Humbol concurred, "Especially when his name's Cletus!"

Remaining self-possessed and unaffected, Cletus delicately washed one iridescent eye with the back of a scaly paw.

He, at least, knew the wisdom of silence.

Returning to the task at hand, the sky above lit by the continued explosions and destruction of alien vessels whose inexorable advance was made possible by the cover of darkest Night, Humbol observed, "Time ta lay low fer a bit. No sense remainin' an easy target out in tha open when only their immediate interest in fendin' off Tellanon's defenders keeps 'em from retaliatin' and rainin' destruction down upon us.'

As wreckage, smoke, and debris fell all around them, Humbol guided the ship downward, directly above the densely canopied forest stretching below. Maneuvering the craft away from the strife, blending in with more protective cover, he put his intent to action while temporarily leaving the tumultuous conflagrations above to those remaining engaged in the aerial battle.

SPIDER'S HEART

A pair of sparrows
squawk and swoop frantically
to the hawk's dismay.

Now that the room's darkness had passed, Yip could see that the expansive chamber was ideal for housing massive congregations of worshippers. Though all but a few signs of their practice and beliefs were now overthrown, struck down, or faded by time, the numbers of worshippers that would have made use of such a capacious space here at one time must have been truly monumental.

He did not understand the significance of the building's layout, however, for this vast antechamber covered but one-quarter of the large spherical dome. Whether each segment was alike and served similar purposes, what he assumed to be general worship, he could not know. Whether all served as large service chambers leading to more selective inner worship halls at the temple's heart, he could only conjecture as well.

If they had the time and their quest met with success, he could ask Wrindanneth or Aroganji to conjure a vision of the services that had once transpired here, but, without further study and time, even then he would have little understanding of the meaning behind the visions revealed by the magic.

Ahead, now within a stone's throw of the large arch leading to the temple's heart, the decorative ornamentation around its rim defaced and faded, he wondered what doom lay in wait beyond the threshold.

The passage of evil, thick and viscous like some loathsome oil, had rushed out of the room, perhaps surprised or seeking a more advantageous position, with the coming of Orogast's ascension. Where that Darkness had gone, what it now contrived, where it lay in wait, he could not say for the chamber beyond was closed to him.

The answers to these questions would come soon enough, he feared.

With every scintillating fiber of his being, he sensed that the impenetrable dark, a Darkness colder, fuller, and more encompassing than the lightless gulf between the farthest stars, was now waiting just a short distance away through the yawning portal ahead.

With each step toward the threshold, he gathered more and more *chi* within, a nimbus of concentrated energy surrounding himself in a pure wave of pellucid force. He felt his friends making similar preparations. Slate gathered and intensified the holy pyre of Brendle's fires. Aroganji and Wrindanneth each prepared complementary spells for immediate use and release upon entering the chamber. Spreesprocket's exosuit shifted and transmogrified into an implement of grim destruction. Daerdros's unbroken song continued to build within her lungs, each breath, each note, sending shivering pulses of euphonious musical energies through the air. A deepening of the absorptive field, a warped region of singularity around Raour'Saqan, marked his readiness for battle just as the effusive radiance around Eidelion grew and deepened in turn. Llyewia bathed in a halo of starshine, the energy very similar to Yip's own.

Consideration of these efforts were now secondary to his own.

With but a few last steps, each beat echoing valiantly, though muted, against the staggering walls, the companions crossed the final archway into madness.

An immense chamber opened up before them, the high dome of the room's outer walls continuing its steady march skyward unbroken, culminating in an open apex almost lost in the vast distance of the empty space.

So enormous was the chamber, its size increased by magics beyond his understanding, that Yip thought that an entire city could have resided, if one of sane mind would ever choose such a place for a city, within the central room's curved walls.

At its apex, visible through a large circular opening within the temple's sloped roof, the vortex of black energy so visible from the skies twisted and surged, a tornado of extradimensional force sucking away the life of this world, belching out the energetic refuse of another. Within the chamber, no longer fully protected by Orogast's boon, he felt the energies of his own world rushing past and into this maelstrom, just as profane extradimensional forces surged outward around them and onward beyond the building's walls.

If they stayed within the shadow of this vortex for long, it would inexorably draw the life away and out of them, slowly sapping their strength and vitality. In the presence of this current, the Heart of Yere grew warmer against his chest, offering him some small degree of solace.

At the room's center, immediately below the opening in the temple's roof, at the bottom of a gigantic open depression, rough-hewn from the raw rock underlying the temple's foundation, a black pit yawned. It was this pit from which the vortex originated, it was into this pit the lifeblood of their world now spilled, and it was out of this pit that the putrescence of another dimension overflowed.

Of their quarry, nothing was seen.

Yip, however, sensed the Shadow's presence ahead, lurking within the depths of the nadir at the base of the vortex, leeching off the energies that surged past.

For his friends, he merely pointed.

There were signs of acknowledgement all around, just as preparations continued for their impending conflict.

If their foe would not meet them, it was into this pit that they must descend, open and vulnerable both above and below—Darkness up and Darkness down.

Lifting a foot to take a step forward, never getting the chance to complete the motion, Yip met their nemesis face-to-face, mind-to-mind.

And he lost.

The collision, the speed of the attack, was so staggering that he never knew or registered what happened.

Despite the need for absolute readiness, his mind had wavered, distracted by the unnatural, unholy context of their environs, the unexpected emptiness of the place.

Faster than the blink of an eye, quicker than thought or reaction, vaster than supposition, inclusive and undiminished, absolute Darkness erupted forth—a tidal wave of living, entropic, all-consuming emptiness.

The last thing he saw, the last thing he knew, was this utter, total, and complete Darkness.

Night descended.

Everything disappeared.

Sparks flew, miniscule trails of incandescent starlight coruscated around him, more numerous than his ken, the myriad heavenly bodies in the firmament, an argent halo of magical energies grating against the swarming tendrils of Darkness, generating light and heat with the friction of metal upon metal. Within this nimbus of energy, Llyewia stood firm, his radiant spirit untouched by the tsunami of virulence engulfing him and straining against his defenses. Beyond his luminous corona of sanctity, all was Darkness, terrible and absolute.

He must weather the storm.

He must survive the Darkness to restore the dawn.

Feeling the awful tension of the forces pushing inward against him directly through his shield, evil struggling against his own inner Light for purchase, reaching for the Aerya Etherum, the flowing light of spontaneous creation, the genesis of the Aerya within, he gauged the strength of his foe and trembled.

He would survive this onslaught.

He would push back against the wall of Darkness and create a temporary space for Light and hope.

Without succor, however, he would not survive the battle.

Gathering his will, striving to regain the intrinsic Light that had been so forcefully thrust away, Llyewia pushed. He pushed with his mind, he pushed with his heart, and he pushed with that which was part of him, though not bodily, only of spirit. With the effort of aeons, with the patience of time, and with the inevitable will of evolution, he forced back the absolute tenebrosity surrounding him and made some small space to work, a small space to live.

Of his friends, he neither saw nor sensed anything.

Constrained by hungry, mephitic darkness, the Fria al'Othra was almost completely blind.

Within the domain of his control, unable to extend his reach beyond the showering sparks of living energy protecting his inner realm in a cascading fount of stardust, with the skill and subtlety of long centuries of mastery, he began to summon wells of rarifying Light, manifesting the hidden energies of the Aerya, planting the seeds of the Daemon's destruction.

Though he could not sense the origin of the Darkness or attack it directly with his fulgent creations, for his sight was now occluded, his target hidden beyond his ken, he could erode the evil's foundation and lessen its expression.

Until he reestablished contact with his *vyaera* and restored some degree of sanity around him, this was all he could do.

And so he fought.

For long moments measured by the expression of ascendant Light and the thrust of nullifying Darkness, time slowing and exaggerating with each embodiment of power, he strove against their common foe, *ciërna* against *ciërna*, possible futures interlocked in a struggle for final mastery.

Raour'Saqan surged forward, meeting Darkness with Darkness.

Though the life-draining emptiness of absolute Void enveloped him, he ripped forward, an all-consuming singularity given life and purpose, driven by one overarching goal—devour all Darkness.

Darkness without essence is empty.

By consuming it, he was filled.

The numbing tendrils of empty hate that strove to contain him could not hold sway over his rage. Such impediments merely fueled his fury, granting him greater power, increased focus, fueled by his ravenous consumption of the Daemon's essence itself.

In a contest of two devourers of souls, it was the hungrier who won.

Eidelion opened his eyes blearily, barely retaining consciousness through the fog and haze of pain and confusion. He lay twisted and mangled, hurled against a far wall of the massive chamber, Archaeus lay flung across the floor several paces distant, too far to grasp, too weakened to summon.

Though he could not move, though he could not turn his head to survey the room around him, his vision was filled with Light for his eyes yet rested on the White Sword, the Bright Blade of the Dalaren Ka, just as Light yet burned in his core.

It was Archaeus that had saved him. The sword's Light yet sheltered him within its halo.

Utterly enervated, wracked by pain, unable to concentrate or regain focus, incapable of gathering his will for a spell or to command his blade and ask for its blessing, all magics stripped from him, his heart beating fragilely within his chest, each frail flutter sounding weaker than the last, he could only weakly, helplessly, watch his life slip quietly away.

Daerdros struggled against the veil of Darkness seeking to blind her eyes forever and smother her song, now but a faint hum, a murmur left trembling and echoing within the resonant chambers of her heart. Its beat yet remained, barely keeping her alive.

Like Eidelion, she could not move.

Her neck was broken.

She felt the cold numbness of loss from her shoulders down.

Unlike Eidelion, she could see her surroundings. What she saw drained the life away from her as quickly and surely as her catastrophic injuries.

She rested limply against a cold stone wall some fifty paces from the entrance to this fell chamber, her broken legs bent backward upon themselves, twisted under her trunk at distressingly oblique angles.

She lay at the edge of Archaeus's blessed circle of Light, however. That was one of her few blessings.

Within her purview, Eidelion sprawled broken, her champion laid low at the center of the white aegis that had brought them so far. Arrayed like lost detritus cast off by a tempest around Eidelion, Spreesprocket, Wrindanneth, Aroganji, and Slate lay scattered to the winds.

Too weak and bleary to concentrate, she could not tell if any yet lived or stirred, whether her companions were conscious, or if there was cause to hope. Of those that she saw, Slate's fires appeared extinguished, her own magics had been quenched, and none but herself appeared to stir.

Of Raour'Saqan, Llyewia, and Yip, she saw no signs whatsoever.

Should her worst fears be realized, she only hoped that their ends were quicker than her own.

Lolling her head to one side, a gesture she barely controlled as her skull fell nearly to her chest, so weakened and broken by the aftermath of the Daemon's horrendous attack, she could, nonetheless, ascertain the likely fate of her missing friends with what little she could yet see through her limited, bleary purview.

Writhing and churning, a horrid mind-numbing heat mirage, its essence so dark that her eyes watered upon gazing at its amorphous form, so virulent and all-consumptive that she sensed its presence by an absence of transmitted light and energy rather than the actual presence of the pitch mass of Darkness itself. Atramentous despair swarmed and fluxed in front of the arch leading to what she presumed was the chamber from which they had entered. As she watched, this somber cloud of Darkness tumbled and roiled fighting frantically against some inner turmoil.

She hoped the Daemon's agitation was due to her friends standing stalwart against its lurid assault.

If not, then its present frenzy could only be the foul, aroused paroxysms of it feeding on fallen adversaries—her friends and companions.

Regardless of the reason for these violent throes, all she could do was watch in dismay, waiting helplessly to see what doom befell herself and her companions in her wretchedly enfeebled state.

With an utmost mustering of will, she gathered what was left of her song. If indeed her time came as it may have for her friends, then she would give the Daemon something unwholesome to chew on before she too met the darkness.

"Get up ya weak-kneed son o' a sea slug!"

"Ya're nothin' but a lazy, good fer nothin' beardless hag!"

"Yer father cut his beard in disgrace when ya were born at tha shame o' ya!"

Slate's eyes moved in slight recognition but did not open.

"If ya were any duller, I'd have ta sharpen ya myself!"

One eye cracked slowly, weakly, unfocused, struggling against torpor.

"Get up and fight! Get up and fight while ya have tha chance! Get up and fight before fate steals tha choice from ya!"

Harangued and berated, scolded and chastened, Duraeleon's taunts went unanswered. For once Slate could not muster the strength to retort.

Too weakened even to smile, he closed his eyes.

All was quiet, absolute and dark.

Disoriented, unsure of where he was or what he had been doing, Aroganji tried to right himself.

Nothing.

His body did not respond.

Perhaps he had been asleep.

Perhaps that was the cause for his confusion.

He tried to move again.

He tried to open his eyes but could not. He tried to reach up to rub his face and clear his vision but could not. He tried to open his mouth to speak but could not.

He could not move.

Undeterred, he tried again.

And again.

Then again.

No response.

He was trapped within his mind and could not escape.

He remained composed. Becoming anxious or getting excited would do little to improve his situation or help him find a resolution.

Pushing his mind outward, he reached for Wrindanneth. He felt the connection between, strong and firm, a bridge that remained unbroken.

"Wrindanneth?"

He waited patiently for an answer.

"Wrindanneth?"

Still no reply.

His consciousness was filled with silence, the emptiness between them the most tangible sensation he felt.

With all his might, he pushed outward, screaming within his mind, pouring across the gap that separated them, *"WRINDANNETH!"*

Only empty silence heeded his call.

Silence rang loudly in his ears.

Impotent, enervated, and at odds with himself, he struggled to find a way to manifest his will through the Wu-hsing when he had no way to access his full faculties.

Though he could touch and guide the energies inherent within and without himself, with no sense of his body or even his relation to the world around him, he had no way of knowing how to guide, manipulate, and express his will, no way to know how to express or manifest his intent.

Neither was he blind, nor could he see.

Words and symbols, images and sensations, all rushed through his mind in an unbroken torrent.

His training, his knowledge, his triumphs, his failings, all were laid low by the brutal simplicity, by the unyielding severity of his perception.

Wrindanneth saw his life not as an unfolding story but as a series of remembrances taken in all at once, a massive, discordant inchoate mass seeking final realization instead denied fruition.

There was no judgment. There was no judge. There was only the summation of his experience laid bare before his fading mind's eye.

As the intensity of the images grew, his strength weakened.

He was dying.

He did not need any images to tell him that.

The White Sword, called Erudhaerya by those Anuvaerya who first wrought her, who first felt her heft and deemed her good, rose up. The white Light of her essence cast its grace about her, illuminating the broken, stricken forms strewn about the chamber around her luminous silhouette.

Those *vyaera* yet in her charge needed her succor now more than ever. Her *coerdaerya*, her partner in Light, was failing, his situation more grave than any she had yet seen. She willingly cast her protective radiance upon them all, shining like the sun on the day of its birth, unfaltering and unwavering.

She would be their shield and their comfort.

Though she remained firm, resolute, their spirits, their Aerya, dimmed.

She would not let them falter.

Opening herself to them, she let them drink of her Light that they may restore their own.

They were thirsty.

She was full.

She let them drink.

Yip opened his eyes.

Disoriented, he lay on his back, the cool tiled floor firm beneath him, the high arching dome of the temple's antechamber lost in the heights above.

His ears rang in silence, blasted with a wall of sound unheard, sensation unmarked, leaving his ears to ring and his eyes to water in the resultant absence.

A soft golden radiance filled the chamber.

He jumped to his feet, his mind clearing.

There may yet be time!

Casting his mind out, he felt that all of the protections granted to him by his friends had been stripped, wiped clean. The alien shield he wore at his waist was drained of all energy, broken and useless. Of his spells and talismans, what few he had, only the Heart of Yere yet remained fit to offer protection. Without its boon, without the radiance in this chamber, he might not now be opening his eyes, his essence riven from his body.

Far off, across almost the entirety of the entry chamber, he could see the arch through which the company had only just ventured, home to the pit of Darkness, his last waking memories, and to despair.

He had been launched bodily, smote backward and through the archway and beyond, his trajectory sending him heavenward back from whence they had first come to challenge the Daemon at the labyrinth's heart.

Had he been repulsed with similar force directly against the walls of the far chamber instead of through the archway, he doubted he would have ever opened his eyes again. Had he not been fortunate enough to land within the protection of Orogast's boon, the Daemon might have ended their initial clash at its leisure.

Even now, he sensed the vast unholy entity's tumultuous struggle, for he felt Light well and surge within its black heart just as he sensed another darkness, one filled not with the emptiness of the Void or the entropy of chaos but with the focus and pull of a singularity, a devourer of both Light and Dark.

Within the Darkness, he perceived both Llyewia and Raour'Saqan yet struggling. Of the others, he sensed but the weakest traces though they were still within Archaeus's protection.

Filling himself with energy, he burst forward.

There was yet time.

He needed to get within range to strike.

Wreathed in the glowing energies of creation, wrapped in trailing streamers of light, countless vital stars moving in tune with the heart of a living galaxy, with hand and bow, mind and body, Llyewia brought forth Light and heat, combating the Daemon's cold emptiness at every turn.

All around, he watched the slow blossoming of Light within the Darkness, planted seeds of ascension slowly taking fruit. Some blooms thrived, pushing back the Darkness, finding room and purchase in which to restore the vibrant living potential of the Aerya Etherum. Other motes of luminance withered and shrank, fading away within the ravaging currents of evil surging against their radiance, unable to push back the unrelenting tide of chaos hungrily lapping in their presence and vitality.

Pulling back the luminous string of his heart sung bow, he reached in deeply, pulling forth and drawing from much energy that yet remained flowing around him. With a fluid release of his bowstring, a brilliant bolt of concentrated scorching sunlight shot forth toward what he judged was the heart of the madness, burning a brilliant trail directly through the Daemon's dark cloud.

He watched the sun bolt cut its way into the Darkness, tunneling through the impenetrable veil of evil, holding the monster at bay for a time before it once more braved the shimmering void left in the Light's wake. Though his arrow did not hit its true mark, for there was no true center to strike within the Daemon's mantle, the arrow's flight did grant a brief vision of another target.

For but a moment, before the Daemon's vile shroud crashed down within the comet's trail, he looked out from within the Daemon's veil. Granted but a brief view of the inner chamber, his eyes fell upon a heart-wrenching scene of misery and broken dreams.

His *vyaera* lay scattered and broken, strewn about the chamber with careless disregard amidst a vision of wanton destruction. What little life, what little Aerya, yet abided within them was rapidly slipping away.

He had failed in his first charge. He had not kept Yip safe for he had lost him along with all the others within the tumult of the Daemon's onslaught.

He had failed in his second, for he could not destroy this Daemon alone, though he could yet dance with his foe many moons. He had killed many of this entity's forsaken kin, atoning for their presence even as he struck them down, but he had never faced one of such puissance, much less without aid.

He had failed in his third charge for his friends lay at the edge of Eternity and he did not offer them his hand to return.

He could not fail in this last charge. If he could not slay the Daemon alone, he must restore his friends for even if they failed, he would not leave them to suffer without his aid.

Reading the dire need of his companions, he could not fight his way to them in time to grant them a temporary reprieve from their torment before their Lights left them.

His vision clear, knowing now what he must do, Llyewia opened himself fully to the Aerya Etherum, the Light of his essence, the Light of all essences, letting it fill and lift him, a radiance without bound or end.

This Light he gave to his friends that they may live. This Light he gave to his companions that they may realize the *ciërna* he never would.

He watched the passing of this Light, of himself, and was glad.

He saw darkness then, deep and abiding, overcome him.

From within this darkness, there rose the light of dawn and he smiled.

Within his first two strides, Yip sensed he was too late.

Within the nebulous Darkness, Light flared, burning so brightly that his mind's eye filled with unmediated Light, temporarily blinding him to the room and his environs. With the passage of this flash, his heart first sank in bleak, utter sadness and then rose just as suddenly in joy.

He sensed that Llyewia had passed, gone forevermore, another friend lost, but yet remaining somehow still present.

A bright grin beaming on his face, he ran forward to meet his destiny.

His friend had transformed, instantly transitioning to a *jalü*, a rainbow body, a body of Light, thought, and energy.

Despite the circumstance, how could he not be happy?

How could he not be amazed, rapt with wonder?

Sprinting forward on legs granted speed far beyond normal ability, he watched a fog of untold brilliance spring upward from within the Daemon's profane clutches, its luster made all the more profound by the depth of tenebrosity from which it sprang. The essence of morn, dewdrops of pure splendor sublimated upward, briefly brushing against the weakened essences of his friends, brightening their flames, rekindled from its own, who were now buoyed by the Light of the White Sword, restored and cleansed by the magic of Llyewia's passing.

Almost to the inner chamber's entrance once more, his heart filled with grim determination, this divine Light brushed against his own, filling him with pure, expansive peace and joy.

With that last gracious gesture, Llyewia, too, was gone.

Though tears welled in his eyes at the touch of such majesty, his focus remained undimmed for the essence of evil yet threatened his few remaining friends who were still within reach of its vile clutches.

In but a moment, he would be within range to strike.

Eidelion sprang upward, invigorated.

Llyewia had granted them all a boon none of them could ever repay. Along with Archaeus, together, they had granted the companions all the gift of life.

He would spend his judiciously.

Reaching out his hand, his will now his own, he called forth the White Sword whose radiance had kept him from fading away within the shadow of Darkness.

Springing forth to his summons, Erudhaerya snapped to her *coerdaerya's* hand, the depth and fullness of the joy of their joining known only to the two of them, a reunion of heart and mind.

While his newly rejuvenated and restored companions gathered and righted themselves, got their bearings, and prepared to retaliate, Eidelion leapt into action, offering them all a prayer for protection against evil. Then, charging forward, he met the Darkness directly with Light.

As one Light departed, Yip watched as another took its place, the luminous spirit of Eidelion bound inextricably with the radiant White Sword, crashing into the tumultuous Darkness with the force of an avalanche. So powerful and awe-inspiring was this collision that he watched the Daemon's impenetrable pitch Darkness recoil backward, reverberating from the unmitigated force of Eidelion's onslaught.

Over and over Eidelion slashed at the enervating tendrils clasping, enveloping, and reaching for him, seeking to draw him into its deadly fold for eternity. Riven to fragments, each slice of the White Sword cut sections from the unruly mass, temporarily severing and withering the Daemon's essence under the sword's holy Light before the sundered sections rejoined the larger black mass.

Sensing the unassailable fury of Eidelion's strikes, the Daemon began to draw backward rapidly toward the heart of the chamber and the dark cavity from which it first sprang.

With the Daemon's swift withdrawal, emerging from the murk, a submerged monolith revealed with the retreat of the tides, Raour'Saqan reappeared from within the Daemon's churning mass, lunging and tearing, shredding the entity's essence all the while, his claws and fearsome maw ripping into and feeding savagely upon the Darkness with the ferocity of a feral spirit.

Leaping to Eidelion's side, Raour'Saqan joined Eidelion in beating the vile being backward, the paladin's forward march augmented by the wings of prayer and a shadow as dark as the Daemon's own.

Her song now triumphant, her blade slicing in tune to her anthem, each note manifesting the true power and beauty of the Caer'collas, the Q'sharian blade masters, Daerdros rushed forward to aid them, her steps faster than the beat of a frenzied drum. Each motion of her lambent blade cut lines and sigils through the air, her brand singing an aria of enchantment, her actions and those of her sword guided and enhanced by a power beyond the reach and extent of her arm and brand.

Though Yip's steps did not falter, the retreat of the Daemon was faster than his advance. So quick was the Daemon's billowing flight that his steps could not match its pace and the Daemon remained far out of range of his counter, slipping away and down the pitted slope, a volatile, frictionless oil slick.

Summoning his *chi*, he redoubled his efforts to match the Daemon's glide.

By the time he reached the arch of the vast central chamber, the nebulous Daemon had withdrawn halfway across the chamber with Eidelion and Daerdros trailing behind, their magics barely allowing them to keep within striking distance, while Raour'Saqan harried the archfiend from above with both rancorous breath and vicious blows.

Stripped of the magics that would have granted him flight, glowing an incandescent white amidst the flames of the Daerdaana'Duin, Slate charged after the Home Guard with Duraeleon shouting imprecations all the while, his short, powerful legs unable to keep pace even aided by the magics of his armor.

Hair flailing, long, pale legs running at full stride, Wrindanneth quickly overtook both Slate and Aroganji as he sprinted toward the pit where the Shadow sought solace, both he and Aroganji chanting incantations as they ran, their spells quickly granting them much faster, safer passage through the air.

Trailing puffs of rainbow hued smoke, his exoskeleton sprouting translucent metallic batwings, a spinning rotor blade, an umbrella, a beanie, and two shoulder mounted plasma cannons that were ripping off rapid pulses of superheated eldritch gas as he moved, Spreesprocket spun through the air like a balloon with the air suddenly released—zooming through the chamber in erratic spins and loops, all the while never losing sight or shots on his target.

Enlivened and protected by a nimbus of glowing blue *chi*, his feet moving faster than the naked eye could readily perceive, Yip rushed across the irregular, pitted floor with an alacrity known only to those gifted in the use and manipulation of magic.

He only hoped that he would reach his quarry in time.

Ahead, closing the intervening distance quickly, he sprinted toward his friends where they angled through the air and across the ground aiming for the Daemon from where they had been thrown against the room's far walls.

"Far travel, Yip!" Now within range of Aroganji and Wrindanneth's sight and spells, he spotted his desired location next to the open maw of the Daemon's pit, directly beneath the violent vortex of extradimensional power.

Not pausing to acknowledge the efforts of his friends, intent upon reaching the Darkness before anyone else fell beneath its insidious guile, he thrust himself forward once more, a bullet seeking his target.

Even then, he was not fast enough.

Ahead, at the bottom of the convex pit, its retreat complete, the Daemon slithered back into its hole like a rank crab withdrawing before the coming waves, taking shelter beneath the swirling mass of life-sucking chaos at the heart of the temple.

Now standing directly beside the pit where he teleported forward, the overwhelmingly oppressive power of the extradimensional energies a surging whirlpool seeking to draw the life from within his veins, Yip called out in warning to his friends, "Do not press! Hold your advance!"

He read the surging power of the black vortex, the malevolence of the fiend now within its overarching shadow, and was afraid. He did not wish for his companions to press forward into the Daemon's strength, at its locus of greatest power.

But he was too far to be heard by his companions, too late to stop Eidelion, Raour'Saqan, and Daerdros's now futile charge, without the requisite time to offer his own counter for the Daemon's impending assault.

The Home Guard were beyond his words and caution, unafraid of the fell creatures of the night, conquerors of Darkness, without peer or regard for peril, for they had mastered themselves and their enemies more times than could be recalled.

They did not heed his call.

Their supremacy was their undoing.

Their success was their failing.

Their mastery was their weakness.

Cunning and ruthless, the Daemon had gleaned more of each of them in their fall than any would take comfort in knowing. Thus it laid its trap to their strengths, built its counter on the edifice of their own weakness—their ability, their pride, their belief in themselves and their purpose.

Moving on the wings of prayer, shielded by holy Light, his faith and courage an aegis, Eidelion harried the Daemon across the massive chamber, cutting and stabbing, the purity of his blade and belief weakening the abomination's essence with each blow. Despite the power of his blows and the ability of Archaeus to bring cleansing Light where none had existed before, robbing the Daemon of its profane essence and vitality, his efforts were futile unless he could find a way to cut the Daemon off from the pit at the room's center for if it reached the gaping cleft, the Daemon would bath in the purloined essence of this world's lifeblood, drinking deeply and restoring its strength.

His hand was forced.

He could not stop his assault for he must destroy the Daemon before it renewed its power and revisited its overwhelming wrath upon them all.

He could not halt the Daemon's retreat for it was too swift for him to counter.

His advance much more rapid than that of his still-recovering companions, Eidelion found himself almost alone in his fight against the Daemon as it flew across the open expanse. Only Raour'Saqan and now Daerdros were in a position to aid him directly as he ravaged the writhing shadow's flank.

"Cut it off before it can reach the pit!" Eidelion's command saw Raour'Saqan swoop down and interpose himself between the Daemon and the fast-approaching gulf riven at the chamber's midpoint.

Though he breathed a swath of black death that cut through the Daemon's mercurial form, his claws rending and tearing against its escape, the Shadow never wavered, absorbing the direct attacks from the Dracodaeran, washing over him like a flood, its route and speed unchanged by all of the Shaur'Daus's attempts to bar its passage.

Her song an occluding wall of doom crushing inward upon the Daemon from afar as she flew forward, the motions of her sword augmenting each note, Daerdros's magic crushed the essence from the Daemon in a torrent of unassailable sound. Despite the power of her attack, the Daemon pushed through and around her barriers, taking the damage directly just as it had with Raour'Saqan.

Assailed by a barrage of fire from above, Spreesprocket's missiles blasted coruscating gouts of magical fires through the tremulous mass, his salvos augmented by the incandescent fires of Aroganji and Wrindanneth. Though destruction rained down upon the Daemon, no detonations hindered its retreat.

Apprehending the futility of this fractured approach, his voice magnified by the power within, Eidelion's command echoed across the chamber, "To me!"

Despite the urgency of his call, aside from Raour'Saqan and Daerdros, the others were only now moving to positions of advantage after recovering their full faculties and bearings. Even if they thought to teleport to his side or to the yawning trench at its center, by the time their spell was complete, the Daemon would have made its goal.

No matter what he did to hinder the Daemon's vacuous flight, it found a way around the impedance just as surely it did any hindrance Daerdros and Raour'Saqan offered for none yet had the time to destroy it outright. Neither did they yet have full command of the ability to destroy its essence through the creation of Light within its heart.

Though he tried as he ran, he could not duplicate the Dragon's Gate as Yip had shown him. He needed more time to fully cultivate the talent.

Though he had many skills, that was one he had yet to fully master.

And so it was, despite his vain, if valiant, efforts, he watched the Daemon pull away from him and slide into the Darkness swirling at the center of the hall, the black pit from which evil sprang in a maelstrom of gyrating power.

Then Yip appeared beside the wretched pit, waving his arms and yelling a frantic warning barely audible over the roaring vortex of life-eroding power at the chamber's center.

Then the world succumbed to Darkness once more.

ARMADA

A worn bamboo rake
rustles, gathering dry leaves
slower than they fall.

When would it end?

Alaeron quickly wiped the steady stream of sweat falling into his eyes with his forearm. The gesture did not break his focus or his rate of fire.

He had seen more destruction in the past few hours than he had in all the nightmares he had ever woken up from trying to forget.

His arms were numb. His forearms felt like wooden blocks. The tension radiating from his fingertips traveled through his shoulders and down his back collecting in a throbbing ball of fire above his pelvis.

He had fired the negentropy cannon so many times that he could no longer feel his fingers. Though he could barely pull the triggers to unload more volleys of luminescent destruction upon the murderous hordes incessantly erupting from the cloud of Darkness closing in around them, he never stopped firing. Thousands of continuous pulses of fluorescent energy bolts limned trails of volatile carnage between the sites projected directly onto his retinas and the bilious targets he obliterated.

All around, whether embedded into the island's fundament, periphery, or floating in shielded spheres near Tellanon's surface, similar gunners fired their salvos of missiles, bolts, beams, and rockets into the teeming multitudes of alien ships. Each shared his connection with his or her weapon. Each's capabilities were enhanced both by magic and the web of interconnected awareness provided by the Construct. Each's efforts were urged onward by their fellow combatants, their commanders, and the steady guidance of Construct itself.

Despite this ceaseless barrage, wave after wave of ships of myriad shapes and sizes swarmed through the air in volatile masses, continually refreshed in numbers from within the engulfing Shadow. After hours of endless firefights of unrelenting intensity, the character of the invaders began to gradually change. More and more horrific creatures joined these alien ships, twisted and unsightly, throwing themselves against the city's defenses with fearless abandon.

The debris of their annihilation littered the skies as much as his holographic targeting system.

Each mass of writhing atrocities that pushed forward breaking against the city's inviolate shield, each volley of enemy fire that blasted into Tellanon's magical barrier, each tendril of Darkness that brushed against the city's protective sphere, drained Tellanon's defenses of power, slowly taking away the city's ability to protect itself.

Every assault on her fastness remorselessly robbed her of the time she needed so desperately to survive.

Grim resolution locked on his face as he spewed forth streams of unspeakable devastation from the pivoting cannon clinched in his hands, Alaeron was determined to give his city the time it needed to persevere.

His will manifested itself in clouds of superheated magical plasma, the remains of his targets ionized into riotous, multicolored gaseous plumes.

No matter how much chaos and destruction his enemies brought forth from the black heart of their infernal Darkness, he was determined to rain down more upon them. Thus would his world be cleansed and thus would his foes return to the blackness that first spawned them.

SPIDER CATCHERS

Swords raised heavenward
gleaming in the dawn sunlight—
hoarfrost on the ground.

This time Yip was prepared.

Extradimensional fury, utter Darkness, exploded through and around him in a concussive blast with enough force to rip his soul from its moorings and reduce his body to lifeless ash.

Anticipating this trap, reading the movement of energies around him and the Daemon's intent, he became an open vessel, his body and mind without impediment or obstacle for the transmission of this overwhelming force. His mind free and loose within the vaulted chamber, he encompassed the room, relaxed and at ease, a touch of sunlight shimmering atop turbulent, hurricane ravaged waters.

At peace within the pandemonium, prepared for the bedlam, he did his best to shield and divert these same terrible energies from his friends. He sensed their essences as bright points of luminosity within the tumultuous uproar. Unprepared for the attack, not having time to react in order to fully protect themselves, he reached out to these points of lights as beacons warning of a storm to come and offered what aid he could.

These turbulent energies he moved through and away from Slate, Wrindanneth, and Aroganji as if they were not there, pebbles submerged in a stream with no sign or sight of ripples. So attuned was he to their essences, he could react immediately to their needs, without thought.

He did not yet have the same affinity for Raour'Saqan, Daerdros, Spreesprocket, and Eidelion though he protected them as best he could as well.

He offered the same diversion of power from the blast, dissipating and diverting the destructive forces, knowing that they were more resilient and better able to weather even the harshest storms should his protections fail.

This time when the torrent of Darkness passed, all of the adventurers remained standing, rattled and battered, but alert, ready, and still alive.

The time to finish the Daemon had come.

"Back!" Yip yelled out a warning once more. In the eerie silence that followed the outpouring of Darkness, his call was heard and heeded.

Alone and vulnerable, he stood at the edge of the yawning abyss carved out of the chamber's heart, hovering between a living pool of blackness below and a surging vortex of destructive annihilating dynamism above.

This time, instead of reaching out, he reached within. Inward and downward, below the firmament of his being, to the ground of creation he felt. Within this absolute peace, this seamless void of unlimited potential, he brought but a small spark—a spark of will, belief, and hope.

This he lit and the world flared in Light.

The chamber exploded in pure, luminous creation, with an energy so vibrant that the air itself hummed with the fullness and lightness of spring. Eyes closed, arms brought up to cover their faces, though they wished to gaze fully upon the glorious brilliance, each and every hero in the Daemon's dark lair was bathed in the clarity of a new beginning.

Matter and anti-matter, the Light of creation and the Dark of endings, collided, neutralizing one another in a fount of resplendence.

All was, for a brief moment, still.

Time stretched…waiting, expectant.

Just as quickly as the violence had begun, it stopped.

Vigilant and ready, his awareness taut and seeking, Yip read the moment, casting his mind out. Though he sought out the Daemon, it was gone. The air above his head now hung clear and unobstructed, no longer marred by the swirling chaos that sucked the life force from the city, its environs, and the landscape as far as the eye could see.

What would arise from the ashes of entropy's end?

Now, the vortex gone, all that persisted in the air were miniscule dust motes riding atop the currents, catching the gray light that filtered in through the hole in the lofty stone ceiling so far above. All around him, the *chi* settled, calm—a diffuse field lighting the air in a lustrous fog. Together, these motes appeared as phosphorescent incandescence, phytoplankton floating in a luminous sea of energy.

With time, once all of the remaining extradimensional energies had dissipated, free from the vacuum that forever sucked all vitality away, if the other extradimensional entities inhabiting the city could likewise be purged, this place would become a source of vibrancy and life again.

Leaning over, he peered down into the rough-hewn pit at his feet. Its depths were no longer filled with an oily Darkness that lapped hungrily along its edges, greedily sucking in all light and energy, filling the space with wretched power and emptiness nor did an extradimensional torrent spew forth from its depths. Now, this vision cleared, he could see the coarsely cut stone walls blasted from the firmament leading downward into a deep hole lost in the darkness of distance.

There was nothing more.

The Daemon was gone. Its end was as anticlimactic as its first appearance had been overwhelming. The violence of its initial presence had been relegated to the softest light of peace.

Consumed by the Light of the Dragon's Gate, the horrific dimension-bridging energetic funnel was no more, the breach between planes sealed, the passage of energies between worlds stopped, and the portal through which Shadows and their ilk skulked closed.

Though there was much to mourn, though much malevolence remained all around, he did not restrain a smile.

His own fires still burning, he heard Slate let loose a loud celebratory Dwarven bellow, pounding Duraeleon's lucent haft against the stony floor, as his other friends joined in with exhausted cheers and whoops. Relying on the surety of his stout legs, Slate sprinted downhill to rejoin his friends and share in their camaraderie and continued jubilation.

Following Slate's roar, Wrindanneth's exultant cry carried cleanly through the still air. His robes and red hair trailing wildly after him in full flight, he darted back and forth through the air briefly in celebration before angling toward Yip with a rare, joyful smile.

Aroganji's response was subdued. He remained on guard lest another trap catch them unawares, leaving them vulnerable, in a position to lose more than they already had. He did not fly or run to meet the others. He walked slowly, looking around charily, his steady gaze darting throughout the chamber not in appreciation or joy but in steady, measured assessment for the Darkness without the temple remained largely undiminished.

Though the cost had been terrible, the price had been paid and now there was indeed perhaps cause for meted merriment.

The smile still bright on his face, Yip walked slowly, tiredly, toward his friends, his awareness already with them, assured that all were in good, if tired, condition. He wanted to sit and rest, recover for a moment, before venturing outside beyond the temple's walls, once more past the extradimensional shield that had fallen, to see what Darkness yet remained.

He did not, however, want respite within the confines of this tainted chamber. Though much had been gained, too much had been lost for him to wish to linger within its confines.

Before anyone could truly rest, they would need to start looking for a suitable spot for the placement of the new seal that some measure of lasting safety would return to their world. They also would need to see how much more time and effort would be needed to repair the *Shrike*, in order to determine if they should wait for its renewal or continue homeward with their ship in disrepair.

Before any of these things could happen, however they must be prepared should more Darkness descend.

Nearest to him of the companions, waiting for Yip as he walked, thoughts running their course through his mind, approaching him across the coarse floor, Eidelion shared Yip's open smile as Raour'Saqan swooped down beside him. Holding out his hand in congratulations, he said, "You, we, have all done Ea'ae a great service this day."

"Mine are the thanks that go unspoken. Mine are the thanks of the people saved."

Yip bowed in reply. "My honor, duty, and love for Life would have events unfold no other way."

"My thanks are those for the ones yet to be, for the potential and the past denied. My thanks are for our friends and loved ones, their sacrifices, and their futures. My thanks are to you."

His massive shadow cast over both of them, its extent not lessened by Archaeus's glorious Light, Raour'Saqan clapped both of them on the back heavily. "You have done more than Ea'ae alone service on this day. Be proud. You have earned the honor of peace and rest."

Ever vigilant, his concern for the time to come, Wrindanneth called as he neared, "While we have a moment, we must restore our defenses!"

Nodding, Daerdros began her song anew as they gathered.

While Aroganji, Wrindanneth, and Slate hurried over to join Yip, Eidelion, and Raour'Saqan in their triumph, Spreesprocket turned about in the air. Flying back toward the chamber's entry through which they had only so recently passed, he swooped down, much more gracefully than many would give credence for a Gnome, particularly one in flight, and carefully gathered Llyewia's remaining implements in remembrance of the fallen.

The time to honor his friends would soon come and he wished to be ready.

The Elf's remaining belongings stowed within his magical bag where he hoped to be able to retrieve them when the time came, should, unlikely as it was, the Deur Spricken Sprack align in his favor, he then flew back into the entry chamber where he placed a long-lasting stasis spell upon Kazarhan that his people would see him as he had been. Retired in a state of solemn dignity, his visage now calm after the ordeal that took his life, he added Kazarhan's body to Llyewia's implements within his magical Gnomish super sack. He would hand over Kazarhan to his people personally that his end would have the finality and ceremony it deserved.

His duties temporarily complete, the fallen honored and attended, he took to the air once more, his oculars reading and recording the energy currents for future analysis, now ready to rejoin his friends in celebration and the selection of a site for the placement of the new seal.

Flying through the air, examining the ancient, timeworn architecture as he zipped back through the archway to the massive central vault, he was the first to notice something amiss.

Unfortunately, he was too far away from his companions to make any difference.

His mouth open to scream, Spreesprocket's words were lost in the resounding echoes of stones grating and cracking, popping and crashing, as the ceiling which had so long stood stalwart against the unyielding weight of passing time failed, the unholy magics that had sustained its heavy masonry now removed, giving way before the inevitable.

With but the briefest warning, the massive interior dome collapsed inward upon the remaining Home Guard and Four. Only Spreesprocket remained clear of its ruin, a helpless observer tormented by his relative safety near the entrance to the massive room.

OPPORTUNITY

A stacked stone chimney
stands alone in the valley—
remnant of lives past.

Probability collapsed in a massive wave, the enormity of the shift bathing him in a landscape of entirely new possibilities, an overwhelming vista of change and chance, of opportunity and failure.

The Shadow below was no more.

The Temple, its guardian, and the vortex had fallen, lost to all but memory, the lingering cascades of unrealized probabilities, and the reverberating echoes of influenced events yet to arise within the shimmering realm of possible futures.

His prey had completed his quest.

Now was the time to complete his own.

The time to strike had come.

Reading the currents, gazing earthward, the thick gray clouds below swirled round the gaping hole left by the departed energies of the extradimensional vortex, a link to another world now severed.

This channel within the gloom plotted the course of his destiny, showing the road to his future, guiding him toward his purpose.

Readying the ship's armaments, he plunged downward through the clouds.

He smiled, his soulless eyes as black as pitch, untouched by the expression.

Reckoning would soon be at hand.

The time of endings had only just begun.

COLLAPSE

The cracking report
of a tree falling to ground
echoes through my footsteps.

Yip sensed their danger before he heard any sound.

"Cover!" Before the startling cracks appeared above, before the brittle pops and snaps first echoed through the chamber, he had time for one brief call of warning.

Then the world filled with dust and debris, stony missiles thrust heaving from above with the weight of ages now unchecked.

Propelled by a burst of living energy, yet near the arch of relative safety below the central opening in the vast dome above where no stones would fall, wreathed in a shroud of protective *chi*, he exploded backward, his swift steps carrying him back toward the central pit he had hoped to leave behind forever.

Without a second thought, as the heavy stones began to crash downward, the force of their impact sending shuddering shivers and thunderous *booms* through the foundation and firmament with such force that the world itself seemed to be crumbling inward upon itself, he leapt into the maw of yawning darkness that he might find safety.

His trajectory taking him into the Daemon's dark chasm, the world of light quickly disappeared overhead in an ever-shrinking ring of gray light above as he fell. Righting himself, he buoyed himself with energy, slowing his fall to a manageable speed as he descended farther into the temple's depths than he had ever wished to tread.

Yip's warning ringing loudly in his ears, Aroganji and Wrindanneth tied their wills together, simultaneously looking to the first spot of safety they could spy —the crumbling ring around the edge of the temple's roof through which light yet shone. In tandem, weaving their spell together quicker than they could apart, they fixed their eyes on the space at the center of this point and, together, they ported.

Not having the option granted his friends nor the opportunity for them to offer him aid, Slate did what Dwarves do best.

He stood firm.

Raising Duraeleon overhead, he sheathed himself in a dome of force, the axe's magic acting as his own, protecting them both within an impenetrable bubble of power. What would happen after the stones fell, he could not say but, if nothing else, he would live to see the walls of his tomb.

Not having sufficient time, too far to offer her protection to anyone else, Daerdros could only shield herself. Her song overflowing, she whipped her blade overhead, the notes of her winding slash encasing her in a dome of vibrating sound, a vibrant wall of energies that would protect her from anything but herself.

Nonplussed, looking up calmly, studying the clouds moving overhead, Raour'Saqan spread his wings, enfolding Eidelion within their shadow. Unfortunately for the small human, Yip, he had never served at length with a Dracodaeran.

Having served with a Dracodaeran, Eidelion remained at ease within Raour'Saqan's shadow, crystallizing the energies of Archaeus's shield so that his friend's wings would not have to get dusty. Also unfortunate for Yip, he did not realize the full capabilities of Archaeus's shield.

So quick was Yip's departure, his motions faster than thought could register, Eidelion did not have time to inform Yip of his misapprehension.

Thus it was, despite the crumbling chaos raging around them, Yip was the only companion who had immediately exposed himself to further danger by leaping into the Daemon's pit.

Long seconds Yip fell, though the distance was not as great as his sense of time would lead him to believe since he had slowed the rate of his descent considerably. Nonetheless, when his feet lightly touched the ground within pitch darkness, he was some distance below the earth's surface.

How far down he was, how much earth and stone lay above him, he could not easily judge. He had not Slate's Dwarven skills of delving and spelunking. However, by the time he stood once more on firm ground, the only light in the chamber was his own. The circle of illumination marking the rim of the pit had vanished in the distance. Far above, through untold mountains of rock, he sensed the distant glimmers of his friends' essences yet burning despite the collapse.

For this blessing, at least, he was glad.

This far down, the *chi* was diffuse, as living beings were minute and largely tied to the fissures and recesses between rocks, within water and stone. The *yuan-chi* provided the majority of the energy present and, with it, he saw the outlines of the chamber.

He stood at the center of what appeared to be a vast natural cavern. The ceiling soared above marked by the irregular shapes of stalactites and other unusual rock formations—delicate and massive, crystalline and monolithic, irregularly organic and unobtrusively smooth. The floor, however, was unnaturally polished, almost glassy. It had been hewn and burnished to an almost perfect finish.

Though this was once a place of surreal natural beauty, a pall of evil hung over it as well, thick and cloying, the very walls and air stained with the blood of innocents and the presence of the unhallowed.

Immediately beneath his feet, directly below the tunnel mouth leading to the temple's central chamber, perhaps twenty paces in diameter, a massive circle was described onto the stone floor. Blocked rocks framed the circle's perimeter and fell runes of an alien design littered the surface along its edge, making him instinctively avert his eyes. Looking down, the air within the interior of this ring rippled and churned, frothing with the agitation of things stirring violently beneath its surface, struggling to break through.

The virulence of the energy beneath his feet came through the barrier separating his world from another.

This sacrificial chamber must have served as the portal between worlds that had only recently been severed. So tenuous was the break between dimensions that he could see the pressure from the other side pushing outward seeking to restore the erstwhile connection.

His feet at least temporarily on a firm surface, he rejected the overpowering urge to leap away.

If his utilization of the Dragon's Gate had failed, however, assuming he survived contact with the Daemon and extradimensional vortex on the plunge down, he would have plummeted directly into some lightless extradimensional Abyss.

Almost immediately to his side, placed along the perimeter of the portal set into the room's floor, was a large, simply formed stone urn graven with horrific runes that seemed to crawl and skitter hungrily across the container's pocked, dark surface.

Most loathsome of all, floating suspended directly above the sacrificial urn, was a massive, icosahedral crystal, its core dripping with evil as dark and malignant as the Daemon they had just vanquished. Feeling the energy radiating from within, guided by a power that sought to draw him into its dark facets, this crystal must have served to capture the essences of sacrificial victims and as a way to fuel the dark rites that bespoiled these walls.

Struggling underneath the crystal's surface, locked within its dark confines, he sensed the tormented thrashing and heaving of myriad hearts and minds.

Their constant struggle, tinged with an overwhelming sense of fear and pain, radiated from the hellish jewel.

He could scarcely imagine something more horrific.

He did not know how to permanently close the portal, but he knew that the crystal itself must be destroyed. He only hoped that nothing more than the life force of the fallen had been captured within the gem. However, based on his feelings, he feared this was far from the case. He sensed that more than energy alone had been siphoned away by the Daemon and its servants within the confines of the talisman.

He would not wish permanent, suffocating imprisonment on anyone or anything.

Neither would he wish for the essences of the once living to fuel abominable rites.

This chamber, then, must have been both where the ancient fallen priests had performed their heinous rituals and where they first summoned the Darkness that had consumed them.

This was a place to be shunned.

This was a place to be feared.

His entire assessment took but a moment.

Just as quickly, he also sensed that he was not alone.

In that moment, he felt the depths of despair and the enormity of his isolation.

Aroganji and Wrindanneth stayed aloft above the temple roof only briefly. As they watched, the gently sloping dome curving away from them began to crack and crumble, heaving and shifting, an ice flow that had thawed and begun to slowly, inexorably break apart. With the thunderous sounds of joints shattering and failing, they watched countless cracks propagate haphazardly, spreading across the stone surface like jagged bolts of lightning seeking ground where none was to be had.

As the magic supporting its dizzying dome finally failed in a storm of noise, dust, and debris, the majority of the temple's roof caved inward leaving a gaping maw the size of a large chasm in its dusty, shuddering wake.

Not taking the time to let the plume settle, they rocketed downward into the thick, pulverulent air, ready to free and heal their friends trapped beneath the massive heaps of settling rubble.

So rapid was their descent, so quick was their assessment of the situation, so swift was their response, that they did not take time to look to the skies or their immediate vicinity.

Not looking up, not being able to penetrate the gray gloom of the fog if they had, they never saw the dark ship descending precipitately toward them, hellbent on their destruction.

Raour'Saqan shrugged his hulking shoulders and stood upright thrusting his corded arms and wings upward and outward. Massive stones fell away, rumbling and grating in protest to his powerful motion. With the gesture, dust flew into air as thick as the fog lying over the accursed city.

Caring not for the stones' protests, he reached down and lifted Eidelion up onto the top of the thick layer of rubble lying haphazardly across the ground.

Their next task would be to find everyone else and ensure that they remained safe as quickly as possible.

Raour'Saqan pointed. "Daerdros lies there."

Eidelion nodded wordlessly in answer.

Dropping his protective shield, Eidelion strapped Archaeus across his back to better allow him to scramble across the tumbled ruins. Before he got any closer, the stones entombing Daerdros exploded upward from where she stood just as he ventured forth from the lip of his own pit.

Aroganji and Wrindanneth flew past Daerdros toward where Slate must be buried. He would leave retrieving Slate to them. Circling above the shattered stones, preparing to land to aid their friend, the debris erupted upward in a shower of granite as Slate climbed spryly from within another depression.

From afar, Eidelion heard Duraeleon's rant. "I'll not be buried in this accursed place ya black-hearted carrion crows! It'll take more than an avalanche ta restrain me!"

Slate barked, "I've heard enough, rust bucket!"

Duraeleon's boasting quickly stopped.

Eidelion restrained a chuckle. Though he could not be stopped by a mountain, a few words from a surly Dwarf were evidently enough to halt Duraeleon dead in his tracks.

With Slate's release, that left only Yip and Spreesprocket to rescue. Spreesprocket had been tending to the fallen when the ceiling collapsed. He hoped that the Gnome had been clear of the danger with the temple fell.

Calling out, Eidelion gave his orders to Daerdros. "Daerdros! We need you to locate Spreesprocket!"

He need not say more.

The smile on his face quickly returning, Eidelion's request was answered before the task was completed.

"All present and accounted for, sir!" Spreesprocket flew out of the haze toward him, the grin on the Gnome's face matching his own.

Raour'Saqan laughed, the sound booming from within his deep barrel chest. "Now we must find out what trouble Yip has gotten himself into in the absence of our guidance."

His face still bright with a grin, Eidelion nodded and smiled, turning toward the base pit where Yip had so recently descended.

"Come! Let us seek out the Daemon's lair and rescue our fair priest!"

Striding forward, Eidelion took two steps before the earth rang out and a massive orange and red wall of heat and flames enveloped him, detonating in a violent shower of earth and stone, leaving a smoking pit in the wake of the explosion, his broken form flung to the edge of the pit with the detonation.

Before any of his companions could make a move to assist him, the air lit up in a barrage of magical green bolts, each superheated blast melting stone, carving the bedrock, and leaving the ground a molten ruin.

Fearing neither the bolts nor their source, Raour'Saqan launched himself heavenward, the speed and power of his takeoff so momentous that the air rang forth with a peal of thunder, stones shattering and rippling outward beneath his feet in a grating shockwave. Before anyone could blink, he was gone.

Just as suddenly as the fusillade had commenced, it stopped.

Daerdros was the first to Eidelion's side, his eyes faint and wavering as she looked down upon him with a care so deep his eyes locked on hers with silent affirmation. Before he called upon Archaeus for succor or his own prayer of mending, she began to chant, her soothing voice relieving his pain and preparing his body for restoration, her hymn providing a shield that would stave off the destruction from above. Reaching her just as her chant began, Spreesprocket and Wrindanneth joined their magics with hers, gingerly seeking out and restoring all of his hurts, rebuilding and fortifying each minute break and fracture, burn and laceration, replenishing his strength and purpose.

Rejuvenated, Eidelion stood, brought back from the brink twice in one day, saved by his faith, his armor, and, most importantly, his friends.

Reassuring his companions, lessening their tension with banter, he looked skyward apprising the danger as he said, "'Tis time to be done with this accursed place. I do not wish to face surviving another unwelcome surprise!"

Wrindanneth's retort was only partially in jest. "Let us hope that Yip does not find any more excitement for us then!"

He rained death without discrimination, firing round after round of magically enhanced bullets, bombs, missiles, and bolts into the smoking, broken ruins. His targets clear to him through the ship's navigation sensors, their presence delineated by the streaming arches of probability, the accuracy of his shots was assured.

Caught unawares, he had felled one of their mightiest, truncating the luminous stream of possibility marking his passage through time to but a meager few weak strands. The priest's other allies scattered beneath his assault like frightened ants, seeking shelter where there was none.

They, too, would die, finished by the odds they neglected, the risks they did not see.

His gleeful smile spread widely, maniacally across his pale, hollowed face.

Death would soon come.

He would be its agent.

Absent an end, outside his sphere of judgment and ken, for some things are hidden even from the eyes of the gifted, the Durnok never read Raour'Saqan's approach, his presence swallowed within the nimbus of nullification that formed his core, spreading out from him in a hungry mantle. So rapid was Raour'Saqan's advance, so swift his counterstrike, that the Cabal's agent never had time to read his doom, his eyes blind to his end.

Before the wild smile left his lips, the Durnok's world exploded in a sea of flames and flinders as Raour'Saqan blasted through his airship faster than a rocketing comet, his end one of scintillating light instead of complete darkness.

Arching through the heavens, shifting his trajectory earthward once more, Raour'Saqan did not slow or waver, ignoring the refuse left in his wake for some things were beneath his notice. His concern was in returning swiftly to ground, assuring his brothers-in-arms were safe, that their mission was complete, and that they were prepared to embark upon their next journey.

Standing alone in the loathsome pall of the unhallowed cavern, grim realization set in. The Daemon had not been alone lurking within the confines of the temple all these dark, uncounted ages.

The crystal was more than a horrid object bathed in evil used in depraved rites, more than a prison for lost souls. It was the tormentor, keeper, and oppressor of those it trapped and slowly fed on over the centuries. It was the gatekeeper to the abyss, the guardian and presider over the portal to the netherworld.

Though the Shadow had held dominion over the city and its temple, the black crystal hovering forebodingly before him had made that reign possible. It had corrupted those who it had once served. It had granted the Daemon passage into this world. It had assured that the gate between worlds remained open. It had made possible the slow corruption and siphoning away of this world's lifeblood to serve another. It was the source of the temple's evil and the beginning of its corruption.

It wished to consume him as it had all the rest.

He felt the iniquitous vessel drawing him forward, pulling him inward toward its accursed fold—insidious tendrils hovering around his mind, seeking purchase, seeking passage, forcing their way in implacably.

He tried to move, to leap free of its grasp.

His body was already lost to him.

He had not reacted in time. He had not countered, redirected, or avoided the Daemonic infiltration. He had been too slow to recognize his own danger.

He had failed.

Sensing what was to come, he had but moments before volition itself was lost to him, before he, too, was trapped within the crystal prison and forced to serve an unholy master in an eternity of suffering.

His reaction was instinctive.

His mind launched toward the source of his fear, not moving away or shirking from it, attacking the evil at its source, taking the most direct path to his adversary.

This time he did not create Light where there was none.

This time he did not counter evil with its opposite.

This time he destroyed its essence.

This time he attacked its core.

The mind, guided by intent, needs not a hand to strike. The truth, guided by insight, needs not a word to cut through deception.

Silent, his will manifest, he launched his intent forward, countering falsehood with truth, confronting evil with its essence, striking with the Pai-lien touch, the Echoing Fist of the K'un Lun.

The blow of verity reverberated through the facets of the Daemonic crystal, resounding off the walls of its interior, amplifying with each repercussion, strengthening and magnifying with the addition of each screaming voice freed —roars of exultation, howls of revenge—from the lost souls once trapped within its shell.

Soundless, wordless, the crescendo of truth rang through the walls of falsehood, the resonant frequency of the crystal's destruction rebounding outward from within, shattering the black facets into countless shards.

Released, he collapsed to the floor, liberated from the unholy grip that had contained him, not yet fully in control of his body.

All around him light swirled, whirling in a luminous helix, spiraling outward and upward from within the former confines of the riven crystal, the erstwhile seal of Eldre'gheu.

Laying prone on the floor, facing upward toward the shaft through which he had first entered the chamber, temporarily bathed in ineffable glory, he watched as the life force of hundreds, thousands, spun away in resplendent elation, in freedom, before disappearing and dissipating in the far distance.

Slowly recovering himself, he stood wobbly, almost completely enervated by the Daemon's ensorcellment. Head lolling unsteadily, his eyes alighted on the floor as he struggled to take a step.

The Daemonic ring was now black. The gate between worlds had been broken, fully and finally secured.

His purchase firm and assured, he now stood atop a solid stone floor.

Now he just had to decide how best to get out.

"Ho, Yip!" Slate's deep baritone voice echoed down into the open, rough-hewn shaft. Leaning over on hands and knees, even with his Dwarven sight enhancing how far and well he could see into the darkness, he could not discern the bottom of the hole. Neither could he see Yip clinging along the sides of the tunnel.

"Nothin'!" Slate stood, dusting off his knees. "If he's not comin' ta us, we have ta go ta him!"

Eidelion gave a curt nod. "Volunteers?"

Wrindanneth nodded. "I'll go. Aroganji and I can communicate with each other well enough in case of an emergency. If I need more of you to come down, I will relay the message through him."

Receiving another short nod, Wrindanneth did not wait for further comment. Instead, he leapt downward into the darkness, allowing himself to free-fall for a time, enjoying the speed, adrenaline, and rush of freedom and danger before he took flight.

Reorienting himself to face head downward in mid-descent, his eyesight enhanced by magic, he shot downward, relishing the speed, allowing himself to fly faster than terminal velocity would have permitted in free-fall.

A wicked grin on his face, he suppressed the urge to let out a triumphant scream as he flew. Such an outburst would be unbecoming and might hurt his image.

Or cause undo alarm.

He did, however, allow himself a brief chuckle.

In a matter of seconds, he sensed an end to the shaft and slowed his rate of advance. Remaining silent, cautious, he slowly approached the lip of the tunnel. Given his orientation and ability to fly, he pulled himself upward and outward slightly from within the hole to peer into the vast chamber beyond to avoid being positioned upside down.

What he saw unnerved him.

He sensed the oppressive evil of the place right away, the pall of death and dark rituals that clung to the air, growing more vile and rancorous with the passage of time. Pervading the entirety of the space, the overriding taint of fell magics clung. This residual presence brought the hairs on his arms on end.

Though the room, its contents, and past held much evil, he still had to smile at what he saw.

Standing at the edge of some occult ritual circle embedded in the chamber floor, Yip stood looking up at him waving.

From where he floated, Yip looked like he stood atop the ceiling, magically clinging to the chamber's roof. The only giveaway that this was in fact not the case was that Yip's robes remained by his sides and were not hanging over his head.

Sensing that all was safe and well, at least for the time being, Wrin flew downward to rejoin his friend.

With a mixture of humor and admonishment, Wrindanneth said, "You had us worried! You should have called for us!"

Yip laughed. "I wish I had!"

Contemplating the room in its entirety, from a normal perspective, Wrindanneth added matter-of-factly, with only the slightest hint of sarcasm, "Looks like you got yourself into another fine mess!"

Yip did not disagree. "We all have our gifts. Perhaps the others should come see as well."

Wrindanneth wordlessly passed the summons to Aroganji.

"Looks like ya stumbled upon a fine nest o' hornets here, Yip!" Slate touched down with the others as they flew into the subterranean vault, a look of appreciation for the natural beauty of the chamber commingled with a steely eye of disapproving evaluation for what had been done by its former masters.

Yip smiled wearily. "I am afraid I have been stung several times over."

"How's that?"

Yip's arm described the confines of the cavern, moving to each point of interest in turn. "This chamber held the gateway between worlds. A portal inscribed into the floor"—he directed their attention to the arcane ring lined in the bedrock—"served as the entry point for the Daemon and the point of passage for all the energy flowing between worlds. When I arrived, the link was only just ended and tenuously so."

With finality, he added, "It is now closed."

"The gate's guardian and creator was none too pleased at my arrival." He paused a moment before revising his comment, adding with a mixture of humor and evaluation, "Or perhaps it was overjoyed at the opportunity to feed. I cannot say. Such minds and motivations are foreign to me."

Before he went on, Aroganji broke in, "Guardian? What was here, Yip?"

Once more, he pointed, this time to the numerous black shards of crystal littering the floor that thirstily consumed whatever light fell upon their shattered facets. "There was another Daemonic presence residing within a fell crystal near that sacrificial urn. I believe it was, in part, the guardian of the portal. Due to its placement directly above the urn, it must have been used in rites performed here long ago. Perhaps it had served in some way to help open the gate between dimensions and bring forth the Daemon we slew in the temple above."

"I cannot say with certainty but I also believe it was the original seal of Eldre'gheu."

"This crystal housed the life forces of many individuals trapped within its vessel, perhaps through sacrifice or mere contact. Regardless, this entity sought to consume and entrap me as well."

"When it was destroyed, this energy, these presences, were liberated."

Eidelion nodded gravely. "I am glad to hear it, Yip. You have performed a valiant act of retribution."

Yip shrugged slightly, letting the compliment pass. "I am lucky to still be alive."

He paused a moment before adding, in reference to the horrific existence that would have befallen him should he have fell under the Daemon's sway, "In this form."

"Of that you can be certain," Eidelion knew much more of these things than Yip, much more than he cared to know as well.

"Although the gate is broken and its keepers overthrown, there is yet much evil within this chamber." Along with the others, Yip sensed the same overwhelming sense of maliciousness and corruption that lingered over the entire temple housed within the cavern. However, within this room and the central chamber at the temple's heart so high above, this sensation, this weight, was particularly stifling.

Eidelion stated simply, "It will be cleansed."

He then added, "Before we rid it of evil, however, we should examine the chamber as it is that we can glean any information that may be of future use."

Acknowledging Yip's interpretation, he said, "I believe Yip's evaluation is correct. We need to be certain that there is nothing else of interest or danger within the vicinity and that there are no additional traps or difficulties lying in wait prior to proceeding."

Slate muttered a grumbling agreement. "I, fer one, have had enough surprises from this wretched pit. And ya can keep whatever ya find because I'll have none o' it!"

Not even raising an eyebrow, Eidelion did not respond.

Spreesprocket fluttered around the chamber like a moth drawn to multiple flames, unable to decide on a particular destination or landing. Back and forth he flew, recording energy currents and patterns, measuring the energetic fingerprints of magical objects and ritual devices, all for future analysis and understanding. His was the task of complete interpretation and the development of long-term counter strategies based on his findings. The room was so rich in history and detail, opportunities for his study, that he did not restrain himself in the slightest.

While the others carefully navigated the chamber, cautiously evaluating each unusual ritual article they found, Spreesprocket hummed a joyous Gnomish tune, buzzing frenetically over their heads, a bee that had been lucky enough to find the world's richest field of newly unfurled flowers.

While their investigations continued below, Raour'Saqan returned to the surface in order to stake a position along the shaft's broken edge. With the advantage of positioning, he would ensure that no other creatures of Darkness interfered with their work while they yet remained within the bowels of the fallen temple.

Despite the horror of the place, Aroganji was barely able to restrain his enthusiasm with the opportunity to explore, albeit briefly. Though he did not wish to disturb Spreesprocket's work, he, too, wandered busily about, seeing what items of interest he could unearth, an archaeologist let loose on a long-lost, untouched remnant of knowledge and civilizations past.

Working directly with his friend, Wrindanneth scoured the vast recesses of the chamber as well. Together, they covered more ground than both could have individually without their shared connection. While Aroganji was largely guided out of curiosity and a desire for understanding, he looked for opportunity and knowledge that may be of direct benefit in his own studies.

Dark or Light, he was an equal opportunity learner.

Yip stood in position where he had first seen Wrindanneth emerge from the tunnel above. He had not destroyed the horrendous urn that rested alongside the summoning circle nor had he ventured far from his original landing spot.

He saw and felt everything he needed to of this place without moving. Profane objects remained littered about the chamber, of no use to the Daemon who had taken its possession. He had no interest in those. This place was soiled and in need of cleansing. Until that time came, he had little desire to further expose himself to the putrescent corruption that continually washed over him, radiating from nearly every object he laid eyes upon.

Other than their mission to restore a seal to this region of the world in order to prevent further incursions by similar hostile entities and groups like the Cabal, little incentive remained for him to not push onward. If they were lucky enough to find some link, some clue, regarding the Cabal's ultimate location from within these ruins, then he would count such a discovery as a momentous gift, but he doubted any such linkage or information would be found.

So he watched and waited, allowing the *chi* to restore his reserves, replenish his strength, and purify the Daemon's taint.

Like Yip, Raour'Saqan was eager. In his short time back on Ea'ae much had been accomplished, much had been learned, and much promise remained for the future. The time to depart was near at hand. The time to pass his knowledge on to others of his kind that the seeds of Light could continue to spread would soon arise.

There was little that now held him here.

His obligations had been met.

He would leave the world in good hands.

Éremon would be much pleased with their progress.

Slate barely moved, albeit for different reasons than Yip. He avoided touching the objects around him religiously that their taint would not become his own. He moved from foot to foot anxiously, rocking back and forth from boot to boot, eagerly awaiting the opportunity to purge the extradimensional evil from this hall. Then the fires of the Daerdaana'Duin would light this place with Brendle's true vision and all would be made well.

That is, of course, what did not melt.

He smiled with the thought.

Like Yip, Daerdros was ready to be on. Though the immediate danger here may have passed, they yet had a duty to restore what had been broken. She cared little about the rest. If the task laid upon any of the other adventurers, champions, and Home Guard to restore the other seals had been as fraught with difficulty as their own, she wished them bounteous luck and success. Much of their own survival had been due as much to chance as skill.

Once the seal was restored, she wanted to return to Tellanon as quickly as possible that she could learn the outcomes of their counterparts' endeavors. If the others failed, Ea'ae remained in grave danger and others would need to be marshaled and sent forth as quickly as possible.

Though she did not wish to leave Tellanon again, she would if her city and its people asked it of her.

Eidelion was patient.

Though there was much yet to be done, much yet to be wary of, he wanted his companions to have a brief, if necessary, respite from the trials that had already cost them so dearly. This delay would only take a moment within the relative scope of their quest. The benefits, however, could be far-reaching.

The time to cleanse would come soon. Tightening his grip on the warm pommel of Archaeus, he looked forward to the opportunity.

Finally, after he had mapped the entire space across multiple dimensions from energetic to locational and had categorized and analyzed every object found, Spreesprocket flew back to Eidelion to give his report.

For a Gnome, he kept it short. "Initial multidimensional analysis indicates a lingering sustained infiltration of 3rd order malicious extradimensional energies. These residual forces pose a category IIa Life Threat Rating on the universal hazard scale."

"Sufficient information has been accumulated to reconstruct the locus in its entirety. No additional need remains for the persistence of any extant ritual implements or objects that warrants exposure to the high risk associated with their presence."

"Further analysis and in-depth assessments of concatenated causation including both pre-and post-manifestation prevention will be performed upon return to Tellanon's research facilities."

"No additional traps, chambers, or hidden objects remain within the areas of highest measured corruption."

"The area is, therefore, both ready and amenable for thorough, broad-spectrum Type 7 purging."

Eidelion nodded patiently in understanding, always impressed with Spreesprocket's succinct phraseology. "What is your final recommendation?"

"Burn it!" Sometimes even Gnomish circumlocutions fell away in times of great need, import, or urgency. At other times, even Gnomes allowed themselves the rare opportunity to express a bit of excitement directly.

Standing beside Eidelion within the arch of Archaeus's glow, Slate grinned wickedly, having waited far too long in his mind for the decision. "That can be arranged easily enough!"

Nodding in assent, Eidelion summoned them forth with a wave of his arm.

Once completed, Yip took to the air with his friends under the wings of Daerdros's spell of flight.

While his friends returned to the surface, Slate wreathed himself in the coruscating white fires of Brendle's flame and commenced to turning the entire room and all of its implements into molten slag. When he finished and all the items and objects of evil had been cast down, he, too, flew up to the shattered temple ruins.

Returning below with Slate's arrival upon reaching the surface, Raour'Saqan descended and finished what his companion began, filling the chamber from end to end with his black, annihilating breath.

Between them, when they were finished, all objects of Daemonic origin and taint were less than ash.

His great wings flapping as he left the chamber, all memory and history of evil within the vault passed with him.

Once Raour'Saqan rejoined them, while everyone stood around the lip of the pit, Yip asked, "Where shall we place the new seal?"

Eidelion took but a moment to answer. "Though the central evil in this city has fallen, much of its stain and ruin remains. There are other powers here, too, that warrant direct intervention but time is short. Ridding the city of this wickedness permanently will be the work of generations, if undertaken at all."

"We must find a position of relative purity and safety beyond the confines of the city and its reach. Though the suffocating fogs yet remain, dissipating over time, we should find a place well beyond their shroud for Darkness travels just as well as Light."

"Though the ward is resilient and resistant to fell magics and manipulation, we should also find a location beyond the reach of the Orcs as well."

Slate clapped his mailed hands together with a resounding thump in mock excitement. "Nothin' like more traipsin' through tha wilderness!"

Daerdros replied for Eidelion. "We have other means to evaluate the surroundings rather than on foot or by air. Spreesprocket, Aroganji, Wrindanneth, and myself all have the means"—here she paused and looked at Yip, correcting herself—"and Yip, I suppose, all have the means to evaluate the local environment. Before we go anywhere, we should first assess these spots magically."

Aroganji asked, "Should we work from here, the *Shrike*, or another place entirely?"

Wrindanneth briefly summarized his thoughts. "We are no more or less safe here than anywhere else in this accursed place. The remaining Shadows are aware of what has transpired with their master and his lair. They will doubtless be about regardless of where we may be."

Wrin paused before adding, "In fact, I am surprised they have not descended upon us already."

Yip spoke next. "We should go to the *Shrike*. Those who are not searching for suitable locations to restore the seal will then have the opportunity to work on repairing the ship—collecting debris, sorting through wreckage, looking for any items that may be lost, and placing parts in their proper place to aid in the ship's regeneration."

Spreesprocket clarified Yip's comment. "If the wards have held and the *Shrike* remains free from evil, the sentry drones should be well on their way to organizing the various parts and wreckage left after the crash. That is not to say, however, that our presence would not be of assistance."

"Anyone else?" Eidelion looked around to each member of the Home Guard and the Fists. Voicing his decision, he said, "Our interests will best be served at the ship. We will need to return there before we can go to Tellanon. Time remains of the essence. By going to the ship, we will be making ready for our return and restoring the seal simultaneously."

He finished, "While the mages are about their business, we can gauge the state of the *Shrike* and determine how much additional work needs to be done before she is operational once more."

Wrindanneth pointed back across the rubble dramatically, over the heaping slabs of stone and debris, retracing their route inward, unexpectedly calling out exuberantly, ready to be reunited with his ship. "To the *Shrike!*"

A motley flock, both large and small, native fliers and those requiring arcane assistance, they took to the air, leaving behind the blighted ruins of Eldre'gheu forever.

Rising above the fractured stones, the irregular jagged lip of the temple's wall, all that remained of the once immense dome, as if a massive Dragon had hatched from within, leaving the broken fragments of its shell in its wake as it took to the skies. Though the air remained thick, the fog had thinned; the wind chill and damp on Yip's face. The putrescent, nacreous green magical dome had fallen with the temple, its master, and the vortex contained within.

Though he still sensed the presence of Shadows and their brethren within the city, they had scattered or disappeared, a tether binding them broken with the Daemon's fall, their numbers diminished from the unassailable wall of thousands upon thousands to the few and far between. Without restoration or continued vigilance, other Shadows could eventually take their place.

Though the air and city remained oppressive, the shadows still dark and deep, the ruins yet threatening, he could imagine the glory and grandeur of the city at its height so long ago. Looking down upon the tumbled stones and vestiges of structures on their slow, inevitable journey back into the earth, he saw these remnants as the foundations for so much more—aspirations striving for the heavens, idealism prior to its fall, and hope before its end.

Lost in an inner recreation of what may have been, the journey to the wreckage of the *Shrike* passed as smoothly as the wind upon his cheeks.

Had they not known where to look, the location of the *Shrike's* crash was easily found. Freshly turned earth, lengthy furrows cutting across otherwise unbroken ground, stood in stark contrast to the ominous, undisturbed cityscape.

The appearance of the ship itself, was another matter entirely.

When they had left, the *Shrike* was only so much flinders—hull shattered into pieces, broken apart, masts snapped, sideboards and rigging destroyed—little remained intact beyond a vision of what once had been. Now, however, in the relatively short time since they departed, though it seemed weeks had passed in the space of a day, she was once more taking form.

The remaining sentry drones buzzed about carefully lifting fragments of wood and rigging, setting these pieces in place with the steady attention required to restore a massive, intricate puzzle. As the drones set these parts in place using intricate spatial mapping and pattern recognition algorithms, the magic of the ship began its work, restoring what had been broken, realigning pieces as needed, recreating the strength and structure that had originally kept the ship intact.

Expecting to see broken fragments, Yip's face lit in joy and amazement when he saw that the entire structure of the ship had been rebuilt and much of the finish work of the deck, hull, and interior was complete.

Though they would allow for some time to finish the restoration once everything had been set back in place to allow proper mending and to prevent further damage in places not fully repaired, with the help of the drones, restoration that might have taken weeks if left to the ship's own magic would be accomplished in days.

Always surprised by the wide wonder of the world beyond what had once been his sheltered monastic walls, Yip shook his head, appreciative of gifts, even those he could not fully comprehend.

Though his surprise was muted, Slate's was not. "By Freyda's frock, won't ya look at that! We'll be takin' ta tha air before nightfall tomorrow!"

Wrindanneth sniffed. "Don't get ahead of yourself, Slate. We'll need at least an extra couple of days before the deck is sturdy enough so that you don't fall through when you trundle aboard!"

Slate harrumphed. "I'm lighter on my feet than a mountain goat. Ya're tha one about as graceful as a blind, three-legged mule!"

"Don't fear, Wrin. I'll be there ta catch ya when ya fall. All I ask is that ya wait 'til tha ship is repaired so ya don't risk fallin' too far!"

Before Wrindanneth could retort, Yip interposed, "The time has come to find the seal a new home. All of our efforts will be needed to reinstate the ward to its rightful place."

Still glowering at one another, their conversation not yet finished, Wrindanneth and Slate kept their argument silent, communicating as effectively with glares as with aspersions.

SEAL'S ASCENT

Spider web strands spun
through the tops of bushes
catch the morning sun.

Their initial assessment of the *Shrike* complete, all gathered within the ship's surprisingly intact shadow, Aroganji asked, "Are we ready to begin our search for the seal's new home?"

Not having received explicit direction from Éremon on the seal's exact placement, Wrindanneth asked, "What exactly are we looking for in a location to place the seal?"

Eidelion answered this question for him. "Without straying too far, perhaps within a hundred leagues of our current location, we should seek a place that is pure, with undisturbed magical energies. The area should be isolated, away from possible risks and dangers, at least as safe as can be hoped within the untrammeled wilderness. Furthermore, the site should be inconspicuous. Without defenders or extensive protections beyond those inherent to the seal itself, avoiding notice will help shield the seal from both the curious and malicious."

Understanding their orders, Wrindanneth, Aroganji, Spreesprocket, and Daerdros prepared themselves as they saw fit to begin their reconnaissance. Given the magicians' skills and capabilities, Yip did not join them in their search, instead choosing to remain on guard should anything unforeseen arise.

Though connected through their respective talismans, Wrindanneth and Aroganji did not search in tandem, rather they choose to use their talents individually while remaining in constant contact during their search. Despite choosing to explore on their own, each relied upon the other to examine and evaluate potential points of interest.

Sitting alongside Aroganji next to the other casters in the *Shrike*'s irregular shadow as the sentry drones flew busily overhead assisting in the reconstruction, Wrindanneth began a clever invocation that granted him the ability not only to see extreme distances as clearly as if he were within a stone's throw away, but also allowed him to examine the region in more detail with all of his senses. Though he did not send the entirety of himself across the landscape, he projected his awareness with the same effect of teleporting to new locations with each glance. Each jump allowed him to quickly assess the region and discern whether any points of potential opportunity may reside nearby.

Allowing magic, the currents of energetic transformation, to be his guide, Aroganji floated upon the tides of transition and expression, reading the flow of the fundamental forces, letting them lead him toward potential oases of stability and purity outside the confines of the city. Drifting like a leaf upon a river, he slid across the landscape searching for those points where the Wu-hsing were in balance, unaltered by malevolent disturbances, replenished by the wells of creation.

His magical instrumentation projected over the landscape like a vast net, a lattice interpreted by his capacious intelligence, Spreesprocket relied upon the extensive sensory capabilities of his exoarmor to augment his search capabilities. Scanning all around, both near and far, the armor's artificial intelligence engine, along with his own, jointly sorted and evaluated each point along several decision parameters, returning those locations ranked as the most favorable for Spreesprocket's additional analysis. From brook to knoll, wood to dale, he registered each point of interest for further discussion with his fellows.

Daerdros sat quietly and began to hum. She sang of peace and safety, surety and stability, lasting endurance and resilience. She sang of purity and hope, purpose and will. She sang of desire and beauty, assurance and perseverance. She wove these sentiments together, creating a vision, a sensation, of place. This impression she gave to the wind, letting the creation of her will find its mirror, letting her anthem return the reality of this vision to her on the wings of melody.

Minutes passed, slipping into hours. Finally, one by one, each spellcaster released their concentration, returning to the group to discuss what they had found, hoping to arrive at a consensus based on the evidence they had uncovered.

Seeing Daerdros open her eyes at the last, her work completed, Eidelion initiated discussion. "What have you found?"

Spreesprocket called up a three-dimensional representation of the surrounding landscape including the complete topography and land cover. Overlaid on this true-to-life representation were glowing white dots scattered at random over the surface. "According to my analysis along several decision and evaluation paths, there are multiple locations within fifty to one hundred leagues that should qualify for placement of the seal for their multi-layered congruity within our evaluation parameters."

Moving his index finger over the projection, placing his finger lightly on each white light in succession, brought up a highly detail-rich enhanced depiction of every qualifying location. "As you can see from these variables illustrated for each area, we can also establish a relative ranking of all designated positions."

With this final comment, each point adjusted intensity from soft white to scintillatingly bright.

Wrindanneth shook his head. "And how exactly do you propose we input our findings within your decision criteria?"

Spreesprocket smiled. "Simple! Magic!"

When Wrindanneth's face remained blank, not for lack of understanding but to signify that Spreesprocket's answer was insufficient, he clarified, "I will overlay the data from your individual determination matrices onto the projection to concisely and simply summarize a complete multi-dimensional decision tree."

With a bright smile, he finished, "Then the answer will be clear for all to see!"

Slate groaned. "Hopefully clear'n yer explanation!"

Though he remained silent, Wrindanneth could not agree more.

"Hold on just a minute!" Never one to rely on a simple spell when a complex device could perform the task in more time with more work, Spreesprocket opened his boundless bag and began to rummage around excitedly, buried up to his elbow in the magical pouch.

After a minute or so of digging, he whooped, sweeping his arm upright dramatically, proclaiming proudly, "Here it is!"

Decidedly unimpressed, Slate merely grunted, his eyes returning to examination of the projection.

Spreesprocket flashed his magical instrument before them with as much pride as a parent at an awards reception held in their child's honor. "Behold! The wondrous C^3!"

Shaking his head, Wrindanneth smacked his forehead and held back a laugh.

For all his excitement, Spreesprocket appeared to be brandishing a shiny tinfoil cap molded into a somewhat regular conical shape with several randomly protruding haphazard antennae in various shapes and angles. For his part, Wrindanneth could not decide if the hat looked like an elaborate dunce cap for the mentally challenged or a lightning rod intended to self-select the wearer directly and mercilessly out of the gene pool.

Maintaining a straight face, albeit with some difficulty, Aroganji asked, "And what exactly is the C^3 and what does it do?"

Spreesprocket practically beamed at Aroganji's question, the glowing look on his face that of a teacher appreciating an astute question from a particularly adept, favorite pupil. "I'm glad you asked! The C^3, better known as the Cogitation Clarifying Cap, registers, displays, and analyzes thought processes and patterns."

Tapping his tin cap lovingly with the flat of his left hand, he gushed, "We merely have to interface the C^3 with the extant multi-dimensional decision tree and we will have a robust, refined solution to our search for the future location of the seal!"

Cautious, Wrindanneth asked, "And what exactly do we have to do for this tin cap to work its magic?"

His face lit by a smile, Spreesprocket replied, "Why wear it of course! The cap will take care of the rest!"

Nodding solemnly, arriving reluctantly at a decision he had hoped could be avoided but that he knew he could not, Wrindanneth muttered, "I feared as much."

Undeterred, Spreesprocket asked effusively, "So who wants to be first?"

His countenance less than enthusiastic, Wrindanneth grumbled, "I'll get it over with first."

Breaking off his connection with Aroganji, Wrindanneth reached for the proffered magical tinfoil hat. Taking the cap in his hands, he felt the cool metal beneath his fingers and a faint charge, the sensation one of a surface laced with unreleased static electricity. Placing the cap gingerly on his head, he felt the same tenuous charge begin to dance atop the surface of his scalp as the electrical impulse transferred to his hair and skin beneath the cap.

As Wrin placed the C^3 atop his head, he watched as his long red hair began to stand on end, floating in a vibrant nimbus around the periphery of his vision where it was not restrained by the contours of the metallic hat.

His hair still floating in all directions to the front, to the sides, and to the back, he felt a slight tickling as the energies of the cap transitioned to his skull, slowly working their way deeper and deeper inward, receiving an oddly soothing, internal electrical massage.

Examining the process intently, Slate watched Wrindanneth transform into something resembling a gigantic, fuzzy red-topped flower. By the time Wrindanneth set the cap down fully atop his head, small arcs of blue energy resembling guided electrical discharges or grounded lightning bolts began to jump and skitter to and fro on the irregular antenna scattered about the hat's surface. At this point, he had no idea what Wrindanneth resembled.

Wrindanneth did, however, appear hilarious.

Nor could he restrain himself from laughing any longer.

Letting out a thunderous guffaw, he held his full belly with one hand and pointed with the other. "Ya look a bit like a wilted flower that's been struck by a bit o' particularly persistent lightning!"

Not feeling the need to constrain himself, confident that his retort would not interfere with the C^3's analysis, Wrindanneth barked, "And you look like a roach infested, heaping pile of bat guano!"

Watching Wrindanneth's head bob back and forth angrily, his hair refusing to budge with the agitated motions, perhaps reinforced by a batch of particularly resilient Gnomish hair styling gel, the electrical arches only accentuating the comicalness of his anger, Slate's laughter rapidly turned into a series of unrestrained guffaws as he shook his head and pointed at Wrindanneth in mute hilarity.

Unable to talk through the laughter, Slate said no more.

Glowering sullenly, Wrindanneth waited patiently for an opportunity to exact revenge, using the time the C^3 worked to think of a particularly suitable retaliation.

What would it be? A forked, swollen tongue that prevented further conversation? Perhaps a particularly nasty case of oozing Troll pustules? Skunk sweat? Explosive hemorrhoids?

The list of possibilities floating through Wrindanneth's devious mind could curse an entire army several times over.

Whatever he chose, he would do it at night while everyone slept. That way, Slate would have to suffer through the curse at least until the morning when someone would be available to offer him a cure.

Within the space of a few short minutes, his hair fell back down around his shoulders and he knew that the cap's work was done.

Smiling welcomingly as he reached for the C^3, Spreesprocket said, "That wasn't so bad was it?"

Glaring at Slate who had finally returned to sputtering bouts of normalcy, Wrindanneth spat, "Not so bad as the company."

"Who's next?" Blithely untouched by Wrindanneth's comment, Spreesprocket cradled the silver cap to his chest while he waited for the ensuing volunteer.

Curious about the whole process and having significantly less hair than Wrindanneth, Aroganji blurted, "I would like to go next!"

The smile never leaving his face, Spreesprocket handed the tinfoil hat to Aroganji.

In quick succession, the C^3 analyzed both Aroganji's and Daerdros's thoughts and their attendant magical analysis.

With significantly less hair, Aroganji lacked the comedic effect that Wrindanneth displayed so graciously under the C^3's magic. He spent the few minutes wearing the cap simply enjoying the novel sensations cascading about and within his skull and mind without distraction.

Having significantly more hair than Aroganji, Daerdros did have an appearance very similar to Wrindanneth's as she wore the C^3, her head wreathed in a halo of floating hair as the cap's magic took effect.

No one dared make any comments about her, however.

Without Wrindanneth's flair for drama, Daerdros remained quiet throughout the experience. Her poise, focus, and attractive features lent her an air of the beatific while the cap worked its magic.

Nodding sagely as he took the C^3 from Daerdros after the scan had concluded, sharing what he had already seen, Spreesprocket swept his hand across the three-dimensional landscape hovering before them. As his arm moved over the image, each point of interest adjusted intensity once more, combining the information provided by each magician's search heuristic into one final, summary analysis of the most desirable locations for the new seal.

Resting on the far southern edge of the rendering, shining above all others, its radiance that of a guiding star alone and without peer in the night sky, one point clearly stood out. This locus was to be their destination.

"There you have it! The solution to our collective analyses lies there!" Spreesprocket's small index finger only accentuated the point where all of their eyes were already focused. With a swish of his finger, the image grew larger, fully revealing the details of the location where the seal would soon be placed and restored.

"That's it?" Slate's incredulity was balanced by a strong desire to move onward and be done with this whole affair. He had seen enough death and Darkness in this ill-begotten city to grind his axe on.

"If there's no further discussion, then I would surmise so." Spreesprocket hopped from foot to foot in his eagerness to personally assess the solution of their collective evaluation.

Spreesprocket magnified the image floating in the air with a wave of his hand, allowing for a much clearer representation of their next destination. The picture showed, most surprisingly given their current bleak environs, a landscape both serene and pristine. A moderately sized waterfall surged over large, stepped stones tinted green by submerged plants. Overhead, ancient trees bedecked in vibrant, multicolored crystalline leaves bowed inward as if trying to drink in both the moisture in the air and the beauty of the place. Lush vegetation crowded the stream's edge, completely obscuring the bank. Butterflies, bees, dragonflies, birds, and numerous other magical creatures flitted through the air in shimmering clouds of iridescent motion.

Yip could almost hear the birdsong.

He could almost feel the vibrancy and life of the setting.

Eidelion waited a few moments to allow everyone to study the image, granting opportunity to voice any pertinent concerns prior to proceeding. "If this spot satisfies all of our requirements, then I see no reason to delay further."

Slate stood, dusting off his breeches, though the magic within them kept them free of dirt. "Agreed! Let's be on with it! If we take much longer, tha ship'll be fully repaired by tha time we return!"

A clear vision of their destination in mind, Daerdros unsheathed her blade, a fluid motion that sent dancing motes of power streaming through the air. With an elegant half-moon cut, she stepped through the image, slicing through the projection with the same skill and precision she would if cutting down an enemy. As her blade whistled through the air, a golden arch of blinding light followed the sword's circuit, the burgeoning energies of another world gushing forth unrestrained from within the cut.

Her motion complete as quickly and economically as it began, a portal danced and wavered in the air, a doorway opened by the fleeting movements of her blade's edge. Sheathing her sword, she gestured everyone through with the motion of one hand. Beyond, they could all see the reality of the image brought within footsteps by the power of her brand.

Peering first from the portal then to Daerdros and her sword, Wrindanneth eyed the Caer'collas with admiration. Though far traveling would have worked just as well, he certainly had to admire her style.

Dipping his head briefly in respect as he walked past, Wrindanneth was the first to take Daerdros's offer and step through the golden-limned portal to the magical panorama waiting for them on the other side.

Stepping through the portal after Wrindanneth, Yip stopped in place immediately upon passing through, gripped in amazement, to take in the beauty now enveloping him. Spreesprocket's representation, though vivid, true to life, and more vibrant than the clearest visualization, could not capture all the dimensions of wonder set in full display so brilliantly around him.

He truly had stepped into another world.

Given the desolation, dearth, and decay of Eldre'gheu so recently departed, these sensations were only heightened by the abrupt transition.

He stood on the edge of an embankment overlooking a clearly flowing ultramarine waterway. Streamers of verdant aquatic plants swayed rhythmically beneath steady currents traveling downward from a small series of cascades murmuring over large flat boulders farther upstream.

Plants of more colors and descriptions than he could classify bunched and pushed eagerly toward the light, magic, and water, both of the crystalline and vascular varieties, the combination of photosynthetic and aeryasynthetic organisms rubbing against each other in the steady breeze creating irregular and harmonious arrangements of musical chimings, rustlings, and susurrations. Over the soft chorus of variegated moving plants, the humming, buzzing, chirping, and trilling of birds, fey creatures of all sorts, and insects fleshed out the interlaced melodies shifting regularly above the refreshing sounds of the wind and watercourse.

Here the music of the senses soothed the mind and heart.

Rushing more vibrantly than the stream and all the organisms crowded in its proximity, energies shifted and roiled raucously through the air and ground, a kaleidoscope of potential, enlivening and empowering all that he felt and saw.

There was too much to appreciate, too much to absorb, so he watched filled with curiosity and awe.

"Ahem!"

He blinked at the deep, irritated sound of Slate's voice, so lost had he been in the scene's beguilements though his fascination had lasted but seconds.

Quickly recovering himself as Slate's low, terse grumble behind him broke his reverie, he stepped aside to let the others through.

"Ya'd think we were on some kinda holiday with ya, laggin' about starin' like a wide-eyed, star-struck yokel!"

A spontaneous grin coming to his lips, Yip made way for the remaining companions with a bow, allowing them to pass through the arcane gate free of his distracted obstructionism.

The others through, he returned to his observation. Such a gorgeous place would be a fitting location for an object of as much importance as the seal. That a place so lush and vibrant could remain intact within the long shadows of Eldre'gheu brought no small amount of joy to his heart. That the Orcs or some other fell creatures had not despoiled this portion of the wilderness only strengthened these sentiments.

He was as eager to restore the new seal to its rightful position as this location was beautiful.

Slate whistled appreciatively to his right, the high note blending in with the many sounds and sensations shifting all around. After a few moments, he added quietly, "I can understand yer distraction, Yip. 'Tis a wonderful place."

Yip need not nod in agreement. He stated simply, "We chose well."

Eidelion walked to Yip's side, his tall shadow falling unnoticed amidst the light reflected and radiated from numerous sources around them. Placing a strong hand on Yip's shoulder, he responded simply, "We did indeed."

When Yip smiled in reply to the comment, Eidelion asked, "Are we ready to begin?"

Yip bowed simply in turn.

Reaching into the inner folds of his robes for the sealed magical pocket that had carried Éremon's protective case all these long leagues through so many dangers and hostile encounters, he gingerly retrieved the delicately crafted oaken box hidden within. Without opening the chest, through the many wards placed upon its case, he sensed the warmth and power gathered within, emanating outward with the heat of the sun on a warm spring day. Not only did the seal's radiance warm his body, it warmed and soothed his mind as well.

Unsure exactly how to proceed, where exactly to place the seal, or what was expected of him, for Éremon had given few instructions or clarifications other than to place the seal in a place of purity, he released the hasp holding the wooden box shut and let the light from the clear stone spill forth from within.

Intending to reach forward, pick up the seal, and gently rest it on the ground, he never had the chance. Before he could place the seal within the palm of his hand, it began to glow brighter and brighter, floating up into the air all the while, higher and higher—a small star returning to the heavens, blazing a brilliant trail for all to see.

A chorus of comments, some whispered in reverence, some outbursts of excitement, greeted the seal's ascension.

"Would ya look at that!"

"Absolutely brilliant!"

"The elements will soon be restored to proper balance!"

"What an amazing symmetrical concordance!"

"May the Light of the seal burn away all Shadows that venture forth on this land, protecting Ea'ae from further advance."

"With this seal, the bonds on Ur'Daus's cage tighten!"

Yip, however, remained spellbound in the deep silence of true, heartfelt appreciation.

He need not do anything.

The magic of the seal would take care of itself.

Burning brighter and brighter, the light and warmth of its radiance spreading ever farther and more intensely, the seal rose heavenward in the glory of rebirth and renewal.

Too bright to gaze upon directly, he averted his eyes, feeling the seal's power growing within the confluence of life-giving energies suffusing the land and air.

With a blinding flash, as surprising as its ascension began, the seal disappeared even more quickly, the afterimage of its resplendence still burning on their retinas once its light had passed.

Within this flash, bathed by the seal's metamorphosing energies, at the heart of a newly arisen interlinked planetary matrix of force, Yip was engulfed, somehow yet connected to the seal, cast upon a vast surging conduit of power, transported within a dimensionless wave of energy.

He was simultaneously a part of this overwhelming current, yet concurrently aware of his individuality. The juxtaposition added another layer of dichotomous interconnectedness upon his awareness of simultaneous immersion within and separation from the all-pervasive *chi*. Riding atop this cresting wave of power, surreally aware of his body standing at the edge of the stream, and yet also aware of the tide of energy's destinations and interlinkages, he was cast away upon the flows of global forces rushing between Ea'ae's protective seals—both a mote and a river.

Though he remained himself, he was indeed the protective energies girding the planet, the self-reinforcing forces organized and channeled to prevent extradimensional incursion, these forces and their destinations, the world and its manifestations. With the newly restored seal, he sensed the eleven active seals harnessing and guiding these ley lines of force, immense nexuses of power shielding the world from outside interference. He also felt the gaps and weaknesses within this matrix, the places where the seals were altogether missing, broken, corrupted, and otherwise compromised.

Their work had just begun for the other seals had not yet been restored. There remained three in need of replacement and several others in need of restoration. The worthies who had attempted to repair these others had either failed or not yet reached their aim.

He desperately hoped for the latter.

Though Ea'ae would never be truly safe until the seals about her perimeter were restored, so, too, would she never be secure until the Cabal were overthrown and cast down from their place in the heavens, laid low by those they wished to destroy. Thus, two combating needs synchronously tore him in opposite directions.

Granted this glimpse, this brief oceanic view of the world at large, given a much deeper appreciation of the role their quest played within assuring its safety, perhaps because of his role as the new seal's steward and as the one who restored its position within the global web, he snapped back into his body, a tether that would not be cut.

He would aid in protecting Ea'ae and restoring her seals so long as they knew not where to seek the Cabal.

He only hoped that the two paths led to the same end for if he walked one, he may not be able to walk the other.

"Yip?"

Aroganji had been talking and he had not responded. There was a note of concern in his voice. "Yip, are you all right?"

"I am." The extra layers of sensation leaving him, his awareness returned to himself, the place, his friends, and the energies emanating within and radiating from without, a drop in the sea aware that he yet remains a droplet in the ocean.

"You had us worried for a minute there!" Wrindanneth's face was etched with rare lines of concern.

"The seal gave me a brief glimpse of its destiny. I gave it my full attention."

"What d'ya mean?" Slate's thick eyebrows furrowed on his brow, crosslinked like the branches in a bird's nest.

"I felt the seal's place among the others, its connections to its peers, the forces binding them together, and I experienced the gaps in that network, the holes and points of weakness. I learned that though we have done much, there is even more yet to do."

"Ya mean tha others have failed?" Slate's mix of raw disappointment and concern sounded much harsher than he had intended against the soothing backdrop of the fey stream.

"I cannot say. I can say that they have not yet succeeded."

Aroganji's assessment was matter-of-fact. "Then we have more yet to do before we can return to our quest for the Cabal."

"Perhaps. Perhaps one will lead to the other. Perhaps one will occur in tandem with the other."

Wrindanneth laughed. "Perhaps, if we take long enough, the Paratechnologists will decipher the alien command sphere."

Slate joined in, offering, "Perhaps, if we take long enough, tha Cabal will die out and we can leave this whole accursed mire behind us!"

Eidelion finished this line of conversation, his voice a mixture of jest and command. "Perhaps we should get back to the ship so that we can begin our journey home."

"Aye! I'll drink a tankard ta that!" Slate stood up from where he had been settled on his haunches, eager to be off.

Turning to Yip, he said, "Ya know, I'd expected tha seal ta stay in place, remain here, markin' this location so ya could see it and touch it. I never thought it would go away after we spent all this effort ta get it here."

Though he could still feel the echoes of the seal's presence, for the confluence of energies it realized and brought together were beyond conception, the sensation remained distant for the seal's magic prevented tampering or alteration with its function.

Like Yip, it was both separate and a part.

"Nor did I, Slate."

Standing off to the side, his small form partially occluded by the shadow of a crystalline tree that split the sunlight into myriad dancing prisms, his eyes both on the dazzling clearing and the spacious world opening within, after remaining isolated for the entire course of their journey, Spreesprocket renewed full contact with his internal world.

Taking flight, his mind weaved through a world of luminous intelligences, each vast and interconnected, webs of awareness tied to each other and the fabric of the metaspace in which they inhabited. This world of information, bounded only by thought, served as the medium through which he moved, the cosmos to which he restored connection.

This realm of the mind, the world of accumulated knowledge was, as much as his breath or body, the foundation of his existence. That he had remained separated from it for so long spoke to the gravity of their quest, the urgency of secrecy, and his willingness to aid in whatever ways possible.

That he returned so eagerly spoke of his own desires.

Within this space, a macrocosm created solely for the inhabitation of melded intelligences, minds merged and brought together through a single medium, he experienced the full glory of abstraction, consciousness revealed in its unbounded clarity. Through immense distances only separated by thought, like intelligences floated through the aether, commingled, and parted, sharing observations, insights, and truths, each a star, a galaxy, and a universe unto itself, each an atom in a much larger molecule.

Though he would soon fully partake in this interaction once more, there was, however, one mind he sought out above all others, one sentience whose light he wished to share.

The need of his will, the aim of his mind brought him to his goal, crossing the entirety of the noosphere in an instant. Before him, a shifting, swirling multi-dimensional nebula of supreme beauty and order beckoned.

To this he returned.

To this, the mind of the Construct, he shifted, extending his awareness to his destination in an instant, for all of Tellanon needed to know of their success and all of her people needed to share in their joy.

All the while, he smiled with his friends in the clearing, sharing in their triumph and the fruition of happiness within their hearts at this success that ensured, at least for a time, their world's continued safety.

While Daerdros drew her sword with a high pitched ring as it left her sheath in preparation to take them back to the ship, Aroganji said, "Maybe the other seals are different. Perhaps they remained tangible after placement. Maybe Éremon, through long study and after careful contemplation, altered this seal's magic to help prevent against the type of corruption and alteration that befell the seal of Eldre'gheu."

Knowing more than them of the seals, their history, and creation, Eidelion stepped forward toward the shimmering gate Daerdros cut through the air with her singing blade, the outline of the *Shrike* visible through the glowing luminescence on the other side. Turning his head before he stepped through the gap in space and time, Eidelion replied with a fleeting smile, "Perhaps you are right."

NOVAS

Wind rushes through trees
rustling last autumn's leaves.
My eyes close, night falls.

Humbol gazed heavenward through his telescope, unable to tear his eyes away from the raging battle above. Watching the conflict unfold over the uncounted hours, his heart sank to the bottommost pit of his stomach.

The battle was not going well.

Though Tellanon's forces fought admirably, mowing down untold swaths of alien ships, wheat falling at the harvest before a sharpened scythe, no matter how many vessels Tellanon's defenders brought to end in founts of fiery destruction, more ships seemed to emerge from the churning Darkness.

No pursuit had followed their flight from the scene of strife. After much evasive maneuvering above the treetops, he and Hoyt had finally settled along the edge of an unnamed wood next to a small river, the water's soothing sounds in direct contrast to the distant sounds of thunder rumbling and threatening from above.

With this temporary reprieve, though they lost track of the passage of time surveying the interminable firefight above, Humbol and Hoyt had taken up watch side-by-side, staring upward into the deepening night as the battle continued to rage onward.

Now, his eyes grown tired from peering through his magical telescope, weary of the sights of destruction, Humbol passed the instrument back to Hoyt, unwilling to bear witness to more devastation.

"The tide is inevitably turning."

He spoke of the steady advance of the alien fleet behind the seething wall of Darkness, its outlines now only inferred from the absence of stars behind its vast stain.

As he watched, he could see Tellanon's shields flickering briefly, failing for a short time before being restored. These moments of failing were due to the relentless enemy fire and allowed more ruination to pass within. Some of this devastation would be countered by secondary and tertiary defenses, but, as time wore on and damage mounted, more and more volleys and invaders would break through.

He did not wish to consider the consequences any further. He felt sullied, watching an aggressive, implacable form of cancer slowly consuming its target without hope of cure or amelioration.

Walking away from Hoyt without a word, his emotions too strong to speak, he stalked off from his friend taking up position by the railing. Resting his forearms on the cold wood, leaving his back to the fray though he was still aware of its presence, he tried to lose himself in the soothing waters flowing below the ship.

Though he tried for interminable minutes, his efforts were to no avail.

In the end, he would wait, as he had done before, until Hoyt grew tired of watching his home being laid low and passed the telescope back. Then he would resume his position of reluctant watch, observer of Tellanon's inevitable fall.

Such ceaseless broodings were a source of further dismay.

The days and months ahead, should they survive, would be filled with much more.

"Humbol! Quit yer sulkin' and come here!"

No longer aware of how long he had watched his sorrows drift by on silvery strands of starlight glistening on the waters reflected beneath the ship's wavering shadow, Humbol returned wearily to his friend's side.

As he neared, Hoyt held out the telescope eagerly, though to Humbol he looked like a snake or basilisk oil salesman trying to lure him into some clever trap, one he wished very much to avoid.

Placing the warm metal in the palm of his hand once more, he brought the telescope up to his eye warily, expecting to be bitten after the steady stream of horror it had already revealed to him.

Nothing had changed. Ships flashed and flared, short-lived stars granted a violent end in brilliant flashes of light and heat. The Darkness remained present—a horrific blot erasing a large, irregular expanse of the heavens.

Taking the eyepiece away quickly, for he was as yet not ready to view more, he growled at Hoyt, "Why d'ya want ta show me more? I've seen enough!"

"Then look again!" Hoyt was insistent.

Humbol, however, was equally resistant, merely shaking his head with finality. "No."

"Look again more closely, ya recalcitrant mule! The tide's shifted! Tellanon's forces are beatin' 'em back once more!"

How, in his mother's own name, had that happened?

Slowly bringing the telescope upward once more, Humbol did indeed look more closely. Watching carefully, taking the battle's measure over long, patient minutes, ever so slowly, he saw Hoyt's point. The pace of the invader's assault, the speed of their advance, was waning.

If he did not know any better, if the long hours passed witnessing just the opposite now proved false, to his eyes at least, he would guess that the alien armada's limitless font of ships had dried up and was no more.

With a dawning look of comprehension, a face filled with wonder, he brought down the telescope filled with a mixture of shock and excitement in equal measure. "Has tha Darkness been cut off from its source? Have tha invadin' ships' points of entry been severed?"

Sharing the same look of growing excitement and surprise, Hoyt grinned, offering, "Perhaps tha Four managed ta restore tha seal!"

Humbol nodded solemnly. "Against all odds, they might've done just that!"

His eyes filled with a mixture of excitement and pride, with the joy of one whose very own children had somehow against all odds accomplished a rare event worthy of note, Hoyt replied excitedly, "That'd be my guess!"

The look of wondrous incredulity still on his face, Humbol replied, "Let's just hope that ya're right and that tha damage done ta Tellanon and her citizens has not been too grievous."

Nodding solemnly, Hoyt replied, "Let's hope we all have a home ta come back ta and our friends can rejoin us."

Now eager to gaze through the telescope and gauge the scene of combat, the sorrow and weight of the past few hours lifted with the dawning of their realization, Humbol and Hoyt passed the telescope back and forth through the night, watching the tide turn as one Night gave way with another.

HOMEWARD

Sweeping ebon night
littered with silver stars
broader than imagining.

After all their work, after all their hardships, after all their triumphs, Yip could not believe their journey together was almost at an end. Thinking back to everything that had transpired since they left Tellanon such a short time ago, he also could not believe that their futures would, in all likelihood, entail so much more.

He smiled inwardly.

Proper endings often led to beginnings even broader.

"What're ya smilin' about?" Slate's gruff voice came from behind him where Yip had just returned through the portal. This time, however, Yip did not need admonishment to move out of everyone's way.

"The future." Yip's answer was as simple as their possible courses of action were broad.

"And ya're smilin' fer that? More traipsin' through Brendle-forsaken haunts filled with Daemonic nasties Abyssbent ta consume yer essence?"

"Nights spent on tha run from ravagin' hordes o' soulless savages tryin' ta eat yer heart?"

"Fruitless quests ta overthrow corrupt civilizations whose warped views o' reality will never change?"

He turned to Slate to address his friend directly, the golden outline of the portal fading in the air even as they spoke, merely an afterimage of what was. "I am smiling for the possibility the future entails."

Slate nodded shortly, returning Yip's smile with his own. "My sentiments exactly! A Dwarf can never have too much ale, gold, or head smashin'! Adventure tends ta reward tha discernin' with all three!"

Walking a few short steps toward the nearly completed outline of the *Shrike* where the Home Guard gathered, Slate turned his attention to Eidelion, Daerdros, Raour'Saqan, and Spreesprocket. "Now that we've saved tha world, will ya be goin' back without us while we wait fer tha ship's restoration or d'ya care ta spend a bit more time in tha pleasure o' our wondrous company?"

Eidelion had already given the *Shrike* an inspection upon his return and was even now standing in the ship's shadow. He laughed briefly at Slate's hyperbole. "If we did not return, who else would spread word of your miraculous feats?"

Wrindanneth took up Slate's tone of joking bravado. "Excellent! I've always wanted a herald!"

"Now you will have three!" Eidelion's bright smile flashed like the sun emerging from behind thick clouds.

A moment passed before Aroganji understood the import of Eidelion's comment. "Three? Why? Will someone else not be returning?"

Slate joked, "Perhaps one o' tha Home Guard has tha good sense ta stay with us and avoid their duties a bit longer!"

When Slate finished, Eidelion said simply, "Those questions are for Raour'Saqan to answer, not I."

"Has your time here come to an end, Raour'Saqan?" Yip felt a tinge of sadness at yet another parting, as their fellowship slowly broke apart, individuals no longer united by a common cause.

Hunched next to the other Home Guard, his massive form made all the more obvious given his imposing size relative to his companions even while crouched, Raour'Saqan's deep, grating voice replied, "The Shadows in Taerris'thule are broken. Though some yet linger, the Light will soon return."

"Though there is much yet to be done on Ea'ae, the remaining seals, should they remain uncompromised, provide enough protection to guard against the evils that may threaten."

His gaze heavenward, Raour'Saqan continued, "Though I may still be of some use here, I may offer more elsewhere."

"And so I must leave."

Each statement was firm, confident, and uttered with complete finality.

Yip studied the fearsome Dracodaeran Shaur'Daus carefully. Of all the mighty heroes he had traveled with, Raour'Saqan alone could stand solitary and defiant against almost any foe they may face on an equal or greater footing. His was a power to be feared with a purpose to be respected. Though his essence devoured energy, both Light and Dark, he defined himself by furthering the cause and opportunity of all life and the potential it engendered.

In such savage hands was the future gently cradled.

"You have done the peoples of Ea'ae and beyond great honor by aiding in our cause just as you have honored your own." Yip offered a deep bow of gratitude to the stalwart Dracodaeran.

"I do what I must as do you."

Raour'Saqan was correct, though there was more than necessity behind all of their actions. Yip acknowledged this comment and sentiment with another bow.

"Though I leave, I may yet return. We should all hope such a course is not necessary, however."

There was no need for further comment.

Waiting but a moment, testing the brief silence with his reply, Slate sighed, "And then there were three."

Raour'Saqan laughed, a terrible sound that instinctively engendered a deep, enduring fear that sank through and down to the bottommost pit of the stomach even in those who were familiar with the expression. "There remain yet six, though we be apart. True fellowship does not end with the parting."

This time, Slate allowed no pause before comment. "Six?"

Now Slate was confused.

"Orogast and Llyewia yet remain. Though Orogast has departed for realms other than these, as will I, Llyewia yet abides."

Aroganji was indeed interested for he knew little of Elves, their magic, their rituals, or their life cycles. "How so?"

Wrindanneth was inquisitive as well for intimations of power, immortality, and transformation were of particular interest to his studies and his desired ends.

Raour'Saqan growled, his deep voice hushed, "Llyewia has returned to the starshine from whence he came."

Knowing more of the Elves than Yip would have thought possible, versed in so little himself, Raour'Saqan added with a thickly toothed grimace in what might pass as something of a rueful smile amongst his kind, "Before his parting with this world, Llyewia will speak with elders of his race, the Aeryn D'al, and sing his last songs to his kin. The knowledge and Light he lived will not be lost nor has it been diminished."

"He is now Anuvaerya, a being of pure thought and Light. His spirit yet burns and grows brighter."

Placing one thickly scaled hand on Yip's shoulder, his long fingers reaching almost completely across Yip's chest as they rested lightly over his front and back, the Dracodaeran grumbled, "Your gift, Yip, will not be lost to the Elves nor to their allies."

"Though he has not truly passed, you must gather his remaining implements and return them to his people in Tellanon. Items from the Elves should be restored to them unless freely given for they hold a special place in the hearts and minds of Elven peoples. They will, perhaps, plant his bow in memory of his passing."

Looking briefly in the distance somewhat wistfully, he added, "In time, when next I return, perhaps I will visit the grove planted in his honor, mayhap started by his Aeryn Sh'al."

Imagining just such an Elven grove sown in the fullness of wonder—lofty alabaster trees coursing with life caressed by sunbeams angling though the air alighting atop a rich loam of silver and golden leaves, the deep peace of silence resting tenderly upon the boughs—Yip appreciated the simple beauty of such a place, such a memorial—a fitting end and a beautiful beginning.

Looking to Spreesprocket, his black eyes glittering, Raour'Saqan continued, "As a representative of the Home Guard, Spreesprocket should accompany you when you return Llyewia's effects to the ground from which they sprang, giving fitting memory and representation to his people."

Slate laughed. "Assumin' he can find 'em in that pack o' his!"

Raour'Saqan acknowledged Slate's jest with a nod and a kind reply. "The implements have not gone far. Just give him time enough to find and arrange them before you visit the Elves. Though the Elves are patient and live long, they, too, may tire and run out of time waiting for Spreesprocket otherwise."

Slate's smile did not leave his face with the jest.

Spreesprocket added, "I will ensure that Kazarhan receives similar treatment among his kith and kin."

Slate sighed and shook his head. "Ya'd better do that one alone. Dwarves can be particular when it comes ta their own. 'T'would be more fittin' if ya came with a formal contingent o' Guard."

Spreesprocket nodded in agreement and offered a weak half-smile and jest, missing his friend greatly. "I will do my best to make certain I can retrieve him with the dignity he deserves from my pack."

His curiosity only partially sated, Aroganji followed another line of thought, adjusting the path of the discourse to suit his need for understanding. "Why are you telling us all this?"

Aroganji asked the question that had not yet been voiced.

"The Elves may be of further service to you in your quests. Their vision and reach are long. Their sages, guided by the Fria al'Othra, may help steer your course."

"They should also know that you have earned their abiding friendship."

"The true and lasting friendship of the Elves is a gift without measure having few equals."

"A fitting reward for your efforts."

Raour'Saqan paused for a moment, sitting in steady, unyielding silence for a time, before adding with a hint of finality, "My oath-bond here is ended with Eidelion's blessing. He has granted me leave."

Smiling fearsomely once more, he said, "I, too, will return to the starshine."

"Before I depart, I will tell the Dalaren Ka personally of our triumph! Taerris'thule has housed and harbored many of their enemies of old. They must know the victory Eidelion has helped grant them."

"The Dalaren Ka will wish to come to Eidelion and then help restore this place. There is much yet to be done here as elsewhere on Ea'ae."

"Perhaps they, too, will be of assistance to you in your quest both on Ea'ae and abroad."

"Eidelion will offer his recommendation should it be required."

"Should Éremon have need of me again, I shall come, but"—here his savage grin returned—"I fear other worlds are not so ably defended against the rising tides of Darkness."

He looked to each of the standing companions, those few that yet remained, in turn with something akin to pride, for he was loath to praise. "The Shaur'Daus, those few of us that yet abide, must know of the Dragon's Gate as well that we may become the Dauren'Kas!"

Raour'Saqan clenched one mighty, stone-crushing fist. "With such a gift, even Ur'Daus the Black will tremble!"

Yip bowed in respect and farewell to Raour'Saqan, not wishing to delay his departure any longer for his needs and aspirations were elsewhere. "May the Light of Life guide you to a future of peace and joy."

Raour'Saqan stood to his full formidable height, looming over the other companions and rested one massive hand upon Yip's shoulder. "May we all be graced by such a blessing."

Slate stepped forward and offered, "May your claws be as sharp as your wit!"

Raour'Saqan bowed his head in acknowledgement. "May your blade never dull."

Aroganji offered his own farewell, saying, "May your future be as rich as your past!"

Raour'Saqan grinned savagely in reply. "And yours as fulfilling."

Wrindanneth spoke simply, knowing how much the Dracodaeran had seen in his many long years. "When next we meet, there must be a telling of tales."

Raour'Saqan's black eyes sparkled briefly in response, lit by his inner fires. "Indeed we must!"

The valedictions complete, Raour'Saqan finished, "Until we meet again! D'orauk managua al'zurka!"

Having already said his goodbyes to the Home Guard, Raour'Saqan leapt into the air, the ground folding beneath his powerful legs as he shot upward, gaining height and speed so rapidly that after but a moment all the remaining companions could see of him was a flashing trail of superheated gases—a comet returned blazing and triumphant to the heavens.

Washing his hands together briefly, looking after Raour'Saqan's passage wistfully, Slate joked half seriously, half in jest, "Fer all o' our sakes, I hope that he's right." Though they had done it before, Slate did not look forward to facing the creatures of Darkness without Raour'Saqan and, far too quickly, the other intrepid members of the Light's Guard.

He knew, however, that time would come soon enough.

Resting the blade of Archaeus directly on the uneven earth along the perimeter of the ragged clearing housing the wreckage of the *Shrike*, Eidelion let the blade of his sword cut deeply into the soil, allowing the magic from his blade to flow freely into the ground. Walking in a large circle, the edge of his brand described a boundary in the dirt.

As he strode, the power of his blade filled the ground and air above it, blazing white Light spilling from the holy sword. When he finished, blessed energy scintillated in the gray light, white fire burning upward from the ground in a translucent haze encircling the ship, Archaeus's radiance warded the clearing from supernatural incursion.

When Eidelion completed protecting the ship, this divine boundary provided a line of demarcation over which extradimensional beings would not cross.

While Eidelion worked with Archaeus, Daerdros unsheathed her own sword in the shadow of the *Shrike*, the blade humming musically with the smooth motion. Holding the blade up to her lips, she called forth her magic and then blew, allowing the sword's enchanted blade to slice the energy in twain. Breaking her own arcana apart, splitting away the weave of her enchantment, she began a spell cleaving her magic into its constituent components. Over and over she breathed across the blade, riving her weavings into finer and finer parts. Though she fashioned her own magic, with each breath, she worked on cutting down any hostile, intruding magics that may contact the ship into its essential parts, dissipating the energy and potential of inimical magical attacks, and protecting against further assaults.

Staying with Aroganji, Wrindanneth, Yip, and Slate, Spreesprocket offered his own direct protection. "While Daerdros and Eidelion offer their boons, I am going to offer my own."

"Uh oh! I'm not sure what I'm more scared o', tha Daemons or havin' yer magic cast on me!"

Ignoring Slate's comments, Spreesprocket said, "Since your shielding devices were shattered by the Daemon's magic, I am going to offer several wards to minimize the risk of physical and magical harm in their absence."

Pulling out a multicolored, irregularly shaped wand, one end holding a faceted prism and the other decorated by the bright plumage of a phoenix, Spreesprocket made ready to begin his work.

Seeing the wand, Slate snorted, stifling a laugh. "Ya're gonna use that?"

Merely raising an eyebrow, Spreesprocket replied flatly, "And you have something better?"

Quieted by a simple forced confrontation with the truth, Slate made no reply.

The interruption at an end, Spreesprocket began. Interlacing several layers of enchantment around each of them, a halo of iridescent light basked the companions in a cloud of magical energies. When finished, the only residue of his magic was a faint shimmer in the air visible in the right light from the proper angle.

Taking his eyes from the dark gray heavens, his wards complete, no longer able to follow the friend he may never see again, Eidelion returned to the ship where the others gathered, looking upon the Four with the light of compassion in his bright eyes. "The time of leave-takings is upon us, though our parting will be but temporary."

"We must return to Tellanon to apprise the council of our success and begin discussions of what may follow. The *Shrike* should be fully repaired within the next few days. With the return stone, you will be able to rejoin us in short order."

"Then you, too, will be summoned before the Protectorate and asked to tell your tales."

"Though Taerris'thule is yet cloaked in Darkness, your Lights will offer the protection you need to remain safe and free of fear."

"Will ya need yer things before ya go?"

Eidelion gave a brief shake of his head. "Daerdros has already summoned those items we brought with us that remain undamaged from within the wreckage. Spreesprocket now has the remnants stored safely in his bag."

Slate laughed. "Ya'll be lucky ta have it back by tha time we return then!"

Turning to Spreesprocket, Slate remarked, "Be sure ta get Llyewia's goods in order when ya retrieve yer own. That might be a bigger adventure than the one we just finished!"

"You're one to talk, Slate." Wrindanneth oozed sarcasm as he spoke. "You're chiding Spreesprocket about his magic bag when you couldn't find your beard in ours. Talk about the cauldron calling the kettle black!"

Smiling politely, Spreesprocket replied accommodatingly to Slate while reaching for the small sack hanging tied at his side, "You are welcome to go in and get things organized."

Alarmed, reacting with the intensity of a tangible threat made directly against his life, Slate barked, "Not on yer life! I already have one o' those bags ta tangle with and that's enough! 'Tis a curse Brendle himself would forswear!"

Surrounded by a wall of laughter, Slate smiled with his friends glad to share in a bit of humor even if it was at his expense.

He minded little for his pockets were deep.

Stepping forward before their departure, Daerdros bid them her own brief farewell. "You have all acquitted yourselves with courage and distinction. Should ever any of you desire a place in the Guard, you have but to ask. We would all be honored to have you as companions working and fighting at our sides."

"If that is not a position you seek, you are welcome to share our halls and camaraderie whenever you wish. Should you need the advice or recommendation of the Guard, you have but to ask."

Yip bowed deeply. "You are most gracious, Daerdros. We thank you for the honor of your offer. I will look forward to walking the galleries of the Guard when our own work is done."

"As will I," chimed in the others in an almost perfect chorus.

Smiling, she bowed elegantly in return.

"If ever you would like some of the world famous Goldpulley Roasted Rutabaga Surprise, just let me know!"

When Wrindanneth wrinkled his face instinctively in distaste, Spreesprocket continued, "Or, if you ever need any Paratechnological advice or assistance, my toolbox is but a call away!"

Bowing once more, Yip answered, "Thank you as well, Spreesprocket. We may need your expertise in the times to come. Your offer is most gracious."

Laughing, Slate joked, "Don't ya ever get dizzy or lightheaded from all that bowin', Yip?"

Smiling, he replied, "Only when the air is too thin from too much talking."

Patting Slate reassuringly on the back, Wrindanneth said, "Never cross a Dragon or a baldheaded man. Particularly if they wear robes."

"Bah! Looks like I'm outnumbered even amongst my friends! Where're tha Shades when ya need 'em?"

A smile showing his brilliant white teeth, Eidelion offered, "You have been a joy to travel with and have done more to aid in the cause of the Light than any would have hoped possible. We are privileged to call you friends and allies."

"The honor is ours." Yip bowed yet again.

Slate laughed. "Yip, if ya don't stop deflectin' all our compliments, no one'll ever want ta aid us much less talk with us!"

Motioning for Spreesprocket to move forward, Eidelion said, "If you will do the honors."

Reaching for the elaborate umbrella angled across his back, Spreesprocket stepped away from the group toward the hull of the *Shrike*. Holding the crook handle of his umbrella in one hand and the central tube in the other, he released the top spring with a quick flick of his right hand with the motion of one shaking off raindrops from the canopy. Snapping open, the umbrella's ribs and stretchers began to glow beneath the fabric in fantastical neon lights. Spinning the umbrella about its central axis, perhaps in preparation to begin a particularly unique Gnomish dance, he thrust the umbrella forward in a kaleidoscope of swirling lights.

With the motion, space warped, visibly stretching and attenuating. Continuing the impetus forward, when space-time could apparently extend no more, his umbrella's ferrule broke through a point that expanded with the pressure of its release, broadening into a view of open blue skies and unsullied clouds.

The open air above Tellanon beckoned warmly full of reassurance.

Leaving their feet on the invisible wings of magic, Eidelion, Daerdros, and Spreesprocket floated upward, slipping through the portal and beyond into the skies adjoining Tellanon, the gateway closing behind them as rapidly as Spreesprocket's parasol first opened.

"And then there were four." Wrindanneth stared after the closing portal only briefly, just as glad to be on their own once again without having to pay consideration to others.

Slate grinned. "Tha Four!"

Yip joined in his friend's smile. "As there were in the beginning."

Slate shook his head. "With all this portin' about, ya'd think tha Home Guard would've just opened a portal ta home long before we got here and brought a whole regiment or battalion through ta clear out tha city and ease our way through ta tha Daemon."

"Don't get started thinking now, Slate, after all these years! It will only get you in trouble!" Though his friend had a point, at least in part, Wrindanneth was loath to give him credit or due consideration. Such actions would come soon enough.

Eying Slate wickedly, he added, "And give you a headache!"

Aroganji laughed, although not in derision. "After all this time traveling together with the Home Guard, why did you not ask them this question yourself earlier?"

Slate scratched his head. "Dunno. I figured they had good cause. 'Sides t'would've been a lot less excitin' if someone else did all tha work fer us!"

Wrindanneth laughed. "There you have it! Forget the fact that they have never seen the place to teleport here!"

"They knew we were expendable. Who in their right mind goes charging off to try and overthrow a doomed city with only a handful of like-minded goons, after all?"

"Why would they send more if only a few crazed lunatics could do the job?"

"Aye." Slate gave a nod, smiling.

More seriously, Wrindanneth offered, "From Tellanon's perspective, and those of its leaders, the fewer resources expended the better—more return on the city's capital. Besides, I'm sure Eidelion, Daerdros, or Spreesprocket would have contacted the council for assistance if they felt the task was beyond our capabilities."

Slate snorted. "I dunno. Maybe they like challenges as much as we do. They volunteered after all."

Aroganji nodded in partial agreement at least with Slate. "I am sure the Home Guard did not cultivate and hone their nonpareil skills, and earn a fearsome reputation for such, by taking the easy way out. Anyone who can stand toe-to-toe with a greater Daemon in single combat isn't exactly the type to take up position at the back of the ranks."

Aroganji paused for a moment before adding seriously, "And we traveled with several."

"And what does that say about us?" Not to be slighted, Wrindanneth countered with a pointed question.

Aroganji replied simply, "We are where they were at one time, perhaps...far away from where we wish to be."

Finishing the conversation as quickly as it began, Wrindanneth replied tersely, taking on the mantle of captain once more. "Wishing we were somewhere else isn't going to help us get our ship repaired any quicker. Now that we have a bit of time, we need to start helping the drones, and our ship, in their repairs!"

"Before any of us go scouring about for wreckage, we all have earned some rest. We need to recover before we are in a position to be at full capacity. Although it might make our lives easier in the long run, I won't have Slate wandering around this haunted city so groggy that he can't tell the difference between a Shade and a shadow."

"Who's up for some sleep and some dinner? Not necessarily in that order?"

Slate plopped down immediately, his arm already shoulder deep in his bag searching for cooking implements when he answered, "I thought we'd never stop! I reckon I've lost a quarter o' my weight since last we ate a meal worth tha name!"

"Looks as though you could stand to lose a bit more, but who am I to judge?" quipped Wrindanneth.

Knowing that he could go without food longer than any of them save Yip who only swallowed air and tea, Slate answered in kind, "If ya don't want ta go hungry yerself, or if ya want ta rely on yer own magic and imagination ta supply yer meal, keep on yappin'. Otherwise, simmer down so I can get our supper cookin'!"

Smiling with his cantankerous friend, Wrindanneth joined Slate and Aroganji around the cookfire he was adroitly preparing. Taking the opportunity to enjoy the company of his friends, Yip sat down alongside Wrindanneth in the shadow of the *Shrike*'s hull ready to enjoy a bit of camaraderie and lightness within the forbidding gloom and dread of Taerris'thule.

On guard while his friends slept, sensing the Shades that slid through the darkness hungrily around them, kept at bay by the ship's surviving wards and Eidelion's perimeter, now pushed only by their own hungry malevolence, more cautious perhaps since their overlord had fallen, Yip stood alert over his friends' prone forms. The sounds of his companions' breathing and the tireless work of the sentry drones repairing the ship were the only noises breaking the evening's stillness.

Though Darkness yet closed in around them, its heart and mind had been struck down along with much of the overwhelming sense of doom and fear that had hung thicker than the gray pall choking the city's turbid air. Within this lingering pall, he yet sensed other greater powers but none were as awesome as the fallen nor had any yet taken its place.

As the moon slipped invisibly behind clouds, the passage of time marked only by the gentle cadence of his inhalations and exhalations, he remained as serene as the night sky.

When they left Taerris'thule, with luck, they would move toward an even greater challenge in the Cabal. For that trial, they would need much more than fortune on their side. If the Paratechnologists had not deciphered the alien command sphere; if the Cabal were too numerous, widespread, or dispersed to fully neutralize; or if the location of the Cabal's center of operations remained hidden, even if they had but one single focal point from which they mounted their attacks, then their quest truly was only at the beginning.

Much depended on chance and the outcome of others' labors.

Conversely, much of their success had been attributable to fortune and outside effort as well. If the insights of the Paratechnologists failed, there were others who would help and may now be more willing to aid directly given the success of their mission to restore the seal of Eldre'gheu and the Cabal's tangible resurgence. Elven vision remained long and keen and may help pierce the veils hiding the Cabal beyond Ea'ae's borders. The Council of Light, hidden though it may be, Éremon and Goran among them, should show them favor and be willing to at least provide assistance if not direct guidance. With Eidelion and Raour'Saqan's recommendation, the Dalaren Ka with their long-standing history of battling agents of evil also may be of service, although he knew not how.

Though the path ahead remained unclear, at least there were now multiple ways to follow, many trails to explore to guide them forward, and those who would journey with them along these paths.

Though their futures remained yet uncertain, in flux as much as the waves of transient fog that continuously roiled around them, he relished the opportunity to sit in deep and sustained peace.

Seated slightly away from their camp with his back resting against the *Shrike*, Yip watched each of his companions arise from their bedding in turn, repeating the evening's arrangements in reverse and commencing their eating rituals in the pale light of morning amidst the long shadows of the broken ruins in preparation for another day within Taerris'thule's gray shadows.

Their mission complete, at least for the time being, they could now focus on their imminent return to Tellanon, hoping for word of the Cabal upon their arrival and the timely repair of their vessel.

Slate held back nothing in his labors for breakfast. He attacked the cooking implements with the same ferocity and intensity as one engaged in the fierce fray of battle. Pots danced and rattled over flames, knives feinted and darted turning over meats and vegetables, the air was thick with smoke and the smells of cooking, signs of the Dwarf's war waged against hunger and time.

Looking askance at Yip who remained watching silently, Slate said, "Nothin' like tha smoke and flames o' breakfast ta lift a Dwarf's spirit in anticipation fer tha day!"

Quickly doling out servings on small metal plates, two in equal measure, the third for himself, a heaping pile larger than the other two combined, Slate called out, "Come on ya lazy varmints! Time's a wastin' and yer food's coolin'! Stop huggin' yer bedrolls like yer mamma's and get ta eatin'!"

Finishing rolling his bedroll and tossing it back on the ship, Wrindanneth scoffed, "You must be about as hungry as you are impatient, Dwarf! Do not fear, Slate, your trough of food isn't going anywhere!"

His gear already packed and back on board the *Shrike* Aroganji added lightly, "Now that the Shades' master has been defeated, you both stay prepared for battle by fighting each other!"

Slate barked a brief laugh as well. "Is there another way?"

Wrindanneth joined Slate in laughter. "Yes, but the alternatives aren't as fun!"

Picking up his meal, the time for talking over, for he was not going to be interrupted while eating, Slate hunched over his plate and began shoveling food in voraciously.

Not starving or inclined to act like they were, Wrindanneth and Aroganji took a more demure approach to eating and actually engaged in casual conversation.

Though their breakfast was short, Slate's was much shorter.

Enjoying watching the unstoppable eating spectacle that was Slate devouring any food thrown his way, Wrindanneth joked, "I think you learned to eat from a Dragon!"

Pausing for a moment, he added, "Although I would imagine a Dragon chews more and has better table manners!"

Ignoring the comments, for he was too focused on the task at hand, Slate continued his one Dwarf onslaught on the mountain in front of him, steadily wearing the mound's unstable heights down to but a few irregular patches of grease.

Standing up with a great stretch from the meager scraps of breakfast remaining after his morning assault, Slate wiped his thick beard with the back of his hand, clearing away the crumbs nestled securely within the recesses of his tangled mane. "Ah! Nothin' like startin' tha day with a hearty meal amongst friends!"

Cleaning both Slate's and his own dishes and cutlery with a flick of his wrist and a quick spell, Aroganji replied lightly, "Even if it's at the heart of a Daemon infested metropolis?"

"All tha better!"

Still working on his meal, Wrindanneth warily looked to Slate who was now licking each one of his fingers to make doubly sure he got every last morsel and said, "I'm just glad I didn't lose a hand!"

Smacking his lips hungrily, Slate growled, "That can be arranged!"

Wrindanneth waggled his fingers enticingly in front of Slate. "Try and you might get indigestion for the first time in your life!"

"Bah! I cut my teeth on sterner stuff than yer sickly flesh!"

Glad for the verbal repartee, always willing to engage in a bit of intellectual sport, Wrindanneth quickly shifted gears and focus to the events of the morn. "Enough of this foolishness!"

Setting his own thoroughly cleaned plate down, he finished his breakfast and laid out the orders for the day. "The time has come to get moving! We have a ship in need of repair, a journey that remains as yet unfinished, and another quest to start. Until the *Shrike* is in order, none of that will happen!"

"We need to find any parts that may be missing from the ship, those not located yet by the drones, and incorporate them into the *Shrike*. The more pieces in place we have, the faster the repair will be completed by the ship's regenerative repair system and the sooner we can leave this dismal ruin."

Nodding, Aroganji said, "That can be accomplished easily enough. I will use a simple retrieval spell to do the work for us, though it will take some time for all the fragments to come."

"What're ya thinkin'?"

Aroganji walked over to a small pile of broken ship pieces the drones had assembled in scouring the immediate vicinity. The drones continually selected parts from this and other piles to piece the ship back together like a gigantic jigsaw puzzle. Picking up one piece from the pile, he said, "I will place a spell upon the wood from the ship for like to attract like, so long as the parts are loose or not incorporated within the *Shrike*. These pieces will, effectively, act like magnets for one another with the greatest attraction or pull generated by the mass of the ship itself."

"So our ship'll have flinders of wood stuck ta its sides?"

"Only while the spell lasts."

"Then we can be about other business while we're here!" Wrindanneth was already looking ahead at the day's activities eagerly.

"What d'ya mean?" Slate lifted his thick eyebrows inquisitively.

"While Aroganji's magic gathers the broken bits of the ship, we can set about exploring the ruins for relics, artifacts, and other items of worth!"

Aroganji laughed, replying, "You mean those that have not been corrupted, despoiled, accursed, or otherwise degraded by a thousand years of disuse and exposure to fell magics?"

"Exactly!"

"Now we've gotten ta tha rub! No better way ta spend tha day than seekin' after treasure while we wait!"

Sharing Slate's enthusiasm in true adventurer fashion, Wrindanneth laughed, "We should never come back from a journey empty-handed!"

"If someone's not payin' ya fer a job, there's nothin' better'n payin' yerself!"

Raising an eyebrow, Yip asked, "Do you think that wise?"

The city was yet overrun by Shades and worse. Just because they were not currently under attack did not mean venturing forth away from the ship's protections was a good idea.

Slate shrugged. "What's life without tha risk? Nothin' gambled, nothin' gained."

Unconvinced, Yip asked, "Are there not more important matters to focus our attention on?"

Nor was Slate. Unswayed by Yip's argument, Slate retorted, "Have we not earned tha chance fer some fun?"

"Given the risks relative to the importance of our aims, the motives for the question pale in comparison to those of the appropriate answer."

Aroganji placed a reassuring hand on Yip's shoulder. "All will be well, Yip. We will use caution and return at any sign of danger."

Having already lost several companions, Yip was less than convinced.

While Wrindanneth and Slate plotted eagerly for their imagined rewards, Aroganji picked up two small pieces of wood from the pile of assorted wreckage ready to be incorporated into the *Shrike*. Holding them apart, he began weaving energy between them, increasing the flow as he brought them closer and closer together. Once released, the two pieces of wood snapped together like two objects drawn together by a strong magnetic field. Setting the pieces of wood back on the pile, the magic of Aroganji's spell induced an effect similar to a strong magnetization of the wooden materials in the pile, an effect which rapidly spread to both the ship and other loose pieces of wood nearby drawing them together and reinforcing the strength of the field as more and more wood came together.

Watching the process unfold, as Aroganji set the pieces of wood down, the fragments rested at first on top of the pile of stacked wood. Within the space of a minute, the pile had begun to shake and shiver, rattling on the ground as pieces of wood rapidly shifted positions and realigned. Much quicker than would be expected, this magical field jumped to the ship itself, causing all of the bits and flinders of wood, including those in the original pile, to jump to the hull of the *Shrike*.

Nodding in silent satisfaction, Aroganji spent the next several minutes casting a complex series of self-reinforcing enchantments to gather the remaining ship parts scattered throughout the city. Adding another layer of additional complexity, he incorporated a bit of intelligent self-seeking to the magical field such that, at least for the duration for the magic, the attraction between pieces of wood would not only self-reinforce its strength, but also seek out other fragments of wood from the ship and then draw them to the central pile.

Unfortunately, at least while the spell's magic lasted, any repair work by the drones would be impeded by the now randomized pieces of wood scattered on the sides of the ship, although the tendency of the pieces to attract could be of benefit while setting parts in place for regeneration.

Staring at the *Shrike*, her sides now grown fuzzy and irregular with the random accreted bits of wood, like a magnet attracting brown bits of metal, Aroganji said, "It will take some thought, but when we return I should be able to modify the spell such that not only are the bits of wood attracting each other but those pieces originally set together will be more strongly attracted to each other as well. Thus, we should accelerate the self-assembling reconstruction of the ship with the broken parts seeking their mates and proper place."

"Anythin' ya can do ta get us outta this crumblin' pile o' dust works fer me!"

"That sentiment holds for all of us!" Wrindanneth was ready to begin the next phase of their journey as well as returning to Tellanon to see what, if any, rewards may be bestowed upon them for their service to the people of Ea'ae. Though altruism and accolades worked for some, he preferred tangible recompense. Whether in the form of knowledge, magical artifact, or coin, he was an equal opportunity recipient.

Motioning for them to close in around him, Wrindanneth said, "Gather round. I will ward each of us for protection against evil before we depart."

Waving his arm in a circle through the air, streaming golden light following his gesture through its spiraling course, Wrindanneth cloaked them each in holy wards against creatures of Darkness.

Feeling the magic settle about him lightly like the faintest dusting of cool morning dew, Yip said, "I will remain with the ship to aid in the repair and organization of the wreckage while you are gone."

Yip did not feel the need to scour the ruins for artifacts. He had had his fill of the city. Nor did he feel such a trip was worth the risk when so much was at stake. He would rather work, especially if he could be of assistance at the crash site and speed their return to Tellanon. The faster the repairs on the ship were done, the sooner they could leave. More importantly, the quicker they returned, the sooner they could begin the next facet of their quest lessening the long-term potential risks the people of Ea'ae faced from the Cabal.

"Fair enough." Wrindanneth was ready to get started. He also welcomed the opportunity to freely explore without Yip's presence reminding him of the pressing needs of others at the expense of his own desires. Everyone could use a distraction now and again. After what they had been through, despite the risks, he certainly enjoyed taking a bit of time to follow his own whims while the repairs were underway.

Finished with making a few final adjustments to the scavenging enchantment, ready to scavenge himself, Aroganji enjoined, "Let's begin!"

With that comment, the four split up, Yip remaining at the site of the wreckage to guard the ship while trying to assist the drones in the organization and placement of the debris, while Aroganji, Wrindanneth, and Slate departed to explore the ruins and discover where their wits and curiosity would lead them.

Sauntering away from the camp, for the immediate vicinity remained clear of fell influences with Eidelion's shield yet in place, Slate asked, "So how do we wanna do this?"

Raising an eyebrow, Wrindanneth countered with his own question. "What do you mean?"

"How do we wanna proceed? Are we gonna use magic ta guide us, set out fer a particular place, or what?"

Looking down at Slate who stood immediately by his side, Wrindanneth answered, "Why don't we just see where walking takes us? We have had plenty of directed searching, much assisted by magic, so why not see where chance and our own interest leads us?"

Nodding as he ambled on Wrindanneth's other side, Aroganji said, "I agree. Is there anywhere that you saw in our flight in or out from the temple that intrigued either of you? If so, that could be a general target. From there we can see what we encounter along the way."

Thinking back, Slate said, "There was one buildin' we flew over that had a roof that shouldn't be too far. Seems about tha only other place around here that still had its roof was the temple itself. Per'aps there's somethin' special about it."

Wrindanneth smiled, saying, "For once, I think I agree with you, Slate!"

Wiping his brow in mock relief, Slate said, "I can take that off my list of things ta accomplish before I die!"

While Aroganji laughed at Slate's joke, Wrindanneth countered in turn, "I didn't know you could write!"

"Let's take to the air then!" As soon as he finished his comment, Aroganji began weaving the spell that would allow them to fly, not letting Wrindanneth and Slate's bickering continue.

Willingly relinquishing control for a moment, Wrindanneth said, "We'll follow your lead, Slate!"

With the completion of Aroganji's incantation, they leapt upward, feeling the cool, damp air rush past their faces as they spiraled in a circle above the camp while Slate got his bearings. Pointing eastward, their direction determined by Slate's unerring Dwarven sense of orientation, they sped off above the ruins, relatively safe from potential ambush by any remaining Shades daring enough to challenge them.

Left below, Yip looked up only briefly at their passage.

Yip spent the better part of the morning scrambling alongside the drones who had the benefit of flight, working as best he could to assist in the ship's reconstruction. For some, the work would have been tedious. For him, however, it was contemplative.

Much of his youth, much of his training, had been spent performing simple menial tasks, learning to develop a perspective that was simultaneously relaxed and alert, clear and insightful, the cultivation of which he gradually learned to carry to all activities including the continued development and refinement of his awareness. From weeding walkways, natural areas, and gardens to repairing walls, buildings, and ornamentation, he had actively practiced awareness his whole life.

Toiling beside the drones around the incomplete skeleton of the ship offered a welcome window back to the days and experiences of his youth.

Clambering through and around obstacles, over loose boards, around incomplete beams, on broken planks, he darted across the ship with the skill and dexterity of an adroit spider. Keeping his relaxed, open frame of mind, he challenged himself physically without any reliance upon *chi* to perform and achieve, to push and hone his coordination and agility. As much as his morning was spent in making restorations, the majority of his effort was spent in dedicated practice and preparation.

He welcomed the physical release just as he welcomed the sense of purpose and focus that accompanied it.

If asked, Slate could never explain exactly how he knew which direction to travel belowground to reach a particular destination nor could he tell how the same principle applied above ground. He only knew that, if he had been to a particular spot before and thought about it, he had a general idea of where it lay in relation to his current location.

This sense allowed him to know, at least roughly, which direction to travel to reach a given point. Though the directional sense was not always a surefire solution belowground, for not all tunnels led where you wished even if they headed in the right direction at first, given enough patience and perseverance, two traits Dwarves held in great measure, at least when required, he could get where he needed to go. Aboveground, where the intractable obstacles of monolithic walls of unyielding stone need not necessarily apply, this guiding sense of direction proved far more beneficial.

Though he would never voice it, for he did not wish to acknowledge the comparison, he often thought, that is when he thought about it at all, that his locational sense must be very much like those of birds of flight, those species accustomed to long migrations across continents and over vast seas moving to and from their ancestral feeding and mating grounds. Compared with the epic navigational skills and abilities employed by other species, his Dwarven sense of direction hardly seemed out of place or particularly worth noting.

However, when the time came to find treasure, return to a place he had visited, or even move toward where he thought a particular destination should be based on his current location, this sense provided an unerring compass to steer his movements.

He particularly enjoyed the building feelings of commingled joy, anticipation, and greed as he honed in on a spot that he thought contained treasure or other items of worth.

These were the excited feelings coursing through his veins as he flew through the air above the gray rubble of Taerris'thule.

Beard whipping against his chest, his eyes remained on the horizon as their destination neared and his excitement mounted.

Eyes locked forward, the buildings immediately below a gray blur as they flew swiftly above, Slate spied the growing bulk of their destination just as his directional sense began to hum warmly in anticipation.

The irregular dome held little resemblance to the massive temple of Eldre'gheu aside from an overarching gray pall and cloying sense of deeply ingrained corruption. The building Slate, Wrindanneth, and Aroganji now sped toward was composed of irregular, bulbous minarets, towers whose unusual organic geometries improbably defied time and dissolution. The degree of architectural complexity of the building was only heightened by the surrounding crumbling desolation.

No other buildings, walls, or monuments remained standing within the glowering building's immediate vicinity.

Slate pointed ahead toward the malformed structure erupting outward from the barren soil like some warped fungus or misshapen mole. "We're headin' fer that!"

Looking over toward Slate, the distaste all too visible in his eyes, Wrindanneth grumbled over the wind whipping between them, "You would pick a place that looked like some misshapen growth on your body."

Slate chuckled lightly. "And I thought they'd used yer nose fer tha model!"

Wrindanneth laughed and shook his head, his long red hair whipping in the wind as they closed in on their destination. "Only Dwarves and Trolls have noses like that!"

His already loud voice even louder as he yelled over the cool, moist wind, Slate barked, "Bah! I can tell a witch's nose from a warlock's and ya're tha only warlock I know!"

Shaking his head in a combination of disagreement and dismay at their target, Wrindanneth sighed. "You certainly can pick 'em, Slate!"

His eyes never leaving the looming building ahead, Aroganji indicated, "This building is more than it seems. We must use caution."

Noting the concern in his friend's tone, Wrindanneth asked, "Are we capable without the Home Guard and Yip?"

Aroganji shook his head. "I do not know. We must be prepared. Many evil currents gather and circulate at that place."

"Let's stop here." Wrindanneth pointed downward and quickly followed his gesture with a spiraling descent, choosing what might have once been the fallen courtyard of a long forsaken building to land in and prepare.

They touched down in an open area amidst loose stones and debris that had been incorporated into the ground over time, most of which were now covered with sickly gray lichen and rust covered moss. From their vantage surrounded by a sea of broken stones, the building they now sought rose upward within a few hundred paces of their landing spot.

The monolith clawed its way out of a landscape of shattered stones and fractured rock, the last relic that had survived some terrible blast long ago—so long ago, in fact, that only the building itself remained intact as witness to the event.

This close, over the sere landscape in between, the building resembled a nightmarish combination of human handiwork and cancerous outgrowths. So old was the structure, however, that they could not tell if these malignant masses were original or added at a later date.

Regardless, the sickening menace of the physical structure was subsumed by a mixture of dread and malice that weighed down upon their shoulders unbearably, overriding the feelings of disgust at the building's appearance with those of fear and revulsion.

Settling down, the feelings of horror sank through them, urging them to bend to their knees under the gravity of the pall. Inhaling strongly to stave off the horrific feelings, giving them just enough time to assess their immediate environs, Wrindanneth asked, "What do you notice different here? In this general area?"

Aroganji and Slate surveyed the region, looking around cautiously, eyes drawn continually to the unavoidable baneful edifice, before Slate finally whispered, "There're no Shades!"

"Exactly!" Speaking urgently, Wrindanneth said, "Whatever claims this place has scared off the Shades!"

Offering an alternative, Aroganji said, "Or bars their approach."

Raising an eyebrow, Wrindanneth replied, "I doubt anything good has survived here long enough to keep out the Daemon-kin."

"I never said anything about artifacts of Light surviving within this city nor am I suggesting that bygone protective magics have remained untouched since the time of the city's ancient fall."

"Then what're ya suggestin'?"

"We know the city is home to many evils. The one or ones laying claim to this building may prefer to keep the Shades and their allies at bay."

Aroganji continued guardedly, "If the entity or entities within that building have established their own sanctuary within the borders of Taerris'thule, keeping the Shades and other greater entities out, surviving in the presence of the Darkness we just destroyed, then perhaps we should reconsider our attempt for they must be beings of great power."

"If, as you say Wrindanneth, the Shades and other Daemons give this place berth without any wards barring their entrance, then this assessment holds as well."

Aroganji let his doubts come to the fore as he looked between them and the cruel structure. "We had difficulty enough with the evil at the city's heart when we brought our full strength to bear. Now, we are but three."

"So ya're sayin' we should quit?"

Wrindanneth looked questioningly at Aroganji as well. "You do not think we should try to rid the city of another evil?"

Aroganji shrugged. Stating his views matter-of-factly, he said, "Our mission here is complete. We left the *Shrike* to pursue our own personal interests while the magic necessary to finalize the ship's repairs ran their course. Our ultimate goals remain unchanged."

"We were not charged with purging the city nor do I feel we are capable of doing so. Our overriding goal remains to bring down the Cabal and secure Ea'ae. Though cleansing this city is necessary, we need not risk our own cause, our own futures, to do so. That duty was not laid upon us."

He finished flatly, echoing Yip's concerns from earlier, "Now that I gaze upon this place, there is too much risk."

Trying one more time, testing his friend's resolve, for he felt the same way, Wrindanneth asked, "Even if we go back for Yip?"

"Yes. Yip's caution appears quite warranted. We need not put our quest in jeopardy, and everything that quest entails, for an uncertain reward against an unknown enemy."

Slate, however, was crestfallen, his visions of treasure and artifacts shattered. He had been listening so intently to his own inner feelings of anticipation and excitement that he had lost sight of the reality, of the danger, now rising before them. "So ya want ta go back?"

Aroganji smiled wryly, the gesture an effort within the oppressive emanations of the horrific citadel. "I'm not saying that..."

Sharing in his strained smile, Wrindanneth and Slate nodded and took to the air.

The day passed quickly for Yip though he could see little of his own hand in the inexorable progress of the *Shrike*'s repair. The drones, with their ability to map, diagnose, categorize, and characterize the ship's parts, moved so much quicker and more effectively in their repairs than he could. After a short time, he recognized that he served the reconstruction efforts best by staying out of the way.

What few placements he had made within the ship's structure were relegated to the larger, more obvious pieces that he could more readily identify and determine the proper point of origin and final setting position with his own rather limited skill sets.

However, though his attempt at repairs had not gone as well as he would have hoped, he had enjoyed the effort and exertion of the morning. Also, though he had not endeavored to follow their travels directly, he was also quite encouraged that he had not sensed anything out of the ordinary with Aroganji, Wrindanneth, and Slate. Thus, their absence of a few hours did not fill him with any degree of concern for they had not, at least not yet, been in grave danger.

There were, however, several more hours in the day.

If there was one thing he had learned in this journey, it was never to underestimate anyone, especially his friends. Smiling ruefully at the thought, there was still plenty of time for them to make amends for this potential shortcoming.

If that were indeed the case and they actually needed his help, he only hoped that he could come to their aid in time. Understanding their capabilities, he doubted this would be the necessary, but, given their fortuitous combination of drive and desire, two traits that tilted chance in a rather precarious direction, he knew better than to make any presuppositions.

Settling down into an afternoon of breath and energy work, he knew better than to interfere—either with his friends or, now after a few futile hours of trying, with the drones as well.

"Ho, Yip!" Slate, Aroganji, and Wrindanneth spiraled downward out of the low, darkening sky, the cinereal afternoon fading into a steely, fog enshrouded night—the difference only in the relative shade of gray.

Remaining still while his friends approached, Yip felt the vibrancy of their miens and knew all was well. The piles of wooden fragments around him were much larger and more numerous resting against and near the ship's hull after the magic of Aroganji's spell had run its course, driftwood returned with the tide.

He returned Slate's greeting with a nod and a smile while his friends landed nimbly nearby.

Examining the mounds of wood scattered along the base of the ship like debris left after a storm, Wrindanneth said, "Looks like Aroganji's magic finally did something useful!"

Smiling lightly, Aroganji responded, "Let us hope that my luck continues with the other portion of the spell!"

"I would guess ya've managed ta gather just about every bit o' wood, limbs, twigs, leaves, and random ship parts left in tha city!"

Slate's keen eye noted that the moving bits of wood, both large and small, from Aroganji's enchantment had brought more than ship parts alone to the crash site. Small bits of debris and other loose objects had also found their way to ship, drug along and over the ground with the rest of the wreckage.

Slate laughed as he looked from fore to aft of the *Shrike*. "Looks like tha ship crashed into tha center o' a large pile o' refuse!"

Nodding, Wrindanneth said, "She's perched like a bird on an unstable, swept-up nest of sticks and twigs!"

"Couldn't have said it better myself!" Slate stood with both hands on his hips appreciating the surreality of the moment.

Addressing Yip after inspecting the ship, Aroganji said, "It appears your day was about as fruitful as ours."

Yip answered simply. "Much was done although not much is apparent."

With this answer, Wrindanneth laughed out loud uproariously, saying, "Only you, Yip! Only you!"

Sensing what was coming, not rising to the bait, Yip replied innocently, "Yes?"

"Only you can take a simple question, answer it just as simply while clouding the answer with an air of mystery and obfuscation fit for a long forgotten riddle…all the while not conveying one iota of useful information!"

Yip shrugged. "The truth is in the perception."

At Yip's response, Wrindanneth laughed even harder.

Once he had control of himself, Wrindanneth replied with some difficulty through the last fits of humor, "Point proven!"

Yip bowed.

Understanding his friend's sentiments exactly, Aroganji replied in similar fashion, "You have only to open your eyes to see, Wrindanneth!"

"Now it's both of you! You're like evil twins!" Laughing in hysterics once more, Wrindanneth struggled through the convulsions racking through him as he said, "Back to the aphoristic lexicon that spawned you!"

Gazing back and forth between Aroganji and Yip on the one hand who both remained calm and poised and Wrindanneth on the other, Slate uttered with simple aplomb, "I think he's lost all tha bat's in his belfry!"

Aroganji shrugged. "I think it is just becoming more and more apparent that he never had any."

Unable to carry on any longer, consumed by delirious gaiety, Wrindanneth was completely unable to defend himself.

Turning to address Yip and Slate together in all seriousness, Aroganji said, "This gives me an idea for my next line of magical inquiry—Wrindanneth's Racking Revelry. We will incapacitate our foes with debilitating laughter!"

Glancing briefly at Wrindanneth, Slate said in all seriousness, "Looks like ya've already had yer first successful application!"

Also looking at Wrindanneth, his face alight with a grin, Yip said, "I am certain Wrindanneth would be proud to have a spell named in his honor."

Nodding sagely, Slate offered, "T'would be fittin' indeed!"

Still smiling at Wrindanneth, Yip asked of Aroganji and Slate, "And what of your endeavor? Did your journey meet with success? What transpired after you left the ship?"

Slate grinned wryly, washing his hands eagerly as he did so. "Thought ya'd never ask!"

Turning briefly to Aroganji before he continued, Slate continued, "This city's full o' more hornet's nests than a beekeeper's apiary! We might've laid tha queen bee low, but there are more than enough hives with queens o' their own waitin' in tha wings ta take her place!"

"We must've stumbled on at least four separate ruins I wouldn't set foot on without Raour'Saqan's long shadow at my back! And those were tha safe ones!"

Aroganji nodded in assent. "This city harbors more malevolence than I would have dared imagine. We may have made Ea'ae safe from the primary threat in these ruins but there are many dark powers here lying in wait for their chance at greater influence and opportunity."

"I'd say we should lay tha entire city low by explodin' tha drones but then we'd never get home!"

More seriously, Slate added with a tinge of melancholy, "Unfortunately, I doubt that their explosions would make a dent in some o' tha protective enchantments we've seen!"

Aroganji nodded. "Though the Shades have lost a bit of their fanaticism, the longer we stay, the greater our risk. We have been noticed. We have shown that we are a threat. It is only a matter of time before these other powers deign to move against us."

Slate growled, "My axe may not be sharp enough ta mow 'em all down, but it'll try!"

There was a muffled rustling and call of assent from Duraeleon where it remained sheathed across Slate's back.

Yip understood his friends' concern, he sensed the evil radiating around them directly, without any filters.

Sitting amid the ruins next to the *Shrike* in the company of his friends, his mind floated in space, adrift amongst the antithesis of stars. All around him, more numerous than the constellations visible in the heavens, were pools of Darkness, singularities devouring any and all Light encountered. Within these regions of Darkness, there were locations of greater concentrations of evil, places that were home to entities of untold power and hostile intent.

Though these Daemons' dominions were temporarily localized, the extent of their range curtailed by the unholy fiend that had until recently resided within their midst, a new balance of power would emerge. Soon, when these extradimensional entities moved to expand their influence, there would be conflict. Though these remaining beings were not of the same strength as their former master and their powers were curtailed somewhat by the severing of their extradimensional nexus, they were formidable nonetheless and had the potential to grow more so. The struggles that would soon ensue would consume the city in violence.

They would need to be out of Taerris'thule's borders before the remaining Daemons marshaled their strength and tested the limits of their control.

He feared, however, that the repairs of the *Shrike* would take too long, that they would not be clear before the violence began anew.

Already he sensed the stirring of evil and the manifestation of these entities' insatiable hunger and thirst for power.

Gazing slowly from one friend to the next, he said in all earnestness, "We must make every effort to strengthen the wards protecting the ship and this clearing. I fear we haven't much time."

"We must grant the time required for the drones and the ship's magic to complete the requisite repairs to return to Tellanon. We must provide them with the space to operate and room for us to take flight once the restoration is complete."

Though he wanted to rest, Wrindanneth understood immediately and pushed for action. "Aroganji, begin the next phase of your magical repairs. The ship must be prepared to leave as soon as possible. The return stone will not work until all the parts of the ship are made whole."

"I will open the ship's systems to you so that you can work unimpeded by the *Shrike's* defensive systems. This will allow you to integrate and interface your magic most efficiently with the ship itself to best facilitate the necessary repairs."

"Slate, are you capable of the Karaduen like those cast on the ship by Kazarhan?"

Slate thought a few moments, considering the request carefully before answering just as cautiously, his tone measured, "I believe so, though tha castin' will take me longer'n it did fer Kazarhan."

"Excellent! We'll need the entire clearing protected to supplement the wards on the ship and the enchantments afforded by the Guard."

"I'll offer Maeth Onai's own blessings to yours along with several other wards against Daemons and magic."

His mind already lost in the nuances and calibrations required to formulate the desired effects for his repair spell, Aroganji added airily, "I will add my own protections as well if I can get the enchantment working properly to help restore the ship."

Clapping his hands together exuberantly, Wrindanneth exhorted eagerly, "Let's get started!"

His own talents not in direct service, Yip remained on silent guard, his awareness a shield against the coming Night.

Through the mental link connecting them, Aroganji heard Wrindanneth's steady voice. *"When you are ready, the ship is fully at your disposal."*

"Thank you."

Aroganji was indeed ready.

He had a plan, a solution, in mind. Now he need only turn his vision into reality.

Although easier said than done, there were few other real options. If he failed they had but a few choices—wait, try again, or supply the ship with more power to try and boost its recovery.

None of those options were as efficient as the one he wished to attempt.

He closed his eyes and relaxed, opening himself up to the energy currents flowing through and around the ship, distinguishing between those used by the ship itself and its systems and those intrinsic to the environs in which the wreckage resided. Going deeper, guided by Wrindanneth's understanding, a doctor examining and evaluating a living being, he traced the forces guided by the ship's command sphere for the repair of the vessel.

With the ship's system opened to him by Wrindanneth's command of the control sphere, Aroganji was afforded an internal view of the *Shrike*'s workings that normally would have been blocked without efforts to break through its defenses. He now had a level of direct access and input that would have been summarily denied.

He studied how the ship utilized magic to regenerate and repair damaged sections based on a thorough, systematic recreation of an internal multidimensional representation of itself. Watching the continual accretion of material and the bridging between fractured sections of fragments, he gradually came to understand how he could apply his magic to interlink with and facilitate this regenerative process, recovering and guiding the damaged ship parts to their appropriate positions.

To this effort, he would need to add a spell to sort the damaged ship parts, returning them to their point of origin in the proper orientation.

With the aid of the ship's visualization along with his own intent guided and manifested by magic, he should be able to create the solution he envisaged.

Then, with his magic in place, he would let that vision unfold and the *Shrike* would repair itself in a much shorter period of time.

Slate walked within the perimeter of shimmering holy energies described by the white flames of Archaeus's blade, a burning ring of power dancing atop the ashen soil. Within this protective barrier, he began his own series of enchantments.

Though he did not have the power or flexibility in magical craft of his companions, with Kazarhan's brief tutelage, he did have access to runic magic which would offer them additional layers protection. Like the overlapping scales on a Dragon's protective coat, these runes would help extend and reinforce the defensive barrier surrounding the ship granted by Kazarhan's original Karaduen and Daerdros's magical shield while providing an additional barrier inside Eidelion's holy circle. His magics would also afford a complement to whatever supplemental enchantments Wrindanneth and Aroganji placed.

Together, the Karaduen Hürn and Loess that he prepared to inscribe would guard against evil and ward off supernatural influence. Even if one of the Daemonic denizens of Taerris'thule did manage to break through Eidelion's barrier, Slate's own wards, when complete, would weaken the extradimensional presence, causing it horrific pain and disorientation.

He smiled evilly at the thought.

Rubbing his hands together with the fervor of one cold and trying to regain heat, he first inscribed his rune in the soil. Then, kneeling down directly over the glyph, cupping his hands over the inscription, he bent down, bringing his lips to his hands, and blew warm air into the folds of his palms, giving the life from his lungs to the runes he wrought. Each Karaduen glowed a faint blue when fully realized, fueled by the fires of the Daerdaana'Duin that gave them life.

Alternating between Hürn and Loess, he inscribed a staggered series of protective runes around the wreckage. By the time he finished, over two hours had passed and he felt more drained and exhausted than if he had been fighting or running for several days on end.

Plopping down beside Yip after slouching wearily back over to the ship, he understood a bit better how Wrindanneth and Aroganji must feel after working with particularly complex, demanding enchantments.

Never again would he mock the work of mage or the frailty of a spellcaster.

Never again would he offer the example of a Dwarven warrior as the pinnacle of strength and will.

Never again would he belittle the efforts of his friends when compared to his own.

Never again would he lose sight of empathy.

At least not until he had a good opportunity.

Then he would gladly forget about his efforts and readily lose the ground of understanding that may have tempered his humor.

Turning wearily to Yip who merely watched him calmly and steadily while he sat down beside his placid friend, Slate muttered weakly, though on ears deaf to his plight, "By Brendle's blade, I need an ale."

Shaking his head recriminatingly, he added, "What am I doin' mentionin' my needs ta ya? Ya wouldn't even know what ale tastes like much less understand tha desire ta have one!"

Yip remained silent. His friend's solution was simple. If Slate wanted something to drink, he need only get it.

"Only thing I want as much as an ale is ta sit down!"

Joining Yip in silence, already committed, at least one of his desires readily at hand, he would see which urge ultimately won out.

Wrindanneth need not follow Slate around the circumference of Eidelion's divine enchantment for he did not need to move to work his own magic. He did, however, follow Slate with his eyes for a time, appreciating his friend's effort, his steadfast concentration, and his mounting difficulties as he worked.

Seeing Slate persevere, though each protective rune gradually wore him down, stirred a pleasant mix of emotions in his heart. Though he would not readily or openly admit it, he was proud of his friend for trying such an ambitious task after so little time in practice and study. He admired Slate's effort and perseverance.

Though he was proud of Slate's efforts, on the darker side, however, he also enjoyed watching Slate labor while attempting something he often mocked, having on many occasions noted his vocal preference for the methods of the blade over the methods of the mind.

Seeing Slate struggle also offered him a sense of misdirected happiness. He felt rewarded by Slate's difficulties in much the same way as he felt after getting the better of his friend in an argument.

Though not pleasant, those emotions were in place as well, ingrained after many altercations and petty disagreements.

Waiting another few moments before starting the invocation for Maeth's blessing, he savored the thought of reminding Slate of the ease, and he would only use that term loosely and with the proper mocking tone, with which the Dwarf had handled his first independent act of magical spell casting.

Now ready to begin, after all his internal denunciations of his friend, he only hoped Maeth Onai would hear him and grant the boon he was about to request. The irony of the fact that his lord may treat him even less kindly than he now thought of Slate was not lost on him.

Once he sorted out the one relationship, maybe he could resolve the other.

Just because he had been treated sorely over the years did not mean he need necessarily treat others similarly. Every man was capable of rising above his upbringing and his current circumstance.

Of course, it was so much easier not to do so.

And often so much more fun.

Those thoughts fresh upon his mind, he began his invocation of the divine, an appeal he avoided whenever possible, for it put him face-to-face with his master, a mirror that reflected too darkly upon his failings and weaknesses, a relationship that only highlighted his shortcomings and need to change.

Joining Yip and Slate, after completing, evaluating, and checking their own spells, Aroganji and Wrindanneth finally settled in tiredly beside their friends.

"Ya look like I feel." Slate smiled wanly, his Dwarven constitution having returned much of his strength although he still felt drained.

Though the opportunity was there, wide open for him to take, for once Wrindanneth refrained from insult, tempering his reply with a bit of empathy. After the chastising he had taken from Maeth, he could do without further argument. He was too tired to joke and in no mood to start bickering. At least his request for a boon had been granted. They should remain safe from the terrors that now freely prowled the darkness, unchecked by the horror that had fallen. "I'm sure that's not very good then."

In no mood to seek an opening in Wrindanneth's weakened defenses, Slate refrained from a sardonic reply as well. He smiled a bit grimly. "We can only get better."

"With all the spells we've layered about the ship and this clearing, I think we'll be granted a bit of time to recover at least.'

Aroganji was not as drained as Wrindanneth or Slate, he was actually feeling rather invigorated after the successful implementation of his spell and the sense of discovery that a new magical application engendered. He laughed in reply to his friends' difficulties, playing light of the situation. "Unless we attract unwanted attention to ourselves!"

"Bah! They've seen what we can do. Tha shadows that creep and crawl will be better off just waitin' and lettin' us leave when tha time comes!"

Aroganji smiled at Slate's bravado. "They shouldn't have to wait long then. The *Shrike* should be whole within a day. Then we can use the return stone to port back to Tellanon."

Perking up with the thought, Slate responded fervently, "And reap our just rewards!"

Wrindanneth laughed wanly. "More likely they'll ask us to go off on some other fool errand to help save the world."

Yip smiled. "If the Paratechnologists have not deciphered the alien command sphere and located the Cabal, that would be to my liking."

Shaking his head in mock disbelief, his long red locks waving back and forth about his face, Wrindanneth muttered, "If ever there was any question, here we have further proof of your insanity."

Yip bowed slightly in reply. "In your world perhaps."

"My world ends for the day." A bit of his sarcasm returned as Wrindanneth continued, "Though engrossing, I must bow out of this conversation. I need rest. The morning of our departure will soon be upon us."

Waiting a moment, Wrin added, "I suggest you all try to get some sleep." Here his personality returned in full, his words laced with innuendo. "That is everyone normal enough to slumber."

Yip replied simply, "Good night, Wrindanneth. I will see to it that your dreams are untroubled."

Wrindanneth barked a brief laugh as he moved away to the shadows of the *Shrike* to unroll his bedroll. "That is a boon I wish you could grant." Turning his back to the group, he skulked away into the darkness.

He would hear more from Maeth Onai this night.

His eyes following his friend, Aroganji said, "I will take a brief repast before I, too, join Wrindanneth in repose."

His excitement and energy returning with the thought of food, Slate replied eagerly, "I think I'll join ya! All this spell castin' has gotten me hungrier'n a Koerdian Cave Bear after wakin' up from a long winter hibernation!"

Glad to see his friends in good cheer despite the growing shadows gathering and moving about them, Yip merely smiled, sitting quietly and watching while his friends bustled about the camp gathering the food and implements necessary to take a brief, simple meal.

He would have much time in quiet solitude tonight. For now, he would enjoy the comfort and vibrancy of activity amongst companions however brief.

There was much joy to be had in the peace and camaraderie of being amongst friends.

Sparks flew—embers in the night.

While his friends slept—time counted by the even pace of their breath; their snorts, snuffles, and shifting bodies; the time between movements—Yip watched.

There was, as always, much to observe.

As the night deepened, turbulent Shadows gathered fervidly beyond the luminous spheres of variegated protections afforded by the combined wards of Eidelion, Wrindanneth, Aroganji, Slate, Kazarhan, Daerdros, and the ship itself.

Where an unsettled calm had fallen briefly over the city after the fall of the nightmarish Daemon, a feverish pitch of excitement and intensity now burned within Taerris'thule's shattered ruins. Those Shadows that had fled or hidden appeared to have reemerged replenished in force, gathering in untellable numbers, surging in ebony waves about the thin barriers warding the *Shrike* and her guardians.

As he sat in silent vigil, these Shadows burned.

The Shadows in the night were the embers that Yip now watched, bursting in violent incandescence when approaching too near to Eidelion's flaming line of divine demarcation. Granted a semblance of beauty in their final moments of destruction, the pitch horrors roiled and torched, ultimately succumbing to their doom, the last remnants of their essences flitting irregularly through the air, glowing cinders given a brief moment of transformation and sublimation by Light.

Watching the ghostly Wraiths press forward, shifting in waves, it was only a matter of time before the relentless surging tide that now pushed forward eroded their defenses and finally broke through.

Though terrible, the Shadows themselves were not what captured his attention. Nor was their brief transformation from Darkness into Light the sole object of his scrutiny. Within the depths of their shifting masses, greater powers now roamed freely and widely. Already these entities moved against one another. He sensed their clashes like the forces of continents colliding against one another—awesome and frightful.

Any one of these newly risen powers could move against the frail beings encased within their fragile womb of defensive magics.

Without the Home Guard, they were exceedingly vulnerable.

Should their wards fail, they would not be able to fight off countless hordes of Shadows when greater entities now prowled their ranks while waiting for the ship to mend.

If they were to have any hope of escape, they must flee before these transient wards collapsed.

The *Shrike* must be made whole.

Allowing his mind to explore the ship's confines, he was glad to see that the repairs were nearing completion. Aroganji's magic had worked wonders in speeding her recovery.

Sitting alertly, his attention spread outward in a broad halo of readiness, he sensed the approach of a being of some might. Darker than the void of space and much colder, this malevolence strode forward toward them with the surety and strength of a shark among minnows.

Shades slipped away from it in fear, avoiding its presence lest they incur its wrath. As it neared and the density of Shades increased, pressing forward to clear its vicinity, the ripples of its presence pushing through the swarm lessened with the Shadows swirling more and more tightly around the entity's periphery.

When he was sure that the Daemon was, in fact, heading directly for them, he sounded the alarm. "Be ready! A Daemon approaches amongst the Shades!"

Warned, Aroganji, Slate and Wrindanneth sprang to attention.

Harsh red light arched between Wrindanneth's hands as he jumped up from his bedroll. Beside him, his arms wreathed in blue flames, Aroganji leapt to his feet as well. To Yip's side, his actions accompanied by a deep growl, Slate rolled out of his blankets simultaneously drawing Duraeleon as he spun to his feet and burst into white flames.

Scowling as he scanned the line of divine energy dividing the clearing from the seething Shadows, Slate cursed, "Blasted blackguards! Can't a Dwarf get some sleep!"

Eager for the taste of Daemon flesh, Duraeleon remained silent in his hands.

Not bothered by the disturbance, for he lived for these challenges, Wrindanneth spoke shortly through tight lips, "Let it come!"

While Yip sensed the Darkness drawing nearer within the field of his awareness, the unnatural gravity of its presence weighing heavily upon his senses, its impending approach was not lost upon the others. As they stood at the ready, a deep chill grew in the air causing their breath to hang thickly in the darkness, each exhalation marked by a cold fog. This chill slowly settled about their arms and legs, touching their skin through their clothing, directly exposed to winter's chill. With this unsettling frigidity, their limbs grew increasingly heavy and lethargic until only their iron wills and magical wards prevented them from being locked in place in the turbid fear of inaction.

Arrayed in a deadly crescent, each stood shoulder-to-shoulder prepared for the Daemon's assault as it drew steadily nearer and nearer.

"It comes!" Finally, Yip gave his friends a brief warning before the Daemon reached the perimeter of their defenses, giving them time to react before the Daemon pushed through.

The assault never came.

Shielded completely behind the writhing Shadows, its presence a horrific stain upon the fabric of Creation, the Daemon stood still, the profound weight of its gaze heavy upon them.

Then, turning, its vile form still hidden by the countless writhing Shadows encircling it, the Daemon walked along the edge of Eidelion's divine shield, a blight unseen but undeniably real.

"My blade is eager ta drink yer essence, Daemon!" Slate called out a fool-hardy challenge to the dark night, his words only receiving deafening silence in reply.

For moments they watched, the air filled with their tension and the force of their readiness. Then, through the Darkness of the otherworldly Shades, a terrible light, gross and garish, the heart of a dying sun doomed to oblivion, emerged slowly from the masses burning violently along the edge of Eidelion's divine shield. First one, then two, then three, until finally four terrifying lines of sputtering, sparking flames flared across the surface of Eidelion's shield.

Enthralled, no one said a word for they distinguished exactly what was happening as they watched appalled.

With the ease of one running a blazing torch cutting through metal, sending sparks flying through the air as a jet of flame traveled over super-heated material, they stood watching while the Daemon languidly ran its foul claws casually across the exterior of Eidelion's barrier amidst a haze of holy heat and embers, its hulking form hidden within the churning cloud of stygian Shadows.

Tracing a path over a quarter of the shield's perimeter, circling around the sanctified clearing like a hungry shark, as abruptly as it began, the hellish fires stopped as the Daemon retracted is claws and the overwhelming, tenebrous presence vanished once more amongst the Shadows.

Still holding Duraeleon in hand, his grip tighter now that the threat had passed, at least for the time, Slate snarled, "If we weren't just tested, taunted like lowly wastrels, then I'll lay down my arms!"

"Evidently we are not yet worthy of further attention but that will change soon enough once the Daemons have established a new order!" Aroganji let the fires wreathing his arms subside with his internal focus and intensity as he sat back down upon his bedding, allowing the dread and fear to wash away with each steady breath.

Nodding, Wrindanneth said, "I suggest we all try to get some rest while we may. Remain vigilant and at the ready. That thing, or others like it, could come back any time. We had best be prepared when they do."

As they all settled back down, the adrenaline coursing through their veins slowly subsiding along with the Daemon's foul chill, Yip said simply, offering his friends the peace and repose they would need to rest, "I will remain on guard."

He would remain vigilant.

Returning his full awareness to the heaving Shadows, Yip observed and waited, knowing time grew short. With this first pass, they had been lucky.

Perhaps they had only been tested out of curiosity. Perhaps they had been evaluated for future investigation after other matters were attended. Perhaps the Daemon wished to check on prey it would hunt after a new order in the city had been established. Perhaps the visitation had been part of some elaborate game that he could not discern.

He knew not. Regardless, time grew shorter by the moment.

His mind fully engaged in the building masses of Daemonic energies converging around them, hours passed in the steady silence of his absorption. Within this bubble of serenity, his mind encompassing the clearing as much as the air or *chi*, an idea came to him unbidden but welcome.

There was, he realized, a way to secure this city for generations to come.

There was a way to overthrow the remaining Daemonic entities without ever engaging directly in combat, without hoping that the life-giving *chi* would eventually drive them away now that their master had fallen.

There was a solution that would prevent further lives from being lost in the effort to rid Taerris'thule of its ancient evils.

The solution was as elegant as it was simple.

Filling his mind with the shining rays of undreamt possibility, he only hoped this idea was attainable.

The lone way to achieve this vision was to manifest the potential in his mind's eye. He must make the possible actual, the achievable real. He must do what, based on his own limited experience, had never been done before.

Closing his eyes, visualizing his aim like a mandala in all its full complexities and glory, with his complete attention and focus, he began.

And, like any beginning, he started first with the breath.

He would breathe his vision into reality just as he breathed thought into action and tangible result.

Slowly, steadily filling himself with *chi*, letting the scant pure energies suffusing the clearing build through and within him with each breath, he commenced. He let these energies grow unhurried, carefully tending them like he would the first precious embers of a fire in the darkest heart of winter, his breath fueling their flames, allowing these sparks to swell and enliven, burgeon and thrive.

Then, after much time had passed, the clearing still silent save for the few sounds of his sleeping companions, when these energies filled him with great warmth and vitality, he tried something he had never attempted before, never thought possible, though the simplicity of the thought, the clarity of the insight now revealed to him filled him with hope and compassion.

He had opened the Dragon's Gate before, but never had he allowed it to flow freely. He had created the energy of life, an infinitesimally scant spark amidst the brilliance of the *yuan-chi* enlivening the macroverse, but he had never let this spark burn.

Now he would try.

He would allow the energy of life to foster and sustain itself, to become a wellspring that would grow from mere drops to a fount of wondrous life-giving force.

Not only would he attempt to create Light from the primordial void of potential, he would encourage It to create Itself.

He would create a self-sustaining Lightwell.

Just as the black Daemon's vortex had spilled forth virulent extradimensional energies that ran rampant on this dimension, debasing the city and corrupting its inhabitants, this new origin would bring forth a source of purity and Light within the forsaken walls of Taerris'thule, a source of hope and vivacity that would run counter to its current perversion and decay at the hands of unholy forces and entities.

Just as extradimensional beings had brought about the city's fall, this well of Light would bring about its resurrection and its purification.

With a final exhalation, he brought forth a spark of *yuan-chi*, creating a manifestation of pure potential. Within this flicker, summoned from the pure, expansive potential of his mind's eye, a flash of Light amidst the breadthless emptiness of peace pervading his inner vision, with the careful attention of an artisan attempting to realize his vision, he roused the reservoir of *yuan-chi* he cultivated.

Allowing the power he stored and the energy he created to commingle, he encouraged the two expressions of possibility to come together—fuel and flame—so that, united, they could burn.

With an explosive flash so bright he was blinded, unable to see with either his inner vision or his eyes, the world obscured by a scintillating pillar of utmost white, he was unable to look directly upon his creation.

He was, however, able to feel its effect.

The warmth of untold life-giving suns spilled over him with all of the vivification and little of the heat. So overwhelming was the presence, he had to force himself not to involuntarily raise his arms to protect himself from the all-encompassing Light.

He knew not how long this first attempt would abide but, sitting calmly in its glow, he knew that, for a time at least, the well of generative force was self-sustaining.

White Light filling the clearing in heavenly radiance, the peace and stillness he had briefly enjoyed did not last long.

Jumping up suddenly, his motions appearing all the faster given his full battle regalia, simultaneously drawing his axe that complained just as loudly, thinking that his slumber had been interrupted by a sudden magical assault from the Daemon that had so recently departed, Slate barked, "What devilry is this!"

Its words mirroring Slate's concerns, Duraeleon growled loudly as it whistled through the air, "Yarr! Who's there? I'll keelhaul ya!"

Just as quick to react, but remaining settled in their bedrolls, Aroganji and Wrindanneth did not fully rouse, though Wrindanneth grumbled, "If you're going to start summoning lights, could it at least wait until the morning?"

Curious and not upset in the slightest, for the effulgent warmth and radiance, as beguiling as a siren's call and as beautiful as a new dawn, drew his attention to its lustrous heart as surely as a moth to flame, Aroganji asked, full of wonderment, "What, exactly, is that?" He sensed the energies shimmering gloriously before him as an expression of multiple perfected layers and transformations of potential, the Wu-hsing alive, the summation of a rainbow.

Whatever it was, despite elusive hints of familiarity, his mind could not fully encompass its presence or significance.

Beyond intellection, he basked in the empyrean brilliance, full of rapture and amazement, the awe of ultimate incipience full upon him.

Plopping back down on his blankets after sheathing Duraeleon despite the axe's continued threats and protests aimed at an unseen enemy, Slate groused, "Seems like ya could give us some warnin' next time ya're gonna start makin' fireworks!"

Tempering his tone a bit as he took stock of the situation and began to fully understand what lay before him, Slate added thoughtfully, reflecting upon the majesty of the resplendence in hushed, respectful tones, "'Bout like Brendle's forge I'd imagine."

Yip bowed. "Yes. I would imagine so."

"Maybe Brendle can turn His Light down a bit before it draws all the Daemons on this side of Taerris'thule to its flame!" Rolling over, covering his head with a blanket though the sheet did not protect him from the fullness of the energies bathing over and through him, Wrindanneth tried his best to get back to sleep.

Replying to his bluster with calm, Aroganji answered, "I believe the idea is to leave this Light on, for the good of the city and for the good of the futures of any who would come here."

Throwing back his covers angrily, admitting temporary defeat in his battle for sleep, at least for the moment, Wrindanneth snarled, "You think that Yip's glorified torch, no matter how sublime, is going to stop those Daemons?"

He shook his shaggy head. "They feed off energy. That's why they did so well in our world, why they thrived, and why more came. That's why they created that hellish vortex…to suck away the energy of this world into their own Lightless pits."

"They spewed the effluent of their warped dimension into our own to make this place more habitable and to deter others from interfering."

"No divine torch will stop them."

It was Slate who responded first to Wrindanneth's diatribe, not Yip. "Don't be shortsighted, Wrindanneth! If my simple wards, small as they be, can keep back tha ravenous Shades, then a manifestation o' tha same power on a much larger scale should behave no differently!"

Aroganji nodded his agreement. "If the Daemons grew in strength here by drawing the life away, substituting their own foul taint in its place, then it only stands to reason that a wellspring of divine energies would slowly dilute their power, undermine their strength, and beat them back!"

"And what if they corrupt this power and use it for their own ends?"

Aroganji disagreed. "Something so pure, so powerful cannot be corrupted."

He turned his gaze from Wrindanneth to look upon the otherworldly beauty that bathed him in perfection. "Such purity fosters, cleanses, and furthers life's inherent potential. It is the bane of those extradimensional beings who have claimed Taerris'thule as their own."

Reluctantly turning his gaze away from the font of clarity, Aroganji finished, "Do not confuse this force with the energy of life created by living beings like us. Though similar, they are yet different as Yip can most certainly attest. You are correct. These Daemonic creatures do feed on the energy of living beings but energy such as this is of an entirely different magnitude."

"What if it just pushes them away, visiting their evil on some other unsuspecting place?"

Slate grunted, "Then they'll be weaker fer it and more vulnerable."

Yip added simply, "The light of the sun will warm one's skin on a cool day. Magnify that warmth, or venture closer to its source, and the sun's soothing light will become unbearable, deadly."

"Though this Light warms our skin, for the Daemons it is like one of us swimming unprotected through the heart of the sun."

Wrindanneth was silent for a moment before he grumbled, pulling the covers over his eyes in his unwavering attempt to get more rest, "Let us hope, for all of our sakes, that you are indeed correct."

The light of a thousand suns bathing them in ineffable radiance, a fulgence so bright that their hearts and minds were lifted to the heavens though they could gaze upon its untold brilliance without fear of being blinded, Slate, Aroganji and Yip sat peacefully about the well of Light for the rest of the evening until the coming morn, basking in a campfire transported directly from the highest of Heavens, their bodies and spirits replenished and enlivened by its presence. Wrindanneth, granted the peace of the deepest unbroken sleep, passed the remainder of the evening in dreamless repose, awaking refreshed and in good cheer, his heart made light and new.

Wrindanneth swept his mind over the ship one last time. All was in order. The *Shrike* had been made whole. Finally, the time to return to Tellanon was upon them.

Turning his eyes away from the burnished hull of the *Shrike*, the beauty of her form restored with her integrity, Wrindanneth called out to his companions who were in various states of activity around the ship, "Everyone ready to leave this ashen wasteland for a place with a bit more hospitality?"

He, for one, was looking forward to a nice, cool draught of spirits at a pub without distraction from friend or foe.

Slate was of like mind, so eager, in fact, was he to leave that he was already onboard the ship, forsaking the ground and stability for a prompt return. Calling down from the deck after spending the morning reorganizing what was left of their stores and supplies in the hold, he replied cheerily, "I'm ready fer a pint or two o' well-earned Dwarven mead!"

Wrindanneth laughed, sharing a smile with his friend. "Just two?"

"Two is where I'll start. I'll stop when I can no longer count!"

While his friends checked and rechecked the ship, ensuring that all was in order, Yip remained sitting dispassionately, his mind aloft, watching the immediate environs around them. He observed not only to ensure their safety, not only to gauge the level of risk threatening, not only to be prepared should an unforeseen event interfere with their anticipated departure but because he wished to do nothing else.

Wrindanneth had been wrong.

The proof unfolded miraculously, haltingly around them.

With the wonder of watching the glory of spring unfold for the first time, he sat in rapt attention gazing upon the agitated mass of otherworldly bleakness, the countless seething mass of Shadows, slowly receding in the presence of the life-sustaining Light.

This retreat was not fast by any means. The boiling wall of Shadow remained yet within a stone's throw of Eidelion's divine ward.

The retreat was steady nonetheless.

The landscape revealed by the Shadows' reluctant abandonment was not made brighter or more wondrous by their absence. Too long had the land been under the wretched boot of the extradimensional invaders, but it was, however, now free of their taint.

The restoration of the land abandoned by the Wraiths would slowly return Taerris'thule to vibrancy. Perhaps a single sprig of green would be the first sign of life to break the unyielding gray depression left in their wake. Perhaps the organisms of the soil would finally reclaim the drifting, forlorn leaves abandoned from a forgotten season aeons past. Perhaps a brave seed, carried on the winds of hope, would pioneer a new path for others of its brethren. Perhaps the surrounding land would reclaim what had once been its own gradually moving inward in a steady march from the city's margins, a triumph only delayed by the span of seasons. Perhaps some intrepid souls would brave the wilds and facilitate the rejuvenation.

He could not say.

Nor could he guess how long such a restoration would take place, only that it would happen at a pace measured by the slow wonder of renewal.

Studying the reluctant retreat of the Shadows, he knew not how long the rebirth of Taerris'thule would take, only that it would happen.

"Yip! Come on! Ya're holdin' us up!" Slate's enthusiasm to take off was a welcome surprise. "Our glorious return ta Tellanon awaits!"

Standing slowly, his eyes taking in the retreating wall of Shadows one last time before walking up the gangplank, Yip bowed to his friend. "My apologies for interfering with your hero's welcome."

"Just don't let it happen again!" Slate smiled as he walked away from the railing, the thick gray sky breaking in occasional patches to reveal small, ephemeral patches of jewel-like blue.

Returning to the deck for the first time after the ship's complete reformation, Yip walked to the aft and the quarterdeck where Slate had just rejoined Aroganji and Wrindanneth by the *Shrike's* silvery command sphere.

As Yip mounted the steps to join his friends, Slate called to him, "Are ya ready ta finally return ta civilization?"

Before Yip could answer, Wrindanneth replied, laughing, "You know he would be as happy sitting on a rock as returning to one that floats in the sky. Here or there, it's all the same to our friend the dispassionate sage!"

Yip's reply was succinct. "My wants have little to do with our imminent return. There is much yet I must do whether I wish or not."

Wrindanneth laughed. "You mean you actually have feelings?"

Returning his friend's jibe with one of his own, Yip replied in a deadpan, "Not that I acknowledge."

Aroganji laughed at Yip's rejoinder. "Both truth and humor in one response, Wrin! The line between the two is left for us to draw!"

Slate grumbled, "Bah! I never was any good at drawin'. I always preferred cuttin'!" He patted Duraeleon's sheathed blade as he spoke for emphasis.

"Another who prefers to cut to the heart of the matter!" His face lit with rare good cheer, Wrindanneth said, "Then we had best be off, lest we incur the wrath of our two bel esprits!"

Grinning in turn, Slate clapped his thickly callused hands together. "Now ya're talkin'!"

Letting his friends' jests continue without him, Yip gazed one last time upon the Lightwell he had created, its ineffable radiance filling the clearing with the warmth and cheer of birth and ascension, a small ember glowing amidst a sea of gray ash.

Who knew how long its fuel would burn?

"Get your last look, Yip! We're off!"

With those words, Wrindanneth invoked the power of the return stone and their universe stopped, collapsing into emptiness, exploding into totality.

ONE NIGHT FOR ANOTHER

> Gray cloudbanks looming
> roiling over the green plains,
> storm shadows dancing.

The joy that now swelled in their hearts, that had only begun to take refuge and flower, was short-lived.

Above, as Tellanon's forces drove the invading fleet back, returning the ships to the Darkness from whence they sprang, another tableau began to emerge before Humbol and Hoyt's eyes.

Those alien ships on the forefront of the attack redoubled their efforts, raining wrath and destruction down upon Tellanon's valiant defenders. The vanguard's furor and intensity could not be maintained, however, nor need it. Sacrificing themselves in violent conflagration, those enemy ships on the front-lines of battle forfeited themselves in devastating distraction that those ranks in the back yet clouded in the remaining fringes of Darkness could flee into the night sky.

One battle lost, these ships sought another.

Under cover of violence and strife, magic, and extradimensional Shadow untold invading ships sped away through Ea'ae's undefended skies, their menace and inimical intent undiverted.

Though Ea'ae's defenders had won the night, victory was not yet theirs.

Hoyt and Humbol could not imagine the devastation these ships would bring upon Ea'ae's innocent populace.

They could not let these ships get away.

They could not let the Cabal's warships succeed in whatever nefarious purpose engendered their flight.

The Cabal's ships must be stopped and their intent averted.

"By tha last hair on my head, we've got ta stop those blasted ships! Few are tha places on Ea'ae that could stand up ta such an onslaught as was seen by Tellanon. Our world will be theirs fer tha takin'!" Humbol's ire burned like a newly minted star. He would not see Ea'ae fall to interlopers just as her seals were restored.

Understanding the odds and their limitations, Hoyt and Humbol came to a difficult decision, if they could not stop these ships themselves, then others would have to do it for them.

Hoyt's words were heavy. "We must turn back, though we wish ta go forward. We must retreat that those who advance can meet with success."

Humbol growled, gritting his teeth, hating that Hoyt was correct, his eyes never leaving the trail of ships arching to the horizon.

Though they could not hope to stop the ships single-handedly, they could divine their purpose.

Sharing his friend's intensity and intent, Hoyt said, "Hail the Construct. Tell it of our intelligence. Let the Construct know that soon we will divine these ships' purpose and find out their destination for they would not quit so easily if other plans were not already in place."

A large grin on his face, eager for the challenge and the role they were to play, Humbol asked anxiously, "What other tricks d'ya have up yer sleeve?"

Flicking his wrists outward dramatically, revealing his bare, pale white forearms, Hoyt laughed. "Haven't ya learned yet I don't need any sleeves?"

Arching an eyebrow, Humbol replied, "Or tricks?"

Already working his magic, Hoyt remained silent.

ALSO BY JOSEPH J. BAILEY

Joe is also working on something else but really cannot say more on the matter at present.

HELP SPREAD THE WORD!

I hope you have enjoyed reading this book as much as I enjoyed writing it.

Whether these words transported you to another place, one you enjoyed wholeheartedly, or pushed you away without lasting impression, I would welcome your review wherever you may choose.

If you truly did appreciate this book, feel free to spread the word to your friends, family, and random acquaintances. I would also love for you to visit me at either my website or like me on my Facebook Author's Page.

If you would like to learn about future book releases, please consider signing up for my book announcement newsletter. I promise to use this information judiciously.

Many thanks and happy reading!

Joseph J. Bailey

.

GLOSSARY OF TERMS
PEOPLE, PLACES, AND THINGS

Abyss – a general name often used for extradimensional regions home to Daemonic creatures of Darkness and despair. Also called nether realms.

Adamantium – an exceedingly strong magical metal.

Acolyte – an Initiate of the K'un Lun that has shown some attainment but has not yet been accepted as a priest.

Adar – a Paratechnologist from Tellanon.

Adrael the Black – an ancient Black Dragon slain by Ithilieon while wielding Duraeleon.

Aerdos and Aerlyn – Elven twins and heroes from ages long past.

Aerie – a name commonly used for the peaks and summits claimed by Dragons as their homes.

Aeromancy – the study of the air and its currents, the manipulation of its energies, and the fashioning of airships.

Aerya – literally, 'Light' or 'air.' An Elven term for the living energy of the universe. The concept of Aerya encompasses all forms of magical energetic expression in a single totality from the universal source to the personal creation—both *chi* and *yuan-chi*. See also *yuan-chi* and *chi*.

Aerya'ana – literally, 'those who bring the Light.' An elite Elven contingent named in honor of Yip Chi Chuan, trained in the ways of Light discovered and shared by Yip, commissioned to spread knowledge and sanctity across the cosmos.

Aerya'anan – literally, 'Light Bringer' or 'one who brings the Light.' An Elven name for Yip Chi Chuan.

Aerya Etherum – literally, 'highest air' or 'highest breath.' Alternatively, 'first breath' or 'source of breath.' An Elven term for the source of the Aerya, the formless, boundless Void, source of limitless potential. See also Wuji.

Aeryaology – the study of living creatures that utilize magical energies as the basis of their constitutions.

Aeryasynthetic – a general term used to refer to those entities that utilize magical energies as the basis for their metabolism.

Aeryn – 'tree' in Elven. Also, a large, silver-boled tree named after the legendary Aeryn D'al for its similar, if diminished, appearance.

Aeryn D'al – literally, 'tree lord' in Elven. Also a derivation of 'magic lord' or 'Light lord.' A legendary, highly accomplished race of sentient trees. Original teachers of the Elves on Ea'ae.

Aeryn Sh'al – literally, 'tree heart' in Elven. Also a derivation of 'magic heart.' Enchanted wood sung from the heart of trees by Elven Iyela and fashioned into implements ranging from bows, swords, and armor to household goods like furniture, utensils, and living structures. Stronger than adamantine and able to carry powerful enchantments, the material of choice for Elven-wrought magical artifacts. Sometimes called Witchwood or Weirding Wood by Men.

Afternoon's Shade Inn – an inn in Shady Vale.

Age – any extensive period of time. Typically thought of as representing one thousand years though events of particular significance may also define its limits.

Airship – magically powered ships in as many shapes as the mind can imagine found plying the air currents and trade routes throughout Ea'ae and beyond. See also aeromancy.

Alaeron – a junior Paratechnologist on Tellanon.

Alain Ar'laen – member of Tellanon's guiding Protectorate, leader of the Home Guard, Tellanon's Master-at-Arms and principal defender, general and Champion. Once a man and a famed warrior, now a synthetic being joined with the Construct whose form and presence are owed as much to his imagination and will as his original physical form. First and foremost of the NUMEN. Also called Brightblade.

Aldael – the Indural's name for the Green Run.

Alderan – a guide, ambassador, and lorekeeper of the Elves of Yenaria.

Aleron – Elven noble and lorekeeper. Father to Llyewia. Husband of Nydia.

Allomorph – a being capable of taking on various shapes and guises, potentially augmenting its own intrinsic abilities, while retaining its primary core awareness, sense of self, and intelligence. The Jira S'al Alann are one such example.

Al'Marr – the homeworld of the H'era.

Aluran – literally, 'Green Glade.' The jungle village of the H'era Al'Marr.

Amakar – an ancient volcano located in the Drake Spires.

Anjali mudra – a gesture of salutation with both palms together at the chest.

Anubaraëthi – literally, 'Spawn of the Shadow,' or 'Shadow made manifest.' A general Elven name for greater sentient Daemons. Sometimes called Dread Lords.

Anubavaeri – literally, 'Spawn of the Flame,' or 'Spawn of the Fire.' An Elven name for powerful Daemons of flame.

Anuvaerya – literally, 'Children of the Light.' An Elven name for those Elves who have willingly left the bounds of the body to explore the realms of the mind and spirit. The existence of Anuvaerya is a closely guarded secret, known only to a few Elf-Friends outside the Elven people.

Anuvatali – literally, 'Children of the Dawn,' or 'Children of the New Morn.' An Elven name for the half-Elven children of Men and Elves born on Ea'ae.

Anuvatari – literally, 'Children of the Sun.' An Elven name for those Elves who first came to Ea'ae.

Anuvatari'aliana– literally, 'of one voice with the Children of the Sun' or 'friend-kin of the Children of the Sun.' An Elven name for those people of any race taken in by the Elves and taught something of their ways or those who are trusted and respected as Elf-kin.

Archaeus – the holy sword of Eidelion, forged from the rarified light of the sun, glows white when wielded by one of pure heart. Also known as the White Sword and the Bright Blade. Originally called Erudhaerya by the Elves.

Archfiend – a general name for a Daemon, particularly in reference to powerful Daemons that have usurped dominion over lesser representatives of their own kind.

Archlich – a particularly powerful Lich, often a powerful deceased practitioner of magic. See Lich.

Archmage – a highly accomplished or powerful magician.

ARMED – Allomorphic Recombinatorial Multidimensional Extravehicular Drones. A flexible, multi-faceted, shapechanging drone system invented by Spreesprocket. Also called sentry drones.

Aroganji – a Fang Shih from the lands of Chang Sen. A practitioner of magical proscriptions and formulae and friend to Yip, Wrindanneth, and Slate. Member of the Four.

Ar'thas – literally, 'Black Mountain Orcs.' A tribe of evil Orcs and their allies, hidden deep in the heart of the Drake Spires.

Aruene – desolate continent to the west of Dharia.

Aspect – a fragment of the Construct. Used to perform specialized duties for the larger Construct in Tellanon. Like a hologram, an Aspect is a smaller, self-aware representation of the whole functionality of the Construct contained entirely within the larger system but granted broad freedom, flexibility, and independence. Often given to and used extensively by citizens of Tellanon. Also called a Fragment.

Aurana – the deep-seated mental link shared between the H'era and the H'era D'ur.

Auros the Golden – along with Uzsanthal the Grim and Glaudron the

Many Hued, one of the most powerful benevolent Dragons in all of Ea'ae. Father of Azaelle.

Ayle'ine Sea – the western boundary of Dharia. A vast expanse of open water dotted with wild, isolated islands.

Azaelle the Golden – a young golden Dragon of Auros's brood.

Azagothe – a Daemon lord of the nether abyss.

Baërn – literally, 'Berserker's Bane.' A magical ring given to Slate by Hoyt.

Baera – 'Brendle the All-Father' in the tongue of the Dwarves.

Baera'Dur – literally, 'Brendle's bulwark' in the tongue of the Dwarves. Called Dreadnaughts by Men.

Baeradun – a legendary Dwarven hero known to burst into flames.

Ba Duan Jin – the Eight Pieces of Brocade. A widely practiced and highly respected series of *qigong* movements with many associated benefits to health.

Bang tui – leg ties used to secure pants or stockings.

Barnaby Bilantré – a famous craftsman, aeronaut, and world-class aero-mancer. Also known as Barney Black Eyes.

Beast Riders of Al'Marr – name for the feline beast riders of the Forlorn Forest who count their mounts as their brothers. Called the H'era in their own tongue.

Beyond – a general term for other dimensions in the multiverse, often in reference to the nether realms. See Abyss.

Blade Master – a highly proficient teacher of hand-to-hand combat in the Home Guard.

Blade Singer – see Caer'collas.

Blaeken Wode – literally, 'dark, bleak, or black wood' in the tongue of Men. An ancient forest on the continent of Kilaeron. Within its reaches, the Keep of Garen Muer houses the seal of Weis'liuhath.

Body of Light – another term for the *jalü*, celestial body, or rainbow body.

Bor'Banna – literally, 'bearded demon.' A name for the Dwarven masters of the axe, imbued by the remnants of power from Brendle's fire.

Borus – Head Magistrate, lead Justicar, and Adjudicator for the city of Tellanon. Member of the Protectorate and famed invoker.

Bot – short for robot, particularly with regard to Paratechnological clock-work devices made by Tinkerers that may or may not manifest synthetic intelligence capable of independent thought.

Braemen – captain of the airship *Shrike*, member of the nomadic R'yn Daer.

Brendle – The All-Father. Dwarven god of the forge and, in the eyes of the Dwarves, the creator of the known universe. More often than not, the brunt of Slate's curses. Called Baera in the tongue of the Dwarves.

Brendle's Flame – see Brendle's Spark.

Brendle's Spark – the remaining embers from Brendle's original flame and forge when Brendle first wrought the universe under hammer, anvil, and flame. The remaining embers even now bring forth life and magic into the universe.

Also, the fires at the heart of the Daerdaana'Duin, the Bor'Banna's highest known skill, where the exponent merges directly with Brendle's flames. Also called Brendle's Flame. An analogue to Aerya and *yuan-chi* in Dwarven cosmology.

Brendle's Tears – the finest of Dwarven ales. Reputed to be so wondrous and flavorful that Brendle himself cries tears of joy and amazement with each sip.

Brightblade – see Alain Ar'laen.

Byear – literally, 'heart of flame.' Magical robe once worn by Mandros Gray Beard, famed archmage, now worn by Aroganji. Able to deflect a blade as well as allow full spellcasting, among other wardings.

C³ – the Cogitation Clarifying Cap. A Gnomish Paratechnological device capable of reading and analyzing both simple and higher-order thought processes. Much more complex, convoluted, and cumbersome than using mind reading spells, the C^3 benefits from a certain Gnomish style and sense of eccentricity. Because of its complexity, convolution, and cumbersomeness, the C^3 is sometimes referred to as the C^6 or, more often, the C^0.

The Cabal –A sinister alliance of dark mages, fallen priests, extradimensional beings, and other creatures of might bent not only on domination but power. Known by many other names including the Order of the Lidded Eye, the Fallen, the Light Fallen, the Order of the Burning Eye, and the Order of the Hooded Gaze. Called Liúxīng Làngrén by the Priests of K'un Lun. Often symbolized by a blazing sigil of a closed eye.

Caelebeor – literally, 'Shadow's Grace' in the tongue of the Elves. A magical ring given to Slate by Hoyt.

Caer'collas – a Q'sharian blade master. Often called Blade Singers by those who watch their masterful interplay of magic and blade work.

Celestial body – see rainbow body, body of light, or *jalü*.

Cersaegian – Liege and eldest of the Fiersayne. Keeper of the Ghrem Weard. An ancient Black Dragon abiding in northern Maeron.

Champion of Light – a general honorific for those who have earned great esteem fighting the forces of Darkness. Also, a title for one of great accomplishment within the Dalaren Ka.

Master Chang – an exalted teacher of the K'un Lun.

Chang Sen – an ancient land of empire and intrigue home to unique ways and traditions found nowhere else in Ea'ae. Homeland to Aroganji and the Fang Shih along with Yip Chi Chuan and the K'un Lun.

Chen-jen – a true human being. Seen as the ideal figure in philosophical and religious Taoism. Chen-jen refers to someone who has apprehended the truth within herself and thereby attained the Tao.

Chi – *Qi*; breath, air, or vapor of particular significance in Taoism and Eastern medicine. From a Taoist perspective, the *chi* is the vital energy or life force that enlivens and pervades all things. *Chi gung—chi kung* or *qigong*—are exercises to build and strengthen *chi* flow. Along with *shen* and *ching*, one of the Three Treasures essential to human life. A less subtle and refined form of the *yuan-chi*, the universal potential. The fire that does not burn.

Chih-jen – a perfected human being. Another term describing an ideal person. A Chih-jen has realized unity with the Tao and is free of all concepts and limitations.

Ching – *Jing*; the germ or source of life. Along with the breath or vital energy (*chi*) and the mind or consciousness (*shen*), one of the life forces essential for the preservation and prolongation of life in the Taoist view.

Chuan – *Quan*; Fist.

Chutefunnel Knobwhistle – member of Tellanon's governing Protectorate, head of higher learning, intercollegial understanding, cross-communication, and numenal exchange, facilitator of intellectual prosperity, and citizen enlightenment.

Ciërna – literally, 'vision of the world to be' in the tongue of the Elves. An expression encompassing and embodying both how one would hope the world will unfold and arise, either individually or as a collective, and what may be required for the realization and actualization of this reality.

Circle – a powerful ritual magic employed by the leaders of Tellanon as a last resort. Used to invoke the Loel'dara.

Class M Fire – a general fire category used by Paratechnologists to describe fires of magical origin. There are multiple subtypes depending upon source, intensity, and required quenching response.

Cletus – Hoyt's pet Fairy Dragon.

Clockwork – a general name for a particular branch or type of Paratechnology focusing on magically animated contraptions of any shape, size, and function often resembling machines and robots but not limited to any specific shape. A particular specialty of Gnomish Paratechnological Tinkerers.

Coerdaerya – literally 'partner in Light' in the tongue of the Elves. A term used to describe two individuals bound together inextricably by *ciërna*, common vision, and common love.

COG – the Construct Organization Group on the island of Tellanon. The Paratechnologists in COG have direct responsibility over the Construct and its attendant artificial intelligence subroutines including the various Aspects and other specialized intelligence engines in addition to the management of the Construct's subordinate functions.

Common – see Common Tongue.

Common Tongue – a universal language used across Ea'ae to facilitate nonmagical communication. Also called Common.

The Construct – a powerful, centralized, multi-faceted sentient intelligence created by the Paratechnologists used to oversee, understand, envision, and facilitate activities in Tellanon. Administered and overseen by COG.

The Council – a secretive, informal band of wizards, priests, druids, and other wielders of arcane power from many different races focused on ensuring Ea'ae's continued safety and prosperity. Sometimes called the Council of Light.

Although an entirely different body, the ruling Protectorate of Tellanon is also referred to as the council or High Council.

The Council of Light – see the council.

Cozy Cabbage Inn – an inn in Tellanon known for its Gnomish delicacies.

Craft – higher magical skills. An umbrella term inclusive of various branches of magic including unique talents and abilities native to particular races, guilds, and tribes.

Cycles – the Elven equivalent for the lunar year. Based as much on the turning and changing of seasons and the ebb and flow of life as Ea'ae's revolution around the sun. Called Soerlyn in the tongue of Elves.

D'al – 'Lord' in Elven.

Daeja – a trade city in central Var'Kera.

Daemon – a general name for extradimensional creatures with hostile intent or for those otherworldly creatures that feed and prey upon the energies of the living. Also called Infernals.

Daerdros – lieutenant of the Home Guard and Master at Arms. A Caer'collas, a Q'sharian blade master.

Daerdaana'Duin – literally, 'to become the heart of fire' or 'to become the heart of the forge.' One of the highest skills of the Bor'Banna, wherein the practitioner wreaths himself in the flames of Brendle's forge, becoming a direct manifestation of Brendle's power and one with its heat, energy, and vitality. In times of old, these warriors cloaked themselves in flames, striking down foes directly with Brendle's might. See Brendle's Spark.

Daer'Duin – literally, 'heart of fire' or 'heart of the forge.' Given Dwarven name for Slate Flintforge.

Dagron Iron Beard – a famous Dwarven Dur'kazak of old.

Dalare – 'Light' or 'One Light' in the tongue of Tol Aeron.

Dalaren Ka – the 'Knights of the One Light.' A chivalrous order whose members follow the ways of the Dalaren Mere, the Light's Path. Guardians of the Star of Elendial.

Dalaren Mere – the 'Light's Path.' The way of chivalry, faith, and the sword through the expression of the Light of Life.

Darkness – a general term for those beings opposed to the Light and Life it engenders and who would subvert, pervert, or otherwise mar Its presence and manifestation. Also a general term for the corruption of the energy of life, the Light, itself.

Dauren'Kas – 'the Bringers of Light.' A name taken by those Shaur'Daus who bring forth the Light of creation to negate the energy voids and Darkness brought forth by Ur'Daus and Its minions.

Dawrac di Gaydial – an alien Paratechnologist resembling an Ogre composed largely of stone and crystal.

Delving – a general name for any Dwarven city or outpost. See also undermount.

Deur Spricken Sprack – Gnomish for 'the Omnispark.' See also Phlogiston and Omnispark.

Dharia – the largest continent on the world of Ea'ae.

Dharma – cosmic law or truth.

Dhwer'werde – literally, 'Fate's Door' or 'Fated Forest.' A cursed forest surrounding the lands of Taerris'thule.

Dhyana mudra – a meditation *mudra*. To form the *mudra*, two hands are placed on the lap, right hand on left with fingers fully stretched and the palms facing upwards.

Diaspora – a general name for the large-scale exodus of various races of humanity from Ea'ae with the development of *faerviage*. Although not native to Ea'ae, Elves participated in these departures alongside Men, Dwarves, Gnomes, and other sentient races of Ea'ae. Many of those people who left have since reestablished contact with Ea'ae thereby encouraging interstellar trade.

DISCO – Daemonic Irradiating Stroboscopic Catastrophe Orb. A multifaceted Paratechnological orb capable of emitting multiple streams of high intensity magically amplified light suitable for the destruction of extradimensional creatures of Darkness...and dancing

Dizzywig Paddlepulley – member of Tellanon's Protectorate, Gnomish Paratechnologist extraordinaire, and leader of the Sliced Bread Society.

Doerdaana'Duin – literally, 'the dance of the heart of fire' or 'to dance in the heart of the forge.' One form of Dwarven axe work known for its fluid strikes and counters, commonly used by particularly adept Bor'Banna.

D'orauk managua al'zurka – literally, 'may your blood flow strong and pure.' A Dracodaeran expression of well-wishing for health and vitality, strength, and power. Often expressed at times of parting.

Dracodaera – a race of humanoid Dragon-kin. Hunters of Daemons and other creatures of Darkness. Originators of the Shaur'Daus.

Dracodin – an extraplanar being of some power resembling a humanoid Dragon.

Dragonflight – a group of Dragons living and moving together.

Dragons – along with the Aeryn D'al, one of the oldest races of Ea'ae. Steeped in magic and power, Dragons are feared by all who cross their path. As complex as they are storied, Dragons are as diverse as their characters and can wield power only rivaled by the gods themselves.

The Dragon's Gate – the way of energy creation, concentration, and direction taught to Yip by Azaelle the Golden.

Drake – Dragon.

The Drake Spires – also the Spine of the World. A series of lofty peaks running down the center of the Dharian continent. Named after the many Dragon lairs and aeries scattered throughout its heights. Ancestral home of the Yeren people.

Dread Lord – a general name for higher order, more powerful Daemons granted intelligence and power far beyond their peers. Called Anubaraëthi, Children of the Shadow, by Elves.

Dreadnaught – a Dwarven warrior specializing in heavy combat. Utilizing enchanted, rune-etched full plate armor along with two-handed axes, hammers, and maces, Dreadnaughts earn their place at the fore of the battle-field by fighting against the most implacable foes. Famous as much for their rallying battle cries and songs along with their fear inducing chants and dirges as their blades. Called Baera'Dur in the tongue of Dwarves.

Dread Steed – the otherworldly flying steeds of the Fyrskal.

Dream Stealer – Wrindanneth's own name for Maeth Onai. A reference to Maeth coming to Wrindanneth in dreams to partake of the choicest lore uncovered or discovered during his travels and research.

Drogu – an Orcish commander.

Drothman – a famous Dwarven hero.

Druids – protectors of the wilds, guardians of nature, and lovers of freedom. First students of the Indural.

Dunédâne – literally, 'deep delver.' Name for the Dwarves among their own kind and the Karadüm.

Dûnedar – a Dwarf from Slate's hold.

Duraeleon – 'The Light Bringer,' bane of Adrael the Black, ancient axe of Ithilieon. Wielded by Slate Flintforge.

Durden – literally, 'valiant heart.' A Dwarven rune that serves to protect against fear and indecision when properly enchanted.

Durin – a famous Dwarven hero from times of yore.

Dur'kazak – literally, 'fire shaper.' A Dwarven master smith skilled in the art and craft of metallurgy, elemental magics, and rune crafting known as Karaduen.

Durnok – literally, 'possibility reader.' One skilled in the reading and interpretation of possibility and chance, probable futures, cause and effect, and the outcomes of events. Often used as trackers, mercenaries, bounty hunters, and assassins.

Duuna'Dan – literally, 'rocks of the father.' The Dwarven name for the Green Run. The old, rounded hills, worn mountains, and boulders of the Duuna'Dan are thought to be the original handiwork of Brendle as he formed Ea'ae from the Void with the careful molding of his hands. Although no longer under their control, many Dwarven mining communities and outposts still dot the wilds in this region.

Duurn'Laden – a large northern Dwarven delving known for the depths and richness of its mines, the skill of its Dur'kazak and the quality of their craftsmanship.

Dwarves – along with Elves, Gnomes, and Men, one of the four most prominent races on Ea'ae. Dwarves are short, hearty, and solidly built and known for their ability to work metal. They excel at reading the earth and mining.

Their keen knowledge of metals and runes allows for the creation of powerful works of Craft. Also called Dunédâne.

Ea'ae – 'The world.' Home to magical creatures and races of many shapes, cultures, and forms.

Echoing Fist – see Pai-lien Touch.

Ectoplasmic Reconnaissance Goggles – Gnomish Paratechnological visual enhancement device allowing the viewing and analysis of supernatural energies. Commonly referred to as ERG's.

EGAD – see the Every Gnome's Anti-Intelligence Device.

Eidelion – knight-captain and officer of the Tellanon Home Guard, leader of the Light's Guard, paladin of the Light, initiate of the Dalaren Ka, bane of the wicked, and wielder of Archaeus the White Sword. Known as Night's Bane, True Heart, and Dawn's Light.

Eiryna – a particularly fleet and agile Elven airship.

El'alen – literally, 'old home.' The Elven name for the Green Run. Named after the ancestral homes of their allies of old, the Dwarves.

Eldre'gheu – literally, 'old god.' One of the fourteen seals protecting Ea'ae from extradimensional incursion. Also the temple to the god once serving as the focal point of Taerris'thule.

Elf-friends – see Elf-kin or Anuvatari'aliana.

Elf-kin – Those people of any race taken in by the Elves and taught something of their ways. Sometimes called Elf-friends or Anuvatari'aliana in the tongue of the Elves.

Elixir field – energy fields in the body. See *tan t'ien*.

Elves – a fey race at home among the trees and dells of Ea'ae. Elves are a race of great Craft and knowledge that made peace with the land long before the coming of Men and Dwarves and many other sentient races. It is said that magic is the lifeblood of the Elves. Often called Lords of the Wood or Tree Singers by Men, although not all Elves are indeed Iyela. Those Elves on Ea'ae are the Anuvatari.

Embodied Cloven Crystallization of Refined Essence – A sentient crystalline entity with significant psychic ability. Also a well-respected Paratechnologist.

EMMA – a NUMEN serving Tellanon. Short for Energetic Mapping, Monitoring, and Analysis. EMMA's specialization is developing predictive models to visualize the magical energy currents flowing across Ea'ae.

Empen Wastes – coastal wetland wilderness of west-central Dharia composed of bogs, fens, swamps, lowland forests, and associated rivers, deltas, islands, and lakes. A vast, largely uninhabited region home to fey creatures and unusual beasts.

The Enemy – Ur'Daus, the Darkness between dimensions. Also known as the Creeping Shadow, Destroyer of Light, the Umbral Lord, the Devourer of Worlds, among many other names and curses.

ENNIS – see Epistemic Noetic Numenetic Integrating Summator.

Epistemic Noetic Numenetic Integrating Summator – a multifunctional Gnomish device with capabilities ranging from measurement and systematic evaluation of phenomena, data analysis, computation, and communication to independent reasoning, learning aid, and thought transference. Also called ENNIS for short.

Éremon – Exarch of Tellanon, august Consul of the ruling Protectorate, Fifth of Thirteen.

ERG – see Ectoplasmic Reconnaissance Goggles.

Erudhluin – literally, 'Heaven's Home.' One of many sacred groves tended and held sacred by Elven Iyela.

Erudhaerya – literally, 'Heaven's Light' in the tongue of the Elves. One of many names for the White Sword Archaeus.

Essence – the essential energies. The energies of life and magic and the source of their origination, especially when viewed wholistically.

Eyrdeas – the White Blade of Morn. The storied sword of Maeven D'lanaran. Called Taliaerya, Morning's Light or Dawn's Light, among the Elves.

Every Gnome's Anti-Intelligence Clandestine Apparatus version 3.1, Corvette Class – see the Every Gnome's Anti-Intelligence Device. Also EGAD.

Every Gnome's Anti-Intelligence Device – a Paratechnological defensive system suitable for espionage, surveillance, and camouflage added to items ranging in size from personal armor to airships. The Every Gnome's Anti-Intelligence Device replicates the surrounding environmental variables and superimposes them over the object protected by the defensive system rendering it indistinguishable from its surroundings. Sometimes referred to as EGAD or, more specifically and to add to the general air of confusion around Gnomish devices, as the Every Gnome's Anti-Intelligence Clandestine Apparatus version 3.1, Corvette Class.

Faerviage – magical voyage. A name for the magical ships capable of interdimensional and interstellar travel. Ships vary in form and function based on magical technology, need, and culture.

Fa jin – also sometimes called '*fa jing*'; a sudden wave of energy that surges through the exponent's body and into an opponent. A spontaneous energy release; to issue and discharge power.

Fallen – the Cabal or Liúxīng Làngrén.

Fang Shih – literally, 'a master of prescriptions'; a magician in Chang Sen. Traditionally, the precursor of Taoist sages and priests skilled in the use of various supramundane arts including astrology, astronomy, spirit healing, prophecy, geomancy, arts of love, the use of talismans and drugs, exercises for prolonging life, and enlisting the aid of gods.

Fang Shu – magical arts, especially as practiced by the Fang Shih.

Far travel – see traveling.

Fay Long – the Celestial Courtyard, highest peak in the K'un Lun.

Fiersayne – the brood and broodmates of Cersaegian.

The Fists – see the Flaming Fists.

Fizzlemiz – a Gnomish Paratechnologist. One of the foremost experts on alien technologies among the Paratechnologists.

The Flaming Fists – an honorific name granted to the adventuring band composed of Aroganji, Wrindanneth, Slate, and Yip. Sometimes called the Four, the Fists, the Four of the Flaming Fists, among other honorifics.

Forlorn Forest – the Emerald Jungle. A vast wilderness adjacent to Jenyuan Shulin and the Drake Spires. A region largely unknown and unexplored by most races. Home to the H'era.

Four Lands – a general reference to the four principle continents of Ea'ae. Although there are many smaller islands and land masses scattered across Ea'ae, Dharia, Maeron, Aruene, and Kilaeron are the largest and most prominent.

The Four – see the Flaming Fists.

Fraeü – literally, 'shadow's heart.' Magical robe once worn by Mandros Gray Beard, famed Archmage, now worn by Wrindanneth. Able to deflect a blade as well as allow full spellcasting, among other wardings.

Fragment – another name for an Aspect. A personalized portion of the Construct assigned to and intended to assist citizens of Tellanon in various capacities.

Freyda – Brendle's wife. Known for her patience and virtue.

Fria al'Othra – literally, 'eyes of true vision.' An Elven term for the universal perspective of the Iyela.

Fu – literally, 'return.' Returning to the root or source, the Tao. In Taoist meditative practice this return is synonymous with realization. The perception of the firmament from which the dynamic energy processes of *chi* flow, emerge, and return. An experience of the primal Emptiness or spacious void expressing the fundamental unity and equality of all things. See also Wuji and Taiji.

Fueron Mountains – a range of southern mountains near the city of Taer-ris'thule.

Fu-lu – Magical talismans, especially strips of paper, metal, or bamboo inscribed with symbols for protection employed by the Fang Shih.

Fyrskal – Guardians of the seal of Mihtig'leht and founders of Morowen. A chivalrous order of ages past that held to the ways and teachings of the Light.

Gaesia – sea-covered homeworld of the Jira S'al Alann.

Garen Muer – an ancient keep located in the heart of the Blaeken Wode.

Ghrem Weard – a common name for the nearly impenetrable northern cliff boundary of Maeron.

Gideon Goldsprocket – Flight Master of Tellanon. A Paratechnologist skilled in the ways of *faerviage*.

Gil-alan – a member of the Home Guard.

Gilaethe – literally, 'the light born.' Son of Nienael and a Wyaera of Tueran.

Gnomes – a race of short stature but of broad mind known for their creativity, imagination, and Paratechnological aptitude. Originators of Paratechnology, famed Tinkerers, often unable to leave well enough alone. Distant relatives of Dwarves.

Gnomeproof – a Dwarven colloquialism for foolproof.

Goran – a forest giant skilled in the ways of the Indural.

Gorthäk – a shaman of the Ar'thas.

Göerden – an armsman of some repute aboard the *Shrike*.

Grast – an evil Orcish tribal leader.

The Green Run – Man's name for the wilds of old, rounded mountains and ancient deciduous forests spanning the region from the western feet of the Drake Spires to eastern Var'Kera. Untamed and largely unsettled, this region is home to ruins, outposts, and creatures of every description. Called Duuna'Dan by the Dwarves, Aldael by the Indural, and El'alen by the Elves.

Gristnast – an Orcish sentry in the desolate wastes of Maeron.

Gromdek – a tribe of Orcs known for their skilled magic-wielding shaman.

Gruendan Weirndan – Champion of the Gleaming Blade, knight and commander of the Fyrskal.

Gründen – Thane of the Flintforge Clan. Kinsman of Slate.

Guai Lo – a Lung-wang, or Dragon king, from Chang Sen's past. Many artifacts of power have been made from his remains as well as his horde.

Guàn – monastery.

Guernden – a magical Dwarven hand cannon similar in appearance to an ornate rifle. Sometimes referred to as Dragon's Gullets for the fire contained in their bellies.

Günda – literally, 'Dwarf excrement.' An Orcish curse.

Guor' Uenaqe – literally, 'forge of our spirits.' Name for the harsh, volcanic homeworld of the Dracodaera.

Gyarxon – a race of psychic warriors who use their mental powers to travel interdimensionally seeking conquest.

Halls of Choosing – special locations spread throughout Tellanon that allow the visitor to select the pocket dimension of their choice to visit.

The Heart of Yere – a blazing red stone talisman that protects and guides its bearer. An artifact of the Yerens' and a piece of their heart and home.

Hellforge – a Daemonic smithy capable of producing fell items of great power.

Hellforged – a reference to Daemonic items made in a Hellforge. Most commonly weapons, armor, or arcane artifacts.

Henosis – a theurgical practice whose ultimate aim is unification with and expression of the Divine Light.

H'era – short for H'era Al'Marr.

H'era Al'Marr – the name of the beast riders of Al'Marr in their own tongue. H'era means 'children of the twin skies,' a reference both to the green canopy of their jungle home beneath the blue skies of Ea'ae and in remembrance of their homeworld of Al'Marr. Al'Marr means 'green sea.' Taken together, their name shows how the H'era find their compass and direction somewhere between the earth below and sky above their home—current and remembered.

H'era D'ur – 'Brother of the H'era.' Name of the sentient cat mounts with whom the H'era share a deep mental affinity, the so-called Aurana. Treated with much honor and respect, these mounts are an integral part of the H'era family groups and are considered an equal member in H'era society.

High Conservator – leader of the Dalaren Ka.

High Council – Tellanon's governing body of thirteen Paratechnologists and citizen representatives. Sometimes referred to as the council. See also Protectorate.

Holder of Secrets – a keeper of esoteric knowledge within the Home Guard. Also Keeper of Secrets.

The Home Guard – elite squadron of Tellanon's defenders and champions led by Eidelion.

The Home Reach – the fortress of the Home Guard located in Tellanon's center, part of Illdrassil.

Homeworld – planet of origin or primary habitation for a race, species, or group.

Hoyt – shop owner, gossip, and guide in Tellanon. Purveyor of fine goods, staples, information, and oddities. Wizard of some repute. Most often seen in his store, Hoyt's – Oddities, Found Goods, and Sundries.

Hröthe – literally, 'divine healing.' A Dwarven Karaduen offering a one-time boon of healing from a grievous or debilitating wound.

Hsiang Lung – a lush mountain range in eastern Chang Sen bordering the Q'ia Shan Sea. Home to Xian Shi, the school of the Fang Shih.

Hui-yin – an energy center located at the perineum called the Gate of Mortality and the Door of Life and Death. The seat of *ching*, the generative reproductive energy.

Human – see humanity. A general name for all sentient races on Ea'ae.

Humanity – a general name for all humanoid races on Ea'ae. Men, Dwarves, Gnomes, Indural, and other sentient races of Ea'ae are included under this broad description. As a naturalized race, Elves, too, are considered part of humanity although they are genetically distinct from the other humanoid races.

Humbol – a traveling merchant and airman. Friend and former adventuring partner of Hoyt. Captain and owner of the airship the *Rare Aer*.

Hürn – literally, 'evil's bane.' A Dwarven rune used for protection from evil.

Iera – literally, 'brother of the heart' in the tongue of the H'era. Uuraja's H'era D'ur.

Ilidian – Watcher of the Drake Spires.

I'ldaerya J'al Ishentaré – literally, 'the art of unbroken change.' An art unique to the Jira S'al Alann that encompasses an unending range of physical and magical transformations in response both to an opponent and the energies expressed by past and present teachers and adversaries.

Illdrassil – literally, 'Spire of the Heavens' or 'Tree of Heaven' in the Old Tongue of Men. The home of the High Council, Tellanon's ruling body and the Home Guard. A vast repository of magical energies that empowers the city in the sky.

Illendial – the North Star in the tongue of the Elves. Sometimes used as an invocation to guide and protect the spirit from assailment.

Imperial – centralized unit of currency used in many lands across Ea'ae.

Incirrinaen – highly intelligent cephalopodic organisms widely known for their heightened cognitive and mental abilities.

Indural – one trained in the magic, lore, and woodcraft of the forest giants.

Infernal – a Daemon.

Initiate – an ascetic just accepted into the K'un Lun.

Irielia – an Elven city in south central Dharia.

Ithil'alen – literally 'elden home' or 'eldritch home.' Elven territory in northeastern Dharia.

Ithilieon – a legendary Elven hero. Wielder of Duraeleon and slayer of Adrael.

Iyela – an Elven lorekeeper, wonder worker, tree singer, and shaper. Known for their ability to commune with the spirit of trees and request the boon of their heartwood, the Aeryn Sh'al. Called Tree Singers by Men.

Jae'elthos – member of Tellanon's Protectorate, Iyela, Lorekeeper of the Anuvatari, the Children of the Light.

Ja'lal – literally, 'dearest one' in the tongue of the H'era.

Jalü – a rainbow body. A spiritual attainment allowing for the direct transition and ascendancy of the body to Light and Mind. Also called celestial body, rainbow body, or body of light.

Jarvis Jenkins – a tailor of some repute in Tellanon known for his functional clothing, craftsmanship, and ability to meet his customers' expectations for unique garment properties.

Jenkins – a trader and merchant from Shady Vale.

Jenta – literally, 'to call' in the tongue of the H'era. To call oneself is *jentara*. To call a group or a people is *jentaro*.

Jenyuan Shulin – literally, 'forbidden garden forest.' The Forbidden Forest, ancestral home of the Aeryn D'al. See also Noes Al'amroth.

Jian Lu – one of Aroganji's teachers at the arcane institution Xian Shi in Chang Sen.

Jin – literally, 'power.' Also an opponent's experience of the energy manifest by another.

Jing – *ching;* literally, 'essence.' Along with *qi* and *shen*, it is considered one of the Three Treasures. *Jing* provides the material basis and fuel for the body and transmits genetic heritage.

Jing luo – the invisible system of channels or pathways through which *qi* circulates throughout the body. Also sometimes referred to as vessels and collaterals, conduits or meridians.

Jira S'al Alann – literally, 'People of the Imagining.' A race of changelings able to shift their guise and abilities depending upon their magical development and attunement. See also allomorph.

Jueran'al – literally, 'brothers-in-living-ideation' or, more simply, 'brothers in ideals' in the tongue of the Jira S'al Alann. The term refers to a particularly organic way of looking at those who share a common ground of thought and ideation created by shared goals and ideals reinforced through each other's commitment and communication to the continual development and expression of these underlying intentions.

Ka – 'Knight' or 'Paladin' in the tongue of Tol Aeron.

K'an and Li and the esoterica that follow – literally, 'water and fire.' In some schools of internal alchemy the interchange of *k'an* and *li* represent a combination of *yin* and *yang* whose interchange corresponds to the functioning of the Tao, both the macrocosm and microcosm, within an individual. After completing the large heavenly cycle represented by the microcosmic orbit and the fusion of the five elements, thereby opening all the energy channels within the body, the Taoist adept is ready to begin the process of energy sublimation of *k'an* and *li*.

Through various stages, the *ching*, the generative energy, is converted into *chi*, the life force energy. The power of the reproductive hormones is thereby transferred into the whole body and brain. The process is similar process to the yogic awakening of the Kundalini, except in the Taoist process the resulting energy is directed throughout the body continuously along the meridians instead of being directed solely upward to the head.

During the initial stages (lesser enlightenment of the *k'an* and *li*) this interchange focuses on the cultivation of the root, the *hui-yin* or perineum, and the heart *chakras* while the *ching* energies are transformed at the navel.

The next stage, Ta K'an Li (greater enlightenment of the *k'an* and *li*), involves increasing the amount of energy drawn up through the body while bringing the energy up to the solar plexus. The increased energy in this stage results from the adept drawing energy directly from Heaven (Yang, above) and Earth (Yin, below) while adding the elemental powers to those of the adept's body.

The following stage, T'ai K'an Li (greatest enlightenment of the *k'an* and *li*), involves further mixing of the *yin* and *yang* powers at a higher energy center in the heart.

From here the adept has several potential stages to follow. The adept goes through a process of sealing the five sensory organs to prevent energy loss. The *chi* is then converted into mental energy (*shen*), or the energy of the soul, to preserve and purify the body and spirit while controlling the emotions.

There are still other formulae available for the adept to practice. Among these are the congress of Heaven and Earth immortality. At this stage, the adept mixes *yin* and *yang* energies at the crown of the head to preserve and cultivate the body to allow the spirit to achieve immortality. As the energies circulate, the body, soul, and spirit mingle and unite with the universe. The spirit thereby returns to nothingness or the source.

Finally, one last formula in the adept's development is the reunion of man and Heaven resulting in a true immortal man. At this stage, the internal alchemist has overcome reincarnation, developed an immortal spirit and an immortal body to house the spirit and soul, and is reunited with creation.

Karaduen – a Dwarven word meaning 'Light's ward' or 'Light's seal.' Special Dwarven runes and symbols often employed by Dur'Kazak and Kor'-Dannan in the crafting of artifacts and the creation of spells and enchantments.

Karadüm – a type of particularly powerful stone giant in tune with the ebb and flow of the land's development and unfolding; usually guardians of a particular sacred place. Distant kin of the Indural.

Kazarhan the Stout – Dwarven lieutenant of the Home Guard, Kor'Dannan, and Dur'kazak. Wielder of the great hammer Raurdros. Master of Karaduen.

Kazzak – literally, 'marks of honor' in the tongue of the Dwarves. Symbols, tokens, and items of repute woven into a Bor'Banna's beard as badges of honor and accomplishment. Also common among other Dwarves.

Keep of Terraboer – the Citadel of Light. Home to the Dalaren Ka, the Knights of the One Light, and the Star of Elendial.

Keeper of Secrets – a select group of the Home Guard charged with guarding and maintaining Tellanon's secrets, hidden lore, and artifacts of repute. Also Holder of Secrets.

Khuerkanna – a famous Dwarven general known for his triumphant last stand against the Orcs and their allies in the Battle of the Broken Blade.

Kiervos – a large city-state in the plains of Var'Kera.

Kilaeron – wild continent to the east of Dharia.

Kiloboulder – a Gnomish unit of force, energy output, and weight.

Kor'Dannan – Dwarven Priests of Brendle given the keeping and wisdom of his fires, Brendle's Spark. Fierce warriors equally adept at healing and providing succor.

Koerdian Cave Bear – a species of gigantic cave bear particularly respected by Dwarves for their strength, perseverance, and indomitable spirit.

Kordas – Orcish blood beer.

Ku – pants.

K'un Lun – a mountain range often portrayed as a Taoist paradise, home to immortals. Home to the Priests of K'un Lun.

The K'un Lun – mystical priests from high in the mountains of Chang Sen. Also the Priests of K'un Lun.

Lael'darnael – literally, 'mission-view-survival-path' in the tongue of the Jira S'al Alann. A shared view and purpose developed organically together from the dictates and exigencies of the requirements for survival and success for an entire group providing the basis and direction for future action.

Landeiss – a large island nation to the south of Dharia.

Liao Qua – a large city in Chang Sen.

Li – literally, 'principle'. The expression of potential in form; the manifestation of inherent order distinct to each and every thing; the order of flow; the Tao in motion. Also pattern.

Lianel – literally, 'bowyer's heart.' A bow crafted by a master bowyer of the Elves melded and formed from his spirit and the spirit of a willing tree.

Lich – undead beings sustained by twisted magical energies.

Life – all living beings taken as a whole.

The Light – the ambient energy of the universe; the energy of Life enlivening all of existence. Considered holy, sacred, and heavenly. See also Aerya, *chi*, *ching*, *dalare*, Deur Spricken Sprack, Omnispark, Phlogiston, *shen*, Brendle's Spark, and *yuan-chi*.

Light Fallen – the Cabal or Liúxīng Làngrén.

Light's Grace – theurgical religious group on Tellanon led by Magdalia Miera whose activities focus on henosis, unification with and expression of the Divine Light on Ea'ae and beyond.

The Light's Guard – an elite force within the Home Guard led by Eidelion.

Light's Swath – the brilliant center of the galaxy encompassing Ea'ae.

Lightwell – the spontaneous, self-sustaining creation of life-giving energies formed through deft manipulation of the Dragon's Gate and the spontaneous creation of Light from limitless potential.

Master Liu – a revered teacher of the K'un Lun.

Liúxīng Làngrén – literally, 'falling star vagrants.' More figuratively, 'those fallen or straying from Heaven's path'. The Cabal, and those fallen priests associated with it, that have strayed from the path of Life, as referenced by the Priests of K'un Lun.

Llyewia L'oerllana – literally 'spring's first breath' or 'first breath of spring.' A lieutenant of the Home Guard. Elven Iyela, lorekeeper, and ambassador.

Loel'dara – literally, 'the Light's shadow beckons.' Tellanon's weapon of last resort and final line of defense.

Loesia – a cold, rugged region of lakes and mountains in the heart of the Northlands. Home to Wrindanneth and seat of Maeth Onai.

Loess – literally, 'Heaven's shielding.' A protective Dwarven rune meant for use against supernatural forces.

Master Loquan – a respected teacher of the K'un Lun.

Lords of the Wood – see Elves.

Lotus – see Pai-lien.

Lueciane Sea – the sea to Dharia's south. Lying directly between Dharia and Maeron, it surrounds the island nation of Landeiss.

Luereal – literally, 'troll's bane' or 'evil's bane' in the tongue of the Elves.

The black wand of Q'ia'Li. Once in the possession of Hoyt, given to Aroganji. An exceedingly rare Anuvaeryan wrought artifact of witchwood.

Luerdan – literally, 'troll dung' in the tongue of the Dwarves.

Lung – a Dragon in Chang Sen.

Lung-hu – literally, 'Dragon and tiger,' symbolic of *yang* and *yin* respectively, and the fusion of *k'an* and *li* in the Taoist alchemical tradition which leads to the realization of the Tao. The Dragon rises from the fire and is therefore associated with *li* while the tiger arises from the water and is therefore associated with *k'an*.

Lung-hu-i tao – literally, 'way of the Dragon and tiger.' A colloquial description by exponents of other alchemical traditions for the mystical traditions practiced by the priests of the K'un Lun.

Lung-wang – Dragon kings; mythological Taoist figures. Dragons (*lung*) also correspond to the *yang* principle in Taoist iconography.

Macrocosmic orbit – the energy path encompassing both the internal and external energy paths. Completion of the macrocosmic orbit is signified by opening the energy gates completely to the passage of *chi* which ultimately leads to unification with the energies of creation.

Macrocosmos – see macroverse.

Macroverse – the totality of multi-dimensional existence, inclusive of all planes, alternate universes, and extradimensional regions. See multiverse. Also megacosm or macrocosmos.

Maeglan – a Dwarven Dur'kazak of the Flintforge clan. Uncle to Slate.

Maer'Din – a loremaster of the H'era. Keepers of the tribe's dreams, aspirations, and history. Their knowledge is brought to life through the dance of the Seura.

Maeron – a largely tropical continent on the southern side of Ea'ae.

Maeth Onai – a god of magic. Wrindanneth's exemplar and ultimate guide. Depending on his mood, sometimes referenced privately as the Dream Stealer by Wrindanneth.

Maeven D'lanaran – a champion of the Dalaren Ka and exemplar of the Light.

MAFS – see Magical Air Foam System.

Magdalia Miera – member of Tellanon's ruling High Council, eminent Theurgist, and leader of the Light's Grace congregation.

Mage armor – enchanted armor for magic users that allows the freedom and flexibility to cast spells while also offering some protection against physical or magical assault. Often made from robes or clothing typical of a given magical tradition.

Magic – the translation of the possible into the actual, the imagined into the real. The three primary components of magical practice are often understood as belief, faith that an individual can take an active part in universal creation; intent (or will), the shaping of this belief can guide in creation; and imagination, the vision or desired outcome made possible by belief and shaped by intent.

The wellspring of magic is universal energy. Depending upon the tradition, this source is known as *yuan-chi*, Brendle's Spark, Phlogiston and the Omnispark, Aerya, and Light among others. This universal energy is often understood as the source and fuel of life, the *chi*. Sometimes broken into greater and lesser magics referencing the differentiation between the universal source energy—*yuan-chi*, Phlogiston, Aerya, Light, and celestial or divine magics—and the intrinsic ambient energies of life—the *chi*.

See also *yuan-chi*, *chi*, Brendle's Spark, Phlogiston and Omnispark, Aerya, and Light.

Magical Air Foam System – a magical Gnomish Paratechnological fire extinguishing foam. Particularly effective against Class M magical fires. Also known as MAFS.

Magnus Flintforge – a distant relation of Slate. Innkeeper of the Afternoon's Shade Inn located in isolated Shady Vale.

Major and Minor Shielding – a complex combination of spells serving to protect the recipient from arcane damage and hostile spells, the Major Shield, while also guarding against physical damage, impacts, blows, cuts, and the like, the Minor Shield.

Mandros Gray Beard – a once renowned archmage known for his great enchantments and wondrous Craft.

Mantaed – a massive mantid native to Landeiss. One of the preferred mounts of the Wyaera.

Mazithras – a leading Paratechnologist.

Megacosm – see multiverse or macroverse.

Men – the youngest and most prolific race of Ea'ae. Native flexibility and intuitiveness allows Men to excel in many fields, progressing quickly through their chosen arts.

Mere – 'Path' or 'Way' in the tongue of Tol Aeron.

Meridians – see *jing luo*.

METS – see Multidimensional Examination Tracker Survey.

Microcosmic orbit – the primary channel for the circulation of *chi* within the body. From the perineum, the pathway follows the spine up the back, over the crown of the head, past the brow, across the tongue, down the throat, past the solar plexus and navel, back to the perineum. This energy meridian passes through several major energy points or *chakras* along its route.

The microcosmic orbit is divided into two primary channels. The governor channel runs from the perineum along the back up the spine to the crown and down to the roof of the mouth. The tongue touching the roof of the mouth serves as a bridge between the two channels. The functional channel continues downward from the mouth through the throat, the heart, the navel, until ending in the perineum.

When energy flows freely along the microcosmic orbit joining the two primary energy routes, the practitioner has completed the small heavenly cycle. When the circuits along the arms and legs are open and flowing in conjunction with the small heavenly cycle, the practitioner has then completed the large heavenly cycle.

See also *jing luo* and macrocosmic orbit.

Mihtig'leht – literally, 'mighty light.' One of the fourteen seals protecting Ea'ae from extradimensional incursion. Housed in a bastion in the far reaches of Aruene in the keep of Morowen.

Mithril – a particularly light, yet strong, magical metal.

Molly Flintforge – Magnus's wife and co-owner of the Afternoon's Shade Inn.

Morowen – the bastion protecting the seal of Mihtig'leht. Keep of the Fyrskal.

Mudra – literally, 'seal or sign.' A spiritual gesture and an energetic seal of authenticity. A physical posture or symbolic gesture meant to connect outer actions with spiritual concepts. In Mahayana and Vajrayana Buddhist cosmography, *mudra* help actualize certain inner states, anticipating their bodily expression, creating a connection between the practitioner and the Buddha or experience visualized in meditation.

Mui Fa Jong – literally, 'plum flower poles.' Vertical poles used in martial practice to train balance, focus, coordination, relaxation, and agility.

Multidimensional Examination Tracker Survey – an active evaluation and classification system for the type and origin of energies used by Gnomish Paratechnologists. Also known as METS.

Multiverse – the entirety of multidimensional space inclusive of alternate universes, planes, and dimensions. Also macroverse and megacosm.

Neana – a rainbow-hued magical tree species whose glimmering, diamond-flecked trunks soar to the heavens.

Negentropy cannon – a Paratechnological cannon that locally reverses the process of energy dispersal associated with a given object's entropy at the cost of localized energy injection into the targeted system. In essence, the targeted object explodes into a highly energized cloud of superheated plasma. Sometimes referred to as the Energy Accumulator or the Particulate Plasmifier.

New Unified Mental-Energetic Noesis – NUMEN. A synthetic Paratechnological being of great mental and physical capacity able to take on many shapes, forms, and functions. An extension of the Paratechnology developed in the TAMERS units without need of an operator as the NUMEN is guided by its own intelligence. Also, a play on words among Paratechnologists for their magical-technological creations that may one day supersede them.

Nether realms – extradimensional planes home to Infernals and other fiendish creatures. See Abyss.

Nienael – a lord of Tueran. Father of Gilaethe.

Noeldri – literally, 'flowing water.' A Dwarven rune granting grace and agility both physically and mentally.

Noes Al'amroth – 'the land where tears do not dry.' Elven name for the home of the Aeryn D'al. Called Jenyuan Shulin by the people of Chang Sen. Bordered by Ithil'alen, the ancient homeland of the Elves on Ea'ae.

Noosphere – the realm of the mind, the collective consciousness, or the sphere of thought. A general name for the metamagical plane allowing for the shared existence and interaction both within and between various synthetic intelligences. A Paratechnological creation of the highest order. Also references the sphere of thought, mind, or knowledge itself.

Noumel – member of the Protectorate of Tellanon. The city's chief diplomat, head of interspecies and interstellar diplomacy and trade.

Novice – an aspirant not yet accepted into the priesthood. Upon acceptance into the K'un Lun, the novice becomes an initiate.

Nüaerblun – literally, 'Dragon dung' in the tongue of the Dwarves. Often used as a Dwarven insult.

Nüaer'Daer – literally, 'life's heart.' A Dwarven term for Dragons.

Nüaer'Duin – literally, 'Dragon fire' or 'life's fire' in the tongue of the Dwarves. Among the Dwarves, Dragon fire is respected for its magical properties and power so like the heat of Brendle's forge.

NUMEN – see New Unified Mental-Energetic Noesis.

Nydia – Elven noble and Iyela. Mother to Llyewia. Wife of Aleron.

Oedenara – literally, 'Daemon's heart.' A crystalline gem found at the heart of some Daemons with powerful magical properties and of much practical use.

Omnispark – Gnomish conception of the ignited or expressed source of life unending, ever-changing and evolving, fueled by Phlogiston. Deur Spricken Sprack in Gnomish. Also called *yuan-chi*, magic, Aerya, Brendle's Spark, and Light, among other terms, by other races.

Orcs – a large, prolific evil race spread through the wilds and caverns of Ea'ae. Orcs are strong, aggressive, and full of guile, a race of warriors and shaman. Working in league with Trolls and Ogres, Orcs often lead their slower-witted brethren on the field of battle.

Oroende – Paratechnologist, member of the Protectorate, and Ueralen, leader of the Thelios.

Orogast – one of the lieutenants of the Home Guard under Eidelion. A Jira S'al Alann, able to change shape and form at will. Also known as Orogast the Elder.

Quju – a type of *shenyi* worn primarily by women

Pai-hui – crown energy center corresponding to the Sahasrara *chakra* in some yogic practices. The Yellow Palace. The spirit door.

Pai-lien – White lotus. The lotus is a significant symbol in the Buddhist and Hindu cosmologies. The lotus can represent a symbol of beauty; the various centers of consciousness (*chakras*) located throughout the body; the lotus floating in water can be seen as a symbol for non-attachment—as the lotus floats in the water and remains dry, the spiritual seeker lives in the world and remains unaffected by it; in Buddhism the lotus is also a symbol of the true nature of beings.

Pai-lien Touch – White Lotus Touch. A method of intervention developed within the Priests of K'un Lun that gives the recipient a chance to reform and remake themselves by granting visions of the summation of their experience, akin to a near death experience. Also called the Echoing Fist because the energies of the Touch echo through the chambers of the recipient's mind. Also called Shakyamuni's Palm because a master can use the Touch to cut through falsehood.

Paladin – a holy warrior dedicated to and empowered by the Light, vanquishers of evil, banishers of the unholy, adjudicators and arbiters, healers and almsmen. Many variants exist, some dedicated to particular deities and powerful entities, each with different talents, specialties, and ethos. The Dalaren Ka are one such group.

Paratechnology – literally, 'beyond technology.' The study of making the imagined real and actualizing the impossible. The art and science of applied magic and magical technologies. Paratechnological apprehension is shared across many races, however, the Gnomes' natural curiosity and creativity have brought Paratechnological expertise to its current refined state and have helped to spread its knowledge throughout the cosmos.

Pattern – the unique movements and shapes of *chi*, of limitless potential, indicative of the particular life force of an individual—the fingerprints of the soul. See also *li*.

Peran – Vicar of the High Lord Éremon.

Perfectly Polished Particulate Propeller – Beta Naught Mark Seven – a Gnomish frictionless toothpick invented by Spreesprocket.

Phlogiston – called Deur Spricken Sprack in the tongue of Gnomes. In Gnomish reckoning, the invisible spark of life pervading the universe akin to an invisible metastate of gaseous energetic conductance. Once ignited, Phlogiston fuels all life as the Omnispark. When manipulated by will, the Phlogiston gives rise to magic. Also called *yuan-chi*, magic, Aerya, Brendle's Spark, and Light, among other terms, by other races and traditions.

Plane – one of many distinct layers of existence in the larger macro or multiverse. Often synonymous with universe or dimension.

Plains of Kadoor – open grassy plains on the western section of Dharia. Part of Var'Kera.

Pocket dimension – a miniature space or reality created expressly for a specific purpose. In the case of the myriad pocket dimensions of Tellanon, these represent miniature universes intimately connected to Tellanon itself, extending its breadth and depth. More often, pocket dimensions are used to extend space within a given region, for example, to make the space within a bag or room larger.

Port – a shortened term for teleport.

Powers – beings of great might, often extradimensional in origin.

Priest – one who has been accepted fully into the Order of the K'un Lun. See Priest of K'un Lun.

Priest of Maeth Onai – an order of magicians from the cold Northlands that practices a unique blend of mundane and divine magics whereby divine energies are channeled to perform traditional and inimitable spells.

Priest of K'un Lun – an order of mystics dedicated to the practice of various esoteric and martial traditions found nowhere else on Ea'ae. The way of the priest is geared toward continual transformation and development within and without through the evolving practice of internal alchemy, meditation, and physical cultivation.

Projection – a general term for a multi-dimensional representation of an object. A magical hologram or depiction. Also a reference to life-like, immersive news feeds displaying current happenings and items of worth.

Protectorate – Tellanon's governing body composed of thirteen elected Paratechnologists and other citizen representatives governing matters of security, trade, diplomacy, research, and city form and function. Also called the High Council or council.

Current members include Éremon, Oroende, Rowena Bowspirit, Dizzywig Paddlepulley, Jae'elthos, Vaendoer Thunderhammer, Whirlygig Sparksocket, Magdalia Miera, Borus, Noumel, Salia Proventure, Chutefunnel Knobwhistle, and Alain Ar'laen.

Psion – a being gifted mentally and psychically.

Psionics – psychic mental powers and abilities as expressed by a psion.

Qì – *chi.*

Q'ia'Li – a highly regarded Elven magician of great power that transitioned to Anuvaerya in order to defeat an exceedingly powerful Anubaraëthi in single combat. Creator of Luereal.

Q'ia Shan Sea – eastern border of Chang Sen. A vast and sometimes turbulent body of tropical water dotted by islands and many atolls.

Qigong – literally, '*chi* work' or 'life energy work.' Generally, exercises to build and strengthen *chi* flow.

Qìxīnquán – literally, 'life essence-mind boxing' or 'life energy-mind boxing.' Another term often ascribed to the martial style of the K'un Lun.

Q'shar – A kingdom in far southern Dharia known for its fierce nomadic warriors.

Quai-lo – A widespread race of semi-intelligent insectoid predators. Large and ferocious, they resemble nothing more than vicious humanoid mantises.

Radok – war chief of the Ar'thas, the Black Mountain Orcs.

Rainbow body – a body of pure Light, a celestial or energy body. Called a *jalü* in esoteric tradition. See also *jalü.*

Rare Aer – Humbol's airship.

Rakshasa – a race of powerful feline Daemonic sorcerers in league with the Cabal.

Raour'Saqan – a Dracodaeran Shaur'Daus. Lieutenant of the Home Guard.

Raurdros – literally, 'evil's bane.' The great rune-etched hammer of Kazarhan, forged by Dwarven smiths of old, empowered by ancient runes of power, Karaduen, and other workings of enchantment.

Return stone – a magical crystal of concentrated energy used to transport the bearer to a predefined location—generally the starting point of a journey. Often used with airships to allow passage home without a portal.

Rhyllia – literally, 'the Mother Tree.' An ancient tree in the grove of Erudhluin held sacred by the Elves. One of the few surviving Aeryn D'al beyond the borders of Jenyuan Shulin.

Róucí – literally, 'pliant or soft poetry.' A simple three-lined poem consisting of five to seven syllables per line. Meant to capture the essence of a moment or the central character of an event, a few words to capture the entirety of an impression. Oftentimes, but not always, the final line heightens the moment of clarity provided by the poem through a sudden, unexpected transition, change, or image.

Rowena Bowspirit – Tellanon's foremost Aeromancer and fleet commander, member of the Protectorate, master pilot and craftswoman.

Ruena O'reine – archmage nonpareil, a principal magical instructor of the Home Guard, and a Holder of Secrets.

Ruen'elde – a name for the cadre of Archliches ruling Garen Muer.

R'yn Daer – a people at home in the skies as much as on the land. Native fliers, swashbucklers and rogues, they wander the skies of Ea'ae in search of fame and fortune.

Saedeus – Lich king, ruler of Garen Muer. Formerly an archmage of great repute and guardian of the seal of Weis'liuhath.

Salia Proventure – member of Tellanon's ruling Protectorate, citizen advocate, and voice of the community and its concerns.

Sarugauth the Red – a primeval Red Dragon allied with the Cabal. Bane of the Yerens.

SAVERS – see Self Actuated Variable Emergency Response System.

SBS – see Sliced Bread Society.

Sceaduwulf – literally, 'shadow wolf.' A spectral wolf.

Scierdyas – literally, 'Spectral Dragons.' Energetic beings very similar in appearance to Dragons summoned from the unholy nether realms of the darkest abysms.

Scimerian Gate – literally, 'Shimmering Gate.' A magical portal allowing entry into Tellanon proper from the loading docks. Also known as the Weirding Gate.

Seals – fourteen magical wards of untold power scattered equidistant across the planet forming a magical barrier protecting Ea'ae from extradimensional incursion and extraplanetary attack.

Seiza – a sitting position commonly used in Buddhist meditation along with the lotus and half-lotus positions. The practitioner sits on her knees with feet tucked under the buttocks.

Self-Actuated Variable Emergency Response System – a Paratechnological clockwork emergency response bot of Gnomish invention capable of independently responding to, assessing, and reacting to multiple life-threatening situations. Called SAVERS for short.

Senea – a massive, thickly trunked forest giant. Its magically reinforced wood is among the strongest on Ea'ae.

Sentry drones – a general name for Paratechnological defensive drones. See also ARMED.

Seura – the 'dance of dreams unborn.' A form of moving knowledge and history transmitted by the Maer'Din of the H'era.

Shade – a nebulous creature of Darkness.

Shadow – a general term for creatures of Darkness and their ilk. Those opposed to the energy of Life in all its manifestations and who seek to subvert, pervert, consume, or otherwise destroy the Light in all its manifold expressions.

Shadowkin – a general term for creatures of Darkness. See Shadow.

Shady Vale – a small hamlet in the western wilds of Dharia deep in the heart of the Green Run.

Shakyamuni – literally, 'sage of the Shakyas.' The historical Buddha Siddhartha Gautama, born into the Shakya, or Lion, clan before realizing the Four Noble Truths and discovering the Eightfold Path as a means to end suffering.

Shapers – see Yerens.

Shaur'Daus – literally, a 'Stalker of Darkness' in the tongue of the Dracodaerans. Draconic warriors wreathed in the fires of Heaven that do battle against the creatures of Darkness across the cosmos and beyond.

Shen – a deity or spirit; also the personal spirit or mind of an individual. One of the three essential life energies of man along with *chi* (*qi*) and *ching* (*jing*). In the Taoist meditative tradition, *shen* refers to both *shih-shen* and *yuan-shen*. Shih-shen refers to ordinary consciousness—thoughts, feelings, perceptions, and the senses. In contrast, *yuan-shen* refers to the spiritual consciousness that exists before birth and is part of the energy that pervades the entire universe (the *yuan-chi*). Meditation, or inner-alchemy, allows the Taoist practitioner to reestablish contact with her spiritual consciousness while eliminating the influence of the ordinary day-to-day consciousness.

Sheng-jen – a sage or saint. Taoist terms for an ideal man who has achieved perfection.

Shen-jen – a spiritual man. Another term used to describe an ideal man, a person who has realized the Tao.

Shen Po – master of the void palm, one of the fallen founding fathers of the K'un Lun, member of the Cabal, and one time teacher of Master Wei.

Shenyi – a long garment of Chang Sen much like a full-body robe with flowing sleeves tied by a sash at the waist. *Zhiju* are worn by men. *Quju* are worn women.

Master Shi – T'ien-shih of the K'un Lun.

Shih – master or expert.

Shrike – airship of Braemen, later of the Fists.

Shuǐ lù xiàn – literally, 'the way of the water course or water's path.' An inner teaching of Xīnyìquán embodying *wu wei, wu bu wei,* and non-resistance, the effortless passage and redirection of force and intent.

Singers – see Yerens.

Skael – a people of nomadic traders who travel the skies in airships plying their wares.

Slate Flintforge – a Dwarf of the land, Bor'Banna, and adventurer of some renown. Friend of Yip, Aroganji, and Wrindanneth. Member of the Four. In the tongue of Dwarves, known as Daer'Duin.

Sliced Bread Society – a Paratechnological think tank dedicated to furthering the depth and breadth of magical and material knowledge and understanding whose study spans the breadth and depth of the mundane and mystical. Driven by the motto, "It doesn't get any better!" Also called the SBS.

Soerlyn – Elven years. See Cycles.

Span – a unit of distance roughly equivalent to a league.

Spreesprocket Goldpulley – a lieutenant of the Home Guard, Gnomish Paratechnologist, and warrior nonpareil.

Squarepeg Springwidget – highly skilled Gnomish Paratechnologist of Tellanon.

Star of Elendial – a magical artifact of great power housed in the Keep of Terraboer. One of the fourteen seals protecting Ea'ae from extradimensional incursion.

Star of Illdrassil – small crystalline fragments of Illdrassil that grant magical boons to members of the Home Guard.

Stasis box – a magical storage box, often enclosing a pocket dimension for added storage space that ensures the freshness of stored food.

Super sack – a magical Gnomish bottomless bag. Super sacks are often cluttered, disorganized, and very difficult to retrieve items from within, especially within a short, highly critical period of time.

Synthetic intelligence – a Paratechnological term for the sentience resulting from the merger of two different intelligences. Typically, one intelligence is natural and the other is artificial, one is organic and the other is disembodied or a metamagical complex arising from technical sophistication, or one intelligence is formed explicitly to merge with and augment another. Far different from the Abstract and Construct's relationship with citizens, for example, wherein one intelligence serves another directly and indirectly, synthetic intelligences are the result of a complete union between two disparate awarenesses, the resulting union having complete access to the knowledge and capabilities of both. Most typically, one intelligence is created explicitly to merge with and augment another, extending the field of sentient consciousness into directions and dimensions only limited by the imagination.

Also a reference to any created intelligence.

Sythaeran Quadrant – a region of space containing the planet known as Al'Marr.

Taerris'thule – literally, 'old home.' Formerly a religious city and home to the seal of Eldre'gheu. Sometimes referred to as the City of the Fallen Gods.

Taiji – alternatively, Tai chi or T'ai chi. Literally, 'supreme ultimate' or 'great absolute.' Undifferentiated or unlimited potential. The source of existence. The primordial state of emptiness from which potential and existence arose and returns. The great, undifferentiated beginning. The wellspring and return of possibility.

Taliaerya – literally, 'Morning's Light' or 'Dawn's Light' in the tongue of the Elves. Known as Eyrdeas, the White Blade of Morn among the Dalaren Ka. The storied blade of Maeven D'lanaran.

TAMERS – see Transmorphic Actionable Multidimensional Exo-Robotic System.

Tan t'ien – an elixir field. The primary energy centers of the human body located at the navel, chest, and forehead. Often a specific reference to the elixir field near the navel. The seat of the *shen*. Alternatively, *dantian*.

More generally, *tan t'ien* can also refer to various energy centers throughout the body through which energy is successively refined. Depending on the alchemical system, the number and purpose may vary. Typically, one *tan t'ien* is located at the navel, another is found at the heart, and one is situated between the eyebrows. Most commonly, the lower *tan t'ien* at or below the navel transforms sexual essence, or *jing*, into *chi*. The middle *tan t'ien* in the center of the chest transmutes *qi* energy into *shen*, or spirit. Finally, the higher *tan t'ien* at the forehead, or on the top of the head, transforms *shen* into Wuji, the infinite space of void.

Tao – literally, 'Way.' Also refers to the way of Nature or Heaven. The mysterious, elusive source and guiding principle behind the phenomena of the universe. The unnamable spring from which *chi* and all existence flow. Also Dao and Wuji.

> *The Tao that can be told is not the eternal Tao;*
> *The name that can be named is not the eternal name.*
> *The nameless is the beginning of Heaven and Earth.*
> *The named is the mother of ten thousand things.*
> *Ever desireless, one can see the mystery.*
> *Ever desiring, one can see the manifestations.*
> *These two spring from the same source but differ in name;*
> *This appears as darkness.*
> *Darkness within darkness.*
> *The gate to all mystery.*[5]

Tao-Shih – a Taoist priest in religious as opposed to philosophical Taoism.

Supervisors of various religious rituals and ceremonies, leaders of congregations, and scholars.

Tellanon – literally, 'Heaven's Landing' in the Old Tongue of Men. A spectacular floating island city in the sky, a center of commerce and diplomacy, and a starting point for both interstellar and interdimensional travel. Home of Illdrassil, the Home Guard, and Paratechnologists on Ea'ae.

Temple of Eldre'gheu – see Eldre'gheu.

Terala – a massive, sentient man-eating spider.

Thaelos – an Elven-trained archer aboard the *Shrike*. Braemen's second.

Thaiel Lui'nost – Elven lorekeeper and sage.

Thane – traditional leader of a Dwarven clan.

Thelios – a guild of Paratechnologists focused on material transformation and alteration led by Oroende.

Therion – an ancient hero known for many exploits including cleansing the seal of Eldre'gheu.

The Thirteen – euphemism for the council.

The Three Pillars – a code of ethics or core tenets of the K'un Lun which guide and support their actions and activities. These moral pillars fall into three general categories reflective of the three primary regions of human endeavor: morality of deed, morality of mind, and morality of spirit.

Furthermore, within each ethical pillar, actions are elucidated by additional secondary tenets. Morality of deed includes expressing humility, loyalty, respect, righteousness, and trust in all actions. Morality of mind entails evincing courage, endurance, patience, perseverance, and will in thought. Morality of spirit includes internalizing, manifesting, and actualizing contemplation, insight, compassion, wisdom, and serenity through freedom of thought and expression.

Three Treasures – the three essential substances of the human body. The three treasures are *jing* (*ching*), the material essence; *qi* (*chi*), the vital energy; and *shen*, the spirit or soul.

The Thunderhammer Clan – a clan of Dwarves residing upon Tellanon known for their technical expertise and cooperative working partnership with Gnomish Paratechnologists.

T'iao chi – harmonizing the breaths. A Taoist breathing technique that serves as preparation for further Taoist development exercises.

T'ien – celestial; Heaven.

T'ien Ming – the celestial mandate or mandate of Heaven. The right to rule granted by Heaven to just emperors.

T'ien-shih – celestial master. Also a title borne by the leaders of some schools of Taoism.

Tinkerers – Paratechnologists focusing on clockwork devices melding magic and technology in forms often resembling complex mechanical devices. Most often associated with Gnomish Paratechnologists due to their strong imaginative mechanical tendencies.

Tol Aeron – a lush, temperate mountainous island far to the south and west of Tellanon off the western coast of Dharia. Birthplace of Eidelion, home of the Keep of Terraboer, the Citadel of Light and the Dalaren Ka, the Knights of the One Light.

Transmorphic Actionable Multidimensional Exo-Robotic System – A multi-functional, transforming exoarmor system created by Spreesprocket. Also known as TAMERS.

Traveler – a magic user capable of teleportation.

Traveling – teleportation or any other form of instantaneous travel whether inter- or intradimensionally.

Tso-wang –meditation characterized by objectless attention or pure awareness coupled with inner and outer stillness—the universe expressing its own enlightened true nature. One of many contemplative approaches employed by the K'un Lun.

Tueran – a largely Anuvatali city that is also home to humans, Dwarves, Gnomes, and Elves located on the southern island nation of Landeiss.

Tuio Shou – literally, 'pushing hands.' A name for the two-person training routines utilized in some internal martial arts.

Tyraethe – homeworld of the Tyraethians.

Tyraethian – reptilian humanoids originating from the planet Tyraethe known for their extreme physical prowess, highly developed code of honor, cultivated ethical systems, and complex moral conduct.

Ueralen – title for the leader of the Thelios, a band of Paratechnologists focused on transmutation and alteration of matter.

The Umbral Lord – see the Enemy or Ur'Daus.

Undermount – a general name for any Dwarven city or a Dwarven occupied region. Typically located in the bedrock beneath mountains. Dwarven fastnesses and attendant halls and byways that grow within the roots of the hills. Also called delvings, though delvings are typically smaller in scale.

Ungar – literally, 'earthen might.' A Dwarven rune granting physical strength and endurance.

Uraera Al'on – literally, 'strengthener of intent' or 'gatherer of will.' A form of magic practiced by the Anuvatali that weaves webs of enchantment around allies, augmenting and expanding upon strengths and abilities.

Ur'Daena – literally, 'the axe's lament.' The uniquely Dwarven art of the axe. Many styles and forms are known, each generally ascribed to a specific family, clan, or thanedom. Variations in styles from the use of great two-handed war axes taller than a man suited to the openness of the battlefield to forms of double-bladed combat better suited to the close quarters of a mineshaft are all practiced with distinctly Dwarven fervor.

When practiced by a master, a Bor'Banna, these styles rely as much on channeling the remnants of Brendle's original creation magic through the axe as physical prowess for their efficacy. When wielded by a true master, the axe of the Bor'Banna is said to glow with the light and heat of Brendle's original forge.

Ur'Daus – literally, 'The Darkness.' Also known as the Enemy, the Creeping Shadow, the Devourer of Worlds, the Umbral Lord, the Great Devourer, and many others. A fathomless Light consuming Darkness trapped between dimensions in ages long past.

Urduen – large Dwarven-fortified city-state of north central Dharia.

Uuraja – leader of the beast riders of Al'Marr, feline lords of the Forlorn Forest. Father of Uuraru.

Uuraru – young son of Uuraja, hereditary lord of the Al'Marr. Named Evensong for his skill in weaving music and magic.

Vaellorea – a grand Elven tree of wondrous form and silvery hue. Kin to Aeryn D'al.

Vaendoer Thunderhammer – member of Tellanon's ruling Protectorate, Dur'kazak, and thane of the Thunderhammer clan.

Vanduen – literally, 'divine regeneration.' A Dwarven Karaduen that enhances healing capacities, speeding recovery and repair from exhaustion and injury.

Vapor of Golden Quintessent Life – a sentient gaseous Paratechnologist with significant psychic ability.

Var'Kera – a land of open grasslands and rich, rolling forests, home to many great kingdoms, and the typical mooring below Tellanon.

Verakesh – a mage in Braemen's employ, pilot of the airship the *Shrike*.

Vöer – Troll in the tongue of the Dwarves.

Vöerdan – literally, 'Troll saliva or spittle.' A Dwarven insult.

Void – the wellspring of creation. The limitless potential underlying all existence. Source of the Tao and *yuan-chi*. Also Wuji.

Void palm – an unassailable attack directly upon the life force of an opponent.

Vorath – an amorphous, mist-like intelligent predator that reads the thoughts of its prey and feeds on their essence.

Vradek – Orcish gruel made from ground bones simmered in blood.

Vyaera – literally, 'wanderers along the path.' An Elven term for those sharing the same path, quest, purpose, or journey.

War of Shadows – one name for the first war with the Cabal and their dark allies waged on Ea'ae in the distant past.

Warren – a general name for the complexly convoluted and often interconnected structures typical of Gnomish homes. Also a name for large, extended Gnomish families.

The Watcher – elusive denizen of the Drake Spires; Ilidian.

Master Wei – an accomplished teacher of the K'un Lun. Yip's primary instructor and guide through the ways of the priesthood. Teacher of the Five Excellencies, master of the Moonlit Mind, keeper of the Echoing fist, and Sheng-jen.

Weirding Gate – see Scimerian Gate.

Weirding Wood – see Aeryn Sh'al.

Weis'liuhath – literally, 'wise light' or 'light of wisdom.' One of the fourteen seals protecting Ea'ae from extradimensional incursion. Housed in a fastness secluded in the lost forests of Kilaeron in the keep of Garen Muer.

Whirlygig Sparksocket – member of the Tellanon Protectorate, Paratechnologist, and lead Designer and System Administrator of COG, the Construct Organization Group.

Wieru S'al Alann – literally 'Way of the Imagining,' 'Way of the Imagined,' or 'Way of Imagining.' The path of self-transformation and actualization taken by the Jira S'al Alann. This way encompasses the techniques, knowledge, and skills necessary to live, survive, adapt, and change in a mutable world.

Witchwood – see Aeryn Sh'al.

Worgs – massive wolves used by Orcs as mounts in lieu of horses.

Wrindanneth – friend of Yip, Aroganji, and Slate. Priest of Maeth Onai. Member of the Fists.

Wu – literally, 'nonbeing; emptiness.' The fundamental characteristic of the Tao. Also refers to a Taoist imbued with the Tao so that he has become free of all passions and desires (empty). Also the absence of qualities perceivable by the senses.

Wu bu Wei – literally, 'not left undone.' The creative completion and natural accompaniment to wu wei. Knowing when and how to act and not to act in intuitive harmony with the Tao. The active, creative complement to the passive stillness of *wu wei*. Taken as a whole, by not acting, nothing is left undone.

Wuji – alternatively, Wu Chi. Literally, 'boundless,' 'ultimateless,' 'limitless,' or infinite. The Ultimateless, Void, or Infinite before the Great Ultimate, Taiji, before differentiation. Synonymous with Tao.

Denoted in Zhan Zhuang standing meditation *qigong* practice as the initial and fundamental stance for practice.

Wu Wei – literally, 'without action' or 'non-action.' A description of 'effortless doing,' 'action without action,' perfect equilibrium, or harmony with the Tao. The complement to *wu bu wei*, or 'not left undone'. Together, *wu wei* and *wu bu wei* form the creative, harmonious passivity and intuition needed to know when and how to act or not to act.

Wu Xin – literally, 'energy gates,' points in the body where internal and external *chi* come into contact. The five primary energy gates include the face, the center of the palms of the hands at the Laogong points, and the Yongquan points on the bottoms of the feet. Energy can also enter through the navel at the *tan t'ien* and through the skin at the pores through special *qigong* practices (i.e. via Fu Xi or skin breathing).

Wu-hsing – alternatively, the Wu Xing, literally 'the five movers,' 'the five elements,' 'the five virtues' (Wu-te). Also represent the five phases of transformation or the five energies that determine the course of natural phenomena.

These 'elements' correspond to abstract forces and act as symbols or metaphors for basic characteristics, properties, and interactions of matter. The five symbolic elements are water, earth, fire, metal, and wood.

Master Wuping – a venerated teacher of the K'un Lun.

Wyaera – literally, 'wanderers along the sky,' or, more loosely, 'sky striders,' or 'cloud walkers.' The Riders of Tueran.

Wyrm – an ancient or powerful Dragon.

Xi Wue – a Fang Shih and respected teacher at Xian Shi.

Xian Shi – a school in Chang Sen dedicated to the arcane study of *fang shu* and *fu-lu* and the development of young Fang Shih. Located between the Hsiang Lung Mountains
and the Q'ia Shan Sea.

Xīnyì – literally, 'mind-to-mind,' 'mind to intent,' or 'mind to thought.' A higher order of teaching rarely employed by the Priests of K'un Lun in which a priest directly shares his knowledge and experience with another.

Xīnyìquán – literally, 'heart to mind fist,' 'mind to thought or intent boxing,' or, more loosely, 'mind-to-mind boxing.' The term used to describe a primary component of the martial tradition employed by the Priests of the K'un Lun. Not so much an internal or external martial style, practitioners read and feel the *chi*, the intention and spirit of their opponent, anticipating, redirecting, and manipulating their opponent's energies and intent before and during expression.

Yaozi – a term for 'kite' in Chang Sen.

Ydrael Faer'Leirn – a fabled archmage and author of a magical tome of high magics given to Wrindanneth and Aroganji by Azaelle.

Yenaria – literally, 'House of Dreams.' Elven city linked to Tellanon.

Yerens – a noble race of yeti-like creatures. Singers of the worldsong. Called the Shapers of the True Song, Shapers, and Singers.

Yi – any open cross-collar garment worn by both men and women in Chang Sen.

Yin-T'ang – the gateway to Heaven; a primary energy center of the body. The point between the eyes along the brow corresponding to the Ajna *chakra*.

Yip Chi Chuan – an Acolyte of the K'un Lun. Friend of Wrindanneth, Aroganji, and Slate. One of the Flaming Fists. Called Aerya'anan, 'Light bringer,' by the Anuvatari.

Ylldel – literally, 'Mountain Father.' The Indural's name for the mountain home of the Karadüm in the Green Run.

Yrien Al'nori – member of the Home Guard, Anuvatali Uraera Al'on.

Yuan-chi – the primordial energy, the inherent unrealized potential, of the universe; the celestial or divine *chi*. In some Taoist cosmologies, the personal spirit *shen* is thought to arise from the union of *ching*, the essence, with the universal primordial energy of *yuan-chi*. The *shen*, the result of this union, enters the newborn infant with its first breath. The *shen* resides in the body in the *tan t'ien* (navel), where it determines thoughts and feelings until leaving the body at death.

Yuan Ser – a journeyman amongst the Fang Shih. Not yet a fully accomplished master or archmage in the rites and traditions of the *fang shu*.

Yuan-shen – universal, original, or primordial awareness, spirit, or mind.

Yu-jen – literally, 'feather man.' An alternative designation for Tao-shih.

Zabuton – a flat padded mat used for sitting. Sometimes positioned under a *zafu* in meditation.

Zafu – a round cushion used for seated meditation.

Zhan Zhuang – standing like a tree or post; a form of standing meditation used in various systems of *chi gung* (internal energy work).

Zhiju – a type of *shenyi* worn primarily by men in Chang Sen.

Zhiyuan – a term for kite in Chang Sen.

REFERENCES FOR MORE IN-DEPTH
INFORMATION AND FURTHER STUDY

1. Blofield, John. *Taoism - The Road to Immortality*. Shambhala: Boston. 1978.
2. Chia, Mantak. *Awaken Healing Energy through the Tao*. Aurora: Santa Fe. 1983.
3. Chuen, Master Lam Kam. *The Way of Energy*. Simon & Schuster, Inc.: New York. 1991.
4. Cleary, Thomas (trans.). *Opening the Dragon Gate*. Tuttle: Boston. 1996.
5. Gia-Fu Feng & Jane English (translators). *Lao Tsu/Tao Te Ching*. New York: Vintage Books. 1972.
6. Liang, Master Shou-Yu and Wu, Wen-Ching. *Qigong Empowerment - A Guide to Buddhist Taoist Medical Wushu Energy Cultivation*. Dragon Publishing: East Providence. 1997.
7. Schuhmacher, Stephan and Woerner Gert (eds.). *The Encyclopedia of Eastern Philosophy and Religion*. Shambhala: Boston. 1989.
8. Suzuki, Shunryu. *Zen Mind, Beginner's Mind*. Shambhala: Boston. 1973.
9. Watson, Burton (trans.). *The Complete Works of Chuang Tzu*. Columbia University Press: New York. 1968.

ABOUT THE AUTHOR

Through such simple questions as, "What if we lived in a world where our beliefs were real, tangible, and actualizable?" Joe explores the possible through thought, fantasy, wit, and character.

Including influences such as Shunryu Suzuki, Tolkien, Krishnamurti, Iain M. Banks, Laozi, Stephen R. Donaldson, Philip Kapleau, Raymond E. Feist, Edward O. Wilson, Dan Simmons, and David Bohm, Joe creates existential fantasy filled with rich worlds, concepts, stories, and ideas.

Joe holds an advanced degree in environmental management from Duke University, where he also studied religion with a focus on meditative, experiential, and transformative traditions. Additionally, Joe graduated with (dubious) honors from the Tellanon Institute of Noetic Knowledge, Education, and Research (TINKER), but has yet to put this knowledge to good use.

When not at play with his family, he enjoys reading, writing, and relaxation. When he can, Joe also practices various martial traditions in which he has attained the victim level of proficiency.

Joe's website

ACKNOWLEDGMENTS

I would like to thank my wife for her patience, love, and support; my beta readers for their willingness to enter worlds unlike any other; my friends for listening to my all-too-frequent updates and ideas; Ashley Davis, my editor, for helping realize my vision; and all the readers who took a chance in reading my work.

Thank you!

Second Edition: December 2014

ISBN: 978-0985390747

This is a work of fiction.
Names, characters, places, ideas, and incidents either are the product of the author's imagination or are used fictitiously. Any resemblance to actual persons, living or dead, events, or locales is entirely coincidental.

Cover design by Joseph J. Bailey
Map Copyright © 2012 by Joseph J. Bailey

For more information, please visit:
Joe's website

www.ingramcontent.com/pod-product-compliance
Lightning Source LLC
Chambersburg PA
CBHW020241030726

47499CB00001B/20